LET A SOLDII
and shocking novel, forged out of the
author's personal experiences in a violent and shocking conflict. It joins such novels as THE 13TH VALLEY, FIELDS OF FIRE and GOING AFTER CACCIATO as classics of the Vietnam war, and ranks alongside such all-time war classics as CHICKENHAWK, THE NAKED AND THE DEAD, THE YOUNG LIONS and ALL QUIET ON THE WESTERN FRONT.

William E. Holland was born in Nebraska. He also attended college there, and graduated from the University of Nebraska with a degree in Civil Engineering. He went on to receive an English degree from Oxford University, a Ph.D. from Stanford University, and a J.D. from Stanford Law School. His college career was interrupted by a three-year stint in the army that included a year flying helicopters in Vietnam. William E. Holland is now back in Nebraska, practising law.

LET A SOLDIER DIE is his first novel.

'Whether avenging angels or angels or mercy, helicopters are what made Vietnam's tactics so different from every previous war's . . . LET A SOLDIER DIE is the best and most thought-provoking book so far about a chopper pilot's life over there. Holland's book flies'
C. D. B. Bryan, author of *Friendly Fire* and *Beautiful Women, Ugly Scenes.*

'Enthralling and sharp and terrible. Holland's ability to make vivid the particularities, the atmosphere of this aerial war is awesome'
The Kirkus Reviews

'Undeniably powerful. Worked into the military action is an unusually gentle love story . . . LET A SOLDIER DIE is as much about the emotions of a soldier who flies a chopper as it is about the machine itself'
Publishers Weekly

William E. Holland

Let A Soldier Die

CORGI BOOKS

LET A SOLDIER DIE

A CORGI BOOK 0 552 12659 4

First publication in Great Britain
Published by arrangement with Dell Publishing Co. Inc., New York, New York, U.S.A.

PRINTING HISTORY
Corgi edition published 1985
Corgi edition reissued 1985

This book is set in 10/11pt Baskerville

Corgi Books are published by Transworld Publishers Ltd., Century House, 61-63 Uxbridge Road, Ealing, London W5 5SA, in Australia by Transworld Publishers (Aust.) Pty. Ltd., 26 Harley Crescent, Condell Park, NSW 2200, and in New Zealand by Transworld Publishers (N.Z.) Ltd., Cnr. Moselle and Waipareira Avenues, Henderson, Auckland.

Made and printed in Great Britain by
Hunt Barnard Printing Ltd., Aylesbury, Bucks.

Let A Soldier Die

The helicopter slid slowly from the sky, as if reluctant to touch the darkening earth. In the glass-smooth air no thump of its blades announced its coming: it sighed from the sky in a long, slanting glide. As it neared the earth, the last weak sun, fighting through gathering evening haze, blazed the cross painted in dull red on its door. It crossed the line of surf where the South China Sea broke on the coast of Vietnam, on the rocks and reefs at the foot of the cliffs of Ky Ha. It skirted the seaward edge of the parking apron, checkered with revetments where the ships of two assault helicopter companies stood. In a last flurry of blades it settled on the helipad at the field hospital sprawled on the southernmost cliffs of Ky Ha.

The big side door of the ship slid back, and a corpsman got down and walked to the hospital; but no one came to meet the ship. It stood on the pad, the engine whistling, the big blade swishing softly, until the pilot shut off the fuel and the engine expired with a final sigh. The blade continued to turn, but more and more slowly, until at last it teetered to a halt. The copilot climbed out then and, with a long hook, caught the eye at one end of the blade, pulled the blade down to the tail strut, and tied it there by the cloth band tied to the hook. The pilot still sat in the ship.

The copilot walked to the pilot's door. 'You coming, Trung-úy*?' he asked.*

'Go on ahead,' the pilot answered. 'I'll wait here till they come.'

After the copilot had gone, the pilot climbed stiffly down from the ship. He sat down in the open side door at the feet of the two bodies lying across the floor of the ship.

One of the bodies wore black-embroidered aviator's wings above the left shirt pocket and a major's oak leaf in dull gold thread on the collar. The other was covered from waist to chin by the armored chest plate of a helicopter pilot. The plate was cratered in the center where a bullet had struck. This body lay closest to the pilot as he sat in the door. One of its boots was missing. The pilot, sitting there, laid his left hand on the stockinged foot. He grasped the foot roughly and shook it, then shook his head. He stood up and walked a little way from the ship to wait.

It was dark when the graves-registration truck jolted down from the hut at the end of the cliffs. The blackout lights of the truck made hardly a mark on the night. The truck groaned to a halt beside the helicopter, so close that the driver and his assistant had no need to take even a step to transfer the bodies.

The pilot would have helped them lift the bodies onto the truck, but there was no room, so he stood back and watched. When they had gone, he slid the big door closed. Its rumble echoed down the silent ramp, among the revetments where the helicopters stood. He stood a long time, holding the handle of the door. Then he, too, went into the night.

1

The early afternoon sun of the dry season baked the fuel pits at Landing Zone Baldy. The fuel pits were a broad stretch of olive-drab pierced steel plank littered with thousand-gallon rubber bladders of jet fuel. The air above the planking shimmered with heat.

Among the bladders two helicopter gunships were running their blades up to operating speed.

Spec-Four Cripps dragged the fuel hose away from the lead ship and stepped gingerly back across the planking, which burned at the soles of his jungle boots. He climbed into the back of the ship, plugged his helmet cord into the intercom, and picked up his machine gun.

'You up, Cripps?' the Bear asked over the intercom. He was lounging in the right front seat, fanning himself.

'Up, sir,' Cripps said.

'Okay. Think you can get us out of here at this weight, Cov?'

'That or die trying,' the copilot, Warrant Officer Covington, answered.

'Don' say that, sir!' This came from Sergeant Handy, the door gunner, who sat in the rear door, opposite Cripps, also cradling a machine gun.

'You know this isn't the strongest ship in the world, Handy,' Covington said. 'If you'd toss off a hundred pounds of that ammo, we might have a chance!'

'Hey, don't insult Cripps's ship,' the Bear said, looking

into the back with a grin. 'This is a good ship, right, Cripps?'

'I didn't say it wasn't a *good* ship,' Covington pointed out. 'I said it wasn't a *strong* ship. Old ninety-seven back there' – he motioned with his head back toward the second ship of the fire team – 'can get off the ground easy at this weight, no hotter than it is today, even with no wind at all; but *this* ship . . .'

'Give it a try,' said the Bear.

Covington made an elaborate show of settling himself at the controls. He simultaneously stretched out his legs, resting his heels on the floor with the balls of his feet just touching the pedals that controlled the tail rotor; took in his left hand – the 'power' hand – with an elaborate curl of his wrist the collective-pitch stick that angled up from the floor at the left side of his seat; and gently settled his right hand – the directional-control hand – against the grip of the cyclic-pitch stick, which rose from the floor between his knees. He paid particular attention to his right hand. His right forearm rested on his right leg. He flexed the fingers of that hand as if he were a pianist preparing to play. He took the grip of the cyclic delicately between the thumb and fingertips.

'Great style so far,' Bear said.

'I learned from a master.'

Twisting the motorcycle-style throttle on the grip of the collective stick, Covington brought the engine and blade speeds up to the bottom of the operating range, then nudged them up to flight speed by thumbing the governor button at the end of the collective stick.

He pulled up on the collective stick, at the same time pressing the left pedal to counteract the increased torque that would try to spin the ship around to the right as it came up off its skids. The skids slanted so that, at rest, the ship sat slightly nose down. As Covington pulled in pitch, the ship rocked slightly back and rested on the heels of the skids. It danced there, just touching the steel planking, ready to fly.

'You set?' Bear asked.

'I'm ready.'

The Bear was slouched back in his seat. He was preparing Covington to become an aircraft commander, and so he was not going to follow through on the controls, however heavy the ship was. He keyed the radio with the foot switch bedside the pedals: 'Two, are you ready?'

'We're ready,' came the answer from the second ship.

'Wolf Lead coming up.' Bear held out his left hand to Covington, thumb up.

Covington pulled the collective even higher, at the same time easing forward the cyclic, to keep the ship from skidding backward, and pressing the left pedal farther forward.

The ship rose straight up, maintaining its heading without a quiver. But it stopped a foot above the ground.

'She's not gonna do it,' Covington said. 'A foot's all she has in her.' As he had lifted the ship from the ground, the tachometer needles had sunk from their normal sixty-six hundred rpm to sixty-four hundred. For a normal takeoff the ship was supposed to hover at three feet above the ground; but the higher the hover, the more power required; and his engine had no more power to give.

Covington concentrated all his effort on holding the ship, trying to will it to rise higher. Sometimes, with Bear at the controls, he had thought that Bear's will alone was what made the ship perform. He willed the ship to go higher. But it went no higher.

'If you can get her to translational lift, she'll fly,' Bear suggested.

'And if cows had wings, they'd fly, too, Bear. But translational lift happens at eighteen knots, and we're standing still.' Translational lift was the sudden increase in lift that would occur when the airflow through the rotor rearranged itself, when the ship changed from a fast hover to flight.

'Maybe you could bump her off.'

'Maybe. Or maybe I could catch a skid shoe in the PSP

and turn the ship over.'

Pierced steel planking had a way of catching skid shoes in its perforations. Being snatched sideways was unpleasant in a ship carrying eight hundred pounds of jet fuel and six hundred pounds of ammunition and rockets.

'You want me to take it?' Bear asked this without looking at Covington.

'No.' Beads of sweat formed along the line of the helmet, above Covington's eyes. He could do nothing about those, but he flexed the fingers of his right hand to relax them, without disturbing the cyclic stick still resting lightly between thumb and forefinger.

He eased the cyclic forward - a half inch, no more.

The ship moved forward. As it moved, it descended, gliding off the cushion of air that helped support it at a hover. A heavy ship could sometimes be coaxed to translational lift by easing forward off the ground cushion, bouncing off the ramp, using the resulting altitude to get a little more airspeed, and so on in a series of bounces until she flew - or didn't fly.

In a ship less heavily loaded, Covington would have pulled up the collective, increasing the power to hold altitude, while simultaneously adding left pedal to counteract the increased torque. Today, the ship had nothing more to give. And so Covington held the collective steady, gave back the altitude, kept the ship pointed straight ahead. He did not even glance at the airspeed indicator. It would not register speeds this slow. If he got to translational lift, he would know it. If not . . . With a great grinding crunch, the ship hit the PSP and lurched to a halt.

'Way to go, Lead,' said the radio.

'Don't mind us,' the Bear answered. 'We'll figure this thing out yet.'

Covington looked at his aircraft commander in resignation. He was not embarrassed. He had given it a good try. The ship could not be got off. 'You want to take off some ammo?' he asked the Bear.

'How about if we pump out some fuel?' Sergeant Handy

suggested. Handy hated to give up any of his ammo.

'We can't spare the fuel,' Bear said. 'We'll be short of time on station as it is, even if the Mustangs aren't as late as usual.'

'*You* gonna try it, then sir?' Handy asked, addressing the Bear.

'Let Cov give it another try,' Bear said.

'Bear, this sucker is *not* going to fly at this weight!' Covington said. 'Not even for you!'

'Probably not. But what the hell . . . let's give it a try.' The Bear laid his hands and feet on the controls. 'I got it.'

'You got it.' Covington shrugged, and sat back to watch.

'Let's see if I can remember what old Tate showed me in flight school,' Bear said. He picked up the ship delicately but without hesitation, bringing it straight to a hover a foot and a few inches above the ground. He did not test the controls, did not bring them to one position and then ease them to a final setting. He moved them to a position, and there they stayed. He got no more power from the engine than Covington had, but the efficiency of his movements took the ship an inch or two higher than Covington had taken it.

He moved the cyclic forward, three-eighths of an inch exactly. At the same time he brought the collective up another eighth of an inch and added a sixteenth inch of left pedal. The ship bowed forward; the tachometer began to ease back down through the green arc – the blade was slowing because Bear was asking for more than the engine had to give. But the ship settled more slowly than it had for Covington. It gathered speed. It kissed the steel of the ramp, bumped into the air, settled again, but moving faster. The low-rpm warning pinged through the pilots' earphones.

'Better set her down, B,' Covington said, but the Bear held steady. The ship bounced again, rose again, moving still faster.

There was that sudden, wonderful, carnival-ride lurch to the pit of the stomach, and the ship began to climb.

The Bear felt the lift come in. The low-rpm warning was still pinging. He lowered the collective a fraction of an inch to let the blade start winding back up to operating speed while not giving back the altitude he had gotten. They needed five feet to clear the concertina wire surrounding the LZ: they had five feet, but nothing to spare. The ship flew with the jerky wallow of a bicycle ridden too slowly. He gave up a foot of altitude, outside the wire, to build up airspeed and rotor rpm. The controls smoothed out. The ship felt alive again. He eased back the cyclic. The nose came up, and they were climbing.

'Hoo ha!' said the Bear happily.

'You son of a bitch!' Covington said.

He said it with admiration.

Handy and Cripps lounged knowingly in the back.

Number zero nine seven, the stronger second ship of the fire team, lifted out of Baldy without fuss and slid into position a quarter mile behind the lead ship and an equal distance to the side. Its pilot called, 'Wolf Lead, two is up.'

'Roger, Two.' Bear turned to Covington. 'You ready to take us to the LZ?'

Covington got back on the controls. 'I've got it.'

'You've got it.'

With Covington flying, Bear leaned back in his seat and closed his eyes. He looked, to Covington glancing over at him, less like a bear than like a seal asleep on a beach. His mustache bristled as he unconsciously puffed out his upper lip. But Covington knew that the Bear was not asleep. He was concentrating on the feel of the ship, to see what was new in the way it flew.

The ship had the same shuffle-bump as always, resulting from a chronically out-of-track blade. Bear opened his eyes and studied the instruments. They showed one auxiliary fuel pump out, as usual. Everything else was operating. At length Bear took out a map from the case beside his seat. The map covered a hundred and fifty miles of the coast of South Vietnam, from Da Nang to Qui Nhon, with a breadth of fifty miles from the coast. Bear had pasted it up by hand from a dozen separate maps. It was much folded and marked with the notes of a hundred missions.

'Do you have the place in mind?' Bear asked Covington.

'Yup.'

'The slicks will be coming in from the south.' A slick was a helicopter without the external weapons of a gunship dragging in the wind – a 'slip ship.' Today the slicks would be carrying troops. 'Let's fly over the inbound track, and then check out that village to the north of the LZ. You know the one?'

'Yup.'

'What's it called?'

'Van Tay.'

'You're a good man, Cov.'

The name of the village didn't matter. The landing zone was specified by the map coordinates, and not one pilot in a hundred would show any interest in the name of the village a mile away. But Bear was pleased that Covington knew the name. It showed respect, to know the Vietnamese names for places. After all, it was their country.

'Someday I'll be able to fly this thing, besides remembering names,' Covington said.

'Mr Covington,' Handy said from the back, 'there ain't a pilot in the country who could of got this turkey off the ground back there, except for the Bear.'

'Hey, don't call Cripps's ship a turkey,' Bear grinned. 'Right, Cripps?'

'Yes, sir,' Cripps said.

As Covington flew, Bear tended to other business. He studied the ground for likely cover or concealment where Charley might have installed a weapon. He did not expect anything: after months of flying this area, he knew where trouble was to be found. It wasn't at Van Tay, or en route there. Division was even using the area as a training ground for brigades new in country, before those soldiers went on to harder stuff. But still Bear was cautious and tended to his business. Some pilots felt that the business of gunships was to kill people; but to Bear, his business was to keep his slicks from being fired upon. So he studied every paddy dike tall enough to hide a dug-in machine gun, every clump of palm trees, every peasant following a buffalo and plow.

Tending to business did not prevent the Bear from enjoying the ride, however. Bear loved flying; but, unlike many pilots, he also loved riding, as long as he was up front where he could get his hands on the controls in a hurry if things got hot. Like all pilots, he hated riding in back, where even the best pilot was only another piece of cargo – a 'pack,' as helicopter pilots referred to live freight. On a day like this one, though, even riding was a treat.

It had been a hot, dry day in the fuel pits at Baldy; but as they flew nearer the coast, a sea breeze rose from the northeast – a cool breeze promising rain, not today, but sometime in the future. The northeast monsoon – the wet monsoon on the Indochina coast – had been teasing for weeks, blowing up intermittent showers and then dying away in a series of Indian summer days in whose afternoons, the peaks of the Annamite chain dwindled away into the blue distance in the west, while to the east the South China Sea burned like a blue jewel clasped in the curve of silver beach. The land seemed to wait breathless for the seasons to rearrange themselves, for the breathing of the whole Asian continent to alter, to settle into the winter rhythm, that brought rain and life to the coastal plain east of the mountains, the plain which had parched while the highlands only fifty miles to the west had been inundated with the summer rains borne up from the Gulf of Thailand on the southwest wind.

Bear slid back the armor plate at his shoulder, the better to look out of the window of the ship. Because the ships were traveling, not hunting, Covington was flying at fifteen hundred feet, above the top of the Dead Man's Zone where small-arms fire was effective.

The plain was alive in the sunlight. On Route One long chains of trucks crept on the highway. Motorcycles dodged among them, scattering peasants on foot or on bicycles but giving wide berth to the water buffalo swinging their curved horns on the margins of the road. On both sides of the highway the plain was subdivided into irregular paddies separated by low narrow dikes. All but a few of the paddies were dry now, awaiting the coming monsoon, their soil red as though rusted from disuse. Some paddies were tiny, no more than a few square meters in size; some stretched for half a mile and would have held a thousand helicopters.

The plain was not a patchwork of squares and rectangles, as it would have been in a younger land. Instead the paddies grew in rings and swirls, starting from small villages, from single farm-houses, or even from nothing at all. From the air they seemed to be cross sections of living creatures that had spontaneously burst into life and added layer on layer of flesh until their growth was checked by collision with a growing neighbor. These cellular patterns fitted into one another in complex mazes that took up the whole of the plain between Route One and the sea, except where they eddied around the shoulders of isolated rolling pastures, or where ragged clusters of palm trees marked a village.

The landing zone for the mission was a broad open paddy on the south side of a low rise. The rise was topped by a pasture holding a few scraggly cattle. At the very top was an old graveyard with narrow vertical Buddhist gravestones crowding among more ancient round stone tombs. North of the rise the palm tops of Van Tay stretched in an arc three-eighths of a mile long and a hundred yards wide.

The mission briefing had been for the slicks to land north, to drop their troops, and to turn east coming out of the LZ so as to avoid flying over the village. There was plenty of room for the maneuver. Nevertheless, Bear waved Covington on toward the village. 'Let's do a high recon. Villages make me nervous.'

They flew the length of the village from west to east and back. There appeared to be no reason for nerves. There were the usual numbers of people, chickens, pigs, and dogs. Covington swung out over the paddies to the north. They were dry and empty except for one where a man was plowing behind a water buffalo. A tenuous trail of red dust followed him across the field, drifting slowly southward on the light breeze.

As Covington turned back south, Bear took the controls again. 'Let's have a closer look at the village. I've got it.'

The two gunships came down in a long, curving dive that ended ten feet above the treetops at the east end of the village. The boom of their blades sent pigs scuttling and chickens flapping wildly. A woman turned, startled, to stare at them, clasping her broad conical straw hat to her head as the two children behind her grinned and waved at the ships. Bear rocked the ship to them and grinned back. He wrenched the ship into a hard right turn and, at a hundred and forty knots, rocketed westward the length of the village. As he passed the far boundary ditch, he pulled the cyclic stick back to cash in his speed for altitude in a steep climb that took him back to fifteen hundred feet. There he nosed the ship forward again, pulling in power to get back speed without losing altitude. Satisfied, he rolled out on a southerly heading to set up and await the slicks. 'If there's a weapon here,' said Bear, 'I'll eat it on television.'

'There could be anythin' in that village,' Handy said hopefully. 'You could hide a elephant in there.'

'Sure, Handy,' Bear answered. 'But who'd pull his trigger?'

Bear's laugh was a cackle which shook his belly and lit up his face. In the helicopter it could only be seen and not heard above the din of the machine itself, all flapping blades and screaming engine and whining gears; and even the shaking belly was covered by the ceramic armor plate strapped to his chest; but the mere idea of Bear's laugh, as much as the joke itself, sent Coverington and Cripps into unheard laughter, until Bear finally grumbled, 'Listen, why am I doing all the work here, anyway? Fly this thing, Cov.'

Still laughing, Covington got promptly on the controls and went through the change-of-control ritual: 'You got it?' 'I have it.'

Bear relaxed in his seat. 'Anyway, Handy,' he said, careful of Handy's feelings, 'Captain Martin said he flew cover for two sweeps through here this week already, with the new brigade. Nobody's taken fire out of this place yet.'

'We're flyin' cover for the Mustangs, don't forget, sir,' Handy said. 'They take fire from anyplace.'

'Don't remind me,' Bear said tiredly. 'Those assholes would claim they were taking fire on short final for the officers' club. And they're worst of all when Baker's leading them.' Captain Baker was a platoon leader in the helicopter company – a sister company to Bear's own – whose slicks had the call sign 'Mustang'. 'But I'll guarantee you they won't get any fire out of *this* LZ.'

At Bear's direction Covington set up a pattern to the west of the LZ itself, flying an elongated figure eight north and south so that the gunships were never turned completely away from the landing zone. With the second ship lagging a half mile back now, one of the two was always inbound. They paralleled the flight path the slicks would be slow, easy targets for any nearby weapon. But it would take a brave gunner to open fire with two gunships on station. As his ship turned inbound at one end of the figure eight, Bear studied the number two ship coming toward him. It flew nose-down like a tracking hound. Weapons hung heavy from its sides: on each flank a six-barreled machine gun on a flex mount, and below it seven rocket tubes in a bundle. Above these main weapons, in each door a crewman harnessed to the ship on a strap carried a machine gun, the crew chief at one door and the gunner at the other.

'Wolf Lead,' the radio said, 'this is Mustang Lead.' Bear knew Baker's voice.

'Go, Mustang.'

'Wolf, Mustang Lead with a flight of ten is, oh, three minutes out. How's the LZ?'

'Roger three minutes out. The LZ is cold.'

Mustang made no response.

They flew the northbound leg of the figure eight again, and when Covington rolled out, the slicks were there below them.

To the Bear there was nothing so beautiful as a formation landing of helicopters – not only for the physical beauty of the formation's geometric order, but for the determination and purpose they showed, driving downward into whatever might lie ahead. He had felt it in the first company formation he participated in back in flight school, which seemed ages past. He felt it again, seeing the Mustangs cross below him, even though this was only a routine lift into a cold LZ.

There were ten slicks, flying V's of three in trail, with the tenth ship in the slot at the rear. They were in tight, so that the lead ship of each V slotted into the opening of the V ahead, making three perfectly linked diamonds. A slick driver was known by how closely he could hold a formation on a combat assault, and like every pilot in Vietnam, these intended to be the best. The main blades were slicing not five feet from the tail rotors ahead, even though the slightest touch between blades would surely knock one ship, and probably both, from the sky – if not half the formation with them.

There was no need for them to be so close: the landing zone would have held ten times their number. They could have flown fifty yards apart, and in safety.

And yet, because they were close, they were a beautiful sight, those ten ships driving down as one. The diamonds glistened, as the sun caught the rotor blades, like the pattern on a snake's back.

The diamonds wavered as the ships flared a hundred feet above the ground to bleed off speed for their landing. The noses of the ships came up: the whole formation shivered, seemed about to disintegrate, then consolidated again as the pilots adjusted. Bear could see door gunners and crew chiefs leaning out the open side doors, scanning the paddy for any sign of enemy fire.

As the ships reached fifteen feet above the ground, dust began to lick beneath the formation. The first wisps grew to a rolling cloud that enveloped the ships as they touched down. Troops were jumping from the doors.

This was the hard part, Bear knew. The slicks had to get on the ground, get the troops off, and lift out again before their self-created dust storm became so intense that the pilots could not see the other ships. The pilots were pulling pitch now: the red cloud of dust rolled around the rear half of the formation in dense vertical curls. Blades flashed through it, then became suddenly clear again as the ships burst up into clean air.

'They're up, Two,' Bear said over the gunship radio channel to his second ship. Two answered with two clicks of his microphone switch, to show he had heard.

'Follow them when they turn east,' Bear said to Covington. But the slicks did not turn east. They continued straight toward the village. '*Now* what the hell?' Bear muttered.

'Hey, they're putting down fire!' the voice was Sergeant Handy's.

The door gun of the ship on the right side of the first V was firing on the village. Tracer rounds arced down from it in short bursts, like tossed baskets of coals. Other ships began firing, by ones and twos, until within seconds the guns of half the formation were in action.

Bear was on the controls instantly and broke toward the village while Covington pulled down the flex-gun sight from its stowage clip above the windscreen. 'Mustang,' Bear called urgently, 'where's your fire?'

Baker's voice came back: 'Mustang's taking fire from the village. Request you suppress.'

'Why is the horse's ass over the village?' Bear said over the intercom. Over the radio, he said, 'Where's the source of the fire, Mustang?'

'Right out of this village!'

'Where in the village?' Bear asked.

No answer came back.

'I don't see a thing,' Covington said. Bear had turned to fly along the south side of the village, to avoid drawing fire in the direction of the slicks.

'Two, do you have anything?' Bear asked over the gunship channel.

'Negative,' came two's answer.

The ground troops Mustang had just inserted certainly were taking no fire: they had stopped and were standing in the paddy watching the show.

Bear was not about to fire at random into an inhabited village. 'We haven't located the source of your fire, Mustang,' he called.

'Well, shit, it's from that village!' Baker responded. 'Hose the whole place down, dammit!'

'Screw you and the horse you came in on!'

If radio silence could be shocked, the silence that followed was. It was broken after some seconds: 'What did you say?'

'I say again,' Bear repeated, 'screw you *and* the horse you came in on. Sir.'

'Wolf Lead, I'm in command of this mission, and I'm ordering you to suppress that fire!'

'And I'm saying I don't see any fire to suppress. Are you ordering me to fire at random on the village, sir?'

When Baker finally replied, his voice was shaking: 'I'm ordering you to suppress enemy fire that my flight is taking!'

'Request again you identify the source of the fire,' Bear said instantly.

By this time the flight was out of range of the village, and the slick's machine gunners had all given up. When the reply came, it was: 'Wolf Lead, I'll see you in the pits at Baldy.'

'Roger that,' Bear said.

Bear flew low over the village. There was nothing to be seen but palm trees and thatched roofs. Even the pigs and chickens were out of sight. But at least there were no bodies. Bear ranged out to the north. The farmer plowing behind his water buffalo had not even looked up as the slicks roared low over him, their machine guns firing; and he did not look up now. That was not unusual, either. For an unarmed peasant, safety was in not noticing.

Bear wished bitterly that he could land, could enter the village, and see what had happened there. *Had* there been a weapon? It certainly wasn't impossible: plenty of colder LZs than this one had suddenly turned hot. And pilots didn't always know from where they were being shot at. But Bear didn't believe it. None of the signs were there. It hadn't escaped Bear's notice that half of the slicks in the formation had not fired. Someone in the formation should have been able to tell Baker, if he didn't know himself, what they were shooting at. The troops on the ground should have shown some reaction. And Baker shouldn't have tried to weasel out of an order, if it was legitimate.

More important than the weapon, or lack of it, Bear wondered who had been hurt. Probably he would never know. The troops on the ground, when they swept the village, might learn there had been casualties, or might not. Either way the word would almost certainly never get back to the pilots of the gunships.

The Mustang slicks had already refueled by the time Bear's fire team made its approach to Baldy, but Mustang Lead was still there, his ship tied down at one side of the fuel pits.

Bear did not report to that ship; he led his flight directly to the fuel pumps and left the ship running as Cripps refueled it.

Mustang Lead, Captain Baker, came to the Bear.

He was a lean, stoop-shouldered senior captain with a Vietnam mustache and fire in his eyes. He stepped up on the gunship's skid at Bear's door and motioned for Bear to remove his helmet. Bear did so.

'I'm going to have your ass, mister,' Baker said. 'And that's not a threat: that's a promise!'

'You know what you can do with my ass.'

This was not exactly what Baker had expected from a junior warrant officer, and he stepped back and, in doing so, nearly fell from the skid. He sputtered as he tried to find words for his rage.

'Careful, sir,' Bear said solicitously. 'You might hyperventilate.'

Baker stood back in astonished rage. Fists clenched, he appeared to be considering inviting the Bear to step outside: but if he was, he thought better of it. At last he merely pointed a shaking finger at Bear. 'Your CO is going to hear about this, mister!'

Even over the noise of the helicopter Bear imagined he could hear the steel planking ring under Baker's boots as he stalked away.

'Do you think that was a good idea, B?' Covington asked after Bear had put his helmet back on. Handy and Cripps were wide-eyed.

'Probably not,' Bear said. 'Who the hell cares?' He had been cool enough in his insubordination. Now he pounded the cyclic stick in rage and frustration. 'Let's get the hell out of here.' He pulled pitch and whirled out of the pits, not even calling to ask two if he was ready to depart.

What the Bear felt was often written on his face; but Covington could not at the moment interpret what he saw there. It was a striking face, though far from handsome, a broad face with heavy brows, a bristling wide mustache, and rolling, wild eyes which, together with the stout frame and muscular shoulders, had led Lieutenant Arp, their section leader, to give Bear his nickname. Bear could be morose, as Covington had just seen, and then he had a cutting tongue; but he was subject to fits of uncontrollable good humor. When he was in a happier mood his face was likely to creep through a range of animal imitations: he could look like any sort of beast, real or imaginary. Even at rest his face, with its bulging eyes and mustache bristling, had a walruslike expression. But now it had a disdainful look, as if the walrus had tasted a bad clam.

It took a long time for Bear's number two ship to catch up coming out of Baldy. Bear climbed out toward the seashore before turning south toward the company's home ramp at Ky Ha. He passed through a thousand feet, through fifteen hundred, and kept on climbing. The ships crossed the beach at three thousand feet and swung south, but still they climbed, higher and higher into the glassy air, until the beach narrowed to a thread below them, while to the west unsuspected mountains rose behind the coast ranges, muscular giants thrust from the silent forest. Among them slender wavering threads of smoke arose at wide intervals. Over a thirty-mile radius a dozen such columns were to be seen. Villagers near the farthest smoke might never have seen the sand and the sea above which the helicopters flew with such remote ease. Over that precipitous land it was a month's walk to cross the distance that, from the Bear's ship, was contained in a glance. But the smoke did not rise from any of the villages which dotted the maps of that area, small clusters of huts that flashed startlingly into view from low above the trees and vanished instantly. The mysterious whispers of smoke rose from unbroken green forest where even maps were silent. They were aloof utterances of unknown men proclaiming only, but beyond mistake, 'We are here,' or 'Here we have been.'

Bear had climbed the ship with his eyes fixed on the land, studying the mountains that were on most days hidden by rain or a blue humidity haze, but which today sparkled as though new-minted for him to see. But wherever he looked there was smoke, there was distant burning, and no knowing if it were friend or foe.

But it was the sight that met his eyes when he turned from the land that tore a gasp from him. There on the left, the inverse of the ghostly smoke rising from the solid earth on the other side - like the reflection of a material universe in some fourth dimension, firmament rising from the emptiness where sea paled into sky without ever becoming horizon - an island hung, a rock in the void, a dream of peace removed from the burning land.

Its name was Cu Lao Re, and it was real. Though it was on his map, he had never seen it before, for haze and the distractions of war hid it on all but the rarest clear days. He was a mile above its highest peak, but it seemed to hang at his own level, for there was no horizon against which to place it. The sea, so fiercely blue below, paled in the distance to silver even as the blue sky overhead paled as the eye left the zenith, so that there was no meeting at all, no line of demarcation between the two, but an intermingling of sea and sky, of being and not-being, and in that space hung Cu Lao Re, the rock in the void, shimmering.

He felt a sudden dizziness, for his eye, bereft of the customary marks of up and down, high and low, led his brain into confusion. He had felt vertigo before. He knew – something of the pilot in him knew – he must tear himself away, seek a reference on which to orient himself. But he did not. He stared at the apparition, enchanted.

The voice on the radio brought him back. 'Lead, if we're going to San Francisco, we could use some fuel first.' His eyes snapped down to the gyro horizon on the instrument panel: the ship was in a left bank and turning out to sea.

Five thousand miles away, somewhere in the void in which the island hung, lay the continent of North America, with nothing between but the curve of the sea.

Bear turned his ship back down the line of the beach. He did so with a sigh which could not possibly be heard above the thousand noises of the aircraft; but he thought Covington looked at him strangely.

2

'Well, Martin,' Captain Blood asked as they left the hospital, 'what's your date of rank?'

'February,' Martin said.

'This year?'

'Yes.'

They climbed into the gun platoon three-quarter-ton truck. Martin had driven down to the hospital direct from the gunship ramp the minute he landed.

'What day?' Blood asked.

'What?'

'Your date of rank – what day?'

'I don't remember. Who cares?'

The truck ground and protested up the steep red-clay road. The road was dusty now, though rutted from past rain.

'What d'you think about Carlsen's hand?' Blood asked, bracing his own hand against the windshied frame to keep himself from being thrown against the roof.

'Couldn't tell much under all that bandage. I don't think he'll lose it, will he? You were there before I was. Did the doctors say anything?'

'Not to me. It don't matter if he doesn't lose it, though – he won't be back here, anyway. Carlsen is *short* in this country.'

'It might matter to him,' Martin said.

'Is it before the thirteenth?' Blood asked.

'What?'

'That's my date of rank – the thirteenth. Yours before

that?'

'Christ, I don't know! What difference does it make?'

'Every Ringknocker knows his date of rank, Martin,' Blood answered with a satisfied grin. 'You can't shit an old trooper.' His fingers, curled over the top of the window-frame, drummed slowly on the taut canvas roof.

Lieutenant Arp put down his tray on the mess-hall table and lowered himself into his chair, cautiously, with a simultaneous downward motion of his left hand like that made in lowering the collective-pitch stick of a helicopter to put the machine on the ground.

'A little rough,' observed Warrant Officer Carter, who was sitting across the table, 'but not a bad landing for a gunnie. Given some time and practice, you could do something with it.'

'The aviator's art,' Arp replied, 'is in *flying* the machine, not sticking it into the ground.'

'I'll remember that next time I try to get eight packs into that hole they call a helipad up at Three MAF. I'll fly over and boot them out at treetop level. "Sorry, guys," I'll tell them. "The aviator's art is in *flying* the machine. But you're capable folks – you figure out the rest." They'll like it.'

Arp agreed enthusiastically: 'Yes, by God, spoken like a true lord of the air! The earth is too lowly for the likes of us. Avoid it! Avoid it!' He turned to Warrant Officer Carlisle seated between them at the end of the table. 'Apparently Cap'n John didn't avoid it far enough, Hitch. What hit him?'

Carlisle had been copilot in Captain Carlsen's ship when the bullet came through: through the door, through the cyclic stick, and through the middle of Carlsen's right hand.

'Hitch did the Blood a favor,' Carter said.

'I didn't know they were such great friends.'

'About as close to being friends as Carter is to being funny,' Carlisle said. Unconsciously he passed a hand over his bare scalp that glistened under the mess-hall lights. At age twenty Carlisle was nearly bald, and, resigned to this, he shaved short what little hair he had left. For a while after he had joined the company he had been called Chrome, but Arp had given him the cognomen Trailer Hitch, now generally shortened to Hitch or T H.

'Hitch put Captain John in front of a bullet,' Carter said to Arp, 'and now the Blood will be executive officer.'

'God forbid!' The voice came from someone at the next table. Arp crossed himself and rolled his eyes theatrically ceilingward.

'God Himself couldn't keep Blood from grabbing for that job!' Carter insisted. 'There's nothing to do but grin and bear it.'

'Grin and bare his ass for kissing,' Carlisle muttered.

Sensing some tenderness in Carlisle, Arp asked more gently, 'How is Cap'n John, Peter?'

'Fair, considering that he's missing the middle of his right hand,' Carlisle said without looking up from his coffee. It was not his favorite drink, but it gave him somewhere to keep his eyes.

'Jesus, it's not *your* fault, Hitch!' Carter insisted in quiet exasperation. 'You weren't even flying the ship; and if you had been, you couldn't have done anything. If a bullet comes through where someone's sitting, he's going to get it! There's nothing you can do about it.'

'Not unless your prayers are more combat effective than mine,' Arp agreed. 'The trouble with Carlisle,' he said to Carter, 'is that he doesn't see enough gore, being a slick driver. He hasn't had a chance to get used to it. We should send him out with the Bear a few times.'

'I've seen enough blood,' Carlisle said evenly. 'I've brought in three dinged aircraft commanders in two months, and two were evacuated to Japan.'

'Why, T H, that's not *blood*!' Arp said. 'I've *killed* more men than that in one pass! The Bear kills more men than that every morning before breakfast!' Although Arp pretended not to notice, the subject of this compliment had come through the mess line and was standing behind him.

'Not *our* men,' Carlisle said.

'Well, not on his better days,' Arp admitted. 'There's no telling what he'll do when the ravenous mood is on him, though. Oh, *hel*lo, Bear!' He gave a friendly pat to the Bear's belly as the Bear pushed past him. 'Eat well. Keep the old fires stoked. Keep the blood lust burning.'

'If Hitch wants to see some blood,' the Bear said, 'he should fly with the Mustangs.'

'You et 'em up today, eh, Killer?'

'We didn't. But it wasn't for lack of readiness on their part.'

'Again? What was their excuse this time?'

'When did they start needing excuses? Sir, Captain Martin's got to stop sending me out with those bastards!'

'Darn it, Bear, you're going to spoil all my efforts in building up your reputation! Who's going to believe you eat babies for breakfast when you come in complaining like this? What have the Mustangs been up to now?'

'It doesn't take a genius to guess that one,' Carter put in. 'If you have three companies flying an assault in the same landing zone, the Mustangs will be the only ones to take fire. Every damn time. So then they proceed to shoot up the surrounding countryside. Right. Bear?'

'There was this village over the hill from the LZ,' the Bear said by way of answer. 'On the way out one slick opened fire on it, and everybody followed. I didn't see anyone hit on the ground; but I didn't see any unfriendly fire, either. Mustang Lead asked me to suppress.'

'And you said?'

Covington, who had come up behind the Bear, answered for him. 'He said, "Screw you and the horse you came in on. Sir."'

'I told him there wasn't anything to suppress,' Bear said.

'In your words, or Covington's?'

'You know how my memory is,' the Bear said. 'But I think there was a horse mentioned at some point.'

'Oh, the old man's going to love you today,' Arp said

with a grin. 'You do such a job of coordination with our sister companies.'

'I already told Major Hart,' Bear said.

'And *he* said?'

Carter interrupted, '*He* said, "That's easy enough to figure out. Whatever you think is right, Don." Major Hart is okay.'

'Someone's been tampering with Carter's rheostat again,' Bear said. His eye scattered the accusation generally over the gathering. 'You're a lot brighter than the average warrant officer, Carter.'

'That's why you get sent out with the Mustangs,' Arp told him. 'Somebody's got to keep the wild beast in line. To listen to your sob stories,' he added, but still grinning, 'a body wouldn't realize you were the most efficient killer since Typhoid Mary.'

'That's all right, too,' Bear answered, following Covington to an empty table.

Captain Blood would have given much to be known as the most deadly killer in the division. He could not envy the Bear: it was beneath the dignity of a commissioned officer to envy a warrant officer. But he knew that, given the chance, he could distinguish himself beyond anything done by the Bear. Blood yearned desperately for the chance to command the gun platoon and show what he could do. When he had arrived in the country five months earlier, the gun platoon had been under the command of a well-established officer, Captain Stoddard, and Blood had been given an airlift platoon. He took no satisfaction in commanding slicks. If the platoon was making combat assaults it might have been different, but this company's slicks were flying mostly administrative flights and 'ash and trash' – resupply and other once-around-the-park things that brought no medals to the man in charge. Blood's ships helped with other companies' combat assaults but flew none of their own. His leadership talents were water on desert sand, or so he told himself. The Bear's nonsense jingle ran in his head despite his distaste for the author: 'Kill 'em dead'll win a medal.' But Blood killed no one, and the Bear, a fat nobody who spent his free time chattering at the hooch-maids in what Blood doubted was Vietnamese, had two Distinguished Flying Crosses, while Captain Blood had none. So Blood watched the gun platoon commander like a hawk, and visited Major Hart regularly with recommendations for tactics, for operational improvements, for ways to improve the company's figures on hours flown, passengers carried, enemy killed. He laid snares for Glory, but always she continued to elude him.

'What do you s'pose Captain Blood is after today?' the company clerk asked, staring out the screened window of the orderly room.

The first sergeant looked up from the weapon he was cleaning, a Chinese-made AK-47 assault rifle that one of the flight crews had brought in. He snorted at the clerk. 'Now, I just don't know why the Blood would be comin' to see the old man on the very same day Captain Carlsen got his ticket back to the world. When Captain Stoddard got his orders, it took a whole day for Blood to get over here and work on getting command of the gun platoon. Either he's ahead of schedule, or he's making a social call. I leave it to you.'

'I guess he's more desperate than he used to be,' the clerk said.

Blood came through the door talking. 'Hello, First Sergeant. Where'd you get the weapon?' Without waiting for an answer he took it from the desk. He would have given it a proper, squared-off military inspection, but he had trouble opening the bolt. As he fumbled, he asked, 'Is it Chinese, or East European? The NVA get weapons from both places, you know.' Blood had an answer for every unasked question on things military. He did not always waste them on noncoms, but Major Hart's feet were visible below the plywood screen separating his small office from the orderly room proper. As he continued to examine the weapon critically, Blood asked in an offhand manner, 'Say, is the major in? Ow! Shee-it!' The bolt had slammed shut on his thumb.

'Yes, sir, he sure is, sir. Just go right on back. I think it's Chinese, sir,' the first sergeant added as he took the weapon back. 'It's got all these little chicken-scratches here on the barrel, you see . . .'

Captain Blood departed sucking his thumb.

'Del, it's a sad day.' Major Hart waved off Blood's salute and pointed to the chair beside the desk. 'We lost a good man. Thank you for going up to see him. I just called the hospital, and he's resting now; but I'll get up there later this evening. Maybe you could get a few of his things together: we don't know if he'll be evacuated yet, I understand.'

'Anything I can do to help, sir. Let's hope he won't go; but he don't look good. But you know how those Minnesota Swedes are. They'll get him to Japan, get some of that cold air on the wound, and it'll fix him right up. Not like us southern boys. Me, I'd do better staying right here in the heat – and in the hot of it.'

'You think he'll be evacuated, then?'

'Well, he was lookin' a mite peaked, sir, as my momma used to say.'

The major rubbed his short-cropped silver hair and pursed his lips in silence.

'Of course,' Blood offered, 'if it looks like they'll only send him to Qui Nhon, say, and he'll be comin' back to the company, why, I can come over and get out his paperwork anyway. Say, wouldn't that be great, if he *could* come back? Of course, it takes a while, after a fifty goes through your hand, before you're up to snuff . . .'

'It's kind of you to offer, Del. There'll be time enough to think about what to do, once we're sure what's happening.'

'We can't reckon on getting another XO in from outside,' Blood supposed, with regret in his words and hope in his heart, 'the way replacements have been running. The ol' pipeline has just about dried up, it appears to me, ever since the company got switched out of the Aviation Group and into Division. Twenty pilots came in last week, but *they* all went to other units.'

'There's a lot in what you say, Del,' the major admitted. 'I expect we'll have to move somebody up. Tighten up the belts down below.'

'It's a shame, but I reckon it's true, sir. Well, as I say, if there's anything I can do . . .'

'Believe me, Del,' Major Hart said, 'you'll be the first to know.'

Captain Blood was whistling as he walked to the mess hall.

As he strolled with Covington across the parking ramp, evil muttering creatures appeared and disappeared on the Bear's face. He was reliving the afternoon's emotions, Covington knew. 'Thank God for a night off,' Covington said, hoping by pleasant anticipation to break his friend free from unpleasant memories. After four days on standby alert, awaiting the call from Division that would send them to anyone needing gunship help, for one night at least they could walk to their own hooch, air out their sweaty sleeping bags, get their clothes off, and sleep in their own beds, without having to tune one ear for the scramble horn.

'Praise Him,' Bear agreed fervently. Covington smiled presently to see by the Bear's face that his storm-wracked thoughts had sailed into calmer waters.

Covington took off his cap and let the wind blow through his hair. In the middle of the ramp he stopped. 'Tell me something, Bear,' he said, 'what were you thinking about, when you turned out . . . toward the island?'

'That wasn't me,' Bear answered. 'It was the prisoner in me, trying to escape.'

'No dramatics, Bear. You were thinking how close we were to home, weren't you?'

'No. I absolutely wasn't. Or hardly any at all.'

'I was. Home never seemed so close as right then, Bear. I was just thinking how to tell Pinky about it.' He added after a moment, 'There's nothing between here and home. Did you ever think about that? You could walk right down the beach and swim away, and walk up the other side in California.'

'Nothing but the curve of the sea,' Bear said. 'And that's nothing at all.'

'Nothing at all. I think I'm going to be homesick tonight, Bear. I almost wish I hadn't seen it.'

'Those who fly too high get their feathers burned.' He tried on the face of Icarus falling. All the way down he was thinking how different their impressions had been of their one transcendent flight: he and Daedalus.

Covington laughed at the face. He thought Bear was being a lobster.

The laugh was a cold plunge into the sea. 'You're lucky to have Pinky to be homesick for, Cov,' Bear said. 'I hope I get a chance to meet her someday.'

'Ah, she'll love you, Bear. When we get back to the world, you and I, you're going to come stay with us, and get a chance to know her.'

'And she will introduce me to her equally delightful, stunningly beautiful, sexually incontinent friends . . .'

'No, nothing like that. I want her to have a good opinion of you.'

'Well, Cov, any wife who would send her husband's company a subscription to *Playboy* can't be *all* prudish.'

'She's not prudish. She's . . . well, shoot.' Covington thrust his hands in his pockets and walked on in sudden, real, despairing homesickness for his distant wife.

The Bear, ambling beside him in rueful helplessness, could think of nothing to ease his friend, and as a consequence was left to rake the embers of his afternoon's anger against the cool bank of the vision they had seen together, if not shared.

Captain Martin smiled at the sight of the two coming toward him. Covington, slender twig of a youth, feeding his straggly boy's mustache on serious thoughts and lover's yearnings; and the Bear, muscular but clumsy-looking, with his jigging walk like a fish fighting the line. He could not imagine how such a pair came to be soldiers, but soldiers they were. The Bear, this wide-eyed monster, filled a commissioned officer's position as acting gun section leader, and filled it as well as any man could.

The Bear, as he again raked over the afternoon's events, had begun to glower and gnaw the ends of his mustache. 'What's the matter, Bear?' Martin asked, wanting to laugh at the procession of expressions across the Bear's face but successfully avoiding it. 'Your after-action report says you drew a blank today. Is that it?'

'*We* drew a blank,' Bear admitted. 'No KIAs, no rounds expended. I wish I could say the same for our hosts, the horses' rears. But they're such rotten shots, they didn't kill anyone that I noticed.' He added, as an afterthought of no importance, 'I told that Captain Baker of theirs what I thought about it all. He didn't like my opinion.'

Martin's face became serious. While he shared the Bear's opinion of the Mustangs' tactics, he could see only trouble from bringing it up directly. 'And it was such a nice day, too.' He sighed. 'Okay. I'll let the old man know after I have some chow.'

'I did that, sir.'

'Major Hart was in Operations when we came in, sir,' Covington said with a shrug. 'He asked how we did, so we told him.'

'Okay. Okay.'

Bear saw that Martin was displeased. He said hotly, 'Shooting up villages won't win any hearts and minds, sir.'

'You don't need to tell me that, Bear. But we're supposed to be protecting *our* people, too. That's what you were sent along for.'

'I always thought we've done a fair job of that, when there's anything to protect them from!'

'Yes. You have, Don. I can't complain about that. Well, I'd better check with Major Hart anyway.'

Martin knew well that Covington and the Bear sometimes embroidered their tales of one another's adventures; but this all had the ring of truth about it. 'Just go away and let me handle this,' he suggested. 'If there's any more, I don't want to know. It's hard to fabricate a good story when you're bound by a lot of facts.'

Although a damp wind had come up, the evening pleased Blood mightily. He sat on the deck of the officers' club with his feet up on the rail, listening to the sergeant of the guard post the sentry in the bunker twenty meters below his feet. He could not hear the words, but the voices pleased him for their timeless exchange of confidence in duty, for their promise of peace in the night. There came the rapid rattle of a field phone being tested in the bunker. Then the sergeant and his little skein of guards passed on down the perimeter. Down the hill, beyond the double-apron fence that stretched along the military crest of the hill, beyond the ancient graveyard with its circular tombs like military earthworks, the lights of a village flickered in and out of sight as the wind moved the palm leaves. They came and went in silence like fireflies on Alabama nights. Beyond them lay the dark waters of the bay whose name Blood had never learned. Beyond that, Route One ran in the darkness up the narrow plain between the mountains and the sea. Both the island in the bay and the shore along the highway were heavily populated, but they were dark at night.

'*Cô*, where the hell is my drink?' Blood called even though he saw that the girl was bringing it. If he had not called, she would have been even slower. Even beautiful Vietnamese annoyed him, and this one was not especially pretty. She arrived with a rustle of her white *áo dài*, complaining querulously, 'I come *beaucoup* fast. Too many officer here. Carry *beaucoup* drink, get *tí-tí* money.'

'*Cô* needs *tí-tí* boot up her ass to make her move faster,' Blood said scornfully. But he dropped a half-dollar tip . . . an undersize orange paper military scrip half-dollar . . . on her tray. It was more than the drink cost, but he enjoyed overtipping the girl. 'You no forget to change that before you go home, you hear?' He knew that if she could get off the post without changing it into piasters, she would.

He sipped at his Scotch and soda. He preferred gin, but he had not ordered that since a general's aide told him it was a plebeian drink.

As she returned to the bar, the girl nearly ran into Captain Baker, who had dismounted unsteadily from his barstool and was coming toward Blood's table.

Blood had known Baker slightly for years, as a result of their serving together on several posts without ever being in the same unit. He remembered Baker chiefly as a fixture in the officers' club bars. Blood had been careful never to be associated with club bar fixtures; but he was feeling expansive this fine evening. He waved Baker to a chair.

'That cunt will be buying grenades to roll under your bunk with that money, Blood.' The years had not improved Baker, Blood noted with satisfaction. Blood was always most comfortable where he felt superior.

'She loves my ass, Baker. Just be firm with 'em, that's the secret with women. But you wouldn't know anything about that, would you? What are you up to – out seeing how the upper class lives?'

'Out trying to find out what makes this outfit you fly for so fucked up. I'll let you know, if I ever find out.'

'After flying with the Mustangs as long as you have, Baker, doesn't fucked up just look normal to you?'

'At least we don't send out a gun escort just to fly around at a safe distance and let the other people take the fire.'

'I didn't know that was SOP anywhere,' Blood answered blandly, 'although I can see where somebody might reasonably not want to risk his rear on a bunch of Mustangs.'

'I'm beginning to think it's SOP in that rinky-dink outfit you poeple call an assault helicopter company,' Baker returned scornfully. 'You've been flying generals around so much, you get nervous if you have to do more than run up and down the coast delivering letters.'

The indignation in Baker's voice departed so far from ordinary intercompany insults that Blood concluded he was serious. 'You really had trouble with our gunnies today?' he asked with sudden officiousness.

'I don't know why you call them gunnies. They didn't do much gunning as far as I could tell. That bug-eyed turd you people sent out with a fire team just stood off and bitched that we were goin' to hurt somebody! Who are we fighting this war for, anyway?'

'Baker, I'll report this to Major Hart, sure as hell.' Blood took a notebook and pencil from his jacket pocket to reinforce the promise. The commanding general at his first post had demanded that all officers carry notebook and pencil at all times to write down whatever flashes of genius might strike them, and he had been known to stop young officers on the street and demand that these implements be produced for inspection. Blood had carried them ever since.

'Your Major Hart already knows about it,' Baker told him. 'I reported it the minute we got in, and the old man called Major Hart while I was in the office.'

'What time was that?'

'I don't know – seventeen hundred maybe. Know what your major said? He said he'd talk to the men involved to find out what the deal was. As if he couldn't take my word for it! Christ, Blood, if any of our pilots tried a stunt like that, our old man would have 'em up for a general court before they could get their blades tied down!'

'Major Hart's had some other things to think about today,' Blood said uneasily. He had seen Major Hart since seventeen hundred hours. As the new executive officer he ought to have been informed. But of course it wasn't certain yet that Carlsen would go – or at least Major Hart wasn't certain of it. 'He might have put it aside for now because he was worried about other things. Our XO got shot up today, and things are kind of crazy.'

'Who's that, Carlsen? Stopped a round, did he? Well, you can't make an omelet without breaking some eggs.'

'Not quite *stopped* – it went through his hand. They'll evac him out of country. The docs haven't said so, but I was over to see him, and he won't be using that tater-hook for much.

The old man was going up to see him – I reckon that's kept his mind off of other things.' Blood could not forbear adding, 'You'll see some action on this gunnie thing tomorrow, I promise you. I'll remind the old man. A little push from the XO can't hurt.'

'I thought Carlsen was being shipped out?'

'There'll always be another XO, Baker,' Blood said.

His significant tone slowly penetrated Baker's mind. 'And you're it, eh? Well, Blood, Christ, congratulations! Your very own company, almost, eh? Won't the shit fly now?'

'Won't it?' Blood laughed. Baker had a proper understanding of his abilities. He offered to buy Baker a drink. 'O' course,' he added, 'it's not official yet. The orders can't be cut until Carlsen goes. But it's never too early to celebrate.'

'Never too early to celebrate good fortune,' Baker agreed. He shouted at the girl to bring him a gin and tonic.

On the ramp a gunship slouched complacently under the baking glare of a portable spotlight, enjoying the attention of a half-dozen mechanics and maintenance technicians who poked in and around the cockpit console and the clusters of rocket tubes on the flanks of the aircraft. The square clusters of tubes, twenty-four tubes to a side, were the only armament on the ship except for the crew chief and door gunner's light machine guns. A ship with that armament was known as a 'hog'. True to its name, even its indolence had a certain ferocity, as if it might willingly bite the hand that ministered to it. The technicians worked carefully around the rocket tubes as they raced to finish before the coming of the rain that the wind promised.

Martin, standing within the circle of light, did not see Major Hart's jeep stop behind the aircraft. The major did not disturb the work. Not until the technicians had begun packing their tools did he move down into the light.

'Tell Operations we've got another ship up, Sergeant Magruder,' Martin said to his platoon sergeant. 'And have them roust another crew out of the rack. It's a good night for business with Charley.' He saw the major then. 'I went to your hooch to look for you, sir but you weren't home.'

'No. I went over to see John.'

'Had the shock worn off yet?'

'I don't know. He was pretty disturbed. To be expected, I suppose – he doesn't think he'll ever use his right hand again. And the surgeons think he's probably right.' He added, 'I guess I'll have to ask you to do some packing tomorrow, Ben.'

'Sure. I'll get his things together in the morning.'

'I'd be grateful.' Major Hart often treated acts which he had power to command as if they were personal favors. In another commander this might have seemed an affectation. In Major Hart it sprang from honest appreciation based on more years' service than he now cared to count as enlisted man and company-grade officer. But even as a second lieutenant he had never been able to convince himself that his power to send men even to their deaths was his by divine right. He still looked on it as a magical gift which might vanish if not cautiously used. 'I didn't mean I wanted you to pack only his things, though,' the major went on. 'Pack yours, too.'

'Mine, sir?'

'I'd like you to move into my hooch,' Major Hart explained. 'It's customary for the executive officer to room with me. Unless you'd rather stay where you are. You *do* have better quarters, I'll admit.'

'No . . . it's not that, sir.' In his surprise Martin fumbled for words. 'But what about Captain Blood? Doesn't he have date of rank on me?' Despite Blood's doubts Martin *had* forgotten his own date of rank. And he had been willing enough to concede the position to Blood on that basis.

It would not have surprised Martin to be promoted over Blood, date of rank or no date of rank – he was convinced of his own egotism – but he knew that Blood had visited the major before dinner, and Blood's self-satisfaction since then could have meant only one thing.

Beyond that, Martin had not come down from Group staff only to sit behind another desk. The Army would see the change to XO as a step up, and Martin would take it if he had to take it. He was not in the Army to retire after twenty years with a tombstone promotion to colonel. But he did not want it badly enough to have trouble with Blood. Blood needed the boost. For himself Martin expected better things in due course. Egotism again, he told himself.

'No,' Major Hart answered him. 'Blood doesn't have an earlier date of rank. In fact, you both have the same date.' He added. 'I want you to have it.'

The major was less innocent than he sometimes seemed, Martin reflected. He knew the bait to use. 'All right, sir.'

'Will you be needing the light, sir?' It was Harper, one of the electronics technicians.

'No, you can take it, Harper. Thanks. And good night.'

'Good night, sir.'

Under the light it had been warm. With it gone, the night closed chilly and damp about them. The wind eddied around the sand-filled steel plank walls of the revetment that protected the helicopter.

'I said I came up to see you. I wanted to talk to you about the Bear,' Martin said, in the confidence of the darkness. He added with a laugh, 'Maybe I should have done it before letting you offer me the job as XO.'

'You surely haven't been having any trouble from the Bear, Ben?'

'No, *I* haven't. But I gather that the Mustangs were not so pleased with him today.'

'So he told me. And then, I had a call from that . . . from their company commander. Isn't it strange how incoherent some folks get when they're upset, Ben?'

'What do you think ought to be done?'

'You realize I don't have the power to dispose of the affairs of other companies,' Major Hart said, 'though God knows they need it. I don't believe there's anything to be done *here*. Unless you have a suggestion?'

'No, none at all.'

'You're going to be an easy XO to work with,' the major said. 'Always give the old man his way.'

'Only when he's right,' Martin answered.

A crew arrived with a tug to move the hog to the arming pits. The ship was quickly jacked up on ground wheels and dragged off into the night.

'You'd better get some sleep on your last night of standby,' Major Hart advised. 'Tomorrow you're going to have to start working days. No more of this lying around all day, flying all night.'

'Thank the Lord. And who gets the honor of commanding the gun platoon? Arp?'

'Blood,' the major answered.

Although Captain Blood had purposely returned to his quarters early to receive the major's call, the coffee-grinder rattle of the field telephone excited him. He answered in his best military manner: 'Blood here.'

'Del, if you have a minute, could you come up to my quarters?'

'I'll be right up, sir.'

The major's hooch was not very grand, Blood noted with a possessive eye. It was in fact not even comfortable. Captain Carlsen had brought in a television and a small refrigerator. Those would be packed and sent wherever it was he was going. There was an ancient civilian table left behind by the marines who had formerly occupied the building, and a spindly metal chair. Against the side walls were two metal wall lockers and two steel-frame bunks. Beyond those the building was starved of comforts. The skeleton of its studs and rafters threw shadows on the outer plywood skin and galvanized iron roof. Many of the pilots' hooches were finer. They were lined with flamed plywood and insulated with Styrofoam packing from rocket boxes. Some even boasted elaborate bars, bookshelves, and cupboards whose ancestry could be traced through the same line as the insulation, for on their days off from flying, officers with nothing else to occupy them turned housekeeper. But the commander's hooch had been occupied by only two men, and as the two had seven-day-a-week duty, the luxury of space remained mere vacancy. Nevertheless, it suited Blood. Important emptiness was a better thing than insignificant comfort.

The major sat on the edge of his bed, leaving Blood the chair, a soft-iron thing badly welded by a Vietnamese entrepreneur for sale to the Americans. 'Del,' the major began, 'Captain Carlsen is going to be leaving us.'

Blood began a sympathetic eulogy, but stopped at a wave of the major's hand. 'I know you've been unhappy, tied down to a slick platoon flying ash and trash.' The major would not hear Blood's objection, but went on, 'I'd probably feel the same myself in your place – want a chance to do bigger things. Anyway, as you expect, we'll have to make some changes because of Captain Carlsen. You'll be one of the changes.'

'I can't say I wasn't expecting it, sir,' Blood admitted. He tried to achieve just the right mixture of humility and self-confidence in his tone. 'I can report for duty first thing in the morning, if you like.'

'Good. Get together with Captain Martin and—'

'Martin, sir?' Blood asked, perplexed.

'Yes. You'll be taking over his platoon. You'll want to inventory the platoon property with him. And then get with Lieutenant Harris – he'll take your platoon for now. God knows if we'll ever get another captain.' Seeing Blood's confusion, he added, 'Don't worry. Martin has left you a good-working platoon. I'm sure there'll be no problems.'

'No,' Blood mumbled. 'No. I'm sure there won't.'

Martin came in the door carrying clothing in a parachute bag. Seeing Blood there, he excused himself and began to back out. The major stopped him: 'It's all right, Ben. You live here, after all. I was just congratulating Captain Blood on having inherited your platoon. There are no secrets passing.' If the major did know of any strain between his two captains, he looked over the top of it with the serene gaze that excluded any hint of awareness that there could be an objection to what he had ordained. He waved off the lingering salute Blood gave him in parting.

Blood's idea, when he first left the major's hooch, was to have a drink, perhaps many drinks. Not that he felt any need for alcoholic anesthesia. But, in the same way that habitual indulgence seemed to him improper in an officer, intoxication seemed the proper response now. Blood had never liked alcohol and never really desired it. He had had no contact with liquor until he joined the Army at seventeen. He took up liquor, as he had taken up the Army, as a manly way of life. But like many an unimaginative man he mistook his idea of the conventional response for a personal desire. He concluded that he wanted to be drunk.

For months Blood had tormented himself with thoughts of the glory that would be his if he were commander of the gun platoon. Now the plum had fallen into his lap, but, in that moment, he had stretched for something still higher. And when he found that promised to another, he returned to his old desire only to find it withered and worthless. The juice was gone out of it.

Strong drink was called for.

But then he recalled that Baker would still be at the club. Blood was not eager to provide a laugh for gin-drinking fools at his own expense.

Blood kicked angrily at the steel plank of the helicopter ramp. Martin was junior to him; but somehow Martin had cut him out. And Blood knew how: West Pointers stood together, the damn Ringknockers! He had once seen a West Point graduate jokingly knock his ring against a table and whisper across the ring: *Knock-knock. Calling Washington! Calling Washington!* They stuck together, and they knew which way was up. Somewhere up there another Ringknocker had heard Martin. Blood cursed and beat his fist against a steel revetment.

Martin was hanging his uniforms in the metal wall locker.

'You should have brought over that fancy wardrobe Stoddard left you, Ben,' the major said, watching him.

'This is good enough, sir.'

'I'm ashamed not to offer you better, after you gave up

the big city for us.'

'We had mildew in the closets there, too.'

A metal locker was all Martin wanted. He had come down to the company from a staff job at Aviation Group headquarters. Most officers, if they ever reached that high, arrived at a staff position only after six months in a line company. Group staff, subordinate only to First Aviation Brigade and MACV itself, was the nearest thing to heaven that Vietnam offered. The higher headquarters sweltered in Saigon, out on the sticky mudflats of the Delta, while Group was headquartered in the old French resort city of Nha Trang on the central coast, on a site of stunning beauty between the mountains and the sea.

Martin had gone there at the beginning of his tour because the adjutant at Group knew him and wanted him there. The adjutant had been his company commander at Martin's firsty duty station after West Point. It had taken four months for Martin to convince the man, who meant well, that he really did want to go to a line company. 'If I'm as good an officer as you keep telling me I am, sir,' Martin had argued. 'I *should* be sent down. That's where the war is.'

There certainly was no war at Group staff. Life at the staff level bored Martin, and angered him. Papers bred like rabbits in his desk at night. Reduce their offspring to manageable numbers in the evening, and by morning they were back to their old strength. And none of them mattered. Awards for meritorious service, PX thefts, even procedures for maintaining files, by God! When he was appointed files control officer for the Group, he knew it was time to get out.

His friends thought he had lost his senses. 'If you're not getting a company, Martin, you're better off here. Command of a unit looks good on your two-oh-one-file, but you're not going to get a command as a captain. You'll only get a platoon in the boonies someplace. Better stick here. The adj likes you. You'll get a great efficiency report.'

Martin could not stick. Tennis at noon. Sunday afternoon on the beach, dinner at La Frégate – these were killing him slowly, but as surely as were the papers raging over his desk. It was not the way to run a war. Nor was a room in a beachfront villa, with a live-in cook, private bar, and roof-top garden where the Air Force nurses came to dance on weekend nights. Beach Road for five miles was lined with villas facing the broad bay. Once they had been filled with the families of French planters. Now they were occupied by American master sergeants.

Even in the boonies it was not always different. The grunts slept on the ground, true enough, but back at the home base the colonel had his trailer air-conditioned. Martin had told a colonel how to win the war once: 'Put every man in the Army, from Westmoreland on down, in a tent, and tell him he's going to stay there until it's all over. Close the PXs and the clubs. Send every man's pay home to wait for him, except for the wages a peasant gets for farming his land. Send home the hooch-maids, the cooks, and the laborers. Besides saving the country's economy, it'll get us all home before Christmas.' The colonel was outraged.

Martin tossed the empty parachute bag under his bunk.

'That's not exactly the most extensive wardrobe I've seen in country, Ben,' the major said. The locker contained only the three issue sets of jungle fatigues and the khakis in which Martin had arrived in country. 'Did you wear out your party clothes in the big city?'

'Those are my party clothes,' Martin answered.

3

The northeast wind lunged landward out of the grey South China Sea, whipping the wild rain before it and pressing long rolling waves down a thousand miles of open sea to crash at last against the Indochina coast. All fluid elements conspired against solidity. The earth melted and ran in rivers of mud inch by inch toward the sea. The mountains were reduced, were grounded by microns to powder, ran riverward. The plain was awash, with paddies brimful and their dikes sloughing off at the edges. But through it all, greenness endured in the sprouting rice, life struggling skyward even in darkness.

Out in the rain the gunships crouched. Their wet flanks, glistened darkly in the revetments, glinting under the distant light from the hospital beyond the long, level ramp. The wind gusting over the revetments made them shudder like live things dreaming of the hunt. Because of the angle of the skids and the main rotor mast, they stood on the ground in the nose-down attitude in which they flew, with the tense readiness of tracking hounds.

Unprejudiced eyes might have found them less than handsome. They were C-model Hueys, with oversized tailblooms appended to short fat bodies, like mongoloid tadpoles. They entirely lacked the lean grace of their D-model relatives, the slick ships. And, like all helicopters, although they could be flown with great precision by a skilful pilot, they flew at all only by dint of the most frantic exertions, as when some fat barnyard fowl hoists itself aloft for a triumphant moment. A helicopter is a collection of moving parts each trying to tear off and throw away every other, and these could be coaxed to fly two days running only through the dedicated ministrations of a retinue of maintenance men. To control them in flight required the use of two hands, two feet, and singleminded concentration that through long practice finally became second nature, but could never be relaxed. Unlike other aircraft, a helicopter untended would not fly itself. It preferred to crash.

But, though clumsy on the ground, the gunships were hunters; and they were ready. Before night came, each had been lovingly prepared by its crew. Helmets now were plugged into the communications system and placed on the seats; shoulder harnesses were adjusted and laid over the seat-backs; searchlight and landing light were positioned and tested; weapons were tested, loaded, and safetied; the throttle was rolled to the starting position, the start fuel switched on, the rpm governor beeped down; the radios were set for departure frequencies; the panel light switches were on and the rheostat set to keep the lights to a dim glow; the position lights and anticollision beacon were switched on. All the electrical systems would come to life at a touch on the master switch. At a squeeze of the starter trigger, fire would rush through the turbine engine, and within sixty seconds from the time the cockpit door opened, the ship could be airborne.

While the ships stood in the rain, the crews waited in the alert hooch. The alert hooch smelled of sweat and mildew. It had been slept in by too many bodies in too many wet clothes on too many soaking nights. The plywood shutters that completely covered the glassless screened windows were down all around to hold back the driving rain; but every chink on the windward side leaked a constant fine spray. The two bare light bulbs dangling from the ridgepole glowed weakly through humid halos. Rain rattled like shot on the metal roof. Below the cliffs the ocean hammered the beach. The wind ripped at roofs, at shutters, at doors.

Cripps on his mildewed cot struggled through disconnected snatches of dreams, washing in and out of sleep like a body tumbling in the surf. From the end of the hooch under one of the light bulbs came the click of cards, murmured words, occasional shouted oaths as the cards hit or failed. Players groped for their cards in the dim light. Through the darkness of lost years came the sounds, the sounds of his father's friends playing poker downstairs, and on the shingles the rain tapping. Rain on the metal roof, a ghost of the past asking to be let in. His mother writing to an aunt somewhere, somewhere up North where, they said, snow came, and stayed on the ground. Not rain. Her pen scratched over the hard shiny paper as he lay drowsing on the floor beside the table. 'They're family, even if they are Yankees.' Firelight flickering warm outside his closed eyelids.

The bare bulb danced as a gust shook the hooch. Through the slits of his eyes he could see the line of the filament. The horse-blanket smell of a too-much-used sleeping bag seeped from under his sweaty back.

Mr Covington, on the next cot, was sitting with a book on his lap for a table, writing. He wrote to his wife every night. Married, and no older than Cripps was himself. Cripps smiled at Covington's serious face laboring over his work.

Beyond Mr Covington, Sergeant Handy snored on his cot. Moisture glistened on his black face, below the hat he had pulled over his eyes.

Democracy reigned in the alert hooch. The assigned quarters might be segregated by rank; but here, where the gun crews spent half their nights, officers, NCOs, and enlisted men alike slept shoulder to shoulder, played cards, traded lies, dreamed their dreams.

In search of a better-smelling spot on his sleeping bag, Cripps rolled the other way. The Bear was seated cross-legged on the next cot like a khaki Buddha, hands folded in his lap. Their eyes met.

'You sleep beautifully,' Bear said.

Cripps blushed.

'Cov, did you ever notice how beautifully Cripps sleeps?'

'Often,' Covington said, not looking up from his letter.

'Hey, no, I'm serious.'

'So am I. Cripps, you sleep more genteelly than any person I've ever seen in all my born days.'

'Your sleep, Cripps, is something to behold,' the Bear told him. 'The most pleasant smile comes and goes, and your nose twitches. I wish I had your dreams.'

'You ought to,' Atterburn said. He had come up the aisle from where he had been watching the poker game. 'A good wet dream is as close as you'll ever get to any real stuff, Bear.'

'Now, Atterburn, you know Cripps wouldn't have any dreams like *that*!'

'A stud like Cripps? Who are you kidding? Just look at him! A little scrawny, maybe, but . . .'

Cripps rolled facedown without answering, and closed his eyes. Cripps never answered, although he was frequently the butt of lewd pleasantries from Atterburn. Cripps did not like Atterburn. But he admired the Bear, and sometimes went so far as to hold a hurried conversation with him. Cripps would have died for the Bear, or done anything else short of holding an extended conversation.

Seeing that Cripps was not to be baited, Atterburn turned to Covington. 'What's this? Letter to Pinky? You haven't written to her since noon. You must have a lot to say by now.'

Covington did not reply. He had heard this before.

'You going to tell her how many Dinks you got today?'

Covington shook his head.

'Why not? Man. I'll bet she'd like to know that! Doesn't she want to know about your work?'

'Since I told her about the round that came through the floor and took the earphone out of one side of my helmet, back while you were still in flight school,' Covington answered, 'she doesn't want to hear any more about shooting.'

'Well, hell, what else is there to write about? I don't see how you can fill up your three letters a day, Covington. Around here, you can't even truthfully tell her you went to town and screwed the bar girls. Excuse me, I forgot you were being faithful to Pinky.'

'It's only fair,' Covington said. 'She's being faithful to me.'

'So you say.'

'She is.'

'Well,' Atterburn admitted, 'if she's being *fair* to you, she is. Except for that doughnut dollie that was at Colt last week, I haven't seen a round-eye in two months. I'm getting horny enough to ask Suzie for a little boom-boom.'

'Suzie's been too old for that sport for fifty years,' Lieutenant Arp put in from his quiet corner at the front of the hooch.

'Well, I'll ask Yan, then.'

'You'll waste your breath,' Arp said.

'Arp wants Yan for himself,' Covington said to Atterburn. He had begun to copy the conversation for Pinky, and he wanted to keep it moving.

'If the major catches anyone making free with the hoochmaids,' Arps said, 'we lose them; and then you'll do your own laundry, or send it to town to be washed in buffalo piss. Besides,' he added, 'Suzie watches Yan like a hawk. You'll never catch her alone.'

'The famous Bear has her alone in a corner every day he's off standby,' Atterburn said. 'Of course, he doesn't know what to do with her. He thinks "good relations with indigenous personnel" means talking friendly. One of these times I'm going to show her what really good relations are.'

'It's a fat rooster that has a pecker as big as his crow,' Bear observed.

The scramble horn blasted the reply from Atterburn's lips. Half-dealt hands fell on the card table. Covington stuffed his unfinished letter into his sleeping bag as Bear fumbled with the zippers on his boots. 'Christ,' Atterburn objected, 'we're not going to fly in *this* shit are we?'

'It's only a shower,' Arp told him comfortably, settling deeper into his cot. He grinned at the gesture which was Atterburn's only reply. Arp's fire team was on secondary standby. Shower or storm, he would not have to fly in it for a while yet. After the rush had cleared the door, he pulled on his raincoat to go to Operations and learn where the mission had gone.

Blood was first to the ships. He muttered one of his favorite military sayings to himself as he slung the blade tie-down hook under his seat and climbed in: 'You got to lead from up front.' He said it again as Atterburn piled directly into the left front seat and switched on and pulled the trigger: 'You got to leap from up front, boy.' The blade was revolving slowly while that on the Bear's ship in the next revetment was still being untied.

The low cry of the turbines spinning up carried only faintly across the wind to the Operations hooch. Arp hurried inside out of the rain and then stayed at the door, watching the steady flash of the red anticollisions beacons. He checked his watch. 'Not bad time,' he said to no one in particular.

'Captain Blood ought to be quick.' The duty sergeant laughed. 'He makes me wait for him to locate the coordinates and get out the door before I can blow the horn for the rest of you. I think he wants you to get all the sleep you can.'

The duty officer came up to the door beside Arp. 'Think they'll get far in this weather?'

'I didn't notice any webbed feet on the ships.'

'Blood had the hero lights flashing in his eyes. They're going someplace for sure.'

Arp turned to study the large-scale chart on the wall.

Covington had already pulled the trigger when the Bear climbed aboard. The steady snap of the spark plug was slowly obliterated by the rush of the turbine, like fire in a distant chimney, that climbed steadily to a harsh whistle. The Bear fastened his harness and pulled on his helmet. His hands raced over the switches on the panel and the overhead console for a last check, and then he laid his hands on the controls. The ship was rocking rapidly as the main blade, which had begun with an almost imperceptible inching rotation, blurred toward invisibility. 'I've got it.' Covington released the controls and began strapping himself in. 'You up in back?'

'We're up, sir,' Handy answered.

Bear rolled the throttle fully on and touched his thumb to the rpm governor button to ease the engine to operating speed. He tested the controls gingerly, lifting most of the weight of the aircraft from the skids as he waited for the call to come on the radio.

Blood's voice came on the VHF, the radio on which the gunship crews communicated among themselves: 'Two, are you up?'

'Affirmative,' Bear answered.

Then Blood was on the UHF, calling the tower: 'Ky Ha, Wolf Lead for hover and takeoff; request left break.'

'Wolf Lead, clear for departure with left break. Winds zero-seven-zero at twenty-five, gusting forty.'

Blood again: 'Roger. Two, you copy?'

'Affirm.'

'Lead coming up.'

The slap of the blades rose to a sudden pounding, the unmistakable sound of a Huey coming to operating rpm. Arp came back to the door to watch the ships depart. They rose into the air and eased slowly backward from their revetments, turned, and bobbed delicately down the ramp three feet above the surface. The solid thump of the blades came as a series of physical blows to the chest. The ships rocked with the gusts but maintained a steady slow pace to the takeoff lane. Hovering across a strong gusting wind was an adventure in itself, for the ship fought continuously to turn its head into the wind, or to slip sideways into the immovable flank of a revetment.

At the takeoff lane the two aircraft pirouetted, made their obeisance to the wind, and still head-down, battled forward in flurry of blades and climbed rapidly out over the sea. Their lights winked out in the rain.

*   *   *

A mixture of rain and salt spray steamed over the windscreen. 'Do you want wipers?' Covington asked.

'Yes.'

The wipers hardly helped. The screen filled with rain faster than the wipers could throw it off. The lights of Blood's ship ahead were a cluster of colored blurs. 'Get on the instruments, Cov,' Bear said. 'We may lose him before too very long.' It took time to transition from visual flight to instruments. Close to the ground the crew could not afford to lose time in the transition. If they lost sight of the lead ship, which at the moment was the only mark on the darkness, they could be into the ground before they could reorient themselves. Bear could feel Covington's touch on the other set of controls.

Blood swung in a broad arc back over Ky Ha, and for a moment there was a visual reference again, with the ramp lights rain-washed below them. The powerful lights of the jet runway, only a mile distant, were not to be seen.

'Think he's going to tell us where we're headed?' Covington asked.

'That's Blood's little secret.'

They climbed out over the hooches on the ridge, over the lights of the officers' club, bright but blurred by rain, and swung northwest over the coastal plain. As they crossed the Chu Lai perimeter, all lights vanished behind them. They had flown into the void.

Bear increased power to draw within twenty meters of Blood's aircraft and settled into a position close off the starboard quarter. 'Put out the beacon,' he ordered. The rotating beam was reflecting from wisps of cloud which they plunged through, obscuring the lights of the lead ship. With their own light off it was easier to keep Blood's lights in sight.

On most night missions the Bear would have flown several hundred meters back and well to one side of his fireteam leader. He would have flown lights out then, too, but for tactical reasons rather than for safety. At night slick ships flew with their beacons off, marked only by three dim position lights with the bottom half of the lenses painted out to make them invisible from the ground. Slicks huddled together in the darkness like chicks without a mother hen, so as not to lose one another. Gunships flew low and loose, the lead ship with lights blazing, arrogantly daring onlookers to fire. Those who go armed do not fear footsteps in the night, especially when they have a friend for security. The second ship, lights out, stalked the leader through the night, ready to rain fire on any attackers from the security of its own invisibility.

Tonight Bear huddled in behind his leader like a slick, so close to the lead ship that one burst of ground fire could destroy them both. But he could not risk losing sight of the other aircraft. Once visual contact was lost, they might be unable to find one another again, or risked finding one another so close at hand that a collision could not be avoided. A helicopter could take a few bullets without great danger; a collision was deadly.

They flew scraping the cloud bases. The puffs through which they plunged became larger and larger, turning to great walls of cotton that blanked out even the rotating beacon of the other ship for seconds at a time. 'I don't like this one little bit,' Bear said at length. They were being forced lower and lower as they went north. There was high ground downwind to the west. They could be drifted off course – what the course might be Blood still had not deigned to tell them – and into a mountain without ever seeing what it was they hit. 'We're below five hundred feet.'

They had flown in bad weather before, but never in ignorance. It was different, knowing where you were bound, and being able to watch the needle swing on the navigation aid which told you at least the direction to fly. Leading flights of his own, the Bear had always briefed the second crew on locations and radio frequencies, so that they could find their own way if the need arose. But he no longer led missions. Blood's first act as platoon commander had been to replace him as section leader, and now he followed Blood like a duck on a string. He did not especially mind that, so long as he knew where he was supposed to be going. But flying into nowhere was agonizing. Finally he radioed on the VHF: 'Lead, can you share the ground frequency and destination with us?'

The answer came eventually in Atterburn's voice: a coded set of coordinates and a coded three-digit number that was the FM frequency.

'Nothing like being halfway supercareful,' Covington said. He worked out the code on his clipboard. 'That's forty-six point three on the Fox Mike. Ground location' – he took up a map from the map case at the rear of the central console – 'outside Tam Ky. Province headquarters?'

Bear switched the FM in time to catch the tail end of a transmission by Blood: '. . . about five miles south, if we can get under these clouds.'

A strange voice: 'Roger. We've still got beaucoup Charlies coming at the wire. Arty has kept 'em outside so far.'

Bear watched the directional needle on the FM homing device as the voice spoke. It hung slightly to the left of center. Because the aircraft were crabbed into a crosswind from the right, it meant that they were almost directly on course to the location of the ground station that was transmitting.

'Blood must have been homing on that guy for a while now,' Covington said, 'Nice of him to tell us. If he'd lost us in a cloud out here, we might have busted our rear ends on a rock.'

'You talk like we were there already,' Bear replied. 'If that guy on the ground has artillery coming in on his position, we should have seen it by now. There's nothing ahead but black.'

'You think there might be a little cloud between him and us, I'll bet.'

'Might be.'

'Speak of the devil.' Hitting the cloud was like tearing into a deep feather pillow. The lights of the ship ahead did not dim gradually: they simply vanished. But the darkness suddenly brightened, for now mixed with the heavy driving raindrops were swirling water droplets that reflected the helicopter's own position lights, so that they moved in a faint aurora, green on the right, red on the left.

'Lead, we've lost contact,' Bear called urgently. 'Put on all your lights!' There was a chance that, if the cloud were not wide, the landing light and searchlight of the other ship would mark it well enough for them to follow while still keeping clear.

'Lights are on,' Blood answered.

There was not a mark on the sky. Bear had instinctively slowed when he lost sight of the lights ahead. The gap between them had widened, and there was now no chance of closing it. His eyes went instantly to the attitude indicator. The ship was still flying straight ahead, but climbing slightly. He began a gentle turn to the right, feeling Covington's hands light on the controls. 'Lead, are you still in cloud?'

'Affirmative. We're letting down. I think we can break out. Follow us down.'

Bear ignored the order. 'Making a one-eighty to the right.'

'Negative one-eighty,' Blood called. 'It can't be far down through the ceiling.'

'Not lower than the ground, anyway,' Covington said over the intercom. 'What's he trying to do, the crazy fool?'

'Watch the altitude,' was all the Bear said. He continued the turn, descending slowly. After a hundred and sixty degrees of turn he rolled the aircraft out. He was allowing twenty degrees to compensate for the crosswind: he did not want to the be blown west of their original course. The moutains were there, and the clouds might be lower as well. Better to end up too far east, where at least the ground was flat.

Flying in the cloud was like being packed in gauze. Although there was no danger, so long as they could stay on the back course and not descend below the height of any obstacles, still they flew with racing pulses, and with a sense of being slowly stifled. 'Don't let me go below three hundred feet,' Bear said.

'Roger three hundred.'

There was little chance of hitting anything down to about fifty feet above sea level. The plain was almost at sea level here, and the trees were low. But there was always the chance tall tree; or the altimeter could be wrong because of air pressure changes in the storm; or they might overlook a loss of altitude for an instant too long. A hundred things could kill you in a low cloud. But they had been flying clear of clouds at five hundred feet a moment before. Three hundred should be low enough to put them in the clear on a back course.

Blood came on the radio again: 'Two, Lead is descending through three hundred, on heading three-one-five. Still in cloud. Do you have us in sight?'

'That's negative, Lead. We've made a one-eighty. We're now at three hundred fifty.'

'Two, I said negative on the one-eighty! Do you copy?'

'I copy.'

'Well, do we go back?' Covington asked.

'Wait a bit,' Bear answered. 'If the crazy bastard breaks out in the clear, we'll go back.'

'There's a tree!' It was Atterburn's voice on the VHF, torn with panic. Then silence.

'Lead, are you all right?' Bear called quickly.

There was no answer.

'Wolf Lead, Wolf Lead, do you receive Two?'

Blood's voice replied, shaking at the beginning: 'Ah, Two, this is Wolf Lead. We're making a one-eighty to the left. What's your present position?'

'Don't we wish we knew,' Covington said on the intercom.

The halo suddenly faded from about their ship. 'Get the searchlight on,' Bear said. The beam, aimed down at a forty-five degree angle ahead, fired a myriad of water drops to silver shooting stars; but at the bottom of the shimmering column which they formed, a patch of red earth could be seen. 'Lead, Two is in the clear at three hundred fifty. We have our searchlight on, and we'll be making a left circle.'

'Roger.'

They circled slowly at the same altitude. Once they brushed the flank of the cloud. It lurked in the rain, invisible until touched, and deadly to incautious pilots. They moved their circle farther south.

The voice from the ground came on the FM. He had been forgotten until now. 'Wolf Lead, this is Cold Turkey. What's your position?'

Blood took a moment to answer. 'Ah, Cold Turkey, say, we can't get through this little cloud south of you. We'll try to find a way in.'

Blood's country drawl was a jarring change from his crisp radio procedure of moments before. 'That must have really puckered his ass.' Covington laughed. It was easier to laugh beyond the grip of the cloud.

Before the Bear had completed another three-sixty, Blood called out, 'Two, we have you in sight at ten o'clock.'

'Aircraft at eight o'clock, sir,' Handy sang out at the same instant. 'About a quarter mile.' It was the first time since take-off that Bear was aware of anyone but Covington with him in the aircraft. He and Covington communicated through the machine. Through it their actions were one. But Handy and Cripps were mere spectators, brooding on foreign thoughts. It was why all pilots hated to ride in back, as passengers.

He tightened the turn, and the blurred splash of light that was Blood's searchlight swung up across the windscreen.

'Two, join up, and we'll try to get around to the east.'

Since they could not fly on instruments together, only two choices were left to them. They could probe along the edge of the cloud, as Blood was suggesting, hoping for an opening; or they could fight the cloud separately on instruments, hoping to home on the ground radio and let down overhead. If the overcast were high enough, they would be able to rejoin at that spot. If it were not, their weapons were useless in any case. Blood was proposing the safer course, Bear knew; but with their fuel burning away at nearly five hundred pounds an hour, time was of the essence. But when Bear suggested the second course, Blood's answer was chilly:

'Negative. We'll get around to the east.' Blood's voice had regained its procedural formality.

'He doesn't like that cloud so much as he did,' Covington said.

'I'm not so fond of it myself, Cov.'

They probed along the side of the cloud as low as two hundred feet for several miles to the east; but each time they swung north, the wall of mist closed around them, and they were forced to separate and turn back to rejoin outside. The pilots traded off flying every few minutes; but still the strain of searching through the rain for the lights of the other ship and of holding position in the turbulent air began to wear at them; and there was no true rest between stints of flying, for the one not actually controlling the aircraft still remained at the controls, his eyes on the instruments, ready to take over when the other ship disappeared.

'Wolf Lead, this is Cold Turkey. How you comin'?' Cold Turkey's voice had gone southern, too. Knowing what the man was facing, Bear admired his dispassion. From his tone he might have been merely solicitious of Wolf's health.

'We're still trying, Cold Turkey. There's a little bit of weather between us.'

'Roger. Hope to see you soon. Charley's rippin' and snortin' out here.' Machine guns punctuated this transmission.

The fuel gauge swung slowly toward the bottom of the dial, until less than four hundred pounds remained – less than an hour's flying time at most. They were fifteen minutes from home, and it was imperative to keep at least a half hour's reserve, for there was no knowing what weather might lie between them and home. Blood continued to poke at the listless cloud, but it refused to roll aside for them. If anything were to be done for Cold Turkey, it must be done at once. At last Bear called again, 'Lead, suggest again we try to go in separately. We can home on his transmitter at different altitudes and hold on station while one of us tries to let down below the ceiling.'

'Roger, Two. Do you know there *is* a ceiling?' Having

tried once and failed, Blood was consumed with scorn that anyone should think that course was possible. He flittered along the cloud until the fuel gauge passed three hundred pounds, and there was no hope. 'Cold turkey,' he called, 'this is Wolf Lead. We can't get in. Wolf Lead turning for home.'

When Cold Turkey eventually answered, his words were hard to make out. The continuous impacting of artillery rounds sent the microphone diaphragm into convulsions and broke up the transmission. The words they could make out were 'Thanks for trying.'

'How many did you kill?' Arp asked as they straggled back, wet and listless, to the alert hooch.

'Not any, unless we ran them down in a cloud without knowing it.' Bear sat unhappily on one end of his cot, pondering his wringing-wet jungle fatigues and his merely damp sleeping bag, and wondering what Cold Turkey was doing.

'At least,' Covington said, 'we got back alive.'

'That is a point in your favor,' Arp agreed.

Atterburn came in shaking his poncho and cursing the rain. That done, he grinned at the Bear and said, with satisfaction only partly hidden, 'The Blood would like to talk to you in Operations.' As Bear rose from his cot with a sigh, he added, 'I wouldn't make him wait. I may be wrong, but I'd say he has a case of the red ass.'

Besides Blood standing at the counter completing the after-action report, the duty officer and sergeant, two off-duty slick drivers, and an Operations clerk were in Operations. All of them were silent – not merely silent, but inoperative, with the significant silence of an electrical machine whose power has suddenly failed as the storm closes around.

Blood slashed a signature on the report and pushed it across the counter. He motioned with a sideways turn of his head for the Bear to follow him to the far end of the hooch, saying as he went, 'There seem to be a lot of people in here without any business in Operations.' The clerk and the off-duty pilots began to gather their rain gear for the wet walk to their quarters. They were gone by the time Blood sat down on a desk at the opposite end of the hooch.

When he was angry, Blood's face became a pictogram of his name. The change of color in his face as he progressed was matched by the climb in pitch and volume of his voice from the near whisper in which he began: 'Mister, if you don't know this you had better learn it a lot faster than I think you can. When I am in command of a mission, I expect that what I say goes! I don't need any wise-ass warrant officers who think they know better to go off making their own flight plans and thinking they can laugh up their sleeves about it. If leading flights gave you such a big head that you can't take orders anymore, then it's way past time somebody dragged you out of command of that section. I thought it should have been done long ago, and what I saw tonight just convinced me I was right. If you haven't got the balls to fly in bad weather, then you're in the wrong line of work, let me tell you! I don't want to be on my way to a target again and find out I'm all alone. For two cents I'd ask the old man to ground you! But I'm not going to do it – not yet. Because I can't stand the thought of you sitting around on your rear, safe on the ground, while better men are risking their flying missions. But there had better be one whole hell of a lot of improvement, let me tell you! This is going into your efficiency report, believe me. And if you ever had any thought of making the Army a career, you'd better start learning to fix shoes or whatever the hell you're fit for!' Blood stalked back down the length of the hooch and erupted into the rain, leaving the Bear still suspended at the dark end of the building. After he was gone, the duty officer remarked to the sergeant, but loud enough for Bear to hear, 'I'd think you lifers would learn sometime, Sarge, that the only one you can threaten with a bad efficiency report is another lifer.'

'I ain't no lifer, sir.' The sergeant laughed. 'I got a little used-car business with my dad back in the world, and if you put me out on a bad conduct this minute, I wouldn't argue!'

Muffled voices, like the chirping of languorous birds, woke the Bear where he had fallen asleep in his fatigues on his own bunk after coming up from the alert hooch. The room was dark, although daylight picked idly at the corners of the plywood shutters. The air was clinging and sour. From the taste in his mouth he thought at first that the birds might be hidden there, but after a few deep breaths he realized that they were really only the hooch-maids sociably doing laundry on the porch. One came inside to hang a set of fatigues over a bunk rail, where they would remain slowly transpiring for days, until either the sun showed itself or they were put on still damp and dried by body heat. While the door was open, a shaft of light struggled down the center of the hooch, but without sufficient conviction to light the whole interior. The storm had passed over, leaving a residue of low cloud to darken the afternoon.

He struggled to his feet eventually, feeling too used up to be revived even by sleeping the day away. Staying ready to go out and kill was a stultifying business. He strapped on his pistol and started out to see what the day had left to him.

As he reached the door there was a little shriek out on the porch. The door burst open, and Yan thumped headlong into him. She caromed off into the darkness beside one of the bunks, to the accompaniment of a great deal of soprano laughter outside. Arp came to the door.

'You no let him in,' Yan pleaded from the corner.

'Lieutenant, how come you're chasing my hooch-maid?' Bear demanded. 'If anybody gets to chase her, it should be me.'

'I was just taking a picture,' Arp protested, holding up his camera to attest to his good faith.

'I haven't heard *that* one before.'

'You no let him in!' Yan repeated.

'It's too dark in here anyway, Yan, if all he wants is a picture. Relax.'

'You want picture, I bring you picture,' Yan said to Arp. 'You no take my picture now.'

'I take your picture,' Arp affirmed. 'I take *beaucoup* picture, put them up all over my wall. Yan number-one girl: she *làm dep*.' He said this laughing.

While Yan showed no objection to being called very pretty, she was not coming out of the corner, and finally Arp relented. He and Bear stood on the porch, feeling the sea wind, still northeast but warmer than before. 'It's really strange how she won't let me take her picture,' Arp said. 'Do you suppose she's afraid the camera will take her spirit? The Montagnards are supposed to believe that.'

'She offered to bring you a picture,' Bear pointed out.

'But you don't know that she'll *do* it. You've seen Vietnamese soldiers walking hand in hand. They say that's to keep them safe from spirits. Who knows what Yan believes about cameras?'

'I always thought the handholding was just friendliness.'

'Atterburn would say it was just being queer. But it's not. Maybe it's not just friendliness, either. But there are lots of things I don't understand. For one thing I don't understand how you can snore away the whole of his sparkling day while others are out working.'

'I thought I heard your flight go out this morning,' Bear said. 'So you got to fly in that little shower after all.'

'It was all over when we got off the ground,' Arp said. 'The very clouds roll apart for me. You know that.'

'Sure.'

'While your lazy body was supine, we paid a visit to Cold Turkey. Just a recon. It's a pity you didn't get through. I understand he called in artillery on himself. Very few friendly casualties, surprisingly enough; but the American advisor was one. All we could get were Vietnamese voices on the radio. Dustoff came in for him while we were there.'

'Was he alive?'

'No.'

Bear studied the grey sea for the space of several seconds. 'Well, I tried.'

'Yes. I understand Blood had a different opinion. But it's not one that's widely believed.' Arp said this as if it were an after-thought; but Bear saw that the whole exchange had been leading up to this reassurance. His business accomplished, Arp turned the subject aside by saying briskly, 'If you're not going to help me lure Yan out into the light, I'm going to leave you to the company of these fair ladies.' He made a motion as if to take the picture of the two old women squatting over their washbasins. The camera held no terrors for them: they cackled at the gesture.

After Arp had left, Bear hunkered down on the porch with the two. Suzie was Yan's mother. The other was an old crony of hers. Both were wrinkled old prunes, the remnant of too many years in the sun. Yan, twittering and fearful, hovered inside the door until she was sure that Arp was gone.

'*Chào, Bá*,' Bear addressed the two old women, using the reverential term 'grandmother'. They in turn called him *Dài-úy*, which meant 'captain,' for they were very polite old women not much concerned with the *Ngu'ò'i Mỹ* distinctions of rank.

The Bear spent a good deal of time chatting with the hooch-maids. Although he was fighting a Vietnamese war, and had seen from the air a large pårt of the Vietnamese landscape from Saigon to Hue, he had little contact with the people themselves. He wished sometimes he could land in a farmyard and simply talk to the people there. His Vietnamese was not good, but he would have liked to try. Instead he was confined to talking to those who came onto the American installation, those who swept his floors, made his bed, laundered his underwear – who in short were familiar with every detail of his personal life, although he had no conception of theirs. But they knew only his life in Vietnam, a monastic and harried existence that bore no relationship to life in America. What could they think of his own country, who saw only its weapons and its underwear?

'It seems your daughter fears the lieutenant,' Bear turned his head slightly toward the door where Yan still lingered, listening.

'One who flees does not always fear,' Suzie answered. Her

friend cackled in glee. After a moment Suzie added, smiling, 'The lieutenant tells Yan she is pretty, but she is more pretty in her finer clothes.'

The simplicity of Yan's mother's statement caused Bear to pause. He looked up where Yan's mother was looking, at Yan in the doorway, and he understood. He had seen Yan always as she was now, in her black silk trousers and white blouse, with sometimes a light jacket or a conical straw hat. Today she had spent the afternoon scrubbing clothes in an aluminum washpan, and a few strands of long dark hair fell across her face. Even as he glanced up at her, she brushed them back with one hand. Yan in her work clothes *was* very pretty: but she was in her work clothes. And he had not even considered that she might have better.

He was ashamed, for he had thought of Yan as only a servant, in whom vanity was unthinkable.

He would have apologized to her mother, but he did not know how.

He was spared the need by a low warning from Suzie: 'The captain with the loud voice comes.'

Blood had been watching for some time from the back door of his own hooch. 'Don't that make a picture, though?' he remarked to Lieutenant Rauch, the Operations officer, who shared the hooch. 'A damn warrant officer squatting there on his heels with the Slopes, just like a turd on a plate. I've told him more'n once about keepin' up our dignity with the indigenous labor. But he don't amount to much where takin' orders is concerned. There he is, in there gabblin' like a turkey till you can't tell him from the rest of 'em.'

'You goin' to chew him out *before* you get his signature on your recommendation, or *after*?' Lieutenant Rauch drawled. He grinned to see Blood squirm at the question.

'Neither one,' Blood said at last. 'I reckon it's good for relations with the locals. Let him talk to 'em, if he wants to.' The importance of the indigenous personnel had risen considerably in Blood's judgment that very day, since the battalion awards officer had called down with the news that the Vietnamese Army wished to give an award to the crews of the gunships that had made such a valiant attempt to reach the provincial headquarters during the storm the night before. The details of the mission were to be provided by the officers and men involved. The thrust of the awards officer's message had been 'Send us some fancy language, and get the pilots to sign each other's recommendations.'

Leaving Rauch grinning, Blood went across to the Bear's porch, where he propped one foot up casually. 'Winning the hearts and minds of the people again, eh? Well, Westy says that's the way to win the war: I reckon there must be *some*thing in it. If we get the mama-sans on our side, maybe they can pussy-whip their husbands into stayin' home at night, and we won't have to make any little trips like that last one.' Blood laughed loudly at this, although he laughed alone. It had been drilled into Blood through a long course of officer training that a loud voice is the chief characteristic of a leader, and he prided himself on never forgetting a lesson learned. The nature of what he had to say next might have softened his voice, except that such a result would have made it appear that he hesitated to ask what was after all only a matter of right. He therefore spoke even more loudly as he launched onto his main topic: 'Say, that reminds me, Battalion sent down a message that the Vietnamese unit we were looking for wants to put us in for some award. I guess Rauch's clerk is typing up the recommendations. ARVN awards don't count for a hell of a lot; but maybe it would be a good thing to get them for the crews. I told Rauch I'd get you to sign some of 'em. Whenever you get time. I don't want to interfere with your part of the war effort.' He went away grinning, as if they shared some lewd secret. He was highly pleased with his diplomacy.

'So,' Lieutenant Rauch said, 'you're goin' to sign Blood's promotion ticket, are you? If he gets enough of these, he might make major yet. If he lives that long. I hear he tried to kill you all last night. That's all we need, is to lose two gunships. Division's already on our ass to get more ships in the air than we own, let alone have flyable.'

'As I understood it,' Bear answered, 'this was to be for the benefit of our crewmen, who're feebleminded enough to pay attention to these trinkets.'

'You haven't seen what Blood had me write about *him*. 'Course, if you want an award to get through channels, you got to make sure it sells.' He took a form from the clerk and read at random: "Heedless of his own safety, led his flight into perilous weather which had stopped all other attempts to reach the ground position . . . showed outstanding leadership ability and skill as an aviator in locating the friendly position under impenetrable clouds . . . bravery above and beyond . . ." He forgot to say anything about dumb-ass attempts at suicide, but you can't remember everything. Here.' Rauch tossed the papers across the counter. 'Sign there.'

Bear's face took on the features of Astonishment Cast in Bronze. 'I thought I was signing for my crew.'

'You'll get those, too. But you can't expect Blood to sign his own award, now, can you? And you're the commander of the number-two ship. Sign the mother.'

'If I'd known we were going to get a medal, I'd have actually gone in and placed some fire for them, at least. I don't feel like they got their money's worth.'

'One day one of them big fifty-caliber rounds is goin' to come right through where you're sittin', and they probably won't give you a medal for that at all, even if there's someplace left to pin one. Just figure it's all evened out ahead of time. If you're worried about tellin' lies for Blood, forget it. It's all arranged, right up through Division. They got to get rid of their quota of Vietnamese decorations, or some damn thing. This thing will go through like castor oil through a baby. Now sign the mother and let me get rid of it. So it was all a mistake, so what? You all risked your asses, and if Blood was along for the ride, he's only getting the same medal as the rest of you. Look, he signed yours. See there?'

'What do we do for the Medal of Honor?' Bear asked, signing.

4

The air being squeezed out at the edges of the cold mass over the continent of Asia swung in a long, right-hand spiral over the South China Sea until it collided with the Indochina coast, where crags and trees tore its lower layers to turbulent shreds. Flying at a few hundred feet became like driving a hilly road paved with cobblestones. Vertical gusts hammered at the three ships flying in a loose trail formation. They nodded up and down, and shuddered with the smaller gusts.

The aircraft seemed to be guided by no purpose. They wandered the mountain valleys as if their pilots were lost or witless. The leader was far ahead of the other two, which hung closer together but still a long quarter mile apart. A sharp eye, if any human eye existed in those remote valleys, would have seen that the first aircraft differed from the other two. The two in the rear were gunships, but the first was a slick. A knowledgeable eye would have noted that it was no ordinary slick. A narrow pipe extended in front of the nose and ended in a crossbar extending almost the width of the fuselage.

The slick was a flying bloodhound. In the crossbar were chemical sensors sensitive to the odor of human beings, a technological nose delicate enough to scent men below the jungle canopy three hundred feet below.

The slick flew a meandering course, drawing gradually toward the cup of a pass, still open below the clouds, that debouched into another wandering valley leading to the coastal plain and home. 'It looks like Snoopy blew this one,'

Bear said. He parked the gunsight, put his feet up on the panel, yawned, and grinned in imitation of a Cheshire cat on its day off.

'I don't know what you've got against Snoopy,' answered Martin, who was flying right seat. 'I thought you liked animals.'

'I wouldn't have Snoopy up my rear if I had room for a snow-plow,' Bear answered flatly.

'Maybe Snoopy's got a cold,' Sergeant Handy suggested.

'I'm s'prised if he don't have n-n-newmonia, if h-h-he's as much out in the w-w-wind as w-w-w-we are back here,' Cripps's voice came over the intercom.

Bear's face crinkled with laughter. 'Cripps, is that *you*? Your very first speech on the intercom! And all you can do is complain about the cold. You're farther south here than in Tennessee.'

Cripps was seated at the back of the open side of the ship, with his machine gun cradled in his arms, shivering.

'I tol' you to wear your long johns this mornin', Cripps,' Sergeant Handy said, 'but what do I know?'

'I don't have n-n-none.'

'Never knew you'd need 'em in Vietnam? Well, if you're good maybe Santy Claus will fetch you some.'

'I tell you what, Cripps,' Martin said. 'I'll fly a little out of trim to put you out of the wind. Handy's dressed for the weather, so he won't mind.' He increased the pressure on the left rudder pedal to swing the nose to the left until the ship was flying cocked twenty degrees to the left of the line of flight. Icy wind poured through the ship from the right side.

'God damn!' Sergeant Handy had no intention of suffering to save face. He shrank away from the open door to the end of his monkey-strap and huddled behind Bear's seat.

'Chilly, ain't it, Sarge?' Bear said.

'Feels just f-f-fine to me,' Cripps said cheerily.

Blood, who was at that moment stretching his cramped legs while Atterburn flew, happened to glance back from the leading gunship. 'Look at that!' he exclaimed, in the tone of one who expected to find a fly in his soup and has just been proved right. 'Our glorious leader's been sitting behind a desk for a month, and he can't even fly straight anymore. If he can't do any better than that, he ought to leave the missions to people who can.' Blood was in a sour mood because Martin had pushed himself in to fly this mission. It was pure coincidence, of course, that Martin chose to fly the one on which Snoopy was being tried out. Of course. When there was a little free publicity to be had, the Ringknockers would gather. The general himself would probably want to see the results of this one. Martin knew how to get his name in the right places.

A voice on the radio cut through Blood's gloom and Martin's laughter: 'Wolf Lead, this is Snoopy. I have a reading.'

Blood came on the radio instantly: 'What do you have, Snoopy?'

'We just flew over some warm bodies, Lead. We'll make another pass and let you know.'

Bear quickly refolded his pasted-up map of the operational area to the segment that covered this valley. Martin had brought the ship back into trim, and Handy was back in his seat, looking eagerly out and to the front, where Snoopy was making a turn a half mile distant. The slick ship, now very low, crossed at right angles to their path.

'Bear, where are we?' Martin had been following Blood. He knew the way home, but was uncertain of their exact location over the ground. Below, everything was the uniform dark green of jungle canopy, slippery with rain.

Bear looked up from the map. 'Hill Four Seven Three, sir.' He pointed where the slick was crossing. A low mound, barely discernible from their altitude, bulged from the narrow valley bottom. 'We're just inside the free-fire zone.'

The slick was crossing the mound. 'Wolf Lead, we have a strong reading. He's right on top of this hill. Do you have us in sight?'

'Affirmative. Two, do you copy Snoopy?'

Bear had the flex gunsight down in position and was lowering his helmet visor with his left hand. 'Affirm,' Martin answered.

While Blood dived gently and loafed in over the hill a few hundred feet above the trees, Martin made a fast diving swing to the right to approach lower and from another direction. Snoopy had gone on and now was taking up a left-hand circuit a mile beyond the hill.

On the hill there was no sign of movement. The canopy of the forest was unbroken. Bear remembered the still columns of smoke rising from nowhere into the clear dry-season air. 'If he's down there, he can't see us for the trees,' Handy said. He added, 'I still think Snoopy has a cold.' They flew on until the whirling dark spot that was Blood's ship turned back. 'Two, did you get anything?'

'That's negative,' Martin answered.

'Let's try it again.'

They came back in the opposite direction. The crew in back leaned from the doors out into the biting wind, searching for any chink in the canopy. Not even a patch of earth flashed between the trees.

'We ought to put a few rounds down to stir them up,' Handy suggested.

'Maybe we're going to fly in circles till we run out of gas,' Bear said the words casually, as though chatting over the intercom; but he pressed the mike switch in to the second detent, so that the words went out over the radio for Blood to hear. He knew he was skirting the edge of danger by saying it; but he could not resist the temptation to needle Blood with what the words would bring to mind.

Blood's face flamed. 'Either the turd didn't learn anything the last time,' he said to Atterburn, 'or Martin put him up to that.' On the whole he found it more satisfactory to blame Martin. 'Golden Boy knows he's going to need a better body count than he's got so far, to impress the general. If you wonder why he didn't bump himself up to lead ship, I'll tell you: it's because that way his name's not on the report if we don't get anything; but if we come through with a big body count, you better stand aside, because he'll be coming right to the head of the line! The bastard thinks I'm too dumb to figure it out, because I'm not a Ringknocker. Well, let him stew awhile.'

They went around again, lower this time, and even slower. The wind whipped at the treetops; but what was below that, they could not tell.'

'Where does the free-fire zone end?' Martin asked.

'About a mile up. Across the next stream.' Beyond that was a second small stream, and then the pass and the valley leading home. 'If anybody's down there, he shouldn't be.'

'Well, there's no use carting all this junk home.' Martin radioed, 'Lead, how about dumping our ordnance here? We'll be lighter going home.'

Blood's answer came quick and cold: 'Two, you sure have my permission if you need it. I was just going to call you and ask if you didn't want to.'

Shy doubt fluttered for an instant toward the front of Bear's mind. But he could not really bring himself to believe that there was anyone at all on the ground. The hill was miles from the nearest village, more than a day's travel on foot over the precipitous terrain; and the whole area had been cleared by infantry and leafleted from the air as a free-fire zone. Anyone there should know he was subject to being shot on sight, or, apparently, on smell. And it had been a long dull day chasing Snoopy over wet jungle, through weather too bad to be pleasant but not bad enough to be exciting. His buttocks told him of every reticulation in the mesh seat. All small certainties joined to turn doubt aside. Then Blood's aircraft arrowed in, lacing the air with fire, and the sight of it sent doubt winging for cover.

Bear pushed the switches to 'arm' and laid the glowing pip in the gunsight on the base of the hill as Martin followed the lead ship up in a tight climbing turn to five hundred feet. Martin leveled out toward the hill. 'Anytime,' he said.

To the Bear the flex guns had a sad voice. The six rotating barrels sent one bullet after another so quickly that the individual shots could not be heard, only a long bronchial rasp, or a groan. But the individual bullets could be distinguished. Seen from behind, a short burst was a bushel of glowing embers thrown to the wind. They fell in a long graceful arc and vanished among the trees. Hold the trigger down longer, and a long stream of red jetted forward, wavering, like water from a shaken hose. Shift the glowing dot of light in the gunsight, and the stream could be played onto the target on which the dot fell. It was a marvelous toy.

Against the tearing sound of the flex guns played the steady hammer of the slower-firing machine guns in the hands of the crew, who strained against their monkey-straps, leaning out to aim their fire under the very belly of the ship or even to the rear. And, finest of all, the Fourth-of-July *whish* and bright fall of the rockets as Martin touched his thumb to the red button on the cyclic stick. Their white stars dwindled and then flashed bright again as the warheads exploded on the heavy upper branches of the forest: a flash, and a lingering white blossom of smoke which quickly passed beneath the helicopter as it turned away to meet Blood coming back in.

Inbound again, and smoke was seeping up from below the treetops. Blood's rockets had pierced the crown and exploded somewhere below. 'Going out in style,' Martin announced. With his left hand he set the rocket selector switch to 'all'. He had fired only two pairs on the first pass: five pairs remained in their tubes below the flex guns. He corrected the rudder pedals to center the bubble of the rocket sight, put the glowing dot halfway up the hill, so that the rockets would not pass over and be wasted if he shot long, and gently thumbed the firing button. The aircraft shuddered, although no more than from the gentlest touch of air turbulence, as the ten rockets flashed free in a white ripple of fire. Bear held down the flex-gun trigger. The stream of fire sank without a trace into the unmarked hillside.

They passed over the top of the hill and followed Blood straight on toward home. Bear pushed the gunsight up against its latch. When he took the controls for a moment the ship, empty of ordnance, felt strangely light and free. His heart felt the same. The fruitless afternoon had burned up in the fires of the attack.

Snoopy, who belonged to a company at Da Nang, reported that he was breaking off to return home. He signed off their radio frequency and vanished up a side valley to the north.

'Do you s'pose there was anybody down there?' Sergeant Handy asked after a time. 'I'd like to go back on the ground, just to see what happened.' Handy took delight in his work. A field full of bodies was a fine sight to him. He was a true sportsman, who would if possible have put endless time into hunting down the last cripple rather than leave him to suffer. Target practice was better than carrying ammunition home, but it was second-rate business. 'It's like shootin' through a curtain,' he mused. 'I sure wish I knew who was behind it.'

'If it was anybody,' Bear said, 'I pity him.'

'Well, sir, I'm *sure* glad it was him instead of me!'

Martin slid his seat back to stretch his legs and watched the wet jungle roll by below. Beyond the pass ahead, the light was already fading from the east. With the coming of evening the overcast would be lowering. He would not like to find the pass closed. But once over that, and it would be home again, home again, jiggety jig, as the Bear put it. The blade of Bear's ship, still chronically out of track despite the best efforts of the maintenance unit, gave the whole ship one vertical shake per revolution of the main blade, and an imbalance gave a two-per-revolution horizontal shake. The combination made the ship fly with the hop-shuffle, hop-shuffle of a little girl at hopscotch. The effect was soporific at the end of a day's hunt.

Martin was snapped from his meditation by the radio, by an urgent voice calling: 'Any helicopter in the vicinity of Bravo Tango two-six-zero zero-two-five, please come up on guard. This is Covey Two-three on guard. I say again, any helicopter in the vicinity of Bravo Tango two-six-zero zero-two-five, please come up.' The transmission was loud; it came from close at hand. As Martin snatched up the area chart, Bear affirmed, 'That's us.' When there was no immediate radio response from Blood, he added, 'Do you suppose His Leadership heard that?'

'If he didn't he's the only pilot in country not listening to guard,' Martin said. The guard channel was the emergency radio frequency, automatically received on all military aircraft UHF receivers unless the pilot turned it off. There were no transmissions on guard except when immediate help was needed.

The coordinates were those of a river junction they had just crossed, not far from Hill 473. Martin switched his transmitter to the UHF guard frequency. 'Covey Two-three, this is Wolf Two. Go ahead.'

'Wolf Two, I'm Forward Air Control, standing by near An Lau. Arty just monitored an emergency call from a company somewhere in this area. They couldn't read the exact coordinates, but they're on Fox Mike frequency forty-six point twenty, call sign Battleax. They've taken heavy casualties and need an emergency medevac. Can you contact them?'

Before Martin could reply, Blood came on the radio: 'Covey Two-three, this is Wolf Lead. That's affirmative. We're gunships: I don't know if we can help on a medevac. But we'll try to raise them.'

'Okay, thanks. I'll be monitoring guard, if you want to keep in touch.'

'And we're out of ammo!' Martin lamented over the intercom. He was bitterly sorry now for the attack they had wasted. They might have been of some use as gunships, if not as medical evacuation helicopters. 'How long will it take us to rearm and get back?' he asked Bear, switching hurriedly to the FM channel and turning back to the map at the same time.

Blood called on FM, and a young, shaken voice came up immediately, loud and almost shouting in panic. 'Wolf Lead, Wolf Lead, we gotta have some help! The old man and the first sergeant are both dead, and two of the platoon leaders, and a whole lot of others hurt bad . . .'

'Battleax, what's your location?' Blood demanded. 'I don't have your coordinates.'

'Uh, roger, I hope you can get in here; we're at, uh, just a minute, it's on top of this big hill . . .'

'Never mind where they are, damn it!' Martin muttered. 'Find out if they're still under attack!'

'We're just . . . we're on top of this big high hill right here . . .'

'All right, Battleax,' Blood radioed, 'we'll find you. Just keep talking to me. We're not far away.' Blood's ship swung into a gentle turn to the left. Bear followed him around. He had the FM homing indicator on, but Battleax stopped talking before the needle centered.

Impatiently, Martin called, 'Battleax, this is Wolf Two. Are you still under fire?'

'Ah, Wolf . . . Lead, ah, this is Battleax. Negative, they've gone away. But we've got people in real bad shape here . . .'

'All right, do you have place where we can land there?'

'Get off the radio, Two.' Blood's voice. 'Battleax, 'what's the terrain like around you?'

'I don't know, there's just trees . . .' Another voice came on. This one was young, too, but steady. 'Medevac, this is Battleax. We're cutting an LZ. It'll be ready in ten minutes. Do you have our coordinates?'

'This is Wolf Lead, Battleax. Negative on the coordinates. Are you still taking fire?'

'No. No, it's all over. Coordinates of our location are Bravo Tango two-two-five zero-two-zero. Do you copy?'

'I copy. Look, we're not medevac. Did you get a call in for Dustoff on your net?'

'That's affirmative. We don't care who you are, Wolf Lead, if you can get some of our people out.'

'We're on our way in.'

'Roger. I think I hear you. There are helicopters off to the east of us.'

During the exchange Bear had centered the needle on the FM homer. The two ships, bound directly toward Battleax, were retracing their course of a few minutes before.

Martin snatched up the map and searched frantically for the location of the coordinates Battleax had given. A low hill bulged up before them in the distance, beyond the metallic ribbon of river. 'It can't be!' He stared at Bear, who was chewing the ends of his mustache as he flew. Bear said nothing, but his face told that he knew it already. There was but one hill ahead of them in the direction from which Battleax's radio transmissions had come. 'A high hill,' the voice on the radio had said. The one ahead was not much of a hill, but to a man on the ground, under the trees, unable to see the mountains towering around, it might seem high enough. It was Hill 473.

As the hill rose, Martin's heart sank, knowing where they were bound. 'They're in the free-fire zone!' he said weakly. Battleax was on Hill 473. They had just attacked friendly troops.

It seemed impossible that anyone should be there. The smooth green canopy, still unbroken, sealed off the ground, covered whatever had happened there as though it had never been.

As they flew over, a tree fell. Its fall opened a hole in the canopy, removed a spot of green, replaced it with a spot of black without yet showing the ground. The edges of the hole moved back as other trees were dropped, but still no person was visible.

The second voice from the ground came on the radio: 'Wolf Lead, this is Battleax are you circling us?'

'Affirmative, Battleax.' Blood's voice was strangely soft.

'Is that a big enough LZ, Wolf Lead?'

The hole in the treetops looked hardly big enough to spit in, let alone squeeze in a fifty-foot helicopter blade. 'What do you think, Bear?' Martin asked.

Bear's voice, too, was broken. 'We can try it,' he said. 'We have to.' They had been flying longer than planned already. They would be burning their reserve fuel long before they could hope to reach Chu Lai, the nearest hospital. They could not wait. All of that was summed up in his few words, and was understood without discussion. And more: at their hands, men lay dying.

Martin did not press Blood for an answer, knowing he was thinking the same thoughts. The answer came: 'Battleax, we'll try it. Give us a smoke.'

The two ships circled the hill again before a puff of yellow showed at the bottom of the hole. It spread to fill the bottom without showing any drift: there was no wind there. A thin veil of yellow rose along the trees on one side, and at the top it was torn away to the west.

'I have a yellow smoke,' Blood said.

'Affirm on yellow,' Battleax replied.

'Two, I'm going in. Stand by.'

Martin clicked the mike switch twice. As he swung the helicopter away from the hill, Martin asked, 'How many packs will the ship carry, Bear?' It was the Bear's ship: he knew its performance better than Martin, who was only out for the day.

'Low on fuel, no ammunition' – at this the young officer seemed ready to weep, or to laugh: his face crinkled, and he turned away – 'with the ship this light, maybe four. Maybe three. That's a deep hole.'

'Battleax, how many casualties have you got?' Martin radioed, ignoring Blood's earlier demand for silence.

'Ah, you'll have to stand by one, Wolf. We're getting a count. Maybe thirty.'

'Jesus!'

'We can get rid of the rocket pods,' Bear said. 'That would add one body at least.' The rocket pods were not permanently fastened to their mounts. They could be jettisoned in flight in an emergency. But to release them over the jungle would mean the loss of weapons which might not be replaced for days. The ships would be crippled for missions. The guns, on quick release latches, could be removed by hand on the ground. 'We'll kick them off in the LZ,' Martin said. 'The guns, too. That should give us one other pack.' He switched to his VHF transmitter and called, 'Lead, this is Two. Suggest we jettison the weapons in the LZ to get as many casualties on as we can carry.'

There was no reply from Blood, who was closing on the landing zone. The nose of his ship came up as it slowed. It hung for an instant, sank toward the trees. Then its nose went down, and it began to climb. Blood was going around.

'Battleax, Wolf Lead. You'll have to take out more trees.'

'Wolf . . . Wolf Lead, stand by.' It was Battleax's first voice. In a moment the second came on: 'Wolf Lead, we're out of C-four. We'll have to cut some trees by hand.'

'How long will it take?'

'I don't know.'

'We're low on fuel, Battleax. We can't wait long.'

From a half mile out the hole in the treetops had not even been visible. They had closed within a quarter mile before Martin could see it again. He began slowing the aircraft. The jungle crawled underneath. Now it was not a blur of leaves, not a lumpy green carpet, but individual trees, reaching for the aircraft. The Bear was on the other set of controls now, but Martin could feel him there only at intervals, only the merest hint of resistance as the cyclic moved. The airspeed fell to forty knots, thirty, twenty. At twenty knots airspeed the ship was almost stopped over the trees. It inched into the strong headwind that whipped the leaves to a froth. Martin eased the ship forward over the hole. Through the chin bubble beneath his feet, faces stared up from a hundred feet below. Arms were waving. The aircraft hovered, almost at full power. 'Is our tail rotor clear?'

'I think you're clear, sir.' Sergeant Handy.

'Coming down.'

He eased the collective-pitch stick downward. The ship seemed reluctant to descend into the dark hole, as if it had a mind of its own and dreaded what waited there. 'Down, damn you!' Martin hissed under his breath, remembering flight school, ages ago: make a perfect approach and, at the critical instant, the ship would unaccountably refuse to land. But it was all, all, in the pilot's mind and hands. The ship would behave, if one had the will to master it. He willed the aircraft to descend into the hole, with sweat trickling from under his helmet.

'Clear over here,' Bear said. He was following on the controls and not turning his head, but looking to the side from the corner of his eye.

'How's the tail?'

'Still clear, sir.'

At fifty feet above the ground, with a quick *whap-whap* the main blade struck off a protruding branch and cast it into the darkness among the trees; but the ship continued its steady descent.

The trees had been blasted off as low as possible, but the stumps a foot or more high studded the clearing. Their mangled ends stuttered white exclamations of shock against the mud. There was no place to land. Martin dared not look down to check his height, for fear of drifting from the center of the hole and slipping the blade into a solid tree. 'How high are we, Handy?'

'Ten feet, sir.'

'Tell me when we can't get any lower.'

'Yes, sir.'

'Just a couple more feet, sir.' Handy was suddenly formal, under the strain of the descent: suddenly respectful to the man who held all their lives between the thumb and forefinger of his right hand. A movement of a quarter inch of those fingers could turn the delicately poised machine into a tangle of twisted, burning metal.

Martin could feel the Bear's touch on the controls now, although they did not move except when he himself moved them. It felt as though the ship were communicating to him the touch on the other stick, saying, 'No, this way,' when he tried to make a false motion.

Faces came into his line of vision at the edge of the trees. He could not see that there was solid earth there, nor bodies to stand upon it. There was nothing but faces, white among the white columns of the tree trunks. Jungle fatigues and helmets blended with the night which already lurked among the trees, but the faces stood forth like masks nailed on the darkness.

'Get 'em on.'

Handy waved an arm, but they were already coming. Four men scrambled over a fallen tree, ducking to miss the blade, trying not to drop the poncho on which a fifth man lay. They passed out of sight around the side of the ship. The aircraft lurched to that side. Martin fought the stick – with all his strength, it seemed, though it was but a fraction of an inch of movement to regain control, a pressure measured in ounces. 'Tell 'em to keep off the skids!' he said through gritted teeth. 'Tell 'em to get the men on and get back!'

More faces outside. Bear was talking to someone outside his window. 'How many do you want, sir?' he asked.

'How's our power?' Martin did not dare glance down at the N_1 tachometer, which would tell what percentage of their maximum power they were using already. Whatever it read now, they would need more to climb out of the hole. It was a hundred feet to the treetops. If they tried to climb out with too great a load, the ship would only give up the ghost and settle back to kill itself on the stumps or in the trees. But there were men dying here, at his hands. He did not dare look down at the instrument, for fear of slipping into the solid trees. He flew and sweated, as the Bear checked the gauge.

'We can't take any more.' Bear added, 'We've only got three on.'

'Cut the pods off.' From the side of his eyes Martin saw Bear's hand leave the control stick and move to the yellow lever beside his own seat, to pull it up through the safety wire. The ship was suddenly buoyed up. Martin pressed it firmly back down. 'Rocket pods away,' Bear said.

Cripps's voice, so seldom heard, seemed strangely lost and out of place on the intercom when he spoke. 'Sir, I could get off. You'd be able to carry more men.' Bodies were still being carried out of the darkness, assembled along the edge of the clearing. They came out of that night draped in dark ponchos like black spirits, with faces white as death. 'No, Cripps.'

'But, sir, I can't do nothing for these guys. I'm just so much weight. You can get me later.'

Martin knew Cripps was right. His own reaction was wrong. But it was like leaving one he knew among the dead to leave Cripps buried in this dark place. Yet Cripps was right. 'All right. Handy too. And take off the guns. We'll be back for you. If Dustoff comes in sooner, come out with them.'

'Yes, sir.'

'Handy . . .' There was no answer on the intercom. Handy was gone.

A movement beside his head caught his eye, and he turned toward the movement for an instant. Beside the ship they were tearing the guns away. Another body came aboard. 'We've got seven on,' Bear said. 'That's all.'

Martin tested the collective stick, the lever in his left hand through which he must lift the whole weight of the ship. It seemed to him that he could feel every pound collecting in the palm of his hand. The ship did not want to come up. 'Bear, take us out,' he said.

'I've got it, sir.' Martin remained on the controls, but the weight passed from his hand. The feeling of the life of the aircraft drained from his right forefinger and thumb. He was suddenly but a passenger. His eyes went to the N_1 tachometer. It stood fixed at 95.6%. MAXIMUM POWER, the placard next to it proclaimed, 95.8%. That was at sea level. They were fifteen hundred feet higher here: the engine was putting out all the power it had.

He felt the collective ease upward. The N_2 tachometer, whose twin needles told engine speed and rotor speed, crept back. The ship had hovered at normal engine output-shaft speed, sixty-six hundred rpm. As the pitch in the blade was increased to lift the ship, the drag increased, and with no more power available, the blade and engine slowed. The tachometer needle crept downward across the green arc. At six thousand rpm engine speed the tail rotor, geared to the main rotor, would no longer be turning fast enough to compensate for the torque of the main blade, and the tail would obey Newton's second law of motion by beginning an inexorable drift to the left, a drift which could be stopped only by reducing power or by striking some solid object. The needle crept below sixty-four hundred. The low-rotor-speed warning flicked on, driving its frantic pinging through their headphones. But the ship was rising along the tree trunks. 'Strong-hearted ship,' Martin said to it, to himself, 'be strong.' The tachometer stabilized at the bottom of the green. Martin watched each branch of the trees in front sink past. At fifty feet the blade clipped the same branch. The light increased as they climbed. At eighty feet he radioed, 'Wolf Lead, Two is coming out.'

'Roger, Two,' Blood's voice answered. 'We're inbound. How is it?'

'Tight. And the bottom's full of stumps. We've left our weapons and our crew there.'

At the top of the hole the blade reached the wind above the trees. The Bear eased the stick forward as the skids cleared the treetops and in a flurry of blades they were released from the grip of the earth and climbed swiftly away.

'Lead, we're on the way to Chu Lai,' Martin radioed.

'Roger, we'll catch you.'

'I'll take it now,' Martin said.

'You've got it.' Bear had been surprised when Martin turned the controls over to him. He had flown with men who would sooner have crashed than do that. It was as much as to say, 'I know you are the better pilot.' Among pilots that meant the better man. The gesture impressed Bear. It made him admire Martin in a way he had not done before.

When Blood reported himself out of the LZ, Bear put on the position lights. Night was coming up from the valleys, and against the clouds they would now be almost invisible. Within a few minutes Blood's ship drew up alongside. Martin fell in behind.

It was then that Bear looked into the back of the ship for the first time. Four of the wounded were able to sit up. They had been perched on the bench seat which stretched across the back of the cabin, where they remained as motionless as statues, as medieval exemplars of the ills of the flesh. One's head was swathed in a turban of bandage which wound down over the left eye; another had one sleeve of his fatigues cut off, and the arm wrapped from wrist to shoulder; a third showed a splash of bandage under his half-open shirt. But it was those on the floor of the ship who caught Bear's eye. They were laid head to toe, but the floor was still too narrow for three, so one had been laid half on top of another. The feet of those sitting up had been worked between and around those on the floor as well as possible, but still they could be accommodated only by propping up an arm here, a leg there. The central man on the floor was conscious. He stared up at the cabin top with unmoving eyes and bit his lips, first the top one, then the bottom. Watching him, Bear was made acutely aware of the roughness of the ride. At every bump and jiggle the soldier's body shook. His shirt was off; his chest had been bandaged all the way around, and blood had soaked through the bandage. One hand hovered always near his chest, but he seemed never to dare touch it. There was a catch in his breath, evident in the labored movement of his chest even though it could not be heard above the din of the machine. Bear supposed he must be moaning.

The third soldier, the one stacked closest to the front seats, was the first who had been carried out on his poncho. He was on it still. He lay with his eyes closed, his hair matted over his forehead, his arms limp at his sides. There was a band about his left thigh, over the trousers. It was a belt tourniquet, twisted with a stick which had been tied to a belt-loop at his waist to keep it from loosening. A ring of dark blood soaked the trousers from the knee to the ankle. It was some time before Bear noticed the strange way the leg rolled, like a log in a heavy sea. As the aircraft bounced, the leg and foot rolled, but the upper leg did not. The trouser leg had been severed at the ring of blood, and when he looked closely there was no knee there at all. What remained of the leg had come along with the soldier, still in the boot; but it was not part of him. As the ship moved, as the moaning soldier bit his alternate lips, the bodyless leg lay rocking, rocking, rocking. Bear turned away.

To Chu Lai from the hill was little more than twenty

miles. The route could not be flown quite in a straight line, for the low cloud base made it necessary to wind down the river valley which debouched into Song Ben Van, the inland bay at the north perimeter of Chu Lai. But at a hundred and twenty knots, with the collective-pitch stick pulled as high as it would go, the distant grey of the sea soon came in sight, and the lights of Chu Lai just coming on against the evening. They whirled out onto the plain. Blood still had not called to alert the hospital that they were coming. They were near the control zone when Martin radioed to remind him. 'He was just going to do it,' Bear said grimly.

'Ah, Two,' Blood replied, 'I was just going to do it.'

Chu Lai tower rogered Blood's call and in a moment called back to give them the medical evacuation frequency for the hospital. By the time Blood could call on that frequency, the tower had alerted the hospital. A black southern voice answered his call: 'Wolf Lead, are you comin' from Battleax?'

'That's affirmative, and there's more casualties out there. Did you send Dustoff out?'

'Negative on that, Wolf Lead. We got three ships out on another mission. As soon as one comes back, he'll be on his way. It shouldn't be more'n twenty minutes.'

While that was taking place, Martin had called company Operations. His hope was to find some of the slicks on the ground, either to send out in addition to their own ships, or to trade for them. The slicks would at least carry more bodies. But in that he was disappointed. Lieutenant Rauch answered in his unhurried buttery voice: 'Man, we had a big CA come up, and *everything* has hit the fan. Everything we got is flyin' but the hangar queens. What's your problem, Wolf?'

'An emergency medevac's our problem! Haven't you even got the general's ship in?'

'You ain't goin' to get blood all over the general's ship?' Rauch did his best to sound shocked.

'I am if it's on the ramp.'

'Nope – he's out, too, watchin' the big show. Medevac's a little out of your line, anyway, ain't it, Wolf?' Rauch had recognized Martin's voice, but not his seriousness.

'Then get us a fuel truck,' Martin ordered. 'We'll be on the ramp in five.'

'Sure. You want to rearm?'

'That's negative.'

'Roger the fuel truck.'

They crossed beyond the main runway, low under the jet departure pattern, popped up over the ridge beside the officers' club, and together whirled to a fast stop on the pad outside the doors of the medical evacuation hospital at the end of their own parking ramp. In their months of flying from the same ramp, it was the first time any of them had been at the hospital pad. They had all of them a strange sense of dislocation, landing at the wrong end of the ramp, seeing the wrong end of the buildings and the canvas maintenance hangars swelling like deformed whales out of the darkness toward Ky Ha.

Before they were solidly on the ground, corpsmen in gowns or green T-shirts were running toward them, pushing litters on wheels. The men sitting up in back had first to have their feet disentangled before those on the floor could be moved. For a moment the two ships were the center of a milling mass, as if ants had converged on scraps of choice carrion. Then the bodies had suddenly vanished: the ships were empty. Bear did not see what had become of the soldier with the severed leg. He did not look back to see. When the last of the litters had vanished through the swinging doors, Martin pulled pitch and whirled down the ramp to the parking area, where a fuel truck had pulled out to await them.

They refueled with the engines running. The truck driver, who had never refueled before with the blade cutting overhead, handled the hose clumsily. He gaped about looking for Handy and Cripps. Martin pounded the cyclic impatiently as this went on. He waved off the driver when they had taken on only six hundred pounds of fuel. It would cut their reserve to the bone, if they should have to make a detour; but they could carry more casualties that way than with a full tank.

As Blood was being refueled, Lieutenant Rauch, who could see them from the Operations doorway, came on the company frequency: 'Say, Wolf, what happened to your guns?'

'We'll talk about it later,' Martin answered.

'God damn, you must of got into something big! I'll write you up for a medal!'

'Sure. You do that.'

'Listen, where you bound for, Wolf?'

Martin gave him the coordinates and then switched off the frequency. He called to Blood that his ship was ready, and in a moment Blood picked up to depart. They climbed out over the ocean and turned quickly downwind toward what little remained of the day, west behind the mountains.

Darkness met them at the railroad beyond Route One, short of even the foothills fronting the big mountain. Rain began to spit against the windscreen. They crossed above the two villages named Thanh My Trung, but there were no lights. The Bear had put the panel lights on at their dimmest setting. The soft red glow of the gauges was no brighter than a remembered dawn. The only other mark on the universe was the lights of the lead ship. Without their guns they flew in uncomfortable awareness of what might be on the ground. The beacons were turned off, and Martin moved in close off the leader's port quarter.

As the cloud base lowered, the ground level rose beneath them, and the mountains were hidden giants on either hand. Into the narrowing funnel of earth and cloud they plunged on until they dared risk flying in darkness no longer. Blood switched on his searchlight.

Despite the open invitation to whoever had a weapon to try it on them, they all felt instantly more confident. Bear noticed it in Martin, who loosened his grip on the cyclic stick as he slid the ship farther back from Blood's. There was no danger now of losing sight of the other aircraft, and with the searchlight picking out the thread of river below, there was no danger of plunging into a mountain in the dark, at least until the time came to cross over the pass above Phu Tho, into the valley of the westward-running river beyond.

They found the pass still open. If the hill itself were not already buried in cloud, they would be able to reach Battleax. In answer to Blood's radio call Battleax spoke calmly from the darkness. It was the second voice that had replied that afternoon. Martin supposed it was that of the young lieutenant he had seen glance out once from the trees. The old man – the company commander – was dead, the other voice had said. And the first sergeant and the two platoon leaders. Their attack had killed nearly the whole command structure. He wondered whose the first voice had been. The radioman's? Or simply someone who had picked up the set, after the radioman was killed with the commanding officer? The lieutenant had been calm from the first. He must be a good officer. He had a future. Martin wondered if the lieutenant knew that he was speaking to his attackers.

'Battleax, how many wounded have you got left?' Blood asked.

'I've got eight. The Kilo India Alphas can wait.' That was phonetic alphabet for KIA – killed in action.

'How many KIA?'

'Twelve.'

It was some time before Blood spoke again. 'We can't take them all, Battleax.' On the first trip they had got out twelve on the two ships. 'Have you heard from Dustoff yet?'

'Negative, Wolf.'

'He's supposed to be on his way by now.'

'Roger.'

How was it that a man could talk calmly to persons he did not know, about the death and anguish of those he did know, who lay in the wet dark around him, waiting for deliverance?

They homed again on Battleax's voice. The homing needle flicked over as the hill pushed up into the circle of light from Blood's searchlight. The landing zone was bigger now:

Battleax had been busy cutting trees. Martin swung out into the darkness to let Blood land.

Outbound, he turned on his own light. As the beam stabbed into the night below them, a glowing aureole formed about the whole ship in the damp air. Their eyes ached suddenly as glare washed out everything beyond the windshield. Bear reached overhead to the rheostat that controlled the panel lights and turned it until the red gauges could be seen again through the glare. Waiting for Blood to call that he was coming out, they turned and flew slowly back toward the hill, brushing aside fingers of cloud which dangled from the overcast. At a half-mile range Blood's light popped suddenly into view. They tried to remember the spot but soon lost it. Bear manipulated the searchlight ahead as they descended, until the LZ was there, a black hole caught in the circle of light in which individual trees now cast hard shadows.

'Landing light,' Martin said. The landing light was housed beside the searchlight in the belly of the ship. Stowed, it pointed straight down. When they were over the hole, they would need both lights, one to light the ground, the other to shine forward on the trees for a horizon reference, so that the ship could be kept level. Bear switched on the light.

The well of darkness slid under them and was suddenly filled with light.

The searchlight marked their inch-by-inch descent along the tree trunks. The tree whose outer branches they had struck before was no longer there. A light drizzle had slicked the clay between the stumps at the bottom. Poncho-draped forms, ghosts in mourning, slipped and stumbled toward them in crippled haste. In this scene from an everyday hell the spirits bore their sins on their shoulders in the forms of their tormented brothers. Among the bearers were Cripps and Handy. Handy grinned through the windscreen as he rounded the front of the ship. The thickness of Plexiglas which separated them seemed the breadth of eternity.

Bear watched the bearers hobble back beyond the reach

of the lights, back to the night that pressed in all around. He pitied anyone driven into that night.

As Handy reached the edge of the trees, he turned to give them a thumbs-up sign. Martin pulled pitch and sank that hell behind them.

Blood had taken out all but three of the wounded. Those three were aboard, and to make up the load three bodies had been stacked on the floor. Martin saw the bodies when he turned the ship over to Bear to fly. They might have taken out Cripps and Handy instead, he thought. What was night in the jungle to one already dead?

They had not gone far when they heard another aircraft calling, another lone wanderer in the void. It was Dustoff at last, calling Battleax. He was still east of the pass, where Battleax could not receive him. Blood answered.

'Hello, Wolf,' Dustoff said in reply. 'I hear you've been to Battleax. Can we still get through?'

'Affirmative, Dustoff. We've got the last of the wounded aboard. There's still some KIAs for you.'

'Thanks a lot, Wolf. Glad you left some for us. I'd hate to come out here in this dark for nothing.'

'Why doesn't the s.o.b. pass his chitchat on another channel?' Bear muttered on the intercom.

'If you've got room, Dustoff, we've got four crew in the LZ,' Blood added. 'Can you bring them in?'

'Ah, how many bodies still to go, Wolf?'

'Two, how many have you got aboard?' Blood asked. 'There should be nine more.'

'Oh, that's dandy, Wolf. I'm a flight of two, so no problem on your crew. You can pick 'em up in the emergency room. You hear that, Ski?' The last remark was apparently meant for Dustoff's trail ship. The only answer was two clicks.

The flight back to Chu Lai was the longest in Martin's memory. After other missions there had been easy chatter on the intercom, winding down from the excitement of an attack, or staving off boredom after an empty patrol. Now there was no word spoken. Sunk in black private thoughts, they journeyed together, separated by a gulf of guilt and shame, hating where they were and yet wishing this flight might have no end, rather than face the inevitable ending. While the Bear flew, Martin sat, hands folded in his lap, watching the light from Blood's ship tumble down the valley toward a horizon that never arrived.

It meant his career: he saw that. He wished not to think of it, for it seemed to him ignoble, to think of his career when at his back lumps of battered flesh gasped for life itself. But he could not help it: he did think of it. Martin was not vain or self-deceiving. He had always seen himself as one marked out for eventual high rank, but only because others also saw that in him. He did not deceive himself now. He saw that it was over. There was no overlooking a mistake so great.

He leaned back and closed his eyes, and for an instant there came to him a vision, he did not know whether of hope or of despair, a waking dream that was to come over him many times in the weeks ahead, at moments when he was not guarding his thoughts – a vision so intensely real that when he returned from it he was startled to find himself still seated in the ship. He dreamed, for an instant, that he was indeed dreaming, in his quarters in his bunk, and that he was about to awake, relieved, from a shattering nightmare. Instead, he awoke and, twisting in his seat, found himself staring into the glittering eyes of one of the soldiers on the floor.

The soldier was dead. He lay on his back, facing half toward Martin. The poncho around him would not close because his right arm was raised, with the hand palm-out over his forehead as if to ward off a blow that would never fall. The eyes were half open and glittered back the light of a red map-light overhead. Martin reached back to push down the arm, but the soldier was already stiff. The arm was wet, not with blood, but with rain. One of the wounded men sitting above the body watched stonily, moving no more than the body on the floor. Martin turned away in confusion.

* * *

Entry into the emergency room was a frantic resurrection, a traumatic spillage from the dark, jolting metal womb of the helicopter into the chill uproar of the ER. Litters were manhandled onto trestles; hooked scissors ripped wet jungle fatigues from torn bodies; orderlies and medical corpsmen, nurses and doctors, milled for an instant in troubled eddies before falling into an orderly stream of procedure. There was no plan: each joined in at the point where he found himself. Yet, although the uproar did not diminish, their efforts suddenly coalesced, as the milling frenzy of a startled flock of geese swings, without direction, into a single V pointing north.

The soldier who had lost his leg came in through the swinging door and was installed beneath an overhead bar where bottles of clear fluid hung waiting like crystalline jellyfish dangling their plastic tentacles. There happened to be a doctor there. Nothing distinguished him from the corpsmen. Like many of them he wore a green sleeveless surgical shirt. Others, doctors and assistants alike, poured into the emergency room in fatigues or T-shirts and fell straight to work. Because he was at hand, the doctor turned first to the soldier with his leg off.

The bearers dropped the litter on the trestles and ran for the door, for another body. The litter rocked, and the leg rolled over the edge. It was not fully severed. A strand of skin and flesh still connected the calf to the upper leg. The boot and the bloody pulp above it dangled below the litter, swinging and slowly revolving, stretching slowly toward the floor. The soldier's eyes were closed. He was pale-faced, his skin clammy.

The doctor took the soldier's wrist. The pulse tapped weakly at his fingertips. 'Give him two units of low-lite O straightaway,' he said to the nearest corpsman. 'He's shaky.' The corpsman shouted to the rear of the room and put up his hands to catch a bag of blood which came through the air as if delivered from heaven. Another bag followed. The corpsman caught it between one hand and his stomach. While the doctor put a needle into the soldier's arm, the corpsman slipped a bag onto an overhead hook and attached the intravenous tube. 'Get his pressure,' the doctor said. 'I'll be back.' Without a word the corpsman began taping the tube to the soldier's arm.

The census officer, a little man wearing fatigues with captain's bars, stopped beside the soldier's head. He did not look at the face. 'His number's seven-five-five,' he announced.

'Can't be,' the corpsman grunted, inserting another needle. 'I just gave that to the sucking chest.'

'Now, don't tell me we're going to have the numbers game again!' The census officer detested the insubordination of medical people during a mass casualty.

'When did we have a mass cal that we didn't get into the numbers game?' the corpsman asked.

'We simply cannot go on this way!' the captain insisted. 'The colonel's going to hear about this! All right, number seven-five-six?'

'Fine by me.' The corpsman fished a blue felt-tip pen from a shirt pocket and wrote the number on the soldier's forehead. He emphasized it with a heavy underline which neatly connected the high arch of the eyebrows.

The doctor had gone to number seven-five-five, the sucking chest. A major whose name, according to his name tag, was Kant, was poring over the soldier's naked body while a nurse held the remains of a foil bandage below the soldier's left nipple. 'Dan, my eyes are going bad,' Major Kant said to the other doctor. 'I can't tell the shrapnel holes from the mosquito bites.' The soldier's torso bore several tiny red spots. A few continued to ooze thin streams of blood. They were all that showed where the bits of jagged metal had slashed into the body 'That's the zit that's sucking,' Major Kant added, nodding toward the spot the nurse was covering. A tiny fragment piercing the right chest had allowed air to enter and collect around the outside of the lung when the soldier inhaled. When he exhaled the hole closed from the inside like a valve, sealing in the air, so that the lungs steadily increased the pressure that was collapsing them. Before he passed out, the soldier had felt the incubus Death enter with the air. It had set up quarters in his chest and was slowly elbowing his life aside.

Major Kant held a long hollow needle against the chest wall and with the heel of his hand thrust it forcibly between the ribs. The air sighed out. The soldier no longer labored for breath. 'That's better,' the major said, 'but there's a zit in the throat, too, below the larynx, and one that could have got the spleen. His pressure's only eighty over. I want him first for the OR, unless there are some more outside that I haven't seen.'

'He's the only airway,' the other doctor agreed. 'We've got some bad bleeders – the amputee over there's fairly shocky, but he can wait once we get him stabilized. There's one for neurosurgery back there. He took a frag over the eye. We'll have to get films to see where it wound up. Were these the only choppers?'

'Apparently not. I don't know who's bringing them in, but they went back for more. They're not our choppers.'

'Well, there are six for the OR, counting the one for neuro.' A fragment in the brain had low priority for the operating room. A man could live long – until the infection set in – with a fragment in his brain. It was the less spectacular wounds which demanded haste – any interference with the air supply first, then unchecked bleeding, and so down through the gamut of injuries, through fragments of steel in the brain, and ending with lowly fractures and other wounds which, although painful, never killed anyone quickly. Pain took a place in line when a mass cal poured through the door of the ER.

'This one's ready to go,' Major Kant called out. 'Chest and abdomen films first, then to the OR.' Two orderlies appeared. They fastened tall rods like fishing poles to the litter, transferred the blood bags to the poles, and with the litter between them hurried out the door at the back of the emergency room.

A nurse hovered uncertainly in the vacancy where the litter had been. 'You can take care of the one over here,' the doctor said to her, 'unless you've got something else pressing.'

She had not. The rest of the medical people had by now fallen into task forces that had stabilized for better or worse. What needed doing instantly was being done. She followed the doctor.

The doctor glanced at two other wounded men on his way back to the soldier with the leg off, but he did not stop. From a shelf he took a clipboard, which he rested on the soldier's stomach. The nurse's eyes stayed on the leg which swung alongside the litter. 'You can put it back up,' he said. 'What's he got, Dean?'

'Pulse one-forty. Blood pressure sixty over ten with a unit in. We just started the second unit.'

'That's better. But you'd better put a pressure cuff on the bag and push it in faster.' He began unbuttoning the man's jacket. 'Get his trousers off,' he said to the nurse, 'and let's see what else he's got, before he gets to the OR.' He handed her a pair of scissors from a pocket on his gown. 'I'm Rawlinson,' he said as he handed over the scissors. 'Lieutenant Porter, I presume?' She was wearing fatigues with a new black-printed name tag.

'Alice Porter.'

'I just got back from Hong Kong,' he said, 'but I know you weren't here when I left. When did you show up?'

'Yesterday . . . no, the day before.'

'Mm. New in country?'

'Yes.'

'Devil of a time to leave home, right before Christmas. Devil of a time to see your first mass cal, too. You have to see one sometime, but they don't always fall on you the first day.' Dr Rawlinson said all this quite absently as he studied the soldier's body for zits. He forestalled any answer by slipping his stethoscope into his ears.

She struggled to cut the soldier's trousers free without loosening the tourniquet on the thigh. She felt exasperatingly inept. She had not completely shaken off the effects of her flight halfway around the world two days before. Instead of the change to tropic heat she had expected, she had gone from a warm dry California winter to the chilly damp of the winter monsoon. The dry chill of the air-conditioned emergency room did not steady her hand. She had seen mangled bodies before, but so may at once was something new even if not unexpected. Twelve maimed young men together were, somehow, more than a cumulation of so many cases met on a ward. And another shipment was due to arrive within the hour!

She was determined to be a proper nurse, and so she was almost pleased to see something that did need attention. 'We need more blood,' she said, looking up at the bags hanging limp overhead.

'I'll get it, ma'am.' The corpsman hurried toward the back of the room, where one of his fellows was standing by with a cart of blood units.

The doctor unplugged his stethoscope and began scribbling on his clipboard. 'You can clean up the stump a bit while he's waiting to go in,' he said. He left without another word.

She began cleaning the debris and dead tissue from the soldier's leg. The outside was blackened and burned where the trousers had been torn away. There were ragged scraps of cloth glued on with dried blood, leaves, and bits of stick; and the splintered bone had somewhere gouged into red gritty earth that was packed up inside like petrified marrow. The trouser leg was stuck to the slender strip of flesh still holding the lower leg to the rest of the man. She knew the leg would be removed anyway, but she left it attached to him. Before she had finished, two corpsmen came to bear the litter away. She stood for a moment watching the empty blood bags swaying overhead after he was gone.

As the soldier with one leg began the trek up the corridor toward the operating room, his friend with the sucking chest wound lay under the hands of the surgeon. His chest wound had been probed, cleansed, and closed, with a tube inserted to reinflate the lung and keep pressure from rebuilding around it. The surgeon had only begun with the soldier, but already he felt good about him. The big problem, the immediate problem, was solved. There remained only the tedious job of sorting through yards of bloody gut, tracking down the perforations in the wake of steel fragments. 'Let me see those films again.'

'There's one near the back, there,' said Rawlinson, who had come in to assist. 'Another one over here on the side.'

The abdomen was hard under his fingers as the surgeon began to cut. It was distended with internal bleeding from the many perforations of the intestine. He finished pulling back the skin and muscle, cut into the abdominal cavity. Dark red blood welled instantly from the incision.

'Jesus, there must be three liters in there!' Rawlinson exclaimed. 'Is it a spleen, do you think?'

'Doctor, he's going into shock,' the anesthetist said.

'Now what?' The surgeon looked from the perforated gut to the soldier's face, which was going suddenly pale. He looked back at the incision, hooked a finger under the first loop of intestine, and stared. 'Christ, it must be the vena cava!' He held out his hand for a scalpel which appeared with agonizing slowness because of this break in routine. When it came, he slashed the incision down nearly to the pubis and threw down the scalpel to paw frantically through the yards of slippery guts, trying to reach the bottom in time. Blood poured from the incision, slopping out bits of floating feces. It was chilly blood that had only now been forced into the soldier from a bag. As fast as they had forced it in, it had been running out the perforation in the vena cava, the major vein at the back of the abdominal cavity, until so much blood had collected there it squeezed the vein closed and shut off the flow. Then the soldier's condition had appeared stable. But when the surgeon cut, the pressure was released and the flow resumed, draining the blood from the soldier faster than it could be replaced. Knowing that it was now the only hope, the surgeon plunged for the bottom, ignoring the perforated guts in the way, hoping to shut off the flow before the soldier died. He failed.

The soldier who had taken the zit through his head lay

staring at the ceiling, and at the many obscene things dangling from it. Those bags, now, full of red goo like ketchup out of the refrigerator. They hung there sweating. They didn't have to do that. He could do his own sweating, even if the room was cold. Christ, was it ever cold! Why didn't they turn down the air-conditioning?

The bags sweated because, although the room was chilly, they were chillier, having just come from refrigeration. There was no time to warm the blood. The soldier was cold because the blood going into to him was cold.

Mainly, the soldier thought about his wound. Not the one in his head – he did not even know that there was one there. The one he thought about was in his left calf. A machine gun bullet had gone through, taking a good piece of flesh along with it. He had begged Dunstable, the company corpsman, for morphine, but Dunstable, the son of a bitch, would not give him any. Zenakis, which was the soldier's name, did not think that was fair; but he put up with it, because he knew morphine was in short supply in the boonies, and there were plenty of other people who really did need it. Patulski, the poor bugger, was minus a leg. He got morphine. But in the hospital now, there should be plenty of morphine or whatever else he needed, but no one would give him any. That really did not seem the way to treat a guy who had just given his leg – well, a piece of his leg – for his country. And it hurt. It hurt more the longer he lay there.

He tried biting his lips and then his tongue, but now his tongue was bleeding and the leg hurt anyway, so he quit.

'Can I do anything for you?' The nurse's face came into his view. It was a long time since he had seen blue eyes on a woman.

'Ma'am, please, can I have something for my leg?' It embarrassed him to have to ask. It was an admission that the pain was stronger than he was. But since she had asked . . .

She read the tag on his litter. 'I'll get you something.' She was a beautiful nurse, Lieutenant Porter.

She brought him a Darvon and a glass of water. Not

knowing what it was, he took it gratefully. Another thing he didn't know was that, because of the head wound he did not know he had, he could not be given any morphine-based drug. The drug could mask the symptoms of brain damage. Zenakis swallowed his pill and lay back hopefully to wait for it to work.

She felt bad about giving him the Darvon. She knew the pain from the wound he had would not be teased away. She hoped the Darvon might help a little.

Zenakis thought the pain was only being stubborn, and for a while he gritted his teeth and told it to go away, half embarrassed now and half anguished, 'Please, do you suppose I could have a little more? I don't think it was enough.' When she said no, he was mortified. But the pain did not care. The pain was stronger than he was. It drove out his scruples. The next time, he pleaded, 'Ma'am, please! Please give me something!' He thought, when tears came to her eyes, that she would agree. But he was wrong.

Lieutenant Porter was too sympathetic to leave the soldier alone, and not hardened enough to be unaffected by his pleas. So she hovered around him, feeling guilty because she was unable to help. Zenakis and his head wound were far down the list for the operating room. He lay for another half hour. At the end he was pleading steadily, 'Oh, please. You could give me something, couldn't you? It's just not fair! Please give me something!'

He was taken away just as the second flight came in from Battleax.

The helicopters landed with a pounding roar that shook the bare walls of the building and set loose bottles dancing on the shelves, until the aircraft were throttled down to a low flapping whistle. A second avalanche of bodies poured through the swinging doors.

Preparations had been under way for this moment for nearly an hour, so that the turmoil of the first arrival was not repeated in full. But uncertainty as to the condition of the men who would be arriving led to a moment of confused scrambling until the triage was well under way. Although she was near the doors, it was some time before Lieutenant Porter noticed that a soldier had wandered alone in the ER. She took him at first for one of the walking wounded. He was pale, and his large eyes glared strangely. He said nothing, but walked back and forth pushing nervously with one hand at his bristling mustache. 'Sit down,' she said. 'We'll have time for you in a minute.' But instead he turned and rushed out.

On the helipad Martin turned in his seat to watch the last of the bodies unloaded. He turned back to find that the Bear had vanished. Only his helmet remained, perched on the left seat and still connected to the intercom cord. Martin knew where he had gone. To visit the wounded was at least an honorable gesture, however worthless to them. He waited for a short while, expecting Bear to return. Finally he picked up the ship to hover back to the company parking ramp.

He could see the lights of Blood's aircraft stationary in its revetment. As he hovered, Blood came on the company radio to report the flight down.

Rauch answered at once. 'Hey, Wolf, glad to see you back! You better haul ass up here. Six has been waitin' for you.' He meant that Major Hart was there: 'six' was radio code for a unit commander.

After the main blade had run down at last, Martin caught it with the hook. He was tying the tapes to the tail stinger when Blood and Atterburn came down the ramp from their ship. They stood back a few feet until Martin finished. Then Blood cleared his throat.

'Well?'

'Well, Martin, what are we going to say?'

'Why don't you just turn in a body count of thirty, Blood, and we'll all go to bed with no more said?'

'How good a chance do you think that has?'

He had not expected even Blood to take the remark other than ironically. His tongue was thick with disgust. 'About as much chance as Battleax had once we cut loose. There's only one reason the old man can be waiting for us.'

'Well, God damn it, Martin, you don't have to put on that high-and-mighty act with me! You were the ranking officer on this expedition, you know! If you're going to butt in and tell me when to dump my ordnance and when not to, you could at least be man enough to stand up and admit whose fault it was!' This accusation was not founded on anything Martin had yet said; but it represented Blood's accumulated sense of the unfairness of everything; and it was near enough the analysis that had been lurking about the back of Martin's mind that he found himself unable to answer. Blood saw his advantage and pressed it: 'We both know you only came on this flight to get your name in front of the general. I expect you'll be able to weasel out of it, since it didn't turn out the way you expected; but, by God, don't think I'm too dumb to know what you're up to! It's no accident that the first time you've had your sweet ass out of that swivel chair since you've been XO is a mission the general has his eye on!'

Blood's ambitions had always been apparent; but Martin was genuinely surprised at the depth of the bitterness now revealed. Blood failed to recognize that it was this rather than any accuracy in his charge which kept Martin silent now. So he began in a more conciliatory tone, hoping to press the advantage he thought he held. 'There's no use our getting at each other's throats, Martin. It's not your god-damn fault that Battleax was in the free-fire zone, and it's not mine either. For all we knew, they could have been Slopes down there. If they're going to blame it on anybody, let 'em blame it on Battleax Six, for getting his troops in there in the first place.'

'He's dead; it won't hurt him,' Atterburn said. He had moved farther and farther back, so that his voice seemed but a parenthesis to the whole matter.

'That's right. He's right, Martin.'

Atterburn was, of course, 'right' so far as any right was to be found in the tale of errors. But Martin knew that was not the end of the tale. With thirty men dead or wounded, there would be little enough credit handed round. Martin found the whole subject offensive – not least because he himself was not far short of casting blame on a dead man to keep his own record clear.

'If we keep together on this, Division doesn't even have to know,' Blood said. 'There's no way for Battleax to know who hit them. Snoopy's out of the division – word of this may never get back to them at Da Nang, or if it does, they may not remember where we fired off our ordnance. We chased all over hell today. Christ, it could have been anybody in the world who hit them!'

'If you believe that,' Martin answered, desperate not to listen, 'you're dumber than you think I think you are.' He turned and strode off toward Operations.

If none of them knew quite what to expect in Operations, none of them expected quite what they found. In addition to Rauch and Major Hart there were two clerks and Lieutenant Harris. Major Hart, who had been seated beside Rauch at the desk, rose up open-armed. 'The conquering heroes come!' he said. The three of them stopped, astonished. 'Tidings of great joy from on high, gentlemen. The division commander called personally to say that awards recommendations for all of you will be on his desk tomorrow morning. So just tell us what you did, and I'll get these fellows' – a wave of his hand explained the presence of the clerks and Harris, who was company awards-and-decorations officer – 'to work on them.'

Despite his mock-heroic tone, it was obvious that Major Hart was pleased, and even excited. He was old, for a major, having joined the officer ranks late, after service as an enlisted man. He had been once passed over for promotion to lieutenant colonel. The major was not a greatly ambitious man. Left to himself he would have been pleased to finish out his twenty years' service in some quiet assignment and retire – or even continue in that quiet assignment, if that would have been permitted. The major liked the Army. He liked flying. If he had been a warrant officer, expected only to fly or to perform low-level supervisory duties, he would have finished out his career in great happiness. He was not an incapable officer. As company commander he was liked by his men, who saw to it that the company's missions were performed well enough to reflect favorably on the old man. But he had no quality to catch the eye of his superiors, to make it appear that he must be promoted to positions of even greater responsibility. Worse yet, he had an inborn kindness that never failed to show through; and however pleasing a quality kindness might be in itself, it was not thought to have any great merit in one whose business was to order others to kill. It was not among the character traits evaluated on an officer efficiency report form. So, as an officer in an army which demanded that every officer go up or go out, Major Hart was well aware that his most likely course was out, and he was pleased at having come to the attention of the commanding general through the deeds of his men.

But Major Hart was not moved only, or even primarily, by thought of his own credit. He was pleased for his men, even for Captain Blood, whom he did not really like very much although he tried to hide that fact from himself. 'If Major Hart doesn't like a man,' the Bear had said once, 'you know he's got to be an original-manufacture son of a bitch.' Major Hart would have liked to see Captain Blood succeed simply because Blood arched so greatly for success.

The major brimmed with pleasure. 'What kind of medals would you like? I guess it's carte blanche. DFC . . . Medal of Honor . . . The general didn't say, darn him. What's appropriate? How many Charlies did you get?'

'Not any,' Martin said softly.

Blood flushed, and said, sounding as if he would choke on the words, 'We . . . flew a medevac.'

'Yes, I heard that. But too late for the action? That doesn't sound like my boys. Well, but you did the main thing – you got our men out. How many did you evacuate?'

Major Hart, so pleased at their accomplishment, took the ensuing silence merely as a pause to calculate. Blood said at last, 'About twenty-five, sir.'

'Twenty, sir. Plus three dead. Dustoff is bringing nine more KIAs.' It was the Bear, who had quietly entered the hooch unnoticed and was standing behind Blood. The number burned in his brain.

'My God!' Major Hart exclaimed. 'Almost an entire platoon!'

'We flew two medevac flights,' Blood said quickly. 'Dropped our guns and crews in the LZ. Dustoff's bringing them in. They had to cut an LZ for us. There was just room for one ship. . . .' Blood's voice showed more and more excitement as he went on. It took the puzzled Martin several seconds to realize that Blood really did believe that a medal should rightly come out of this. And, on the part of the tale which he told, he was right. The story was an awards-and-decorations officer's dream. Only the prologue killed it. But Blood had forgotten the prologue. It was of no consequence to him. Martin heard him out before he said quietly, 'Blood, you are crazy!'

'Shoot, there ought to be a medal in that!' Rauch objected.

'If only we could go back and kill all the witnesses, there would be,' Bear said. 'But we blew our chance at that already.'

'I don't follow you, Ben . . .' Major Hart ran his fingers nervously through his thinning silver hair. His forescalp glistened under the bare light bulbs.

'Sir, how did the general get into this?' Martin asked heavily, not having the heart to answer directly.

'I told the crew on his ship, when they called about more guns for the big do up north, that you were still out medevackin',' Rauch said, 'and I reckon they told him. Hell, if you don't want the medals, I'll take 'em. I could use a DFC – I'm never goin' to get one flyin' this desk!'

'There won't be any medals, can't you get that through your thick head, Rauch?' Martin exploded. 'There won't be any at all because we killed those men!'

Major Hart's smile was replaced by a quizzical incomprehension. He looked from Martin to Blood to Martin again, while Atterburn looked at the floor, and the Bear gnawed his mustache and pounded a fist steadily against the doorframe. Then there was absolute silence in the hooch.

Outside, the footsteps of mechanics on the way to the flight line rang in the damp air, and a voice sweet and thick as syrup: 'You see them gunnies come in? Lost they rocket pods somewheres. I hear they was doin' a medevac. Thought they was s'posed to kill folks, not save 'em.'

Major Hart smiled again, but now a reflective sad smile marking the end of one more hope. One of the clerks quietly placed the cover over his typewriter.

Blood, when Martin first spoke, had turned to him fiercely, his face flaming with anger. But now he turned back to Major Hart and said with forced composure. 'I wouldn't have sprung it on you like that, but it's true, sir.'

'How? How did it happen?'

'When we were bound for home, Snoopy got a reading just inside the free-fire zone, and Martin ordered me to dump our ordnance.' At this there was a snort from the Bear. Blood turned to Martin, his face flaming again: 'Isn't that true, Martin? Are you going to deny it?'

'No. It's close enough.' He had in fact been the ranking officer. He could have ordered whatever action he chose, and he certainly had chosen as Blood said. He could not escape the blame. All he might do would be to drag Blood down with him. It hardly seemed worth the effort.

'We all should have known better,' the Bear said. 'All of us.'

'It was my decision,' Martin said, feeling as if he had stepped into a long hall whose end he could not see, and heard the door lock behind him.

Major Hart picked up the field telephone. 'Give me Battalion – no, make that the battalion commander's quarters.' To the clerks he said gently, 'You boys can go on to bed. Thank you for coming.'

Lieutenant Rauch sat behind his desk shaking his head. 'We are into some deep shit,' he said to no one in particular.

5

The investigating officer, an infantry lieutenant colonel, arrived promptly at nine hundred hours the next morning. He and his assistants had already been to the hospital. They interviewed the crew members one at a time in the back of the Operations hooch while the others waited in the alert hooch. The crews that would have been there on alert on other days had drifted away early, to the ships or to the steps of a nearby hooch - anywhere to avoid the chill silence. Except for Covington, only Arp remained, having to be near at hand to Operations in case a mission came down. He was in charge of the platoon now, until the investigation was closed. When the Bear came back from his turn before the investigating board, Arp was lying on his bunk, reading *Catch-22* with a look of sour pleasure.

Atterburn paced the floor, while Handy meticulously cleaned and recleaned his machine gun to the accompaniment of a humming moan that flooded and ebbed about him with the endless surge of the ocean out on the reef. Covington and the Bear sat apart, sometimes talking and sometimes not. Cripps lay on his back on his bunk to one side of them. He lay with his hands folded on his belly and his eyes closed, as one laid out for his own funeral. His breathing was so shallow that he might have passed for dead, in the grey light; but he was listening to Covington and the Bear, when they spoke, and the rest of the time he day-dreamed.

Sometimes Cripps wished he were an officer, so he could be friends with the two of them. They had never said anything that would keep him at a distance even though he was only their crew chief, but the constraint of military custom, however thin an overlay it might be, when added to Cripps's own shyness formed a wall he did not dare attempt to breach. Cripps would particularly have liked to say something comforting to the Bear, whose stricken look when he thought no one was watching was more that Cripps could bear. Cripps tried not to look at him, except when someone else was there to harden the Bear's face into one of his masks. Except with Covington. With him the Bear lapsed into a bemused sadness, his eyes like those of a hound that has finally lost a trail already long grown cold. Cripps envied them their friendship.

They were talking of the night before – or rather, the Bear was talking of it, trying to talk of it, in brief strangled phrases while Covington tut-tutted with helpless good intent. Once Covington turned to him, to Cripps, and asked, 'What was it like down there, Cripps? You were there.' That was after the Bear had attempted to convey the horror of the pit in the trees, but had tumbled to a halt. Cripps had only mumbled a reply that made no sense and then had turned away because the Bear had looked at him with fierce interest, awaiting his answer. Now, with them fallen silent, Cripps was rehearsing the answer he might have given.

When the helicopter rose away and its blade winked out beyond the edge of the hole in the trees, he had felt the forest edge closer around him. It was still daylight then, at least it was daylight above the trees. In the landing zone it was grey twilight while a few steps back from the clearing it was already night, a night echoing with the groans of men dying.

A fine mist settled gently in the clearing. Under the trees the water fell in great drops that had collected on the jungle canopy. When the helicopters came back, the turbulence in the treetops released a downpour along their flight path. Cripps had finally borrowed a dead man's poncho, but the smell of blood was still hot inside it, and he cast it away. Handy took it to cover the guns.

He and the other crewmen drifted around the clearing for a time, like swimmers testing the water, not wanting to plunge into the darkness that lay beyond. He offered to help the corpsman who had collected the wounded near one side of the LZ; but the corpsman had long ago run out of medical supplies, and he only answered, 'All there is left to do is fan 'em and give 'em ice water, buddy.' At length the lieutenant who was now in charge of the company (the commander lay in the trees with a poncho snapped around him) became aware of them and sent them with their machine guns down the perimeter in place of some of the wounded. The lieutenant himself wore a dressing on one arm, and his face trickled blood from many small cuts.

The men on the perimeter looked at them wide eyed once, as they stumbled past in their flight helmets, and then turned back to the more important matter of the darkness. He and Handy crouched in a shallow foxhole – it might have been a grave – while helicopters came and went ('Stay down there until I call you,' the lieutenant had said. 'I'll let you know when they're ready for you.') but the night stayed. They hoped the lieutenant's word was good. No one had asked them who they were, or how they came to be there. No one asked what part they played in this small tale of horror. But the first time the helicopters returned, Cripps heard a man in the next foxhole begin to breathe heavily – tremulously gasping breaths, half sobs, as if he were in the grip of some nightmare of anguish. 'Take it easy, buddy,' a voice said softly. 'They can't hit us in the dark.' Later the sweet burning-hay smell of marijuana drifted down through the night.

How the Bear imagined it Cripps did not know. Maybe it was better not to tell him. Knowing might only make it worse. Cripps wished he himself did not know.

But one thing that the Bear had said circled through his mind. 'They asked me if I remembered anything else,' the Bear had told Covington. 'God yes, I remembered so much else – but how to say it? So I told them, I remembered Handy taking the guns off, carrying them away into the trees. And when they were gone, how the ship rose up, how light it felt – lighthearted. The colonel said he didn't catch what I meant.'

Cripps understood. When the ship had risen away from

him, he had thought for an instant how different it looked without the guns. How beautiful and clean. He wished he had said that much to the Bear.

One by one the other crew members came back to the hooch, Blood and Martin last of all. It became very quiet. At last Major Hart came in. He asked Arp and Covington to leave while he talked to the others. His message was brief: the investigating team had gone; the enlisted crews were to report for duty; the officers were grounded. 'I wouldn't worry,' he said. 'It's only a formality until Division gets the report. The general will lift it after the investigation is complete.' The words were kindly meant, but no one believed them.

After the major dismissed them, Blood caught up to Martin. 'Well, Martin, it's all hit the fan now. That light colonel's going to try to make his eagle out of our hides. It looks like we'd better all pull together on whatever strings we can find.' Martin walked on and left him standing.

Martin had told the investigators that he himself had insisted on attacking the hill contrary to the advice of all the others. ('Don't pride yourself on it,' he told himself afterward. 'It's only egotism again. If you're going down anyway, you know how to make it seem it was only because you tried to rescue others, don't you.')

The emergency room was the front entrance to the hospital. Its double swinging doors opened directly onto the helipad, and the long corridor giving access to the sprawling wards led back from the other side directly opposite the doors. It was a convenient layout, for all the hospital's business came through the emergency room. Daily, helicopter loads of bodies arrived at the swinging doors, were disgorged into the chill pandemonium of the emergency room, were sorted, patched up, and held until it was safe to move them to a treating hospital. Then they were evacuated. The least injured went to the treating hospital on the cliffs of the next headland, a mile to the south. The more severely injured went to Qui Nhon or Da Nang. Those who needed closer care but might still return to combat before their year's tour of duty ended were flown to Japan, while those for whom the war was over went back to the Land of the Big PX, the United States. They were not always the lucky ones. Some made the trip in a body bag.

The emergency room was but an echoing cavity that afternoon, full of nothing but sunshine so wasted and consumptive that it seemed sustained only by the memory of summer. The Bear entered hesitantly, stood just inside the door gazing about in large-eyed distraction.

'What can I do for you, Chief?' He started at the voice. He had not noticed the orderly behind the counter at one side of the doors. The orderly was a lean black man with short curly hair going grey above the ears. He did not press for an answer to his question, but went on penciling check marks against a list on his clipboard. At his elbow the lights on a tiny plastic Christmas tree flashed on and off, on and off.

'You had some infantrymen brought in here last night . . .'

'We got a pot full of 'em, Chief. You looking for any in particular? If you just want to look at an infantryman, take any ol' ward back there' – he waved down the corridor opposite them – 'and you'll find all you can stand.'

'They came in from Hill 473.'

'I don't know where people come from, Chief, or even where they're going. You don't mebbe have an idea what unit they was in? Or mebbe some names? Did they have names? Friends of yours?'

'I don't know. Their unit was Battleax. They got shot up by some gunships.'

'Oh, them! Yeah, we got some of them, if you really want to see 'em. We got some of them folks out already, last night or this mornin', though, the best of 'em, and the worst. Any of 'em in particular you want to see?'

'I don't know,' he lied, 'don't know this guy's name; but I heard he was with them. . . .'

'You're not with this investigation, then? I thought you was one of them – they been comin' and goin' all day long. Well, it ain't visiting hours, but you can go on back if you want to. The ones that ain't in Intensive Care are in the second ward on the right. And you can look around. Bein' as you're a special friend of mine.' He winked and grinned.

Bear paused at the second ward on the right before pushing through the doors. They swung closed like fate behind him.

It was absolutely still in the room. By the door was a desk with no one behind it. There were some two dozen beds ranged down the ward, with crisp sheets laid over them. Blue pajama sleeves extended over some of the sheets, and on some of the pillows heads had been laid, sunburned or tanned or black. On one there was not what could be called a head at all, but a rag doll of bandages. Beside some beds, limbs were hung at odd angles – a bandaged arm cocked up on a wire frame, a leg in traction. The place had the air of a storeroom for spare human parts or a display of artificial limbs.

He walked slowly down the center of the room. His heels squeaked softly on the waxed floor. A few eyes were open, but none followed: most remained closed. He tried to appear to look for someone, and at the same time not to seem interested in anyone at all. He reached the end of the room, turned, and came softly back. He had almost expected to catch eyes covertly tracing his steps. A hate-filled glance would have been deserved. He thought, comfortlessly, that he would even have welcomed it, if it meant someone to whom he could explain, apologize. He turned back to face the room. A few faces were turned toward him now, faces with unoccupied eyes, faces slack-jawed as though they had been dropped on the beds and by chance rolled to a stop facing toward him. He wondered uneasily if they were all dying, these empty faces whose spirits perhaps wandered in witless dreams while the bodies waited glassy-eyed. These were not the men, the reeking, burned, and battered but undeniably human flesh he had torn from the jungle the night before, but something more horrible still, mere vessels waiting for the breath of life to be poured back, or to fail utterly.

'What do you want?' a voice demanded behind him. He had not heard or felt the door swing open, and he started again, as he had in the ER. It was a woman's voice, low but positive, stating and not questioning. Yet it had the liquid hoarseness of a gravel-bedded stream. 'What do you want? You aren't supposed to be here.'

'I . . . I was looking for someone.' She was not, as he expected from the voice, a middle-aged field-grade career nurse. She was a lieutenant. Her name tag said her name was Porter. He did not know he had seen her before.

She could not place him at first. She felt she had seen his face, but the only scene that came half to mind was a zoo somewhere: the round face, the great sad eyes, seemed for an odd moment to stare at her from behind a wire screen. 'It's not visiting hours,' she said. 'You can't talk to anyone now.'

Although nothing about his face changed describably, the eyes seemed to become limpid with pain. She remembered then – the wild eyes racing over the carnage of the emergency room under the cold sputter of the fluorescent lamps. She had thought for a moment he must be another investigating officer come to badger her charges for statements. She was instantly sorry for the harshness of her tone. She asked, more gently, 'Do you know someone here?'

'No.' He could not face the admission. He started to go past her to the door. On an impulse he stopped and asked, 'There was a soldier with one leg. Is he . . . here?' *Dead*, he might have said.

'Private Patulski? He's still in Intensive Care.'

'Then he didn't die.' As he pushed quickly out the door, she was going to add, 'You can't visit there.' But she checked herself, thinking that perhaps she had said enough already. She did not know quite why she thought that. In part she believed he had saved the soldier with one leg. She had seen the wings on Bear's jacket, and she knew that many of the casualties the previous night had been brought in by pilots of other helicopters before the medical evacuation ships came in carrying the dead.

She sat down behind the desk to face the pain- and drug-glazed eyes and wished for a moment she had not sent him away. Dreams of good to be done were easy; but the flesh was harder to face.

The Bear went on back along the corridor, pausing outside doors but not going through them. He was unable to face the empty eyes behind the doors; but he could not bring himself to leave the place. He wandered the empty corridors until he had completely lost himself.

There were voices behind some of the doors he passed. At times he paused to listen, but he did not open the doors. While they were closed the illusion remained that life, and not death, was in progress here.

The hospital was a rambling aggregation of one-room wood frame buildings connected by enclosed walkways that crossed and recrossed in an immense checkerboard. Once he saw a nurse cross on an intersecting corridor far ahead; but when he reached the spot, the cross-hall was also empty. At last he worked his way completely to the back of the complex. The sea, fitful gray and blue as sunlight fell or vanished, was to be seen beyond the windows of the rear corridor, in the intervals between the separate buildings of the wards.

Turning again toward the front of the hospital, Bear was brought up short by a glimpse of a familiar figure coming toward him. It was Captain Martin.

Although he could have given no logical reason, Bear did not want to be seen here by anyone he knew – as if kindness might need to be explained away. He turned quickly down a side corridor. He waited at the next turning to be certain that Martin had gone past. Then he escaped quickly toward the hospital entrance.

Martin was moving slowly. His walk, normally rapid and purposeful, was now the meander of a stream run out onto a delta, its force suddenly gone. In a way it pleased him to wander about these halls, occupied as they were only by echoes of his movements. They struck him as near kin of his own present condition, a life empty save for the echoes of his acts. For the present the lives of his friends went on behind doors closed to him.

Bear had been sitting by himself at dinner until Covington came in. He had not been the first to the mess hall, nor the last. He had not sat with anyone who was there ahead of him; and, before Covington, no one had come to sit with him. Blood and Atterburn were seated together, a little apart from the other officers then in the mess hall. Bear, for his part, was happy enough with the arrangement. He knew there was no order or plan to separate the four of them from the company: their ill was not contagious. But he was not of a mind, either, to join the conventional round of scatology and carnality that passed for dinner conversation, nor to burden the others with sympathetic silence. Covington, not understanding these grounds for the Bear's own reluctance to join the others, began a loudly incensed harangue about those who were afraid to be seen with people in trouble. Bear shushed him and steered the conversation to the safe subject of Pinky.

'She's fine,' Covington said. 'And speaking of her, let me just look at this letter a sec, okay?' He plunged into his letter, leaving the Bear to watch the top of his head with some amusement at having been rescued from his solitude in this way. Occasionally Covington's face bobbed up to relay a fragment of information.

'Your home life sounds delightful, Cov.' The Bear smiled. Covington had made him feel better after all.

'Yeah, you ought to get married, Bear. It's really great.' This he said without raising his head.

'I believe that's contrary to my nature as a free-ranging creature of the wild.'

'We'll see. When we get back to the world I'm going to fix up your free-ranging frame with a nice girl—' He came to a full stop. His face bobbed up and down twice, but he said nothing.

'Well?' Covington was so totally astonished that Bear could not help laughing. 'What's your wife up to now?'

'I'm going to have a son!'

This was proclaimed loudly enough that every face in the officers' section of the mess hall turned toward them. Among shouted congratulations, someone called, 'How do you know it's going to be a boy?' Under his breath Blood muttered, 'If *he* got it, it's likely to be nothing but a squirt of curdled milk!'

'When is he due, Cov?'

Covington counted on his fingers. 'June. He'll be three months old before I get to see him! Wow! I wonder who I can get to take standby for me tonight, so I can get up to the MARS station and call her?' When he looked at Bear, his happiness burst instantly, for the Bear's face had gone gray with sorrow: now that he and the others were grounded, there were no gun-pilots not on standby. The platoon was already short three officers before the grounding. 'I wish I could,' Bear said.

'Don't worry about it, Bear. I can call another night. Hey, I tell you what. I want you to be the godfather. Would you do that for us? Pinky would love it, too – I know she would. Here, she asks what kind of cookies you like. She's sending us some.' Covington was too overwhelmed by it all to be distracted for long by anyone's sorrow, and his excitement carried the Bear along with it. Covington reached across the table and gripped his friend's arm: 'You'll make a classic godfather, Bear. The mustache bristling in all its prickly glory, like porcupines copulating! What the devil are we going to call the little nipper, now? Give me some suggestions: I want to get a letter off to Pinky tonight.'

The pierced steel plank of the parking ramp could not completely contain the red Vietnamese clay which crept upward through every hole and joint, covering the steel with a fine dust which now had turned greasy in the evening drizzle. The Bear skated arms-out over the rough surface. He had started out for no place that he could name, but he saw that his skating steps were tending toward the hospital. Perhaps, he reflected, that was only because it was downwind, as cattle stray downwind before a storm. But he could not decide whether this was really the path of least resistance for him. The hospital repelled him, and yet something drove him toward it – the same thing, perhaps, which drove men to kill others they had never met, because to do so was their duty. Duty was a porcupine: it stuck you from whatever side you took it. The one-legged soldier came to his mind. Patulski. It was an easy enough name, for being

Polish; but 'one-legged soldier' told all the facts of military importance. If the soldier had been Viet Cong, as he should have been, then duty would have been to put him in the condition he now was in, or worse, and it would have been proper to shoot through the trees without stopping to ask his name. But since he was not Viet Cong, duty was to visit him and pray for his recovery. In all this the name somehow became lost, and not only the name, but everything that made him Patulski and not someone else. Duty did not care that it was Patulski who lay on a starched bed with dangling tubes spitting life into his veins and phantom fires roaring through a leg that had become purely imaginary but ached nevertheless. Yet the fact that he now knew the name made the memory of the soldier the more painful for Bear. Even though he knew nothing else of the man, the name invested him with the trappings of humanity, made him more than duty's anonymous object.

The Bear stopped at the end of the ramp and looked up for a long time at the hospital buildings sprawling under the floodlights. Even the outside repelled him.

As he stood there, a helicopter appeared out of the darkness over the ridge, descended like a whirlwind to the pad near the emergency room doors, swung its tail downwind, and settled to rest. On its doors stood the white square enclosing a red cross. Bear hung back, breathless, but no one issued from the swinging doors to carry away wounded men. He saw then that there was no one in the back of the ship. There was not even a crew chief aboard. The blade plopped steadily for a minute as the pilot let the engine cool down at idle, and then there came the dying whistle as the fuel was shut off and the turbine ran down. As the blade slowed, Bear walked down to the ship. He caught the end of the blade as it teetered to a stop.

The pilot, a short, dark-haired, and quick-moving warrant officer, stepped down from the cockpit to assert his authority over the blade; but seeing the wings on Bear's shirt he handed over the hook and watched as Bear dragged the blade back and tied it to the tail skid.

The aircraft commander was coming down the other side

of the ship. 'Primo, what say we—' He broke off when he saw the Bear. 'God damn, Primo you changed shape on me again! You're getting slick at that.' He extended a hand and a quick grin. 'Thanks, even if you're not Primo. You're not joining this unit, by any chance?'

Bear shook his head. 'I fly with a company down there.' He waved toward the far end of the ramp.

'Too bad. As short as we are on crews, I was hoping you were an FNG.'

'I haven't been a friendly new guy for a long time.'

'Too bad. Too bad. Well, this *is* Primo.' The other warrant officer had come back to join them. His name tag said he was Guiterrez. 'I thought we had a new pilot, Primo; but it's just a refugee from down the ramp.'

'We don't see many of you guys,' Guiterrez said. 'You ought to come visit.'

'Well, he's visiting now, Primo. Just in time for a root beer.'

'A what beer?'

'Root beer. We may have places to go yet tonight.'

'Couldn't be any worse than last night,' Guiterrez answered. 'C'mon . . . what's your name?'

'Bear.' He was so rarely called anything else, except by Major Hart or sometimes Captain Martin, that he gave it without thinking. 'That is, Don.'

'Bear, that is Don? What kind of name is that?'

'We can eliminate Polish and Spanish,' said the aircraft commander, whose name was Wolchesky. 'Scandahoovian, maybe? Leave it to the Swedes to call someone "Bear". Well, we're about to have a beer, Bear. Come and join us. Do bears drink beers?'

'In fabulous quantities.'

'Then it's a good thing I'm not buying. Guiterrez is buying. Thanks, Primo.'

'I distinctly didn't hear that part before, *Trung-úy*.'

'Must have been the radio, then, because right when we were on short final I heard a little voice say, "Primo is buying, Lieutenant." The voice specified fabulous quantities.'

'I'm much obliged to the voice,' Bear said.

'Don't mention it,' said Lieutenant Wolcheski.

Guiterrez mumbled under his breath.

The Bear turned with relief to an offer of company who would not feel obliged to sympathize. He was normally gregarious as a seal, but among those who knew of his trouble he felt like an iceberg, chilling everyone around him even if he only lurked in his bunk. Talking with Covington would mean sitting in the alert hooch with the rest of the platoon. The movie at the officers' club he had seen years before, and he did not want to sit in the bar, where Blood and Atterburn would be putting a brave face on the situation. But being alone only forced his thoughts back over the same rutted path again and again. He pretended to be lighthearted and followed the two medevac pilots up the hill.

The hospital officers' club was only a room on the end of a two-story officers' quarters. They hung their weapons on pegs beside the door.

'I thought medevac people went unarmed,' Bear said.

'The ships do,' Guiterrez told him, 'and some of the corpsmen do; but the crews don't.'

'This one sure as hell don't,' Wolcheski said. 'A couple months ago one of our ships went down in a PZ, and the crews had to shoot their way through to the friendlies. In the air we are all tender mercy; but on the ground we are some mean sumbitches.' He grinned at Bear: 'Another illusion crushed?'

'Yes,' Bear said. 'You should be ashamed.'

'I am. No Ba Muoi Ba. American beer is all we've got. But, as my Polish grandmother used to say, "Bread is better than cake anyway, when you don't have cake."' Wolcheski helped himself from the untended bar. He handed Bear a beer, but Bear saw that Wolcheski was in fact drinking root beer himself. 'Eight hours from bottle to throttle.' Wolcheski shrugged apologetically.

'Better take two, Bear,' Guiterrez suggested. 'Fabulous amounts may take a while, a can at a time.'

'Maybe fabulous amounts are better lingered over,'

Wolcheski said. 'Be sociable, Primo, or I won't let you buy next time.'

'You couldn't be so cruel.'

Wolcheski picked his way around a table full of arguing doctors to where two nurses were sitting in the shadows along the wall. He presented the Bear with the air of a diplomat presenting the President to a girls' school: 'Ladies – and I use the term loosely – may I present Mr Bear. Mr Bear, Lieutenant Swensen, Lieutenant Porter.'

Lieutenant Porter's half-smile might have had recognition in it, or only disinterest. She did not speak. But Lieutenant Swensen asked him, 'What kind of name is that . . . Bear?'

'Scandahoovian,' Guiterrez said. When Swensen punched him in the arm, he complained, 'That's what *he* said,' pointing at Wolcheski. 'You know these Anglo names all sound alike to me.'

'It doesn't say Bear on your shirt,' Lieutenant Swensen said. 'Why not?'

'I believe "Bear" is only a temporary appellation,' Wolcheski told her. 'A *nom de guerre*.'

'A *cri de coer*?' Coming from Lieutenant Porter, the words stung Bear. He was sure she remembered him then; but what she knew he could not tell. Everyone laughed at her words, except himself. But when Lieutenant Porter saw that he did not, she stopped, too, with a look of sudden confusion. No one else appeared to notice. 'I won't listen to any more horrid words in Polish,' Swensen said firmly.

'It ain't Polish, dear,' Wolcheski told her.

'Hebrew, then. Those Eastern languages all sound the same to me anyway. But if your name is Bear, Mr Bear, then you are wearing someone else's shirt. Why is that?'

'It keeps his back from the cold,' Wolcheski said.

'But doesn't the real owner care?'

'Of course he cares!' Wolcheski sighed. 'He doesn't want our friend Bear to have a cold back. That's why he lets him wear the shirt.'

'Then he's a very obliging person. Cheers to the owner of the shirt!' Swensen raised her beer can in a toast, and drained it.

'That's not so great,' Guiterrez insisted. 'There are plenty of spare shirts around.'

'Oh, really! Where?' Swensen demanded.

'They throw away hundreds in the ER every day. How about those guys that got medevacked in last night? One of the companies up the ramp brought 'em in. Plenty of spare shirts there. He could have picked up a dozen! I bet you were on one of those flights, eh, Bear?'

Bear saw then that, wherever he turned, there was going to be no escape from that piece of the past. It traveled with him, and he felt as if somehow radiated news of it to everyone around him. Guiterrez, meaning no more than a jest, had found the tender point at once. Bear turned his head and chewed at his mustache. Swensen, misreading the turn of his head, giggled at his expression. 'He's modest. Look, he's blushing! Why, you should be proud, Mr Bear! You saved some of those boys. Not like our "professional rescuers" here' – she tapped Wolcheski on the arm – 'who only got there in time to bring in the leftovers for graves registration like so many sides of beef!'

'For God's sake, Janet!' Lieutenant Porter murmured, lowering her eyes.

'Oh, you can't get involved with a dead soldier, Alice.'

'How about a live pilot?' Guiterrez suggested, gazing speculatively at the ceiling. Lieutenant Porter's eyes remained lowered.

Wolcheski, sensing the discomfort spreading around him and thinking to change the subject, said quickly, 'Our other ship brought in some crewmen and weapons last night. Were those yours, Bear?'

The Bear nodded slowly.

'Then it was quick thinking on your part, if you were flying a gunship. You couldn't get many casulties out on a C-model, with a full crew and guns aboard.'

'Oh,' Swensen said brightly, 'do you fly a gunship? I think it's wonderful, then, that you rescued those boys. Maybe you don't know that some of them were wounded by gunships? All those investigating people were coming and going all day! And Alice was very cross about gunship pilots when she heard it. Now, see there, Alice? They're not all so bad.' She flung a friendly arm about the Bear's neck.

'They were hit by guns?' Wolcheskui said. His voice trailed like smoke vanishing, and he stared thoughtfully at the root beer can as he rolled it between his palms.

'Boy,' Guiterrez said, 'wouldn't that make you feel like day-old shit?'

'Yes,' Bear agreed, 'that's just about it.' He thought Lieutenant Porter looked at him more closely as he said it.

'Those things happen,' Wolcheski said, now with the tone of one who is positively changing the subject.

'Not if you're careful,' Bear said. He felt principle should be defended by someone, even if it had to be himself.

'There's a war on.' Wolcheski shrugged. Wolcheski had a fondness for only Army sayings, though he only said them ironically.

'It ain't much,' Bear answered, 'but it's the only war we got.'

Wolcheski was surprised that Bear understood the irony – few officers did. 'You can't make an omelet without breaking some eggs,' Wolcheski tried, with just a touch of a grin.

'There's three ways to do things,' Bear responded. 'The right way, the wrong way, and the Army way. But,' he added, 'I don't know that any of them include shooting up your own troops.'

'You do your best, and hope it works out,' Wolcheski said – not ironically. He found himself liking this strange warrant officer, and he had a feeling that a certain amount of kindness – although he was uncertain what might be looked on as kindness – would be well bestowed at the moment. 'You cut corners when you have to, and hope it works out. We had a ship try to get out of a pickup zone with one KIA too many and end up killing eight live guys, besides two dead ones.'

'At least he was trying to save someone,' Bear said.

'I guess the gunnies are, too.'

'I guess that's the theory,' Bear said. 'I guess.'

Bear had been crumpling his beer can. He now pushed it

slowly endwise between his hands until they almost met.

'That's great,' Guiterrez said. 'You could do that with Victor Charley, and save the cost of ammo.'

Wolcheski laid a hand on Guiterrez's shoulder.

'Primo, buddy, nobody has called us yet, but we'd better stroll back to the ready room and be ready, for a change.'

'Maybe tonight you can bring in some live ones, instead of leaving your work to poor Bear here,' Swensen said.

'Swensen, you're sweet but you sure don't know when to keep your mouth shut. Why don't you just walk down with us, huh, and stay out of trouble? But you have to say "May I?"'

'May I?'

'You bet your sweet—'

'Your sweet censored,' she said, putting a hand over his mouth as they all rose. 'Bye, Bear. Come again.'

'How come Bear gets left with the new nurse?' Primo asked.

'I don't know, buddy,' Wolcheski said, 'but there it is.'

'How come,' Bear asked after they had gone, 'Bear does get left with the new nurse?'

'I don't know, but there it is.' It might have been only shyness that caused the hesitance now, as it might have been what caused the harsh words of the afternoon. Her voice, though still rough-edged, was gentle. A part of a smile came and went from her lips, as if undecided where to break out next. She had a kindly look about her – not maiden-aunt kindly, but kind-to-all-small-harmless-things kindly. He suddenly wanted her to like him; but he was afraid to allow it. She would be too easy to like in return. He felt his face about to put on a small-animal expression, and suppressed it ruthlessly.

His face was treacherous: he could not always tell what it was doing. From the fading of her unborn smile he feared the worst. 'All right,' she said, 'I apologize. So now there's that, too.'

'Apologize? For what?'

'You know for what.'

'If it's for saying bad things about gun pilots, they all

deserve worse than anything I've ever heard on a lady's lips.' He put all the gun pilots of the world into his remark as a screen between them.

'I'm not apologizing to them,' she said. 'Only to you. You know it's not for that, so don't ask me to play the fool, please.'

He did not feel worth the contrition in her voice, and now wanted only to make her smile again. 'Yes, sir!' he answered quickly. 'Uh, yes, *ma'am*!' His eyes, when he said it, grew large as saucers, and his mustache bristled. She laughed. He had not willed it, but the walrus had come to his rescue.

He had started doing the walrus to amuse his hooch-mates, but it had taken on a being of its own and sometimes came out when he was not even aware it was in the neighborhood. It seemed to thrive on a woman's laughter.

As for the Bear, if a woman's laughter sent bells ringing through him, well, bells were fine. However, he said sternly as he stroked his mustache into place, 'You shouldn't laugh. I gave myself hemorrhoids, straining to grow this thing. At least have a little respect.'

'I am sorry,' she said, still laughing.

'You should be. If a woman won't respect a man's mustache, what will she respect?'

'I really am very sorry.' Her words were for more than the mustache. Softly, touching his arm, she sounded as if she did mean it. How strange to find her voice, her touch, so soft after all. He sank helplessly in her words, words he did not merit from anyone, and struggled not to forget what had led to his hearing them.

They talked for an hour without ever mentioning the night before, or the afternoon, but those were always at the back of his mind. He did not have to avoid the subjects. They were avoided for him. But when at length she told him that it was nearly time for her to report for duty, she added, as if it were a joke on herself, 'I turn back into the wicked stepmother now. You can walk me there, if you're not afraid.'

'I am afraid. Not of that,' he added.

'I hope not. I wouldn't like to think I was so terrible – so terrible as I was to you this afternoon.'

'I've deserved worse.'

'Like all gun pilots?'

'No – just like me.'

'You don't seem to be such a bad person,' she said, with a gentle smile that had found where it belonged.

The drizzle had ended for the moment, although the air still tasted of rain. A moon glanced through breaks in clouds fleeting southwestward. It silvered the sea in spreading patterns of moon dapple. They had twenty minutes to spend before she must report to her ward. It was a night for walking on the beach; but the beach was not theirs for walking. At night it spread under the glare of the floodlights above on the cliffs. Within the dark ring behind the floodlights squatted cubical bunkers, great sandbag piles with slits for machine gun barrels. They walked along the cliff behind the line of the bunkers. 'At home,' he said, 'we stacked hay bales that way. And we used to drag out bales to make blockhouses, just like those, to play war. I remember once when a bale broke and buried my brother. We dug him out, but we made him be dead for the rest of the day because his bunker had been bombed. Or we tried to. He thought it was too long to be dead.'

'You were wicked even in those days.'

She felt him shiver. 'Don't tease.'

She faced him, and with two fingertips wiped a stray pearl of rain from his cheek. 'No, I shouldn't have. You're really not a bad person.'

'Good or bad – do they apply in this country? Or can you be a good man when you've killed . . . more than enough men?'

'Does it depend on why you did it?'

'I've been told that.'

'It couldn't have been all wickedness,' she said, smiling again at the word. 'I didn't see that in your eyes.'

'A bear's eyes are notoriously deceiving.' He took shelter in light words.

'Yours weren't last night, in the emergency room.'

He stopped. They had come to the end of the headland, to

where the earth fell away at their feet. 'Were you there?'

'Yes.'

'You understand what it meant – what Wolcheski said, about bringing in my crew, and our guns?'

'It means that you cared enough about . . . what happened . . . to go back.' Her soft voice has the rasping catch of a wave dragging down the beach, seaward.

'To go back. And before I went *back* – can you know what happened then, without hating me?'

'I can hate what happened, without hating you. Last night I thought, how terrible it is, that these beautiful young men should . . . But there's nothing in you that could have caused it.'

'Something in me agreed to it.'

They stood above the cold rolling sea whose waves died on the reef below. A gust whistling in from the sea cut like cold steel across their cheeks. Lieutenant Porter shivered inside her rain jacket. 'I hate to be a spoilsport, but I have to go to work,' she said. Her breast brushed him as she turned. His hands hovered indecisively about her shoulders, then fell to his sides. 'Curse you,' he said to his hands.

From the nearest bunker between gusts of wind floated a summery murmur of voices, the words lost on the wind, but the drawl there, thick as molasses on grits. A laugh, and the murmur renewed. Bees in the magnolias, and kudzu vine spilling over the ditch banks; hot sticky afternoons at Fort Rucker, waiting for a helicopter, for his turn to fly. Flying, flying. The blue humidity haze blotted the horizon, while low forested hills rolled below on all sides. They slipped in and out of one-ship clearings, with grass belly-deep to the ship. Flying at night, forty miles out to locate three tiny flare-pots lost in wilderness, land, take off again, and fly home. Flying with the air full of ships all around, snuggling closer, two blade-widths, one and a half, until the IP said, 'Let me show you how we did it in Nam,' and moved the ship within a half blade-width of the ship bouncing through the turbulent afternoon out the port windscreen. 'Now hold it there.' Sweating with the strain of holding the other ship so close and yet *away*, right hand in an aching death-grip on a cyclic stick that a finger's touch could move. And blasting home to the tactical base after the mission, skimming the treetops in trail formation like ducks on a string, bursting out suddenly over the open field, lowering the collective pitch, pulling up the nose and floating, floating out to a soft, satisfying landing. Waiting for Vietnam.

None of them had known what to expect, or what they were expected to expect, of Vietnam, the big field exercise. The tactics instructors, those for the final stage of flight school, were all just back. They were there to tell the new pilots what to expect. Each one told something different. Mr Jackson, round-faced and balding. He had flown a Piper Cub for a gas-line company, before joining the Army. Every day he made a three-hundred-mile patrol, checking the pipeline. For a change of scenery he went to Vietnam. 'What was it like? Glad to have seen it. You boys go have a look now.' A ground-school instructor in gunship tactics was going back. 'That's where the medals and the combat pay are, and that good flyin'.' His voice caressed the words – "goood flyin'" – as his handsome black face glistened under the lights of the classroom. His sports car had the cyclic-stick grip from a gunship mounted on the gearshift lever, with its switches wired to the light and the horn. The rocket trigger flashed the lights.

The voices in the bunker brought it all back. And gone again before it could be grasped. What had been in their hearts then?

'A penny for your thoughts.' She was half sorry she had said it; a startled small creature flashed across his features.

'They're worth less than that,' he said. 'I was recalling Alabama. Flight school. All those Suthun voices.'

'They must have been worth more than a penny. You sound nostalgic.'

'I loved flying.'

'Loved?'

'I'm grounded.'

There seemed to be nothing to say to that.

The two of them stopped beside the emergency room entrance. 'I must go . . . Bear.' She used the name shyly.

'Isn't there another name I can call you?'

'I have been called Don.'

'I must go, Don.' She added after a moment. 'If you come again, I promise to be friendlier.'

'A promise like that could seal your fate forever.'

She squeezed his hand and vanished through the swinging doors.

6

Major Hart hunched over the table on his elbows with his shoulders up against his ears like the wings of a grounded vulture. He watched his executive officer swirl the dregs of beer around and around the bottom of a glass before putting it aside with a disgusted snort. 'Well, Ben?' The major was wishing to find some opening for a kind word, for whatever a kind word might be worth to Martin.

'Thank God Arp isn't here, to tell us about man's plight, tossed like the foam in the beer glass of life.'

'I know it looks like a tough spot now,' Major Hart said, 'but that will change. The disciplinary letter isn't in your file yet; and you know you're going to get a good efficiency report as my XO. In fact, I've been thinking of putting in a special OER on you anyway, because quite frankly you are one of the best young officers I've seen.'

Martin shook his head. 'Aside from what it would do to *your* career, you know it can't work. You submit a special report on me at the same time the CG gives me a reprimand? The battalion commander would have to endorse that report of yours. Whose line is he going to follow?'

'Ben, by God, something is going to work! You're too good a man to . . .' What Martin was too good a man to do the major did not say, perhaps from that intuitive feeling, which in him never quite became a superstition, that to say the thing might tend to bring it about. Although Major Hart believed in the abstract rightness of everything he said, he felt less hope than he professed. He had tried to take the issue directly to the general, but had been shunted to the chief of staff, who talked wary circles around the incident.

'Wait until the investigation report comes in. We have to have the facts to go on, Major. The general is very concerned about this matter: very concerned.' So Major Hart avoided any concrete reference to possible outcomes. But Martin's grim determination to stand up to whatever came, and damn it all, did not hide his inner turmoil from the major, who had all day to watch him across the width of their tiny office.

'You take it too much to heart, Ben,' the major said. 'You need to be a little more like Captain Blood.' Before the objection in Martin's face could be formed into words, Major Hart raised a hand and went on, 'Sometimes if you act as if there's only one thing in your head, people assume it's there because there's no other possibility. If Captain Blood insists often enough that he's being treated unjustly, well, someone's going to believe that he is. I'm not saying you have to go as far as he does,' he added, seeing the slow shake of Martin's head.

'The only thing is, whatever happens to me is my own fault.'

'Ah, if everybody suffered the results of all his own choices, Ben . . .'

'Yes?'

Major Hart this time shook his head sadly, as if the result would not bear contemplation.

'If you don't want to suffer the result of your own choice,' Martin advised, 'you'll take the chief of staff's hint and get rid of me yourself.'

'Nonsense! You may think I'm keeping you out of some sense of loyalty, but that's sentimental humbug. I'm only doing it because it *looks* like that's the reason. The real reason is that the general admires loyalty to subordinates, even if he doesn't admire the subordinates. It's not costing me anything.'

'You almost made that sound reasonable,' Martin said dryly.

'Thank you, Ben. But somehow I have the feeling this is all going to turn out for the best.'

Martin went back to swishing the remains of his beer.

'The question is, for whom?' He thought of broken soldiers being dropped like fallen logs into the back of his helicopter.

The struggle the major sometimes surprised in Martin's eyes upon looking up quickly from the papers on his desk was fiercer than the old man knew. Martin had always wanted to be a soldier. He could have been anything, and knew it, but he did not want to be anything. He wanted to be a soldier. Soldiering was a hard life, when it was real soldiering. He knew that. His father was a brigadier, dead in Korea, not of wounds but pneumonia. Some who knew Martin would have said that was the reason he wanted to be a soldier – to meet the worst head-on, and not flinch. In some part they were right. But Martin did not have a Marine mentality. Up the hill into the teeth of the guns was not for him if there was a better way. God gave man brains as well as guts, and gave them both for use. There were softer reasons that weighed more heavily with Martin, although he did not speak of them. If his reasons for being a soldier were all boiled into one image, it would have been West Point on a clear autumn evening as the flag was struck and the bugle played 'To the Colors.' God gave man heart, too. It was not that Martin loved ceremony. Forms long empty were less than nothing to him. He had incurred the deep suspicion of at least one colonel by suggesting that the Red Chinese army had done a good thing if it had really abolished all badges of rank. But there were traditions, too, that grew brighter with use. And there was comradeship. It was a word he never used, for many in his society had thrown it away. But the thing itself hung on here and there. Whenever men banded together in face of duress and danger (even self-imposed, as duress and danger often are) there it existed still, although unmentioned because the word was in disrepute; but except for such odd sorts as these, it was hardly to be found in that part of the population which had passed the age of majority. In the army it still flourished unnoticed.

Martin wanted to be a soldier for those reasons, and others like them that he was equally unwilling to name. His inability to think yet of any other life led him back again and again over Blood's suggestions: there were ways out of this, if he would look for them. During this time Martin lived among haunting dreams, for it was still possible to believe that Blood might be right. Yet Martin was determined to face the wrong he had done, for that was the only way to preserve what he valued. To be what an officer and a gentleman should be was more important than to be an officer and a gentleman. But it was a hard position to hold against the assaults of rationalization. It was to cut off his own escape that Martin had admitted full responsibility for the accident. But he still caught something within himself wondering at times if there was not reason to hope. He was forced to struggle against hope, for if there was hope, there was reason to help hope along; and that was the harder struggle. And sometimes, as he sat at his desk nodding over reports or as he lay in bed listening to the ships with pre-dawn missions running up on the ramp, there came to him like a glimpse of salvation that always faded before his eyes could take it in, the dream: it has not happened – soon I will wake.

Martin considered himself lucky in one way: he still had duties to perform. The others had not even that consolation and were reduced to fluttering about the edges of the company either hoping to be unseen or like the ancient mariner demanding the ear of all who could be stopped to listen.

Blood was still platoon commander for ground purposes, but his ground duties were few. Nevertheless, he adopted the pretense that it was a good thing that he had some time on the ground for once, to catch up on the many things that demanded his attention. He elaborated this thesis at great length for the major, the first sergeant, Lieutenant Rauch and the Operations sergeant, Mr Rowland the supply officer, and his own platoon sergeant. Sergeant Magruder had successfully managed the enlisted men and the equipment of the platoon without the help of the platoon commander under both Captain Blood and Captain Martin, and under Captain Staddard before them. Blood's eye over his shoulder now had him so bedeviled that he swore to the first sergeant he would pitch Blood over the cliff into the sea the next time he came down to the pits to tell the crews how to rearm a gunship. 'We got only so much time in a day, Top; and there ain't much of it put aside for listenin' to pep talks on how to cut down our turnaround time. We spend more time listenin' to that these days than we do gettin' the rounds in the ships! And maintenance! My God! Let a ship be on the ground ten minutes, and here he comes with his clipboard, wantin' the windscreens waxed, wantin' a light bulb changed, not because it's out but because it's too dim, wantin' the wolfheads touched up, for Chrissake, in case the general happens to see one of our ships on the ground somewhere! As if nobody had any more to do than he does himself. Christ, if the general don't get him off the ground, and off my back, I'm goin' to shoot myself in the foot like that gunner over at the Mustangs last month! Only I'd be afraid he'd end up at the hospital, tellin' the docs how to cut my turnaround time there, too!'

If, in this estimate of how Captain Blood spent his days, Sergeant Magruder failed to give credit for the time Blood put into convincing the world that grounding him was a foul injustice, the sergeant was right in his complaint that Blood stalked the ramp making work where none had been before. On the third afternoon they were grounded, Blood hailed the Bear crossing the ramp. 'Now, how come it is that you're leaving the company area so much? Every time I see you, you're off down the ramp. What is it down there that attracts you? I wish I was a young officer with nothing to do but run off somewhere and diddle myself. If nothing else I can get you a detail of men to refill our revetments; some of these barrels are leaking sand.'

Sergeant Magruder, whom Blood had been dragging along to inspect the ships on the line, quickly put a stop to that with 'I don't know what you'll do for men, sir. We ain't got an enlisted man that's not flyin'. And you know Major Hart wants all details sent through the first sergeant.'

'Yes, of course I know it. Well, where is it that you're going, Mr Bear?' This combination of the Bear's nickname and the proper military form of address to a warrant officer was ridiculous, and was meant to be.

'I was going up to the hospital, sir.'

'The hospital! What in hell for?'

'Well . . . there are some people up there we know.'

'There's nobody from the company there . . . You don't mean the troops from Battleax? Oh no you don't! You're not to leave the company area, and that's an order!'

The order was short-lived. Blood broke into Major Hart's office with the haste of one who has just uncovered quicksand beneath the foundations of his house. 'It's that damn fool of a bug-eyed warrant officer, Major! He's been running off to visit the troops we medevacked to the hospital!'

The major did not immediately see what harm that might cause.

'Why, damn it, sir! There's an investigation on! If that infantry lieutenant colonel finds out that one of our pilots is hanging around there to see those troops, what can he think but that someone has a guilty conscience? How will that reflect on the rest of us? I told him not to leave the area. But God knows how much trouble he's caused already!'

'You know, of course, that I went to visit them myself two days ago?' Major Hart said quietly.

Martin, listening in a quiet rage from his side of the office, was as surprised to hear this as was Blood himself.

'That's a different thing,' Blood said at last. 'As company commander you've got a duty, of course, when an incident happens . . .'

'I think, Captain Blood,' the major said, as close to openly angry as Martin had ever seen him, 'that if one of your officers wants to visit those men, we should just let him do it. I don't think that's doing any harm.'

After Blood had left, Martin said, 'I didn't know you had gone to see the men, sir.'

'Now, that's strange, Ben. I knew *you* had. Who'd think an old codger like me would know more than you sharp young officers?' He put on his best paternal smile and seemed unusually pleased with himself the rest of the afternoon.

* * *

Finding the ward silent, the Bear turned to step back out into the hall, but a voice from the far end of the ward turned him back. Its rattling hollowness was in the silence so like a voice from the graveyard that it made his mustache bristle although it had only wished him a Merry Christmas.

'There's nobody here to greet visitors,' the soldier rasped. He spoke with broken pauses, as if the words tore at his throat. 'In fact, it seems sometimes like . . . there's nobody here but me.' Walking to the back, the Bear saw that the one who had spoken was a red-haired boyish soldier he had seen here before, but always asleep. His open pajama top showed a dressing about the chest. 'Well,' the soldier said in some surprise, 'I didn't expect to . . . see you again, sir.'

'You remember me?'

'Oh, yes, sir. I couldn't hardly forget.'

'No, I don't guess you could.'

'Not after the way Lieutenant Porter . . . run you out of here . . . the other day. Was it yesterday? I lose track.'

He did not remember the attack, then.

'Longer than that.'

'Longer than that. It's not like . . . being out in the boonies. There, you forget what day it is . . . but at least you know . . . when it's day or night. I guess they had me out for a while . . . when I came in here. I won't forget . . . seeing Lieutenant Porter run you out, though. *Chieu hoi!* I'm glad it was you instead of me. But she's really pretty nice. I wish they hadn't . . . sent her away.'

'Did they?'

'To another ward. You never came back . . . when she was on . . . did you?'

'No.' Not because he had not wanted to see her. Perhaps because he *had* wanted to.

'She talked to me for a while . . . that night . . . when she came back on . . . 'cause I didn't feel like sleeping. You ought to talk to her again.'

'I guess I should.'

'She's number one.' The effort of so much talk seemed to exhaust him. He shrank back on the pillow gasping, but his eyes remained on the Bear's face. 'Didn't I see you someplace before . . . before that? I know! You were flying the medevac!' He gasped for air again. 'Damn! I'd buy you a beer, sir . . . if there was one to be had . . . in this place.'

'I'd buy *you* one. It's the least I could do.'

'Oh, Jesus, no! You saved my rear! After the gunships came over . . .' He stopped there, rasping air into his lungs.

'What?' Bear asked, found himself asking without volition. 'When the guns came over . . . ?'

The soldier shuddered visibly. 'I dreamed about it. That's kind of how it was . . . like a dream. Not even a real dream . . . like a dream you see . . . in a horror movie. Where they run and run . . . and never get anywhere . . . and they don't know what they're running from. I never had that kind of dream before. That's . . . kind of how it was. I was supposed to be diggin' in . . . for the night. With Lewis – that was my buddy. We had a two-man foxhole. But I was up the hill . . . taking a whiz. When the choppers went over – passed on by us – I heard Lewis cuss . . . 'cause there wouldn't be any chopper . . . with hot chow and beer . . . 'cause we were so far out in the boonies. And then they come back. You know how they sound . . . when you can feel them coming . . . all the way through your guts? I felt them, way off someplace . . . but coming closer. And then all of a sudden . . . a big round went off . . . right up at the top of the hill . . . and somebody yells, "*Incoming*" . . . and I hauled ass for the foxhole . . . but I tripped over something. I got up to run again . . . and when I come up . . . I saw Lewis sitting there looking dumb . . . so I shoved him into the hole. I didn't know where the fire was from. I thought it was just Charley . . . potting a few mortar rounds at us again . . . until I heard the guns. You ever heard one of them . . . the kind they have on gunships?'

Bear nodded, biting at his mustache.

'That's what I dreamed. The guys shouting for medics . . . and Lewis lying there looking silly . . . in the mud. I didn't even know he was hit . . . until they come around collecting casualties. And that sound coming down on us . . . coming right overhead . . . and you couldn't see anything but treetops. It was like . . . something up there hated us. And then the tracers came down . . . through the canopy . . . streams of them, bushels of them. I jumped for the foxhole . . . I guess I had been standing there . . . kind of dumb, like I'd never seen incoming . . . when the tracers walked all round me . . . and I got hit. I remember lying there . . . with Lewis . . . wondering what the hell. I still didn't know what it was . . . until I heard somebody up the hill . . . holler that it was gunships . . . for somebody to get on the horn . . . and report we were being hit by gunships. Then I heard them coming back . . . and I just shriveled up and prayed. I dreamed that – the waiting and the sound. I hope to God . . . I never do again!'

Bear nodded again, remembering the evil voice of the guns.

The soldier closed his eyes and gasped.

'How are you now?' Bear asked. It was a helpless silly question, of no use to anyone, but the soldier answered, sounding pleased: 'Every day I'm getting better. That's what this hospital . . . is here for. Pretty soon . . . I'm going to take up my bed and walk. It doesn't hurt now . . . just a little hard to breathe. It must be this bandage . . . they got me in. Right at first . . . it was like a hot poker . . . had been laid across my ribs. That sucker almost missed me . . . just one bullet . . . took a piece out of a rib. Half an inch over . . . and he'd have missed me clean.'

'And how's Lewis?'

'He died.' He said after a moment, 'No reason for you . . . to trouble over it, sir. It's not your fault. It wouldn't have done any good . . . to get him here sooner. He was dead . . . before the medic got to us. I said to him . . . "Lewis, buddy, I'm hit. . . . How you doin'?" . . . but he didn't answer. We carried him up . . . in his poncho. He was the third buddy . . . I've had killed out of my foxhole . . . in seven months. Probably a good thing I got it too . . . this time . . . or I'd have been going it alone anyway. People already were kidding Lewis . . . you know? – "bad luck to be with McWade!" Ah! Bad luck! There's not one of them . . . wouldn't trade with me today. A few days ago I had five months to do . . . and now I'm short.'

'But they wouldn't trade places with Lewis.'

'Well . . . at least they'll wait their turns . . . for *that*, sir. No rush.' His arms relaxed over the blanket, and he lay dozing. 'Merry Christmas, McWade,' Bear said under his breath. He tiptoed out.

'Merry Christmas, Bear!' It was Carter. He went bursting through the hooches like a monsoon wind, sweeping officers before him. 'You coming to the Christmas Eve party up at the club?'

The Bear was lying on his bunk studying the curve of his mosquito net overhead. 'I don't think so, Carter. Not right now.'

'Not right now? Does that mean, "I'll be there for sure later"?'

'Maybe I'll come later.'

'Maybe! Look, Bear, you don't have to be a hermit, just because you're grounded. We still love you! Come on!' When the Bear didn't move, he added coaxingly, 'Tonight we're all equals anyway, because with the truce tomorrow we're *all* grounded. You can be a hermit again the day after. Starting tomorrow night.'

'The guns are on standby tonight,' Bear said. 'Cov won't be at the party.'

'Okay, you're right. And not everybody will be sitting around to open presents tomorrow. I'm flying myself. But why take that out on your poor tired bod? Flying or no, it's the season for mellowness and good cheer and good will to men.'

'And peace on earth.'

'And absolutely peace on earth! Listen!' He cupped a hand behind one ear and struck a pose of absurd expectancy.

'I don't hear anything,' Bear said.

'That's it! Peace on earth! Divarty shut down at sunset. That's peace you hear out there, Bear, or don't hear. All over the land, nobody dying. Not a single poor soul for you to worry about. Now, come on, Bear - come help us be happy.'

'After a while, Carter. I'll come up later.'

'Ah, Bear, you're a hard man! Promise you'll come?'

'Maybe.'

'Wonderful! Now I've got to go before I catch your enthusiasm.' Carter bounded out the other door. Bear heard him calling to the other slick pilots as he hurried to catch up.

When he could no longer hear their voices, Bear went out the opposite door. He really did not want to join their party. Or perhaps more accurately, he did not think he should want to, and did not think his company would be of much cheer to them. He wandered along the edge of the cliff staring off into the emptiness where the ocean rolled listlessly.

There *was* a great silence, all around. Now that he listened for it, it astonished him. Nowhere was there a roll of artilllery. No jets rumbled, over the ridge of the main airfield. No helicopter beat the night sky. Against that great silence smaller sounds could be heard, sounds that ordinarily would have been lost – the sounds of human voices. Across the ramp in the enlisted men's area there was laughter. A snatch of song floated down from somewhere up on the ridge. Far down the ramp from the direction of the club there was a single distant burst of happy noise, as if a door had opened and closed on a room where a party was in progress. Only the sea kept on in its old pattern.

Suddenly he was more lonely than he could stand.

'I wasn't going to come.'

'That's certainly a complimentary thing to say.'

'Not because I didn't want to see you. More because I did.'

'I understand perfectly.' She said this ironically, as if to show that she didn't understand at all; but he had the feeling that she did understand perfectly.

They stood in the darkness outside her hooch above the cliffs. The only sound was the slack surf washing at the reef below.

'There's a Christmas party up at the officers' club. Would you like to go?'

'I'd like to be with you. But I go on duty in an hour. And I don't feel very Christmasy, somehow.'

'Christmas does need snow.'

'Not for a California girl. Christmas needs family and friends. I'm glad you came along.'

'Are you from a big family?'

'Four sisters.'

'That'll be tough for me to do.' He tried putting on a sisterly face, but he couldn't make it work. 'Nope, that isn't it. Can you make do with one friendly soldier?'

'A friendly soldier is what I was most hoping for.'

'You came to the right country.'

A faint glow spread about them. He barely noticed it at first; but her fine face, lean and beautiful, came slowly out of the darkness, seemed itself to glow, to stand out from the surrounding night. She was wearing jungle fatigues, as he was, and he could hardly see her in the darkness, except for her face and her short pale hair. For an instant there came to mind the faces in the darkness of Hill 473. Then they were gone.

Some sound caught his attention. Turning, he saw that the light was a distant flare, so far off that the battery that fired it had been almost unheard. Its single star hung alone in the sky, flickering slowly for uncounted time.

'A star in the east,' she said. 'We could follow it.'

'If He's come back, He's got a big job ahead of Him.' The light went out. 'There, it's gone.'

'Let's go see.'

She took his hand, led him along the rocky cliff edge.

Near the end of the cliffs, beyond the bunkers and the floodlit beach, the darkened shape of the graves registration hooch squatted at the very top of the rock.

'No business for them tonight.'

She seemed to know whom he meant, although he did not look up at the building. 'No business for any of us,' she said.

'I could probably stir some up for you, if I was flying.'

'Stop it.'

'You're right. I'm just trying to get you to feel sorry for me.'

'No, you're trying to feel sorry for yourself. I *do* feel sorry for you. But that's different.'

'I don't want you to feel sorry for me.'

'Why not? Something bad happened to you that you don't deserve.'

'Something bad didn't happen to me. Something bad happened to McWade, and the rest of them. I'm okay.'

'I hope you are.' She took his arm. Her grip was firm.

'I was in to see some of them, this afternoon. When you weren't there. I talked to McWade.'

'How was he?'

'I don't know. How can *I* tell? I wanted to ask you.'

'Is that why you came to see me?'

'No.'

'McWade will be all right.'

'He sounded terrible. Like he was drowning.'

'He has some fluid in one lung. He'll be all right.'

'Is it okay if I feel sorry for him?'

'I hope you do. *I* do.'

'I don't see how you can feel sorry for both of us. It isn't fair to McWade.'

'Stop it.'

'You were a lot easier to talk to the other night.'

'So were you.'

'I was never good at talking to girls.'

'You were the other night.'

'Was I? I must have been in shock.'

'It affects some people that way – makes them suave and debonair. That's one of the first things they teach in nurses' training.'

'Don't tease the troops, Lieutenant.'

'Teasing is the conversative course of treatment for absurd self-pity.'

'And if it doesn't work?'

'Ve haff means.' As she said this she stroked her upper lip with the thumb and forefinger of one hand, as if stroking a mustache. 'Ve haff means.'

He could not help smiling. 'I won't make you resort to heroic measures.'

'Darn! Just when we were getting to the fun part!' Her eyes were laughing at him.

'In that case,' he said, 'maybe heroic measures are called for. How do they work?'

Her lips grazed his cheek.

'That's it?'

'Moderate dosages, to begin with.'

'I think they could be addictive.'

'Trust me.'

He turned to face her, took her arms in his hands. 'Alice,' he said seriously, 'this conversation has got to stop. You're getting all the good lines.'

Then they were both laughing.

A moment later he was kissing her earnestly. She returned the kiss, but only for a moment. She stepped back, and her eyes searched his.

'It's all right,' he said. 'I understand that you're only acting in a professional capacity.'

'Am I?' she whispered. 'That *could* be addictive.'

They stood looking at one another for a long time. He broke first. 'Merry Christmas, Lieutenant Porter.'

'Alice. I won't be kissed by anyone who calls me Lieutenant Porter.'

'Merry Christmas, Alice. I wish I had a gift to give you.'

'It's a gift to have you here, on Christmas Eve with no guns firing.'

'You don't even know me.'

'I know your heart.'

'Nurses' training?'

'Intuition.'

'If you do, I'm definitely in trouble.'

'Pretending to be wicked won't save you.' She kissed him lightly, but dodged anything more serious. She took his hand and started along the cliffs again. 'Now let's stop talking about sad things. There are enough good things in the world.'

'All right. What do you want to talk about?'

'Tell me about flying. Flight school. You were nostalgic for Alabama. That must have been a good thing.'

'Flying.' He pondered. 'Yes, that's a good thing: good flying is. Old Tate would never forgive me if I denied it.'

'Old Tate?'

'He was my first instructor. In Texas, not Alabama. I never had another one like him; but he was enough. More than any pilot deserves.'

'*Was* he old? I thought all pilots were young and bold.'

'As they say in the Army, "There are old pilots, and there are bold pilots; but there are no old, bold pilots." I don't know how old he was. He was old for what he was doing. Or maybe he only looked old. Old Tate was a cowboy who happened to be one of the great helicopter pilots of the world. He looked like a fence post with a couple of knots for eyes, and was about that lean and weathered and hard. He was a civilian instructor, not a soldier. Always wore a cowboy hat, indoors and out, except when he was flying – he hated the Army for making him wear a helmet even then. He looked seventy, but I don't guess they'd have hired him if he was. Or maybe he never had a birth certificate and didn't even know his age. Or maybe his first name really was "Old" – I don't know. That's what everyone called him – not "Tate," but "Old Tate." Even to his face: "Hello, Old Tate, how you doin' today?"

'Old Tate had been a fixed-wing pilot before he took up helicopters, and he'd flown every aircraft known to humankind. Show him a picture of a Fokker trimotor, and he'd say, "Hell, I flew one of them in Bolivia back in thirty-two." And he wasn't just blowing smoke. He remembered the numbers. "That ship was the meanest cuss to fly that ever was put together in sheer spite!" he'd say. "Stalled at sixty-three knots, and wouldn't fly more than sixty-four." And you'd look it up in some book nobody had opened for thirty years, and the old coot would be right!

'Mostly, old fixed-wing pilots don't take well to rotary wing. They can't think in three dimensions, and slow speeds scare them. But Old Tate could think in every dimension at once, and nothing scared him as long as he could reach the controls.'

'You sound like you loved flying with him.'

'The first two weeks, he had me scared to death.'

'How could that be?'

'You have to understand what it's like to fly a helicopter. I suppose it was helicopters that had me going, and not just Old Tate.

'The way you start out learning to fly a helicopter is one control at a time. There are three – four, counting the throttle, which pretty much takes care of itself on a Huey, but didn't on the trainers. Four controls: collective pitch, for up and down, in your left hand; cyclic pitch, for forward, backward, and sideways, in your right hand; two pedals for turning the nose left or right; and by then the average pilot has run out of appendages and still has the throttle left over. So they put a twist grip on the collective, and you twist that with your left hand to control the power. There are a few other things, of course, like microphone switches and trim buttons, and, on a gunship, triggers for the guns and the rockets. But not so many you can't work them with one finger or another. The things you might need in a hurry have to be on the cyclic or the collective, where you can reach them without letting go of the controls, because a helicopter isn't like an airplane. An airplane will fly itself, if you just let it alone. A helicopter you have to actually hold right side up.

'The hard part is that all the flight controls are interconnected. The ship is just dangling under the disc of this whirling blade, and it drags along in whatever direction the disc is tipped. The cyclic stick controls the tilt of the disc. But when you tilt the disc, some of the lift that was holding you up goes into dragging you along, so you have to add more power unless you're willing to lose altitude. So you pull in more collective pitch – the collective stick is the up and down control. But adding more lift with the collective requires you to have more power, or the blade will slow down, so you have to roll on some throttle at the same time. But rolling on throttle increases the torque being applied to the blade – that's what keeps the blade from slowing down – and so up pops Isaac Newton and informs you that the blade is going to twist the engine just as hard as the engine is twisting the blade – see Newton's second law – and since the engine is attached to the fuselage, if you don't do something quick the ship will be spinning just as fast as the blade is. So to keep the nose pointing straight ahead you add a little left pedal, which increases the pitch of the tail rotor that pushes the tail to the right and keeps the blade from spinning the whole ship. But having the tail rotor push the tail around takes power, too – there's no free lunch – and takes power from the main blade unless you add still more throttle . . .' Bear halted, panting as if out of breath. 'And so on. Getting it all together is complicated.'

'How do you ever do it?'

'You don't think about it. It's like riding a bicycle. You just do it. Of course, right at first you *don't* just do it. In fact, you'd swear it can't be done by any single human being. That's where Old Tate comes in.

'You learn to fly a helicopter by trying one control at a time. Pedals first. Old Tate gets you out in a big open field with plenty of room all around and set up at a three-foot hover with the nose pointing at a tree over yonder. Then he says, "Okay, I'm going to hover this thing, but you have to keep the nose pointed at the tree. That's all. Feet on the pedals, and keep off the other controls so we don't die in this thing." Well, that sounds easy. So you get on the pedals, and Old Tate gets off them, and for about three seconds everything is dandy. And then the nose starts to turn to the right, for no reason at all. You push in a little left pedal – what seems like a little – and the nose shoots to the left, and Old Tate's trying to bring in enough throttle to keep the ship from sinking through the surface of the earth, and about that time you poke the right pedal, and the ship jumps fifteen feet in the air, spinning at the same time, and Old Tate hollers, "I've got it, dang it, before you kill us!"'

'It sounds like as much his fault as yours.'

'It's just that two guys can't fly a helicopter. But it'd be even worse if he gave you all the controls at once, right off the start. You'd die in fifteen seconds. Actually, it's *not* as much his fault, because after about, say, three hours, you *can* actually keep the nose pointed more or less in one direction, with Old Tate on the other controls. You can do it quicker with Old Tate than with most instructors, because Old Tate is as smooth as a spanked baby's behind.

'After those three hours he gives you the collective, and you go through the same thing, in the vertical instead of the horizontal, for a few hours more.

'Eventually, you get to the place where you can almost control the whole ship, most of the time, as long as you don't need any major power changes. For taking off or landing, though, you do need major power changes. As the Marines say, "The difficult we do at once; the impossible takes a little longer." I remember learning to land the ship. Along about the time I should be ready to solo, I got blocked. I would set up a beautiful approach - fly level until the landing pad comes down to the right spot on the windscreen, adjust power, nose up to slow the ship, just hold it and let it fly down the path to the landing pad - and at about forty feet, the ship would start to slide off to the right. Bring it back, and it would slide off to the left. But it wouldn't go down. Push down the collective, and it would bounce right back up. You've seen the ads on TV with the "invisible shield"? That's how it was: no human force on earth could make that damn ship fly through the invisible shield protecting that landing pad!

'Old Tate would get real impatient. He didn't use profanity; but he did express impatience rather well. He would say, "Dang it! Why don't you get on down there? You see a snake there, or sumthin'?" But he wouldn't help. Because there is no help. Sometimes you'd swear there was someone else on the controls, blocking every move you tried to make. You look over there, and there's Old Tate, leaning back with his arms folded, grinning like a possum. He must have seen this a thousand times. And you'd know that there was nothing keeping that ship in the air but you, yourself; and you still couldn't get it on the ground.'

'How did you get over that?'

'Grace.'

'Grace?'

'One day, there you are fighting that damn ship, trying to

poke it through that invisible dome over your landing pad, and all of a sudden the dome isn't there. She just flies on down, sweet as can be.'

'"And that," says Old Tate, "is when you're a helicopter pilot. Not by works; by the grace of God."

'Old Tate knew how far I still had to go then. I didn't. But he had me convinced I was going to make it.'

'He sounds like a character.'

'He was a lovely man. He convinced me I could fly. "By God, boy, you are sumthin'!" he'd say. "All the equipment to make a first-rate pilot, packed in this silly-lookin' carton! It's like findin' a damn movie star in a box labeled *dwarf*."'

'Whatever he was, he wasn't very kind!'

'He was a grand gentleman. He'd never say anything he thought would hurt you – not hurt you when you'd thought about it. He didn't mind letting you know how screwed up he thought you were at any given moment, but he was gentle of what counted. And by God he convinced me I could fly! I'd never been especially good at anything before that. Raised a little hell, took what came. I've got a brother—'

'The one who didn't want to play dead in the hay bales?'

'That one. He's a genius. Everybody loves him. He went off to Stanford. Haven't heard from him for months – he's against the war now. Well, who isn't? I'd sure as hell quit if Charley would! But when he went to Stanford, I decided to go into the Army. They gave me some tests to see what I was good for. When I qualified for flight school, I think everybody really figured they got the wrong scores under my name, and I'd be out again soon enough.

'Instead, Old Tate made me a pilot. He had me at the head of my flight class in no time. When we moved on to Alabama for the advanced stages, it sort of stuck with me. I guess everybody had got used to me as the ace pilot by then. I don't think I ever flew as well as I did for Old Tate, though.

'"Good flyin' is important," Old Tate would say. "Flyin' right is like livin' right. You don't do it because it's fun – though it is – and you don't do it because its healthful – though it surely is that, or a lot more so than bad flyin'. You do it 'cause anything less would be a cheat on your Creator, who gave you the gift to do it right. You got that?"

'That was Old Tate's sermon: the only one he had.' Bear shook his head in sad admiration. 'I loved the old coot. I hope he's got students worth his while.'

'It sounds as if he had one, at least.'

Bear blushed. 'I didn't mean to brag quite so much.'

'I don't think it was bragging, except on your teacher. And everyone who's good at something should brag on his teacher.'

'Old Tate was one to brag on.' He sighed. 'I wonder what he'd think of it all.'

'Of what?'

'The killing; the dying. I don't think he was much in favor of either of those; though we never talked about it.'

'No one's in favor of those.'

'Not of dying.'

'Surely no one likes killing.'

'Some do. Handy, my door gunner. If Handy gets a VC in the open, he'd chase him across the paddy with a trail of bullets, and get him right at the end.'

She shook her head. 'I can't imagine it.'

'Don't try.'

They had come eastward to the end of the cliff, and then north where it skirted the parking ramp of Bear's company. The blades of the helicopters angled up from the revetments in stiff Roman salute. A guard, passing among the revetments, did not see the two of them.

Below the ramp, out of sight of the hooches, a road had been graded down the low cliffs to the beach. A roll of concertina wire followed the edge of the cliffs, connecting to the bunkers farther up; but the road was left open. At its foot there was only a short strip of beach between two coral reefs, where crew members could swim when not on duty. Alice turned down the road.

Bear poked at the concertina with one foot as they passed, curious at its misshapen bulk. A vine had climbed into it. The vine wound comfortably through the coils, issuing leaves among the thorns of steel.

'There's your truce,' Bear said. 'Peace is having friends with weapons.'

'You're a wicked cynic.'

'It's an occupational hazard: it comes from killing people.' He wished he had not said so much. He had forgotten himself, talking about flight school. Now he was back.

They stood at the shoreline in the darkness. The waves were low and slack. There was no star.

'If you waded out,' he said, 'you'd find nothing but water from here to San Francisco – nothing but that and the horizon. And that's nothing at all.' What change could it work, a mere curve of the sea, a mere nothing at all? How could it make a difference in good and bad? 'What's to keep the war from just walking down the beach some night, and walking up again in California?'

'War isn't carried by water,' she said. 'The only carrier is the human heart.' She laughed, embarrassed. 'They teach that in nurses' training, too.'

'I wonder if it's in mine,' he said.

Some piece of wavedrift bobbed in the broken water, alternately surging landward and being dragged back. Happiness was like that, he thought; washing in and out, but never quite making shore.

'We've got to do something about the Bear,' Carter said. 'He's not even going to show for the Christmas Eve party.'

'Why not shoot him and put him out of his misery?' Atterburn suggested.

'Shut up, Atterburn. It's just not like old times without the Bear,' Carter said to the rest of those at the table. He pointedly turned his chair away from Atterburn. 'We need to think of some way to cheer him up.'

Atterburn didn't notice Carter's hint. 'If he's sorry, it's his own fault,' he insisted crossly. Atterburn was just on the edge of being drunk, and it made him feel like a man. He was not old enough to drink back in the world.

'He needs to fly,' Carlisle said. 'He'll rust away, sitting on the ground.'

‘We’d *all* still be flying, if it wasn’t for him,’ Atterburn said.

‘Atterburn,’ Carter suggested, ‘why don’t you go have Griggs teach you how to do a carrier landing.’

‘What’s that?’

‘If you weren’t so new in country, you’d know. Go ask Griggs.’

Those of them who had been there in the early days – back when the Marines still inhabited part of Ky Ha – had all been initiated into carrier landings. Carrier landings were a party game in which a body in a state of drunkenness sufficient to convince it that it could fly was coaxed into taking a belly-slide down a series of beer-slicked table tops. Griggs, who was much like a Marine himself, had taken it on himself to pass on the art to the next generation of helicopter pilots.

‘Maybe he’ll overshoot and break his neck,’ someone suggested hopefully.

‘You can never count on Atterburn to do the right thing,’ Carlisle muttered. He returned to Carter’s subject: ‘The Bear is about to go nuts doing nothing. But I don’t see what’s to be done about it. He can’t fly until that investigation board clears him for it.’

‘Maybe,’ Carter said thoughtfully.

‘What you mean, maybe?’

‘Maybe he could if he was somebody else.’

‘If I was the general, I could let him fly. But I’m not. You’re too deep for me, Carter.’

‘Think about it, T.B. You and I are flying the goody run tomorrow with Christmas dinner for our starving troops in the field. Right?’

‘Sure.’

‘Well, then it’s easy. You’ve always wanted the day off anyway.’

Carlisle frowned. ‘I see what you mean. But what if you go down? If it’s me that’s killed on the ship, then the me back here will have to be the Bear for the rest of my life.’

‘It’d be a big step up, I admit, but . . .’

‘I don’t think I could hack it.’ Carlisle tried rolling his

eyes, but they were too small to have much effect, and his mustache would not bristle.

'It's a beginning,' Carter said sympathically.

'Well,' Carlisle agreed, 'if it might save a dumb animal's life. . . .'

'Wake up, Bear.'

It was dark in the hooch. Bear grumbled and blinked at the darkness. He had gone to bed early, but he felt as if sleep had come only that instant. Some sounds would wake him instantly – an incoming round or the scramble horn – but Carter's voice was not one of those.

'You didn't come to the party,' Carter said.

'Oh, Carter, I'd just spoil it. Don't drag me over there now.'

'I'll drag you out, all right, but the party's long over. It's time for Santa's little helpers to be on their way, if the troops are going to have their Christmas turkey and mail. Get your helmet.'

Bear sat up and shook his head energetically, as if to rid his ears of water. 'My helmet? You're going to feed the troops out of my helmet?'

'No, dummy, we're going flying.'

'You're crazy.' He lay back down and pulled the blanket around his neck.

'I thought you'd like to do a good deed for your fellow man.'

'I would. But I don't know how, except by not getting out of bed.'

'I'm telling you how. I'm flying resupply this fine Christmas morning, and you can come with me.'

'Unless you know something I don't, Carter, it'd be everybody's rear if I do that. The general doesn't approve of my flying.'

'What the general doesn't know won't hurt him.'

'But if the general does know, it could hurt you and me both.'

'Well, Bear, I'm old enough to decide for myself what will hurt me, and I don't know why you should worry about your position.'

Bear sat up again. The sleep was gone from inside his head. He had decided Carter was serious. 'Who's your copilot supposed to be?'

'Carlisle.'

'It's not just to cover for a drunken wojug, then,' Bear said.

'Drunken wojug! How you talk about poor Hitch when he's only trying to do you a favor!' Carter exclaimed in delight. 'Drunken CW. Two, maybe. Now, if you're coming, let's haul ass. We've got a six-thirty take-off.'

'I'll beat you to the ship if you don't get moving.' Bear was on his feet before the words were out of his mouth, and his fatigues were going on his body. 'What are we flying?' he called to Carter, who had started for the door.

'Number ten thou.'

'I'll see you there.'

When Bear reached the flight line, Carter was atop his helicopter with a flashlight, inspecting the rotor head. Theirs was the only early mission. Bear tried out the right seat. It felt strange to him, after so many months in a gunship. The D-model sat on the ground at the wrong angle. 'This is crazy,' he said to Carter as Carter climbed into the left seat.

'What is?'

'Letting me fly this mission.'

'We'll pray for light loads and good weather; and I'll keep a hand on the stick.' Carter was pretending to misunderstand.

'I didn't say letting me fly this *ship*. I was driving D-models around Nam while you were still chasing clouds at Rucker. But isn't it going to look funny for Carlisle to be sitting around the company area while his mission is taking care of itself?'

'I don't know what you mean, Carlisle. Do *you* understand what Mr Carlisle is driving at?' Carter asked, turning to the crew chief, who was mounting his machine gun at the back of the cargo door.

'No, sir. Not me,' the crew chief said. 'Merry Christmas, Mr Carlisle,' he added, grinning at the Bear.

'I can tell you that the Bear will be mighty scarce around

the company area today,' Carter said, 'but that's not unusual these days, I understand. Last night he said something about going off to visit one of the Marine officers' clubs for the day. Now, then, Carlisle, are you ready to crank this thing for me? No sense in the aircraft commander doing all the work.'

'Yes, sir,' Bear said.

The day passed in a series of twenty-minute jumps. In twenty minutes a helicopter could reach nearly any point in the division area of operations from the main post. They shuttled back and forth from the Division Artillery supply point to all the lonely hilltop outposts where little groups of tents and bunkers clung like barnacles to the rock. On the broader hilltops howitzers stared silently skyward from sandbagged shallow pits. On the narrow ridges – some so narrow that the helicopter's skids overhung both edges as it perched on the top, and the engine could not be rolled back to idle as the cargo was unloaded – mortars leaned idly on splayed legs. Everywhere, soldiers in wet, mud-caked fatigues scrambled toward the helicopter. The cargo of insulated containers, with dinner hot from rear-area kitchens, vanished within seconds. The helicopter would dive over the side of the mountain, with Carter's hearty 'Ho, ho, ho!' ringing in the headphones, and be off for Chu Lai and another installment of Christmas dinner.

And the ship – the ship felt alive in his hands. Picking it up from a pinnacle, Bear could feel the weight of it in his left hand – not heavy, but somehow there, all of it cupped in his palm and rising at his will. And through the cyclic stick the fingers of his right hand felt the whole being of the ship to the very tips of the blades, and at the touch of his fingers it bowed and went where he willed. With swift and untouched grace the ship passed over the miles of warring land.

Between the mountains stretched winding stream-laced valleys. On the seaward side the valleys stair-stepped down in long flights of terraced paddies until they opened on the plain. The white circles of peasants' hats winked up at the helicopter from the steely luster of paddies that glittered back the gray of the sky. On the landward side the valleys were choked with jungle. Nothing was seen to move there; but the guns brooded over those dark valleys. Their keepers turned with relief toward the glimpse of sunshine down over the plain toward the sea, or turned inward in the silence, and tried to forget the dark forests where the rain, the artillery rounds, the light itself, seemed to be swallowed as they fell. Bear flew uneasily over these valleys, knowing they were less empty than they seemed.

But even there over those black lands he felt lighter at heart than he had for many days. Toward noon the clouds began to break above Chu Lai, although they still hung low and heavy over the ridges to the west, and by early afternoon each trip back to the supply point was a plunge into haze-silvered sunshine. When there were no more supplies to be carried, Bear said to Carter, 'You've made a new man of me.'

'You're not done yet,' Carter said.

'No? What now?'

'You'll see.' He took the controls and headed the ship around the south end of the main airfield to the division headquarters pad.

'You're going to show the general that you've rehabilitated me,' Bear suggested.

'Close, but no cigar.'

At the headquarters pad a mixed group of Air Force officers and airmen came aboard. One signaled to Carter that there were no more, and Carter took the ship away over the headquarters buildings scattered among the low evergreens at the edge of the sea. He continued south at five hundred feet until they had passed beyond the jet traffic pattern and then turned directly across the bay toward the peninsula that curved into the sea beyond the mouth of Song Tra Bong. The ship climbed rapidly, and the rocky peninsula dwindled in the haze below them.

'You're taking me to California?' Bear asked.

'You're getting closer.' Carter put the peninsula behind them without changing heading, and then Bear knew where they must be going. Short of California, there was only a handful of islands. The nearest was Cu Lao Re.

As they flew out to sea, the haze thinned but did not disappear. The coast vanished behind them, but no land came in sight. There was blue above and blue below, and silver all around. Only a narrow circle of wrinkling waves directly beneath them marked down from up. To the Bear, who had seen the island only as if it had been a mirage, it seemed almost an act of faith to leap off from the earth in this way. The island might be only a mark on the charts, and not really exist at all. Carter flew by the instruments, unconcerned, and the slap of the blade carried them across the silver chasm.

The island materialized from the mist.

It glowed in the sunlight. From afar it had seemed but a single peak; but now he saw that there were three crescents – the shells of old volanic craters whose sides the sea had broken – joined by a low shelf. The whole island except the tallest crescent – that on the east – was quilted with hedged-in fields and pastures. Some were plowed, and burned a rich reddish brown, while others glowed golden or emerald green. These fields climbed even the sheer sides of the two smaller crescents. Rooftops were scattered among them. On the south shore of the island the roofs condensed into a series of towns spread under fluttering palms. The eastern crescent towered over it all. It formed nearly a complete circle. Its outer slopes were grassed, but within the shell was cupped a dense unmarked jungle.

There was a grassy shelf on the northwest side of the tallest crescent, not far below the rim. A few tin roofs glistened at its edge, beside the dish of a parabolic antenna. The Air Force maintained a radio relay station there. Carter made a low pass over the buildings. By the time he turned the ship back, a smoke grenade had blossomed from the grassy shelf. Carter circled and landed into the light northeast wind.

Several airmen strolled down from the buildings as Carter shut down the ship. One came to his door. 'Can you wait, sir? Some of the guys going back with you haven't come up from the beach yet.'

'Are we likely to get attacked here?' Carter grinned.

'Not hardly.' The airman laughed. 'Not hardly at all. There's no war here, sir.'

As if to prove his point, a jeep came bouncing up the narrow track around the side of the crater. There was no road – only a set of tire tracks through the deep grass. At some places the jeep was almost awash in the grass; at others it clung to bare rock and seemed in danger of rolling down the outside of the crater. In the jeep were four men in swimming suits. The air was cold, but it would be warmer on a sunny beach out of the wind. The men were shouting and laughing. None of them carried weapons.

'They wanted to get in one last swim,' the airman explained. 'They won't get much swimming back in the States, this time of year.' He didn't say 'back in the world', as everyone did on the mainland. 'I'll go get them moving for you.' The airman walked back toward the buildings where the jeep had gone. Like the men in it he carried no weapon. Bear saw that there was a barbed-wire fence below the buildings; but the gate was open, apparently permanently.

'They say the island is a VC rest camp,' Carter told Bear. 'I flew a doctor out here once. There's a medical station of some kind down in the town for the Vietnamese. He told me they see a lot of wounds, one kind and another. No use asking what kind. They always pretend not to understand. It's always "*Come bic! Come bic!*" He said he thought they were Charlies, come over from the mainland to get fixed up. But the police say no. They don't want to push it as long as it's quiet here.'

'That's a funny attitude,' Bear said. 'Haven't they ever heard of duty?' He got down from the ship and walked out across the meadow. They had landed in a shallow saddle between the main crater and a projecting knob somewhere below the rim. Bear walked out toward the knob. The grass clung about his knees. It was green and shining, and it whispered back at the gentle wind. At intervals spikes of yucca-like cactus thrust out of the grass. He wound among them toward the top of the knob.

Beyond the knob the hillside fell away, too steep even for walking, in a great cascade of green all the way to the blue sea hundreds of feet below. But at the very edge of the drop there stood a small bare tree. Its dense gnarled branches formed a globe perhaps ten feet across, perched atop a twisted trunk. There was not a leaf on it. It had the look of immense age, of an old man gnarled and lined; and yet it seemed extraordinarily alive. Against the bright silver haze it glowed even more brightly, as if it were wholly carved out of light, and each branch a stroke of lightning. The grass flashed about its feet. Behind it the sea wrinkled and glittered. But the tree, as the spirit of the place, gathered all elements into itself, contained them all, as if in its dry age it contained the secret of renascence. Bear sat down in the grass, enchanted. 'What *do* you know, Tree?' he asked. He knew the tree had a message, if only he could hear it.

He heard the jeep coming down the track behind him once more. Turning his head, he could see it beside the helicopter. Carter was waving to him. He went back down the knoll feeling he had all but touched the Happy Isles.

'What did you see?' Carter asked him.

'Grass, and haze, and the ocean, and a tree.'

'It *is* empty up here,' Carter said. He was a little disappointed. He had expected the Bear to like the island. That was why he had held it back as a surprise. 'But it's a nice setup they have. You could sleep all night without one hand on your weapon and the other on your boots.' He said this with a hopeful eye on the Bear, but he saw no reaction. He shouted, 'Clear!' out the side and pulled the starter trigger. The engine whistled, the blade pounded, and the deep grass slid away behind them.

The Bear said little until the helicopter was on the ground at Ky Ha. Clouds had closed back over the coast in their absence, and on the ramp it was almost dark, but Carter parked well down the ramp to be out of sight of Operations. They sat on the ship waiting for the blade to stop. Carter was filling out the log book. 'Do you want to sign it?' he asked the Bear. 'That'd shake up maintenance, if they ever read these things.'

'Only as Carlisle,' Bear said. 'You risked your rear for me, Carter, but let's not leave any record of it.'

'Maybe we should - a memorial of our Christmas in Nam. The Bear Memorial Ash and Trash Run. It'll become a company tradition.'

'If they're all as good as the first, I'll come back annually,' Bear said. 'You saved my life, Carter; or at least my mind.'

'Ah, it's all right, Bear. If I ever need anyone killed, I'll call on you.'

'I wouldn't do that for just anybody, Carter. But I would for you.'

The blade had stopped. Bear got out to help the crew chief tie it down. What remained of the day was fading. A thread of smoke still issued from the tailpipe. It vanished against the heavy sky. He hoped the memory of the island would not vanish in the heaviness of his mind.

The crew chief's eyes followed his to the tailpipe. 'She's sure a smoker, sir, old ten thou,' the crew chief said. 'And gettin' worse.'

'Your engine's going to go, then,' Bear said. It was easy to slip back into professional matters. They relieved him of remembering for a little longer.

'That's what maintenance said,' Carter told him. 'But she's still a strong ship. I'm going to fly her until she quits.'

'Thanks for telling me before we got over the water,' Bear joked. *Number ten thou* - a bad sign, slang for the *the worst possible*, infinitely worse than *number ten*. Today the number had been no omen. Even if Carter had said the engine was about to fall out, Bear knew he would have gone anyway. They left the ship to the darkness and went up the hill. Somewhere far to the northwest a series of explosions rumbled down the hills. It was past sunset. The truce had ended.

7

The nurse on duty was a friendly weathered old captain whose jungle fatigues hung like Spanish moss from her limbs. She peered up at him with a slow puzzled gaze, but at last she remembered him from some earlier day. 'We only have one of your friends here today,' she told him. 'One came down from Intensive Care; but one we had here was sent there last night. McWade was his name. Oh, I think he's in no danger,' she added quickly.

The one who had come down from Intensive Care was Patulski, the soldier with one leg. He lay with the blanket drawn up around his shoulders against the air-conditioned chill of the ward. His eyes were closed, but when the Bear stopped at the end of his bed, he asked without opening his eyes if there was anything he could do for his visitor. He did not sound as if he intended to comply with whatever it might be.

'I just came to see how you were.'

The eyes opened. 'You're not one of them investigation jerks? They keep coming around and around, nothing better to do than bug a wounded man with stupid questions. I haven't seen 'em for a day or two, and I hope I'm rid of 'em. What do *you* care how I am?'

'I brought you in from the field,' Bear said. But his answer, sliding over the initial fact as it did, made him think of Blood in the Operations hooch that night, and he fought down a spreading blush.

The soldier seemed to take that for a sign of modesty, and he became less unfriendly. 'A pilot, huh? Well, if you medevacked me, you're the only one that did me any good.

Those investigation people keep asking me what happened. I don't know why they didn't listen the first time. You know what happened to me? Some dumb-ass pilot came along and shot my leg off. This chaplain was in to see me. "Could be worse," he says. Well, it could be better, too. I didn't ask to have my leg shot off. That dumb s.o.b. Carpenter, I heard he only took a few frags through the legs. Shipped him off the next day, and now he's in Conus. Talk about a million-dollar wound! He'd think it was worse, if it was his leg.'

'Well,' Bear said, 'it could be worse.' He did not intend to laugh at poor Patulski, who was lying there one-legged and rightly angry. But from somewhere inside him a bubble of the humor which would have laughed at self-pity in himself escaped without warning. Patulski unaccountably took the remark as a friendly gesture, a sign of common contempt for the chaplain. He broke into a grin which had no pleasure in it, other than that of shared ill-will. 'He was a damn poor excuse for a chaplain,' he said.

Talking to Patulski was for Bear like being dragged over the rocks of his past. Yet he did not tear himself free. He listened as the soldier crisscrossed the injustices of his present condition. 'Excuse me not knowing you – you being my medevac pilot, I mean – but I was flat out cold when you brought me in here. It's not really so keen, being short a leg. Last thing I knew, I was leaning up against this tree, supposed to be digging a foxhole, listening to the choppers buzzing around – I was thinking how nice it would be to go home every night and sleep in a clean bed with no mosquitoes, and here we were, out four nights with not even a chopper to bring us hot chow or a beer – when I heard this noise, *whish!* just like that, and I was laying on my back and there was this little fountain coming out of my knee. And then I was in the other room up there, all that stuff dangling around me like spaghetti, and Charley grinning at me.'

'Charley?'

'Yeah, there was this little Slope in the next bed, just grinning like a loony, or at least I thought he was grinning. I thought, what the hell, Charley's got me and put me in a hospital. We blew up one of those places a few weeks back. It was all underground – must of been forty foot deep. Well, that's where I thought I was, until I saw this round-eye nurse. And then I thought, Patulski, you're short. Jesus I was happy! And then my foot hurt like a son of a bitch, and I looked down, and there wasn't any foot there at all! But it hurt anyway. Is that fair, that the damned thing should hurt when I haven't even got it anymore?' As he spoke, Patulski alternated between great animation and deep sullen brooding. He ended in a slow angry voice, 'That's what Charley was grinning at. And when I looked him over better, *he* had both legs gone.'

'I guess they get some Arvins in here,' Bear said, to fill the silence left as Patulski's voice trailed off coldly. His words reignited Patulski's scorn: 'Naw, he wasn't no Arvin! He was Victor Charley. They come in with an armed guard after a while and took him out. I heard one of'em say he was off to the security ward. And I laid there all that time with him watching me. He could of got up and stuck a knife in me when I was out cold – except he didn't have his legs. No telling how many of my buddies he's killed, even if he didn't look like much. They're little shits, but they're tough. But then I thought, shit, no telling how many of his buddies I might of killed, either. And who was it got me in the end – me and more of my buddies than Charley ever got? Some dumb-ass officer in a gunship!'

'Lord, forgive him,' Bear said, but only to himself.

'If you want to know what a dumb shit he was,' Patulski continued, 'you ought to talk to McWade. He didn't get hit right off, and he was awake through it all. Not only did the gunships shoot us up once, they turned around and came back to make *sure* they got us! Talk to McWade; he'll tell you. He was in here last night when I come in here. We talked some, and he told me. But he didn't feel too good, and they took him out.'

'I saw him one day,' Bear said.

'Yeah, McWade didn't get it near as bad as I did. He never was in Intensive Care. I don't know where he is now – they took him out while I was asleep, I guess. Maybe they shipped him out. I don't know.'

'I'll try to locate him.'

'Yeah, we're the last ones here, he said. Everybody else has gone on. Carpenter went out the first day – right straight to Japan, McWade said. I suppose he'll be going next, and then it'll be just me. Son of bitch, that leg hurts!' He was slamming his hand on the bedcovers as Bear left him.

He had not thought to check who were the nurses on duty in the Intensive Care unit. When he stepped through the door, Alice was there.

The ward had filled with new bodies. They stretched behind her desk, two neat rows of beds festooned with tubes and hoses and straps and frames. A few balloons, and they would be ready for a party. One near the front had an oxygen tent erected over it. He recognized McWade's red hair inside it.

The rows of beds took his eyes beyond her; but she rose to meet him. 'I didn't expect to see you here.'

'I came to see one of your customers.'

She knew that one he meant: she led him to McWade's tent. He was asleep, and breathing heavily with the short gasping breaths of a swimmer surfacing after long submersion. 'He has shock lung,' she said, before he could ask.

'What is it?'

'The bullet that struck his ribs bruised the lung, and fluid is collecting in it. He's on Demerol. That's partly why he's sleeping.' The rippled Plexiglas tent made McWade look like an aquarium specimen, on underwater display.

'Is he dying?' He could not manage a more positive question. Though it had been only two days since she had told him McWade was all right, McWade did not look all right.

'No. This condition comes on a few days after the wound. The other lung will get him through. He'll stay here until he stablizes; but he won't die.'

'How many have?'

If she heard the question, she pretended that she had not.

She stepped out into the hall behind him. Through the windows the sea could be seen. It stretched and wrinkled in the pale sunshine.

'I didn't know you were on this ward,' he said.

'I'm not. I only stopped by to see McWade, too. The poor guy. He's so sweet and brave.' When she saw Bear flinch, she added quickly, 'He'll be leaving so soon, I'll almost be sorry to see him go.'

'I don't see why I couldn't have met a harder-hearted nurse,' he said.

'I'm sure you couldn't find another nurse who would throw a kindhearted officer out of her ward for trying to visit her patients. But I'll make it up to you.' She held out her hand to him. 'You can come visit the ward I'm on now. There's no one you need to worry about there.'

She led him along the corridor toward a back corner of the hospital. A soldier with a rifle was leaning back in a chair opposite the doors to a ward. He smiled and waved them inside. Another guard was posted inside the door. He stuffed a magazine quickly behind himself as they entered. 'Caught you again, Johnson,' she said. It smoothed away his sheepish grin.

'This is my ward, for this week at least.'

The patient closest to the door turned to watch them. Haunted eyes gleamed out from deep hollows above the cheekbones, while the mouth at one side was pulled back into a perpetual grin by an old scar that meandered up the cheek toward the ear. He propped himself half upright, his forearms lifted clear of the bed, leaning on his elbows rather than his hands because there were no hands. He was protecting stumps that ended above the wrists. He wore pajamas with the legs pinned over, for his own legs ended above where the knees had been. But the eyes – the eyes were screens behind which nothing moved. Bear recognized with a shcok the true figure of Patulski's drugged perception. 'Charley,' he said softly.

'Yes, he's VC. This is a prisoner ward.'

The ward was half full. All the patients – prisoners – were Vietnamese. They lounged on their beds empty-eyed, as though they, like the American patients, had resigned their bodies to this place but sent their spirits elsewhere for the duration. None of the others paid any attention to Alice and the Bear – except for one. At the far end of the room was an old woman sitting on her bed. Her eyes were fixed on them as if she sought to penetrate to their very hearts while guarding her own thoughts. She had sparse white hair floating about her head like whisps of cirrus. She had no eyebrows. Leprosy had mined her bones until the wrinkled flesh collapsed into the subsurface channels, leaving a flattened nose below the heavy bare brows that stretched up to a forehead arched in the taut curve of a drawn bow. It was a stern, almost fierce face, a leonine face, majestic even in ruin.

'All VC?' Bear asked. 'Even her?'

'Yes. She was here before I was, but I was told she was found stalking through the jungle with her AK-47, half starved and eaten by mosquitoes, but not ready to give up until she ran out of bullets. There's nothing we can do for her, but the prisoner compound won't have her. So she stays here. Her name is Phuong.'

She did not move even her eyes when they spoke her name, But, though the body she occupied seemed but the relic of a human frame, the fire in those eyes had survived the disease that had consumed her. 'She looks like Mother Courage herself,' he said.

'Mother Courage! It's exactly the name for her! If she's as indomitable as she looks, she'll endure forever.'

'If anyone can, in this land.' He looked back at Charley, who had fallen back now on his pillows, exhausted by the effort of propping himself up. He was shivering. Alice went to draw his blanket over him. The terrible grin etched across his face masked whatever emotion might burn behind those eyes. Was there any less courage to be found there than in the old woman, because her trials had left her outwardly fierce, while his had made him only terribly, foolishly grotesque? The lips moved, but no words emerged. Bear saw then that the scar down the cheek extended all the way into the throat and out of sight inside the pajama top. Whatever had struck him had taken his voice as it furrowed his face and jaw. 'Lord,' most would have asked, 'what could have done it?' But Bear could name a dozen things that could have done it. He had seen them in use: most of them he had used himself.

To kill or be killed was not so hard a choice. But daily to face the true product of the choice seemed to him now to require a different order of courage. 'I don't envy you your job,' he said to her. Charley was the ideal product of the art of war – not a dead man, but a casualty, useless in battle yet eating up resources that could go to keep his fellow soldiers alive. But he had by some twist of his fate fallen into the hands of his maker, and there he remained, little more now than a trophy.

The kindness Alice showed made him admire her the more even as it made him more acutely aware of how limited was his own compassion. His own desire, he recognized with shame, was to turn away. To face this daily, without tears and without callousness, surely required a strong rein on one's soul. He forced himself to watch her trying to make the broken body comfortable. 'Were you good with pets when you were a little girl?' he asked. 'You have kind hands.' He did not mean the question to belittle her patients, nor did she understand it that way.

'My father says I was. Puppies and kittens at least, and a pony.' She added, 'I never had a chance to be kind to a Bear.' She touched him lighly on the arm, smiling.

It was then that his will capitulated. His heart had done so days before. 'This one would take it kindly if you had time to see him tonight,' he said.

She considered for a moment. 'I'd be pleased.'

The hazy afternoon ended in a cool humid evening which lingered beyond the Grandfather Mountain, Nui Ong. In the side door of one of the gunships on the line, Bear and Covington sat talking. Covington had got onto his favorite topic, his son-to-be. Bear was pleased enough with the subject, since it relieved him of any need to speak. His own life seemed to him to be a subject best left alone.

'I don't know what to do about Pinky,' Covington said. 'She says she's still smoking. I told her two weeks ago that I thought she should quit. That can't be good for a kid, can it?

To have the mother smoke while she's pregnant, I mean. Do you think she didn't get my letter?'

'Maybe not by the time she wrote. What was the postmark?'

'It was a week ago. She should have had my letter. Maybe it got caught in that attack on Da Nang. Wasn't that about two weeks ago? I'll bet it was on one of those C-130s that was hit on the runway.'

'Why don't you tell her again?'

'Ah, you don't know how women are, Bear. Little things set 'em off. Especially when they're pregnant.'

'Of course, you've impregnated thousands.'

'Well . . . I *was* quite a performer in my bachelor days.' Covington lay back on the floor of the ship, grinning with what Bear thought might pass for wickedness in Iowa. The claim, however, was greater than Covington's slender nineteen years could carry. And Bear had heard from him more than once that he had never considered, never even dated, any girl other than Pinky. Their parents had been against the marriage, which came so shortly before he left for Vietnam. But he had great stubborness for so small a frame – he was mere apostrophe of a man – and he had had his way. Only he was sorry he would not be home in time to see his son born. 'I don't think she should smoke anyway,' he said, 'but she only does it when she's nervous. Now she claims the whole thing makes her nervous, with me here and her there. You know how women are.'

'You just told me I don't.'

'Well, you don't, except when they're nervous.'

'Why don't you suggest she wait up until you get home?'

'Thanks a whole lot, Bear.' Then he sat up again. 'Hey, you know what would be neat?'

'No, Cov, what would be neat?'

'Your DEROS date is in April.'

'I'm not going around hollering "short" yet, but you're right again.'

'Well, my son is due around the end of Arpil; and what would be neat is if you were around – you're going to be on leave then anyway, and you can't go anywhere in the States without going through Iowa, believe me – you would just stop in and see my son and my wife for me, and tell them both how lucky they are to have me for a husband and father, and how much I miss them . . .'

'Come on, Cov, let's not make yourself all lonesome again tonight.'

'I won't. Cross my heart. I had enough of being lonesome on Christmas while you were off pretending to be Carlisle. But Pinky would just love to see you. And you could write and let me know how they both are. I wouldn't mind an unbiased opinion on how handsome my son is.'

'Pinky might have better things to do than entertain soldiers, being a new mother and all.'

'"Entertain soldiers" sounds like something illicit. But no, she'd really like to meet you. And she's thinking about beautiful girls to introduce you to. I told you about this friend of hers who's going to a modeling school?'

'Cov,' Bear said impulsively, 'I'll be glad to visit your bride for you. But it's too late for the girls.'

Covington stared. 'Too late for girls? What the devil does that mean? I don't recall that you took a round between the legs while *I* was flying with you. What have you been getting into on the ground these last few days? Listen, you haven't really got something going with Yan, have you? The major won't go for that.' Although he admired the Bear's ability to chatter with the hooch-maids, Covington half-shared Atterburn's opinion that there could be only one purpose in it.

'No, Cov, I don't mean Yan. She's just a little girl.'

'Well, you could fool me, but I've only seen the wrapping, not the package. But I wouldn't have thought Suzie or any of the other grandmothers were to your taste. And there's nobody else around. Carter said they flew some doughnut dollies out to Colt the other day, but they live way up at the headquarters compound, and you said you've only been between here and the hospital. Unless you found something out in the boonies . . . Oh.' He squinted one eye at the Bear. 'You haven't been going to see someone besides wounded grunts at the hospital, have you?'

'I haven't,' Bear said, 'not really, but I thought I might.

Shoot, I don't know, Cov. I met this nurse down there . . .' He stopped. He wanted to tell Cov about Alice Porter; and yet he did not know what he could say about Alice Porter, did not know what he felt about her, knew only that whatever he thought of her he felt that she was squeezing out of him some element of compassion that ought to be there instead of her. But he could not help thinking of her.

'You met this nurse down there,' Covington prompted him.

'That's all. I met this nurse.'

'That's all? "No more girls," he says, but that's all. He met a nurse, just a friendly handshake, but it's too late for the beautiful model. Jesus, Bear, tell old Daddy Covington about it!'

'Don't make a big deal out of it. She's a nice girl, and I like her. I'm going to go up and see her for a while this evening. That's all.'

'Ah, the Bear strikes again! While the rest of us swelter in the ready room, the Bear is out romping with a friendly nurse!' Covington seemed transported by the thought. He lay back in the ship with his eyes closed and a wide smile on his face.

'What have we here but two leisured gentlemen?' It was Lieutenant Arp checking the ships that were on standby. Washington, the crew chief on this ship, was with him. 'They're holding down my ship so it won't blow away,' Washington said.

'No insults now,' Covington insisted. 'Don't forget who's flying this thrashing machine tonight, Washington. Your life is in my hands. That's one leisured gentleman,' he said to Arp, 'and one working man.'

'Mr Covington's working, sir.' Washington grinned. 'He's straining to grow a mustache.' Washington stroked his own Mexican-bandit growth.

'It appears to me that he's given up on it,' Arp said. 'Or else it's dying of loneliness.'

'Maybe you could give him lessons, Washington,' Bear suggested.

'He couldn't use my method, sir. It's not fit for a married

man.'

'You'd better teach it to the Bear, then,' Arp said. 'He needs something to pass the time. Now if I were you, Bear' – Arp paused to cross himself – 'I wouldn't be spending my time down here on the ramp sitting in a gunship. You're going to be doing enough of that when you come back on flight status. You'll pull duty for two weeks straight just to make up the time Covington and I have put in for you. Here we are on our sixth day of twenty-four-hour standby, and you add insult to injury by hanging around showing off your freedom. Why don't you go get drunk with the animals?' He meant Blood and Atterburn.

'Little does he know,' Covington said with satisfaction. Bear shoved his heel into Covington's ribs.

'Know what? That the Bear's drunk already? You know, Bear, if I thought I'd get away with it, I'd sneak you into my bunk and just run on up to the club to watch the horror movie.'

'Just give him your cap, *Trung úy*, and nobody will know the difference.'

'He couldn't pass for me,' Arp said with a grin. 'I'm not as ugly as Carlisle.'

'I've heard that debated,' Covington answered. 'But the insult I meant was that, with a different bar on his hat, Bear would run this outfit to beat all hell. But I will say the flying end of the platoon has been running one heck of a lot better since you've been doing it than when Blood was. Maybe the trade we should make is Blood's hat for yours.'

'Don't be heretical,' Arp said. 'I'll have to report you up the chain of command.'

'So what can they do – ship me to Vietnam? They couldn't even bust me or ground me, because either way they'd lose a pilot, and then there wouldn't even be enough people for standby.'

'Rationality will get you nowhere,' Arp said. 'Not in this army.' He went on up the ramp.

'Everybody in the company seems to know about me and Hitch and the Christmas run,' Bear said.

'Only people who are safe. Don't fret.'

'If everybody knows about Alice, I'll know how the news got out.'

'Anybody but you would be shouting the news from the rooftops, Bear. But *I'm* not going to tell. No, never. Wild horses couldn't drag it from me.'

'If it matters *that* much to anybody, Cov, you can tell them. But nothing less.'

'Tame horses?'

'No.'

'You're a hard man, Bear.'

He had arranged to meet Alice at the hospital officers' club, but he found her there with Janet Swensen and Wolcheski. Wolcheski was off for the evening and had borrowed a jeep. The four of them drove down to one of the huge officers' clubs built by the Marine Air Groups on the main airfield.

The club was a towering hall of lashed bamboo, walled with plaited mats and thatched with palm fronds. The columns were single poles of bamboo as thick as a man's thigh, and the rafters disappeared into a smoky darkness. The seaward side opened directly onto a broad white beach where the sea flapped idly beyond the reach of the lights. It had been built by Seabees as a dream of tropic architecture, the dream of the tropic isle transposed to an American scale.

A band led by an off-duty sergeant in civilian clothes hammered out hard rock while Vietnamese serving girls in *áo-dàis* threaded among the tables. On a semicircle of open floor, fighter-bomber pilots were dancing. They danced alone. There were no women in the club.

Alice and Janet's entry provoked a barrage of stares, but no one, at first, approached to ask them to dance. Those who were already on the floor went on as they had begun; and when a song began that seemed to be a favorite of the house, the floor was instantly crowded with men shaking in stylized abandon, while those sitting around them shouted out the chorus: 'We gotta get out of this place,/If it's the last thing we ever do . . .'

'I thought only Greek men danced alone,' Janet sniffed. 'It's disgusting.'

'She hates to see anything in trousers going to waste,' Wolcheski said to the Bear. Janet pounded his arm. When one of the Marines did come to ask her to dance, she went off with only a sidelong look of triumph at Wolcheski. He shrugged. 'Why not share the wealth? I'm the one who's taking her home.' When she returned, she held his hand and worried about the edges of his serenity like a puppy trying by being a nuisance to draw attention to the fact that it is now prepared to behave.

It was the strangest evening Bear had spent in Vietnam. While Marines danced alone to a rock band, jets boomed off the runway just across the main post road, drowning all conversation until they turned out over the sea to begin their long swing to the north. Between jet departures they sat over drinks and talked quietly of nothing to do with the war. That was the strangest part of all – when it was like an evening in real life.

He danced with Alice eventually. Within the slow music her body touched his lightly. And in the jeep going home she had no objection to being kissed.

Outside her door she reached up and touched his mustache with one finger. 'Share with me,' he said, when she laughed.

'You bristle.'

'You've discovered me. Most people don't know that I'm the walrus.' He had taken hold of her finger, and he kissed it before letting go.

'As far as I can recall,' she said, 'I've never been kissed by a walrus before.'

'Many strange experiences lie before you,' he murmured. 'You will live a rich full life—' He broke off abruptly.

Sensing the reason, she said nothing.

After a long time he said, 'You know, I could just as well have met you under some other circumstances.'

'I wish you had, if that helps.' She turned and looked out over the cold dark sea into the depth of emptiness. He looked off in the same direction, as if somewhere their eyebeams might intermingle, in some neutral space far removed from this where they were caught within the wrong lives.

'I don't know why you wish that,' he said. 'I'm just the ugly Bear, and you're a fair princess of a lieutenant.'

She touched his hand. 'Poor Bear.'

'It's not fair,' he said. 'Why should I have met you because of . . . because of my damned stupidity? While they . . .' Gone into the earth. And he could not mourn them with his whole heart, as he should, because his heart was sliding into love.

He walked up the still ramp in the sea mist, hearing the distant boom of the jets regular as clockwork, seeing the damp blades of the silent glistening gunships angling up into darkness, troubled by how easily he might forget.

A poker game was still going forward in the little empty hooch that was the company officers' lounge. A half-dozen pilots from the lift platoons were slumped about the battered card table. The game had started early and now only inertia kept it going. They greeted him with slow bored turns of the head: 'Hey, Bear.'

'Get some of that fresh money in here and liven things up,' Warrant Officer Griggs muttered. Griggs had not been losing, but he was never pleased with less than elimination of the other players, and he was frustrated by a long evening in which he had gained no edge.

'The Bear won't play poker,' Carter said. 'He's saving his pay to buy a pink Cadillac when he gets back to the world. With a stove and refrigerator in it.' Griggs had once informed Carter that a pink Cadillac was the pinnacle of motorcardom, and Carter would not forget.

'Up yours,' Griggs snarled.

'Originality will get you nowhere,' Carter said happily. He was never so pleased as when he was ragging Griggs, whom he detested.

'Deal those mothers!' Griggs demanded. He shook his head as if to dislodge Carter from his ear.

As the cards flicked out around the table, Lieutenant Harris, one of the slick platoon commanders, came in the door at the back of the hooch. 'Missions.' He tossed a sheaf of mission assignment sheets onto the table as the cards went around the far side.

'What kind of shit did you stick me with this time?' Griggs asked him. He folded his cards and leaned back as if daring the lieutenant to give him the wrong answer.

'How would you like artillery resupply?'

'What?' The blow of Griggs's hand on the table bounced off the bare walls. 'God damn it, Lieutenant, I haven't had a day off in thirty days now! Do you know how many hours I've flown this month? When the hell do I get a day off, I'd like to know?' The strength of Griggs's sense of injury was matched only by the loudness of his voice.

The lieutenant only smiled. His lean freckled hatchet face had wrinkles about the eyes when he smiled. 'I thought if I let you fly ten hours tomorrow, you'd be over the limit and I'd have to let you rest for a few days,' he said seriously; but he winked at the dealer.

'You know, Lieutenant,' Griggs said, as if explaining to a child, 'I'll get over there at oh-six-thirty tomorrow, and I'll wait an hour for some supply sergeant to haul his ass out of the sack, and then I'll spend half the day screwing around while they try to find out where this next load of C-rats is supposed to go, and there's no way in hell I'm going to get ten hours tomorrow. I'm on alternate flare ship tonight besides. What if I have to go up? I can't see dragging my own rear out of the sack at four thirty after being up all night.'

'Charley won't be out tonight,' Jones observed. 'There's not enough weather to keep the gunships down. If he didn't come in all that weather last week, he won't be out tonight.'

'Leave it to a New Guy to tell you how the war goes,' Griggs snapped. 'What I want to know, Lieutenant, is why the hell you pick me for all the shitty missions?'

'It's because he knows you were in this Army when he was still a gleam in his daddy's eye,' Carter put in, echoing one of Griggs's favourite Army sayings.

Griggs, although not that old, was an ex-sergeant who knew his rights and stood on them. He had no use for lieutenants. 'Why?' he demanded.

'I always try to suit the mission to the personality of the pilot,' Harris answered with a shrug, to the laughter of everyone except Griggs. He handed the mission sheets around. 'You're on a standby tomorrow,' he said to Griggs, who smirked in triumph.

'Damn it, sir, I need some hours,' Carter said. 'Why don't you let me fly artillery resupply tomorrow.'

'Can't. I have to take this young stud up' – he pointed a thumb toward Jones – 'and give him a workout. He'll never make aircraft commander, if somebody doesn't take him in hand.'

'Give him to me,' Griggs said. 'I'll make an AC out of him.'

'Or see that he dies trying,' Carter said.

'Speaking of dying,' Griggs said, grinning about the room before he looked at the lieutenant, 'did you hear about the Dink I got today?'

'I saw the report,' Harris said.

'We got that son of a bitch just bigger than shit. He thought he had it knocked when he got two fields between him and the infantry. But I wasn't about to let him get away. And then he thought he'd get out of it by dropping his weapon and putting his hands up. That Rogers is a sweet gunner! He holed him on the first burst. I'm having him paint a Chinaman on the ship.'

'Why didn't you capture him?' Harris asked. 'He might have known something that infantry company wanted to know.'

'Christ, he had a weapon! If we tried to land, all he had to do was pick it up and blast the crap out of us!'

'You couldn't keep him pinned down until the infantry got there, I don't suppose.' Harris said, with the tiredness of one who had been through the routine before.

'Low on fuel, sir,' Griggs answered pleasantly. 'Anyway, one more dead Slope makes the war that much shorter.'

'It could be true,' Harris said. He turned and walked out abruptly.

'You in this game, Bear?' Griggs demanded.

'No.' He went out into the damp night air. 'Deal me out, too,' Jones said behind him. 'I've got to fly tomorrow.'

'You going to let the lieutenant scare you off to bed, are you?'

'Well, Griggs, we don't all have a late standby tomorrow morning.'

'I handled him all right on that, didn't I?' Griggs sneered. 'The bastard might make a decent officer, if he wasn't so rubbery. He wanted to stick me with that resupply, but he didn't have the guts to stand by it.'

'I notice he had your name on the standby mission sheet already,' Carter pointed out.

'Sure, and probably on the resupply, too. You notice he didn't let anybody else see that one.'

'Why should he? He's flying it himself, as usual.'

'Suck-ass trick,' Griggs answered scornfully. 'He thinks Major Hart will notice. The old man's been around. He knows who's worth a shit and who's not.'

'Too bad we can't say that for everybody,' Carter said.

The Bear lay on his bed, dressed only in his OD undershorts, feeling the mosquito net breathe gently as the night land breeze sliding down from the mountain passed through the hooch. Someone came down the walk behind the hooches. The walk was made of a mixture of pallets, steel and wooden, left from some company move so long past that almost no one was left in the company who could recall it personally. The unit had moved up the coast from near Qui Nhon more than a year before. A year was forever here, where men arrived, grew to maturity in their jobs, and departed, all within a year, leaving only a name to be remembered for six months more by those to whom had been an old hand when they arrived and now were old hands themselves. Then they, too, departed, leaving their own names to linger for a little while on the lips of other soldiers. A few stayed on for an extra six months as volunteers in exchange for thirty days' extra leave in some other part of the world. Only a very few, like Sergeant Handy or some generals, stayed on and on unable to give it up.

The pallets of the walk rang under the steps of one more set of feet soon to become a faded name. They stopped behind the hooch. The officer, whoever he was, had stopped to feel the air, to judge the dampness against the chance of rain by morning. Another came down the walk. 'Why are you still up, Jones?' he asked. Lieutenant Harris's voice.

'Just looking at the weather, sir. It should be good flying tomorrow.'

'You'll be too tired to enjoy it. Young officers need their beauty sleep.'

'Don't worry, I'll be down on the ship before you are, sir.'

'I sure hope so. These six o'clock takeoffs will be the death of me yet. I don't like 'em any more than Griggs does.'

'Griggs! I don't know how you can put up with that ass, sir.'

'Well, he's a body in an airplane. You have to have enough ACs to fly the ships.'

'What you need is more ACs, then. How long do you think I'll have to fly right seat before I get my own ship?'

Harris laughed softly. 'I don't know. Not more than a year, at the outside. We'll see how it goes tomorrow. You've got plenty of time to fly.'

'Never enough time for that, sir.'

'Remember that when you're short, Jones.' Lieutenant Harris had a soft pleasing laugh, Bear thought.

When Jones came into the hooch he turned on his small lamp inside his mosquito net and moved softly about, prolonging the last moments before sleep as much as possible. He pulled off his boots slowly and placed them loosely laced beside the head of his bed, ready for quick use. His pistol belt he hung on the back of a chair next to the boots. He stretched and scratched and grinned to himself. Bear remembered the night before his own check ride for aircraft commander. For a combat pilot that was graduation.

Jones became aware that he was being watched. 'Hell, Bear, I'm sorry.' He blushed. 'I was trying to be quiet so I wouldn't wake you.'

'I wasn't asleep.'

'I don't feel like sleeping, either. Isn't this a great night?' He tactfully said no more, supposing that his grounded hooch-mate might not wish to be reminded of his own misfortune by chatter about check rides. They slipped into private thoughts, not speaking, listening to the sea worry the beach below the cliffs. Bear thought of the sound of the surf below the Marine club, and of Alice.

Out of the still depths of the night, not loud, yet close at hand, as if they could reach out and touch the sound itself, came a low hollow thump like a wood mallet striking an iron pipe. It was a small drop of sound falling into a sea of sounds – the rustle of surf, muffled voices from the poker game, the groan of a truck on the main post road, the distant boom of Phantom engines testing. It was a sound no civilian in real life would have noticed. It brought them both bolt upright in an instant.

'Did you hear that?' Jones asked. But Bear had already snatched up his boots and pistol belt and was off for the door, with Jones at his heels, both bawling like demented cattle: 'Incoming! Incoming!' They fled across the slippery clay and into the mouth of the sandbag bunker between the hooches.

There was a sudden dead silence. The voices from the poker game had stopped; even the jet had shut off. Griggs's voice cracked the mirror-surfaced stillness: 'Who the fuck's that?'

Jones hesitated at the mouth of the bunker, suddenly uncertain what he had really heard. He knew if he were wrong it would be long before the subject would be put to rest.

The mortar round they had heard coming out of the tube impacted on the ridge of their hooch with the flat spreading crash of a chest of drawers being toppled on an upstairs floor. Instantly there was the thunder of boots over plywood floors and the sticky slap of bare feet on clay. 'Who's blocking the door?' Bodies scrambled urgently over the Bear's legs inside the low, ninety-degree angled entrance to the bunker. 'Get the hell inside!'

The bunker was low, only high enough to sit in – hardly higher than a coffin, someone had remarked as it was being built – as wide as a man lying down, and twice as long. The walls were a double row of sandbags, cross-laid and braced by steel fence posts. The all-important roof was a layer of steel plank over heavy timbers, topped by two layers of sandbags. It had been built in the heat of summer, by men whose backs ached, and other men now prayed that they had not thrown down their tools before the job was truly done. None of those inside had ever seen a bunker hit directly by a mortar shell. They did not know what it might do, and so they expected the worst.

Someone switched on a flashlight. There were seven faces. Their eyes were mere walls of blackness as the flashlight shone obliquely down the length of the bunker. Outside, the alert siren began to wail slowly up from the bottom of its throat, sounding far away.

'Did everybody get out of the hooches?' Lieutenant Harris's voice was calm.

'I think so.' 'There was nobody inside ours but Jones and me.' 'The lounge cleared out, but some guys must have gone to the other bunker.' 'Where did that mother land, anyway?' 'Close, man! Close!'

After that rapid burst of words a long silence set in. They listened.

A vehicle started up nearby and roared away to the north on the road around the ramp. 'Some crazy bastard,' Griggs muttered.

'It's Captain Martin going over to the perimeter.'

The vehicle was gone, and still nothing.

'What the fuck?' Carter said. 'Is that all?'

'A one-shot Charley,' Griggs snorted, as if disgusted at having been bothered.

Three rounds fell almost together – *ka-bom . . . pom* – far off, like flour bags falling onto a hollow board floor.

'Four-shot,' Carter said.

Bear tried to guess how far they were, but he could not judge the sound from inside the bunker. They could have been as far off as the hospital. But surely she would have a bunker there. As for McWade, and Patulski, and the rest . . .

Another round dropped, closer.

'Oh, Christ.'

'They're going for the ramp.'

'I hope to shit they don't come after me!'

The siren wailed alone, its high steady scream desperate in the darkness.

Harris had switched off his light. The darkness within the bunker was absolute: a narrow right-angled tunnel of sandbags meant to stop shell fragments closed off all view of the outside. Waiting was the three-dimensional Chinese water torture, waiting for the drop to fall and wondering where it would be, as well as when. The plodding giant steps of the incoming rounds crashed back up the ramp toward the area they had first leaped over - *pom!* at the gunship ramp - *pam!* the Operations hooch - WHAM! Shrapnel rattled through the tin roofs on either side of the bunker.

The inside of the bunker was suddenly like a tomb. It had even the smell of death about it. It etched on Bear's mind suddenly the dark prison of the LZ on Hill 473. He ached to be outside, even if only to die under the open sky rather than be buried before life ended.

'Come on,' Griggs muttered. 'God damn it, fall!'

Pam! It was beyond the major's hooch. The rounds had walked on by.

'I forgot my damn weapon,' Lieutenant Harris said.

'At least you brought a flashlight. You can blind the little dears if we get a ground attack.'

'Hell,' Carter said, 'Bear doesn't even have any clothes on. You're obscene, Bear. And who the hell was in the door? I damn near broke my neck on him in the dark.'

'Jones was right behind me,' Bear said.

'Was that you, Jones? Jones? Hey, Lieutenant, switch your light on.'

Jones was seated just inside the door where Carter had pushed him. His knees, encircled by his arms, were drawn up to his chest, and his head bent forward to rest on them. Carter put out a hand to shake the young officer gently by the shoulder. He drew it back covered with blood. The sweet cloying smell filled the bunker. 'Jones!'

The note of the siren broke to a rising and falling wail, the signal to report to Operations. 'Carter, stay here with him,' Lieutenant Harris said. 'I'll get a medic up here. Everybody else get your flight gear and get moving.'

Outside, all the lights were out. Every hooch was black; the ramp lights were extinguished; the hospital floodlights beyond the ramp were not to be seen. Bear rushed into the hooch – the door did not hang straight – and struggled into his clothes. With his helmet bag in one hand he ran for the Operations hooch, joining a current of dark shapes moving in the same direction. Up from the ramp floated the whistle of the gunships cranking. Lieutenant Rauch was shouting from the Operations room door: 'Spread out, damn it! Spread out, but stay in the area. We're not goin' to evacuate the ships yet, so spread out!' The pilots wandered about with the curious nonchalant bravery of men in the open air and not yet under fire, each believing that the first round will not land at his own feet.

The four gunships, as each came up to operating rpm, whirled in a rapid arc past the takeoff point and climbed out beyond the cliffs. One slick fell in behind them; but when they broke off and swung low toward the north, it climbed on. It was the flare ship. 'Griggs! Where's Griggs?' Rauch was shouting.

'Right here!'

'Griggs, get the number-two flare ship loaded! And be sure the damn thing is fit to fly before you take off!'

Bear worked his way back to a point near the corner of the Operations hooch, where he could hear the radios in the bunker. The voices from the gunships crackled out of the dark cave of the bunker, metallic and emotionless, as did that of Carlisle in the flare ship clearing his flight path with the artillery control center.

From high up beyond the naval yards at the end of the peninsula came the chest-thumping beat of the flare ship's blade as it turned inbound. 'He's close!' a voice said from behind Bear. The voice meant Charley.

'He wasn't shooting from far off,' Bear said. 'How far up did rounds land?'

'I don't know.'

He asked the anonymous voice from the shadows, 'They didn't hit the hospital, did they?'

'I don't know.'

A soft white glow spread over the sky above the island opposite the naval yards. A few seconds later came the gentle pop of the flare igniting. The guns were hunting up and down the island but not firing.

The island was a sickle-shaped flat spit of land built up in the mouth of the broad Song Ben Van. Its brilliant white crescent beach faced the sea in a curve from the high rock at the end of the island two miles away. The whole island covered an area of nearly a square mile; but beneath a dense cover of palm fronds, villages sprawled over most of its surface. The mortars were somewhere among them, where the gunships could not fire.

A second flare popped toward the far end of the island. The flares drifted down on their parachutes, leaving long fluffy columns of smoke that slowly dissolved into the damp air. The two pairs of guns cast about the island, plaiting their patterns from side to side, watching for the flash of a weapon. The sound of their rotors broke like waves over the compound as they turned outbound on each pass. The flare ship passed back and forth above them, steadily ejecting the magnesium flares which carried downwind to hiss out at last in the sea. One fell onto the small sandy speck of land beyond the main island, where it lay for a long time like a distant bonfire.

A field ambulance, driving with only blackout lights, rumbled down the rutted clay road to the ramp and accelerated away toward the hospital.

As the minutes wore on, men began climbing up onto the Operations vehicles and the hooches for a better view of the gunships. The Bear worked closer to the bunker. He had heard Covington's voice on the radio, but he could not make out the words. He was about to join the men on the top of the bunker when Covington's voice again startled the silence: 'Lead, we're taking fire.' It was a dry impassive announcement. But it was instantly followed by an exclamation which might have been meant only for Boroff, who was flying right seat with him, transmitted by mistake in the excitement of the moment: 'There he is! There's a muzzle flash at nine o'clock!'

At Covington's words the crowd atop the bunker stretched and craned for a better view. Almost at once there was a low concerted gasp. 'Oh, Jesus, will you look at that! He's on fire!'

Bear scrambled for the top of the bunker. He stood up in time to see a fireball swinging rapidly seaward. The pilot might have been trying to land in the shallow water just offshore, or even to turn back to the beach, to land facing upwind. Instead, Covington's voice came again over the radio, steady but faintly disgusted: 'Shit, we're out of control.'

'Cov, get your nose up! Get your nose up!' Arp's warning cry on the radio had no effect on the path of the fireball. It arrowed earthward until suddenly, irrevocably, it winked out.

Three brilliant stars – the gunships searchlights – blossomed above the sea, now fading as the ships searched in another direction, now bright as the star of the Magi.

Bear was alone atop the bunker when the ships turned homeward at last. Lieutenant Rauch and the major had shut off the bunker radios and moved back into the Operations hooch. Lights were back on in the company area and around the ramp. Captain Blood, who had been in the officers' club at the other side of the ramp, had come puffing across and installed himself inside Operations to wait for the flight crews. Only when the landing lights stabbed out of the night, burning their dazzling streak through the white haze, did the Bear climb stiffly down. He slung his helmet bag over one shoulder, hooking a finger through the straps, and walked slowly down to the revetments where the ships were shutting down. He stopped at a little distance and waited as the crews tied down. Arp left the ships first, walking slowly and alone. He stopped and did not speak for a moment. Then he hooked both thumbs in his pistol belt at the front in a characteristic gesture of anger. But his voice was soft, almost apologetic. 'He's gone, Bear.' he said. 'They're all gone.'

'I saw it happening.'

'I don't know where the weapon was. I turned back and there he was, burning.'

'Were there any bodies?'

'Nothing. Not a trace. Not even any wreckage.'

To stand on the shores of a strange land quietly discussing the death of friends would have seemed to him a year before to be an act of despair or callousness. Now he found it was neither, but perhaps only a substitute for both.

'Oh, God, I'm sorry, Bear!' Arp put out a hand and touched him on the sleeve. Then he went on up the ramp to Operations to complete his duty by turning in his report.

Bear turned aside from the rest of the crews who were beginning to leave the ships. Down the ramp he stumbled on a torn patch in the steel plank. One of the rounds had landed there. It had left a jagged hole not more than six inches wide, with the metal edges curled up. The round had barely penetrated the surface.

At the end of the ramp a guard challenged him. When he gave the password, the guard stepped forward nervously from the shadow of the revetment, beaming a flashlight. 'Oh! I'm sorry I didn't know you, sir. I should of known.' It was Cripps. Bear had seen him only rarely since he had been grounded. He had supposed Cripps was flying.

'Weren't you up tonight, Cripps?'

'Oh, no, sir. The ship's down for inspection, and I drew guard duty besides.'

'Did you hear . . . ?'

'About the crash? I seen it, sir. But I didn't hear anything. Do they know who it was?'

'It was Covington.'

'Oh, Jesus, sir! Oh, Jesus God!' Cripps shouldered his rifle and turned away. After a long pause he asked, with an effort to control his voice, 'Was there anybody . . . ?'

'They're all dead.'

'Oh, why him, sir? His poor wife!'

'I thought you went in, too, Cripps,' Bear said. 'I forgot . . . forgot he had a different ship tonight. Let's give thanks you're still with us.' He in his turn gripped the soldier by the arm, as Arp had done with him. The touch of a friend was little enough, but it was more than nothing.

'If not me, then somebody else,' Cripps said. 'There's no thanks in that. It just changes who suffers.'

There were lights in some of the nurses' quarters at the hospital, and voices eddied out through the screens, talking of the attack. Alice's room was dark, but she answered immediately when he knocked, and in a moment she came to the door. Seeing him there, she gasped and hugged him. 'You're all right!'

'I'm all right,' he said. 'I was worried about you.'

'*I* was worried about *you!* Nothing happened here. But all those explosions . . .'

'We took a few mortar rounds.'

'But you're all right!' She hugged him again, as if to be sure. 'Was anyone hurt?'

'They brought at least one of our pilots up here.'

'You want to find him. Let me come with you.'

'If it's all right?'

She was already dressed. They went around by the wooden sidewalk to the emergency room. The sound of their feet was the sound of hard earth falling on a coffin. 'What happened to him?'

'He took some fragments from the first round. I think it was bad. I don't know.' He added, as if by afterthought, but his voice gave away his feeling, 'We lost a ship, too.'

'Oh, no!'

'Covington – my friend I told you about . . . you'll never get to meet him.'

'Oh, Don!'

'He went into the ocean with his whole crew.'

She stopped him and held him close to her for a long time. She could hear his heart pounding in his chest. Then they went on.

Dawson, the orderly who had directed Bear to Alice's ward, was on duty in the ER. It was empty except for him. 'Casualties, ma'am? I ain't heard of any casualties, praise the Lord?' – Dawson crossed himself, and grinned as he made the gesture – 'and I sure would of known if they'd come through the swingin' doors.' He added, 'You might try graves registration.'

Graves registration was where they found Jones. Inside the small white building the walls were lined with square doors like lockers in a bus depot. Each was the end of a drawer. The drawers slid into refrigerated cabinets. Bodies were laid in them for keeping until they were shipped back to the world. 'Jones,' a sleepy spec-four repeated. 'Oh, yes, he's here. The one who came in after the attack. Wasn't that something? I'm too short for that crap. I'm going to be out of here by New Year's. My bags are already packed. You aren't here to identify Jones already?'

'No. Only to find out what happened to him. Thank you.'

'Any time, sir.' He put his head back down on the desk.

Outside her door she asked, 'Do you want to come in?'

'Yes,' he answered. 'Yes, but . . ..'

'You can. The head nurse isn't watching.'

'Don't you have to work in the morning? I forget about things like that, since I'm out of a job myself.'

'I'm not asking you to spend the night.' She smiled, squeezing his hand to show that the remark was meant kindly.

'I'd better not.'

'All right. I hope I see you tomorrow.'

'You will.'

As he went back up the ramp, Blood was out with the platoon sergeant inspecting the ships for damage. They had a portable generator with a spotlight and were going over the aircraft inch by inch. A tiny fragment in the wrong place could sever a control cable or pierce a hydraulic line, leaving the ship nearly uncontrollable. 'Well! Mr Bear,' Blood said. 'Where have you been?'

'Out on the ramp. I wanted to be outside.'

'Be careful Charley doesn't catch your rear end out on the ramp. He may not be through for the night. We ought to put up another ship, if we had a crew.. We would have, except for this half-assed investigation. I had to make a heavy fire team out of the three we've got left. Might not be a bad thing for *us*, though – you and me. Division wants two fire teams from us, and we don't have the bodies to do it, they've let us go so far under strength. If they need the ships bad enough, they just may let some people fly who can't now, eh, my friend?' Blood chuckled at his own cleverness.

When Bear walked away, Blood's friendly manner vanished. It had risen only from his hopes for a quick change in his own status, and it collapsed when Bear appeared to doubt his dreams. 'Don't wander out of the area!' Blood called heatedly. He fell back into recalling that the whole business was at least half the Bear's fault for insisting that they all deserved some blame for Hill 473. It was hard enough to keep ahead of the Ringknockers on fair terms, without having pansies in your own platoon drag you down.

The Bear's hooch was still empty. Except for Jones, only gun platoon officers had lived there, and they were still in the alert hooch. He did not look into the bunker; but the building itself smelled of death. The door opened under protest. His flashlight showed a ragged yard-wide hole in the roof at the ridgeline. The galvanized iron was blackened around the edges of the hole, and there was the sour smell of burnt gunpowder. The mosquito nets over the beds near the door had been ripped by the shower of metal. The floor and the walls were pierced with dust-shot holes which seemed too small to have been made by anything more dangerous than termites. But what had made them had killed Jones.

His own bed at the far end of the building was untouched. He tossed the mosquito net aside and lay down fully clothed.

8

He awoke to the sound of the dawn patrol taking off. A soft fogdiluted daylight poured through the roof and the plastic-covered screen door. As the two ships hovered up the takeoff lane he could feel each revolution of the blades go trembling through his bed frame, and through the pit in his stomach. The ships beat their way into the rising offshore wind and swirled away along the cliffs toward the island. The hissing whine of the engines lingered far down the wind after the sound of the blades was gone. He rose sour-mouthed and weary and stepped out into the dawn.

The late-night fog was already giving way to the sun and the wind. Shreds of it passed through the low evergreen trees among the hooches.

Other ships were cranking in the revetments now or hovering up for takeoff. They trickled out by ones and twos as he walked slowly along the clifftop. The gray waters were far down the beach and the reef was uncovered.

The patrol soon returned. The two gunships beat low over Ky Ha and swung beyond the ridge before turning upwind for landing. Bear walked down to Operations and sat on the steps until Arp came up from his ship.

'Nothing,' Arp said.

Bear walked back to his hooch.

The deuce-and-a-half truck that brought the hooch-maids to work from the main gate shuddered to a halt in the soft dirt alongside the road below his door. The women's voices flowed among the hooches, broke like water into a dozen eddies that subsided into whispering pools.

He was lying on his bed when Yan came in. She gave out

a soft *Troi oi!*' when she saw the hole in the roof. She set about rearranging Jones's bed as well as she could, clucking softly over the torn blanket. When she became aware of the Bear in his far corner, she caught her breath, startled, and then laughed in embarrassment: 'Oh. You sleep.'

'Yes, I sleep,' he answered, wishing he did.

'You number-ten GI, you sleep so late. Boss no like.' She twittered like a bird about its nest as she went about the beds. When she came closer to him, she said tentatively, 'You no hurt?'

'No.'

'VC number ten,' she said firmly, looking at the hole in the roof.

'You might say that again.'

'*Khong biĕt*,' she said, not understanding him. She added, 'Sergeant at gate, he number-ten GI. He touch me here, and here.' She demonstrated gravely how she had been searched. 'We come late.'

'Better late than never,' Bear said.

'*Khong biĕt*.'

Near midmorning Martin came to the hooch. Bear was in a chair on the low open plywood deck at the back. Martin sat down on the edge of the deck at his feet. The island, all but the near shore, could be seen from there. The beach was clean and bare. Beyond it the white sails of fishing boats dotted the sea.

'He was a hard one to lose,' Martin said after a time. 'They all were; but Cov especially.'

'Do you think they'll be recovered - the bodies?' Bear asked it hesitantly, as though words could somehow still make a difference.

'A Swift boat went out this morning. There was nothing. But maybe they'll come up on the beach: I don't know how the currents run.' He sighed. 'I just finished writing the next of kin. I hate this business.'

'When do they find out?'

'They should know already - at least that they're missing. That was reported to Saigon last night. Division will hold the letters of condolence until they're confirmed dead.'

'Confirmed! Is there any question?' Bear got up and stared at the empty sea. There was the confirmation.

'Not to us. But until the bodies are identified, they'll be carried as missing.'

In Iowa it was evening, and Pinky would know her husband was missing, but not that he was dead. It would be, by the calendar, the evening of the day before, there on the other side of the International Date Line, and she might have learned of her husband's misfortune even before the calender would show that it had occurred. But no one would say he was dead. 'And if the bodies never come up?'

'I don't know, Bear. I suppose the Army will be satisfied some other way.' Martin stood up. 'I have to pack their gear. Do you want to do Covington's?' He did hate this business.

'All right.'

'You don't have to.'

Bear did not want to do it. It was like sealing his friend's tomb. He knew it was time even if his heart was not ready. So he agreed: 'It's all right.'

They stripped the beds Yan had just tightened. The blankets and sheets were to be returned to Supply. Bear sat on the mattress of Cov's bed sorting his possessions into two piles: one for Pinky, one for the Army. In the Army's pile went the jungle boots, fatigues, blanket, helmet liner, and steel pot. In Pinky's, one set of civilian clothes (shirt and wash pants, shoes and socks, no coat and tie), razor, toothbrush, soap, three paperback novels, a thick sheaf of letters, and a picture of Pinky, dark-eyed and short-haired and pretty in the mist-edged dream an Iowa photographer had created. 'What about the letters?'

'The rule says to read all papers. They'll go to his wife. Anything you think she shouldn't see, destroy.'

'I doubt that Cov had much to hide.'

'No. You don't have to look at letters from Pinky. Take a look at the rest.'

There were only a few others, but Covington had mixed them up. Bear came on one of Pinky's in an evelope from

Covington's mother. It begin, 'My dearest darling, When I feel our child just beginning to make itself known . . .' He put it away hurriedly, feeling as though he had stumbled clumsily into some secret place. He did not read any others. He tied the letters into a single packet, put them into the waterproof bag with Covington's clothes, tied that at the neck, and locked it inside one of the duffel bags. All that remained of Covington's life in Vietnam went into the bag, to be locked away like a genie in a bottle.

Covington had lived like a monk – sent his money home – but Jones in his short time in country had assembled a more respectable variety of goods. His tape recorder, stereo, camera, and guitar were scattered along his wall of the hooch, mixed with those of some of the other officers. Martin gestured with his head toward the records and tapes. 'Can you tell me how much of this stuff belonged to Jones?' Bear moved down to help.

'Is this his?' Martin held up a shortwave portable radio he had found on the window ledge midway between Jones's bunk and the next one.

'Yes. Two hundred bucks, I don't think he ever used it.'

'He didn't have much time,' Martin said. He pulled out the telescoping antenna of the radio and switched slowly through the bands. Snatches of Oriental music, ethereal whistles, code transmissions, and foreign words burst forth and were abruptly silenced. Emanations of Malaysia, Indonesia, Japan, Red China revealed their presences. Bear was startled by a voice like Covington's, but it was clipped off. The dead were packed away, and if the room was haunted, it was by the voices of men still living.

Yet, if those speaking were alive, they were no more than ghosts to the Bear, no more alive than Covington who lay silent in deep water. Their lives could not touch him.

There was an English voice – deep, deliberate, sonorous; 'This is the Australian Broadcasting Commission. The time is . . . twelve noon.' Martin left the radio on the station. The anonymous Australian voice read the news: Parliament, cricket, the weather in Sydney (fair, eighty-six degrees), the prime minister said, the price of wool on the international market, forthcoming season at the Sydney opera house.

It had no meaning to the Bear. The voice told echoes of lives uncomprehended, things too far removed to catch at his heart.

Yan and Suzie, scrubbing laundry in flimsy aluminum pans on the next porch, tittered and called out to the neighbors. They, too, haunted the room. This was all of life to Yan and Suzie: by day, a job with the *Nguio My*, the Americans; and by night - what? Suzie's husband was dead, Bear knew, dead years ago of some disease. They lived in one of the villages, but he did not know where. Not on the island, but somewhere around the shores of Song Ben Van. He saw them daily, but knew no more of their lives than of those whose echo filled the room from a six-inch radio speaker. The only thing more than an echo was war, and that overwhelmed everything.

Listening to the same civilized voice from the radio, Martin was struck with surprise that ordinary life was going on all about him. He could almost reach out and touch it. Only an eyeblink away barmaids and stockbrokers were at the very instant passing back and forth under a fair sky, taking their lunches, reading their newspapers, laughing.

The hooch-maids on the next porch tittered and called out. For them, too, this was everyday life. Yan, at least, had grown up with war, known nothing else; but she survived. She laughed. War had not defeated her.

Through the screen in the window Martin could see the fishing fleet from the island scattered like snow across the grey plain of the sea. In any but bad weather the sampans were out by day and sometimes by night. Fishermen's lives were regulated by wind and tide, by the sun and by the clock. Boats at sea after the curfew might be sunk on sight by the National Police, by the Swift boats, by prowling gunships. War regulated their lives, or cut them short without warning. But that was only one more regulation, no harsher than wind and tide.

Martin felt his grip on life tighten, at the same time that the Bear's was slipping. The Bear had always taken strength from outside himself, from people and things around him.

Grounded, he had already lost the place he thought he had found for himself as a man. Now that had led to the first great personal loss he had known, and he was shaken. Martin's case was different. He had never been one to look at life rather than touch it, any more than the Bear was: but ultimately even his belief in comradeship came from within himself; it appealed to him as an idea, and he could take as much strength from what he saw or imagined in others as from what he experienced himself. Whatever happened – and he knew no more than Bear what it might be – he would endure it.

'Jesus Christ, ain't that a purty picture!' Rauch was standing in the door of the hooch. 'Our high-culture hour for sure. Captain Martin, sir, you're goin' to seduce that poor boy yet.'

'Hello, Rauch.' Martin was sensitive enough to the pain lurking in the Bear that Rauch's voice annoyed him. Loud voices did not belong in the house of dead men.

Rauch, who saw none of that, went on loudly, 'Bear, you're goin' to get a flat ass sittin' on the floor like that. Why don't you get up off it and I'll give you a little somethin' to do?' He said this with a broad grin.

Bear looked slowly from Martin to Rauch. 'Whenever Captain Martin's done with me,' he said without interest.

'I'll bet Captain Martin will even let you go for this,' Rauch said. He was almost hidden now by his own grin, like the Cheshire cat.

'What's happening, Rauch?' Martin asked.

'Oh, nothin' much. Major Hart just called over, is all, and told me to get the Bear down to the ready hooch. The chief of staff just cleared him for flight status.'

Bear climbed to his feet slowly, to the obvious puzzlement of Rauch, who had expected more of a reaction. His grin faded.

'The investigation report came out?' Martin asked.

'I don't know about that,' Rauch answered. 'The major just said to tell Bear and Blood and Atterburn they're back on flight status. So get your gear and haul ass down to the flight line, kid. We got a ship nobody's preflighted because we didn't have bodies to man it.'

'What about Captain Martin?' Bear asked.

'I don't know. I reckon the major will tell you himself,' Rauch said to Martin. 'Come on, Bear. I'll see you down there.'

After Rauch was gone, Bear walked up and down the aisle of the hooch. Martin congratulated him, but he only said quietly, 'I don't want to fly until you do, sir.'

'You may have a long wait for me.'

'I don't care. I don't know if I want to fly at all.'

Martin looked at him, startled. No man flew the way the Bear did unless he loved to fly.

'I don't know if I can,' Bear blurted, in answer to the look. 'Maybe it seems like I'm letting down Cov, and the others, if I don't get back at Charley. Maybe I am. I hadn't even thought about it until just now. I don't know. But I thought about this – you didn't do anything the rest of us didn't do. To go back on flight status is like saying it wasn't my fault, it was yours.'

'It wasn't your fault, Bear. I was the flight commander, or could have been. I was responsible.'

'Whatever that means. I killed as many men as you did.'

'But I made the decision.'

'Was there a "decision"? Snoopy made as much of a decision as anybody, and Snoopy's nothing but a trunkful of fuses and wires.'

'For all we know,' Martin said, 'the investigation has cleared us all. I wouldn't be flying anyway. We're hard up for pilots, but the paper-pushers stay with their paper forever.' He knew it was not so. Blood was right about that infantry light colonel: he hadn't come down from the hills for nothing. But he said, 'We've got men who've been on standby for a week straight, and it will be worse now that we're shorter on pilots. Get your helmet and get on down to the flight line.'

At this Bear stopped in the middle of the aisle and stared up at the hole in the roof. 'I guess one man dead flying my mission *is* enough,' he said.

'I didn't mean that, Bear.'

'I know you didn't, but it doesn't matter. I know the truth when I see it.' He picked up his helmet bag and pistol belt from his bunk, pulled on his cap, and plunged out the door.

The radio was uttering something about the Vietnam war. Martin snapped it off turned it upside down, and copied its serial number onto the list of Jones's property.

Bear felt odd and out of place stepping into the alert hooch where he had been a regular inhabitant little more than a week before. It was like stepping back into a life left far behind. The hooch was crowded with the rest of the gun platoon and a handful of slick pilots. When he came in they stood and clapped and cheered.

Bear was ashamed how grateful he felt at that moment.

Blood stood at the back of the hooch wrapping himself in a benign smile. 'Speech by Bear!' someone shouted. 'Speech by Bear!' They were all so raucously pleased that he did not have the heart not to pretend it was not just like old times. He raised both arms in the manner of the pope pronouncing a benediction, and when they were quiet, he said solemnly, 'Screw you all and the horse you rode in on.' It was just the speech they expected from him. They roared and stamped and applauded.

But after others had crowded around and fallen back, and he had sat alone for a moment, he was aware that he was still being watched. Cripps was seated on the bunk in the back corner of the building. He came forward – indirectly – as if he were really bound out the door and stopped only as an afterthought. Cripps's shyness disarmed the Bear's comic defenses.

'Ah, I'm glad you're back, sir,' Cripps said.

'Thanks, Cripps.'

'Not that I mind flying with anyone else so much, but everything's been so serious.'

'It doesn't do to be serious when you're out killing,' Bear said. He wished he hadn't said it, for Cripps's eyes switched away from him. Bear saw that Cripps had prepared a compliment and now felt foolish. He tried to smooth it over with a soft word of thanks, which he meant seriously.

Bear did not see Alice that day, as he had promised, nor for many days after. Duty left him no time for anything other than flying or waiting to fly.

And when he did go flying at last, he could not stop his heart from racing. Arp was flying with him for the afternoon. Arp was delicate about the protocol. Although he was, as senior officer, the aircraft commander, he insisted that Bear take the right-hand seat; and when they cranked for takeoff, he said, 'You fly. I've been doing this too much lately.' They had the Bear's own ship, with Handy and Cripps as crew. Lifting the ship to back out of the revetment was for a moment like coming home, in a way moving back into the alert hooch had not been.

It was an easy mission. They led a light fire team as escort for a flying crane delivering guard towers to Special Forces camps along the Song Tien, west of the first range of mountains. The interstorm monsoon weather was at its best - hazy, cool, with a weak sun silvering the edges of the sky. They flew out and back four thousand feet above the highway west from Tam Ky. They saw nothing but mountain, tree, and haze, except at one point a few tanks pulled off in a paddy beside the highway. While the crane shuttled towers in and out, they circled overhead, studying the roofs of the distant town of Hoi Lam or watching buffalo souse themselves in the marsh at the edge of the rain-swollen river.

They parted from the crane at Tam Ky and returned toward home over the sand dunes on the seaward side of Song Tam Ky, the broad, slow-flowing, many-channeled river which partly emptied into the sea north of the crescent island and partly turned into the Son Ben Van behind it. The plain on the landward side of the Song was paddy and marsh mixed with sandy waste, split by dikes and hedges and pathways; but on the seaward side there was only a broad belt of bare dunes, with a few evergreens tucked into the hollows. Outside that belt was the narrower channel of the Truong Giang, a tidal river lying parallel to the sea, marsh-bordered and separated from the sea by a bare quarter mile of blowing dunes. Fishing villages huddled at wide intervals along this shore. They sheltered among the evergreens behind the first row of dunes from the sea, for during the monsoon the wind blew fiercely, and the boats were pulled far up on the sloping beach that ran straight and unbroken for fifty kilometers from Chu Lai to Hoi An. The villagers' homes were thatched roof and wall, so that they had the appearance of haystacks among the scrubby trees. They were chimneyless and stained black by the smoke which filtered through the thatch. Bear led the flight low down the strip of dunes between these two worlds of farmer and fisherman, over the regular V's of the fishing weirs pointing upstream in the Song, the nets on gin-poles stretched above the surface to dry, and the sampans with painted eyes plodding patiently upcurrent with the wind behind them.

The helicopters broke out over the palm forest of the crescent island. Bear started to swing back inland in a climb which would take them above the ridge behind Ky Ha for an upwind landing, when Handy called out, 'Sir, what's all them people down on the beach?'

Arp, who was on the seaward side, stared out the window for a moment. Although the islanders lived by fishing, there was rarely anyone to be seen on the beach on the seaward side. Their landings were in the quiet waters of Song Ben Van, on the far side of the island. 'Let's go have a look,' Arp said.

As the two helicopters broke out over the edge of the beach, the crowd there dissolved and flowed toward the shelter of the trees, leaving only a piece of seadrift at the high tide line.

'Put it down,' Arp said.

They made a low turn over the water and swept rapidly up the beach. Bear feathered the ship to a quick stop.

The thing the sea had cast up was a body.

It was pale, and shriveled from the water. Sand whipped over it as he put the ship down on the beach beside it. Except for one black sock, it was naked. Some of the clothing had been dropped farther up the beach by the villagers who had been stripping the body. 'Put the gun down, Handy,' Arp said. Bear saw that Handy had raised his machine gun and had trained it in the direction of some conical straw hats which were still visible along the edge of the trees.

'Let me kill the bastards, sir,' Handy pleaded. 'They did it to him, and now they're stealin' his clothes. The sons of bitches! Stealin' a dead man's clothes!'

'I said put down the gun. Now get him on board.' Handy got down and rolled the sea-whitened body clumsily onto the cabin floor. Arp waved him back to collect the articles which had been dropped along the beach by the crowd. The straw hats vanished when Handy started toward them from the ship. He returned with a pair of trousers and a holster with no weapon in it. 'Let's go,' Arp said.

An ambulance took the body from the aircraft. It was not Covington, as Bear had expected, but Washington. His body was unmarked. The arms were rigid, spread slightly from the sides, and the head was pulled forward toward the chest. The skin of the body was wrinkled and bleached white as flour, but the face looked quite like Washington. He looked peaceful and unconcerned about the sea-foam in his fine mustache.

The dusk patrol picked up the body of the pilot, Boroff, who came ashore at almost the same spot as Washington. The patrol also brought in part of an engine cover panel. The paint was blistered, and there were two bullet holes.

Every aircraft that went out made a pass over the island, but there was no sign of another body. Part of the fibreglass nose cone was tossed up on the third day. That was all.

On the fourth day Martin checked with the Navy. A strong tidal current flowed parallel to the shore twice a day, he was told. A body might come ashore miles away, if it came ashore at all. When Martin told the Bear that, Bear asked, 'How long does the Army wait before it decides they're dead enough to tell the next of kin?'

Martin could only say that he didn't know.

That day was New Year's Eve. The Bear spent it in the alert hooch next to Covington's empty cot. He was awake when the New Year came, but he did not mark it. The rejoicing in the clubs around the ramp was lost in the rumble of artillery up and down the plain, where the New Year's truce was going up in fire and smoke.

On New Year's Day the weather held fair, with a light southeast wind and a calm sea. The gun pilots sat on the Operations officer's jeep letting the sun ease out the stiffness of a night of interrupted sleep. Inside Operations, Blood was explaining the tactical situation in detail to Lieutenant Rauch, who cared only about getting his quota of helicopters into the air by the proper hour each morning. When the telephone rattled, Rauch snatched it up at once, but Blood's voice went on, addressed now to the Operations sergeant, who could not take cover behind a telephone.

'Captain Blood says Charley's licked,' Atterburn said. 'It's just mopping up now.' He was half-listening to Blood inside the hooch, although he had heard this analysis a dozen times before.

'Considering what mileage Charley got out of his New Year's truce,' Arp said, 'I can hardly wait for the Buddha's birthday.'

Blood came to the door. 'That was graves registration on the line,' he said. 'They need two officers to identify a body.' He looked straight at the Bear. 'Why don't you go on up and tell them who it is, Mr Bear?' He added. 'I'd do it myself. After all, it might have been my mission he was flying. But I have to be here in case a fire mission comes in. You and Arp go.'

'You're remembering we're on standby, too?' Arp asked.

'Ah, don't worry. It's just up the ramp. Rauch can telephone if anything comes in. You can get to a ship about as quick from there as from here. Take the jeep.'

Atterburn climbed down, and Arp and the Bear drove down onto the ramp and past the tails of the parked ships. 'That didn't make the most sense I've ever heard,' Arp said.

'He wanted me to see the body,' Bear answered.

'Even Blood isn't that much of a bastard.' They both knew it was Covington.

The graves registration clerk said, 'There's nobody here by that name.'

'Somebody just called and said there was,' Arp told him.

'From here? Not from here, sir.' He flipped through the papers on his desk again. 'What unit are you from?' When Arp told him, he threw up his hands: 'Oh, sure! You've got a body here! But his name isn't Covington. At least not as far as *we* know.'

'Not Covington?'

'No, sir. It's Laforgue. That's what his name tag said. He didn't have any dog tags. There were some papers in his wallet that you could still read. They say LaForgue, too.'

'Yes, we had a LaForgue.' LaForgue had been the gunner on Covington's ship that night.

'Well, we're pretty sure that's him, sir. Unless he changed clothes with this Covington before whatever happened, happened.'

'I doubt he did,' Arp said dryly. 'All right, let's see him.'

'Sure. He's outside, sir.' The clerk hesitated. 'You don't have to view the remains if you don't want to, sir. If you don't have any question about the identity, I mean. You can, but . . . he's been in the water a long time, you know, and . . . the fish have been at his face.'

'Who brought him in?'

'The Navy sent him up. A Swift boat picked him up offshore.'

'Let's make sure,' Bear said.

'All right,' Arp agreed. 'But you don't have to come. There's no need for both of us.'

'Not looking won't change things.'

Outside behind the building there was a brown Conex container, a seven-foot-high steel cube used as a shipping container by Army units moving overseas. 'This gives us a little spare capacity,' the clerk explained as he opened the container, 'and it saves handling, on people like LaForgue.'

The container was refrigerated. On either side within there were racks built against the walls. On one of these there was a black rubberized bag. The clerk slid it forward and unzipped the end. An evil odor spread from the open end.

The body could have been anyone. There was no face, only a ragged mass of pulp which looked as if it belonged in the sea, as if it should be growing on a coral reef. The bloated carcass strained at the bag. Arp motioned for the clerk to shut the Conex.

'Let's look at the papers,' he said.

'Anything you want, sir. We're sure they're LaForgue's papers, even if we ain't sure it's LaForgue.'

The wallet contained a few dollars in scrip, a washed-out letter no longer legible, and a plasticized driver's license which was unquestionably LaForgue's. The clerk was right: the body could not have been Covington unless they had changed clothing on the way down. Bear remembered the swift plunge of the fireball. He signed the identification form after Arp.

They drove back in silence. As they crossed past the end of the hospital, Bear looked up toward the nurses' quarters, but no one was to be seen. He had been on standby since the morning after the mortar attack. It was only a few hundred metres from the company to the hospital; but he had not seen her.

Arp went into Operations. Bear remained outside on the jeep. Arp was back outside in a minute. He sat on the jeep and pounded his fist on the hood.

'What did he say?' Bear knew that Arp had reported to Blood.

'Nothing.'

'Don't shit the troops.'

'Well, the first thing he said was "How did Covington look?" in his best egg-sucking voice. So I said, "He looked a lot like LaForgue." Blood said to Rauch, "LaForgue? I thought you told me it was Covington" and Rauch said, "Naw, sir, I said graves registration wanted a couple of officers to identity a body." "What the hell did they ask for officers for," Blood asks, "if they had an EM to identify? They could get the first sergeant for that." As if LaForgue wasn't worth the waste of an officer's time.'

'"Even Blood isn't that much of a bastard,"' Bear said.
'I was wrong.'

Tired of endless standby in the alert hooches, some of the pilots had wandered down to the ships, where they sat restless and bored, watching the sunny patches slide and shift over distant ridges. Warrant Officer Ruth pulled down the gunsight and stared around the area through it. 'I wonder if vis fing works,' he grumbled. He had come into the company two days before, and there had been no action in all that time.

'It works, Rufe,' Arp assured him. 'Have faith.'

Ruth's nickname came from his speech defect. When Blood had first asked him his name he had made a special effort and came out with a clear, 'Ruth, sir.' 'Okay, Ruth,' Blood had said, 'what's your last name?' Arp thought it a shame that Blood had been serious. 'I'd like to hear Captain Blood make a joke before I die,' he said.

After that Ruth gave up on his name. He had a slow crooked smile, the beginnings of a Vietnam mustache, and no objection to being called anything at all that showed he was liked.

'It took me a week and a half to get here from Saigon,' he complained. 'I don't want to spend anuvver week waiting for Charley.'

A Chinook delivering water flapped overhead dangling a five-hundred-gallon rubber bladder from its cargo hook. Ruth watched it with interest, but Arp frowned and said, 'I wish he'd fly somewhere besides over the ramp. I saw one of the buggers drop a ton of lobster into Tam Ky one day.' Lobster was the radio name for ammunition for the 105-mm howitzer.

'Did it go off?' Ruth asked.

'No. But what if it had? Or even what if it hadn't, if it landed on somebody. How would you like to get a five-hundred-gallon bladder on your skull?'

'I'd like to get the Hook pilot that dropped my ship,' Griggs muttered from his seat in the door. Griggs was standing by with a command and control ship for one of the infantry battalions and had come over to Arp's ship while waiting for a call to fly. 'Did I ever tell you about that, Rufe?'

'Not more than three times, Griggs,' Arp said, 'But Rufe's only been here a couple of days.'

'I was on this rat fuck down south,' Griggs began, 'and on short final the whole world went up.'

'That means someone took a shot at him,' Arp said to Ruth.

'Look, Lieutenant, you tell your stories, and I'll tell mine,' Griggs said. 'Okay? Anyway, there we were on short final when the Christmas tree lit up and the engine quit. Well, I put 'er down and we unassed the ship. AK-47's everywhere. We got the guns off and snuggled down in this little gully to wait it out. Finally things quieted down enough that the next lift came in, and we could have gone out then but I wanted to save the ship. That was a good ship, number zero eight five. So we spent the day there after the infantry moved out. We took some sniper fire, but along about dark we got the ship rigged and a Hook came in after it. Carlsen came in and got us out at the same time. Damn good pilot, he was. I hated to see him go. Well, we took off after the Hook, and we caught up with him at about three thousand feet - just in time to see the bastard drop my ship! The thing wasn't even rigged wrong - they just hit the cargo release by mistake, and off she went.'

This story was Griggs's set piece, but he embellished it less than usual because Arp was leaning back in his seat with a bemused look. Griggs did not like being around Arp. 'I wish the Gunfighter would get his ass in gear so we could go get some Dinks,' he grumbled.

'Who's ve Gunfighter?' Ruth asked.

'Who's the Gunfighter!' Griggs said this with pity for anyone who didn't know the Gunfighter. 'He's the commander of the Fighting Forty-ninth infantry battalion, that's who.'

'So called,' Arp told Ruth, 'because his chief delight in life is to take his C-and-C ship down into any firefight he happens across.'

'The man's got a pair.' Griggs shrugged.

'Maybe a little less than the issue amount of brains,' Arp said, 'but balls, yes.'

'He just wants to get his share of Slopes before we run out, sir.' Griggs grinned, pleased to see that he had annoyed Arp. 'Though we ain't likely to run out soon enough to suit me. You made any live Slopes into good Slopes lately, Bear?' The Bear had just come up to the side of the ship.

'Don't worry about it, Griggs,' Bear said. 'We'll keep your tail safe.'

'I'm like the Gunfighter,' Griggs said. 'I never worry about dead Slopes. I just worry about the live ones.'

'I didn't know you were so tenderhearted.'

'That's what I am. I'll tell you how tenderhearted I am. I think we ought to give this fucking country back to the Slopes. I figure if we gave every one of'em about six feet of it, the war would be over in no time.'

'Why don't you take yourself back to your own ship, Griggs?' Bear said. 'I'm tired of hearing your jaw flap faster than your brain works.'

Griggs tried to outstare Bear; but after a moment he gave it up, climbed out of the ship, and sauntered away.

'Don't mind that asshole, B,' Arp said.

'"Mind" is the wrong word to use in a sentence referring to Griggs,' Bear said. '"Asshole" comes pretty close, though.'

'For sure.' Arp sighed. 'Between the assholes and the hearts and minds of the people, this is one complicated war. Well, what's up, Bear?'

'My ship. Handy has the new rocket tubes boresighted. If you can find me a pilot, I'll take it down to the range to test them.'

'Hey, have I got a pilot for you!' Arp clapped Ruth on the knee. 'Rufe has just been panting for some exercise. You take him, and I'll go ask Rauch for someone else to stand by with me until you get back.'

'You think it's a good idea,' Rauch said to Arp, 'to send Rufe up with Bear, his first mission in country?'

'If I didn't, I wouldn't have sent him,' Arp said, a little coldly. 'I wish *I'd* had a chance to fly with the Bear my first mission in country.' He expected backbiting from Griggs, but not from Rauch.

'Nothin' against Bear,' Rauch said. 'But it's the first time he's flown with anybody but you, since Cov went down. I don't know how he'll feel about it.'

'There's nothing special about me.' This was said with considerably more warmth: Arp was grateful that his suspicion had been so wrong.

'I'd be the last to admit there was, for sure,' Rauch remarked, grinning at Arp. 'But you and Bear go back a long ways. Farther even than Bear and Cov. You know how close he was to Cov; flyin' with you wouldn't be so different. But takin' up a Fuckin' New Guy . . .'

'Bear will take care of him,' Arp said. 'Anyway, they're only testing weapons. It'll give them a chance to get used to each other *before* the shit hits the fan.'

At the south end of the five-mile-long Chu Lai beach, beyond the fishing villages clustered at the mouth of the river Tra Bong, the shore hooked back northward in a rocky peninsula that cradled in its arm the bay Dung Quat. The steep flanks of the coastal range to the south trailed off there into a low tumbling ridge that stretched for a half mile into the shallow waters of the bay. From anywhere along the Chu Lai shore fighter-bombers could be seen daily working along the mountains south of the peninsula. On sunny days their wings flashed as they rolled into inverted dives and then upright again before releasing their bombs. Tiny golden flashes would twinkle against the mountainsides, and, when the wind was in the south, a quarter of a minute later then sound would pass by, a weak mutter of distant trouble. The peninsula was said to be a VC stronghold, but that belief apparently arose from the high visibility of the jet strikes, which might, for all anyone in the helicopter company knew, have been training missions, like their own weapons testing.

The ruin of a large house stood at the tip of the peninsula.

Once a rich Frenchman's seaside villa, now its yellowing walls were a convenient mark for testing weapons. A low pass could be made from seaward with no danger that a wild shot would do any harm.

Bear was fond of the building. It stood firm to its daily fate. Although pocked and splintered by machine gun, rocket, and grenade, its walls and even part of its red tile roof still stood. Its bare back was turned on the sands of Chu Lai five miles away: the empty sockets of the windows were turned to the sea, where of old, on the clearest of day, Cu Lao Re might have been seen floating above the horizon.

The gunship came in low over the bay, out of the silver haze that hung between sea and sky. A cluster of fishing sampans lay slack-sailed far offshore in the haze, at the limits of existence. One, bound homeward under power, plowed a silver trail through the blue sea below, its painted eyes fixed on the mouth of the Song Tra Bong.

Ruth drank in these sights. He was still dazzled by the Orient.

A half mile out Bear took the controls and turned in toward the house. 'Ready to arm?' he asked.

'Ready.'

'Okay. Let's go hot.'

Ruth flipped the switches to the armed position.

Bear called out the range to the house. 'There's a thousand meters.' How the Bear knew, Ruth could not say, for the house on the rock seemed to float at the same untouchable distance in the same endless blue. But he took down the gunsight and twisted the bright dot onto the house.

Bear touched the red button of the rocket trigger with his thumb. The ship was enveloped in light. Through the gunsight Ruth watched the twin flares of the rocket motors slide down the hill of air. They looped above the distant red speck of the roof, then against it, then below it, and vanished in a single smoke blossom against the side wall of the house. The smoke drifted away beyond the end of the rock to join with the bright sea-haze. The building still stood.

'Were they short?' Ruth asked.

'Not hardly, sir!' Handy said. He was watching over Bear's shoulder. Handy was pleased. He had just boresighted the weapons. He loved to see the first cold shot be on target.

'Your turn,' Bear said. Ruth squeezed the trigger switch on the gunsight. The steady spray of tracers played about the walls of the house. As they closed within a hundred meters, he released the trigger. Not until he had released it was he aware that the Bear was watching him with an amused smile.

'You never get enough of that in flight school,' Bear said after Ruth had let the guns fall silent. 'Maybe you'll find satisfaction here.'

Ruth had the uncomfortable feeling that he should have broken off sooner. But the Bear was right: he liked seeing the tracers flash on the target.

As the ship broke away short of the house, Ruth saw that the rockets had indeed been dead on, as Handy had known: a fresh scar had appeared on the back wall of the house. One rocket had broken through, and now the sun shone in. 'I'm afraid she's not long for this world now,' Bear said, to no one in particular.

'She's been standing a long time,' Cripps said. It was the first thing Ruth had heard Cripps say.

'All things come to an end, Cripps,' Bear answered. 'The bad with the good.'

Ruth felt as though he were overhearing a part of a private conversation, the key to which he had somehow missed.

Bear turned to Ruth. 'Do you need another pass?'

'I'm satisfied.' Ruth could not tell whether Bear was asking if he needed to fire again to check his sight, or just for the sheer pleasure. Ruth wanted to make another pass and watch the tracers' slow burning fall, but he did not, somehow, care to have Bear know that.

Bear turned the ship toward home, climbing out rapidly over the open bay.

As the gunship turned away, a scout helicopter bored in below. The two fixed machine guns on its skids left a stuttering stream of smoke as the pilot tested his weapons.

The gunner and crew chief, who rode one on either side of the pilot in the three-seat cockpit, were leaning from the doors to fire their hand-held machine guns. Handy leaned out to watch them close on the ruined house. 'Would you lookit them work out!' he called in delight. To Handy there was nothing so beautiful as well-aimed fire pouring onto a target – the more the better.

Bear held the ship steady on course for home.

Suddenly there was a voice on the radio: 'Mayday, Mayday! Skeeter Six-eight is hit and going down on the target range!'

Bear thought at first it was a joke. The point was worked over daily by weapons of all descriptions, and no one had ever taken a round of return fire. The broken rocks offered hiding places in plenty; but a squad of infantry could seal off the peninsula, trapping anyone hiding there. To fire on a gunship from there was suicidal. Yet there was something in the voice on the radio that demanded belief. There was no panic in the voice, but there was that adrenal tension that could not be hidden under orderly radio procedure.

Bear wrenched his ship around in time to see the tiny scout ship flare to a teetering stop at the very tip of the peninsula. 'Switch 'em back on!' he said to Ruth, who sat stunned as the crew of the other helicopter piled out and raced for the shelter of the rocks below the ledge where they had suddenly come to earth.

Ruth later remembered only the lazy way the small helicopter's blade ran down as unseen bullets smashed its windscreen, while the three crewmen scuttled like crabs among the rocks. He could not find the enemy weapon. He threw the switches to 'arm' and reached for his gunsight, but by then the Bear had dived the ship to sea level. When Ruth looked out, he thought for an instant they could not pull up before hitting the water. Then they were racing for the shore below the scout helicopter. 'Any tracers in sight?' Bear was asking. Both Handy and Cripps answered with quick negatives. 'Without tracers that guy could eat our lunch before we find him, alone up here,' Bear said. 'I wish the hell we had a trail ship to keep his head down when we break off.

But maybe if we sneak in low enough, that ledge the other ship is on will block his fire.'

The shelf the scout helicopter had landed on was a few yards above the water. The crew had dropped over the edge of the shelf and were firing their sidearms from among the seaweed-strewn boulders the sea had piled there. Bear drove his ship for those rocks with its skids almost cutting the water, slowed in a rattle of incoming gunfire, swung the tail to one side, and came to a hover with the main blade overlapping the rock shelf but with the body of the ship below the shelf's edge, partly sheltered from the gunfire. He parked one skid atop a boulder, and two of the crew of the scout helicopter stepped aboard dry-footed. Bear started the aircraft hovering toward the third crewman, who had become separated from the others and was now behind a boulder on the far side of a low break in the shelf. As Bear hovered his ship down the shoreline past this break, bullets suddenly snapped all around them. A machine gun was firing down through the break in the shelf. There was a ringing clang from the rear as one bullet struck metal. They could not cross the break.

Bear peeled the ship away and dashed low over the sea until they were beyond small-arms range. A few bullets skipped around them, but none struck the ship.

'Ask the pilot where the weapon is,' Bear said to Ruth.

Ruth leaned back and asked, but the pilot did not know. He stared unhappily down toward the shore, where his gunner was huddling behind his rock. 'He won't last long there!' the pilot shouted. 'If we leave him . . .'

'We won't leave him,' Bear said. He turned back inbound for the point. 'The fuel is low. We have to find that weapon quick.' Bear appeared to be holding a conversation with himself. It took Ruth a moment to understand that Bear was doing more than deciding the best way to proceed. He was pointing out the things Ruth would need to remember if a bullet suddenly left him as the pilot in command.

They came in higher up this time, where they made a clear crisp target against the silvered sky. There was no difference from the approach they had made while sighting in, Ruth reflected, except that now they knew a weapon was waiting. Charley could have potted them on the first run, if he had been ready. Perhaps he had been caught asleep, and they had wakened him in time for him to hit the other ship. Whatever Charley's reasons, Ruth knew that it felt different now, flying down to the muzzle of a hidden weapon. He saw things now on the peninsula that he hadn't suspected were there on the first pass – the folds in the black-veined rocks near the ruined house, the glint of sun from a thousand facets of broken stone, the dry dead bush whose branches might have been the barrels of a dozen weapons. The ship bored relentlessly in.

'If he's smart, he'll wait for us to break off,' Bear said. 'So I'll start a break and then turn back in. Be ready.' He broke off farther out than he might have otherwise, at five hundred meters, barely within machine gun range, unless it was a fifty. 'Let's hope he bites.'

'There he is!' Handy called out. At the same instant the air came alive with the crackling of bullets. Handy fired off a burst of tracers that fell toward a fold in the rock three hundred meters from the house.

'Put it on him,' Bear said to Ruth. In the violent turn back toward the weapon, the main blade now blanked out Handy's fire, and Cripps was facing the opposite direction. Bear's rocket tubes pointed straight ahead, not yet on the target. Only Ruth's flex guns were able to fire. He alone held the defense of the ship in his hands.

He could not keep the sight on the spot. His tracers spewed all around it. He could see the weapon now – a point of sputtering light that stood out from the reflected flashes of sunlight on the rock. He watched it sputter at him. It was such a small thing, hardly larger than the glowing dot in the gunsight. It seemed to have no connection with the snapping fingers of death all around him.

The ship had rolled off target in an instant: it seemed an eternity coming back. Ruth held the trigger down. The guns growled. The stream of tracers swept up the rock, beside the muzzle flashes, above them, back on the other side. They would not settle down.

A hole appeared in the windshield before Ruth's eyes. He did not hear the bullet strike, nor feel the ship rock: but he saw the hole, a neat thing the size of his finger. Nor did he hear the rockets go, but he saw them. Two pairs rippled away, four bright points of light, much brighter than the muzzle flashes toward which they fell. They did not fan out, as rockets would do if fired across the wind of an uncoordinated turn. The ship had come steady for that instant when the tubes were first on target, and the four rockets sped in a tight cluster toward the cleft rock.

For perhaps two seconds the bullets continued to crack about the ship: they had been already on their way when the rockets were launched. Any one of them could have been enough to bring an end to the flight of the ship, and the lives of those on it, even if, when it struck, he who had sent it was himself already dead. For the space of two seconds the living on either end could watch their fates cross, and know that all was now beyond their control. It had been determined already who would live and who would die. There remained but to wait and see.

A pair of rockets blossomed where Handy's tracers had fallen. The second pair exploded within a second of the first, on the same spot.

The rattle of bullets went on, went on . . . and ceased. There was sudden silence, if the pounding, whistling interior of a helicopter could be called silent. It seemed silent to Ruth, who had been hearing only the incoming rounds and the tearing growl of his own guns. Now there was nothing.

'You got the motherfucker!' Handy exulted. 'He is *gone*!'

'Keep an eye out,' Bear said. 'There may be another baddie.'

They prowled the edges of the peninsula, first well out, then closer in, and finally flew directly over the spot where the weapon had been. What could have been a body lay at the bottom of a split in the rock. Handy showered it with bullets as they passed over. 'Don' never hurt to make sure,' he said complacently as he brought the gun back inside.

'All right, let's go pick up that crewman,' Bear said to

Ruth as they made a wide circle beyond the tip of the peninsula. 'One more thing you should know: the hydraulics are out.' For the first time Ruth noticed the stick bucking in Bear's hand. The bullet that had come through the windshield had gone on through the back of the cabin and cut a hydraulic line. With no hydraulic boost the ship could be flown only with the full strength of the arm, and not by the pressure of two fingers. It turned from an obedient, thoroughbred to a kicking rebellious mule as every revolution of the main blade fed an amplified blow back through the control rods to the pilot's hand on the cyclic stick. How Bear could have rolled it out exactly on target, Ruth could not imagine.

The approach to the shore this time was slow, careful, and effortful. Ruth, merely following on the controls, felt the sweat crawling down his ribs. The cyclic struggled in his hand like a wild live thing; but the Bear had the other cyclic locked in his fist, and leaned forward to get the strength of his shoulder behind the strength of his arm. The controls kicked; but the ship was steady as rock. It eased among the rocks; the gunner scrambled aboard; and they were climbing safely away.

The pilot of the other ship pounded Bear on the shoulder. 'Some flying, by God!' he shouted with a happy grin. Over the noise of the ship his voice was but a weak echo of what Ruth was thinking himself.

When Ruth flew on the way home, to give the Bear a rest, the cyclic slammed at his right hand, and the collective was a leaden bar in the palm of his left. The ship flew angrily, as if grudging every second it was forced to remain in the air.

Blood was enraged to learn that the company that owned the scout helicopter had recommended Bear for a Distinguished Flying Cross. 'What do those bastards know about it?' he demanded.

Lieutenant Rauch, who was the only person to hear this performance, went on reading after-action reports. He was unsympathetic but not up to pissing off a senior officer. He could not resist observing, however, 'I expect they've seen a little flyin' in their time.'

'So all right, the son of a bitch can handle a ship! He doesn't have the first fucking idea how to follow an order, and he needs a special delivery telegram from God before he'll shoot. If he gets another DFC, he'll just be that much worse. Why didn't the bastards ask his own company, before they start sending off papers to Battalion? The son of a bitch doesn't need a medal: he needs to be busted to buck private!'

When Bear heard about the citation, he wasn't as pleased as Ruth had expected him to be. He looked mostly tired, like some faded zoo animal that had long since given up hope of escape.

'You deserve it, B,' Ruth urged. 'I fought . . . I fought that was the best flying I've ever seen.'

'Good flying is important, Rufe,' Bear agreed. Old Tate would have liked it. But Ruth did not know quite what to make of the answer, accompanied as it was by an enormous fart, and a sigh which might have been profound physical satisfaction or grief, Ruth could not say which. He tried again: 'You deserve a medal for it.'

'Yes, I guess I do.' Bear's face took on the pensive look of a shorn sheep pondering the winter sun. 'I was brave, resourceful, cool in the face of withering enemy fire . . . It does make a great citation, doesn't it?' Though Ruth did not know it, Bear was quoting from one of his own earlier citations. 'Also, I killed an enemy. Not many, but one can be enough, in the right place. Kill 'em dead'll win a medal. There wasn't any way not to kill him, was there, Rufe?'

The morning the letters came down from Division, Martin was endorsing efficiency reports on the company officers. Every officer was rated at least twice during his year in Vietnam, or whenever he changed duties or changed units, or when his rating officer changed. To a career soldier his rating was everything; but to most of the pilots, who were in the Army for three years of flying it meant nothing. Still, there was no telling what a man would want to do in another year, and so Martin weighed each one with equal care. He resisted equally the desire to be creative and the desire to tell the truth. There was no place in an officer efficiency report for either imagination or truth.

Each report had two parts. The Army believed that one part was subjective, the other objective. On the former the rater or endorser wrote a paragraph describing the subject's performance of his duties. On the latter he gave a numerical rating to the officer with respect to certain specified qualities (tact, forcefulness, decisiveness), and also gave him a numerical rating between zero and one hundred. The number represented the percentile of all officers into which this officer would fall, rated from worst to best. An officer scoring one hundred was to be more effective than ninety-nine others out of every one hundred. There was a nice graph provided, showing rows of angular men at attention, to indicate what proportion of rated officers should fall into each ten-percentile block.

A rating below ninety could destroy a man's career. As a result there were no scores below ninety, unless the rater was bent on the destruction. An unimaginative rater intending to end a man's career scored the problem underling at seventy. One more subtle might award an eighty-six. Since every officer at every level was aware of the inflation of the numbers, eighty-six could be taken as a mark of true incompetence, while seventy was a warning of personal bias. Every man was rated by his immediate superior and endorsed in the same manner by the next higher person in the chain of command, so it was expected that bias would come to light through an inconsistency of scores. Sometimes, in fact, that did happen.

The subjective part of the report was as stylized as the objective. Since all officers were, by the numbers, outstanding or better, the destiny of superlatives in the description became the only distinguishing characteristic. There was a vast difference between 'the best officer I have known' and 'absolutely the best officer with whom it has been my pleasure to serve.'

When Martin had left the gun platoon, he had rated the

Bear at ninety-nine. Now he had in his hands Blood's report rating him at eighty-eight. He was struggling to find a way to make Blood's bias evident without going beyond that point at which it would seem that he was raising the rating only because he himself was biased against Blood. He suspected that the Bear would have found the whole business merely comical; but he nevertheless had spent a half hour poking at the problem. It gave him a grudging admiration for Blood's calculation. Blood certainly knew that a really low rating would fare badly with Major Hart; but the major was not blackhearted enough to believe that an eighty-eight was anything worse than misguided. The major would not pressure one of his officers to change an honest rating, however much he might disagree with it himself.

Major Hart came back from the morning battalion staff meeting with an envelope in his hand.

'We have high-class messenger service this morning,' Martin remarked. The Major stopped at the side of Martin's desk and stood there studying the envelope. Then he threw it down before Martin. 'That came down for you.'

It was from the chief of staff of the division. 'So it got here at last,' Martin said. He picked up the envelope, tapped one end on the desk, and tore off the other end. 'Here's looking at you.'

There were two letters in the envelope. One was the report of the investigation of Hill 473. He read it as carefully as he could. It was hard to read it seriously after endorsing four efficiency reports, because they and this report all sounded as if they had been wrung from the same damp dishtowel, wet with the thin scrapings of real language. The report concluded: 'Command of the flight was taken from the flight leader by a higher ranking officer in another aircraft. This officer, in ordering fire on an unknown target, failed to utilize approved procedures of identification and fire clearance which were adopted to minimize the chance of occurrences of this nature. The recommendation of this investigating board is that appropriate disciplinary procedures be instigated.'

Martin handed it over to Major Hart while he read the accompanying letter from the chief of staff. 'In accordance with the recommendation of the official investigation, I feel that your most unmilitary conduct on this occasion cannot pass unnoticed. However, because of the excellence of your past record, it is my decision that no disciplinary action will be undertaken in connection with this matter. A copy of this letter and the investigation report will be inserted in your records.'

'A brief enough end to a glorious career,' Martin said as the major took the letter from his hand. The major read it, put it back down on the desk, and then walked around and sat down behind his own desk. He sat there leafing back and forth through his mail without reading it.

'I think I'll go out for a little walk, if you don't mind, sir,' Martin said.

'Surely, Ben.'

He did not go far. He left because he did not want Major Hart to have to go on struggling for kind words. He knew that the major expected him to be stricken. He had expected it himself. He could not yet decide why he was not. But he was not.

He went down the hill past the tech supply building and the communications platoon, across the main post road and down onto the ramp. The ramp was nearly empty. The slicks were all out, except for three that were down for repairs and two that were torn down for periodic inspections. The ships were torn down every hundred hours. The slicks sometimes picked up that much time in two weeks, so there were always two or three torn apart.

He went down to the gunship row above the cliff and sat in the door of one of the ships.

A thin watery sunlight poured over the revetments. The early haze was beginning to retreat offshore for the day. It was going to be a beautiful day. At the mouth of Song Ben Van, fishing boats were standing out for the open sea.

For the first time since he had taken his ship down into the LZ on Hill 473, he suddenly felt fully awake. This was no longer a dream from which he might waken. It was real. But now that it was real, he could accommodate it. He could endure it.

As he sat there the beat of a flight of Hueys had been growing around him. He stood up now to see them swinging low over the island. It was Blood and the Bear coming in. Their blades flashed in the sun. Martin wondered, for a moment, why Blood, who despised the Bear, had assigned Bear to fly in his own fire team. Martin could imagine no reason.

The gunships swung wide over the sea and made a low, slow approach to the clifftop landing lane. The heavy thump of their blades ran through his whole body, waking his heart.

The first thing to do, he decided, was to get back on flight status. He set off back across the ramp to the orderly room.

When he came in, Major Hart was behind his desk with his head in his hands. 'Well, Ben, how's your constitution?' he asked without looking up.

'Fine. Don't worry about me, sir.'

'Ah! There are so many people to worry about, Ben.' He turned over a letter on his desk. 'This came this morning, too.' He handed Martin the letter.

It was addressed to Major Hart. The return address said 'Covington.' Martin read it quickly. Mrs Covington had been informed that her husband was missing, but not that he was dead. What, she asked, could Major Hart tell her about him? Martin laid the letter back on the major's desk.

War spoiled soldiering.

'Do you want me to answer it?' he asked.

'You know we can't, Ben.'

'I know we're not supposed to. But he's been dead for two weeks. She should be told.'

'You know how the Army is when there's no body,' Major Hart said. 'You can't chance a mistake.'

'There wouldn't be a mistake. We know he's dead.' Martin had the unpleasant feeling that he was returning his conversation with the Bear, from the wrong end. Or perhaps from the right end this time.

'We know it, Ben, but the Army doesn't.'

'Well, I know it. What if I just happened to write? In my position nothing can hurt anyway.' This remark earned him a quick glance from Major Hart. 'I don't think that's so, Ben,' he said.

Martin supposed it wasn't, but he didn't care.

'I wish you wouldn't,' the major said. 'She may have heard by now.'

'The body hasn't been found.'

'No.'

'It never will be, now.'

'No, it won't.' The major sat back in his chair, rubbing at his forehead with his hands. 'But the Army has had more experience handling these things than we have. It's for the best. I hope it's for the best.'

'I hope it is.' If it were left to him, he would have written to Pinky. He knew the risks. When she learned that her husband was dead, and that the Army knew it but hadn't told her, the next letter would be to her congressman. The Army would be displeased. Martin felt sudden absolute freedom from the tyranny of 'proper channels'; but Major Hart could still suffer for what his XO did. Martin did not feel so free to jostle the old man's delicately balanced career.

9

A week of sun had faded behind the high thin overcast that lowered slowly during the night. It was a gray Sunday morning. They knew it was Sunday because, about mid-morning, the bell beside the chapel rang. Lying on their cots or sitting on the ready-room steps they heard its slow toll fall among the empty hooches, and reëcho from the walls of the hangars mixed with the clatter of tools and the ring of voices.

'Sunday mornin',' Handy said. 'Used to go out for a drive of a Sunday afternoon, back in the worl'.'

'Maybe we'll get a chance today,' Ruth said.

'You'll get all the chances you can stand before you leave Nam, Rufe,' Arp told him.

'Don't pine away waiting, Rufe,' Bear advised. 'Just remember, the pilots that fly together, die together.' He added gloomily, 'When you go over six months your thoughts will begin to turn to new things, like how the devil you can survive long enough to get home. The shorter you are, the easier it is to sit on the ground.'

'Is that an Oriental saying?' Arp asked.

'That's a short-timer's saying.'

But Ruth walked down to the ship to check the switches just one more time, in case they had to fly in a hurry.

Sunday morning was filled with cold northeast wind and long hours of waiting, waiting. Bear drowsed on his cot, dreaming of Alice Porter, unseen for so many days.

The other way they knew it was Sunday was that dinner was special. The cook at least had a list of menus to separate one day from the next. They were midway through ham with raisin sauce when the field phone clattered. Operations needed a fire team. Aboard the platoon three-quarter-ton truck Blood's crew and Bear's lurched desperately from the mess hall to the flight line.

Within three minutes they were pounding southward under the sheet-lead sky, dodging wisps of rain along Route One. By the time they reached the Song Tra Bong, Blood was calling ahead for the ground unit, seeking directions. But even before he received an answer, it became obvious where they were bound. The sky ahead was slashed with distant streaks of red. 'Somebody working over vere,' Ruth said, elaborately casual in his remarks for his first real mission. A puff of smoke issued from the exhaust of Blood's ship ahead as it nosed over and accelerated toward the firefight.

There were two other fire teams ahead, working in long frenzied passes. 'It's the Sharks,' Handy said. The grinning bloody maws painted on the ships could already be seen from a mile away. 'Damn, they must have somethin' good!'

As the Wolfpack fire team flashed out over the open field the Sharks were working, the ground suddenly came alive with running men. A Shark gunship plowed its way through the mass of men, who parted or fell to the earth before it. They were Vietnamese; but they were in uniform. For an instant Bear could see only the bloody uniforms coming out of the dark on Hill 473. Were these government troops? '*Give 'em all six feet of their ground*,' Griggs had said.

'Shit!' Handy exclaimed, 'those are NVA!'

Handy was right: they were enemy, caught between the government troops on the west in the trees, the river Song Pra Khuc on the south, and gunships and open land on the north and east. Blood was on the FM calling for smoke to mark the friendlies, and colored smoke quickly blossomed from the tree line a mile distant, while the Shark leader came on the ground frequency to confirm their location. 'Help yourself, Wolfpack,' he offered. 'There's plenty for all.'

What organized movement there was among the men below was westward, but ten miles of open country lay between them and the mountains, even if they broke through the ARVN lines. They could not even scatter and run – there was nowhere for them to go. The evidence of that lay all around, in fields on every side, where some had already tried. The gunships had ended the escape.

Down along the river a steady slow rain of artillery was falling. The few trees that had stood there were already cut to stumps and shreds. Now air bursts flashed in steady rhythm all along the riverbank.

Charley, trapped, went down before the guns like grain before a reaper.

The Sharks, their weapons dry, left for home to reload. Blood was not being prodigal with their own ammunition. There were too many targets for the ordnance they had on board. He had already called for another fire team, but it would be twenty minutes or more before they could come on station. The Sharks, flying to Duc Pho to reload, could not return for nearly an hour. Meanwhile, to keep the trap closed there was only one Wolfpack fire team. After the first full-firepower sweep up the center, they stood off and worked the edges of the killing ground.

Reluctance to fire was the soundest strategy; but with each pass Bear felt a wrenching sensation inside. There was no way to avoid hitting something. A rocket launched blindly would fall on living flesh. At each pass, a touch of the thumb against the little red button, and a thousand meters away, men died. He could see them dying, see their death reaching for them in its whole long slow arc to the ground. For all his reluctance to kill, men died.

The other fire team arrived. Blood led a last pass to drain the dregs of the ammunition, and his ship and Bear's turned for home. 'Leave us some,' Blood called. 'We're coming back.'

The Sharks were back on station when Blood's fire team returned. They had moved in and were working closer to the river now. On each pass they overflew fields scattered with corpses. The living had dwindled.

As the Sharks again departed, a last remnant of the enemy unit, hopeless whether they stood or fled, pressed a determined attack on the ARVN troops in the tree line and broke through near the river. With all the weapons again empty, Blood broke off and pounded for home. They made the turnaround this time in forty minutes flat. A man running for his life can travel far in forty minutes; but no farther than a gunship can follow in three. The team hunted up and down the tree lines and paddy dikes, flushing a covey here, a single there, and killed them. The other fire teams had done the same before them. The trails of dead and dying men dotted the plain from the breakout point.

It was late afternoon when the ships finally turned for home. There was still a few rounds in the ammunition boxes under the back seats, but there had been no one to kill for twenty minutes past. They cruised slowly back over the battlefield, where the ARVNs were out collecting weapons and counting the dead. They turned for home through spitting rain. 'Wasn't it somefing!' Ruth bubbled. 'Wasn't it great, Bear?'

At home Blood pounded the Operations table as he dashed off the after-action report. 'We must of set some kind of record for one-day kills! Dammit, I'll bet any man here that we get credit for two hundred KIAs! Lord! Wasn't that something? They went down like turkeys on Thanksgiving!'

'You never seen so many dinged Slopes in your life,' Handy told the first sergeant over a beer at the NCO club. 'That was a battalion at least.'

Cripps, lying in his hooch, in his own bed for the first time in three days, said to his buddies, 'Today I killed more people than there are in my hometown.'

'Is that three, Cripps, or four?' someone asked.

'I wish you'd save some for me, Cripps.'

'I'm surprised you got any at all,' another said, 'flying with the Bear. I heard he swore off killing.'

'I don't know about that,' Cripps said. 'I don't know how you do that.'

Dawson greeted him at the emergency room entrance to the hospital. 'Well, Chief, we haven't seen you for a few days, More'n a few.'

'I went back to work,' Bear said. 'I haven't been able to

get here.'

'Well, your frien's are all gone anyways. We shipped the last of 'em out days ago. We don't stockpile bodies aroun' here.' He added, raising an eyebrow, 'Lieutenant Porter, she's aroun'. She ought to be goin' off duty about now. I'll show you how to find her ward – that is, *if* you want to see Lieutenant Porter?' He added with a grin, 'She ast me once if you'd been aroun'. I wouldn't tell you that, Chief, if I didn't like you. You ought to come around more.'

'You'll have to tell that to the Army,' Bear said.

They went around the covered walkways to the prisoner ward. 'Lieutenant Porter? She just left,' the guard outside the door said. 'If you want the nurse, Captain Newton just went up the hall a minute, but she'll be back.'

'Can I go inside?' Bear asked.'

'I don't reckon you're goin' to disturb anybody's recovery much,' Dawson said, 'or bother anybody if you *do*, except maybe Lieutenant Porter. She is the kindes'-hearted person! Me, I wish they'd ship 'em up to the POW camp where they belong, I figure everybody's forgotten they're here. Except you, Chief. Checking up on your handiwork, I guess.' He winked at the Bear.

When they entered the ward, Mother Courage was sitting on her bed, as if she had not moved since he was there last. She studied them impassively.

But the face that drew Bear's eyes was that of the man still lying in the bed nearest the door – the one he thought of as Charley. His handiwork. His handiwork made slow vegetable stirrings on the bed.

'That one might just as well be dead,' Dawson said. 'What can they do with *him*? I don't know why we keep him aroun'.'

Charley tried to move his body to face the door more fully. His helpless embryonic movements, so painstaking and laborious, hardly served to shift the trunk at all. Armless, legless, even voiceless, the mere remnant of a person, he was alive enough to be killed, if found outside the wire. Life was guarded behind the eyes. If man had a soul, one was there. As clay, the weight of him would not have borne down on Bear's heart.

But beyond the wire even that spark would be extinguished. He thought of the bodies he had left strewn in his wake over the fields by Song Pra Khuc.

He went out the side door which Dawson showed him and along the board walkway to the nurses' quarters. When she did not answer his knock at the door, he went down to the hospital officers' club. She was not there, either. He went around the end of the buildings to the cliffs. She was sitting against the rocks down at the edge of the sand, watching the waves come in a curve around the end of the point and break at a gentle angle down the length of the narrow beach. He picked his way down the cliff. When he threw a few a grains of sand on her leg she looked around and saw him. Her face hardly changed, but her eyes went large, and then she smiled. 'I was worried about you,' she said.

'I've had to fly.'

She turned quickly to him and took his hand. 'That's wonderful! I wish you'd told me. I wouldn't have worried about you then.'

'There's something wrong there,' he said, sitting down where she had made room for him on the narrow shelf of stone. 'It's when I'm flying that I get shot at.'

'Oh. Yes, of course I know it. It's hard for me to think of "shot at" as happening *now* to anyone I know, though. It's what happened to someone before I see him. And you wanted so badly to fly.'

'Yes, I did, didn't I.'

'Is something wrong?'

'What could be wrong?'

'Don't be sarcastic,' she said. 'You'll spoil having you back. I did miss you.' She made it sound impersonal, as if the words were just the thing to help the attitude of a difficult patient. He scowled toward the waves.

'Your people are all gone now,' she said brightly after a moment. 'McWade was the last one. We sent him home, and he's going to be all right. I was almost sorry to lose him, he was such a nice person. He had just a golden outlook.' She stopped talking then and looked at him for a long time.

'Don?' she said gently. 'Don, I'm so happy to see you again.'

'I wish you wouldn't sound as if you mean it,' he said.

'I do mean it. And I wish you wanted me to.'

'Your wish is granted, Alice.' He touched her on the head and put on the face of a fairy godmother.

'I just don't think I understand you all of the time,' she said.

'It's just that I feel like two people at once. Like now. I don't know whether to feel like Christmas or the first day of school. I feel like both. If you weren't around I could just feel rotten all the way through, instead of half rotten and half wonderful; and then I wouldn't feel guilty about feeling so great when I should be feeling guilty.'

'You're really a terrible person,' she observed, amused.

'Don't wrinkle your nose at me, lady. You're likely to get kissed for it.'

'That would be nice.'

She left her hand on the back of his neck. He started to tell her how he felt, but what he meant for winged words of love were clumsy as the remembered flight of a penguin, and he quickly tumbled to a halt. She kissed him again gently. 'Do you want to tell me the other, too?' she asked.

'What other?'

'Whatever it is that's on your mind.'

'No . . . I don't think I do. It's just that I killed a lot of men today.'

'Oh.'

'Not Americans this time,' he added. She said nothing, and he was glad for it. After a time he said, 'Mostly, you don't see them, the ones you kill – the *people* you kill. It's just a tactical exercise. The good guys have taken fire and they call for support. You locate them, you locate the enemy, or the place they say he is, you consider the surrounding terrain, you calculate the most effective direction of attack, and you suppress the enemy. "Suppress the enemy." That's a nice way of saying you kill people. If you can. And most of the time you don't even see them. You shoot the hell out of a tree line, a paddy dike . . . The grunts go in afterward and count the bodies.'

They sat again in silence.

'It's harder to kill a man in the open. For the other you're a pilot; but for that . . . I think you'd have to like that, to do it well.

'The hard part,' he said, 'is not being what they want me to be. The complete gun pilot. You can see it in their eyes, the people who like me: "There's the Bear - he's killed a hundred men, two hundred."'

'Have you?'

She was instantly sorry she had asked, for she saw the serpent fascination that troubled him most.

'I don't know,' he said. 'Some pilots claim a number. I don't. I don't count them. I *won't* count them. But I could tell you how many I've seen die under my guns - I remember them all. Until today. There were too many to remember today.'

They walked up the hill to the Artillery Battalion club in the remnant of the day. Rain was curling up over Nui Ong and threatening around the fences of Chu Lai. The wind smelled of it. At sea darkness had already come. They stopped to look back seaward from the quiet yard of the chapel on the hill. The sea wind rattled the broad leaves of the banana tree there. They stood, not quite touching one another, yet each feeling the other's presence as if their hands had met. 'It's so dark there,' she said. The blue lights of the helicopter ramp spread at their feet, bounded on one side by the hospital floodlights and on the other by the yellow slashes of light seeping around the storm shutters in his company area. But those ended abruptly, and beyond was nothing. On a calm night the sea would have been strewn as thick with lights as stars in the sky, where the villagers were fishing far at sea. Tonight the boats were safe ashore, and beyond the cliffs raged the empty black sea. Yet there was peace at sea, while no men were there. Was there peace only in the void? Nothing to hope for but blackness? He turned her away and led her quickly to the club, out of sight of the cliffs and whatever lay beyond.

Inside the door someone called to him. 'It's Janet,' Alice said. 'Over on the balcony.' Wolcheski and Guiterrez were with her. 'Do you want to be sociable? We can pretend we were only looking in.'

'Sociability is better than thought,' he said. She took his hand as they crossed to the balcony.

'Say,' Guiterrez said, 'it's that shaggy critter, out guzzling beer again.'

'I thought you were among the missing,' Janet said to Bear. 'We haven't seen you for such a time.'

'Pull up a chair and tell us some war stories,' Guiterrez offered. 'How's gunning?'

'Busy,' Bear answered. 'Very busy.'

'You should have been down toward Quang Ngai today,' Guiterrez continued. 'Somebody got a potful of them down there today.'

'Don't talk shop,' Alice told him.

The balcony was on the landwind side of the club, out of the sea wind. Mortar flares were dropping to the west. First there came the light, yellow and weak and wavering, too weak even to cast a shadow at this distance. Sometimes the faint plop of the flare igniting reached them, many seconds after the light. Sometimes there was a distant rumble of artillery like the stirring of an uneasy sleeper.

'I hate artillery in the night,' Wolcheski said, speaking for the first time. He had been slouched back in his chair, watching the Bear when he looked at anything at all.

Wolcheski had watched the Bear carefully, although Bear did not know it. Wolcheski was a born watcher. As a small boy, he had been told, he would spend hours watching anything that crossed his path – a snail, a cat, a thunderstorm. He would try to outwait a dead bird, until dragged off to supper. He also loved all moving machinery, not only trains and fire engines, but electric fans, toasters, and jackhammers. Later he had turned scientific. His schoolwork won prizes in physics and biology. Somewhere in his late teens, however, he discovered people, and thereafter he concentrated on watching them – natural enough, since in the absence of angels people showed the most complex behaviour of any objects available. He did not outgrow machinery, however; and so after he was drafted and made his way to Officer Candidate School, flight training was his first stop.

Wolcheski considered himself a failure as a scientist: he tried to be a detached observer, but never could retain his detachment intact. But, while he knew that this was a shortcoming, it was not one that bothered him. Real people were more fun than was theoretically possible, so who needed theory? Real people were also more heartbreaking than was theoretically possible. Wolcheski tried to do what he could about that, but had long since found that he usually could not do much. Bear's sorrow saddened him. He liked Bear, and did not see what he could do about him. He suspected that if anything was to be done, Alice was it.

'I hate artillery in the night.' As he said the words, Wolcheski looked away toward the mountain. Or toward where the mountain stood. It could not be seen in the darkness beyond the pale distant flares. 'When I hear artillery I always expect a call in twenty minutes. I hate to fly at night.'

'Any particular reason,' Guiterrez asked, 'other than that it ain't safe? At least we don't have to fly tonight, *Trung-úy*, knock on wood.'

As if in warning to guard his words, a prolonged heavy burst rolled in from the northwest. 'I wonder where that one is,' Guiteerez went on. 'Probably Tam Ky. They're always after the province headquarters. Anyway I'd rather it was out there than as close as those rounds that came in a couple weeks back. Did they wake you up, Bear?' Guiterrez had a quick grin that came and went when he had said something he thought was ironic. It flicked across his face and was gone. 'I hope you went up and shot their asses off. I take that personally, when Charley starts pegging at me in my own quarters. You ought to be like the Bear, *Trung-úy*,' he said to Wolcheski. 'Carry a gun and when you crank you don't worry about flying at night. If Charley knows you're the meanest mother out there, he leaves you alone. With us, he sees that red cross and cuts loose right now!'

'But when *you* crank,' Bear said, 'you don't have to wonder who you're going to kill.'

'It wouldn't worry me *too* much,' Guiterrez said, 'not so much as who's going to kill *me*.'

'You two should trade places,' Swensen said brightly. Bear stared at the table.

'*Trung-úy* Wolcheski couldn't get along without me,' Guiterrez said. 'Who'd drag him home when he gets lost out there in the dark?'

'Never happen, Primo,' Wolcheski said, sitting up with sudden decisiveness. He added quietly, as if for Bear alone to hear, 'You know we're short a warrant officer in our unit. If you were to put in a ten-forty-nine, you might end up with us.'

Bear shook his head. 'My company's still so low on pilots, they'll never let go of a warm body.'

'Deep down the Bear's attached to his guns,' Guiterrez said. The quick grin came and went.

'Would you check out that shit!' Atterburn exclaimed, coming to a stop inside the door of the club. 'His Bearness himself, sitting with a couple of round-eyes!'

'I never heard of a mirage appearing at night,' Arp said. 'Where's that?'

'Over there!' Atterburn kneaded his cap in his hands. 'The Bear out with a round-eye! How'd he ever get himself into that position?'

'We could ask,' Arp said. He was already on his way. He stopped behind the Bear. 'It didn't take *you* long to get the war off your mind, Bear,' he said. 'I like to see the troops enjoying themselves; but I didn't know you were so widely acquainted.' He pulled up a chair between the Bear and Janet Swensen. 'May we join you? This,' he said to Lieutenant Swensen, pointing to Atterburn, who was hanging a yard away, 'is Mr Atterburn. You can forget about him. He's easily forgettable.'

Swensen smiled at him. 'I seem to have forgotten you, too, Lieutenant. Have we met?'

'We would have, if Bear were doing his duty by his leader. Come on, Bear. These nice people will think I haven't taught you any manners.'

'My glorious leader,' Bear presented him. 'And his

faithful sidekick Attenburn.' He made an effort to sound lighthearted; but Arp gave him a puzzled glance, hearing something strange in his voice, and Alice squeezed Bear's hand under the table. The others were pleased enough, though. Not to spoil their pleasure, Bear began seriously to try to be happy. He drank, he told jokes, and eventually at Attenburn's urging he even ordered drinks from the waitress in polite Vietnamese. But happiness fled with its tail unsalted.

'You're a man of rare talent,' Wolcheski said. 'I wish I could speak Vietnamese.'

'It's easy,' Bear said. 'You just have to give up your inhibitions.'

'*He* doesn't have any,' Swensen said.

'Few,' Wolcheski corrected her. 'Few, but firm.'

'From your Polish grandmother, no doubt.'

'Absolutely. But from her also, my aesthetic sense.'

'Polish?' Arp raised an eyebrow.

'Absolutely. The heritage of Chopin and Paderewski. All that sort of thing. But Vietnamese, now – a lovely language.'

'At least if you spoke the language, you could get laid,' Atterburn said. 'Not that it helps Bear any.'

Alice blushed; but in the dark, who was to know, except Bear?

'A lovely language,' Wolcheski went on, ignoring Atterburn, as did everyone else. 'Even if you don't understand it. *Chu Lai* – a beautiful name. Who cares what it means? Oh *Ky Ha*?'

'Bear was always pointing out names to me, when we first flew together. It's been a long time, huh, B?'

'A long time.'

'He used to chant Vietnamese names as we flew,' Arp said to Alice. 'What were some of them, B?'

Bear closed his eyes. He chanted slowly – slowly, and a little sadly: 'Chu Lai, Dong Xoai, Quang Ngai; Phuong Tan, Vinh Giang, Hoi An; Tam Ky, Khanh My, Que Son.'

'It's beautiful,' said Alice. 'Is it a poem?'

'The list of villages,' Arp said. 'I remember when you composed that. It was longer, though. And there was one for rivers. How did it go?'

'Rivers I can't do on a night like this,' Bear said. 'The names of rivers are sad names.'

'How about "Song Tra Bong"? That's not sad. Any people who call a river a "song" can't be all bad, can they?'

'Song Be,' Wolcheski said. 'There's another. Or Song Ben Van. The whole country sings.'

'How many ways are there to say "river" in Vietnamese, Bear?' Arp asked.

Bear was reluctant. 'A lot. If you count creeks, and water-courses, and tidal streams and the rest.'

'For instance?' Wolcheski asked. Wolcheski saw that Arp was trying to draw Bear out. For the first time Bear seemed ready to forget whatever was on his mind.

'*Sông*,' Bear said. 'And dialect, *tong*. And some others: *ea, ia, ya. Ọ, hô, houei. Bao. Ngoc, or nu'ớ'c* – that's "water." *Tam, nam, rào. Khê.* That's one we all know – *An Khê*, where the First Horse is camped: "river village." *An* means "village."'

'How do you learn all this shit?' Atterburn asked.

'Mostly, I read charts. And think about what's down there. Try it sometime, Burn. Don't think about *who*'s down there, though.'

'All good pilots read their charts,' Wolcheski said, addressing Arp. 'Now Bear mentioned Vinh . . . what was that village, Bear?'

'Vinh Giang,' Arp told him.

'Vinh Giang. How about Vinh Qui Nhon, Lieutenant? Have you ever seen that one on your chart?'

'Qui Nhon we all know is a coastal city. Vinh Qui Nhon, you no doubt expect me to guess, is a village in the area. But it isn't. Vinh Qui Nhon is the bay on which Qui Nhon is located. Very tricky.'

'The two '*vinhs*' aren't the same word, of course,' Bear pointed out. 'Vinh Giang – *vinh* or *viñh* or *vĩnh.* Vinh Qui Nhon – *vinh.* They look the same on the map if you can't see the tone markings; or they sound the same if you can't hear the tones.'

'Don't confuse us with knowledge, Bear,' Arp said. 'It's my turn to ask the lieutenant one. How about this: if Nui

Ong is out there' – he nodded out the open door across the western balcony, into the night – 'where is Nui Ba, and why do I ask?'

Wolcheski pondered. As he did so, he seemed to sink inside himself. His eyes closed. His lips curled down, to match the curve of his dark brows. He shook himself surfacing. 'Don't know,' he admitted. 'They're both mountains; but that's trivial.'

'Nui Ba is on the coast south of Bong Son,' Arp said. 'And I ask because . . .' He pointed to Bear, to cue him.

'*Ong* means "man,"' said Bear, 'or politely, "mister." Or "grandfather." The Grandfather Mountain. And *bà* means "woman," or "Mrs." or "grandmother."'

'You only knew that from flying with Mr Bear, though, didn't you,' Wolcheski challenged Arp.

'Sure. But he was my wojug, in those days.'

'What's a wojug?' Swensen asked.

'Warrant Officer, junior grade. Boy, was he ever new.'

'About as new as a certain lieutenant,' Bear said. 'But how about this one, then? Now that you've got Nui Ong, where is Hon Ong, and why do I ask?'

Wolcheski and Arp both pondered. They glared at one another. Each started to point an accusing finger at the other. 'Well, I'll give up if you will,' Arp said. 'But not before.'

Wolcheski thought a while longer. 'Okay. On three.'

Janet counted: 'One. Two. Three.' They both turned to Bear.

'*Hòn* is another word for mountain,' Bear said. 'And Hon Ong is a mountain not far from the coast, between Qui Nhon and Ninh Hoa. Boy, was I ever new last time we flew by there, Lieutenant. New enough to read the chart.'

'That's a cheat, Bear,' Arp said. 'And if *hòn* is a mountain, how about Hon Tre, that island off Nha Trang? Or is it a different word, in disguise?'

'Same word,' Bear said. 'A mountainous island.'

'Then how about Cu Lao Re, off the coast here? Why don't they call that a mountain island? It is one.'

'I don't know,' Bear said. 'I didn't invent this language. I didn't invent this country or this war.'

Three of those at the table heard the sudden darkness in Bear's voice; but none knew why it was there.'

Alice thought it was the memory of the ocean, dark as endless night, and never a star to see.

Arp, too, thought of the sea, and the fiery fall of a dying ship, a dying friend.

'Is there an island out there?' Wolcheski asked. 'I've never seen it.'

'It's on the charts,' Arp said.

'Have *you* seen it?' Wolcheski challenged.

'No.'

'Some days it's there,' Bear said. 'Some days it isn't.'

'That sounds mysterious,' said Janet. 'If it's there, why haven't you two seen it?'

'Maybe if a guy just had faith,' Bear said. 'To fly off into the blue . . .' The memory of the island, of his vision of it, overwhelmed him.

The Bear was dancing with Alice. They circled slowly off in the darkness toward the other end of the bar. Martin and Major Hart, sitting there far back in the shadows talking quietly, seriously, glanced up more than once at the couple.

Those at the other table also watched Alice and the Bear. 'Who'd of thought the Bear was such a lover, Lieutenant?' Atterburn said to Arp. 'He's hardly met a dollie, and he's off into the night with her.'

'And not the first time, either,' Guiterrez said. 'He did the same thing the first time I introduced him to her.'

'To her? You mean the Bear's been seeing her before?'

'Sure. Weeks ago. But he hasn't been around lately. You kept him out of my way. And it didn't do me a bit of good.'

'The Bear's been pining for a round-eye!' Atterburn exclaimed. 'And I thought he was doping around like he had a turd hung up in his tubes just because he'd lost his nerve after Hill Four Seven Three!'

'The state of his soul is more complex than you apprehended,' Arp told him dryly.

'All that time on the ground he had everybody feeling

sorry for him, and all the while he was off getting some squeezies from a warm round-eye! It definitely ain't fair, Lieutenant!'

'Fair is what you make it,' Arp said.

'Well, I thought he'd missed *his* chance, too, when he was gone so long.' Guiterrez said. 'She's been around Dr Rawlinson pretty much lately.'

'Be quiet, Primo,' Janet said. Bear was coming back leading Alice by the hand. Because the others were watching, he capered at the edge of the floor.

'Is that a blimp coming in for a landing?' Atterburn greeted him.

'It's the walrus bellying up to the ice floe,' Arp suggested. 'Cold! Very cold. You can tell by the way the tummy shivers. Listen, do the walrus for us, Bear. Have you seen the walrus, Lieutenant Swensen?'

'I think the walrus has gone on,' Bear said.

'Gone south for the monsoon?' Atterburn asked. 'What is he, a fair-weather walrus?'

'I guess he is,' Bear said softly. 'A sunshine walrus.'

'A sunshine walrus,' Wolcheski repeated in the direction of the mountain. He smiled. He liked the Bear's turn of phrase.

The sound of shots rang out from the side room off the bar. It was only the cowboy movie reaching its denouement. From somewhere out toward the mountain where the flares were falling, the sliding thump of artillery rolled in around them. 'Cannon to the left of them, cannon to the right of them,' Wolcheski suddenly declaimed loudly. He drew the attention of no one but Arp. Atterburn and Guiterrez were watching Bear talk privately to Alice. Arp had been zeroing his attention in on Janet; but now he turned to Wolcheski: 'I didn't know anyone here spoke Tennyson.'

'Don't pay any attention to him,' Janet said. 'He's always quoting some dead poet.'

'Her main objection to them,' Wolcheski said to Arp, 'is that they're dead.'

'Well, who was that poet who said there's no poem like a real live woman?' Janet asked. 'You told me about him yourself. Doesn't that go for men too?'

'Keats,' Arp said. '"Let the mad poets say what e'er they please/Of the sweets of Fairies, Peris, Goddesses,/There is not such a treat among them all,/Haunters of cavern, lake and waterfall,/As a real woman."'

Bear and Alice had drifted off again to dance. Guiterrez and Atterburn stared after them, and then Atterburn asked Janet to dance. Guiterrez wandered sadly away to the bar.

'You don't like poetry?' Wolcheski called after them, but no one answered.

'You aren't afraid he'll snake your date?' Arp asked, indicating in the direction of Atterburn and Janet.

'If *you* can't do it, *he* sure as hell can't,' Wolcheski said. 'And you can't.'

'I could,' Arp insisted – but laughing – 'but I'd rather swap lines with you. Keats to the contrary, women abound; but how often do you meet a man who knows Tennyson? I couldn't steal a woman from a man I've exchanged quotations with.'

'Very gentlemanly of you.'

'You know how Thucydides told of the Greek generals spending the night before a battle exchanging lines of poetry? That always seemed to me the proper way to run a war. But I never thought I'd have the chance. Do you suppose that's the way the CG spends his evenings?'

'Considering that your Greeks were writing of the blush of color on a boy's cheek,' Wolcheski said, 'I think I won't answer that. You never know who's listening.' He looked around and then said quietly, 'I'll give you a quotation for the Bear, though:

> There *is* confusion worse than death
> Trouble on trouble, pain on pain,
> Long labor unto aged breath,
> Sore task to hearts worn out by many wars
> And eyes grown dim with gazing on the pilot-stars.'

'Meaning?'

'If you're flying guns with him, you should already have

seen it,' Wolcheski said.

'The Bear is the best gun pilot in the company,' Arp said firmly. 'He has two DFCs and a third in the oven, and he earned them all. In fact, he's earned a couple he didn't get.'

Wolcheski shook his head. 'I didn't say he was afraid. I'd like to have him fly with me, anytime. But . . . "Men may come to worse than dust."'

Arp looked toward the Bear and Alice, who swung about one another in an orbit inclined toward the far end of the bar where it was dark, as though together they made up a planetary system that had slipped the bonds of its star and was drawn inescapably toward the darkness from which there was no return.

When he woke, Bear saw the letter on the mosquito netting over his bunk. He had not looked for his mail after the mission of the day before. He had gone first to see Alice. He supposed Ruth had got it for him. He had not turned on the lights when he came home.

There was no return address on the envelope. It had an Iowa postmark. He put the letter aside to dress, wondering who he knew in Iowa now that Covington was dead.

Without buttoning his shirt he snatched the letter up again and tore open the envelope.

Dear Bear [Pinky had written], Dear Bear, I don't feel right calling you anything but that, because Wes always wrote of you as the Bear. I hope you won't take it badly that I think of you by that name. As you can see by the address on the envelope, I know you have another, but Wes's letters made me like you so much by this one that I want to use it.

I suppose you don't think I wrote just to chat about names, though; and you're right. I'm writing to you now because it seems you're the last hope I have of finding out about Wes. You see, the Army told me – so long ago, it seems! – that he is missing in action. But I haven't been able to find out anything more. Wes told me in one of his first letters what 'missing in action' means. If any pilot is reported missing in action, he said, it means he's dead, but they haven't found the body. I believed him. Now I don't want to believe it anymore. Surely the Army, or someone, somewhere, in the Army, must know more than that he is just 'missing in action'? I've tried every way I know how to find out. I even wrote to your company commander. But there has been no answer. Now I am turning to you as my last hope. I still want to hope, but I hardly know how. You see, I still believe what Wes told me, because he never lied to me. I want you to write and tell me there is still some reason to believe that he is alive. But even if there is none, I want to know that. Anything is better than not knowing. Please, write and tell me.

Pinky

Bear raged up and down the aisle of the hooch, cursing silently. He threw on his clothes and his pistol and set off for the Operations hooch.

Lieutenant Rauch was behind the desk, his feet up and his arms behind his head, apparently speculating on the height of the ceiling. He turned his eyes, but not his head, to see who had come in. 'What's up, Bear?'

'I have to go see the old man. And I'm due on standby. So give me a call if we get a mission.' Bear was too much in a hurry to frame a polite request.

'Well, Jesus, yes sir, *Chief*! Anytime. Just let me know. Do you want to take my jeep?'

'Yes,' Bear said. He ignored the sarcasm in Rauch's voice. Rauch did not try to stop him when he climbed into the jeep.

Before Bear could drive onto the ramp, he was flagged down by Lieutenant Arp. Yan was with him. She was crying. 'Well, what are you doing to my hooch-maid now, Leiutenant?' Bear asked. He was annoyed at being stopped. He thought it was only Arp teasing Yan again, until he saw how serious Arp was.

'Bear, can you make sense of what this girl is saying? She came running up to me saying somebody's caught her mama-san, but *I* don't know what she means! Talk to her, will you?' But Yan was not easy to talk to. She was near hysteria. Her Vietnamese rattled past too quickly for Bear to understand, and her English had shrunk to 'He take my mama-san away! She no bad! You tell him bring mama-san back!' To Bear's attempts at Vietnamese questions she only answered wildly, '*Khong biẽt! Khong biẽt!*' Several minutes had dragged past before they calmed her enough to learn that Suzie had been picked up on the ramp by Captain Blood as she was returning from the other side. He had forced her into the gun platoon truck and driven back in that direction with her. One of the other hooch-maids had seen that much and had told Yan, for none of them liked Captain Blood. 'I run quick look for *Trung-úy* Arp,' Yan said.

'Ask her what the devil Suzie was doing on the ramp,' Arp said. The hooch-maids were not allowed among the aircraft.

'She came back from other side,' Yan said. She took questions from the Bear but she put her answers directly to Arp as best she could.

'Then what the devil was she doing over there? She works here, not there!'

'*Khong biẽt!*' Yan wailed.

'Oh, Christ! Ask her, Bear.'

'*Bà dã làm gì dãy?*' It took two tries with this question before Yan understood, because Bear used the wrong tone on the word *dãy* the first time, so that it meant 'here' instead of 'there.' The second time though, Yan understood that he was asking what her mother was doing *there*.

'She lose ID card,' she said to Arp. 'She think friend catch it.'

'If that's all, it's much ado about nothing. Are you going that way, Bear? Check on Suzie, will you? And tell this girl her mother's all right. Yan, mama-san number one okay. All right? Trust me.'

When Bear reached the orderly room, Suzie was there. She was in a chair, quiet and frightened. Blood was pacing up and down.

'There's your Slope expert,' Blood said as the Bear came in the door. 'Let *him* find out what she's up to.' This was a sneer directed towards Martin, who was leaning against the screen that closed off his desk and the major's.

'Intelligence will have somebody down here soon enough,' Martin said. 'Just let her alone, Blood.'

'Sure, we'd send her on home to blow us all to Kingdom Come if you had your way.'

'I'm glad she's alive,' Bear said. 'Yan was all gone to pieces. She thought her mama-san had been kidnapped. What happened?'

'Never mind what happened,' Blood snapped. 'Aren't you on standby? What are you doing here?'

'I want to see Major Hart. But I told Lieutenant Arp I'd find out what happened to Suzie.'

'Well, go back and tell Lieutenant Arp that I'm taking care of Suzie. And since when does he give people permission to leave their duty area?'

'Captain Blood thinks Suzie was pacing off the ramp,' Martin explained.

'Thinks? Why the devil else would she be stopping at every row of revetments? She didn't have any business down there anyway.'

Martin ignored Blood's outburst. 'Someone will come down from Division to interview her,' he said to the Bear.

'Yan said she lost her ID and wanted to see if her friend over here had it.' Without her ID Suzie could not enter or leave the post.

'Then we'd better talk to her friend, too,' Blood said. 'What if she does have it? It's easy enough to rig something like that. If Charley gets the ramp measured off, his mortars will do a lot worse next time than they did the last.'

'It could be true, Bear,' Martin said. 'We have to check on it.'

Since Suzie was apparently in no danger of anything worse than a talking-to, Bear let the matter pass. 'When can I see Major Hart?' he asked Martin. He could see that the major was not in his office.

'He's gone up to Division with the battalion commander. Is there anything I can do?'

'I think I'd better see him, sir.'

'All right. I'll call Rauch when he comes back. You'd better go back across if you're on standby.'

Blood muttered something about disciplining his own troops, but he said nothing else to the Bear.

Lieutenant Arp was waiting for Bear at Operations. He went up to the hooch to tell Yan about her mother, while Bear went down to his ship. Rauch put his head out the door and called after him, 'You're welcome, Bear!'

'Thanks for the jeep, sir.'

'Anytime.'

Ruth was on the ship. 'I've preflighted it,' he said. 'And I set the radios. Everyfing's okay.'

'You're a good boy, Rufe,' Bear said. He began to preflight the ship again. Whatever he felt, the preflight was something he always did for himself. Normally he did without the checklist, but today he got it out and forced himself to read off every item. He knew he would miss something if he didn't read it. His mind was everywhere but on flying. Ruth followed him around, anxiously watching over his shoulder.

'You got a letter yesterday,' Ruth said. 'I left it on your bunk. I hope you found it.'

'Yes,' Bear said. 'Thank you.' He finished the preflight at his door to the cockpit, where he adjusted the seat and his harness and plugged in his helmet. He got down and closed the door. 'You're right, it's ready to go, Rufe,' he said. 'You done good.' They walked together back to the alert hooch. Blood's truck was outside the door.

'There he is,' Atterburn said, 'the sunshine walrus. Where'd you go off to last night, Bear, that took you so long to get home? Captain,' he said to Blood, 'did you hear that the Bear has been getting his squeezies from a round-eye nurse all the time we were on the ground?'

Blood had not seen Alice, but he had his own idea of what kind of American girl would keep company with a specimen like the Bear. He ignored the question, but muttered irritably, 'What's the sunshine walrus business?'

'The Bear's animal imitations,' Atterburn said. 'They've migrated for the rainy season. He's only a sunshine walrus.'

'The hell,' Blood said. 'About time, Bear. Everybody grows up someday, eh?'

He expected Blood to say something about his being at the orderly room; but Blood seemed willing to let it go. In turn Bear asked nothing about Suzie. He supposed Martin had sent Blood away. He knew that Blood would not have left otherwise. Bear sat down on his cot with his clipboard. He was going to write to Pinky. But before he could begin, the scramble horn sounded.

Coming out of the hamlet, the infantry platoon had taken fire from the tree line across a deep paddy. It was light fire, and they returned it and maneuvered toward it. Before the platoon leader realized how deep the paddy was, his men were bogged down or swimming, and automatic weapons fire was coming in on them. They struggled back with heavy losses. From behind the paddy dike they called for gunships.

Bear listened to Blood talking to the company commander on the Fox Mike. Smoke coming out now. A smoke grenade popped near the trees. Green. Damn them – green was hard to see in a planted paddy. But Blood had seen it; he began to acknowledge, when a second grenade popped, far down along the trees. Yellow. 'Well, Panther, I have a yellow and a green. Which one are you?' Blood asked.

Panther said his was the yellow.

Charley had a receiver on their frequency; but he had out-smarted himself.

Or else, Bear thought as they turned inbound, it was some dumb grunt who got his signals mixed up.

Ahead, Blood's ship enveloped itself in a shroud of smoke as a brace of rockets streaked earthward. In the seat next to Bear, Ruth had the gunsight down, and the crew in back were leaning out the doors in anticipation. 'Hold your fire,' Bear said.

'We're in range?' Ruth said hesitantly.

Bear did not answer. The ship flashed down the length of the tree line. There was no fire from the ground. There was no one to be seen. But someone had thrown smoke.

'What's the matter, sir?' Handy asked.

'Did you see anything?'

'No, sir. But Charley's in there. I can all but smell him.'

'Hold on.'

Outbound, they passed the lead ship turning in. As they passed, the other ship lit up with rockets and tracers.

'They sure as hell got something,' Handy said.

Bear was on the radio: 'Lead, any Victor Charlies in sight?'

'Negative, but he's in these trees. Work out.'

Inbound again, there was no one. It was like a hundred other missions. You never saw whom you were killing. Yesterday, seeing men fall, had been exceptional. For standard operations you shot up a target area and let the ordnance kill whoever was there. A rocket had a killing radius of thirty meters. No need to hit a man dead on. And there was someone in the tree line. But who was it?

Out the other end of the tree line again. 'What's the matter, Bear?' Ruth looked at him with concern.

He couldn't say it. Ruth had seen men die in the open, but he hadn't been there at Hill 473. He hadn't been at the hospital.

Over by the place the yellow smoke had been, heads began to pop up behind the dike, American heads watching the show. 'Go get 'em, Wolf,' the radio said. It was the ground commander's voice. So the friendlies were accounted for.

'All right,' Bear said. There was no longer a way to hold back.

With a fierce whoop Handy strained at the end of his monkey-strap as he directed his weapon under the belly of the ship. Ruth squeezed the trigger switch. A-a-a-a-ahh, said the flex-guns- A-a-a-a-a-a-hh.

In the tree line no one moved. But one could die without moving.

As the guns departed, a medevac helicopter called in on the ground frequency, coming for the wounded. It was not Wolcheski's voice; but others flew for Dustoff, too.

Before the blade had stopped, Blood was at the side of Bear's ship. He waited until Cripps and Handy had gone to bring up more rockets before he spoke. He made a point of waiting. One officer did not point out the shortcomings of another with enlisted men present. It was a rule Blood often forgot when impassioned but it pleased him to remember it now. A leader should do the correct thing. After they were gone, Blood asked, 'What was wrong with your weapons?'

'Nothing,' Bear said.

'They didn't work very well, right there at first.'

'I wasn't sure who I was shooting at.'

'I'll decide when to fire and when not to,' Blood said. 'All you've got to do is follow me around, mister. That shouldn't be so hard. You don't need to decide who you're shooting at.'

'I made that mistake at Hill Four Seven Three,' Bear answered.

Blood's face slowly became livid, and his jaw muscles worked; but in the end he said nothing. His nostrils flared wide, and he snorted in disgust and walked away.

Ruth, still in the left-hand seat, was pale and wide-eyed. 'See that we get rearmed,' Bear told him. 'I'm going to the orderly room.'

Major Haert had come back, and the battalion commander with him. Bear sat in the orderly room listening to the low voices from behind the plywood screen. He wondered if the battalion commander was always so friendly with Major Hart. Congratulations were in progress for something; but what it was, the Bear could not tell. The first sergeant was grinning to himself as he played at fitting names onto a duty roster. 'There's something big coming, sir,' he said, nodding toward the back offices. 'Tell Handy to keep his guns cleaned.' When he saw that Bear was not going to answer, he tried a different subject: 'Did you come to check on your hooch-maid?'

Bear shook his head. He had forgotten all about Suzie.

'I thought maybe you wondered what happend when she never came back,' the first sergeant said.

'Never came back? I've been gone. What happened to her?'

'That interrogation team that come down took her away with them. I thought you come to check up on her, sir.'

'Where did they take her?'

'I don't know. Back to Division, I guess. They talked to her for a while, and then they went off with her in their jeep.'

'Christ, what is going on around here, First Sergeant?' Bear's anger would have boiled over then and there, but there was a scraping of chairs from the back office, and Major Hart and the colonel came out followed by Martin. The first sergeant jumped to his feet, shushing the Bear with a quick hidden gesture.

'Let's see that this one goes like clockwork,' the colonel was saying. 'We don't know when the general will be looking in, but he'll be there sometime.' Seeing the Bear there, the colonel stopped. 'Glad to see you're still with us,' he said. The colonel had cultivated a bluff way of speaking that sometimes left it a mystery whether he was pleased or angry, until a slow smile followed, accompanied by an unconscious gesture of rubbing a hand over his bald forehead. 'I lost a lot of sleep over you,' he continued to the Bear. 'I'll be damned if I'm going to let you out of my sight now. You're doing some decent flying, judging by the DFC recommendation that crossed my desk lately. And Hart says you're a good man. I don't know whether Hart knows shit from applebutter; but I can't find anybody to take his job, so I'll have to take his word.' Before his slow crooked smile had faded, he was out the door.

The first sergeant lapsed back into his proprietary slouch behind his desk. 'This young warrant officer came to see you, sir,' he said to Major Hart.

'In case you missed it,' Major Hart told the Bear, 'that was a compliment from the colonel. Well, come on in, Don. Captain Martin said you wanted to see me about something.'

'I wanted to see you about this, sir.' Bear took Pinky's letter from his pocket and handed it to the major. 'But,' he said to Martin, 'sir, what happened to Suzie?'

Martin shook his head tiredly. 'I don't know, Bear. Somebody and his interpreter came down from G-2, and they thought they had to talk to her back there. It just got out of my hands.' Bear could see that Martin was embarrassed by the way things had turned out; but he also seemed annoyed that the Bear should question his judgment. 'Whatever we think of Blood,' Martin added, 'sometimes he's right. She could have been stepping off the ramp, and we can't take a chance. Some things just have to be done. She'll be back to catch the truck home: just look at it as a day off for her.'

Bear saw that there was nothing more to be said.

The major had stood behind his desk during this exchange. Now he sat down and smoothed the letter out carefully. He read slowly, turning the page at the end to see that there was nothing on the back. 'Well, Ben,' he said, 'here we go again.' He handed the letter to Martin and thoughtfully rubbed his nose with one forefinger. While Martin was reading the letter, the major asked Bear, 'Have you answered it?'

'Not yet, sir.'

'Are you planning to?'

'Yes.'

'Of course. You know it's against regulations, don't you?'

'Not officially. Is it?'

'Yes. Now that you know "officially," are you going to answer it anyway?'

'Yes, sir.'

'Yes, sir. You know, Ben, if we had many officers this honest the Army would have to be disbanded. If you're going to answer it,' he asked the Bear, 'why did you bring it to me, for God's sake? Never mind, I know that one. It's because you wanted to take me to task for not answering the letter Mrs Covington says she wrote to me.'

'Not exactly, sir, but I—'

'Oh, hell, if not exactly, then close enough. Well, Ben, what are we going to do with this one?'

'With Bear, sir? Nothing, I hope.'

'No, no, of course not with Bear. What kind of animal do you take me for? They'll be calling all of us by the names of beasts before it's all over anyway,' he said aside to the Bear. 'No, with the letter.'

'I think he should answer it,' Martin said.

'So you said about the last one. It's still against regulations.'

'I know.'

'Is that all you can say? I thought you were going to try to tell me that people are more important than regulations. Who's going to set me straight if my own XO won't?'

'Maybe one of your warrant officers,' Martin suggested with a smile.

Major Hart sighed and removed his reading glasses, 'Insubordination is spreading in the ranks. What's the Army coming to? Well, Don, here is an old man's apology, on behalf of his Army, to you and to Mrs Covington. I thought she would be properly informed in due time. But, as my XO has so persuasively argued, people are more important than regulations, and something has gone amiss. You'd better get your letter off to Pinky. And for his fluency, the XO gets to draft a letter for me, apologizing for my tardiness in answering her. What else can I do for you?'

Bear hestiated. 'Well . . . one more thing, sir.'

Major Hart sighed. 'Name it.'

'I want to transfer out of the unit, sir.' Major Hart stiffened behind his desk, and Bear heard Martin move suddenly at his back. 'It's nothing to do with the letter,' Bear said. 'Or with Suzie.' He was not sure why he had added either of those – or even, now that he had said them, that they were true. Everything had suddenly fallen together.

'Are you having trouble with Blood?' Martin asked.

'No. Well, no more than usual,' Bear said with a shake of his head. 'It's nothing about the company. I want to go to Dustoff.'

'Any particular unit?' the major asked, leaning back in his chair and studying the ceiling.

'The detachment at the hospital' – he gestured down the ramp – 'is short a pilot, sir.'

A long silence followed. Major Hart continued to study the ceiling. Martin sat turning Pinky's letter on his desk, while the Bear looked uneasily from one to the other until the major looked back at him. Then, remembering the bar and the night before, a blush spread slowly over the Bear's face. 'It has nothing to do with . . . her,' he said quickly. He had not even considered, until that moment, that the move would put him in daily contact with Alice.

'But it would be convenient,' Major Hart said. He hated to say it. It was unkind, and, left to his own feeling, he would not have said it even if he believed it was the reason behind this request. But he thought it was his duty to the Army to say it, to examine the Bear, whom he liked, as any pilot requesting transfer from a shorthanded command should be examined. And there was another reason: he did not want to lose a first-rate pilot because every pilot would be needed for the combat assault that was coming in a week, the combat assault that the colonel had come to discuss.

'I hadn't thought about it, sir,' Bear said. He was tempted at first to take back the request, rather than be thought to have asked for that reason. In merely asking he was setting himself apart from his fellows, saying that he should not be asked to do what they would do. But having gone so far, he found himself looking back on the request as a bridge crossed even though he had not known he was approaching it. Finding himself somehow across, he was reluctant to go back.

'You know how short we are on pilots,' the major said, with the tone of one who thinks he should be closing the issue.

'Yes, sir.'

'People will be back on continuous standby.'

'I know that, sir.' He could have offered to wait for a replacement. He thought that was what the major was waiting for, as a way gracefully to allow the major to do what he wanted. But to offer that would be to deny the reason for the transfer, would be to recross the bridge. He was determined not to do that.

'And if you leave now, Don,' the major said, leaning forward across his desk, 'some people may think it's because . . . the incident. I don't know if you're planning to stay in the Army, but these things can follow you, even when they're not your fault at all.' Major Hart flashed an apologetic glance at Martin as he said this.

'That's not important to me,' Bear told him.

'Maybe it isn't now. But you never know what tomorrow will bring. You think about it, will you? I'll tell you now, in confidence, that we're going to need every man we can get during the next week. I can't let anyone go before then. After that . . .' He shrugged. 'We'll see.'

Bear's sudden determination had been a spring blizzard. It melted before his sense of obligation to his friends, and his desire to please a man he admired. He was half ashamed of his request, for he felt still that it was selfish. When he was gone, others would be left to do his job. But the determination melted, leaving him only the feeling that he had lost his way and was alone.

Bear set out to tell Arp what had become of Suzie, but he found that the lieutenant already knew and had told Yan. They both believed that Suzie would be back before the end of the afternoon. But when the truck came to take the hooch-maids to the gate, Suzie was still missing. Yan looked about pale and frightened from the back of the truck.

'Maybe they'll pick her up on the other side,' Arp said to the Bear. They watched the truck roll away. Yan was still staring from the tailgate.

Suzie was not on the other side of the ramp, either. She was returned the next morning, before the rest of the maids arrived, by a sergeant from Intelligence who, according to the company clerk who was the only person in the orderly room at the time, would not say what she had or had not told. She would not walk across the ramp to her place of work, and so she remained in the orderly room until the major and Captain Martin arrived. Martin took her across the ramp in the major's jeep.

She was squatting alone on the back deck when the Bear came up to his hooch for a change of fatigues. She was soaking clothes in a washpan. Her own clothes were rumpled. Bear supposed she had slept in them. She answered him when he spoke to her, but she did not smile. She had a bandage low on one leg.

'We were worried about you, Grandmother,' Bear said.

He felt awkward with her. Because he did not know where she had been nor what had passed, he did not know what to say.

She thanked him politely for his concern and asked him whether Yan had gone safely home.

'She went. She was also worried.'

Suzie studiously massaged the laundry in her pan and did not look up again. At length Bear left her there.

During the day Martin tried to learn what had been done with her, but he had no more success. 'They've got a one-way telephone line at G-2,' he said to Arp and the Bear. 'You can ask questions, but you can't get any answers.' He added, 'I should never have let her go.' But, like the Bear, he could not think quite how to apologize to Suzie herself when he did not know what had occurred.

Yan, too, was subdued that day. She did talk to Arp, but she knew little, or claimed to. She did know about the bandage. 'She says the Vietnamese interrogator tried to scare Suzie with a dog,' Arp said to the Bear, 'and the dog got too close.'

10

Nervousness ran through the company. Although nothing was said openly, everyone down to the cooks and supply clerks felt it. The company was not one, as some were, that led assaults two and three days of the week. Instead, it supplied aircraft for other units' assaults, two or three slicks to fill out a formation, and a fire team for suppression when others' gunships were down for maintenance. The individual pilots were veterans; but the company's joints were tight through disuse. And whatever was coming was not an ordinary company assault. Before the first briefing, while the detailed plans still simmered above in the chain of command, before it had even been said that there was to be an assault at all, that much was commonly understood. The pressure of it could be felt already, like a monsoon storm offshore speaking to arthritic limbs before any cloud could be seen.

Lieutenant Rauch stewed around the Operations room, going often to the large-scale chart of the division area of operations. 'It's gotta be up the Que Son Valley,' he said. He spoke to no one in particular, but both fire teams on standby were there for an audience.

'Captain Blood says it's going to go out of Duc Pho,' Atterburn said.

'Duc Pho! Nobody works out of Duc Pho but outfits just in country, trainin' for the real war! What makes the Blood think it's going out of Duc Pho?'

Atterburn shrugged. 'I don't know. But he has a way of knowing what he's talking about.'

'Is that the Blood we all know and love?' Arp asked.

Ruth put in shyly, 'The night I was off standby—'

'You had a night off already, Ruth?' Rauch demanded. 'You ain't been in country two weeks. What is this?'

'The night I was off standby,' Ruth began again, 'I heard Captain Blood talking to some uver officers in ve club, and he said it looked like Major Hart was going to be leading ve mission, and if vat was so, it was sure to go from Duc Pho because he hasn't had enough experience to lead a battalion operation anywhere else. I fink he said ve major hasn't led a CA since he's had ve company.'

An uneasy silence fell in the room. 'Leave it to fucking Blood to talk out of school,' Rauch muttered, to one side so that Atterburn would not hear.

'He said vat a mission around Duc Pho is all ve major needs to get his promotion anyway,' Ruth went on in all innocence, 'so vey might as well save ve big ones for someone who needs ven worse. But I fink it is going to be a big one: Captain Blood said ve major was going to have every body in reach in ve air vat day, if he had to turn down R and R's to do it.'

'We *know* it's going to be a big one,' Atterburn said. 'The only question is if it's going to be hot.'

'Pray for rain, Bear,' someone said. Everyone laughed, except Arp and the Bear. Arp would have laughed, if the Bear had. But he had been watching the Bear since the night he talked with Wolcheski. He did not think the Bear had laughed since then.

'Captain Martin, sir?' Someone stepped out of the shadow beside the first gunship revetment. Martin thought at first that it was a guard; but the man was not wearing a helmet. 'Who is it?'

'Arp, sir. Do you have a minute?'

'In abundance. They come in bundles of sixty, and every day I accumulate a surplus. I was just trying to burn up some extras by working late.'

'Better store them up for your old age, sir. You'll be glad of them then. All I need is a few from one bunch.'

'When you're looking at it from behind a desk,' Martin

said with a shrug, 'a year in Nam contains more hours than will fit into the average lifetime.'

'You should fly more,' Arp said. 'It passes the time.' He knew Martin was back on flight status, for as company IP he had given him a check ride. But he did not think Martin had flown since then.

'You're assuming I've been offered a choice,' Martin said. 'Napoleon thought an army marched on its stomach, but he was wrong. It's paper that keeps it moving. And it takes more paper to make it fly than to make it march. But – we do what we have to do.'

'Or what we're told to do. But there ought to be a way out sometimes.'

'I haven't found it.'

'I don't suppose you've looked, sir,' Arp said, without meaning any flattery.

'There isn't any.' Martin could not see where the conversation was leading; but he supposed Arp had met him out on the ramp for a reason; and he was less impatient than he might once have been. He lingered there.

'I was hoping you could find one for the Bear,' Arp said.

Martin considered for some time before he answered: 'He's already asked.'

'I suppose that shouldn't surprise me,' Arp said shortly, 'but it does.'

'It surprised *me*,' Martin said.

Without suggestion by either one they began to walk down the gunship row. The empty ships, their doorless sides cavernous in the night, loomed in the revetments, their guns pointing out over the cliffs. Martin and Arp climbed into the back of the farthest ship and sat on the creaking canvas seats. It was a ship Martin had flown often. Number zero-seven-four. He remembered it well, trying to bounce its swollen toadlike bulk off an asphalt ramp on a hot afternoon with its belly dragging too many pounds of fuel and rockets and cartridges. But he remembered it fondly. It smelled of kerosene and cold steel.

'I don't think the Bear wants to quit flying,' Martin said. 'I used to think he lived to fly. If he quit flying, he wouldn't exist anymore. Flying was what defined him. Maybe that's not so anymore.' He remembered Bear and the nurse.

'He wants to fly,' Arp said, 'he just doesn't want to fly guns. But I don't know if what he wants is what matters.'

'Then why are you here?'

'It's not so important that he get what he wants, even though I'd like to see that happen. We've got to get him out of the guns, sir, or it's going to mean his life, or worse.'

'It's meant a lot of men's lives. But how do you mean, worse?'

'"Men may come to worse than dust." Something's gone wrong with the Bear, sir. I don't know if it was Hill Four Seven Three, or Covington, or what. But he's not a gunnie anymore.'

'The Bear always hated to kill people. Is that all that's wrong?' Martin laughed.

The laugh held an irony that Arp did not hear. 'It's serious, sir,' he protested. 'Cripps told me—'

'Ah. If Cripps said something, it is serious. What was it?'

'Cripps is worried the Bear is going to get himself killed. He won't let his crew shoot anymore. Cripps came to me himself to tell me.'

'Is Cripps afraid?'

'Probably. But the only thing he asked me was if I couldn't do something for the Bear. He loves the old Bear, sir.'

'He should.'

'Sir, the Bear's ship has been coming in with three fourths of its ordnance still on board. Handy's been complaining to the platoon sergeant. You know Handy doesn't care about anything but his body count. The platoon sergeant reported it to me, and I didn't say anything; but I know he's been reporting to Captain Blood, too.'

'Well? It's Blood's platoon.'

'Why hasn't Blood sent Bear to the flight surgeon, or to the major, or something?'

'I don't know. Why not?'

'I think, sir, it's because he's storing up things to make a case for charges against the Bear. Blood doesn't want him out of the gun platoon, because that's what the Bear wants. Blood wants to get him court-martialed.' After a time Arp added, 'Even that isn't the most important thing.'

'What is, then?'

'Having to go out every day and sooner or later squeeze the trigger. It's killing him. He's not the same Bear. I've been watching him, sir; and it's like seeing him shrink before your eyes. The crews laugh about it, when Cripps isn't listening. But it's not funny, sir. The Bear is still the best pilot in the platoon. There are so many things he could be doing: why does he have to go on at the one thing he can't do? It's worse than killing him or court-martialing him! You know the Bear, sir: he wouldn't have asked, if it wasn't serious.'

'Then we'd better try to get him out,' Martin said. He knew that Arp was right. The Bear would not have asked if it were not serious. Neither would Arp. He thought of Suzie, sitting in the orderly room awaiting the result of his misjudgment. 'I'll talk to Major Hart.'

Bear was still in his seat filling out the aircraft log book after the mission when Captain Blood came around the tail of the ship. 'Has your crew rearmed your ship already?' he asked, in elaborately feigned surprise.

'No,' Bear said.

'No what.'

'No, sir.' The Bear went on writing.

'Don't you have a lot of rockets left?' The tubes were still all loaded. Bear did not answer.

'If that switch isn't working, you'd better get Cripps to check it out.'

'I'll do that, sir,' Bear said.

Blood stayed no longer. He walked away at his plunging gait like a man charging an obstacle. He was smiling.

Blood was talking to Major Hart when Martin came in.

It annoyed Blood to have Martin listening. He was not worried about anything Martin might have to say: he had prepared his ground too carefully for that. But he did not like being around Martin. Since Hill 473 he liked it even less than before. Martin's Ringknocker smugness was unbearable in a man who had nothing to be smug about. Hill 473 had showed that he was no better than Blood was himself, but still he went around with a superior air, as if he was above being hurt by a reprimand. He had kept the letter of reprimand quiet, but Blood knew about it – there were ways to find out that kind of thing, and any fool knew it had to come. A man with that on his record had no place being smug.

'Ben,' the major said, 'Captain Blood was just showing me some interesting figures.' He handed to Martin the sheet which Blood had given him. There was penciled on it a neat column of dates, and opposite each, two sets of numbers.

'What is it?'

Major Hart looked to Blood. 'Rockets,' Blood said. 'Rockets left on board the ships in my fire team after the last dozen fire missions.'

'Is that significant?' Martin recognized the meaning at once, but at least Blood was going to have to say it.

'The first number is for my own ship,' Blood said. 'As you can see, I've come in with from zero to two pair. And I try not to waste any ordnance, as you may remember. The second number is the number of rockets left on board the other ship. In case you haven't been keeping up with details, Martin, our friend the Bear is AC on that ship. As you can see, he's come in with an average of ten pair unexpended. He hasn't fired a round in the last four missions.'

'Very economical,' Martin said.

'Economical! If the point is to save money, we could all go home and save the whole bundle!'

'Well, what is the point?' Martin asked.

'The point,' Blood said, 'is to kill Charlies. And that AC won't do it.'

'Really? How do you explain that?'

'How do *I* explain it? The question is how does *he* explain it!'

'Isn't he in your platoon, Captain Blood?'

'In my platoon? Of course he's in my platoon! Am I

supposed to hold his hand on every mission because he's in my platoon?'

'Well, have you tried ordering him to kill Charlies?'

'Christ, Martin, what is this? Of course I haven't, not in so many words. You don't have to do that. Did *you* order him to when you were leading that platoon? I've told him when to open fire. He knows the SOP.'

'Then why isn't he firing?'

'Well, I'll tell *you* what he tells *me*,' Blood said, 'if you really want to know how he explains it. He can't see the targets. Or he doesn't know who they are – just like he needs a personal introduction to every man he fires on. Today he told me his selector switch was inop. That was a lie. I had the switch checked before and after the mission and a member of his crew states that the aircraft commander never even armed the system!' Blood played this last statement triumphantly and sat back to watch Martin react. Martin shrugged and looked at the major.

'Well, Ben, I think that just about seals it,' Major Hart said. 'I suppose there's nothing else we can do.' He turned to Captain Blood. 'I appreciate your bringing this out, Del,' he said. 'Captain Martin has been telling me that the Bear was having a hard time; but he's been such an excellent pilot that I was sure he'd bounce back. I can see now that he hasn't. He asked some time ago for a transfer, but I refused him. He wanted to fly Dustoff. I think now it would be best for all to let him go.'

Blood's face reddened. He started several times to speak, but he found no words. His effort was such that the eyes bulged from his head.

Major Hart was musing and studying the ceiling. 'It will take some time for the papers to go through,' he said. 'And I was studying the hours-flown figures today. You've got some aircraft commanders near the limit for this month. We're going to need every ship we have within a few days. You know, I suppose, about the operation coming up?'

'I . . . heard something about it,' Blood managed to answer. 'Nothing definite, sir.'

'Well, it'll be definite tomorrow. Lieutenant Rauch went

out to recon the area today, and I'm going up with the colonel in the morning. You're not to let any of this out, of course.'

'Of course, sir.'

'Well, to make it short, if I ground him now, we'll have to import an aircraft commander to make up our complement of gunships, and since it's a battalion operation, I suspect there won't be any aircraft commanders available anywhere else, either. That could be hard to explain – why we're not using a flyable pilot. There's no sense getting the colonel in on this. Is the Bear's ship of any use at all to you, as things are now?'

'The rest of the crew is fine, sir!' Blood said. 'They do their best. It's hard for them to press an attack home, when the AC . . . when the AC won't fire. But at least there's another ship up there for Charley to have to keep an eye on.'

'All right,' Major Hart said. 'Let him fly, then. Ben,' he said to Martin, 'get the papers started. You can tell the Bear before tomorrow's briefing. And Del,' he said, turning back to Blood, 'thank you. You've made me see what needs to be done. We need more officers who keep an eye out for their men.'

Blood, seeing no better way, took the thanks and bowed out hastily.

As he sought through the file for a form, Martin stole several glances at the major, trying to decide what he really thought of Blood's visit. The major was sucking at his empty pipe. Whenever his eyes met Martin's he smiled benignly.

The helicopters began to gather at the pickup zone before dawn. Companies thundered down out of the darkness and crossed the gray foredawn in tight formations. Gunships ranging the flanks of the formations circled lazily out over the paddies and returned to settle at the edge of the PZ as the slicks dragged in alongside the troops spread across the middle of the field. Arab Six, the battalion commander's ship, came in alone and parked to one side near the head of the column of slicks. Blood left his ship at the head of the five Wolfpack gunships and plunged off across the rutted field toward the command ship in order to arrive before the other element leaders. He slowed when he saw Baker already there. Baker had been promoted to major, and he was XO of the Mustang company now. Blood did not want to have to talk to Baker. He had not seen Baker since Martin became XO, and he did not want to see him now.

In the open ships it was chilly. Cripps huddled in his flight jacket, but Handy sat on the cabin floor running a cleaning rod through the barrel of his weapon.

Arp came back from the ship ahead of Bear's. Bear's was the last in the Wolfpack element. He was flying behind Arp because Blood had sent him out of his own fire team once he saw there was no longer a point in counting leftover rockets. A special maintenance effort to get everything flying for Major Hart's mission had got five Wolfpack gunships up, and Blood was leading a three-ship heavy fire team.

Arp stamped his feet against the chill and studied the eastern horizon. The cloudless sky promised warmth once the sun was up. 'It looks like you get a good sendoff for your last day,' Arp said. He spoke in a low voice. Bear, who had not told anyone of this coming departure, gave him a sidelong glance but said nothing.

'Or,' Arp went on, 'maybe we can call it your first day.' He punched Bear's arm gently.

Captain Martin, coming up from his aircraft at the trail position in the company formation, turned from his path toward Arab Six to pass by the Bear's ship. 'Well,' he said, 'here it is at last. End of the line. Starting this evening you'll be a ground-pounder, until your transfer goes through.' That he spoke in Arp's presence told the Bear how Arp knew.

Now that the time had come, a sense of loss filled the Bear, for the shame of leaving his friends behind to do what he would not was still with him. 'I wish there was another way to do it,' he said.

'If you find one, let me know,' Martin said. He went on toward the leaders' briefing.

The field began to brighten. The briefing was not yet over when Blood came streaming back across the dew-whitened grass. 'I'd better see what that is,' Arp said. He went up to meet Blood beside his own ship. Bear could see Blood's breath condense around him as he huffed violently at Arp, shook his head, puffed again, and finally waved a hand palm-out in disgust and marched off once more. Arp came back to the Bear's ship.

'It all looked exciting,' Bear said.

'Very. The Mustangs are short a gunship this morning. We have to send them one.'

The Bear sighed and pulled on his gloves. He did not want to fly with strangers today. It would be hard enough with men he knew. But he had no doubt that Blood had sent him to the other company and given Arp their own extra ship. 'Where are they parked?' he asked.

'Never mind that,' Arp said. 'I'm going myself. Blood is sending Ward back here to fly with you. You'll be in charge of the fire team.'

'Me?' Bear cried. 'Why?'

'You sound just like Blood,' Arp grinned. He tapped Bear on the shoulder again and stepped down from the door. 'It'll be a milk run. And you deserve your place back as fire-team leader for your last day.'

Bear knew that he could have argued and got out of it. But Arp had argued with Blood for his sake, simply as a kind gesture. He did not have the heart to argue in turn. He gave Arp a thumbs-up sign through the windscreen. Arp waved and walked on away. In a moment Arp's ship began to crank, and Ward's hovered out and moved in behind Bear.

The meeting broke up. The first lift of troops was aboard the slicks. Arab Six had turned on his beacon, and the whole formation began to crank. As the blades spun up in slow drunken swings that gradually vanished into stable transparent discs above the fuselages of the helicopters, the sun leaped from the sea, and the whole field trembled with lightning as the blades caught the sun. Gunships slid away low over the fields and peeled off in their loose teams of two or three. Behind them Arab Six climbed steeply out, and the whole formation took to the air and turned west toward the mountains.

Bear's unease passed as the slicks discharged their loads into the first landing zone. There was no enemy fire. Troops strolled across the open field toward a tree line as the slicks thundered away. It was a cold LZ, and it was the only dangerous one on the list. Two other infantry companies were to be inserted, but they would go into the pacified fields nearer the coast. Bear turned the controls over to Ruth.

With his ship empty Martin gave it to his copilot to fly on the return to the PZ. The copilot was a new warrant officer. Martin knew the face and the name, but he had hardly spoken to the man. That was the worst thing about not flying, for him: his comrades, the men on whom his life might depend, were nothing but names on a list. Martin studied the man as he flew. The ship was in the slot behind a V of three others, and the pilot was nervous. His neck was rigid; his right hand engulfed the cyclic stick. 'Don't strangle it,' Martin said dryly. Then he laughed. The man gave him a sidelong sheepish grin and relaxed his hand. The fingers soon crept back around the stick; but Martin knew that the man would work out his tension now, if left alone. He turned to watch the show outside the ship.

Martin wished he could be with Arab Six high overhead, or in a gunship – not to be able to fire on the enemy, but only to see better. Even from the inside, from the trail ship in the first of three elements, the formation was a beautiful thing, a dense phalanx of aircraft pressing forward as war swirled around it. Gunships crossed and recrossed at different levels, like goldfish swirling in a bowl. Chinooks with artillery pieces dangling from their umbilical connections barged past, while air strikes flashed and rumbled along the ridgelines. Nothing could match it.

The ships refueled after the second sortie. The guns had no need to rearm – no ship had fired a round. They had time to spare, and they shut down in the PZ for a short time. 'Damn dull, this,' Atterburn said. 'I see Arab Six got tired of it and *di-di*'d for home. Let's hope for more action, eh, Bear?'

'If it keeps up like this,' Bear answered, 'we'll all live long happy lives.'

'Not you, damn you. You'll screw yourself to death with your nurse.'

'Thank God it's not contagious,' Bear said. He was too happy to be offended by Atterburn.

'You certainly haven't caught it, anyway, Burn,' Arp said. 'How's it going, Bear?' The Mustangs had shut down at the same time, and he had come back to check on his fire team.

'Quiet,' Atterburn answered for Bear. 'Just the way he likes it.'

'Would we all had as much sense,' Arp said.

'Shoot, Lieutenant, it ain't much, but it's the only war we got,' Atterburn said.

The third sortie had been changed from the original objective. It was to go into the river valley west of Quang Ngai. Bear checked the coordinates on his chart during the wait; but he did not recognize the place until the formation turned the corner of the mountain. Then he knew it at once. The houses were still there, clustered beneath the tattered palm trees like chicks under the ragged wings of a long-legged jungle fowl. It was a village he had seen evacuated, its people moved to 'pacified' territory. The village was to have been burned: there should have been nothing but ashes; but roofs and walls winked at him in the sun. Far ahead a buffalo was browsing along the edge of the paddy.

'Ah, Wolf Lead, do you have that fuck-ox in sight?' a voice asked on the VHF radio, the gunship frequency. It was Block, the pilot of the second ship in Blood's fire team.

'That's affirm.' Blood had on his professional voice.

'Ain't he in a free-fire zone?'

'That's affirmative.'

'Permission to fire?'

'Let's go.' Blood's fire team was on the opposite flank from the Bear, out along the river. A puff of black smoke issued from the tailpipe of Blood's ship as it nosed over and accelerated across the front of the formation of slicks a mile behind the gunships.

'Sir, what've they got?' Handy asked in sudden excitement. He could hear only the intercom on his headset, not the radios; but he had seen the other ships dash forward.

'Vey have a fierce buffalo,' Ruth said, laughing. Blood's ship spat a pair of rockets which arced ahead as two glowing dots that touched the earth and sent two muddy fountains into the air behind the startled buffalo. The buffalo did not stay to chat but broke into a frenzied run in the direction in which his nose was pointed. The second ship was armed with a grenade launcher. It came in low behind Blood, sending out a stream of forty-millimeter grenades whose flashes rippled under the buffalo and threw it rump upward onto the paddy dike beside the village. The two gunships swung away over the paddy and back toward the first element of slicks now beginning a long final approach to the paddy.

'Good shootin',' Handy said enviously on the intercom. 'Good shooting, Two,' Blood's voice echoed over the VHF.

Across Blood's voice Major Hart's said on the company FM frequency, 'Wolf, we're taking fire.' His voice was unmistakable, ancient and craggy but somehow restful despite the urgency of the words.

All the radios were talking at once. The Bear had switched his transmitter to FM: 'Coyote Six, where's your fire?'

'Uncertain, Wolf,' Major Hart said. 'No tracers.'

'They're taking fire,' Bear said on the intercom. Handy and Cripps came to their feet instantly. They hung one-handed in the doors searching the ground ahead as Bear rolled the ship toward the village.

'Ready to go hot?' Ruth asked. Bear affirmed with two clicks of the mike switch, knowing that he should have given the command before that. Ruth flipped the switches to the armed position.

As the ship flashed over the buffalo, they could hear the rattle of a machine gun.

'Where is it?' Bear asked.

'Can't see anything,' Handy answered. Ruth was hanging half out his window. Both of the crew in back strained against their safety straps.

'Wolf, we have fire from ten o'clock,' Major Hart's voice said.

'There! There's somebody down there!' Handy exclaimed. He was pointing his machine gun down into the village.

Bear had seen the figure, too. It was a young boy, unarmed. 'Hold your fire!' he said desperately. Had all the villagers really been evacuated? 'Do you see a weapon?'

'No weapon,' Handy said.

'Wait until we come around then.' He said over the radio, 'Coyote Six, do you have the weapon located?'

'Negative, Wolf,' was Major Hart's answer. Even now his voice had a soothing, fatherly sound, as if to minimize the importance of his problems.

'That's Charley, sir!' Handy protested.

Bear switched back to the gunship frequency. 'Ward, do you have the weapon?'

'Negative,' Ward answered him.

'Dammit, work over the village!' Blood called. His return from the pass at the buffalo had taken him out of range for the thirty seconds in which the Bear's team had been inbound. During that time the slicks had come from a mile distant onto a long straight final approach toward the village. If a weapon were there, the relative motion of the slicks would be almost zero. They would be fat sitting ducks that grew in size with every passing second.

Bear made a short run out and wrenched the ship back inbound. Suddenly gunfire rattled like popcorn around the ship. 'Where is he?' Bear called. 'Where is he?'

'We got to get some fire on the village!' Handy insisted.

'Wait.' Sweat ran down his nose from beneath his helmet. The trap had closed about him. He must fire, somewhere; but he could not fire blindly today, of all days.

Suddenly voices were calling out on the FM: 'Two's hit!' 'Four is hit!' But the formation drove steadily earthward, and landed. Troops scrambled for the cover of the dike. All of the ships were off the ground as Blood's rockets began to fall into the village.

'There!' Ruth shouted on the intercom: 'There!' A burst of tracers had streaked from beyond the edge of the village, from the perpendicular dike at the far end. Ruth had his gunsight trained on the spot without waiting for an order to fire. The flex guns muttered their fierce hate. Bear lined up the rocket sight, leveled the bubble, and touched the red button with his thumb. The range was so short the rockets exploded almost under the ship.

The slicks had nowhere to go except over the machine gun. As they scrambled for speed and altitude, the lead ship dropped suddenly from the formation. 'Mayday, Mayday. Coyote Six going down.' Major Hart's voice did not rise even to the level of excitement. It was his only communication. His ship nosed up and slid to a mud-spewing halt in the next paddy, a quarter mile beyond the village.

'Six, stay close,' someone called. 'We're coming in after you.' The trail ship in the formation had broken away and turned back, racing in low and downwind. But there was now no one on the lead ship to hear. The crew were out and scrambling for the shelter of the nearest dike. Out in the paddy the ship was the center of a storm of bullets.

The Bear heard, and recognized the voice. It was Captain Martin.

The men on the ground had strung out in a line. Major Hart was the last. It was a long run to the dike. Martin's ship jinked twice like a broken-field runner, made a last hard turn, and dropped ahead of the first of them. As it touched the ground, the men began to fall – first Major Hart, then the two ahead of him. None rose again. The fourth, although he was far ahead, turned back. He took the arm of one fallen man over his shoulder and started again for the waiting ship.

Martin saw the tracers streak across the paddy ahead of him. He put them out of his mind. He took his eyes from the men on the ground, too. The only thing that mattered was the one spot on the ground where the ship would touch down. He was running downwind and much too fast. If he overshot the spot, the machine gun might be on them before he could turn and hover back. He pulled the cyclic back against the stop and pushed down the collective pitch. The nose of the ship came up. With the big blade acting as a brake the airspeed indicator unwound: fifty knots, forty, thirty. The ship floated, floated. The tail skid touched the mud. He felt it, as if a guiding hand had brought the tail up for him. He pulled the power back in as the skids touched. The ship slid to a halt.

He did not see the men fall. He did not need to. 'One . . . no, three of them are down!' the crew chief called out. When he had time to look, Griggs was staggering toward the ship with Major Hart's crew chief over his shoulder.

Griggs tumbled the crew chief onto the cabin floor and fell in behind him. 'I think they've had it!' he shouted to Martin.

Martin picked the ship up from the ground, turned toward the two bodies collapsed in the mud. Neither one was moving. He hovered the ship toward them. Something in the air caught his eye. White flakes were fluttering all around him. They came flashing down through the blade and were spread through the air over the paddy. Snow? No, they were butterflies! They dodged and drifted across the paddy, fearless in their innocence. 'Look at that!' he said. Then the butterflies were joined by other white flashes that twinkled across the windscreen.

The pilot flying with Martin did not see the butterflies. He was looking at the bodies on the ground. But he saw the tracers. They snapped around the ship and dug little spurts of mud alongside the bodies. Then they slammed against the ship.

The life went out of the controls. The pilot looked over at Martin. Martin was slumped forward against his harness, and his hand had fallen from the cyclic stick. The stick kicked against the pilot's hand. The hydraulic boost was gone. He pulled at the collective to bring the ship higher off the ground. It took all his strength to move the collective at all. Another bullet hammered through the ship.

'Take 'er out!' Griggs was shouting. 'We can't do anything here!'

The pilot forced the nose over and accelerated away.

Bear saw Martin's ship climbing away, and the two bodies still sprawled on the red mud of the paddy. For one instance he started down after them. Before he was close to the ground, bullets pounded against his ship. A Christmas tree of warning lights lit up the console. He would have gone in anyway, but as he turned toward the paddy he glanced across at Ruth in the left seat. Ruth was on the controls, following him through. His dark visor was down so that the Bear could not see his eyes, but his tongue was licking his tight lips. Ruth did not want to go in, but it was not his place to say that. He was on the controls, as he should be, ready to try to complete whatever mission his aircraft commander chose.

Bear pulled in full power and broke away.

Bear's ship sat alone in the fuel pits as a maintenance team out from Duc Pho for the day poked at its guts, while the ships still able to fly continued the lift. Before the last of the warning lights was extinguished, other gunships and an air strike had pounded the village. The troops had worked their way up on foot from paddy to paddy, and the machine gun had been silenced. Bear and his crew rejoined the company for the last sortie. The sky was clear. Sunlight sparkled from the paddy. The bodies of Major Hart and Durand, his door gunner, lay there, biding their time, ripening in the sun along with the dead buffalo so sportively upended on the paddy dike. A pall of smoke rolled from the village. It had burned at last.

Dustoff had finished their work with the living wounded farther back down the village perimeter and reached the final paddy during this last sortie. The medevac aircraft commander checked in with the gunships during his approach. Bear knew Wolcheski's voice. As the gunships blazed along the tree line, the red-crossed helicopter flashed in low over the treetops, flared to a quick stop, snatched the bodies aboard, and was gone.

The slain buffalo remained, to the delight of its growing coterie of flies.

There was no overhead break when the formation came back from the mission that day. On other days the ships that had flown in a combat assault would fly the length of the landing lane in tight formation at five hundred feet, and on reaching the end would break sharply away one at a time in a diving turn to slide easily over the landing pad at four-second intervals. After a good mission there would be smoke grenades tied to the skids, to be set off by the crew members pulling a wire tied to the pin.

The grenades had been put on the skids that morning, but they were not used. The ships came directly over the ridge and hovered to their revetments. Lieutenant Rauch did not come out of his Operations hooch to watch them land. Aircraft commanders turned in their reports in silence and walked away. Only Griggs and Captain Blood showed any animation. Griggs, who was back from the dead, was licensed to show his relief in ways that would not have been tolerated that day in others. Also, Griggs was a hero, for he had risked his life in turning back to pick up Murchison, the crew chief. Special tolerance was extended to heroes, at least for the first day. Griggs exercised his license by becoming rapidly – almost instantly – drunk and roaming from hooch to hooch recounting the great events in exhaustive detail.

As for Blood, he left the platoon after-action report with Rauch and was off at once 'to get things squared away over at the orderly room.'

'What's to square away over there?' the Operations sergeant wondered.

'He means,' Rauch said, 'that he's goin' to get his rear behind the major's desk and hope the colonel lets him stay there.'

'God help us!' the sergeant responded.

Although he didn't mean to do it, it was Ward who started the speculation that this time the Bear would be grounded forever. 'Why wouldn't Bear let us fire?' he asked Ruth. Ward was no enemy of the Bear. Although he had heard rumors, he ordinarily flew in a different fire team. He remembered the old Bear, and he assumed that there were good reasons for not firing.

Ruth said nothing. But Griggs had heard the question. At the time it happened, Griggs was too busy with other matters to wonder what the guns were doing. Now, safe on the ground, he became alarmed over the value of the skin he had so nearly lost. 'Not fi'? Wh'cha mean, not fi'? What the hell're gunships for if they don't fi'?' he demanded. Griggs, who had no great opinion of anyone's ability but his own, had heard the rumors, too, and had always thought that a reputation as great as the Bear's had been must be overblown enough to leak somewhere. 'Was that bastard not shootin' 'gen? I'll be damn' 'f I'm goin' fly with a asshole who won' be with me when the bullets fly!'

'Don't worry, Captain Blood will take care of that,' Atterburn said. Atterburn flew with Blood day in and day out. He had seen the list of rockets not fired grow day by day. He knew what its purpose must be. But he did not know that the list had already been expended. He assumed that Blood was preparing to use it.

Atterburn was wrong. The Bear was not then in Blood's mind at all. He had thought it all through already, and dismissed it from his mind. There was the perfect case against the man, of course. But Blood knew, without really bringing that part of the matter to his consciousness at all, that if the company had been without gunship support because the Bear's fire team had not fired, someone was sure to ask where the other fire team had been at the critical instant. Out of range chasing a buffalo? What?

Blood sat at the major's desk leafing through the day's papers. The morning report was unsigned: the major had gone out before it was prepared. Blood signed it as ranking officer in the company. But the morning report was not enough. He needed to get the attention of the battalion commander somehow. Time was everything. The colonel was not really high enough, either. The CG would be better;

but he was out of reach. If Blood had been a Ringknocker like Martin, he supposed, he could have done it. They had their ways. But if you weren't one of them, what you wanted you had to get on your own.

Blood pounded the desk in frustration. The company was here, leaderless. It needed him. He could take it over and remake it into what it should be, a superb fighting machine. But first he had to get it in his hands. He *would* find a way to get the attention of the chain of command. He squared the major's papers neatly in the center of the desk, pulled himself into a perfectly rigid military seated posture, and proceeded to think the problem through in a military manner.

'First Sergeant!'

From the time Captain Blood disappeared into the major's office, the first sergeant had been sitting at his desk staring furiously at one sheet of paper. Now he banged it down on his desk, looked at his morning report clerk with a look that, if the clerk had been combustible, would have set him aflame, and forced himself to march to the opening in the plywood screen. 'Sir?'

'First Sergeant,' Captain Blood said, 'have you started arrangements for the memorial service?'

'No, sir. Memorial service, sir?'

'Yes. For the men we lost today. For Major Hart, and . . . the executive officer. And a crew chief.'

'Door gunner, sir.'

'Yes, door gunner. I think a memorial service is in order, for men who made that sacrifice. I want it tomorrow.'

'Tomorrow. Yes, sir. Any particular thing you had in mind, sir?'

'Yes.' Blood knew just the thing he had in mind. He had attended one at another company while he was still flying in the slick platoon. It needed some sprucing up, but he would see to that. It would be a memorial service he would be proud to have for himself, if he were to fall in battle. A company should honor its fallen. That was one of the things this company lacked. It had no traditions. No decent honor for the fallen.

On the wide hover lane of the parking ramp, between the ranks of revetments on the seaward side and the landward, the company was drawn up in platoons abreast. The revetments were nearly all occupied by helicopters: the sun was almost down, and all but the long resupply missions had returned. A forest of blades slanted upward all around the men. A single helicopter was parked across the center of the hover lane at the front of the formation. In its open cargo door three helmets lay in wreaths of evergreen branches.

The men were ill at ease in their long straight lines on the ramp. There had not been a company formation with men and officers together within the memory of any of those present. Although they stood at parade rest, there was shuffling of feet and a low murmur of voices from within the ranks. Parade drills seemed years distant to all of them.

Captain Blood had positioned himself the regulation twelve steps in front of the center of the company, where he was braced at a rigid parade rest as he waited for the battalion commander. Although he did not turn his head, he was aware of the fidgeting in the ranks. The men – and the officers, too – could fight a war, but they had forgotten how to be an army. They needed more discipline and a leader to hold them together and make them a fighting unit and not a mob. Blood pleased himself with the thought until the colonel came down the edge of the hover lane on foot.

With the colonel were the battalion sergeant major, the chaplain, and a major whom Blood did not recognize at first. When they came closer, Blood saw that it was Baker. He did not have time to wonder why Baker was there. He brought the company to attention and greeted the colonel: 'Sir, the company is formed!' His salute had snap to it; his hand vibrated as though the arm contained more energy than could be dissipated by a salute alone.

The colonel tossed off a salute in return. 'All right, Captain Blood. Begin when you're ready, then. The CG sends his regrets.'

'Yes, sir.' The colonel's remark hollowed Blood's reply; but it was not a soldier's place to show disappointment at the actions of his commanding general. Blood executed a smart about-face, commanded 'Puh-raid, *rest*!,' faced about, stepped into line with the colonel's party, faced about again, and nodded to the chaplain to begin their rehearsed ceremony. The company had slid to thankful ease, feet apart and hands somewhere behind the back.

At the chaplain's suggestion a microphone had been set up between the company commander's position and the formation. The chaplain stepped to the microphone and suggested, 'Let us pray.'

The chaplain was wily in the ways of men standing in formation. A merciful God would not hold his men long at parade rest. Nor did the God of Battles care for cajolery. The prayer was short and unobsequious.

When the chaplain had stepped back, Captain Blood marched forward again, but not all the way to the microphone. A leader with a command voice could dispense with artificial aids. He read at the top of his voice from the note cards he had been carrying in the palm of his left hand: 'Major Howard Hart, born 1928, entered the United States Army in 1949. He was commissioned second lieutenant, Infantry, United States Army Reserve, in 1951, upon completion of Officer Candidate School, Fort Benning, Georgia. He served his country with distinction in war and in peace. In the Korean War he was wounded twice and decorated twice for bravery. His awards and decorations are the Purple Heart, three awards, the Bronze Star for valor, two awards, the Bronze Star for service, the Air Medal with ten oak leaf clusters, the Korean Service Medal, and the Vietnam Service Medal, two awards. He died in battle, in the service of his country, fifteen January, nineteen sixty-eight.'

The Bear, buried within the ranks of the warrant officers drawn up in front of the enlisted men, heard out this capsule life of a man whose death weighed on him. Hart was born, he was commissioned, he was awarded, he died. Was it all the Army knew of him? Or only all that mattered to Blood? The records were a sieve too gross to catch the man himself. He had dropped through without a trace. Where were the kindness, the concern for his men, the love of the country in whose service he *had* died? Where was even the concern that he might remain in that service, the concern, Bear thought ruefully, which led him to cling too long to the rotten thread, the man who failed him and so caused his death? He had passed away from all that. That it even had existed, no one now could tell. He was a pile of paper, which told what was of no importance to anyone.

And Captain Martin. Blood marked his milestones, too. It was a shorter life, but brighter as the Army saw such things. Born 1940. Educated United States Military Academy at West Point. First Captain of Cadets. Honor graduate, Ranger School, Fort Benning, Georgia; Outstanding Officer award, Airborne School, Fort Benning, Georgia. Awards and decorations: Distinguished Flying Cross, the Bronze Star for service, the Air Medal with two oak leaf clusters, the Vietnam Service Medal, the Purple Heart. Died in battle, January 15, 1968.

The record said more, that Blood did not say: letter of reprimand, ending his useful career as an officer of the United States Army. And what the record did not comprehend: an intelligent man who felt what some would say no intelligent man could feel - love for the military and its traditions of honor and service, while despising the insensitivity and brutishness that passed, with some, for dedication to duty; an ambitious man who knew what his merits deserved, but did not brag, and who rose by his merits, and not (as Blood's envy told him) by influence (or if by influence, only by the influence his merits earned among those who knew him); a man believing in himself, determined to endure and conquer what would finish lesser men; a man conquered by that which conquers all men.

And the gunner Durand. He was born, he went for a soldier, he died January 15, 1968, having been awarded the Vietnam Service Medal and the Purple Heart.

Blood called the company to attention and present arms. Behind the formation, from behind one of the revetments where a helicopter stood, taps sounded. But as the bugle call rang across the air between the ridge and the sea, a helicopter was running up at the company down the ramp. The sound of the bugle was lost in the crescendo of the blade coming to operating speed. As the men saluted, the helicopter hovered out of its revetment to the takeoff lane and turned to face the sea. Blood cursed to himself and made a mental note to coordinate the next ceremony with the neighboring company; but to the Bear there was nothing about the ceremony so moving as the appearance of his unplanned visitor. It hovered easily in the last sunlight, hanging delicately, impossibly, suspended, like a soul about to depart. As the bugle call died it dipped its nose and moved away to mount the hill of air, leaving behind a long sigh.

'Order, arms!' Blood's voice rang down the ramp. He ordered the platoon commanders, 'Dismiss your platoons!,' took their salutes on one of his own, and turned toward the colonel full of self-congratulation as the company was dissolved behind him. Blood saluted the colonel again. The salute was not required by the field manual on drill and ceremonies. It was merely an expression of good feeling. In spite of the wayward helicopter Blood was happy. The ceremony had made him sentimental himself. He thanked the colonel for coming.

'It's the least I could do,' the colonel said. 'But I'd have been coming anyway. I think you know Major Baker?' He turned to include Baker in the conversation. 'Major Baker is your new commanding officer.'

Blood's happiness dissolved and flowed away like the men streaming off among the revetments.

'I tried to talk Division into giving me two field grades,' the colonel added. 'Or at least a senior captain. We must be the only battalion in country that's underranked. But the buggers wouldn't do it. They said they'd try to get us a first lieutenant next month. Or squeeze the pipeline for a couple of junior captains. So, it looks like you two are it.' He grinned at them at the end. 'It's your company. Try not to wreck it.' The colonel had liked Martin and Hart. He did not like Baker or Blood, either one; but they were the senior officers available, and Division, for reasons that escaped him, would not pry loose an outside officer. The colonel hid his distaste under apparent irony. A reputation for ironic humor could be useful at times: no one knew when you were serious.

'Sir, we're gonna do you proud,' Baker said. Blood saluted again and said nothing.

When he saw his name on the duty roster, Bear set straight out for company headquarters. He walked past the company clerk and straight to the back, behind the plywood partitions where Baker and Blood's desks were.

Blood was alone, staring gloomily across to Baker's side of the room. 'Who the hell invited you in here?' he demanded.

'I saw my name on the duty roster,' Bear said.

'Bingo. You can read. Learn to shoot, and maybe you'll be worth a shit after all.'

'Major Hart approved a transfer to Dustoff for me,' Bear said.

'Don't look like you're gone to me,' Blood said. 'How'd that happen?'

'That's what I came to ask.'

'I don't know anything about a transfer,' Blood said. 'You got your ten-forty-nine?'

'No. But Captain Martin told me it was approved.'

'Oh? It's convenient that Captain Martin is dead, isn't it?'

'For some people it is,' Bear said.

Blood was not to be baited into anything. 'So you want to go to Dustoff, eh?' he asked.

'Yes, sir.'

'Tired of being shot at, are you? Ready to crawl off where it's safe? That's right, Bear, let a *soldier* die.'

He dismissed the Bear with a wave of his hand. But as Bear turned to go, Blood called him back. 'This came down from Battalion,' Blood said. 'Your name's on it.' He tossed Bear a box. It contained Bear's third Distinguished Flying Cross.

'Bear, what are you still doing here?' Arp asked. The Bear

was lying on his side on a bunk in the alert hooch, resting one cheek on the backs of his hands like the reclining Buddha carved on a mountainside east of Saigon.

'I keep asking myself that,' the Bear answered without moving. He fetched up a long sigh, then rolled up to a sitting position. 'The answer I keep getting,' he said, 'is that I'm on standby.'

Arp had just landed from escorting a pickup assault with the Mustangs, and he was tired of war for the day. 'I thought you were done with this business,' he said.

'I guess that makes two of us who were wrong,' Bear answered.

It increased Arp's irritation that Bear showed no concern at still being on standby. 'Aren't you supposed to be on ground duty?'

'That's a matter of opinion. The opinion of the Operations officer is that I'm supposed to be on standby. My day off isn't until tomorrow.'

'What do you mean, your "day off"? You're done. *Fini. Hẽt rôi.*' Heads up and down the hooch turned toward them as Arp said this. What they thought, Arp did not care. He supposed they thought he meant that the Bear was being grounded for failure to fire the day before. 'I'm going to see Rauch about this.'

'Rauch's opinion comes from the CO,' Bear said, 'so you can save that step. And,' he added, 'the CO's comes from the XO.'

'Blood? What kind of horse manure is it now? He knew about your ten-forty-nine! I'll go see him, then.'

'I already did that,' Bear said quietly. He had pulled his legs up under himself on the bed so that he looked more the Buddha then ever, and had folded his hands in his lap. He was meditating on the space between the balls of his thumbs held a quarter-inch apart. The thumbs had a barely visible tremor. 'The Blood doesn't know anything about any ten-forty-nine,' he said.

Arp turned without a word and went out of the hooch. To Rauch in the Operations hooch he said, 'Give me the keys to your jeep. I'm going to the orderly room.'

'If it's about the Bear, I'll tell you for a fact you're wastin' your time, Stud.'

'Probably. Now, are you going to give me your damn keys?'

'Sure.' Rauch tossed them across the counter.

Blood was alone behind the screen in the orderly room. He was sitting with his arms folded, leaning back in Martin's chair, studying the empty chair behind the commander's desk opposite him. Arp's sudden appearance brought Blood quickly down to a more military posture. 'What do you want, Lieutenant?' he demanded, as if in his translation from platoon commander to executive officer Arp's name had been lost from his mind.

'I want to talk about the Bear, sir.'

'Well?'

'He's still on standby in the gun platoon.'

'You *are* his acting platoon commander, Lieutenant,' Blood said. 'If you want him to have the day off, give it to him. Just so somebody flies the missions.'

'You know it isn't the *day* off, sir,' Arp said. 'He has papers in for a transfer to Dustoff. Major Hart had arranged for him to be on ground duty until that came through. He was not to fly guns again. That ought to be honored.'

'As his platoon commander,' Blood said, 'you ought to know how short of pilots we are. As for the transfer, your warrant officer came to see me about that. According to the first sergeant and the clerks, nobody ever gave them one to send up. I know he did request a transfer to medevac. As I hear it, Major Hart turned it down. I think there was a nurse down at the hospital, if I'm not mistaken?'

'You're mistaken,' Arp said. 'Captain Martin told me that the transfer had been approved, and that you know about it.'

'I can't say what Captain Martin might of approved,' Captain Blood said, his drawl deepening as he spoke. 'But I'll tell you this: the only thing that matters is what Major Hart put his John Henry on and sent up through channels; and there ain't been a ten-forty-nine out of this office. Now if

Martin said I knew about any other deals, he was just plain wrong.'

'Then I want to see the CO,' Arp said. He knew already how hopeless that would be. But whatever he had to lose had been cast away already, by coming to Blood, and he was determined now to press the issue to the end.

'Does that mean you're calling me a liar, Lieutenant?' Blood asked.

'Yes, sir,' Arp said.

Blood's next words astonished Arp, who thought he knew his captain through and through. Blood said in a low voice, calm but intense, 'Lieutenant Arp, I'm goin' to forget you ever said that. Okay?'

Arp could think only that somewhere there existed paperwork on the Bear's transfer that had escaped Blood's hands. Arp had no hopes and no illusions of aid from Baker; but a signed ten-forty-nine in Major Hart's hand might embarrass Blood enough to make him give in. So Blood's words only encouraged Arp. 'Forget it if you want, sir,' he said, 'but I'm going to take it to the CO.'

'Then you're a damn fool!' Blood snapped. In fact his reason for the sudden uncharacteristic offer was not fear, or not fear of unknown paperwork. He had already put beyond reach the draft that had been in Martin's desk. Nor was it any concern for Arp, whom he considered an overeducated wise-ass whose rich father protected him from his smart tongue. But he would have traded the chance to court-martial Arp for the chance to separate him from the Bear. Blood could understand why Martin would stick out his neck to get the Bear out of the company alive. Martin and the Bear were both mush-hearted; and Martin owed him something for the mess at Hill 473. But Arp owed the Bear nothing. Having him spurn what Blood meant to look like friendship was like seeing Martin, not even in his grave, come back to life. 'Major Baker will be back from Battalion right shortly,' Blood said. 'You can see him anytime he's got the time to waste on you, Lieutenant, as far as I'm concerned. But don't expect too much.'

The sound of Baker's jeep pulling down over the dirt bank behind the orderly room stopped any reply Arp might have made. Baker came in the back door, talking excitedly before the door was open: 'Blood, there's big times comin'. Big times. It's goin' to be . . . Well. Lieutenant Arp. I didn't know you had the day off. Have you killed all the Chinamen in country so quick?'

'The lieutenant wants to talk to you about one of his officers,' Blood said. 'A bug-eyed one.'

'Oh, yeah? Are you ready to cashier that turd so quick, Arp? It's about time somebody did.'

'I'm ready to get him out of the company,' Arp said.

'A dandy idea. What have you got on him?'

'Major Hart approved a transfer for him before . . . before he was killed. I want to see it go through.'

'What kind of transfer?' Baker asked, putting aside his offhand manner.

'He was supposed to go to Dustoff.'

Baker pursed his lips. 'You know anything about this, Blood?'

'No. No, sir.' Blood had difficulty remembering that Baker now outranked him; but when he did remember, he added the proper tag. 'I know that he asked Major Hart for a transfer and got turned down. He has a girl friend up at the hospital, I hear.'

'That right, Arp?'

'No.'

Baker raised his eyebrows in an exaggerated query. 'No girl friend? I've seen him with a nurse, Arp, with my own two little eyeballs. What kind of dummkopf do you think I am?'

'That part is true,' Arp admitted, 'but Major Hart approved the transfer.'

'Well, show me the paper.'

'I don't have it, sir,' Arp said. He looked closely at Blood as he said this; but Blood showed no sign of knowing more than he was telling.

'Hart sure as hell didn't transfer anyone out without paperwork,' Baker suggested, raising his open hands palm up and shrugging his shoulders. 'God himself couldn't do that.'

'No. But maybe he hadn't forwarded it yet.'

'Come off it, Arp! My XO just said that Hart turned down the transfer. Have you seen any paperwork, Blood?'

'No.' Blood left off the 'sir' this time. He did not care for having Baker call him 'his' XO. 'Neither has the first sergeant,' he added sullenly.

'Well, Arp?'

Arp said stubbornly, 'Captain Blood knows it was approved, sir.'

'He just said he didn't.'

'I know.'

Baker, who had been pacing between his own desk and Blood's, threw himself impatiently into his chair. 'Jesus H. Christ, Arp, what are you after? If I wasn't so damn short of officers, I'd have you court-martialed for insulting my XO! And I'll tell you one thing – even if I had the paperwork in my hand, I wouldn't forward it. *I* have to run this company now, Arp, and I am not goin' to give up any warm bodies until our replacements improve. As I was starting out to tell Blood, there are some big missions coming. G-2 has the word out that Charley is going to be all over this area for Tet. I don't plan to give up anyone who can fly a helicopter; not even as poor an excuse for a gun driver as that one in your platoon. Now, is that clear enough for you?'

'He's no good where he is now, sir!' Arp pleaded. 'For God's sake, let him go where he can do some good! What can you gain by holding him on? If nothing else, put him in a slick platoon!'

'Isn't he the great gun driver?' Baker asked rhetorically. 'I remember him telling me how it was done. Months ago. Let him show me, now.'

When Arp returned, the Bear was still lying on his bunk. Arp almost knocked down Cripps at the door. Cripps had been lurking there watching for his return. He muttered an apology and stepped aside guiltily, but stayed in the vicinity of Bear's bunk.

At the back of the room Atterburn was watching Handy fit together the newly cleaned pieces of a Thompson submachine gun. Handy had got it in a trade, for a Chinese rifle and an NVA straw cap. From time to time he lifted it in his left hand and shook his head admiringly, feeling its weight. It was too heavy for a grunt to carry. That was why the previous owner had parted with it so cheaply. But for a helicopter gunner, that was no objection. Handy loved it as the Bear had loved helicopters. He had no thoughts of sculpture, but he loved each piece of the weapon, loved their fine finish and their shapes and their weight in his hand and the exact way they slid together, because he loved the thing they became. 'Lookit that, sir!' he exclaimed to Atterburn as the bolt slid into place. 'Ain't she a beauty?'

Bear raised his head to look at Arp. 'I see how much satisfaction the great man gave you,' he said. 'I wish you hadn't bothered him. I have enough men's lives on my conscience already, without yours. Even if you would be the first lieutenant in my bag.' A self-deprecating smile sneaked out under his mustache as he said this, as if to show he knew that it was silly to worry about other men's lives. One hand came up to poke at the mustache, driving the smile back into refuge. 'But thanks,' he said. 'Thanks.'

When he smiled, the Bear's face had a mock-angelic look – a cherub with a mustache. Arp was not sorry for having tried to help him. He deserved better luck than he had got from this war. 'There's still a way out,' Arp said.

'I don't believe in suicide.' The smile came back briefly, giving his face the fugitive light of summer lightning reflected on far clouds.

'It doesn't have to be that serious,' Arp said.

'Don't wanna shoot myself in the foot, neither,' Bear said, picking up for a moment the drawl of a southern grunt they had once brought into a field hospital when he and Arp had both been flying slicks, so many months ago. The soldier had displayed a neat bullet hole in his left foot. (He had been left-handed.)

'If you can stand to be serious at all at a time like this,' Arp told him. 'you should consider having the flight surgeon ground you.'

The Bear's face instantly did become serious, more serious than Arp wanted. The hands went back to the meditating position. Bear said after a moment, 'There's nothing wrong with me, sir.'

'I didn't say there was anything wrong with you.'

'Then why would the flight surgeon ground me?'

'There are a potful of reasons for grounding people, Bear. You know that. You're nervous, for one thing – that's reason enough.'

'Oh, no. Nervous is one thing I'm not.' He held up his hands, with the thumbs still spaced a fraction of an inch. 'See there? No tremors.' The hands were steady. 'I can fly like an angel, sir. Check me out with any IP. They'll tell you.'

'Bear, you're no damn good as a gunnie! I hate to say it, but you know it's true. If you keep on, someone's likely to get killed!' His voice was low, but intense.

Bear laughed at that. It was a short, low laugh unlike his old cackle that shook his cheeks and belly. 'Oh, yes, I *am* a good gunnie! I can prove it!' He took out the box Blood had tossed to him, opened it, and held up a medal by its ribbon. 'See there? Certified. USDA Choice. My third Distinguished Flying Cross. Besides, how would anybody get killed the way I've been flying? My body count hasn't amounted to much lately. Ask Captain Blood!' He waved a hand to forestall Arp's objection. 'I know. You mean one of us. I'm sorry, sir, but I've thought it through. Lord, have I ever! When you shoot too soon, you get Hill Four Seven Three. How many men died to teach me that? And when you don't shoot soon enough, your friends die. Captain Martin and Major Hart died to teach me that.'

'That wasn't your fault, Bear,' Arp said. 'No one knew where the weapon was. If you'd done what Blood said and shot up the village, you'd just have been wasting ordnance, and you'd have been out of position to do any good at all. We might have lost *more* men.'

'Nice try, sir, but that doesn't help much. Whenever you

shoot, no matter if it's soon or late, someone dies. I don't know if you ever wonder who's down there, sir, where your rounds are falling. I hope not. But I keep seeing bodies – how they trailed away at Song Pra Khuc.' His voice trailed off. A deep silence had fallen in the hooch. 'Well,' he began again, 'you say, a man can quit. If he's had enough, he can have the balls to say, "Screw it. I've done what you said, and I won't anymore. So take your guns and stick 'em." But it's not . . . I can't get just myself out, sir. If I don't fly, somebody else flies in my place. Somebody dies doing my work. Covington died to teach me that. Ah, Cov! Lieutenant, the Army never told his wife he was dead. Did you know that? Pinky could have gone on from now till Doomsday morning thinking he was "missing." A hundred men could swear he's dead, but nobody told her. I almost didn't have the heart to tell her he died flying my mission. Sir, I don't want to have to tell anybody else's wife that. No one can be a pacifist when his friends are dying. If I'd gone to Dustoff, I'd at least have been sharing the load. But I'm not going to ground myself while I can still fly a ship. Death will still be there if I wash my hands of it.' He stood up, pulled on his cap, and turned to the others in the hooch. He looked them over one by one and then chortled to himself, almost like the Bear of old, and said with a shake of his head, 'I don't know why I go to all this trouble for *you* guys.' He went out and down the ramp toward the flight line. After a moment Arp went out and walked swiftly after him.

Atterburn said after they had gone, 'That Bear sure is a crazy bastard.'

Cripps lay on his cot and stared at the roof. After a long time he mumbled, 'They never even told her he was dead? How could they not tell her?'

Handy went to the door, but seeing Arp and the Bear on the ramp he went back to his table and began oiling the stock of the Thompson. 'Cripps,' he said, 'tell me if they get done down there. I got to get some oil on the miniguns.'

'Who'll ever get a chance to use them?' Atterburn snorted.

Handy shook his head sadly. 'You don't never know, sir,'

he said. 'He could be the old Bear yet.' But Handy sounded dubious. He added, too low for even Atterburn to hear, 'But sharin' a ship with him *is* gettin' to be like livin' with las' year's woman.'

Arp caught up with the Bear near the first ship on the ramp. He caught him from behind the arm. 'Don,' he said, 'you're going to go to the flight surgeon.'

The Bear turned to face him. He had the melting eyes of a llama. 'No,' he said, 'I'm not.'

'That's an order, Don.'

Bear laughed again. 'Court-martial me,' he said.

'Oh, Christ, Don!' Arp said in disgust. 'You know I can't! But you can't take a crew down with you, just to spite Blood and Baker! Or even to ease your own conscience!'

'Oh,' Bear said, as if awakening from a puzzling dream. 'Is that what you thought? No, I can't do that. And I won't. I'm going back to being a gunnie. That's what I meant. Somebody's going to do it anyway, and I can't ask someone else to be executioner for me, just to keep my hands clean. So I'll do it. I'm no better than the rest of humanity, taken as a whole.' He grinned weakly. Seeing the doubt behind Arp's eyes, he added, 'I mean it, sir. I won't let you down.'

Arp knew he had no right to feel let down now, by the mere fact that one of his officers – one of his friends – had said no more than that he would do his duty, would do what others did, what Arp himself did, daily. Yet Arp heard the words with regret, as one recognizes the passing of an unreturned love, or looks back on the loss of the faith of his childhood years. It was better so. And yet . . .

'All right, Bear,' Arp said.

11

To those who learned of it in their newspapers, or those who woke in city villas to the sound of rockets falling, Tet of 1968 may have come as a shock. Farther from Saigon and the pleasant hotel rooms of the war correspondents, the attacks of the Viet Cong and North Vietnamese came on as imperceptibly as a change of seasons or a change in tides. The four-day holiday itself was only the peak of a storm that had wandered the length of the land for years not to be counted without heartbreak. For a few weeks before and after Tet, men killed one another at a rate somewhat greater than usual. That was all.

But for the Bear, it was a time of despair. Daily, almost hourly, as the old year neared its end, his words to Lieutenant Arp were thrown back at him by grinding circumstance. After Hill 473 his return to flying had been a return to hours spent on mildewed cots, in the rain-spattered hooch at Chu Lai or in a baking tent on the asphalt helipad of a fire base, dreaming of Alice and waiting to fly and reliving minute by minute the flaming fall of Covington's ship into the relentless sea. But not killing.

But now was not a time for thought or dreams, good or ill. It was a time to survive, and to keep one's friends alive. To survive meant to pull the trigger, to touch the thumb to the red button. Whenever he did it he felt the light caress of death, touching him back. He had not thought, when he spoke to Arp, that there could be so much killing. He wondered sometimes who brought home the word to the wives of the North Vietnamese soldiers.

The sound of the scramble horn became a horror to him.

He went about leaden-eyed: but, as others were leaden-eyed from want of sleep, he supposed no one noticed him, and he preferred that. Arp, it was true, watched him closely, but more with the regret of one who has seen a fall from grace than with the admiration of one professional killer for another. Arp's strange notions, however, were not shared by many, probably by no one at all except Wolcheski, to whom Arp spoke once when their paths crossed at a fuel dump at Hill 63.

Arp came aboard while Wolcheski's helicopter was being refueled. He plugged his headphones into the ship's intercom, and they talked through the nervous system of the helicopter about things far removed from the war. The ship was too noisy for conversation outside the intercom, and Wolcheski did not have the time to shut down. Before leaving he asked after the Bear.

'I think,' Arp said, 'the Bear has come to worse than dust.'

'Maybe dust is worst of all, after all,' Wolcheski said. 'I've seen enough of bodies for the day.' He put his visor down, not with the finality of one cutting off the subject, but only because the crew chief had withdrawn the fuel hose and it was time to go for still more bodies.

'What did that mean, *Trung-úy*?' Guiterrez asked after Arp was gone.

'It meant that the legendary beast is still flying his gunship – and killing.'

'Shoot,' Guiterrez said, 'I told you a long time ago that deep down he was attached to his guns.'

'You've told me a lot of things I don't believe, Primo,' was Wolcheski's reply.

But there were those who did believe. Alice was with Dr Rawlinson in the officers' club that night when Guiterrez came in. 'I heard news of the friendly neighborhood Bear today,' Guiterrez remarked with elaborate casualness. His quick grin was for the way Rawlinson stiffened, and not for Alice's sudden uncertainty that would not let her quite meet his eyes nor let her look away.

'I hope he's all right?' she said hesitantly, for she had not heard from him since that night he had found her on the beach, although he had promised this time to keep in touch.

'Oh, I think he's fine. Very fine. But he's gone back to his first love. You lost him.'

'I don't "own" him,' she said, with a shrug of her shoulders but not her heart. She added, on an impulse, 'I hope he's happy with her.'

'Oh, it's not a *her*!' Guiterrez answered. 'I just meant he's decided to go on killing Charlies. I knew he wouldn't give it up. Remember?' He left behind another grin for Rawlinson.

She did remember. She would not have believed it then. Although she would have liked him for his company alone, the kindness of his heart was what she had valued in the Bear. She did not think the less of any man for being a soldier: she had, in the abstract, no convictions against one man's killing another. It was only in the flesh that she found it repulsive. But hiding within her was a feeling that could be found as well in nurses outwardly more cynical than she – that it *was* worthwhile to try to limit human suffering wherever it was found. It was why they were nurses. It was why she was a nurse.

She might have loved someone who lacked the tenderness she thought she had seen in the Bear; but in caring for one who showed it, she became unable to accept less from him. And what she had not believed before, she believed now, because he had not tried to see her nor sent word to her, as he had promised, and because it was the easier to believe as the flood of wounded from both sides swelled daily through the ER.

'If you've lost *him*,' Rawlinson said after a silence that was more awkward for him than for her, 'you might fall back on me.'

She placed her hand on his, with a laugh that she hoped was sparkling and told him, 'You're nice, Danny, but I couldn't ever love you.'

'So you've said. But I don't see why not. I'm so much handsomer than your warrant officer, and you're *crazy* about him!'

She smiled. 'You are handsomer than he is,' she agreed, 'but I'm not "crazy about him." I just can't love you. I'm sorry. I tried to when you were so kind to me right at first, and I just couldn't.'

'And you do him.'

'I *could* him, perhaps,' she said. 'But I don't.' She said it with more certainty than she felt, and began making plans to cross him out of her heart.

Whatever glee or disappointment Baker and Blood felt at the Bear's return to military righteousness, they did not communicate it. Probably they felt neither the one nor the other. It would not have occurred to either of them that the Bear had ever wanted more than to escape his past or their presence, unless it was really to join his nurse girl friend. Neither one had lost his dislike of the Bear, but action on that could await easier times.

Some in the company looked on the assault from Duc Pho as a turning point. That was a small view of the war, though not unlike those from Saigon or Washington or Hanoi in which the Tet offensive which came immediately after was seen as a great change in the direction of the war, for better or worse, if one knew which was which. For the company the assault from Duc Pho brought a change of command, a loss of a commander and executive officer, at the moment that the fighting swelled and the deaths mounted. The 'old days' came to mean the time before Baker and Blood were in command – a better time altogether. Only Atterburn ever showed resentment when someone noted that they 'wouldn't have had this shit in the old days.'

The complaints came chiefly over company operations. There had been few large operations in the old days; but the missions that came down were flown well, and the crews were given credit for knowing their jobs. Under the new regime, briefings increased, always beginning with the assumption that no one knew anything, because nothing had yet been told him by the present command structure. Among aircraft commanders with more time in country than either the commander or his executive officer, that did not go down easily. Worse yet, extra duty alert times were scheduled, beyond those assigned by Division. 'Bad enough to work an eighty-hour week!' Griggs thundered through Operations. 'But then to get stuck for an extra twenty hours of sitting on your ass in the company area, just so the BBs can suck up to the brass! Jesus!' For once no one thought Griggs was being a complete ass.

But that was at the end of those days before Tet, when tempers were already short. Then the slicks flew combat assaults daily, and pieced in the spare hours with resupply, while the guns waited from hour to hour for fire missions.

By Tet three men were gone. One, a crew chief named Hobbs, was killed in a mortar attack on the fire base where his ship was standing by. He had always been late getting to the bunkers. The fact that he had once, when drunk, slept right through an attack gave him a feeling of immortality that remained with him up to the moment the round dropped on the tent pole and caught him stretching and yawning. Even after his bunk was dragged outside, the smell of blood was so strong in the tent that the other crewmen sat outside weary-eyed in the dawn rather than go back to bed.

The second and third were Bear's friend Carter and his copilot, the new guy Williams. They were flying number ten thou, whose smoking engine finally did fail as they were racing home alone low level under a ragged sky, hoping to beat rain and nightfall into Chu Lai. They were flying low level – inches above the treetops, or a few feet above the new rice in the paddies – because the cloud base was too low for them to fly above the Dead Man's Zone. Slicks forced to fly in the Dead Man's Zone flew as close to the earth as possible, twisting and turning and hiding behind every ridge and tree line. The earth is every aviator's enemy, but in war it is only his second-worst enemy, and its presence offers some shelter from his worst enemy so long as all goes well with his aircraft. When their engine failed, Carter and Williams did the only thing that could be done – they landed the ship straight ahead. Straight ahead was a Vietnamese graveyard whose round stone tombs reached up to tear them from the sky. Nightfall beat them into Chu Lai.

The maintenance warrant officer, Burgess, had made a

flight that day to Cam Ranh Bay, halfway down the coast toward Saigon, to pick up parts. His ship came in just after dark. It whistled down the hover lane and wound down under under the eyes of the crew chief while Burgess hurried up to Operations.

'Burgey, I ain't seen you move so fast since somebody put that cobra in your bed,' Rauch said to him. 'What's up?'

'That's what I was going to ask you,' Burgess said. 'What's up? Something big's going on, man! Everyplace I tuned in the radio, all up and down the coast, they had an attack going! I couldn't even get into Nha Trang to go to the PX! The tower said aircraft were taking fire in the landing pattern! What the hell's going on?'

'Partyin',' Rauch said. 'Didn't you know? Tet started today. You ought to read the intelligence reports I sent you. Or read *Stars and Stripes*. It'll tell you everything that's in the G-2.'

'If you'd mark your stuff Top Secret, I'd read it,' Burgess said.

'I do, Burgey, I do! Your sergeant's probably been throwin' 'em in your desk drawer again. Clean out that rat's nest once in a while, huh?'

'Top Secret in a desk drawer!' Blood exploded from behind Rauch's filing cabinet. He was checking Rauch's files to see that they conformed to the latest Division directive on filing. 'Who's putting Top Secret documents in a desk drawer?'

'Just a little joke, sir,' Rauch said calmly, winking at Burgess.

'That's nothing to joke about,' Blood grumbled. 'There's a war on, Rauch.' He added to Burgess, 'Don't let a little gunfire scare you. We'll kick Charley's ass around some, and he'll get tired quick enough. You ought to get out and see some real shooting.'

'Ask *them* what's going on,' Rauch suggested, nodding toward Arp and the Bear coming in the door. 'They been out killin' Charley like he was goin' out of style. How many today?'

'Thirty,' Arp said.

'Thirty!' Rauch took the reports they had filled out, scanned them, and tossed them into the sergeant's tray. 'Only thirty ain't worth *my* time.'

'Maybe they're running out of Chinamen,' Arp said crossly. He knew Rauch was joking, but he did not think it a subject for jokes.

'I hope they last at least till I'm gone,' Rauch said. 'I wouldn't want to leave you fellas with nothin' to do when I'm gone. Did you know I was short, Bear?'

'I heard that somewhere,' Bear said.

'Didn't know if I'd told you yet today. Listen, you guys didn't see number ten thou out there anywhere, did you?'

'Carter? I heard him on the radio about sixteen hundred,' Arp said. 'He was on artillery resupply up the Que Son, wasn't he?'

'Yeah, but he ain't come in yet. He had a seventeen hundred release time, too.'

'Divarty always gives you just one more sortie,' Arp said. 'Especially when the ceiling's low.'

'Jesus, get him back!' Burgess interjected. 'The longer they fly, the sooner we have to tear them down.'

'If Carter don't get his rear back here soon,' Rauch said, 'he's goin' to find this place closed. I'm plannin' to get my shit down to that bunker and pull the door in after me. I'm too short to be sittin' around this office after dark, the way Charley's been tearin' around. I don't aim to get caught standin' in the door tryin' to hook my static line when the jump light comes on.'

'Charley won't hit here,' Blood said. 'Division's had patrols out for miles in every direction all week. He might lob in a few mortar rounds. The only way to stop that is to tear up that island hooch by hooch. And that's just what I'd do, if I was running this division. But if you don't want to disturb the Slopes, why, Rauch, you just can't let a few little mortar rounds bother you. There won't be anything big in here, I can tell you that. Nobody's called a red alert for tonight, that I know of.'

'Just the same, I think I'll move down to the bunker. Damn, where is that Carter anyway?' He paced from one window to another staring out onto the ramp.

'He's going to be into periodic by the end of the week again, if he keeps piling on the hours,' Burgess complained. 'And it's going to be a bugger. He needs an engine change, if we had an engine.'

'Keep 'em flyin', Burgey,' Rauch said. 'Keep 'em flyin'.'

Burgess followed Arp and Bear out the door. 'What do you think *is* going on?' he asked. 'This was a wild day!'

'That's like asking a pickle what the sandwich looks like,' Bear said. 'You'd better take Blood's word on what's going on.'

'Don't ask a man for opinions on his night off,' Arp told Burgess. 'Bear's been like that all day. Listen, Bear, do you want to take the three-quarter-ton tonight? You can haul the fair Alice off to one of the clubs. Eat, drink, be merry.'

'For tomorrow you may kill.'

'And tomorrow and tomorrow. But for tonight . . .'

'She could be on duty tonight for all I know,' Bear said. He was not sure he could see her again; but he did not want to explain, even to Arp.

'In a minute you'll have me feeling sorry for you for having the night off,' Arp said.

Once he was beyond Arp's shepherding eye, the Bear ambled toward his hooch with his head bowed. Killing was bad enough business, without having to look as if he could do it forever.

He turned on the light in his hooch. His bed was tightly made, as it had been for the last two weeks. Several days' mail was stacked on it. He ruffled through it and tossed it back on the bed. There were clean fatigues in the locker. At least Suzie and Yan had been at work. He had not seen them, either, in more than a week. He had heard of minor fighting around the villages outside Chu Lai. But there was no way to know what was true and what was not. He could not answer Burgess's question. The fighting he saw, he knew had happened. The rest might or might not be true. Major battles appeared, in fancy dress, in *Stars and Stripes*. Some of them he had been in himself without knowing. But you knew men died when you killed them yourself.

Bear drew a pan of warm water from the maintenance officer's shower – a tall plywood box topped by two jet-fighter drop tanks with burners under them – and began to wash away the Vietnamese countryside from his face. 'What an ugly bastard you are,' he said to the face in the mirror. The face said the same back to him. And well deserved, too, he thought. The face did not seem to be interested in trying on amusing expressions. He moodily began to shave. The mirror insisted on fogging over, and he cut himself. 'That's the first blood I've drawn from *you*,' he said. 'Serves you right.' The face mistily returned the compliment.

The platoon three-quarter-ton truck was parked beside the alert hooch. The crews on standby were spread over the steps of the hooch, except for Atterburn, who was seated on one fender of the truck. 'I suppose you expect me to move, Bear,' he said, climbing down slowly, 'just because you want to go see your nursie-poo.' Atterburn was an aircraft commander now, and the less inclined to give quarter to anyone.

'I'd let you stay,' Bear said, 'but you make a hell of a hood ornament.'

'A night off for Tet,' Atterburn commented: 'that takes real suck with the platoon leader. I just want you all to know,' he announced, turning to the others, 'that tonight's the night the Bear gets to the promised land. I hope nobody told him that last night I took his nurse friend out, though. Did you know she does it for savings bonds, Bear?'

'I know that it's a big rooster that has a pecker as big as its crow,' Bear called down from the truck. 'Bk-bk-b-*gack*!' – the imitation of a chicken with strep throat floated behind as he put the truck in gear and roared away down the ramp.

As he pulled up in front of the hospital a helicopter pounded in over the ridge and whirled to a halt on the main pad outside the emergency-room entrance. He stopped the truck far down the road from the pad. Before he could switch off the engine the helicopter was surrounded by a swarm of litter-bearers who poured from the building at a clumsy run. They snatched the long litters from the racks at the rear of the cabin, at a pace that somehow fell from frantic to deliberate without losing any of its speed. Within seconds the last litter was pushing through the swinging doors. When it had vanished inside, the helicopter rose up and hovered to the parking ramp, where it sat swishing its blade at flight idle as the engine cooled down. The rotating beacon flashed a moving band of red around the inside of the revetment and under the flickering blade.

The Bear remained in his truck until the engine was shut down and the blade had swung to a halt. The crew dismounted. He recognized Wolcheski. He stepped out of the truck then and went down to the aircraft.

'Ah ha,' Wolcheski greeted him. 'Strange creatures walk the night in these parts. It's the very Bear himself, Primo.'

'I bet he's only down here because he ran out of targets,' Guiterrez said. 'When there's nothing else to do, he comes to visit here. Just often enough to spoil the water for everyone else.'

Wolcheski ignored the remark. He extended his hand to the Bear: 'It's good to see you again. We've been worried.' He sat down in the cargo door, making room for Bear beside him. 'If you're waiting for Alice, you may as well sit down. She's in there.' He nodded toward the ER. The cold light of the fluorescent lamps fell from all the windows of the room. The bottom panes of the windows were painted out, so that nothing could be seen through them; but sometimes a swiftly moving shadow fell across their translucent surface.

'Who were they?' Bear asked. He meant the men on the litters.

'I don't know. Just another company out in the boonies. One platoon was overrun just before nightfall. That's what we could find of them. The rest are scattered all over hell, or dead, or gone.'

They sat without speaking, watching the shadows move across the glass and vanish. 'Six was all?' Bear asked at length.

'That's all we found. They had the radio. Platoon leader was dead. Some more will show up in the morning.'

'God, I hope so.'

'They could have done with some gun support,' Guiterrez remarked.

'Do you want me to go tell Alice you're here?' Wolcheski asked.

'No. I won't bother her on duty. I didn't know whether she'd be off tonight.'

'If she was . . .' Guiterrez began. *If she was, there's a doctor who'd have her busy*, he was going to say; but Wolcheski saw that coming, and cut him off.

'She's not on duty,' Wolcheski told Bear. 'But she's always there for a mass cal, and we had two big loads early this evening. I'll tell her you're here,' he offered again, 'so she'll know to come out when she can. I go off standby in an hour. Swensen and I will stand you to dinner. I think it's steak-and-shrimp night at MAG Thirteen.'

'All right,' Bear said. 'But let me tell her I'm here. It's all right if I go in there, isn't it?'

'If you want to.' There was an edge of doubt in Wolcheski's voice.

'I don't,' Bear said. 'But I will.'

'I'll be up at the ready room.'

Bear walked up the hill toward the light-streaming windows. The cold light of that place repelled him with the force of falling water; but he forced his way against it. Outside the door he stopped to collect his breath. Then he pushed the door open.

Alice was the first one he saw. She was standing directly opposite the door, facing him from the other side of a litter. She looked up as the door opened. Her eyes were heavy and dark. His eyes did not stay on hers. They went to her hands, her arms, which were red with blood to the elbows. She was retwisting a tourniquet that had slipped from what remained of the leg of a soldier.

She frowned at him. He signed to her as best he could that he would be outside waiting. She nodded, still frowning, and went back to her work.

When he let the door close behind him, he realized he had been holding his breath the whole time. He leaned against the outside of the building to wait for his pulse to settle.

While he was leaning there, four men burst from the ready room and went racing toward the helicopter ramp. 'Bear!' Wolcheski called. He was one of the four.

Bear ran for the ship. The blade was already turning when he reached the side of the cockpit. 'We're going on another trip!' Wolcheski called down, shouting to be heard. 'Won't be long! If you want to go ahead, leave word with Swensen where to go! She's in the bar!'

Bear gave him a thumbs-up sign to show that he understood, and stepped back from the ship. It rose straight up out of the revetment and climbed out across the cliffs and northward. He watched it until the beacon was gone.

It was a long time before Alice came, but she did come at last. He approached her shyly. What had been between them had been so tentative and new, he was not sure it could be rebuilt. He did not know even if it had been between the people they had become in that short time. He did not know about what Guiterrez had told Alice, nor of what she felt; but if he had not changed in that way, he had changed. Nothing lasted.

They halted, two yards apart. She looked at him guardedly. 'Hello,' he said. It was with a feeling of something breaking that they moved together at the same instant. It was gone in a moment. She embraced him, but dodged his kisses. 'I'm a mess,' she said. 'Let me change.'

'Of course.'

They started toward the nurses' quarters. 'I don't even know if you're free this evening,' he said apologetically.

'I'm not on duty,' she said. 'As for "free" . . . I hope there's no need for my help for a few hours. Sometimes we need everyone in the area. After all, I can't spend *all* my off-duty hours just waiting for you.' She smiled, but it was only a small smile.

'I meant "free" to include "not going out with somebody else",' he said.

'I'm free.' She said it with finality. But she added, as if it were a whole new idea, 'I just wish I knew, when I'm waiting, whether you were alive or dead. But I suppose when you're dead I'll see you sooner than when you're alive, won't I?' The matter-of-fact way she said it invited no reply. But when there was none, she said next, 'I see such a wide sample, you'd think one would look just like another: but I'll know when it's you.'

'I suppose not many walruses wash up on your beach,' he said.

She would not be diverted. 'I'm not surprised at anything that comes in the doors now,' she said without a trace of a smile.

She left him at her door while she changed. She returned shortly, still in fatigues, but freshly laundered ones, and smelling distantly of perfume. 'Where?' she asked.

'Wolcheski wanted us to go with him and Janet, someplace. But he went out on a mission just after. Do you want to go on?'

'Let's wait.'

Swensen was in the club with two doctors. She left them and came to meet the Bear and Alice. She kissed the Bear on the cheek. 'The famous beast!' she bubbled. 'I'm so happy you're back.'

'That's at least two of us,' the Bear said, bemused.

'Two of *us*,' Swensen corrected him, taking Alice's arm. But she appeared to know what he meant. She said, 'Alice thinks nothing will go right in the ER if she's not there. She's been absolutely haunting that place for weeks! Those doctors were just telling me she was there again tonight. Alice, I went to see if I could help, but there absolutely wasn't anything for another nurse to do. So I came right here and drank to that.' She said to Bear, 'That deserves a drink in its honor, doesn't it?'

'More than one.'

'It might if the day were over,' Alice said. 'Ski has gone out for another load.'

'Has he gone? The louse is supposed to be taking me out for dinner.'

'People do die at the most awkward moments,' Alice said.

'They certainly do,' Swensen agreed, ignoring the irony. 'Well, I'll drink my first dinner while I wait for him, then. Will you two join me?'

'Wolcheski already invited us to join you for the second dinner,' Bear said. 'We may as well take in the first, too.'

'This may be the only one for me,' Alice said. 'I don't think I should leave. We can eat something here, Don.'

'Oh, come on, Alice,' Swensen said. 'You haven't been off the hospital grounds in weeks.'

'We could wait and decide when we see what Lieutenant Wolcheski brings in,' Bear said.

'Spoken like a true compromiser,' Swensen told him. She patted him on the back in an almost masculine way. 'Let me play the barmaid. Alice has been waiting on people hand and foot for days on end. Everyone loves her for it, as long as we don't all have to keep up with her. I'll tell myself I'm making up some of it by bringing your drinks. What can I get you?'

'Nothing but a soft drink,' Alice said. 'I may have to go back yet tonight.'

'Alice, you are disgusting, after the speech I just made. Bear, be a dear and drink something to keep me company. If *you* have to go back to work, it'll release your inhibitions and make the bullets go straighter.'

'It had better be a double something, then,' Bear said.

'Spoken like a true killer, dear.' She patted him on the back again.

As Janet walked away from them, Alice made a brief sour face which Bear pretended not to see.

They sat in embarrassed strained silence while Janet was gone. Neither wanted to ask the other what he or she had been doing since they had last been together; but what they had been doing loomed like a dark shape in the night blotting out the constellations of things they had so recently thought they shared.

Eventually, with a feeling of surrender to hard circumstance, Bear asked whether she was still on the same ward.

'The same by number at least,' she answered.

'Is Mother Courage still there?'

Alice shook her head.

'Where did she go? They couldn't have released her?'

'No. I don't know where she is. They're all gone: they

have been for a week. There aren't enough beds now, you see. One day they were just all gone. No one could tell me where. I would have gone to see Mother Courage. I think she liked me, in her fierce old way. But no one could tell me where. Maybe I can find her at the prisoner camp, if there's ever time. The ward wasn't empty more than a half hour. Now it's full. It's full for the third time this week, with different patients.' She rested her elbows on the table and propped her chin on her fists. Although she was on the edge of tears, it was not from weakness. Sadness had only tempered her determination to relieve whatever wretchedness the war might throw her way. Although her eyes went limpid, her face took on the angry defiance that disease had carved on the face of Mother Courage herself.

'Alice, for a girl who hasn't seen her friend for weeks,' Janet said, sitting down next to the Bear, 'you're not exactly the picture of seductiveness. You two are sitting here like an old married couple. Cheer up! Make hay while the sun shines, as Ski's Polish grandmother would say!' She handed Bear a glass. She was just tipsy enough to be aggressive but not unpleasant. 'There's a double something for a thirsty warrior. But it seems to me that Alice needs it more than you do. Alice, can't I get you something better? After all, it's a holiday!'

'What holiday?'

'You're the friend of the "indigenous personnel," aren't you? You should know that it's Tet!'

'Happy New Year,' Bear said, raising his glass.

'I'll drink to that,' Janet joined in. 'Alice? You won't be any fun if you don't keep up with us.'

Alice paused before she raised her glass with a smile and a shake of her head. 'I hope it is a happier new year,' she said softly.

The sound of the helicopter coming in to the hospital pad brought Alice to her feet. 'Sit down,' Janet insisted. 'At least let me go see who they've brought in now. This poor man needs company as much as anyone else does, Alice.'

'We can both go,' Alice said. 'He'll understand.'

'If I'm going to be lonely anyway' – Bear shrugged – 'I

may as well get credit for being noble, too. Go do your duties.' In fact he was pleased that Alice wanted to go, however disappointed he might be. 'You nurse them,' he said, 'and I'll nurse this.' He had hardly touched the drink. He knew how Alice felt, for there was no easy way down from two weeks of continuous readiness. Inside he was still listening for the scramble horn. Whatever a double something might have done for his inhibitions or his aim, he knew what it would do to his coordination, and he could only sip at it uneasily.

'I'll send word if we'll be long,' Alice said. 'I am sorry.'

As she walked toward the ER, Alice thought of the way her feelings ran in gyres. While he was gone, they had spiraled off into a tenuous sympathy for all the broken figures who drifted under her hands, and she convinced herself that what she had felt for the Bear was no more than the focus of that sympathy. She could force herself not to think of him, except for instants when a medevac helicopter stood before the door and she waited to see who would be on the litters it had brought. She could never keep him from her thoughts entirely then. She always expected that sooner or later he was going to appear without warning on a litter. Sometimes she could convince herself that she had no special dread of that. Sometimes her first night in the emergency room came to mind, and she played at wondering whose hand had been on the trigger when the bullet sped out to shatter this bone, when the rocket fell that had mangled this limb. But when he stepped back into her life, all the feelings so carefully sorted out were emptied in a pile on the floor of her heart.

When he stepped into the ER, she had been startled and then annoyed. For an instant she had thought, as when she had seen him first, that he had come in as a walking wounded. When she saw that he was whole, it annoyed her to have him come between her and her duty. He was not coarse and blundering about it, as a killer should be, but polite and sensitive as always, motioning that he would be waiting when she had time for him. And he did not even apologize, for having been gone, for not having tried to contact her, for having defected so easily from the high image she had of him.

She was still imagining these accusations against him when she saw the bodies come off the helicopter. There were aviator's wings on the first uniform. The emotion she had only imagined so often suddenly struck her in reality; with a catch at her heart she forgot for an instant that she had only now left him sitting in the club. The face above the wings was mangled, for it had struck the array of knobs on the panel when the seat was torn from the floor by the force of the crash into the tombstone. But the body was too slender to be his, and the name was wrong. Carter, the name tag said. Her grief drained away at once. Even that saddened her: it seemed wrong to be glad that one man had died, instead of another. But she was glad. She was glad and, suddenly, eager to be with him.

Seeing Janet and Alice outside the ER, Wolcheski tried to wave them over to the helicopter. They could not see him. He gave the ship to Guiterrez to shut down and climbed out.

'Where's the Bear?' he asked Alice as he came up to the two of them.

'We left him in the club,' Janet answered for them both. 'Alice thought maybe we could help. But they won't need us for only three.'

'Two of them are dead,' Wolcheski said. 'Do you know who they were?'

'No.'

'Don't say anything about this to the Bear. They were his friends. Let him be happy for tonight.' He went back to his ship to sign off the mission.

Bear was surprised that the girls came back almost before the helicopter had shut down. 'Nothing?' he asked.

'Wolcheski is slipping,' Janet said. 'They don't need us for just three.' Alice sat down without saying a word. Bear took his cue from her mood and asked no more questions.

Wolcheski came in just behind them. He threw his cap on the table and sat down without removing his pistol belt. 'Janet, my love, fetch us a drink,' he said. He sounded tired. Bear gathered that it had not been a pleasant mission for him.

'We're going out, remember?' Janet said. 'These two are coming with us.'

'I don't think we are,' Bear said, 'but Happy New Year.' He raised his glass. He was startled when Alice said suddenly, 'Let's do go somewhere, Don.' He looked at her with a question in his eyes. 'We have few enough chances,' she said. Her hand was cool and steady on his arm.

'Gather ye rosebuds and so forth,' Wolcheski advised Bear. 'Or whatever passes for rosebuds in this land.'

The club alongside the western runway did business as usual on the first night of Tet. There was no local alert, and short of an attack on Chu Lai proper, outbreaks of fighting in the cities of South Vietnam had little effect on the Marine Air Group to which the club belonged. The pilots there flew Phantoms, and commuted north to a different war. Day and night the club was rattled by heavy jets going out on afterburner. But that and the beat of passing helicopters were almost the only sounds that penetrated the building. Outside in the stillness between takeoffs returning aircraft could sometimes be heard. Overhead in the darkness Phantoms trimmed for landing made weird creaking wails. Inside, the band, singing, shouts from the craps game in the side room, covered all small sounds. It was steak-and-shrimp night at the club, and the war was locked safely outside.

It was easier to be together there, at first, where not to talk was no embarrassment because talking was possible only in the band's intermissions. But Alice felt herself slipping closer to him simply by being with him; her feelings rearranged into the old pattern.

Wolcheski and Janet were off somewhere and the band was resting. She could see the words forming in him long before they came to the surface: his face went through a series of expressions, all serious but all different. He said, 'I want to tell you why you haven't heard from me.'

'You don't have to. I didn't mean to be nasty about it. I didn't know what had happened to you, Don, and I heard . . .'

'You heard . . . ?' he prompted.

'It doesn't matter.'

'It matters to me.' He thought he knew what she was going to say. Wolcheski had picked up Major Hart's body, and Captain Martin's, after the assault from Duc Pho. Bear feared at once, without stopping to wonder how Wolcheski might have known it, that Wolcheski had told her how they had come to die.

'I heard you had gone back to your "first love".' Because she had taken it seriously then, she said it now as if she were teasing.

At first there was only relief; but then slow puzzlement slid across his face, so evidently that she laughed.

'You shouldn't tease an old trooper,' he said stoutly.

'You asked what I heard, and that was it. And it *was* enough to make me want to throw you over.' She could admit that, so long as he wouldn't know it was true.

'Then it was a deadly slander and a base canard. And besides, it isn't true. Who told you I ever had a first love?'

'Guiterrez,' she admitted. 'He said your first love was . . . flying gunships.'

Bear mulled that over with a physical chewing motion. 'Maybe it was,' he said at length. 'Once upon a time.'

'I know.'

'Do you?' he asked. 'Then, why did he say "back" to my "first love"?'

She shook her head.

'I want you to know all the bad things about me,' he said. 'To counteract my notorious deadly charm.' He said the words lightly – as lightly as she had spoken of his first love – but his eyes were serious.

'Well, for my own protection, then,' she agreed, smiling in an attempt to match his light outer manner and turn back the darkness in his eyes.

'It was why I didn't write or send up a smoke signal or . . . something,' he began. 'I wanted to see you. But I thought I was going to be free of gunning; and I wanted to wait until then.' He went on to tell about the transfer; but not about Major Hart and Captain Martin – not yet. 'And then, since it fell through . . . it's been a busy time.' He was dismayed at how inconclusive those words sounded.

'It's terrible of your commander to tell you he'd let you go, and then not do it,' she said. 'How could he?'

'It's a different commander, you see,' he said softly. 'The major and Captain Martin . . .'

She laid a hand on his arm.

'They were both killed.'

'Oh, Don, I'm sorry! I shouldn't have said anything against your commander, not knowing . . .'

'It won't hurt him now. Though, God knows, there's nothing bad should be said about Major Hart. Or Captain Martin. But what did hurt them . . . what got them was a weapon I should have put out of action.'

'It can't have been all your fault!'

'You sound like Lieutenant Arp. "Not your fault, Bear," he tells me. "Nobody else got Charley first, either." I don't know. Could I have got Charley first, if I'd been ready? I don't know. But I wasn't ready. I didn't want to hurt anybody, so I wasn't looking for someone to kill, and so I didn't *find* someone to kill. Instead, two good men died. Those things I know for sure.

'Now you know all about me,' he said at the end, with a short laugh. 'I wish I had better excuses to make for myself. Hey, don't cry! People will think I beat you! There come Janet and Wolcheski. Let's act friendly and surprise them.'

She took his hand suddenly and wiped her eyes with his fingers. 'You don't owe *me* any excuses,' she whispered.

'I don't know that game,' Wolcheski said, 'but it looks like fun. You must teach me how to play it, Bear.' He and Janet sat down beside them.

'Don't be cruel to Alice, naughty Bear,' Janet said. 'Not even if she likes it.'

'We're going to learn that game, Swensen,' Wolcheski said.

'BS, as your Polish grandmother'd say.'

The music began again. A Marine major came and asked Janet to dance. He asked the band for something slow and spun slowly with her crushed against him. 'Let's hope the poor thing doesn't suffocate,' Wolcheski said. 'In a more civilized time there'd have been a war over less than that. I think there's more sense in fighting over women than over ideas. Now we both try to cram our system down the other guys' throat, and when it's over no one's got anything but the exercise. Of course,' he added, 'the same could be said about dancing. Dancing is war by another means, originating in an acting out of victory over the enemy. That poor Marine doesn't know he's only acting – that all he's going to get in the exercise.' He sighed. 'Bear, why are you wasting your life listening to me talk, when you could be dancing with Alice?'

'That's what I was wondering,' Alice said.

It was awkward at first, like all their meetings. But the touch of the music drew them both back into what had been, as if the weeks past were only minor dreams. There was still room in their lives for small corners of happiness. This, at least, was a moment saved from utter loss, until the music faded and their dance dissolved into the blue-lit, smoke-washed stillness that lurked behind the music.

The end of a set found them near the door. It had been left ajar to let in the night wind. With the band silent, the talk hushed for an instant, there edged in at the door a foreign sound, faint and shy, no sooner heard than gone. Music and voices closed over its track. But they both had recognized it. It was the distant wail of a siren.

They followed the music again without a word. What the sound had meant there was no way to know; but they feared they knew. Yet they turned away, as if by their refusing acknowledgment, it could be made not to exist.

The music, and their hopes, were cut off in midflight. A Marine major came to the microphone in front of the band. 'I just want to let you know,' he said, 'that there's a mortar attack on at Ky Ha. Those of you who are nervous types can start for the bunkers now. For the rest of you, Happy Tet, and drink up!' He raised his glass, to a round of cheers from his audience.

The words broke away the shell of happiness that the

thing itself had not been able to pierce. 'Let's go,' Bear said quickly.

Wolcheski was leading Janet across the floor toward them. 'You were marv'lous, silly old beast,' Janet said to the Bear. 'Just marv'lous! Look, he's having a good time, too, Ski. He doesn' want to go! Alice doesn' either.'

Bear and Wolcheski spoke together for a moment. 'We'd better do it,' Wolcheski said, nodding. They started for the door. 'We can't go back now!' Janet was protesting. 'We can't jus' go driving back into it, with ever'one else in the bunkers, and there we come driving up big as you please.'

'It will be over before we get there,' Wolcheski said, 'and then they may need some untouched bodies to help out.'

The four of them were loudly applauded by those near the door as they left. 'Going to the bunkers with the nurses,' someone said loudly. As the door closed behind them, the music was blasting out and Marines were singing lustily, 'We gotta get out of this place,/If it's the last thing we ever do . . .'

The lights on the main runway were out, but all around its borders the clubs and hooches still glittered. The blackout order from Defense Control, if there was an order, had not yet filtered down below the major commands. They set out in the truck around the south end of the runway on the main post road. As they crossed the end of the runway, the lights came back up. 'It must be over,' Wolcheski said. The moment he spoke, a heavy *boom* rolled down the runway. Bear could feel it through the steering wheel of the truck. A second followed almost at once. 'Get over!' Wolcheski said. 'Get off the road!'

'What is it?' Bear swung the truck down into the ditch and fought to a stop.

'Rockets!' Wolcheski spat out the word as if it had a bad taste. He had Janet out the door before the truck had jolted to a stop in the bottom of the shallow sandy ditch.

Bear saw the third rocket impact. It struck halfway up the runway. The explosion printed a dazzling dandelion-head of fire on the night, a three-quarter sphere that laced out to the whole width of the runway, and, at its full size, vanished entirely. The shock wave followed; it struck him in the chest as he came out of the truck. He took Alice's hand and dived for the inner edge of the ditch.

The next rocket they heard coming before it impacted. It came in a long hissing sigh that continued after the fiery bloom of the warhead. The fire was already gone before the hiss was cut off in a heavy shuddering blast. 'They're a half mile off,' Wolcheski said. He had counted the seconds between the visible impact and the arrival of the blast.

A siren began to wail from the direction of the helicopter companies on the southern perimeter. Another answered from the direction of the club the four of them had just left. The lights on the runway were gone again. This time the lights in the buildings along its flanks began to wink out as well.

Another rocket came in behind them, in the direction of the helicopter companies. 'Charley's a darn poor shot,' Bear said – 'or he's got the whole place bracketed.' They pressed flatter against the sandy bank, grasping at roots of grass in an attempt to pull themselves nearer to the earth. But, though the nearer explosions shook the solid earth, few rockets fell at all near. They dropped in a leisurely rhythm up and down the runway and eastward toward the second runway along the sea. Between explosions there was absolute silence except for the mixed chorus of distant sirens.

The Bear peered cautiously over the top of the ditch bank. A fire up along the runway was sending a plume of dense fire-tinged smoke northwestward on the light wind. As he watched, another rocket flashed among the hooches beyond the fire. He rolled onto his back. The low clouds were beginning to glow with the light of many fires. A rocket passed high overhead and fell into the hooches crowded among the dunes behind the beach. They could hear it all the way across the sky. He was glad to be outside, free of the stifling uncertainty of a bunker. He did not want death to find him in some black hole as it had poor Jones. Better for a pilot to die under the open sky. 'I wonder if it's true,' he said, 'that you don't hear the one that hits you.'

'Don't talk about it!' Janet insisted suddenly. 'Please just don't talk about it!' She continued to clutch at the earth, and Wolcheski lay beside her talking to her in a low voice. Alice took her hands and tried to comfort her, but she continued to lie face down, sobbing to herself.

Off to the south the slow beat of a helicopter blade arose. Another joined in quickly. Bear sat up, and he felt Alice's hand on his arm. 'Gunships,' he said nodding.

The helicopters went out to the south and turned back toward Chu Lai along the beach. They could not be seen against the clouds. The rockets continued to arrive in a slow rain from the west. 'Where are they coming from?' Janet asked in a small, shaking voice.

'Nui Ong,' Bear told her. 'The big mountain.'

'But it's so far away!'

'Not more than five miles. That's close enough for rockets.'

'If... if they're gunships' – she looked up toward the sound of the blades over the beach – 'why don't they go out there?'

'There must be artillery out there by now. I doubt they can get through it.' Now that he thought about it, he could even hear it – a low, intermittent roll like surf that crashed in waves about the feet of the mountain. Concentrating on the sound of each rocket as it fell, or waiting for the next, he had not noticed that sound; but he knew now that it had been present for some minutes. North and south, too, artillery muttered and grumbled. The uneasy sleep of the whole coastal plain had been broken. But the rockets continued to hiss and boom along the edges of the night.

Janet's body was shaking with silent periodic sobs. 'Can't we please go somewhere?' she asked toward the ground. 'There must be a bunker someplace! Why don't we go?'

'We're not going to move,' Wolcheski said quietly. 'Nothing but a direct hit can get us here. Charles can put all the rockets he wants to out in the open fields.'

But Wolcheski was wrong. A rack of bombs, on their way from the ammunition bunkers to the arming line, had been left standing when the first rocket came in. The bombs were unarmed. They were not dangerous, left alone. Their explosives was insensitive. They could be kicked, rolled, dropped, or burned without exploding. Only the shock of another explosion would set them off. For that purpose they would be armed with a fuse of more sensitive explosive.

The rocket that fell among them took the place of a fuse. Its detonation took the bombs with it, and the concussion from that blast raced down the arming line and through the ammunition bunkers, through earth and through air, through sandbags and steel doors, waking bombs that had slept soundly through the height of the attack, and would have slept on until they touched the foreign earth.

The Bear was looking up the runway when that rocket fell. He saw the blast coming. It was a sharp line that defined a dome of fire, a swelling orange hemisphere that raced outward as if intent on engulfing the universe. Its outer surface raced through the low scud clouds, and they vanished. Bear threw himself on the ground, pulling Alice down with him. The shock wave hammered over them. 'Get up now!' he said urgently. 'Get under the truck!' He was on his feet and running; but Alice was not with him. He turned back. Janet was still stretched on the ground. Alice and Wolcheski had her by the shoulders and were shaking her fiercely. She would not move. 'Get her up!' Bear shouted. 'There's going to be all kinds of stuff falling here!' Even as he said it, he heard the first pieces thudding around them: broken concrete, shards of steel plank, five-pound lumps of lead bomb fuse. He ran back. 'Let me take her!' He tore Alice's hand from Janet's shoulder, picked Janet up, and got her arm around his neck. 'Come on, Ski, let's get her moving!' As they turned her around, his eyes met Alice's. 'Happy New Year!' He laughed.

She would have loved him forever, for that if for nothing more.

There was a brilliant flash and an instant concussion that staggered him. He was looking into her eyes, and the flash printed her features on his memory like a photograph, forever. 'Go on!' he said, shaking off the impact. She took her hand from his arm.

When they reached the truck, when he turned again, she was lying on the ground.

'What's the matter?' Bear said - cried.

'Something hit her,' Wolcheski said. 'Maybe it's not much.'

But she was unconscious when they got her under the truck. Given a task she understood, Janet threw off the spell which had seized her; but too late. 'I can't do anything for her!' she said. 'She's all shocky!' Janet was crying still: no longer senseless tears, but no less in vain. 'We've got to get her to a hospital!'

The steel rain had ceased. Janet helped them get Alice in the back of the truck. She and the Bear rode in back holding Alice on one of the benches along the side, while Wolcheski drove.

There was no one else on the road. South of the perimeter a few artillery flares were now dropping. They threw a faint yellow glaze over the passing scene. Everywhere buildings had been thrown down. Those still standing leaned away from the center of the bomb dump. One steel maintenance hangar had a dark hole that gaped over half the roof, obliterating the proud sign painted on it by its makers: BETTER BUILT BY CB-12. There were no lights anywhere. There was no one moving.

Wolcheski drove madly. The truck skidded and nearly left the road on the sandy washboard corner near the prisoner compound. Even on the straight stretches Bear could hardly hold Alice on the jolting bench. He shouted for Wolcheski to slow down, but Janet shouted in turn, 'We can't slow down! She won't last if we do!'

The rockets were falling at longer intervals now. Most of them were back near the bomb dump. Once a smaller secondary explosion ripped the dump; but by then the truck was roaring up the twisting road over the ridge that was the spine of the Ky Ha peninsula.

The hospital was blacked out. Wolcheski slammed the truck to a stop outside the emergency-room door and ran for a litter. When the doors opened, the cold light fell out and across Alice's face. Bear thought it was the color of the light that made her face so pale, until he saw the blood spreading on her fatigues.

The litter-bearers appeared almost at once, with Wolcheski behind them. Bear expected them to say something, because they knew her; but they accepted her silently. Janet and the Bear helped them move her onto the litter, and they took her through the doors. Janet went after her. Bear started to follow, but Wolcheski caught him by the arm. 'Why don't you wait out here, Bear,' he said.

'I'm no good to her here.' He struggled against Wolcheski's grip.

'You're no good to her there, either. They'll take care of her. You don't have to see it.'

Bear broke free and pushed through the doors.

The ER was seething. Up and down the floor a double row of trestles bore two ranks of men. The rags of their uniforms were caked with red clay mud: they had not been wounded in the attack, but were grunts in from the field. Most of them lay untended - some bloody and groaning, some impassively studying the ceiling. A few dangled IV tubes. One of those rolled his eyes up as if trying to read the number inked on his forehead. Activity bubbled around six or eight centers in the room, where gowned or fatigue-shirted figures clustered around a man on a litter. Between these a handful of orderlies strolled aimlessly or stood about. Or so it seemed to the Bear. He had not seen a mass casualty in its early stages and could not place this scene in the stream of scenes as the mass cal developed. He did not know that the triage was just over, and that those who needed aid most urgently were receiving what aid there was to give.

Alice was on the litter on trestles just inside the doors. A man in a gown detached himself from one of the groups, glanced briefly at Alice, and went to another of the groups, as if to a point of greater interest. He spoke in passing to a young black spec-five in jungle fatigues who disappeared instantly down the back corridor.

Bear stood beside Alice's litter. Above the collar of her jacket her skin was like marble. It looked the paler because the jacket was soaked from the collar down with blood. It had been cut open down the front, but the flaps had been pulled back over her. She was breathing. He could see that she was breathing.

The spec-five returned rapidly pushing a cart. There were several plasma bags on it. All but one were taken by another corpsman. The spec-five brought the cart and the last bag over to Alice. The other corpsman came up to help him lift the litter onto the cart.

'Where is she hit?' Bear asked. The spec-five spared only an instant to stare at him. 'I don't know man,' he said. He started away with the cart.

Bear followed him to the end of the ER. The spec-five pushed the cart under an overhead bar there and hung the plasma bag overhead. He began to uncoil a plastic tube, but before he had well begun, someone shouted to him from down the room. He looked up, startled, then took down the bag and hurried away with it.

'Where are you taking that?' Bear called. The man hurried on. 'What are you doing? Somebody's got to take care of her!' Bear caught a nurse by the arm from the closest group. 'It's Alice Porter!' he insisted, pointing. 'Somebody's got to help her!'

'Someone will,' the nurse said. But she made no move to go herself. He looked wildly about the room, looking for Janet. He saw her at last where she had joined one of the other clusters about an earlier casualty. The spec-five had gone there with his plasma bag. Bear ran up the line of litters and edged between two of them, brushing aside the hanging IV tubes. 'Isn't anybody going to do something?' he demanded. 'There must be a doctor who can look at her. Do you need so many standing around here?'

Janet bit her lip and appealed with her eyes to the gowned man opposite her. It was the one who had stopped beside Alice. 'Doctor Rawlinson?' she said. Bear understood that it was for his benefit that she had addressed the man as doctor.

'Yes, we do need so many standing around here,' Dr Rawlinson said without looking at the Bear. 'And I did look at her. So did Dr Kant. She's dying. Now get out of the emergency room.' The spec-five was hanging the plasma bag on the bar above the soldier on the litter between Rawlinson and the Bear.

'Dying!' Bear stared up at the plastic bag, full of clear fluid, glittering like a crystal under the fluorescent tubes. 'Dying? You son of a bitch, she's dying and you're going to let her lie there and die?'

The doctor had a scalpel in his hand. He threw it down and looked up at the Bear. No one else except Janet looked away from the soldier on the litter. 'No, I am not going to "let her die"! There is no way I can stop it!' He rubbed the bridge of his nose between his thumb and forefinger. It was a gesture Major Hart had often used when he was tired, or under a strain. Bear forced himself not to feel sympathy because of that coincidence. 'You were going to give her blood! You took that away!' he shouted.

'We had three chopper loads of casualties ten minutes before she came in,' the doctor said evenly. He glanced up and down the row of trestles. 'We've had fifty others through here today. We're all but out of blood, and we have to save it for those who have a chance to live. She doesn't have a chance. Anything we do for her will be thrown away. I was going to throw away an IV, just because I can't help hoping sometimes. But *this* man can live, if he gets blood!' Now the doctor shouted, too, as he jabbed a finger toward the soldier between them. 'Can you get that through your thick ugly skull? I thought a lot of Alice, too, but this man can live, and *she can't*! Now will you get out of here?' He nodded to Janet.

Janet took the Bear's arm and steered him away. She had changed from the frightened girl who could not force herself to stand up in the open air. When she stepped back into her familiar professional setting, some compound of training, habit, and professional pride took charge of her fear. 'I'm sorry, Bear,' she said. 'He really did try.'

Her words would have enraged him if they had come from anyone else. But he did not have in him even then the cruelty to say that it was her fault Alice was there at all. He could see that she was bitterly aware of it, as far as it was true; and how was *he* to lay blame at the feet of another for any such thing?

He went back to where Alice was lying alone. No one looked his way. He ghosted about the litter, sometimes looking at her, sometimes not. He could not tell whether she was breathing now.

The ER began to clear out. Soldiers were wheeled off on carts down the back corridor toward the operating room. The clusters of medical people broke up, reformed at different stations, broke and reformed again. During one of these permutations Dr Rawlinson came back to where Alice lay. He put a hand on her wrist for a moment and shook his head. He looked at the Bear then.

'Go on home,' he said. He added, with a glance that took in the Bear's clothing from ankle to shoulder, 'I take it you're not wounded?' Bear realized for the first time that he was covered with Alice's blood. 'No.' he answered. 'I'm not hurt at all.' The words were bitter on his tongue.

The doctor vanished up the back corridor among the stream of patients. Bear did not go until the spec-five came to push Alice's body away.

He found the truck outside the hospital. He went looking for Wolcheski, to tell him about Alice. But Wolcheski had gone out on a mission, to replace a pilot who had taken a thirty-caliber round through the chest while hovering in the dark above a rice paddy looking for wounded grunts. The pilot was the man who had lain between Bear and the doctor; but there was no one to tell the Bear that.

He drove down the ramp to the company. The sirens had been shut off. Patches of dim light stretched and slid over the helicopters on the ramp where the maintenance crews were out checking for damage. In some revetments there was no need for a light to see by: one ship sat broken like a straw, its tail boom angling to the ramp at one end and its nose touching at the other; another revetment contained only a pile of gray papery ash with the ends of a rotor blade sticking out – a direct hit by a mortar shell had set off the fuel in the tank, and eventually the magnesium alloys of the structure itself had burned like a torch. The Bear passed all this, slowly, without looking to either side.

'Bear, you missed all the excitement!' Atterburn appeared to have been waiting outside Operations just to find someone who had not seen it all, so that he could tell all of it again. 'It was Suzie's Revenge! Those mortars walked up and down the ramp – boom, boom, boom! One every ten yards, and then over to the next row of revetments! They must have had it measured down to a gnat's eyebrow! Jesus, was the old man pissed!'

It was the first time Bear had heard anyone call Baker 'the old man.'

'They got four ships cold,' Atterburn went on, 'just totaled them. And put six more down, that we know of so far. They didn't get the gunships, though. We're still in business, Killer. Too bad you missed it. Did you hear the bomb dump go up, or whatever the hell it was? Jesus, there must not be anybody alive over there!' A long silence as he followed the Bear up the hill among the hooches finally seemed to give rise to an idea that the Bear had not been suspended somewhere during these events, and Atterburn asked, 'Listen, where were you anyway? I bet you were down in some nice quiet bunker with your nursie-poo all the time the shit was coming down, weren't you? Jesus, what a life you have, Bear.'

They were in the middle of the officers' area. Bear stopped, and Atterburn stopped beside him. There was no one else in sight, nor any sound of human movement. 'How many casualties did we take?' Bear asked. He could not imagine where everyone might be.

'Casualties? Oh, hell, not a one. Not a damn one! Except the usual – sprained ankles and stubbed toes. The Operations clerk busted a finger. He was typing a report when the first round landed right outside, and he just shoved his hand right through the keys. All Suzie's work went for nothing.' He laughed. 'They missed everybody.'

'Where is everybody, then?' He ignored the part about Suzie.

'All down on the perimeter. Captain Blood and the old man think there might be a ground attack coming. Captain

Blood's got me up here coordinating. We've got some people down on the beach, and I'm in charge of them. I had to come up to Operations to report in.' Reminded now that he had command duties, Atterburn said, 'You better report to Captain Blood, Bear. We need every man we've got.'

'This is my night off,' Bear said. He turned away and went into his dark hooch.

Atterburn followed him. 'What the hell are you going to do in here?' he demanded.

'Go to bed, or hang myself. I haven't quite decided yet.'

'You got to be shitting me! You mean you're going to just come in here and go to bed?'

'No, Atterburn. I told you I might hang myself instead.'

'Bear, what's your nursie-poo been giving you to drink, anyway? You got to be drunk to talk about going to bed tonight!'

Bear lay down on his bunk in the dark. 'That's right,' he said. 'I'm drunk. And you know, Atterburn, that when I get drunk I step on all the shit I come across. So if you don't want a waffle tread on your ass, get out of my hooch!'

Atterburn sputtered out the door. Beyond his quick footsteps on the metal walk, the deep thump of the bombs in the ammunition bunkers continued to roll over the ridge.

He heard Blood coming within two minutes. The steps rang sharply, as if Blood had somehow contrived to square off the very sound in a military manner.

A light flicked on beyond the Bear's closed eyelids. 'What is this?' Blood's voice demanded.

'This is a man lying on his bunk and minding his own business,' Bear answered without opening his eyes.

'Are you drunk?' Blood snapped off the end of the question between his teeth.

'Sir, when I'm drunk, I step on all the shit I come across. Do you feel anything?' The words had worked so well with Atterburn that the Bear tried them again as an incantation. If they rid of him of Blood for the moment, he did not care what else might follow. He did not really expect them to rid him of Blood; but Blood snapped off his light and walked out. Bear felt neither surprise nor interest.

Blood had never paid enough attention to his underlings as persons to be surprised that the Bear should be drunk; and it never occurred to him that anything else could make a man insult his superior directly. Blood rather liked the idea of the Bear drunk. It was an ordinary weakness. Let him sleep it off where he was. Maybe a rocket would fall on him.

For hours the Bear did lie there, listening to the war go on around him. It went none the worse for his absence, so far as he could tell. A machine gun along the perimeter chattered uneasily, and flares popped beyond the wire. Another weapon took up the cadence, and then another, and soon a whole sector of the perimeter was wild in defense against shadows. After several minutes it all died away. Over the ridge the fire the bombs had begun continued to gnaw its way through the ammunition bunkers, intermittently flinging out with a roar the artifacts of war it uncovered. The muffled explosions went on until near dawn, when a light north breeze sprang up and with a puff of its breath chased the sound back over the Ky Ha ridge.

The breeze poured wraithlike through the screen above the Bear's bunk. Its cool hands passed over him. Bear came near to weeping.

12

There was a soft step on the porch outside the back door. The door opened and Arp came in, followed by the gray light of dawn. He stopped at the foot of the bed. He stood looking down at the Bear, but he said nothing until the Bear spoke: 'I'm alive, if that's what you were wondering.'

'That's not exactly it,' Arp said. 'I heard this strange report that you were blasphemously drunk, and I had to see it for myself. How's your head?'

'About like my heart,' Bear said. 'Empty.'

Arp went to the end of the hooch and switched on the light. Bear's eyes were full of the darkness: he threw an arm over them. 'It's for your own good,' Arp said, laughing. He came back toward the bunk. The laugh was abruptly cut off. 'Good God, Bear, are you all right?' He leaned forward, stretching a hand toward the bloody fatigues the Bear was still wearing.

'No. I'm not.'

'Those asses! They didn't even ask if you were hurt, did they?' Arp stormed. 'Stay there! I'll get the truck!'

'No need,' said the Bear. 'It's not my blood.'

Arp had already started. He stopped, his hand on the door, and turned back.

'It's Alice's.'

'Alice's?'

'She's dead, sir.' He could not keep a little tremble from his voice.

'Oh, God, Don!' Arp switched the light off, as if to cover up in darkness what he had said, his joking tone, his stupidity. He came back to stand beside the bed. 'I'm sorry,

Don. Forgive me!'

'For what?'

Arp had no answer to that. 'Is there anything I can do for you?' he asked helplessly, knowing there wasn't.

'Yes. You can keep me from cutting Atterburn's tongue out when he lets it run off today.' He said it as if joking, but then he sat up on the side of the bed and buried his face in his hands. 'Atterburn is going to have more smart remarks about her than I think I can bear, with her in the hands of strangers.'

'I'll take care of him,' Arp said.

'Thank you.'

All the ships that were combat-ready went out that morning on a combat assault. There was no advance planning, as there had been for Major Hart's assault. At 0730 word came down from Division that the assault would go. The ships that had already departed on missions were recalled. At 0900 they were to assemble at Hill 69, across Route One in the foothills north of Nui Ong.

The event swept the Bear up with the rest. When he took his helmet to the ship, Ruth had already preflighted. He climbed aboard without so much as looking at the main rotor – nodding to Cripps, who stood tongue-tied with the blade hook in his hand – plugged in his helmet, cranked the engine, called the tower and his second ship, and flew away.

As the ship crossed the main runway, Ruth called Chu Lai tower for traffic, but there was none. The main runway was closed. At the far end plumes of white smoke trailed away to the south.

Helicopters littered the tiny pad at Hill 69. The guns parked down along the fence overlooking the rice paddies, and the officers walked up to the briefing at one corner of the pad while the enlisted crews tied down the blades.

There were ships from two understrength aviation companies on the pad. Baker was to lead the flight. He strode importantly beside his helicopter while the pilots gathered.

Those around the Bear looked sidelong at him, or mumbled and edged away. Even Ruth fidgeted in silence beside him. Bear did not care. It was not a sorrow he wanted to share. He could see that the word had spread beyond Atterburn; but Atterburn stayed away. Blood, however, did not: he came down to greet the Bear: 'So, how's the head this morning, eh? Bothered by the noise of a few helicopters? If you want to play, you've got to pay, soldier.' It was the first time that Blood had ever spoken to the Bear in what passed for a friendly way. 'What, nothing but sour faces?' he went on. 'I thought you'd be a real tiger today, after your vacation last night. The sun's not bright enough for you this morning I guess. Nothing but a sunshine walrus after all, ha ha.'

'Sorry I couldn't get to everybody,' Arp muttered behind the Bear as Blood turned away.

There was no sun that morning. Over the coast there was a high thin overcast, but low clouds shrouded Nui Ong. Men looked up uncertainly toward it as Baker began the briefing from the door of his helicopter.

'This morning,' Baker said, 'Charley is up there on the mountain grinning; but he ain't going to be grinning long, because we're going to cut his ass off and keep it for a trophy. Our mission is to pick up an infantry company here' – he pointed to his map and gave the coordinates – 'and put them down here, on the west slope of this little peak.' Ho Cong was its name. It was one of the subpeaks of the big mountain. 'Whoever fired the rockets into the main post last night is going to be running west for the jungle. This company is going to cut them off at the pass.' While Baker was talking, Blood paced impatiently beside the helicopter. When Baker had finished with the details of time, place, and radio frequencies, Blood jumped onto the step on the helicopter skid. 'I reckon I don't need to tell you,' Blood said, ''cause Major Baker said it, that this is an important mission. We're goin' to get out there and romp and stomp, and the eyes of the whole Division are goin' to be on us. Maybe the eyes of the whole country, or the whole world.' (Blood could not know that in the avalanche of attacks which had taken place around the country, the journalists would not have an attention span sufficiently broad to extend beyond those closest to their native haunts, the press bars of Saigon and Da Nang. A mortar shell close to him is always more interesting than a rocket in some remote province.) 'Now, this could be a hot LZ. The slick drivers are gonna expect some good support from you gunnies, and they deserve to get it. I know what it's like to fly support in a really hot landing, and what it's like to need it, too, 'cause I've flown both ends. The guns are gonna have to work close and put those tubes right down Charley's throat before they fire, even if it means facin' down some heavy-caliber weapons. Now . . .'

Blood would have waxed eloquent, except that Baker announced that pickup time was in one-five minutes and he would be pulling pitch for the flight to the PZ in zero-five.

The guns went out early and orbited while the slicks trickled out of the pad to join up in the air in the initial formation for the pickup. There were thirteen slicks and three light fire teams of gunships - the two led by Arp and the Bear, and one from the other company. The slicks were barely in formation before they reached the PZ and Baker's anticollision beacon flashed the signal for landing.

About the mountain itself clouds still hung below the peak. The flight path would have to follow back around the north slope. It was empty, jungle-choked country.

The guns orbited upwind from the PZ waiting for the slicks to load. At each circle the dark bulk of Nui Ong swept across the windshield and vanished astern. 'Nice day for an RF,' someone muttered sourly on the gunship channel. Otherwise there was no chatter on the radios.

The flight started north along the foothills to the west of the Chu Lai perimeter and swung into the broad but rapidly narrowing valley on the north side of the tumbling mass of mountains that was Nui Ong. Few of the crews had come this way before. American units did not often patrol the jungles beyond the head of that valley. The Bear had last come this way on his last flight into Hill 473. The landing zone for which the flight was bound was halfway to that hill, above the peak called Ho Cong. ('Do you reckon,' one of the slick pilots from the other company had said, 'that's because nobody's out there but Uncle Ho and the Viet Cong?') The clouds lowered as the flight penetrated the valley. Soon, at the elevation of the LZ, the ships were scraping the cloud base. While Ruth flew, the Bear studied the ground. The broken valley floor on the right held a narrow stream slashing a streak of daylight through the treetops. On the left the steep flank of the mountain, a wall of black treetops, curved out of sight ahead. They crossed the first, lower, saddle beyond Ho Ngon, into the land where the streams ran north rather than east down to Song Ben Van and the sea. Baker led the formation along the lower slopes, over the almost hidden jungle village of Trung Chanh, and turned upstream above the silver thread springing from the heart of the mountain.

The valley pressed in on both sides. The gunships, which had been flying on both flanks, were forced in below the formation or ahead of it. 'Where do you want to be?' Ruth asked on the intercom. He was staring up at the bellies of the slicks two hundred feet above. The rocky streambed was rising below.

Bear came on the controls and edged the ship out to the right until his rotor was slapping at the treetops. 'Vere's going to be noffing but clouds in a minute,' Ruth said. At the same instant Arp came on the UHF. He was well ahead of the formation, leading the first fire team. He called to ask Bear, at the head of the formation, if the LZ was yet in sight.

'Negative yet,' Baker answered. He sounded annoyed.

Ruth had picked up his chart. 'It's in ve clouds,' he said. 'We're at ve LZ altitude now.' The slicks were scudding in and out of the rags of cloud that looped down from the overcast. The air became turbulent. The main rotor banged through vertical gusts.

'Is that cumulo-granite out there?' an anonymous voice asked over one of the radios.

'It's only a little stratus,' another answered.

'Strato-granite?' asked the first.

'This is Coyote Six,' Baker's voice said vehemently. 'Cut the chatter.'

Arp's call slashed urgently across the banter: 'Six, Wolf

Lead is making a one-eighty. There's no place to go up here.' Bear saw Arp's fire team a half mile ahead break to left and right in hard driving turns that barely cleared the treetops at the sides and bottom of the valley. The two ships came whirling back toward the formation.

'I have the LZ in sight,' Baker announced. His beacon came on. His ship nosed up into a decelerating attitude, but did not descend.

'Negative on the LZ!' Arp called. 'The LZ is in the cloud!'

'Stay off this channel, Wolf.' It was Blood's voice this time.

The formation was then a half mile from the spot where Arp had turned back, groping forward at sixty knots. There were at most thirty seconds before Baker's error became irremediable. Probably there was not half thirty seconds, for although one helicopter might grope through the murk at a near standstill, and so find a way safely back to the clear air below and behind, a formation of thirteen could not. In the cloud the formation would dissolve into thirteen mutual unseen enemies each wielding a deadly blade. But where Arp had turned back the valley was already too narrow to turn the whole formation. And ahead in the clouds the rocks climbed on three sides, perhaps faster than a loaded helicopter could climb.

Bear saw what was coming. He broke instantly to the left and below the formation, then pulled in power to accelerate away from Arp's fire team arrowing down the streambed toward him. He did not see what happened behind him, but he heard Baker call: 'Six going around. Execute bad weather break.'

Baker had not briefed on bad weather procedures. He was not planning to fly into cloud, not with a formation of slicks behind him. But sure of himself, sure of what he thought he saw, sure of the need to put the troops on the ground where Division demanded, he did fly into cloud, with a formation of slicks behind him.

Even without special briefing, every pilot in the formation would have known what had to be done. The bad weather break was a standard flight school exercise, designed to separate three ships which had lost sight of one another. The lead ship in the V was to climb straight ahead, while those on either side turned right or left away from the flight path in a standard-rate turn and at a five-hundred-foot-per-minute climb to the right or descent to the left. With three aircraft this would provide vertical and horizontal spacing while the pilots sorted out what to do next. With thirteen ships in close formation and rocks rising on three sides, it could not be done. Every pilot in the formation would have known that, too. For that reason only the first six aircraft entered the cloud. Those at the rear still had room to turn and dive away, bursting into a startled swarm in which they all maneuvered frantically to avoid striking rocks or trees or one another. All but one managed that. That one turned directly into the path of Arp's gunship. The gunship's main rotor struck off the tail boom of the slick, whose cabin nosed inexorably over and dived into the rocky stream. The gunship's blade, shattered and hopelessly out of balance, tore itself free from the airframe and went pinwheeling through the formation. ('It looked like a telephone pole whizzing by,' one pilot said.) The fuselage dropped through the jungle canopy without leaving a mark.

Atterburn, flying a hundred meters behind Arp, shot through the melee and came untouched out the other side calling out that Arp and another ship had gone down.

Bear turned back instantly in a violent pull-up that shook the aircraft but brought it back to cloud base, above the other ships and headed back up the valley. 'Is Ward still with us?' he called on intercom.

'He's coming up, sir,' Cripps said. It was the first thing Cripps had said all day.

Ward's was the only other ship Bear was responsible for now. Knowing that it was still in the air, he dived away behind the formation to where the cabin of the slick lay cracked open like an egg on the rocks. A body was rolling slowly down the foaming stream. As it bumped and rolled from pool to pool, the limp arms waved meaningless signals to the gunships overhead.

The air at the head of the valley was suddenly empty; but

the radios were cluttered with frantic calls as the slicks in the cloud tried to announce their movements to one another. They seemed to cease trying at the same moment, and into the ensuing silence a single word erupted: 'Mayday!' The silence closed over the word.

Baker came back on the UHF: 'Aircraft calling Mayday, identify yourself.' There was no answer.

Baker had not heard Atterburn's call on the gunship channel. In the cloud himself, he had no time for those who had managed to stay clear. He tried now to gather the ships still in the cloud: 'This is Coyote Six. Any aircraft now IFR, climb to at least forty-five hundred feet and fly a heading for the coast. Contact Chu Lai radar for a steer. The rest of the flight, reassemble at the PZ. Anyone in the cloud who breaks out, return to the PZ. Now, I want all aircraft to check in . . . ah, by your position in the formation. This is lead. Number two?'

Two checked in. So did three and four. There was a long wait. Baker broke it at last: 'Five? Number five, do you read?' Number five failed to answer. Baker called at last for number six, who said quietly, 'Six here. We're in the clear and joining the rest of the formation, in sight.'

While Baker was counting his lost slicks, the Bear had been on the gunship radio, asking where Arp had gone down.

'Left side of the valley,' Atterburn answered. He, too, had turned back and was picking his way through the tangle of slicks.

'There's smoke up there,' Handy said.

A thin trail of white was oozing up from the trees on the valley wall. Bear flew slowly up toward it, through it. The ship was too heavy to hover there. He flew a slow figure eight upslope from the smoke. Even as he did so, the smoke increased. The shock of a heavy explosion rocked his own aircraft, and a ball of fire belched through the treetops. It left a ragged black patch of withered leaves, but the ground still could not be seen. 'We can't get to vem wifout a winch,' Ruth said.

Blood had been flying the last ship in the formation. He

called to Baker now, 'Six, Coyote Five here. We have a flight of six up, and one more in sight. Number twelve is down. Will check him and proceed to Papa Zulu to wait for you. Break. Flight, this is Coyote Five, moving from Tail-end Charley up to lead. Number seven, move back here, and number six, you can join in at the rear. Break. Wolf Lead, what's your status?' Blood's voice was choked with emotion – the voice of a man who has just won the Irish sweepstakes.

Bear watched Blood's ship slip below the truncated formation and bob up again at the front. 'Coyote,' he radioed, 'be advised that Wolf Lead is down.'

'He lost a blade and went into the trees,' Atterburn called. Atterburn was making slow passes over the wreckage of the slick.

Blood acknowledged. 'Any survivors in either ship?'

'Negative survivors in view,' Bear told him. 'Request a medevac with a winch.' The formal phrasing of radio procedure was a great relief to him at that instant. It left no room for emotion. The words had a fitness of their own. They embodied action; and action, even when hopeless, was at least something – something to keep futile despair at bay. Coldness was better than tears. If he could have announced Alice's death over a radio, perhaps it would not gnaw at him so.

They slid into the pickup zone and shut down to wait for the rest of the slicks to come down from the overcast. Two of them had already landed. The others were soon there, except for one that had wandered far to the south and descended over the plain halfway to Quang Ngai. While they waited, Baker had earnest discussions with the infantry battalion commander, who arrived in a jeep only minutes after the flight landed.

Bear looked around to see who was missing. Something was wrong, but he could not decide what for a long time. He got it at last. 'Where's Carter?' he asked Ruth. Had it been Carter's ship in the stream? Bear asked in sudden fear, 'He wasn't flying number five, was he?'

Ruth looked at him strangely. 'No, he wasn't flying number five.'

'Where is he?' Bear asked. He saw the way Ruth was looking at him.

'I fought you knew – his ship went down last night.'

'Carter?'

Ruth nodded. He knew the state Bear was in, and he wanted to say as little as possible.

'What happened to him?' Bear saw that Ruth was trying to avoid an answer. 'Is he dead?'

Ruth nodded again. 'He went down just at dark.'

Bear remembered then. 'He was medevacked, wasn't he? Him and two others.' There had been three on Wolcheski's helicopter. 'Who were the other two?'

'Williams – ve new guy, you remember?' Already, Rufe was calling someone else a new guy. How quickly they went! 'And Rensdorff, the crew chief.'

'Dead?'

'Williams was. Rensdorff is up at ve hospital. Ve gunner wasn't hurt,' Ruth added, trying to end, at least, with better news. 'He stayed wif ve ship until vey hooked it out. But I fink a mortar hit what was left of it, on ve ramp last night.' He laughed a little nervously.

Bear shouldered the loss of two more friends and went back to his ship.

Blood came there as soon as all the slicks had landed. The other Wolfpack pilots had already gathered there. Bear was now the senior officer in the platoon, and they expected him to lead the three remaining gunships. 'We're going back out,' Blood said. 'There's a new LZ if the other one isn't in the clear yet.' He showed it to them on his map. 'You'll have to form a heavy fire team with your three ships. Atterburn, you'll be the lead ship.'

Atterburn's eyes were like a pinball machine.

'So the Burn gets a promotion,' Ward said before leaving for his ship. 'And he's never led even a fire team. How does Blood figure he can take Arp's place?'

'He'll never take Arp's place,' the Bear said.

The alternate LZ was not needed. By the time the formation – eleven ships now – reached the area once more, the primary LZ was in the clear. The formation overflew the crash site. Dustoff was there with a winch, hovering along the stream collecting bodies.

There was no sign of ship number five. It was a ship from the other company. After the second sortie, all of the aircraft of that company returned to search the slopes of Nui Ong for any trace of wreckage. But there was no emergency radio transmission, no signal flare, no scrap of metal on the rocks, no tear in the jungle canopy to mark a grave. The trees on Nui Ong stretched a hundred feet from base to crown, and a ship that went through the canopy would leave no trace unless it burned. If it burned, everyone aboard would die swiftly. If it did not, then injured men might linger for days in the wreckage; but they would never be found.

The sky was dark in the east. The long waves broke slowly on the shore, leaving trains of foam-bubbles that winked out in random order or were crushed by the next wave. The coarse sand slid away beneath his feet and slid back. The sea wind smoothed it into place once more, and his steps were gone. Stars climbed out of the misty edge of the sea and glittered faintly overhead. All around, the land lay under the brief truce of evening. He did not smell the sea, nor feel the wind, nor savor the stillness of the land. His heartbeat raged in his ears, and his thoughts were driven down the wind from a wider sea.

Wolcheski found him there on the shore.

'Sometimes I wish I could vanish the way you do,' Wolcheski said. 'Your Operations doesn't know where you are.'

'If they need somebody killed, I'll be there,' Bear answered.

'I wish you had come to us,' Wolcheski said.

'It's not what you want that makes you fat.'

'My grandmother used to say that,' Wolcheski said. He and Bear both smiled, but there was no joy in either smile.

Bear stuffed his hands in his pockets and worked his boots

into the sand. 'Anyway, I'm afraid if I was in your business I'd see too many people I know. Carter . . . Arp. It can't be that much fun carting in your friends' bodies.'

'It ain't much, but it's the only war we've got.'

'I suppose it beats killing. Lots of things beat killing. Maybe dying does. I don't know. I've only tried the one.'

Wolcheski grasped his arm above the elbow. 'Listen, Bear, promise me you won't do anything rash, eh?'

Bear shook the hand away. 'You're starting to sound like Arp. Jesus, what would I do without somebody to worry about me? You do know about Arp, don't you?' He looked at Wolcheski for the first time.

'Yes. One of our ships went out for him.'

'Why is it the people you like always get it first, Ski?'

'I don't know. That's the way wars are arranged, I guess. "The good die first, and they whose hearts are dry as summer dust burn to the socket".'

'Yeah. Why couldn't *I* have been born with a golden tongue, instead of a puckered asshole? Well, don't worry about me, Ski. I'm not going to drown myself. But I'm just trying to decide why it is that I'm not. Can you tell me?'

'Because you're the only Bear we've got?'

'And I'm not the Bear that I once was. I'm empty, Ski. I've had good friends, more good friends than I'm worth. And they're all gone, or going. It's the people that matter to us that give us substance. If *you* go, maybe I'll just crinkle and blow away in the wind. I'm light-headed already.'

'You've got plenty of friends, Bear. More than you know.'

'Maybe I'll have one less enemy, at least. Baker's been scampering around Division, trying to head off an investigation. Isn't that grand? Blood's grinning from ear to ear. If he grins any more, the top of his head will fall off.' They had begun to climb the trail up the cliff. Bear stopped near the top, near the roll of concertina. The vine now had covered it; but the barbs were still there. Bear shook it idly with his foot. 'I hope you can stand my rattling tongue,' he said. 'I don't know what I can do, Ski. I really don't.' They had talked all around Alice. He saw that Wolcheski was not going to mention her if he did not. But there was no need to say her name. He turned his face seaward once more. 'What's out there? Tomorrow, coming up out of the sea, bringing nothing but more killing or more dying. As far as I can tell, neither one is worth a rat's ass.'

'More living, too, Bear.'

'Is there? I wish I knew that.'

For answer, Wolcheski only pointed. He was pointing at the wire that Bear was shaking. The vine that had covered the concertina was putting forth flowers. They fell in pale cascades over the rusting coils of the wire.

Bear pulled at a spray of blossoms. The petals stripped free and fluttered away like snow. He shook his head.

'Bear, if things get rough, you can call on me.'

'You bet your golden tongue on that, Lieutenant.' He laughed, but it was a dark, mirthless laugh. Wolcheski's offer, an offer of nothing but friendship, moved him; but he dared not let it touch him. He could not clutch at another straw caught in the wind. He turned the offer to its other, unintended, meaning: 'I've got your call-sign on my kneeboard. You'll be the first to know when I need to be carted in from the field.'

'I was right!' Atterburn crowed. 'She didn't come back to work!'

'Who?' Bear didn't look up to ask. He kept his face buried in his pillow so that Arp's empty bunk couldn't stare him down. Besides, he knew who.

'Suzie. That's who. I *told* you it was her, Bear.'

'All right, you told me.' Atterburn's name for the mortar attack had spread through the company. To every man it was already 'Suzie's Revenge.' But today, the day after Tet, was the first day the hooch-maids would return to work, and they had all been waiting.

'Yan came back,' Ruth said, after he had waited for Bear to speak again.

'What's that prove?' Atterburn demanded.

'Well, she's Suzie's daughter.'

'She's probably hanging around to get more information for the next time.'

Bear walked out of the alert hut and through the company area.

Yan was in his hooch. She was ironing a set of fatigues. When he came through the door, she dropped the iron. 'You not hurt?' she gasped. She had washed out the fatigues with Alice's blood in them.

'No, I'm not hurt,' he said. 'I'm number-one GI.'

'I see here' – she raised the fatigue jacket – 'I think you *bi thu'o'ng* – wounded.' She turned away and took something from behind the end of his bunk. 'I bring you,' she said, extending her hand shyly. 'For Tet.' She had brought him a tiny basket of flowers. He took it and turned it in his hands, unable to say anything. She looked away and said in a lower voice, 'I bring for *Trung-úy* Arp, too. You see him?'

He made himself look her in the eye as he answered. '*Trung-úy* Arp *bi thu'o'ng*,' he said. 'No –*tu'-trân*.' He said, 'killed in action.' He did not know the Vietnamese for just 'dead.'

'Ai! *Trung-úy* Arp!' She folded herself onto the bed behind the ironing board and began to weep. At length she wiped her eyes into one of his handkerchiefs and asked unsteadily, 'What happen him?'

'Death happen him. That's all. He's gone. *Tu'-trân*! The dark angel took him! Christ!' He did not know how to tell her in her own language, and he hated the bastard Army patois that was all the hooch-maids understood because it was all that was spoken to them. He thrashed incoherently among the stubble of two languages, unwilling to reduce Arp's death to the ridiculous, unable to raise it to the sublime or even the comprehensible.

'Mama-san be sorry,' Yan quavered. 'She think *Trung-úy* Arp number one.' She began to sob again.

'Isn't your mama-san here today?' Bear asked.

'*Khong biẽt?*'

'Mama-san no come to work today?'

'Mama-san sick,' she said. 'She no come work. She no come work again.'

'What's the matter with her?'

'*Khong biẽt*.'

'Why she no come work?'

'*Khong biĕt*,' Yan insisted, crying harder than ever. It was all she would answer – that she did not understand the question.

Each time he had thought he grasped some piece of truth, it slipped away and left him holding out an empty hand. Now he felt even his old anger on Suzie's behalf slipping away. Surely she would have chosen another day to stop coming to work, if there were any truth in what Atterburn implied? Or did she want them to know? But then, would she send her daughter back? And with flowers? And Suzie *had* liked Arp – he knew that was true. But what would she do, if duty called her?

He dropped the matter from his mind. What difference could it make? Either way, where was Arp now? And Alice? He picked up the fatigue jacket which Yan had dropped on the bed. It was clean. There was no sign of the life that had drained into it. How long would it be before they were all gone from his heart?

13

Cripps rolled over on the sour-smelling, mildewed sleeping bag. The Bear was seated on the next cot, his legs crossed and his hands cradled palm-up in his lap with his thumbs not quite touching. He raised his eyes. They met Cripps's own, and stayed for a moment. 'Cripps,' he said, 'you sleep like a pig in clover. I wish I had your dreams.'

Cripps blushed. 'They ain't much to write home about, sir,' he muttered.

'No? From the look of you when you were asleep there, I'd have said your momma would have been pleased to hear about them.' The ghost of his old gentle smile touched Cripps, faint but warm as candlelight seen through a frosted winter window.

'I'm not so much for writing home,' Cripps said with a slow shake of his head. 'Not like Mr Covington was. He was the one, wasn't he, sir? I don't guess it does any good to talk about it, though?'

'Maybe it's a good thing to talk about old friends,' Bear said. 'Do you think we could keep him alive for a while, if we talk about him?'

'We could use him now, sir.'

'You speak the truth, Cripps.'

'Not that I don't like Mr Ruth, you know, but . . .'

'Rufe is good folks,' Bear said. 'But new friends never quite fill the void.'

'I guess that's it.' After a long silence Cripps added tentatively, 'Do you ever hear from . . . Pinky, sir?' He hesitated before using her name. He would have called her 'Mrs Covington'; but he had never heard her spoken of except as 'Pinky,' and he always thought of her so. He had seen her picture. It was hard to say 'Mrs Covington' about a girl no older than himself.

'I wrote and told her about Cov,' Bear said. 'I guess you know that. I haven't heard from her since. Maybe she didn't want to know, Cripps, not really? Maybe I should have let her think, well, somewhere he's alive. Maybe the Army knew best. But I told her.' He sighed. 'What do you think, Cripps? Was it wrong for me to tell her?'

Cripps was flattered that the Bear would ask his opinion on anything. He did not hesitate to answer. He had the answer ready in his heart. 'You did right, sir.' He would have told her himself, had she written to him. But probably she did not know his name, or even that he existed. 'You did right.'

'Well, one time out of a hundred probably won't spoil my reputation,' Bear said.

'Maybe you ought to write again, sir,' Cripps offered. 'If you haven't heard from her, you don't know that she got your letter. And you don't know that she didn't write back if she did get it. You remember I got just that part of a letter from my momma when that C-130 carrying the mail got hit by a rocket at Da Nang?'

'Cripps, I love your faith. You restore my soul.'

But the words were empty. He knew it. He did not believe anything would restore his soul. He would not write the letter. He was afraid that she hated him because Cov had died flying in his place.

Cripps knew that, too. Bear said nothing about it now, but Cripps remembered.

There was no memorial service for Arp and his crew. Major Baker did not want their end remembered. An investigation of the mission had not materialized, but the wraith of it hung always about the orderly room, and Baker lurked in his back office listening for its first footsteps on his floor. He said little about combat missions now, and made sure that Blood did not, either, at least where he might hear of it. Blood hated losing the combat assaults this way; but he did not say so, at least not where Baker might hear. He did complain discreetly in the officers' club, the alert hooch, the Operations shack; but Baker, if he knew, did not dare to take notice.

Blood had a growing fear that without combat assaults to fly, not only was there no chance for glory, but no chance that Baker would be killed. He might drag on as CO forever, or until the end of Blood's tour of duty.

And Atterburn became acting gun platoon commander.

'Atterburn! God help us!' Ward groaned.

'You say it should have been the *Bear*?' Handy said to Cripps. 'What are you, crazy? Suppose he was to take another spell of not firin' his weapons? How many Charlies would still be alive to shoot up your ass another day? He ain't the Bear he used to be, you know. I admit, he was somethin' to watch, in the old days. I seen him put a dud rocket through Victor Charley's belt buckle at a thousand meters! Sure, he's been all right here lately, but you can't count on him. He ain't the Bear he used to be.'

Atterburn began by pasting on the alert hooch wall a chart showing the running total of kills for each fire team. He personally inspected the weapons of every ship daily. He spoke of applying for a commission. 'Captain Blood thinks I ought to do it,' he said, as if seeking the wise advice of others on that hard question. 'But I don't know. It's a lot of responsibility. Look at Captain Blood – he's got a lot on his shoulders.'

'Not to mention his conscience,' Ward muttered.

'Vat's right, I wouldn't do it,' Ruth said. 'Once you get to be captain, vat's ve end of your flying. Noffing but desk jobs. You wouldn't like ve responsibility. Don't do it, Burn.'

'A lot you know about it, Rufe!' Atterburn answered indignantly. 'You think just because you don't mind being a flunky all your life, nobody else minds. If you want to get ahead, you've got to grab for the brass ring.'

'Well, if it's what you want, ven do it!' Ruth said, perplexed. 'You'll probably like sitting behind a desk.'

'I don't think I could stand it if I ended up just sitting behind a desk,' Atterburn said, shaking his head. 'What do you think, Bear?'

What Atterburn really wanted was for everyone to be aware of the magnitude of the problems facing him. But he also yearned for the Bear to show some envy. By date in grade the Bear should have been acting gun platoon commander. Atterburn was determined to smoke out the hard feeling that must be inside him.

'I think you ought to follow Blood's advice,' Bear said. 'After all, he used to be a sergeant, and look at him now.' He smiled blandly and scratched his rear.

'You don't have to worry about spending your life behind a desk, Atterburn,' Ward told him, 'so you might as well put in for a commission.'

'How's that?' Atterburn asked. Visions of general officer rank danced in his head.

'If you outlast the war, you're going to get riffed out anyway.'

Atterburn grinned uneasily at the laughter around him. They would be slower to laugh once he had his commission.

The numbers on Atterburn's chart grew rapidly. Those under the Bear's fire team grew as rapidly as any. The tide of killing that had begun to flow weeks before Tet was past its crest, but often the guns were out all night long. Bear, coming in after dawn to throw himself on his bunk, would turn away from Arp's empty bed, turn his eyes from the hospital buildings down the ramp, try not to dream of the figures caught in the wire under the fevered light of the flares, caught in the fiery web of the tracers.

One night outside LZ Ross they left a hundred bodies hanging in the wire when their ammunition gave out and they turned for Hill 63 to rearm. A Mustang fire team came on station behind them. Before the Wolfpack ships had gone five miles, one of the Mustangs called out that he had taken a round through the transmission and was going down. The pilot's voice was as calm as if he were announcing a stroll in the park. The ship landed outside the wire, within a hundred yards of unreachable friends. When the Wolfpack returned, the helicopter was standing there in the light of the flares, looking as if it had been parked, except that the blade was not tied down. The next afternoon one of the pilots walked into a firebase three miles away, dressed only in his OD undershorts and T-shirt. He had stripped off his uniform to look more like a farmer out in his fields. He was almost shot by a sentry for his efforts. But the rest of the crew were never seen again. Were they still alive somewhere, Bear wondered, in one of the secret jungle prisoner camps the VC were said to keep; or did only their names now wander the earth, to the torment of their families, kept moving because the Army permitted no empty tombs?

Bear defeated Arp's empty cot by occupying it. As the numbers on Atterburn's chart mounted, he could not bear being where it always met his eye, and Arp's old place still stood empty in the corner. He was not superstitious about the cot. He liked it better than being under the eye of the monster.

He was lying on Arp's cot one morning – he supposed it was a Sunday, for the chapel bell had rung an hour before – when Cripps appeared at his feet. It was one of those silver days into which the monsoon expires, a cool still day with the mountains awash in haze. The shutters were up. The hooch was bright with refracted sunlight, so that Cripps's untanned face floated against the remnant of darkness hiding above the rafters. Cripps was grinning.

'You look like the cat that ate the canary,' Bear told him. 'Do you know something I don't but wish I did?'

Cripps blushed, mumbled, and held out his hand with an envelope in it. 'I got your mail for you' was all he said.

'Cripps, you don't have to do that every day. You're turning into my personal servant lately.'

'It's okay, sir.'

Bear sat up and took the letter. Cripps stayed at the foot of the bed, beaming. Bear looked at the return address. He knew the hand even before he read the words: 'Covington.' It was from Pinky. He looked up at Cripps and then opened it.

Dear Bear [she wrote], I hope you'll forgive what must seem my unforgivable thoughtlessness in not thanking you for your letter to me. I did answer it, but my letter must have gotten lost somewhere between me and you, for I had a note from Sp. 4 Cripps (Doesn't he have a first name? I've written to him asking if he won't write again and tell me, but please you tell him, too) saying that you hadn't received it. I hope this will make up for it. I don't want you to think I'm angry with you for what you told me. You only told me the truth about Wes. It was what I asked, and it was what I wanted to know. I'll always be grateful to you for having the compassion to break the Army's rules (and thank you for explaining them to me – I hope their effect isn't always so cruel as it seemed to me) and share the hard truth with me. I know that Wes's death was hard for you to take, too. All of his letters showed how close he was to you. But you can't blame yourself for his death. You said he was flying your mission; but I know that's not true. If you had been flying, I would only have lost you both. That was why I didn't write to you sooner – not because I didn't think of you, but because I knew that you and Wes always flew together. Every time I thought of you I was terrified that I might write and learn that you weren't there, either.

Dear Bear, I wish you would write to me again. I know Wes asked you to be the godfather to our child, and that you agreed. I'm going to hold you to that. I so much want you to be that. I hope you won't think it silly of me to say that in that way it will seem that some part of Wes will still be coming home to us. Please stay whole for us, dear Bear, and write to let us know that you are.

'Stop grinning, Cripps,' Bear said roughly, as he finished the letter. 'You know I can't stand a show-off.'

'Yes, sir,' Cripps answered, grinning.

'The proper answer to that is "No, sir."'

'Yes, sir. No, sir.'

They both began to laugh. Bear felt that his heart had flowered.

'Share the joke,' Atterburn demanded as he came in the

door. Atterburn could never rid himself of a fear that unexplained laughter was aimed at him. 'What's the joke?' But the two of them only laughed the harder, until he wandered off to mull over the numbers on his kill chart.

14

The carefully nurtured plans of Baker and Blood bore fruit after the sowers had ceased to tend them. The slick pilots no longer treated special standby as anything more than a formality. They read their names on the list and wandered away in the evening to the movie at the officers' club. The only reason there was a full complement of crews available when the call did come from Division for a quick-reaction assault was that the call came at three A.M. The duty officer had some trouble locating the list of standby crews; but by 0330 pilots were beginning to straggle in to Operations with helmet bags and pistol belts in their hands and sleep in their eyes.

The fire team on standby was called last, because the gunships were already preflighted and set up to fly, and also because the duty officer in his distress forgot that gunship escort had to be provided. The crews in the alert hooch slept on uneasily as the mission took shape around them.

Marching feet moved through the Bear's dreams. Dark shapes passed him in the darkness. They bore weapons and carried helmet bags under their arms as they trod inexorably down the hill to where the helicopters waited. He searched among them for a face he knew, but it was not to be found. Every face was turned from him, and there was no reply to his questions.

A low mound of sandbags rose beside him. He turned to it and began to climb. As he climbed a wind arose from the sea. The rain streamed over him. The sand ran beneath his feet, and the faster he climbed, the faster it flowed away. The red star before him winked in time to his footsteps. With each step he took toward it, the star moved farther off. 'What's the joke, anyway?' Atterburn asked him. The star fell heavily into the sea. He sought it up and down the rows of drawers. Each drawer had a name on it. He could not read the names. The drawer handles were cold to his touch. He rattled and pounded at them in vain. They would not open. The clerk laughed at him: 'Why do you seek the living among the dead? He is in his tomb.' Below the cliffs the sea cast spray into the white dawn. 'Go back,' he said to Alice. 'I have to find it alone.' 'You can't,' she told him, 'it doesn't exist alone.' She walked heavily beside him. Her pregnancy made her clumsy on the rough path, but she went on, cool and white as the dawn that trailed its fingers down the sea. 'Look,' she said, 'it's still there. You can see it.' He did see it. The dawn cleared the mist from the sea, and in the space where the mist had been, the space where heaven and earth flowed into one, he saw it. The island floated there, mirrored between sea and sky, a part of both and of neither, untouched by the storms of war – Cu Lao Re, the rock in the void, the dream of peace beyond the bleeding land.

A burning light drove the image from his eyes. Was it the sun that had leaped into the sky? 'Wake up, Bear, wake up!'

The lights overhead had been turned on. 'Time to get a move on. There's a briefing.'

'There goes my night vision,' Ward was grumbling. 'Who turned that on?'

'I did. Get your night vision on your own time.' It was Captain Blood. He was going down the row of cots, jolting men awake with a kick at the foot of each cot.

The scramble horn or an incoming round would have brought the Bear to his feet wide awake in an instant; but he was not tuned to wake to a human voice. Groggy and disoriented, he buckled on his pistol belt and stumbled across to Operations. 'What's ve matter, B?' Ruth asked. 'You look like you saw a ghost.' Bear shook his head, but he could not shake off the dream. The night was clear and chill, but the cold air did not clear his head.

The Operations hooch was filled to the corners with dark-eyed pilots. They talked in low tones among themselves.

There was none of the horseplay that preceded most briefings. 'I just can't get up to operating rpm three hours before get-up time.' Carlisle said. No one laughed.

Rauch was drawing on the plastic overlay to the large-scale area chart. Blood paced nervously behind him, three paces to the right, then three to the left. At each end he consulted his watch. He stopped when Baker came down into the hooch.

Baker smiled about the room at the dim ranks of men in the unlighted rear half of the hooch. His forcibly steady smile bordered on being a grimace. Rauch met him beside the chart and began gesturing toward the Tam Ky coast while Baker shakily lit a cigarette. He blinked off the glare of the match and nodded his head as Rauch spoke to him. When Rauch had finished, the major made an expansive gesture toward the chart with one hand, as if offering the territory all to Rauch, and sat down abruptly on the nearest chair.

'Y'all want to have a seat, and we'll get this thing on the road,' Rauch said. The room subsided into silence.

'As some of your prob'ly know,' he began, 'you folks are all on standby for a quick-reaction force tonight. Well, tonight we're goin' to quick-react – even if not *too* quick.' He glanced at his watch. 'Division says there's a big shootout goin' on up here' – he gestured toward the chart of the coast north of Chu Lai – 'at about three-six-zero, two-eight-zero. There's supposed to be an NVA company, more or less, in contact with an ARVN company. Division wants us to cut off their escape to the north by puttin' two platoons of grunts down on the beach between this here little river – that's a *big* river on the ground, in case you never noticed it – this little river and the ocean. We pick up the grunts north of Tam Ky, right here at three-zero-zero, two-five-zero, at oh-four-thirty, so we got to do some fast travelin'. Ground frequency is fifty-one-hundred on the Fox Mike. C and C will be on company UHF. You got eight ships, formation will be V's of three, and the basic load will be six packs – it's nice and cool out there tonight. Even ol' seven-six should be able to cut it.' Seven-six was a notoriously weak-hearted ship. On a hot day it could not be got off the ground with a half load of fuel and two passengers. 'Any questions?'

'What about lights?' someone asked.

Rauch shrugged and looked toward Baker. 'Sir?'

'Sure, we'll use some lights,' Major Baker answered loudly. There was a scattering of laughter.

'You want position lights on dim in formation?' Rauch suggested. 'No beacons, except to signal liftoff and landing?'

'Sure,' Baker said agreeably. 'Soun's great. Ask Blood there. Blood knows what we want.'

"'That's fine,' Blood said. His voice was neutral; but his eyes sparkled.

'Sir, you got anything else?' Rauch asked the major.

Baker teetered on the edge of his chair. It seemed only a matter of chance whether he rolled forward to his feet or back against the chair back. Finally, he lurched forward onto his feet and took the pointer from Rauch's hand. Jabbing the tip of it at the floor, he stood leaning against its frail length with both palms down against the handle. 'Gen'men,' he addressed them gravely, 'as L'tenan' Rauch said, this is a very importan' mission. Division gave us this one on a ver' short f-f-fuse, and they gave it to us b'cause they know this is the bes' ou'fit in the Division. I expec' you all to do a good job on this, hol' right in there tight while it's dark, you know, an' . . . an' . . .' Unable to think of anything further to say he at last asked if there were any questions. If there were, they went unanswered, for at that moment the overstressed pointer, which had been bowing under his weight, gave up the struggle and snapped in the middle. Baker jigged two steps forward and came upright against Captain Blood sitting in the first row. He straightened up with a shake of his shoulders, grinned around the room as if he had done it all for their entertainment grinned down at the shaft of the pointer still clutched in his right hand, and threw the shaft on the floor.

The briefing broke up in silence. The pilots drifted down the ramp among the dim blue lights marking the hover lanes. Across the muffled tread of boots on the ramp came the clatter of a blade hook dropped by some crewman. Cargo doors slid open with a hollow rumble. Blades were swung out to the side for starting. Overhead, the luminous stars hung heavy in the sky.

Bear had seen and heard all of it a hundred times before, but tonight it all seemed strangely foreign. He looked around, bemused by the dark shapes passing him. 'Hullo, Bear,' one said. It was Carlisle. His face, too, looked strange in the distortion of the shadowy darkness. His bare scalp glistened pale as a death's head as he swept off his cap to wipe sweat from his forehead with the back of one arm. Bear felt it was all still part of his dream. 'Wasn't Baker rare?' Carlisle said. 'I hear he just got back from the club an hour ago. If you ever want to know what it's like to fly with a drunk, ask me when we come back for breakfast.'

'Are you flying with him?'

'Somebody's got to do it.' They came to the tail of the Bear's ship, and Carlisle turned aside. 'Luck, Bear.'

'You too, Hitch. You need it more.'

Cripps was beside the tail boom, waiting to untie the blade. He greeted the Bear with a smile but no words. The Bear climbed into the cockpit and strapped himself in. Ruth was already there. Lights began to flick on up and down the ramp as aircraft was ready to crank. The whirr of the first starter rose up from a revetment. The Bear reached up to turn on his ship's position lights and nodded to Ruth. 'Clear, sir.' Those were the only words he heard from Cripps.

The formation hung off the left flank of his ship, no more than a faint constellation of colored lights, as motionless and unreachable as the stars themselves, which were splashed undimmed across the heavens. Over Song Ben Van the steel sheen of open water stretched below; but after that only faith could affirm that anything at all remained. Not a candle showed from the dark earth until the flight passed Tam Ky. Then, far to the northeast, there arose the distant flicker of artillery.

Two quick flashes of red from the head of the formation signaled that Baker and Carlisle's ship was descending. The cluster of lights dropped slowly away below the horizon. The Bear pointed down for Ruth to descend along one side of the formation's approach to the pickup zone. They were close to the ground before he could make out the faint triangle of lights that marked the PZ.

While the slicks were loading, the guns cast a wide circle around the pickup zone. Then the constellation of lights within the circle extended, turned, condensed once more as the formation left the earth and turned east toward the coast. The formation climbed, and Bear found that while he had been turned away, dawn had insinuated itself over the horizon. At first it spread in a long narrow line on that far edge of the world as if, without touching either heaven or earth, day had dawned in that uncertain space where in the long haze-blued afternoons the horizon hid itself. Then it spread slowly down the sea toward the dark shore. The marshes and sandy waste directly below seemed to feel it before the shore itself: they glimmered up faintly, the merest suggestion of solidity, as if the light afar had called them into being from nothing, but only half succeeded. Ahead, the waters of Truong Giang were dark behind the dunes at the sea's edge.

The artillery had gone out. The shells had been falling from the west until they could no longer be fired without endangering the helicopters. From a distance the shore was peaceful. But as the formation drove steadily closer, the impression of peace was proved false. The remnant of night that hung in the dunes beyond Truong Giang was torn by streaks of fire. The angry flashes spit back and forth in ever-changing patterns. Had not the malice behind them been known, they would have seemed as random as the paths of lightning.

The artillery strike had left a pall of smoke hanging over the dunes. On the windless air it thinned slowly, flowed with the chilled air down the shallow draws and valleys, billowed above the breath of dying men. It thickened and spread where the predawn chill spun a veil of mist over water and sand.

There was a fishing village on the landward side of Truong Giang. Beside the water its dark houses loomed like peaceful shaggy beasts sleepily contemplating the battle that raged on the far shore a half mile distant. Cooking fires within made the houses steam like cattle in a foggy meadow. Nothing moved within the village. The boats were drawn up on the shore, upended.

On the opposite shore men could now be seen moving. Who they might be, no one could tell. They waded the chest-deep fog slowly, sometimes plunging over their heads only to reappear farther on. As Ruth swung the aircraft toward them, they vanished into a deep pool of the mist and were seen no more.

'Were they Charlies?' Handy asked. Bear shook his head to show that he did not know. Up and down the dunes now tracers cut through the deepening mist. But they were fading as the light of dawn reached landward.

As the slicks turned north toward the landing zone, Bear ranged out over the dunes. Machine gun fire rippled up and down the evergreen scrub where two armies of Vietnamese drove one another over the sand. Sometimes he could see the men. Intent on killing one another as they were, none fired on him. He could not say which were friends and which foes. Nor, perhaps, could they. Once a smoke grenade was set off below him. It stained the velvet mist a bloody purple that spread and thinned and ebbed away into the valleys to melt into the remaining darkness. He could not tell what it was meant to mark. He prowled the marsh, the dunes, the edge of the sea. Bodies were bobbing in the low surf. They were dark-haired, uniformed, uniform in the equality of death; and whether they fought for north or south he could not say. Nor could they.

And always, always, the day crept up the sky, and down the sea. Not over the horizon – there was no horizon. But from wherever it was stored, from that eternity where sea and sky did not quite meet, day came back to try again. It was so like the dream, he almost expected to see the island there. He could not see it, but he knew it was there. Cu Lao Re was out there. There were things worth perceiving that the eye could not see. Visible or not, it was there still, the dream of peace. And home – that was there. Lost in the same uncertainty, but there nonetheless, it seemed suddenly close at hand. There was nothing between himself and home – only the curve of the sea, and time, and they were nothing at all.

He turned back to catch up to the formation. Baker had set the final approach path directly over the village. 'He should have gone farver norf,' Ruth said, 'so he wouldn't have to overfly ve village.' The landing zone was nearly a mile farther north in a narrow marsh between the tidal channel and the dunes.

As Ruth spoke, a broken stream of tracer bullets darted from Baker's aircraft toward the dark roofs of the village. 'Wolf Lead,' Baker's voice said from the company radio channel, 'Coyote Six is takin' fire from this village. Reques' to fix 'em. Flight, open up.' His voice, instead of urgency, contained a sly gaiety.

'Not another Mustang trick!' Bear kept Ruth's hand from the arming switches. Only one of the other slicks had opened fire – Blood's, at the rear of the formation.

The roof of one of the houses began to smolder. The slow general seep of cooking smoke from within changed to a dense white cloud boiling from one side near the ridge.

'Six, where's the source of your fire?' Bear asked quickly.

'Down in this village. Lay it on 'em, Wolf.'

'Did you confirm visually?'

'You damn bet! There was tracers all roun' me!' Baker laughed.

Bear made a swing over the village; but he knew Baker was lying – there had been no tracers. The formation drove steadily downward over the channel, out of range of the village. 'They were them invisible tracers,' someone said. It might have been Carlisle.

The roof of the house had broken into open flame; but still no one appeared outside. They might not dare, with a helicopter circling overhead. Bear cursed into his silent microphone and turned to follow the slicks.

Baker had already taken the flight into the thin ground fog that undulated over the marsh. The ships hovered heavily as the troops on board hesitated before plunging into water of uncertain depth. As they hovered, two things happened together: bullets ripped through the formation from the low evergreens clinging to the surrounding dunes; and the mist suddenly began to thicken.

Bear heard Baker's voice on the radio: 'Get 'em off! Get

'em off!' He saw crew chiefs and gunners sending troops out the doors with the palm of their hands. With the first few out, the rest followed. The water was only knee-deep, but the bottom was soft. Slow, sucking steps took the troops away from the helicopters. Those on the dune side of the ships fired toward the sand dunes without knowing where they were firing. Those among the helicopters could not do even that. They waded slowly, slipping into the reddening water, while the whole world slipped away into the fog.

Baker's voice sounded high in his throat as he called out, 'Coming up!' With the horizon vanishing, the ships could not be hovered over water any longer.

When he saw that Baker was taking the flight down into the ground fog, Carlisle got on the controls and then sat as still as he could. He tried to slow his breathing to nothing at all, to keep his pulse from racing. All the instincts of battle had to be suppressed. He did not want to be excited: he wanted to be steady. He knew he would need it. But it was no use: when the fog blanked out the horizon, his heart raced. Still, his hands were steady. Baker's control movements were erratic, going that fraction of an inch too far and then searching back. Carlisle steadied the controls.

The ship came to an uneasy slipping hover. Carlisle could not settle the ship down. All of the world that could be seen was a half-circle of undulating marsh grass and wind-whipped water. It was not enough to steady a helicopter against.

Someone called out that his ship had been hit; then a second called.

Baker did not wait to be told that the troops were off. He called for departure and pulled pitch. Troops were jumping from the skids. To give them a chance to get off, Carlisle tried to hold the collective down. The collective jerked up against his hand before he was ready. As he groped for that, the cyclic got away from his right hand. Baker had jerked the helicopter into the air and shoved the nose down in an attempt to force his way to flying speed. The overloaded engine would not respond so fast. The main blade began to slow. The low rpm warning went bouncing through the earphones.

Carlisle, leaning on the collective with all his weight, could not force it down againt Baker's grip. 'Get off it! Get off!' Carlisle demanded; but Baker had frozen on the controls.

The marsh grass began to spin away to the left. The blades had lost so much speed that the tail rotor could not counter the torque of the straining engine. The ship was in a slow turn to the right. When it came broadside, its speed fell off, and it ceased to fly. The marsh grass spun up across the left windscreen and crashed through Baker's door.

Bear saw a helicopter blade burst through the top of the fog. The ship was not going to fly. It was sideways and pitched steeply down. It slid back into the fog. When it appeared again through a thin patch farther on, the blade was slashing the water.

The aircraft shuddered to a stop under the rolling white blanket. The crew were coming out over the upturned side. Tracer bullets twinkled against its belly. One of the crew fell, but he rose again and followed the others as they waded off to the north.

Other helicopters burst from the fog and climbed away over the channel. Blood's was the last. His ship crossed low over the thin patch and turned toward the downward aircraft as the crewman fell. Then it turned away. The ship left a telltale puff of black smoke as the power came back on.

Bear, still racing in from the village, thought that Blood had not seen the crew get out. He called urgently, 'Five, they're wading north!' At first there was no answer. Then, Blood's voice: 'Wolf, we can't get in.'

'Ve bastard!' Ruth said.

Bear dumped the ship into a power-off slipping dive. The crew, if not picked up at once, did not have long to live. The turbulence of the formation landing had mixed the shallow layer of cold misty air near the ground into the next layer above, producing the much deeper layer in which fog was now forming. The downed ship was already vanishing. The other ships had got out; but landing was harder, with the cold water waiting for any mistake. But if it were not done at once, it could not be done until the fog burned away. And the sun had only touched the horizon.

Carlisle dragged Major Baker free and started the crew moving northward, trying to keep the fuselage of the ship between them and the machine gun until they could get out of sight in the fog. He propped up the gunner, who had broken his ankle in the crash. The crew chief stopped to return the fire with his own machine gun. His foot slipped in the mud, and he fell. He came up sputtering and choking, without the weapon. He could not find it in the ooze under his feet. The other machine gun on the helicopter was buried under the left door. Carlisle fired back with his pistol as they moved off. It had no effect, but it expressed his feelings.

Baker, once they got him started, moved quickly enough and was soon ahead of the others. When Blood's helicopter passed low overhead, he stopped and waved frantically; but when it turned away he plunged on without a backward glance for his crew. Bullets geysered the water at random throughout the marsh. A low sand dune swelled from the water ahead. Baker surged toward its cover. He was far ahead of the others when the Bear's ship beat down through the mist.

The world narrowed suddenly to a hundred-meter circle, with the broken hull of the other ship the only reference mark. The voice of the machine gun was suddenly loud. Handy's weapon answered. 'Where the devil are they?' Bear growled.

'They're coming, sir!' Cripps sang out. Three men were coming toward them in a great flurry of water. The two on the outside ran with the third between them. Bear turned to hover to them. They went down as he did so. Bullets slammed against the ship. A hole appeared in the windscreen before Bear's face. The bullet had come in the open side door, passed between him and Handy, and exited through the windscreen.

One of the men was up. It was Carlisle. He began to stagger toward the ship, dragging one of the others. Bear swung the ship to a halt beside them; but Carlisle could not lift the crewman aboard. Handy dropped his weapon to help. A little way off, the third crewman was face down in the water.

'You've got the ship,' Bear said to Ruth. Ruth had been following on the controls. His face was white, and his gloved hand was rigid on the stick. Bear unbuckled his harness. 'If I don't come back, get out while it'll still fly. And take care of my crew.' He unplugged his phone jack before there was an answer. 'What a fate, to become a grunt at this stage of my career,' he said – to the ship, since no one else could hear. He patted the ship's door, and waded off.

Carlisle had got the gunner aboard and was starting slowly back for the crew chief. Bear started in that direction, too; but beyond that, at the edge of the hundred-meter world, Baker appeared. He was running in high splashing bounds, waving an arm and shouting. The return sweep of the machine gun cut his legs from under him. He came up again to his hands and knees, his head just above water. Bear waved at Ruth, signaling him to fly the helicopter toward the crew chief. He himself started to run toward Baker. His feet sank deep into the sucking bottom. He lost a boot to the mud, but he got his knees up and kept moving.

Blood was pouring from Baker's nose and mouth when Bear reached him. 'You might have told me you were going to die anyway,' Bear said roughly. He took the major by one arm. 'Come on, let's not waste my effort now.'

A tremendous blow to the chest knocked him on his back. The dark water closed over him. It tasted of salt. Cov's tomb. 'Death,' he thought. Just the word: death. But the air touched his face once more. As he came to his feet he saw that it had not been death knocking after all. The bullet had struck the center of his armor plate. The plate was cratered, but the bullet had not come through. He lifted Baker once more.

Something hit his back.

This time no thought carried the message through his brain. Although the armor did its patient work, he was facing away from the weapon, and the armor was on the wrong side of his life. The bullet passed through the body and shattered against the inside of the armor. Its companions snuffed out the life in Major Baker and hammered at the sides of the helicopter hovering over the crew chief. Ruth, seeing them fall, seeing no hope, did as he had been told and took the ship out while it could fly.

The ship with the red cross came down out of the sun in a tight circle. The pilot was careful not to stray far from the secure area close around the American unit. The battle had pushed back to the south, but stray bullets had still winged around the ship on his previous trip in. The risk had been acceptable then, with live casualties to evacuate. But he did not want to die for a dead man.

He took the wind direction from the thin plume of smoke drifting inland from the burnt hooch in the village across the channel. He set his final approach directly into the onshore breeze, well north of the village. He touched the ship down just beyond the edge of the marsh and, after testing the solidity of the spot, put the collective down quickly to let the storm of sand settle back through the blade.

The detail of grunts waited for the sand to fall before they came with the bodies. 'We've got no ponchos for these two!' one shouted up apologetically to the corpsman on board. 'They came without!' None of the living wanted to give up a poncho for the dead.

'We'll take 'em, wrapped or not,' the corpsman answered. Bodies no worse than these he was glad to get. He signaled thumbs-up to the aircraft commander. As the grunts scattered out of range of the sand, the helicopter lifted up over the dunes, across the beach, and out to sea to climb to a safe altitude.

'Hey, Lieutenant Wolcheski,' the corpsman remarked over the intercom, 'a couple of these guys have wings.'

Wolcheski had seen that they were pilots when the grunts carried them out: one of them, though missing a boot, was still wearing a chest plate. Wolcheski supposed that the bodies belonged to the dead slick lying down in the marsh. He turned the controls over to Guiterrez now, and looked back.

Baker's face was still bloody, but the Bear's looked quite at peace. Only the mobility was gone from it. The walrus was nowhere to be seen.

'Something wrong, *Trung-úy*?' Guiterrez asked him.

'No. I always feel like crying on days like this.'

Guiterrez glanced quickly into the back. 'Ah,' he said. He added, in what Wolcheski knew was meant to be sympathy,

'Well, it ain't much, but it's the only war we've got.'

'It ain't much,' Wolcheski said.

After a while Wolcheski took the controls back from Guiterrez. Still heading south, he put the ship into a slow, steady climb.

'Were we goin', *Trung-úy*? You lookin' for angels?' They were at five thousand feet and still climbing.

'Tryin' to keep the meat cool,' the corpsman suggested.

'I was looking for an island,' Wolcheski said.

Guiterrez looked at his chart, then out to sea. 'Cu Lao Re? Yeah, I've seen that. Kind of neat.'

'I've never seen it,' Wolcheski said. 'He told me about it; but I've never seen it.'

'Well, you ain't goin' to see it today. Too much haze.'

'I'll see it.'

The gold thread of beach unspooled out of the haze below them, vanished again behind. To the west the mountains climbed from the plain. Beyond the paddies green with new rice they rose, range upon range into the west, while ahead the wide Song Ben Van sparkled around the crescent island. Ahead were Chu Lai, Dong Xoai, Quang Ngai; behind him the villages Phuong Tan, Vinh Giang, Hoi An; out on the plain Tam Ky, Khanh My, Que Son, whose names the Bear had loved. But to the east the ocean closed with the sky, and if the island was there, he didn't see it. Wolcheski looked and looked, but he didn't see it. He wished he could see it, for the Bear's sake; but he didn't see it.

THE END

Chapter One

The only thing Ben Kinsella ever wanted to be when he grew up was nothing like his father. It was the truth, plain and simple. Some boys wanted to be firefighters or doctors or astronauts, but he honestly couldn't remember ever giving those professions a second thought. Or any occupation in particular. He only wanted to be something more than "no damn good."

So far, he'd succeeded.

Glancing down at the khaki uniform he wore, he grimaced and brushed away the evidence of the cruller he'd wolfed down. There were moments when he could not imagine why any young boy would ever think growing up to be a police officer would be a good idea.

"You all right, Sheriff?"

Julianne Shields, Masters County's clerk/dispatcher/secretary, remained unruffled, as always. Unlike him, the woman was a fixture in the boxy building serving as both the town hall and county offices. He hadn't had to call her to come in. She'd shown up minutes after dawn with a box of the tasty treats—still warm from the fryers at Brewster's Bakery—and started running interference for him.

It hadn't simply been a long night. Two days had rolled into one since Clint Young's mother had called to say her son had never returned from his fishing trip. A quick drive out to the property on Sawtooth Lake later, one of Ben's deputies discovered Clint's lifeless body sprawled across a broken-down sofa in his family's old cabin.

The Youngs' place was little more than a shack, but there was a tricked-out Charger parked on the dirt lane leading straight to the door. And Clint's clothes weren't cheap either. From what Ben observed, they were blood-splattered but pricey. A fella didn't grow up in Ben's old neighborhood without knowing exactly what a trendy pair of kicks cost.

Deputy Schaeffer, a former classmate of the deceased, rambled on and on about Clint having "finally gotten himself together." From what Ben could decipher, Mike believed the victim's steady job as a foreman at Timber Masters, new car and nicer clothing meant the guy was really making it. He supposed he would have thought the same thing at Mike's age. He made a mental note to give the car and clothes more thought in light of Clint's financial circumstances but set those details aside in hopes of securing what was left of the alleged crime scene.

Unfortunately, his deputy hadn't handled the discovery with as much professional detachment as Ben would have preferred, but he couldn't blame the guy. The grisliest scene Mike Schaeffer had seen in his twenty-two years was a three-car accident out on Route 32. He'd never seen a person's insides splattered around like a paintball shot. But Ben had.

Closing his gritty eyes, Ben inhaled deeply and said a prayer the coroner didn't suspect foul play, because his deputy had compromised the crime scene beyond any hope of excavating clear evidence. Still, they'd done what they could.

"Sheriff?"

Ben's eyes popped open. His other deputy, Lourdes Cabrera, appeared in the doorway, and not for the first time, Ben wished Lori had been the one to discover Mr. Young's body. Though she was roughly the same age as Mike and the deceased, Deputy Cabrera was calm and cool. Unflappable. She was former military police like Ben. Establishing order was the first point of business on any scene, and the scene the previous night had been chaos. Mostly because Mike was too young and too green. "Hey, Lori," he said tiredly.

His deputy stood with her hands braced on her hips above her nylon utility belt, an old-fashioned glazed doughnut pinched between her fingers. For one groggy moment, he wondered if she planned to tase him awake.

"Why don't you run home and grab an hour or two, maybe a shower?" The expression of concern she wore undercut the stridency of her suggestion.

Scrubbing a hand over his face, he nodded, grimacing as the stubble rasped his palm. Not only did he feel awful, he probably looked warmed-over. "Yeah, I, uh—"

He trailed off, patting various piles on his desk. He wanted there to be something useful in one of them. But there was nothing. And there wouldn't be anything until Mel Schuler, the county's coroner/funeral director, determined whether the body needed to be referred to the state medical examiner for further testing.

All too aware he was stuck until then, he pushed back from the desk. "Mel should be calling soon," he said.

Lori nodded once. "I'll call you the moment I hear from him."

"Even if it's only an hour or two from now," he interjected sternly. "I need to know what he says more than I need sleep."

Her lips twitched into a smirk as she toasted him with the doughnut in her hand. "Even if it's thirty seconds after you walk out this door, I'll call," she promised, then she took an enormous bite.

"You're only playing into the stereotype there," he grumbled as he sidled past her into the outer office.

"Says the man who demolished two crullers before he even hit his desk chair," Julianne said without looking up from the report she was typing.

"Hey, now, it's not fair picking on me when Mike isn't here to even up the sides." He'd sent the shaken man home directly after he'd recorded his notes for Julianne to transcribe. Ben gave a tired chuckle as he reached for the ball cap emblazoned with the department logo from the coatrack by the door.

He'd just pulled the brim down low when the front door banged open and Henry Masters burst in. Ben blinked hard, willing himself into a more alert state as he rolled his shoulders back and plastered on a pleasant expression.

Henry Masters was the man who'd hired him. One of three men serving on the Pine Bluff town council, he was the owner of Timber Masters, the great-grandson of the man for whom the county was named and the self-appointed ruler of all he surveyed. A slender blonde followed in Henry's wake. She was enough to make Ben blink twice.

The woman was a stunner. Smooth, fair skin that somehow managed to look sun-kissed though she wasn't tanned. Laser-bright blue eyes framed by dark lashes and fierce slashes of eyebrows. She was young and long-limbed, with a spill of honey-blond hair so thick and wavy, it made him think of beauty pageant contestants. But this woman wasn't wearing a sash and swimsuit. Or a smile. She wore a stiff navy blue pantsuit and a grimace.

Her posture was straight but rigid. Every inch of her bearing screamed resistance. Ben couldn't help but wonder if it was him, the dingy municipal building or the man she was with she objected to the most. She shot Henry Masters an impatient glance, and Ben felt fairly confident in crossing himself and the building off the list.

"Mr. Masters," he said with a cordial nod.

"Sheriff," the older man said curtly and returned the nod. He placed a hand on the young woman's arm and forced her to take a step forward. "This is my daughter, Marlee. She has recently finished up at Emory Law and will be working for Timber Masters as she awaits the results from her bar exam. Marlee, this is Ben Kinsella. He's taken over for Bud Walker until the general election in November."

Ms. Masters extended a hand, her expression making it clear she took no pleasure in meeting him. He shook her hand briefly, prepared to be no more impressed with her than she was with him. "A pleasure."

"Sheriff," she said, her voice surprisingly husky.

Ben gave his head a subtle shake as he withdrew his hand from her grasp. He supposed he expected her to have one of those high, whiny sorority-girl voices, the type to end every sentence with a question mark. But no. She'd infused the one-word greeting with enough smoke to make a man long for a glass of good bourbon.

"We've heard about Clint Young. Tell me what you know," Henry Masters stated bluntly.

Surprised, Ben shifted his attention back to the older man and tried to get his sluggish mind to kick into gear. "What we know?" he repeated.

"Yes," Masters clarified, impatient. "What has your investigation uncovered?"

Ben took a half step back, wary. Why would Henry Masters be so upset about Clint Young's death? Sure, Clint worked for Timber Masters, but Henry could have called to express his concern. This early-morning office visit seemed a bit over-the-top. "We don't have much at this juncture," he said, choosing his words carefully. "Mr. Young's body is being attended by the coroner at the moment."

"Right, but the scene," Masters pressed, his agitation rising. "What did you find at the scene?"

In the months since Ben had been hired by the Pine Bluff town council to be the interim sheriff of Masters County, he'd thought he had a good gauge on how to handle Henry Masters. Still, he was surprised the man flat-out posed such a question. He had no familial connection to the victim that Ben was aware of. And if being the man's employer was justification enough, Henry might feel free to violate the privacy of three-quarters of the town's residents.

"I'm afraid I can't divulge any information on what is presently an ongoing investigation," he said, repeating the line Julianne had used to dodge the reporters who'd called already. He made a move to stride past them toward the door. "Now, if you'll excuse me, I'll be stepping out for a bit."

Henry gaped at him, as did his daughter. Clearly they were both accustomed to getting what they wanted.

"Wait a minute," the older man sputtered as he wrapped a hand around Ben's arm to stall him.

Ben looked down at the hand, then raised his head, letting the brim of his hat shield his eyes until the last possible moment. Masters released him without another word, but this time, his daughter moved closer.

"Sheriff, we understand you can't give us any of the particulars," she cut in, her voice as mellow and sweet as raw honey dripping from the comb. "It's only… Clint was a neighbor." She let the statement sink in for a moment. "He was my late brother's best friend growing up," she added. Their eyes met, both of them all too aware she could keep dropping these factoids into the mix if she chose. She might not have lived in Pine Bluff for a while, but she knew the place and its people in a way he never would.

"His mother is…distraught." Something about the way she seemed to settle on that adjective made her father stiffen and the back of Ben's neck prickle. "Word has obviously gotten around town." Her smile was small, sad and no doubt measured to the last millimeter for effectiveness. "People are worried they should lock their doors tonight."

He diverted every ounce of energy he had left in his tank to keeping his expression as unreadable as possible and his pitch uninflected. "People should lock their doors every night. The world is a big, bad place, Ms. Masters."

Her lips pursed slightly, and he would swear he caught a gleam of amusement in those startling blue eyes. "Pine Bluff isn't," she asserted. "Do people need to be worried about a murderer on the loose, Sheriff Kinsella?"

Violent crime was nearly nonexistent in Masters County, but other crimes had taken root. The only reason Ben was there was because Pine Bluff's mayor and the entire county sheriff's department had been swept up in a sting operation run by the federal Drug Enforcement Agency, an operation Ben was familiar with from his time in the agency. His knowledge and experience on that front had been a key factor in securing the job as interim sheriff.

Something about Marlee Masters's demeanor told him she wasn't pleased to be questioning him. She was rigid and annoyed, but she tried to cover it. The blunt questions served up in a syrupy-sweet manner spoke of a woman who wanted to get what she came for and get out. Though it was no hardship to look at her, he found he wished he could give her some answers so she could shed her boring navy pantsuit and run off back to whatever she was doing when Daddy called her home.

Tipping the brim of his cap up so he could meet her frank stare directly, he said, "I wish I had an answer for you. We should have the preliminary report soon."

He cleared his throat to command everyone's full attention as he tore his gaze from hers. Waving a tired hand toward Lori, he directed his comments to Henry Masters when he spoke again. "Deputy Cabrera will call me as soon as the coroner gives us a preliminary." He kept that same hand lifted to stave off any protest the older man might conjure. "I will contact Mrs. Young and you, Mr. Masters, as soon as I have any information, but for now... I've been on duty for nearly thirty-seven hours. Deputy Cabrera will be in charge until I get back."

He pulled his cap down over his eyes again and carefully stepped past Marlee Masters. "It was a pleasure to meet you, Ms. Masters. I am sorry about the circumstances." He inclined his head toward Henry. "Please give Mrs. Masters my best," he said, then made his escape.

He hurried through the door and around the corner to the crumbling concrete parking lot adjacent to the building. The April-morning air was cool but already growing thick with humidity. He opened the door to the SUV marked with the county sheriff's logo but took a moment before stepping in. By the third deep breath, he felt steady enough, awake enough, to haul himself into the driver's seat and plug the key into the ignition.

He had a feeling something big was happening in his small town. Something big and bad. The kind of thing that wasn't supposed to happen in towns where people didn't lock their doors.

He liked this town. The small, quiet life he was carving out for himself suited him fine, even though it was so different from anywhere he'd ever lived. But when he closed his eyes, he saw the shoes Clint Young had been wearing. Those snow-white kicks. God, how many times had he seen shoes like those on dead bodies? Fresh out of the box. The laces were pristine except for the spatter of blood drying from red to rust.

Blinking away the image, he twisted the key and blew out a gusty breath. Trouble had come to town, and he could only hope the dark shadow of the mess he'd made in Atlanta hadn't followed him here.

Chapter Two

Marlee kept her mouth clamped shut as her father blustered then said his goodbyes. She nodded to Julianne, shot Lori Cabrera a rueful smile then trailed her stomping father out the door.

Things certainly had changed in Pine Bluff.

Including there being a handsome new sheriff in town.

She failed to remember a time when Bud Walker didn't have the sheriff's badge pinned to his barrel chest. She followed her father to the car, dawdling as she looked around the town square. The old courthouse had long been converted to an agricultural museum. The civic facility they'd visited was a low-slung midcentury-modern monstrosity made of pebbled concrete. The U-shaped building housed the sheriff's offices and county jail on one side and the district attorney administrative offices and courtroom on the other. The reception areas on each side were walled with floor-to-ceiling glass, a stylistic choice that reminded Marlee of a fishbowl. She shuddered at the thought of working in such a fishbowl.

Since her mother enjoyed trips to Atlanta to shop and visit, Marlee hadn't come home to Pine Bluff often since she left for college. Now that she was back, she saw the town with fresh eyes. New ornamental lamps dotted the walking path at Parson's Creek. The awning over Brewster's was still bakery-box pink, but this one appeared to be new. It hadn't yet been faded by the sun. She noted the cool weather annuals planted in Lane's Antiques's window boxes. They'd have to be replaced with petunias or geraniums soon, she mused as she reached for the door handle. Summer in southern Georgia was no place for pansies.

The lights flashed on the black Suburban her father drove, startling her from her thoughts. Another change. Since when did her father bother locking his car? When she'd lived in Pine Bluff, she used to leave her ignition key under the floor mat of her Mustang. No one would dare to mess with anything belonging to a Masters. Marlee didn't think she'd ever used the key fob until she moved to Atlanta to go to school.

"Get in already." Her father barked the terse order from the other side of his monstrous SUV.

Marlee bristled but did as she was told. Hoisting herself onto the buttery leather seat, she kept her gaze averted. She couldn't let him see how she truly felt about his orders. Or how much she loathed herself for following them. She loved her father, but she didn't always like him much.

She'd been plotting her escape since the day they buried her brother. Their father had stood stiff as a statue, uncrying, unblinking, as they laid Jeff to rest. Her mother had been a wreck, crumpling into herself on one of the white wooden folding chairs provided by the funeral home. She'd watched, tears streaming from her eyes, as Jeff's casket was lowered into his grave. But her father showed no signs of grief or weakness, even though he'd only allowed the immediate family at the graveside service.

Now here she was. Summoned home again by news of a death. She needed to get away. Had to figure out a plan to break free from Masters County and everything lying in wait for her. A life she never wanted was closing in around her, and she had to find a way to wriggle off her father's hook.

A mere female, she'd been granted a good deal more leeway than her younger brother. After all, she wasn't the scion. She wasn't supposed to run the family's timber-and-pulp business. She was extraneous, as far as her father was concerned. As long as Jeff was alive and she didn't do anything to make it impossible for her mama to show her face at First Baptist on Sundays, she could do as she pleased. She was brainy enough to graduate at the top of her class and score a spot at Emory University School of Law. Henry assumed once she passed the Georgia bar, she'd come home and serve as her brother's legal counsel and adviser. That was what they'd told him she would do.

Diploma in hand, she'd hunkered down and immersed herself in preparing for the bar exam. But Jeff's death had blown all their plans to smithereens. She'd thought her father wouldn't notice her staying in Atlanta. She'd hoped he'd had his hands full enough with the business and Mama to keep him off her back for a while. But nothing got past Henry Masters.

"Your mother wants you to go with her to visit Eleanor Young this afternoon." It was a command, not an invitation. "I'd appreciate it if you could encourage her to keep her wits about her until after y'all get home."

Marlee opened her mouth to protest but clamped it shut and forced herself to swallow her rebellion. She had to play it cool. Be a Masters.

"Fine," she said tightly.

He cast a sidelong glance at the pantsuit she wore and wrinkled his nose. "You'll want to change into something more…appropriate."

She glanced down at the tailored coordinates she'd chosen so carefully. This was her interview suit. She'd thought it would be her *lucky* interview suit after she had alterations made. She'd had a meeting lined up at one of Atlanta's hottest law firms. Then her father had called to tell her about Clint's death and ordered her to come home.

"This is perfectly appropriate," she said in a quiet voice, trying to keep the rage bubbling inside of her to a low, rolling boil.

"It's unflattering, ill-fitting," her father said bluntly. "What an actor would think an attorney wears." With another sideways glance, he smirked. "You are an attorney, aren't you? You didn't fib about sittin' for the bar exam and all, did you, Miss Marlee?"

His condescending use of what was once a beloved childhood nickname fanned the flame under her anger. Her ears grew hot and prickly. A flush crept up her neck and into her cheeks. She resisted the urge to press her hands to her scalding face. She wouldn't give him the satisfaction.

"I can show you my registration papers when we get back to the house. I brought my diploma with me too, since you couldn't be bothered to come to my graduation."

He dismissed her hurt with a wave of his hand. "I told you your mama wasn't up for the trip."

She disengaged. There was no sense in arguing. The man believed he was the law, both in the family and in the whole county. Dealing with an ego the size of his was akin to running headlong into a brick wall—repeatedly. One she'd been butting up against her whole life. And he and her mother were a pair. For better and for worse. Looking out the window as they cruised through town, she couldn't resist prodding him.

"You don't seem to care much for the new sheriff," she said, striving for casual observation.

"He's fine. I hired him, didn't I?"

She stifled a huff at the defensiveness in his response.

Henry Masters considered himself an expert strategist, and he hated any implication he might possibly be ruled by a stray emotion.

"Besides, it doesn't matter if I like him or not. The man has a job to do, and as the head of the town council, it's my responsibility to make sure he does."

Responsibility. Duty. Legacy. Those were three of her father's favorite words. And now… Now he wanted her to do her duty to the Masters family legacy and pay a condolence call to the mother of the boy who was once Jeff's best friend. Her stomach tightened into a knot.

"I need you to go with your mother to represent the family, Marlee. I can't send Carolee alone." He cast a meaningful look in her direction. "Maybe you can ask your mama to help you pick out something to wear. That would make her happy."

He spoke in a low, cajoling tone—the same tenor she'd fallen for repeatedly when she was a child. When a simple request from him could make her strive to do better. But she wasn't a young girl desperate for her daddy's approval anymore. And nothing short of Jeff's resurrection would make her mother happy.

MARLEE PASSED THE afternoon grasping a sweating glass of iced tea and watching her mother and Eleanor Young sit huddled together, clasping hands and crying. She'd been pretty teary herself, but when she pulled a fresh handkerchief from her mother's handbag, she'd spotted a silver flask tucked inside. The sight stirred fresh worry that her mother's emotions might be fueled by something other than pure grief. Marlee just hoped that the friends and neighbors coming to pay call were too focused on Mrs. Young to notice that Carolee Masters was listing ever so slightly to the left.

Townspeople came and went, passing in and out of the Youngs' once-chic, but now truly shabby, parlor in a steady stream. The visitors greeted each other in passing, but no one lingered. They reminded Marlee of relay racers anxious to pass the baton.

Her mother touched a hand-embroidered handkerchief to the corners of her eyes. It came away damp but unmarred by mascara or makeup. Marlee realized with a jolt that sometime in the months since Jeff's death, her mother had morphed her mourning into a kind of performance art.

She studied the two women, the more analytical part of Marlee's brain comparing and contrasting. Eleanor Young was a mess. She alternately sobbed and sniffled. Her face was pale but blotchy from crying. If she'd started the day wearing any kind of cosmetics, they were long gone. Tendrils of curling brown hair escaped the clip worn at the nape of her neck. Marlee had been stunned by the streaks of silver visible at the crown of her hair. Going gray gracefully was simply not done in these parts. Rinker's Drugstore kept Clairol Light Auburn 6R specifically for the county's oldest resident, Miss Louisa Shelby. But Eleanor Young seemed to be flouting convention with at least three inches' growth.

"Excuse me, Mrs. Young?"

The request was spoken in a voice so deep and resonant it sliced through the hum of murmured conversation. Marlee looked up to find Sheriff Ben Kinsella standing on the threshold, wearing a freshly pressed uniform and carrying his broad-brimmed hat in his hands. She took in his height and wide shoulders along with a sharp, short breath. The man was impressive.

He noticed her then and gave a nod of acknowledgment. "Ms. Masters."

Attraction flared hot in the pit of Marlee's stomach, and

the sensation made her jostle tea onto her hand. Her cheeks burned as she fumbled for her paper napkin. Had he been this handsome when they were introduced? She must have been too peeved about being hauled down to the station by her father to notice. But how could any woman with breath in her body not notice a man like him?

Dark hair curled close to his head. He was clean-shaven—a fact she appreciated, as it allowed her to map the planes of his face. Tawny skin stretched taut over high cheekbones and a jaw so square he could have been a cartoon hero. But there was nothing flat or two-dimensional about this man. Even standing still in a stuffy parlor, Ben Kinsella personified the word *dynamic*. He appeared to be tightly coiled. Ready to spring into action. Desire snaked through her, moving as stealthily as smoke.

He directed his full attention to the distraught woman on the worn velvet settee. "I'm sorry to interrupt, Mrs. Young, but I'd promised to call as soon as I had news from the coroner," he said, his voice low and sympathetic.

Her mother and Mrs. Young looked up at the same time. They wore matching expressions of apprehensive hope. Marlee had to marvel at the resiliency of the human spirit. What good news could they possibly expect from him? Clint was dead. So was Jeff. The sheriff's presence certainly enhanced the room, but nothing truly good could come from this visit.

"Yes, Sheriff?" Eleanor prompted in a tremulous voice as she started to rise.

"No, no," he said, waving her back into her seat as he strode into the room. "Please, don't get up."

A handful of curious residents had followed him into the Young house. Marlee spotted Trudy Skyler, the woman who ran the local paper, lurking behind Mr. Jensen, the middle school math teacher. But her attention was drawn back to the sheriff.

He stood towering over the settee for a moment, then lowered himself to one knee in order to look Mrs. Young directly in the eye. Something about the gesture tugged Marlee out of her wayward thoughts. Wetting her lips, she leaned forward on her chair, drawn to Ben Kinsella by more than that invisible thread of attraction.

"Mrs. Young, I wanted to come to tell you I've spoken to the coroner." Marlee saw his gaze shift to her mother and back. "He is not going to refer the case to the medical examiner's office. Your son's body will be released immediately and the case closed."

Someone behind the sheriff gasped, but Marlee couldn't see who it was. She only heard a woman whisper, "I told you. It's just like Carolee's boy."

Sheriff Kinsella continued, "Mel Schuler asked me to assure you he'd take care of Clint. He said if you would go down to the funeral home in the morning, he'd like to go over all the arrangements with you."

The moment Sheriff Kinsella spoke her son's name, Eleanor Young broke down in big, gulping sobs and collapsed against Marlee's mother, hardly noticing Carolee Masters was better equipped to accept comfort than to dole it out.

"I am truly sorry for your loss, Mrs. Young," he concluded, his voice lower and gravelly.

Marlee watched in helpless horror as her own mother, having far more experience in playing the part of the bereaved, offered the sheriff a limp hand to shake. "Thank you so much for taking the time to come yourself, Sheriff. I'm sure Eleanor appreciates all your efforts."

"It's the least I could do, ma'am," he replied. "I truly am sorry."

"Thank you," Carolee said, bowing her head as she extracted her hand. "So kind of you to say. You're new to our town, Sheriff. Do come to the house one night for supper," she instructed with a faint upward tilt of her lips. "We'd be pleased to have you."

Marlee rose as the sheriff did, her fascinated stare fixed on her mother. Apparently, it wasn't possible to drown a lifetime of grace and poise in vodka. Glancing over the sheriff's shoulder, she was relieved to note the soul-shaking sobs emanating from the parlor had driven the gossips from the foyer. The implication of what he'd said, of the coroner's ruling on Clint's death, weighed heavy on her heart. She needed to be certain she understood him correctly.

"Sheriff," she called as he pivoted to leave. "Does this mean—"

She pressed a hand to her neck, hoping to calm her own racing pulse. Grabbing his arm, she propelled him away from the weeping women on the couch and toward the now-empty foyer. When they stopped near the Youngs' front door, she couldn't quite bring herself to relinquish her hold on his solid bicep. The man felt strong. Sturdy. Secure. All the things she hadn't felt since her brother died.

Marlee looked up to find him gazing down at her searchingly, his brown eyes dark with sympathy. He covered her hand with his, and her pulse leaped. She looked into his eyes, wondering if he even realized he'd done it. Surely, the gesture was meant to comfort and nothing more. She couldn't stand there and let a total stranger hold her hand, no matter how good it felt. Could he feel how fast her heart was beating?

"Ms. Masters? Can I help you?"

She forced herself to slide her hand from his grasp. Marlee didn't want sympathy. She wanted to get out of there. More than anything, she wanted to be anywhere other than where she was, about to ask what she had to ask. Drawing a shaky breath, she forced the question out in a rush.

"Does this mean Mr. Schuler believes Clint took his own life?"

Her gaze dropped to the badge affixed to Ben Kinsella's uniform tunic as he drew in a deep breath, then reluctantly let it go. "It means we could find no evidence to make us think anyone other than the victim was involved in the shooting."

His careful phrasing snagged her interest. Her eyes widened with the dawning realization the new sheriff had found something about Clint's death puzzling. "'No evidence,'" she repeated. Sheriff Walker had said something similar when he'd talked to her family about Jeff.

"Yes, ma'am," he confirmed.

His use of the word *ma'am* made Marlee flinch, but she refrained from saying anything about it. After all, she was the daughter of the town's most prominent citizen. She'd been called "miss" and "ma'am" and treated with deference her entire life. Even if she hadn't done a thing to deserve it.

Sheriff Kinsella looked as itchy and uncomfortable as she felt, but still he stayed, waiting for her to speak her piece with infinite patience.

She averted her gaze to the fine mesh of the screen door. One push and the lucky man would be free to go. Would she ever be? Drawing a shaky breath, she fell back on the lessons learned in a lifetime of training.

"Thank you for coming by, Sheriff. Shall I pass the message along to my father?"

He hesitated, and she saw his cheeks darken with a flush. "Thank you, but no," he said, donning his hat with a touch too much force, then adjusting the brim to ride low over his eyes. "I've already spoken to him."

The screen door slapped against the old wood casing,

punctuating their conversation. Marlee's estimation of the new sheriff in town clicked up a couple notches. The man was clearly tuned in to who ruled the roost in Masters County.

"Why, yes, of course you have," she said to his retreating back, her fingers tangling in the slim gold chain she wore at her throat as she watched the handsome man stride away from the house. With a tired sigh, she stepped back and closed the heavy front door. The grieving Mrs. Young would not be receiving any more callers.

Chapter Three

"It wouldn't kill Patti Cummings to go a week or two between visits to the Curl Up and Dye," a woman behind him whispered loudly. "I swear, I can hear her hair calling out for a deep conditioning all the way across the room."

"Now, Susie," another woman's voice cautioned, suppressing laughter.

"I'm only sayin' the bleach is turnin' her hair to straw."

Ben tuned out, mentally filing the conversation under "idle gossip" in his mind. He eyed the woman currently condoling with Mrs. Young and cringed internally. The Susie lady hadn't been entirely wrong in her assessment. Patti Cummings had hair the color and presumed texture of sun-bleached wheat.

Biting back the urge to chuckle, he attempted to blend into the back wall of the funeral parlor's viewing room. Of course, he knew trying not to stand out in Pine Bluff was a silly notion. Sure, there were plenty of people of color in the area. They'd tried to welcome him to their churches and socials. But it was hard for folks to get past the sheriff's badge on his uniform shirt. His profession, coupled with the fact that he was city born and raised, made people uncomfortable. Particularly here, where the sweeps made by federal law enforcement had impacted so many families.

Scanning the room, he did his best to put names with

the faces he recognized. The town was small, but he'd only lived there for a few months. He wished he'd asked Lori to come to the visitation. She'd grown up in town and could give him the lowdown.

"Coffee, boss?"

Ben jerked, then gaped at his deputy, wondering—not for the first time—if she was some kind of mind reader.

Lori winced. "Sorry, I thought you heard me say your name."

She pointed toward the lobby. "Coffee? I have to warn you, it's not as good as Julianne's, but it's a sight better than the sludge you brew."

Ben smirked. "Maybe in a minute." He cocked his head to indicate that he was listening to the people around him. "I was thinking I should have asked you to come tonight."

"No need to ask," Lori said, scanning the room. "I'd have been here anyway."

Ben stared at her dumbly for a moment, trying to remember if he'd ever bothered to ask if she was acquainted with the deceased. "Did you know—"

She shook her head, cutting him off. "No. I mean, not well. One of his cousins on his mama's side was in my class. I was a couple years ahead of them." She nodded to a knot of people who bore a vague resemblance to the woman standing in front of the casket. "Doesn't take much to make a connection in these parts."

"You were coming anyway," he concluded.

"Everyone will," she corrected with quiet certainty. "The only people who don't show up for a visitation here are the ones who don't give a damn about what anyone says about them. Reputation is currency in a small town. There's a pecking order, and believe me, attendance is taken."

He pressed his lips together then gave Lori a grateful nudge with his elbow. "Noted."

He spotted some familiar faces. Camille Brewster from the bakery visited with a small cluster of women as they inched forward. Chet Rinker, the pharmacist, stood solemn-faced and stared in a trance at the wooden cross suspended behind the casket at the front of the room. An older woman with bright red hair stood behind him, leaning heavily on her walker but steadfastly refusing all offers of assistance, cups of water and vacated chairs. He speculated she might be *the* Miss Louisa Shelby. People loved to tell tales about the town's oldest and most colorful resident.

"Where's Clint Young's father?"

"Ran off with his secretary about ten years ago," Lori supplied quietly.

"Secretary?"

"He was Henry Masters's right-hand man at Timber Masters until he got bit by the love bug," she reported. "About the time Clint would have been starting junior high, I guess." She gave her head a sad shake and searched the crowd. "I don't think he's here. They moved off somewhere. Tupelo? Tuscaloosa? Some city with a *T*." She shrugged. "Anyhow, it was big gossip for a long time. Still is."

"Really? Even that long ago," he commented, shooting her a skeptical look.

"Gossip moves fast, but people's memories are long." She gave him a smirk. "This isn't the city. Not a lot happens here, so when something does, people tend to hang on to it."

There was a rustling commotion at the back of the room, and the line of mourners shifted, moving to one side of the aisle or the other. Henry Masters made his way into the room, pausing to exchange nods, handshakes, shoulder squeezes and cheek kisses with nearly every man or woman he passed. His wife and daughter followed in his wake but left the glad-handing to him. The women doled out smiles and pats on the arm here and there, but it was clear Henry was the man to be hailed.

When Henry clasped both of Eleanor Young's hands between his and bent his head close to speak to her, Ben remembered something he'd overheard at the Youngs' house. "Do they have a son?"

He felt Lori stiffen beside him and tore his attention from the blonde on the other side of the room to look at her. "What?"

"The Masters," he clarified. "Do they have a son?"

She gaped at him, but Ben simply waited for an answer. Patience was often the most effective tool in getting people to talk.

"Yes. Jeff. His name was Jeff." She cleared her throat, then spoke in a quiet, but infinitely steadier, manner. "Jeff Masters. Why do you ask?"

"Was?" He leaned forward, inviting her to continue.

Lori swallowed hard and said only, "He passed away less than a year ago."

Ben felt an instant stab of remorse. "You knew him."

She huffed a laugh. "I'm sure it's strange to you because you're new here and all, but we all know each other. Everyone." She looked up, meeting his gaze directly. "Some of us better than others, but we all 'know' each other," she said, using air quotes to emphasize the difference in degrees of knowledge.

Something about the deflection pinged his radar. "How well did you know Jeff Masters?" Suddenly, he realized he was asking the wrong question. "Wait. How did Jeff Masters die?"

Lori pressed her lips together and shook her head. He caught the shimmer of unshed tears in her eyes, then she pivoted on her heel and pushed past the guests lingering at the back of the room to get to the reception area. Torn between going after her to press for answers and the uneasy feeling in his gut, he hesitated. The room hummed around him. Quiet conversation charged with a buzz of tension. He looked to the front and found Henry Masters had escorted the old woman with the walker past the people in line and delivered her to Eleanor Young.

He scanned the room and spotted Carolee Masters seated in the front row. As always, she was immaculately dressed in a navy blue suit with black piping. Her slender ankles were crossed and tucked neatly beneath her seat. She sat still and straight, her face pointed toward the casket. Unmoving.

The hairs on his arms prickled as he sought Marlee Masters. Something told him she'd stick close to her mother. He wasn't wrong.

She stood near the end of the front row, her bearing erect and alert. Protective. Clearly ready to run interference for her mother, if the need arose. The air in his lungs grew too full and hot for him to hold. He exhaled in a long gust as he took her in. There was nothing provocative or the least bit suggestive in the styling of the black dress she wore, but the fabric draped and clung to her curves. She wore the same killer shoes she'd had on when she accompanied her father to town hall, but they were miles more lethal paired with the dress rather than the pantsuit.

When he lifted his head, he found her staring back at him, her jaw tight and tilted at a defensive angle.

A sizzle of awareness traveled up his spine, but Marlee Masters didn't back down.

Aware his stare would be considered rude, he inclined his head, then looked away.

A group of young women approached Marlee with a hushed glee wholly inappropriate in the setting. She looked decidedly uncomfortable as they closed around her, chattering and gushing over her, completely oblivious to the fact they were in a funeral home.

"Killed himself, they say," an older man seated in one of the back rows said, his volume making up for what was clearly his own hearing loss.

"I heard he was runnin' with a bad crowd, but..."

The last part of the snippet dangled tantalizingly, but Ben had no idea who gave voice to the speculation. There were at least a dozen women in his vicinity.

"I took a seven-layer salad," a woman to his right said to the woman sitting next to her. The two of them waved paper fans attached to oversize Popsicle sticks in the general direction of their faces. "It's so hard to know what to do. I couldn't just throw together a tater-tot casserole," the first woman complained, pausing midwave to cast a glance at her friend. She sniffed her disdain. "Women like Eleanor and Carolee don't eat carbohydrates. They aren't normal people."

"Lord, no," her friend concurred. "Everyone knows Carolee Masters is perpetually on a liquid diet."

The two women snickered and resumed their desultory fanning. For the first time, Ben noticed how warm the room had become. A rivulet of sweat ran down his spine as he checked the door. The crush of people kept coming.

He wasn't going to be able to make heads or tails out of any of the things he overheard. He'd unwittingly tripped headfirst into a sticky spiderweb of small-town connections. But he had to figure out where he'd gone wrong. He needed his deputy to provide some context. Resolved, he headed toward the lobby, hoping she hadn't decided to leave.

She sat in a small alcove, perched on the edge of a velvet settee looking shell-shocked. In one hand she clutched a napkin with two chocolate chip cookies, and in the other, a bottle of water perspiring only slightly more than he was.

He rubbed the back of his neck. He'd never seen his deputy looking so vulnerable, and he had to say, the look didn't suit her. "How are you doing?"

She peered up at him, then past him. The corners of her mouth tilted up as she nodded to the procession of people waiting to pay their respects. "There's my family."

He spotted a cluster of people who matched Lori's tawny coloring at the tail end of the line. The youngest of the children appeared to be no older than ten. "Oh, wow." Then, realizing his reaction probably wasn't the correct one, he gave a self-effacing laugh. "Sorry, uh, big family."

"I'm the oldest of seven," she said with a low nod. She wrinkled her nose, but a devilish light sparked in her dark eyes. "Cath-o-lics," she said in a stage whisper. "What can you do?"

Ben chuckled. For the first time, it occurred to him Lori was nearly as much of an outsider in this town as he was. The only difference was, she'd been born here.

He nodded to the empty spot beside her. "May I?"

She scooted to the side to allow him more room. "Sure."

"I didn't mean to upset you. I guess I'm figuring out what to ask and what not to ask."

"This town is full of quicksand." He waited while she took a deep pull on the water bottle. His patience was rewarded. "I was seeing Jeff Masters when he died," she said, low and confidential.

"Was it a secret?"

She shook her head, and her lips curved downward. "No, not a secret, but there were plenty of people who didn't approve."

"Like who?"

She snorted a laugh. "His parents, mine, anyone who

didn't think the crown prince of Pine Bluff should be spending time with me," she said, waving the water bottle in an all-encompassing circle.

"Why not?"

"Because I'm not white," she said bluntly. He sputtered a weak protest, but she plowed ahead. "Oh, I'd be good enough for some people but not for Jeff Masters."

"I see."

They lapsed into silence for a minute. Ben watched as people slipped out of the room. A few sidled closer to the exit as they greeted newcomers, no doubt hoping they could sneak out without anyone taking note.

"He killed himself," she said softly. He jerked his head around to look at her, but she kept her eyes fixed on the water bottle in her hands. She picked at the loose edge of the label with her thumbnail.

"I'm sorry."

"We hadn't been together long. And no, I don't know why." Her words were spoken thoughtfully, as though she was shifting through memories in her mind. She gave a short laugh, then took a sip of her water. Straightening her shoulders, she looked him directly in the eye. "I guess I fooled myself into believing we were more than we were. He certainly didn't give me a second thought in the end."

"I am sorry," he repeated, enunciating each word in the hopes his sincerity might ring through.

"Anyway…" She studied the cookies with disinterest. "I'm trying to move on, but now Clint." She sighed. "They say something about how one suicide can lead to others, don't they?"

"There are theories, I suppose," he said carefully.

She bit the cookie in half, then chewed. "It's weird, though. Clint and Jeff used to be friends. They fell out years ago. I don't have any answers for why," she added with a preemptive glance at him. "But I can't imagine Clint being so torn up over Jeff he'd do the same thing."

"Maybe they were unrelated," he said gently.

Lori shook her head, her sadness palpable. "Maybe," she murmured, but she sounded unconvinced.

He wanted to press her to explain, but a pair of shiny, expensive-looking black high heels appeared in front of him. He fixated on them for a moment, then allowed himself the luxury of savoring every inch of Marlee Masters's long, lithe frame as he lifted his head.

"I'm sorry to interrupt," she said. The agitation in her posture clearly indicated the woman didn't have a sorry bone in her body. She wanted their attention, and she wanted it now. Something about her demeanor made him want to shut her down, but then she shifted her focus to Lori, and her expression softened.

"Hey, Lori." She paired the casual greeting with a brief flutter of her hand. "Can you help me?"

Lori met the other woman's gaze, surprise written all over her face. "Um, sure."

Marlee darted a quick glance at him, then shrugged. "I guess you can see this too." She thrust out her phone, and Ben watched as his deputy carefully took it from her.

Lori cradled the device in both hands. He didn't blame her for the extra caution. Replacing that particular model could eat up a mere mortal's entire paycheck—before taxes. Which, he supposed, made sense. Marlee Masters seemed the type to be accustomed to having the latest and greatest.

He tipped his head to the side as he looked at the blank screen. "What's going on?"

"Oh, sorry. Here." She plucked the phone from Lori's hands and unlocked the screen by flashing a megawatt grin at the camera. The moment it sprang to life, she ditched the beauty queen routine and placed the phone back in Lori's hands. "Open the message app."

Lori did, and Ben leaned close enough to see a string of text conversations appear. There were a couple labeled "Dad," one with "Mom" and a whole string of others showing only ten-digit phone numbers rather than contact information.

Lori opened the first of the unlabeled texts. It read simply, Welcome home.

Lori tapped back to the list screen, her expression tightening. "I take it you don't know who this was from?"

Marlee shook her head. "No."

The next message read, Lookin good marlee.

His deputy snorted and clicked off the second message, mumbling, "Too busy for capitalization or punctuation, I see. I guess we can narrow it down to someone who flunked English in school."

Marlee laughed, but the sound was mirthless.

Ben peered over Lori's shoulder. The third and fourth messages were along the same vein. One, a brief approval of the dress she'd worn to visit Eleanor Young; the other, unsolicited commentary on whether she should be eating whatever it was she had been carrying in a Brewster's Bakery box.

"Nunya, you jerk," Lori muttered as she clicked back to the list of messages.

She started to open the next text, but Ben stopped her with a hand on her wrist. "Wait."

Both women swung startled gazes in his direction. "What?" Lori asked, suddenly on high alert.

"They get worse," Marlee said, frustration making her voice low and tight.

"They're all from different numbers," he said, pointing to the list on the phone. "Have you tried to call any of these numbers?"

At last, he felt the full force of Marlee's blue-flame eyes on him. "Yes. They all go to a recording saying the person is unavailable."

Rubbing his chin, Ben shook his head. "Burner phones or some kind of automated thing?" he puzzled aloud.

"No clue. Read the last one. It came while I was in there," she informed them, nodding toward the viewing parlor.

Ben tore his gaze from Marlee's troubled expression, his gut tightening with dread as Lori scrolled to the most recent text and opened it.

Can't wait to see more of you.

He looked up and found Marlee Masters staring directly into his eyes, and the only words that popped into his mind were *Me too*.

GOD, SHE HADN'T wanted to get the hot sheriff involved in this, but the last message had come through minutes ago, and it freaked her out. She'd abandoned her mother long enough to give official condolences to Mrs. Young and settle Miss Louisa Shelby into one of the chairs in the front row, walker close at hand. Her father was still working the room, so she'd picked up her purse and clutched it close as she claimed the chair next to her mother.

She'd felt the vibration indicating an incoming message. Murmuring a weak cover story about needing a tissue, she'd opened her bag and took out her phone. But what had once been a chastisable offense in her mother's eyes hadn't mattered. Carolee Masters's once all-seeing gaze was completely glazed over.

Now, Sheriff Kinsella was looking at her, and she couldn't look away. His dark eyes burned with intensity as he nudged Lori Cabrera with his elbow and extended his hand, broad palm up. "May I?"

She eyeballed him, wondering what his angle might be. After all, he'd been reading along with them the whole time. But now, he was asking permission. Despite what most people thought of her, Marlee was far more accustomed to being told what to do. The question was a formality, but he was giving her the power to say yes or no. The very fact that he gave her a choice made her want to give him anything he wanted.

"Of course."

He took the phone from Lori and began opening and closing the text messages with a detached efficiency she found herself envying. She'd been tempted to delete the messages when they first started, but the better judgment gleaned in three years of law school tempered the impulse. Evidence. Her gut told her these creepy texts from some rando might one day be evidence, so she kept them.

"Do you mind if I write these numbers down?" The sheriff pulled a small notepad and a pen from his shirt pocket.

"Knock yourself out," she said.

"We'll check them out," Lori promised.

Marlee refocused her attention on the younger woman. She hadn't known Lori growing up. They had years and multiple layers of social strata between them, but her brother had dated her. Maybe even spent his last months falling in love with her. From what she'd seen in the days surrounding Jeff's funeral, Lori had loved him too.

"How are you doing?" Marlee kept her voice quiet and gentle.

The other woman raised a shoulder and let it fall. "I'm

okay." She glanced beyond Marlee's shoulder, her gaze straying to her family. "Most days."

"But not today," Marlee answered with gentle understanding.

"Exactly."

Marlee watched as Ben Kinsella noted every phone number, as well as the date and time received, in his notebook. There likely wasn't much he could do with the information in terms of tracing the messages, but having someone else see them, having the information listed somewhere other than in her phone, made her feel more secure.

He finished, closing the notebook and giving the cover a little tap. Despite her father's bluster the other day, she trusted this man. Whether she approved of Ben Kinsella's method or management, Henry obviously did.

"Thank you," she said. "I…" She blew out a breath, and her shoulders relaxed for the first time in days. "I needed to show someone." She gave a self-deprecating wince. "See if someone else thought it was creepy or if I'm crazy."

"You're not crazy," Lori said to her without a beat of hesitation. She gestured to the phone Marlee clutched in her hand. "Super creepy."

The succinct assessment startled a laugh from her. "Thank you."

"If you get any other messages, would you contact me?" Sheriff Kinsella pulled a business card from the same breast pocket where he'd kept the notebook.

She took it, noting the heavy card stock retained the warmth of his body. "Yes. Thank you."

Marlee turned to leave them, but his deep voice stopped her in her tracks. "Ms. Masters?"

"Yes?"

"How long do you plan to stay in Pine Bluff?"

The question cut to the quick, but she couldn't let it show. She wouldn't let any of them see how desperate she was to leave. Her father had her trapped here for the moment, but she'd find a way out. She had to if she wanted any kind of life of her own. But for now, she needed to keep a cool head and not fight the ties that bound her there. Because everyone knew the harder you fought to free yourself, the tighter a snare became.

"Indefinitely," she said, lifting her arms out, presenting herself to them. "I'm home. Take care, Lori." She backed off a step and raised a hand in farewell. She was done with this conversation. "Thanks, Sheriff. I appreciate y'all."

Chapter Four

Home from the visitation, Marlee avoided the cross fire of her parents' lame attempts at conversation by escaping to her room. The door closed tightly behind her, she planted both hands flat on the tall four-poster bed for balance as she stepped out of the torturous high heels. Moaning her relief, she curled her toes into the plush pile of the rug beside the bed and reached for the zip on her dress.

Black fabric pooled on the floor, and she sighed as the cool air flowing from the vents breezed over her heated skin. She unhooked her bra as she moved to the cherrywood bureau. In one practiced motion, she let it fall into the open drawer, then she pulled on the first T-shirt she found.

It was one of Jeff's. She'd rescued a bunch from his room when her mother was in the midst of a grief-fueled purge. The hem fell halfway down her thighs, even though her brother had been only an inch taller. The Greek letters screen-printed onto the fabric were still stiff and uncracked from washing. A reminder of how young Jeff had been when he died.

She ran her fingers along the collar of the shirt, stretching the fabric away from her throat. She shook her arms out and gave her shoulders a couple rolls to loosen her tense muscles as she approached the bed. The leather clutch she'd carried to the visitation lay atop the rumpled coverlet. She opened it and removed the lipstick, card case and her phone. She tossed the lipstick into the depths of the larger handbag parked beside the bed, removed her identification and debit cards from the small leather case and placed them on the nightstand before connecting her phone to its charger.

The screen woke but showed no new notifications. She dropped down onto the bed, drawing one leg up under her as she settled in to relisten to the voice mail she'd received a mere hour after her father called to summon her home. Pressing the play button was the technological equivalent to testing a bruise, but she couldn't help herself. She tapped the screen, and the speaker hummed to life.

"Marlee, hello. I'm sorry we keep missing each other." Jared Baker, senior partner at one of Atlanta's hottest firms, had the kind of mellow baritone voice both women and juries loved. But she'd been impervious to him. All she'd wanted was a job in Atlanta. "I received your message about a family emergency, and I understand completely. I was going to have to cancel our appointment anyway. I, uh, I'm sorry to tell you my partner and I have decided not to take a new associate at this time. I'm sorry to disappoint you, but I wish you the best in your future endeavors. Please give my best to your family."

Her family.

The Masters name strikes another blow against freedom, Marlee thought, her stomach souring.

She blew out a breath that ruffled her hair, then let her head fall back. Staring up at the ceiling, she drew a couple deep breaths to center herself. Here she was, back in her childhood bedroom, doing her father's bidding. Squinting at what appeared to be a small brown water mark on the ceiling above her bed, she concentrated on resuming the natural flow of her breathing as she forced her racing mind to slow.

She straightened her neck and raised her hands over her head with her fingers laced together, stretching every muscle as long as she could make them. When she let go, she fell back across the bed, snatching her phone up as she flopped.

A trickle of trepidation rippled through her as she saw she had an unread text message awaiting her. More than the unsolicited commentary on her daily activities, she truly resented the creep for making her not want to look at her phone. Setting her jaw, she jabbed at the icon to open her message queue. The breath she'd been holding rushed from her lungs when she saw the text was a terse reminder from her father to be at Timber Masters offices no later than eight the next morning.

She wasn't likely to forget.

Marlee resented being called home from Atlanta. Sure, he'd only agreed to pay her rent until she'd sat for the bar exam, but she had hoped she could stretch things out long enough for her to land a job and get a paycheck or two into her account. She promised herself this layover in Pine Bluff would be nothing but a speed bump. As soon as she could, she was getting out of town.

Her phone buzzed and she automatically lifted her hand to see the screen. Another unknown ten-digit number. Feeling more confident having shared them with the sheriff and Lori, she tapped to open the message.

Nobody likes a tattletail

A chill ran down her spine as she sat up straight once more. This time, she couldn't find even a modicum of comfort in the sender's grammatical errors or misspellings. A second later, a different phone number appeared.

I like this outfit even better then the dress you wore earlier

The message came across loud and clear. Whoever it was, they were watching her. All the time. She growled her annoyance at both the arrogance and the grammatical offenses, but the sound tangled in her throat and morphed into a groan when her phone buzzed again.

You should show more skin marlee you have nice legs

Whipping her head around, she checked the window. The blinds were open. Cursing under her breath, she slid off the corner of the bed, scurried to the wall and slid over to the window. Her heart hammered as she twisted the rod to close the slats.

Once she felt certain she couldn't be seen, she yanked the sheer curtains from their decorative holders and closed them over the entire window. Feeling more secure with a few extra millimeters of nylon between her and her peeper, she gripped her phone tightly, willing her hand to stop shaking.

Her gaze caught on the clutch she'd abandoned on the bed. Forcing herself not to lunge for it, she walked over to the bag and extracted the business card Ben Kinsella had given her. A mobile number was listed beneath the office phone and fax.

She dialed, allowing her mind to ruminate on the necessity of a fax number these days as she poked at the screen. Closing her eyes, she pressed the phone to her ear and concentrated on faking a normal breathing pattern until her brain got the message all was well. And all *was* well.

Her parents' house had a state-of-the-art security system. She was safe. Whoever was doing this was nothing more than a creep—

"Kinsella."

The deep, masculine bark startled her out of the circular pattern of her thoughts. She blurted the first thing that sprang to mind. "He's watching me."

There was a beat of silence on the other end of the line. She cringed, squeezing her eyes shut tight in mortification as a rush of blood set her cheeks and ears afire. "I mean, I was changing clothes—"

"Are you home alone?" he broke in, brusquely efficient.

"What? No. My parents are here," she stammered. "I'm safe. A bit…freaked. He texted me."

"He?"

"I assume it's a he," she said haltingly. "I guess, maybe… I'm not sure. Maybe I shouldn't assume, but the things he says are things a perverted guy would say."

"What did he say?"

"He called me a tattletale, said that he preferred what I'm wearing now to the dress I wore to the visitation. He also remarked about my nice legs."

There was a pause, then a small cough as the sheriff cleared his throat. "This is probably going to sound out of line, but I don't have the first idea how else to ask… What are you wearing?"

"A T-shirt," she admitted. "One of my brother's old shirts."

"A men's T-shirt," he repeated, and Marlee got the vague impression he was making another note in his notebook. "And…?" Another awkward moment hung between them, then he exhaled a soft, "Ah."

"Yeah."

"Well, uh…" His words stumbled to a halt.

"My blinds were open," she confessed in a rush. "I didn't think to close them. I came in and wanted to get out of my dress and shoes."

"And then you received the text," he said, a husky edge in his voice.

"Three texts, actually," she clarified. "First, he called me a tattletale. Then the one about the dress and the other about my legs." She sat down on the edge of the bed with a huff, then dropped her head into her hand. "Different phone numbers."

"Answers my next question."

"I figured."

"Do you feel safe? Do you want me to call your father and let him in on what's happening?"

Her head jerked up. "No. No. Do not tell my father," she ordered.

"But, Marlee—"

"I'm serious. I only wanted to tell you what was happening in case I ever felt…not safe. Come to think of it, I never meant to tell you. I was telling Lori. If I wanted to tell my father, I would have gone to him. Don't call my father."

"I won't."

She snorted softly. "Sure you won't."

"I said I wouldn't and I won't." His annoyance sliced off all the softer notes of his earlier agreement.

"Please." She scoffed. "No one keeps anything from Henry Masters. Not in this town."

"You told us in confidence. We will keep your confidence."

She gave a bitter laugh. "I'm going to assume you're so new here you haven't even unpacked, but fine. I guess I have no choice but to believe you."

"If you didn't want to take the chance of your father finding out, why did you tell Lori?"

Pressing her hand to her throat, she let her head fall back. "I," she started, stopped, then figured she had nothing to lose at this point. "I wanted to go on record, I guess. In case—" Clamping her mouth shut, she gave a frustrated squeak of irritation. "Good night, Sheriff."

She ended the call.

Staring at the wallpaper she'd added to the phone's home screen, she swallowed hard. Her brother's smiling face shone up at her, the blue eyes they'd both inherited from their father glowing with amusement. She'd snapped the photo the last time she'd seen him. It had been one of her rare weekends home in Pine Bluff. They'd ditched the house after an excruciating Sunday supper. He'd begged her to hang out with him for a while and she gave in, but only grudgingly.

Regret twisted in her gut, radiating pangs of remorse. Her heart squeezed. She'd resented a couple hours spent with her brother, and weeks later he was dead. Thank God she'd given in. Thank Heaven above she'd climbed into his truck and let him drive her out to their place on Sawtooth Lake.

There, they'd sat on the dock while they daydreamed of a life out from under their father's thumb.

Less than three months later, her brother had been found in the lake house with a bullet in his brain and a gun in his hand.

Ever since the day she'd received that awful phone call, Marlee was aware her time would come. But she'd find a way to face the forces her brother couldn't handle. She didn't have time to be intimidated by some coward who got his jollies sending anonymous messages. And someday, she was going to face her father and tell him she had no intention of staying to help run the family business.

She was going rogue—as she and Jeff had dreamed.

Chapter Five

Ben gripped his phone long after Marlee Masters ended the call. He told himself to stop thinking about how she'd look wearing only a men's T-shirt. Told himself over and over again. But he failed miserably. The image was in his mind now, and there was no shaking it.

He glanced at the plain white undershirt he'd stripped down to upon arriving back at the house he was renting. The place was on the small side but tidy. And furnished. Only two blocks from the town hall and his office. There were days when he felt utterly ridiculous making the one-minute drive to park in the space designated for the sheriff's vehicle, but he couldn't waste time jogging home to get his car in the event of an actual emergency.

He imagined Marlee Masters jogging down his street wearing only a T-shirt similar to the one he wore and her underwear. Blue underwear. Light blue. Bikini cut? Yeah, bikini. Cut to cling to the curve of her hip and colored to match her piercing eyes.

His phone rang again, and he jumped. Heat prickling his neck and cheeks, he checked the display, half-afraid the lovely Ms. Masters might have sensed he was thinking about her in a salacious manner. Thankfully, it was his deputy calling.

"Hey, Lori. You going on shift early?"

"Yeah, I sent Mike on home. He's still pretty shaky," she reported.

"No problem." He cleared his throat, hesitant to bring up the personal stuff she'd been wrestling with at the funeral home but figuring it was better to climb on the elephant in the room and try to ride it out. Emotions were running high all over town. This was another reminder that he wasn't in Atlanta anymore. "And, uh, how are you holding up?"

To his relief, she laughed. "Boy, you suck at this," she teased.

"I do not," he replied, offended. "I'm not used to, uh…" He shrugged, then remembered she couldn't see him. "You know."

She gave another chuckle. "People having feelings? Or, rather, seeing other people's feelings out there on display for the whole town to see?"

He ducked his head. She was dead-on. She also didn't realize how lucky she was to grow up in a place where people actually placed value on feelings, no matter how inconvenient they were.

"Sorry, boss. It won't happen again."

"Don't say you're sorry," he snapped, too on edge to get a good read on his own emotional barometer to control his tone. "You didn't do anything wrong."

"It was pretty unprofessional of me to spill all over you," she began.

He cut off any additional apologies. "It was pretty human of you. And it's not like you were on duty."

She snorted. "I'm sure every time one of your busts went south, you and your old DEA buddies huddled up and had a sharing circle."

"No," he admitted with a chuckle. "But that might also give you some decent insight into how a former agent ends up the sheriff in a rural county." He hesitated for only a moment, then swiped one of the agency shrink's favorite lines. "It's no crime to want some peace in your life."

"I know," she answered softly. "I guess we're all shook up."

"Totally understandable," he said gruffly. "It's natural to think about it, Lori, but make sure you don't dwell. Get me?"

"Yeah. My *abuela* used to tell me not to borrow trouble from tomorrow. There will be plenty to go around when it gets here."

"Your *abuela* was right."

Lori cleared her throat, then slipped back into the brisk, no-nonsense manner he'd grown accustomed to since coming to Pine Bluff. "All is well here, Sheriff. Get some rest. We'll see you in the morning."

"Thanks, Deputy. See you then."

Ben ended the call and sat staring at the television screen without registering what was happening on the cold-case show he'd been watching when his phone rang the first time. Warmth unfurled in his gut. People were starting to trust him here. At least, one was.

The conversations he'd shared with Lori were the easiest they'd exchanged since the day he walked into the Pine Bluff municipal building. He didn't blame her for being wary of him. Aside from being an outsider, he was also a city guy, and a former federal agent. In these parts, those were the kinds of strikes a guy didn't get a chance to swing at often. The realization made him feel all sorts of warm fuzzies he'd never admit to having.

People had warned him when he took the job. Everyone from the resident agent in charge of his old division to Henry Masters himself had told him he'd have a hard time settling in and an even tougher row to hoe if he wanted to actually belong in his new hometown. Locals were still rattled by the drug busts that exposed the seedy underbellies of several bucolic Georgia towns. But the life of a social outcast was something he could deal with if he had to. A life outside of law enforcement was not on the table.

Tossing his phone aside, he reached for the bottle of beer on the coffee table and took a swig, grimacing as the now-warmish brew flowed past his lips. He cradled the bottle between his palms, laced his fingers together and let his head fall back against the sofa cushion. The ceilings in his cozy house were tongue-and-groove knotty pine. To his surprise, it took him only two nights in this new exile to discover he loved looking at them.

Those ceilings provided endless games of connect-the-knots. Some nights, he assigned the spots of burled wood key points in the cases he'd left open when he'd opted out. Others, he traced and retraced his steps through the maze of deals and double crosses ultimately culminating in his resignation. On the darkest nights, he luxuriated in torturous games of "what if," starting with the large black hole of a knot in the corner of the ceiling, and let the twists and turns of his life lead him from one impossible spot to another until the game ended with his childhood best friend, Andre, emptying a good portion of his bumped-up AR-15 into the agents rushing the room where they'd stood. Though he lived to rue his decision for a whole host of reasons, Ben had had no choice but to take his oldest friend down.

A blown cover and the death of the man he'd once loved as a brother would have been reason enough to move on. The bounty placed on his head by the leader of the SEATL—the notorious southeast Atlanta gang whose business he'd been infiltrating—helped move his decision process along.

Ivan Jones was a white kid born in East Point, Georgia.

A maniac with an ego the size of all of Atlanta. In order to survive, he'd spent most of his life telling everyone who'd listen that his family was connected to the Russian mafia. His parents were actually penniless Serbian refugees, but the truth didn't fit the image of the cunning Russian oligarch he fancied himself.

After Ben's cover was blown, Ivan could have had him popped on any number of occasions, but he hadn't. No, he'd wanted to make a game out of it. A hunting game, with Ben as the prey and a quarter-million dollars as the prize. In essence, he'd made sure there wasn't any place in Atlanta Ben might be safe.

The agency had put him on permanent desk duty and wanted him to transfer to another regional office, but Ben resisted, so they cut him loose altogether. His use as an undercover agent was spent. When Masters County found itself without a sheriff due to fallout from a sting operation targeting methamphetamine production, a friend of a friend gave Henry Masters his name. "The rest was history," he said, reaching for the remote control on the cushion beside him.

The screen went blank with the touch of a button, but Ben didn't move from the couch. He was half-afraid to go to bed. What if he spent the night replaying bloody scenes from dead-end streets of Zone 3? What if he lay awake thinking about Marlee Masters's long, bare legs? He snorted at the last thought.

Of course he was going to think about Marlee Masters's legs.

What had Lori said about Jeff Masters's death being too similar to Clint Young's? The two men had been friends once. Or so Lori had indicated. Had they veered off in different directions? Young started working for Timber Masters prior to Jeff Masters's death. Perhaps the two of them would have become friends again. Would Marlee Masters have come back to town if her brother had lived?

With a groan, he shook his head to clear the spiderweb of thoughts, set the bottle on the table, switched the television on again and stretched out on his side on the sofa. Better to spend the evening zoning out on cold cases and waking up with a crick in his neck than to lay awake chasing ghosts and elusive women.

"MORNING, BOSS MAN," Lori called out when he shuffled through the door the following morning. "You're up early."

Ben was dressed and mobile, but he wasn't necessarily awake. He cast a baleful glance at the empty coffeepot. How anyone made it through an overnight without coffee was beyond his powers of comprehension, but he didn't have the energy to question the woman's life choices.

"I'll give you Schaeffer's stapler if you'll make a coffee-and-doughnut run," he said as he trudged past her desk.

Lori narrowed her dark eyes appraisingly. "The good one? The Swingline?" she pressed.

He nodded as he dropped heavily into his seat. "Yep, but I'm holding it in escrow until I get some decent caffeine in me."

She moved to the coffee maker Julianne had banned him from operating in his first week on the job and gave it a fond pat. "I'll do you a double solid if you'll wait until I come in this afternoon to tell Schaeffer about the redistribution," she countered.

"Done."

With practiced ease, Lori set a pot to brewing. "I want to make it clear I'm doing this because I want the stapler, and I want to see Mike's face when you tell him it's mine. Gender has nothing to do with it."

Ben nodded his understanding. "And I want to make it

clear I wasn't asking because you're a woman, but because you are on the approved list of coffee makers."

"Noted," she said as she hit the switch and the machine burbled to life. "Okay, I'll run and grab an immediate infusion for you. Do you want one dozen cliché-makers or two?"

"One," he said gruffly. "And if you order at least one cream-filled, I'll ask Julianne to order some of those colored paper clips."

"Done." She raised a hand as she beat a path to the door. "Okay, but I expect them to be jumbo-sized."

Ben nodded. "Noted." Watching her go, he made one last attempt to gain the upper hand in their dealings. "Make it two cream-filled doughnuts," he shouted after her.

Lori laughed, and he closed his gritty eyes, rubbing them with his thumb and forefinger. He heard the creak of hinges but figured it was the door closing in Lori's wake.

"Wow. Hitting the cream-filleds hard. I take it you didn't sleep much either?"

The plush softness of Marlee Masters's voice set him off like a starter's pistol. He kicked out, sending his desk chair flying across the tile floor. He crashed into the wall, arms flailing as momentum pitched him forward in his seat. He grunted and bit back an oath when the back of his hand connected with a metal filing cabinet. He shot out of his death trap of a chair, cradling his throbbing hand in the palm of the uninjured one. "Ms. Masters," he managed to huff.

"Oh, Sheriff, I'm sorry," she said, moving farther into the room. She drew to a stop just shy of touching him, then looked up into his face. "I didn't mean to startle you. I thought you heard me say hello to Lori," she said in a rush.

"I, uh, no," he managed to mutter. He shook his head, hoping the action would pull double duty by negating her assumption and clearing the fog from his brain. "No. Sorry, I didn't."

"You had doughnuts on your mind."

She wore running shorts. The strappy top she paired with them may as well have been a second skin. To add insult to injury, the mile-long legs he'd spent half the night purposefully not imagining were on display. She had cordless earbuds in her ears, but she wasn't shouting, so he assumed the phone strapped to her bicep wasn't cranking out the beats. He pressed his fingers to his throbbing temple in a vain attempt to block the mental image of her jogging down his street in her T-shirt and panties.

"Were you out running?"

She glanced down at the toes of her running shoes, then pushed a hand to her rib cage as she caught her breath. "Wow, you really do have what it takes to make detective, Kinsella," she quipped. "What gave me away?"

Ignoring her flippancy, he shook his head again, this time in disbelief. "Seriously? You've got some creeper peeping in your windows at night, then you're going out running all over town alone?"

"I'm assuming you mean like a person who jogs for exercise," she said, enunciating each word.

Ben copped to her meaning and cringed as he played the question back in his mind. If he'd had even a couple hours of escape into sleep, he might not have blundered into caveman territory, but damn, her legs were enough to make a man lose his ever-lovin' mind.

"I, uh…" Mortifyingly aware there was no way he could retract or redirect his misstep, he tried a different tack. "It's barely light outside. You shouldn't run with—" He gestured to her ears. Then, his instincts for self-preservation finally sprang to life. Holding up both hands in surrender, he squashed the chorus line of admonishments kicking its way through his mind. "Yeah, I didn't sleep much. Sorry for being old-fashioned." Then, quickly shifting topics, he asked, "What can I do for you?"

The corner of her mouth tilted upward. "Much better."

She huffed a breath, apparently as annoyed as he by the tension between them. Ben admired the effort, but watching her chest rise and fall did absolutely nothing to get his mind right.

"I came to talk to you about my brother," she said, jolting him from his wayward thoughts.

"Your brother?"

"Yes." She shifted her startlingly direct blue gaze to the file cabinet he'd assaulted. "I'm sure you've heard about my brother's death."

It was a statement, not a question. A leading one, but a statement nonetheless. Uncertain how to proceed, he opted for the less-is-more approach. "Yes."

A small harrumph of disgust escaped her. The resigned set of her jaw told him she'd expected nothing less but had still hoped for more.

"Small town," he said gruffly.

"Microscopic," she concurred.

"And I am the sheriff."

"Then, if you are acquainted with the circumstances surrounding my brother's...passing," she said with a hitch in her voice, "I'm sure you've heard that Jeff and Clint Young were friends when they were boys."

Lowering his arms, he nodded. "Yes."

"They hadn't been close in years," she hurried on. "People are making all sorts of assumptions—"

"Assumptions?" he prompted, interrupting her midstream.

"About connections between their deaths," she said, meeting his eyes directly again.

"Deputy Cabrera told me she was involved with your brother. While it's possible for someone to be interested in more than one person, I didn't get the impression there was any question in her mind she was the only one."

"You trust her judgment," Marlee determined.

Though she wasn't asking, he nodded anyway. "I haven't known her long, but in the short time I've been here, I have found Deputy Cabrera to be a quick study and a good judge of character. I trust her gut." He added the last because, to his way of thinking, what she'd said was all that needed to be said on the matter.

He gestured for her to take the seat opposite his desk and waited until she'd settled into the chair, then reclaimed his own. Rolling back to his desk, he bit the inside of his cheek to keep from wincing when he reached into his shirt pocket with his sore hand. He pulled out the notebook he kept there and flipped it open to a blank page. "Was there something you wanted to tell me about your brother's death?"

She wet her lips, then glanced away, her gaze traveling over the postings and notices pinned to a corkboard. "My mother always said he didn't do it."

She spoke so softly, he scooted to the edge of his chair, hoping proximity would improve his chances of catching every word. "Your mother?"

"No doubt you've heard some whispers about her as well."

He had, but he'd be damned if he'd confirm or deny what he may or may not have heard about Henry Masters's beautiful but fragile wife. When he didn't answer, she continued her perusal of the room, refusing to look straight at him.

"My mother drinks too much," she said at last. "She's…"

Again, she wet her lips, but this time she met his gaze head-on. "She's not in the most stable place right now."

"I understand," he assured her. No mother should have to bury a child. He couldn't imagine the pain of it. It was unfathomable.

"She has always said Jeff did not take his own life." This time, her voice was dull, and when he studied her, he saw signs of her sleepless night shadowing her lovely face.

"Has she any—"

"Proof?" she interrupted. Marlee shook her head forcefully. "No. Not one shred. Don't you think if there were any indication of anything untoward in the death of Henry Masters's son, a more extensive investigation would have taken place?"

The edge in her voice surprised him, but Ben was careful not to let it show. "No. I have no doubt."

"He would have spent every last penny he had on an investigation if there had been even a hint of something concrete, but there wasn't. My brother put a gun to his head and pulled the trigger."

Her voice was flat and emotionless, but when he searched her eyes, he saw only the anguish of the helpless there. "I *am* sorry for your loss," he said gently.

She tried to smirk and couldn't quite pull it off. "You didn't know him, Sheriff," she began.

"Ben," he interjected.

Marlee inclined her head, accepting his invitation to use his given name. "He was an ass," she said, a wicked light sparkling in her eyes. "Your typical spoiled, entitled prince of a small town."

Her blunt assessment made him warm to her even more. "But he was your brother and you loved him."

"From the moment they brought him home from the hospital," she said without hesitation.

"So you came here this morning to tell me…what?"

Marlee uncrossed her legs and bit her lip as she slid up to sit on the edge of the seat, rubbing her flat palms together between her knees. "I came here to tell you my mother might be a fragile flower hell-bent on drowning her grief, but I'm not."

"I can see you aren't."

"Yet my mama and I agree on one thing—I don't think my brother killed himself."

"What makes you say so?"

"I feel it in my gut," she said evenly.

He blinked, then shook his head. "Didn't I hear you're an attorney? I'd think the whole thing about evidence would have been covered in even the most basic law class."

She nodded and then stood. "It was. And I don't have any evidence. At least not yet."

The door opened, and they both clammed up as Lori backed her way into the office, a tray of coffee cups perched atop the doughnut box. "The place was packed," she called out without looking up. "Everyone's talking—"

"I don't doubt it," Marlee said with a short laugh.

Lori drew up short, then set her load down on the nearest desk. "Oh. I didn't realize you were coming in here."

"I stopped by to pass a couple messages from the family to Sheriff Kinsella," Marlee answered smoothly. "Today is my first day as chief legal counsel at Timber Masters. I thought I'd get a jump on things." She tugged the hem of her tank down over her hips. "I'd better get my run in before I'm late punching in."

Ben had to use all his strength of will to keep his eyes glued to her face. Her expression was one of calm friendliness, but the intensity in her eyes told him she didn't want to air her suspicions in front of Lori.

"Yes, thank you." He cleared his throat, desperate to

buy some time to figure out what she expected him to do with the groundless suppositions she'd dumped on him. "You'll call if there's anything more I can do?"

"Absolutely."

"Doughnut?" Lori offered, opening the box in invitation.

Marlee peered into the box, then tossed a triumphant glance over her shoulder. "Are those cream-filled?"

He scowled to indicate he wasn't buying the wide-eyed innocent bit. "Weren't you going for a run?"

She narrowed her gaze, and he realized a fraction of a second too late that she believed his reminder to be a challenge.

"Oh, Sheriff, if there's one thing I learned in law school, it was how to eat on the run."

With a smirk, she plucked one of his precious cream-filled pastries from the box and bit into it as she waved her thanks to Lori and hustled out the door.

Chapter Six

Marlee smiled as her father's longtime secretary, Mrs. Devane, came out from behind her desk to greet her with a handclasp. "So good to see you, dear. We're excited to have you on board."

She wasn't on board, but there was no way Marlee could say so to poor sweet Mrs. Devane. The woman had been guarding the executive offices of Timber Masters since Marlee's grandfather ran the place. She settled on something innocuous but polite. "Good morning, Mrs. Devane. I'm happy to see you too."

"Your father is waiting for you," the older woman cooed.

Marlee felt her press something hard into the center of her palm and looked down to find a cellophane-wrapped butterscotch candy in her hand. The kind she used to sneak to them on the rare occasions when Marlee and Jeff came into the offices with their father. Hot tears stung her eyes, and her throat closed. Looking at the polished oak door her great-grandfather had made with his own hands, she felt a wave of longing for her brother threatening to swallow her.

Mrs. Devane patted the hand holding the candy. "You'll be the next Masters at the helm of Timber Masters," she said with quiet conviction. "I suppose it would be more appropriate for you to call me Gladys now."

Marlee gulped the lump in her throat. "Thank you, Mrs. Devane."

The other woman chortled as she headed back to her post. "We'll work on it. Young Jeffrey almost had it down when he—" Gladys's eyes widened as her brain caught up to her mouth, and Marlee noticed the sheen of moisture trapped behind the other woman's spectacles. "You go on in, dear," she said, her voice thick and hushed. "They're waiting for you."

Anxious to escape, Marlee failed to register the plural pronoun prior to opening the door and stepping into the confines of her father's inner sanctum. She drew up short when she saw Henry seated in one of the club chairs facing his desk rather than the massive leather seat behind it. He was sharing a low chuckle with the white-haired man seated in the matching chair. Both men looked up, and Marlee recognized the town's resident attorney, Wendell Wingate, by the polka-dot bow tie he wore with his pale gray summer-weight suit.

"Miss Marlee," the older man called out, admiration lacing the greeting.

He braced both hands on the arms of his chair to rise, but she tried to wave him off. "Oh, no, Mr. Wingate. No need to get up. I'm sorry to interrupt. Mrs. Devane said to come in. It's nice to see you again."

Mr. Wingate pushed to his feet and captured her hands between his. "The day I don't get up when a pretty woman enters a room is the day your daddy can build me a nice pine box." He beamed at her. "Congratulations on your graduation, my dear, and welcome to the club," he added with a wink.

"Thank you, sir." She extracted her hands from his grasp then gestured for him to sit again. "Would you prefer I came back in a while?"

Henry shook his head. "No. I called Wendell in for you."

He rose from his chair, then gestured for Marlee to take it. Tamping down on her disappointment, Marlee seated herself. "Oh?"

"Yes, it only makes sense." Her father settled himself in the executive chair behind the massive desk. "Wendell has been handling the company's legal matters for decades, but now we have you."

A surge of panic had Marlee fighting the urge to jump from her seat. To counteract it, she folded her hands in her lap and waited patiently, exactly as her mother had taught her. "You can't mean that," she said with a nervous chuckle.

"Unceremoniously fired," the older man said with a woeful shake of his head.

Appalled, Marlee gaped at her father. "But after so many years—"

He cut off her protest with a nonchalant wave of his hand. "Stop preying on the girl's sympathies, Wendell," he admonished. Focusing on her, he said only, "This has been the plan all along. Wendell here has his eye on a seat on the bench."

"Oh." She blinked twice as she felt another chance at charting her own course closing down on her.

If the only attorney in town wasn't on retainer to Timber Masters, they'd have to engage someone from another county for counsel. Henry Masters didn't give company business to anyone living outside the county that bore his family's name. She cast about for something to say as her mind fought to recalibrate plans.

"You're closing your practice?"

Mr. Wingate shook his head. "No. My grandson, Simon, has been with a lobbying firm in Atlanta, but he'll be coming home to take over the firm."

Marlee stared at him in shock. Wonder of wonders, Simon Wingate was coming to Pine Bluff. Wendell Wingate's son, Dell Wingate, had been serving the district that encompassed Masters County in the Georgia General Assembly since the year after his twenty-first birthday. Dell's son, Simon, used to visit Pine Bluff for two full weeks every summer, but as far as Marlee was aware, he hadn't stepped foot in the town since the day his teenage rebellion won out over the wishes of his grandparents. Not even for his grandmother's funeral. The snub had fueled the gossips for years after the event. He'd been in college then, Marlee recalled. At Yale. Another strike against him as far as the people around here were concerned.

"Wow. Simon. I don't think I've seen him since I was in middle school."

Wendell nodded, his genial smile fixed firmly in place, though it didn't reach his eyes. "Yes, I think you would be about right." He hesitated a moment, seeming to have lost his usual bluff and bluster. "But, boy, wait until he gets a look at you, young lady." He winked at Henry. "Perhaps we can orchestrate a merger."

Henry huffed a laugh but rolled his eyes. "Keep your sights set on the circuit court. You do more good for us in the superior court than as a matchmaker."

Wingate chuckled and cast a long-suffering sigh in Marlee's direction. "See how it is? His daddy would tan his hide if he ever heard him disrespecting his elders thataway."

Marlee couldn't help being amused at the byplay between the two men and the image of her quiet, kind grandfather ever getting the best of his bossy son. Still, she could play the game too. "Mama always says he's incorrigible."

"An understatement," the older man concurred.

"Enough," Henry grumbled. "Marlee, you're going to

spend some time over at Wendell's offices. I need you to get up to speed as quickly as possible, and I can't pull him away from all the drunk and disorderlies he's set to defend."

"Hey, now, the majority of my clients are employees of this fine company," Wendell shot back.

Her father's gaze drifted down to the stack of folders arranged on the corner of his desk, and Marlee gathered he was losing interest in the conversation now that he'd given his order. "Exactly why I need to get back to running this business."

"I don't want to be in the way," Marlee said, dividing a glance between the two men as she searched for an escape hatch.

"You won't be," they said in unison.

Taken aback by how quickly and efficiently her father had managed to circumvent her every plan, Marlee dug in. "I understand you have a plan," she said tightly. "But I was hoping to discuss something with you in private this morning."

Her eyes bore into the top of her father's head, but he didn't notice.

Mr. Wingate, obviously accustomed to taking his cues from this man two decades his junior, rose from his chair. "I'll give the two of you a moment," he said as he buttoned his suit jacket.

"Not necessary," her father answered, shuffling through the stack of folders, his mind fixed on his next task.

She bit the inside of her cheek to keep from screaming for his attention, as she had when she was a child. But she wasn't a child any longer. And she wasn't one of Henry Masters's many pawns. Tipping her chin up, she drizzled extra honey over her words. "If you wouldn't mind, Mr. Wingate. Please and thank you."

The second the older man opened the office door, her father looked up from his work, impatience etched into every line on his face. "There's no need to keep the man waiting, Marlee. His time is valuable, and you'd better believe he's billing us for every minute of it."

"I understand, but I need to tell you—"

"You think you want to get a job up in Atlanta," he said, cutting her off. He lifted his head and met her eyes with a pointed stare. "But you don't."

"I do," she argued.

"There's nothing for you there," he said succinctly.

The steely glint in his steady blue gaze made her gut twist. Pressure built in her chest. Her fight-or-flight instincts kicked into gear, and Marlee exhaled as she realized her father had somehow gotten to Jared Baker. Her fingertips tingled, but her hands felt tight and numb as she curled them into fists. If he'd managed to poison Baker against hiring her, Henry wouldn't have thought twice about doing the same with every other decent firm in town. Now he had the nerve to sit there glaring at her as if she'd run over his dog then got out of her car and kicked the carcass.

"There's nothing for me here."

"Your place is here," he replied, his voice quiet and uninflected. "That was the deal, wasn't it? I send you to law school, and then you come back here to work for me."

No, the deal had been she'd go to law school then come back to help her brother run the company. But their plan could never happen now. Neither would her new dream of a life free of Timber Masters and all that being one of the Masterses of Masters County entailed. Not as long as her father lived, at least.

Snapping her jaw shut, she rose and stalked to the door. When she reached for the knob, he called after her, "Don't you want to guess what I told them?"

She didn't want to give him the satisfaction, but she needed to determine if the situation might be salvageable. "What?"

"I told them I wanted them to liaise with you on Timber Masters's franchising along the Eastern Seaboard."

Whirling to face him, she gaped at the audacity of the play. "Franchising? We're not the kind of business that can be easily franchised."

"We are aware of that, but Jared Baker doesn't have the first clue about my business. Either way, he was happy to swap a first-year associate for a chance to even talk about it. And I'm such a friendly guy and all," he said, gesturing expansively. "We're having drinks the next time I'm in Atlanta." He picked up his pen and tapped the file in front of him, tsking softly. "So there you have it. You're worth about two fingers of Glenlivet on the open market."

"Wait a minute—"

"No," he barked. "I won't wait another second. I paid for your degree so you'd put it to work for me. And don't you keep Wendell waiting another moment, missy. You hear?"

SHE SEETHED THE entire morning, miles from absorbing any of the words flowing from Wingate's mouth. They hardly mattered anyway. She could read. Once she had the files at her disposal, she'd figure the business out on her own. At the moment, she wasn't the least bit interested in learning anything her father's toady had to teach her.

"Miss Marlee?" he called, gently breaking into her ruminations.

When she looked up, he closed the file he'd been droning on about, then fixed her with a kindly gaze. "Many people would kill to be in your position."

"Excuse me?"

Though she had been woolgathering, Marlee had heard

the man perfectly. She simply wasn't sure how to respond when people said stuff like that to her. People assumed she led a charmed life, but they didn't have any idea how it felt to be Marlee Masters.

"The first thing they taught us in school was to assume nothing, Mr. Wingate."

"We're colleagues now, Marlee," he said, peering at her over the top of his tortoiseshell reading glasses. "Call me Wendell."

She hesitated, transfixed by the warmth and… Did she see understanding in his brown eyes? "I'm not sure I can," she confessed with an apologetic wince.

"Try it on for size. I'm sure it'll grow on you."

He said the last with such supreme confidence, she had to laugh. "I imagine it will… Wendell."

"It's my grandson's name too," he said conversationally.

To her recollection, the Wingates had only one son and one grandson. Puzzled, she gave her head a shake. "Simon's?"

He nodded. "Wendell Simon Wingate the Third," he intoned sonorously.

"'The Third'?" she repeated. "All three of you are Wendell Simon Wingate?"

"Dell nabbed the nickname, and Simon's mother categorically objected to calling her only child 'Trey' or 'Chip' or any of the other inanities used to differentiate generations, so Simon it was."

"I see."

"And I see too." He removed the reading glasses and folded the temples in, then used them to point at her. "I see you clearly. I also saw your brother. I see your mother, your father, and I knew your grandfather about as well as any two men could know one another outside of getting biblical." He halted a moment, his dark eyes steady on hers. "And I too can differentiate between the generations without the use of silly nicknames."

He couldn't have driven his point home harder if he'd used a judge's gavel. Still, the man was quite obviously and unapologetically in her father's pocket. Determined to proceed with caution, she gave him nothing more than a mildly interested, "Oh?"

"You and your brother were wary of your father's plans and machinations. Hell, I often chafe against them myself, but I can tell you one thing—the man knows how to run a business."

"I've never doubted my father's business acumen," she said flatly.

"Only his affection."

His blunt assessment threw her off balance. "What's your point?"

Wendell set his glasses atop the file he'd been trying to go over with her and folded his hands in front of him. "My point is, you can disagree with him, you can rebel and run away, you can denounce the name of Masters at the top of your lungs... Your father is a horse's patoot most of the time, Marlee, but one day you will inherit all of this whether you want it or not."

She blinked, taken aback. "He could leave it to someone else," she argued. "Doesn't he have some second-in-command he can bless with it?"

"He won't."

"He could sell it, stick Mama in rehab and take off for Las Vegas."

"He won't run away either."

"I don't want it." She pushed back from the gleaming conference table, where they'd been seated adjacent to one another.

"He won't care whether you do or not," he reminded

her. "You are a Masters. The last of the line," he added with a sad twist of his lips. "I had a similar talk with your brother when he was finishing up school. You were born to be who you are, Marlee. You can't change who or what shaped you in the past. You can only pin your hopes on the people who come after. Your father has been doing so since the day you were born."

"Since the day Jeff was born, you mean," she said with a bitter bark of a laugh. "He forgot all about me once he had his heir apparent."

Wendell sat back in his chair, cocking his head to the side. "Funny how you never blamed Jeff," he observed.

"It wasn't Jeff's fault."

"True, but rational thought rarely plays a starring role when it comes to family dynamics." His expression grew sorrowful and his eyes misty. "Jeff and I talked about this."

"You did?" She wasn't certain what he was referring to, but she leaned in, hungry for any scrap of the brother she missed so much.

The older man nodded, his gaze fixed somewhere in the distance. "He told me his kids would never wonder if he loved the company more than he loved them. Told me he'd sell it off right down to the last toothpick to reassure them."

"His kids," she whispered, devastated by the tragic loss of her imaginary nieces and nephews. "He wanted kids."

Wendell sat up straighter, shaking his head to clear it. "Yes, well. The what-ifs are what makes it all so sad, aren't they? The might-have-beens."

"Should-have-beens," she corrected.

He nodded. "Yes. It's often the loss of possibilities that breaks our hearts." Picking up his glasses, he deftly unfolded them and shoved them up onto the end of his nose. "But we deal in facts, don't we?" he said, shifting forward in his chair again.

Marlee couldn't resist probing one more time. "Do you think Jeff killed himself, Mr. Wingate?"

The older man reared back, but he couldn't quite pull off the appearance of genuine surprise she assumed he was hoping for.

Narrowing her eyes, she pressed harder. "You don't, do you?"

"What I think does not matter," he chided. "We are only concerned with what the evidence at hand will support. All we know for certain is two promising young men are dead, presumably by their own hand."

"But you think it's odd, don't you?" she insisted. "Jeff and Clint Young were friends once, they both worked for Timber Masters—"

He cut her off. "Their place of employment is hardly a strong connection in this instance. Most of the residents of Masters County are employed by Timber Masters or adjacent companies." She opened her mouth to say more, but he held up his hand to halt the flow. "And we were all friends with our peers when we were young, but we tend to grow apart as our lives progress. I seem to remember you and Mandy Duncan were thick as thieves when you were in high school. What's she up to these days?"

Marlee blinked, thrown by having the tables reversed on her so deftly. "She's still living here in town, isn't she?"

He inclined his head in a half nod. "She is. As a matter of fact, she works for Timber Masters," he added with a triumphant lift of his unruly eyebrows.

Pursing her lips, Marlee inhaled deeply through her nose as she prepared to concede. "Fine. Point taken."

Wendell flipped a couple of pages without looking at them. "But I did hear she had a date lined up with Clint Young for the weekend after he died," he said, glancing up at last. "I find it interesting he'd made plans to take Mandy out but decided to end it all instead."

The implication hung between them for a moment. He pursed his lips, then said, "Perhaps I took the wrong approach with this. Rather than diving straight into Timber Masters itself, maybe we should start somewhat smaller and build up so you can get a feel for the scope of the work."

He thumbed through a stack of folders to his right, then withdrew one bulging with papers. "These are summary files, you understand," he explained as he plopped the brick of a file on the table in front of her. "There are boxes and boxes of documents to back all this up, but I keep the most pertinent facts close at hand."

"Real estate?" She eyed him askance as she flipped open the cover. "You want to start me off with lease agreements and evictions?"

"Among other things," he said, unperturbed by her pique. "I'm sure you are aware your family has extensive holdings throughout the county. Commercial, single family and multidwelling rental properties are held in a separate corporation from the business or personal properties."

Despite her annoyance at being handed the legal equivalent of a bike with training wheels, she scanned the summary pages, her lips parting as she lined up her questions. Skimming to the bottom of the page, she clamped her mouth shut and forced her pride aside long enough to absorb the information. "Nearly all of our tenants in single-family dwellings were evicted two years ago."

"Yes, they were." Wendell beamed at her, and for some reason it made Marlee feel like she'd earned her first gold star.

"Why? They couldn't have all lost their checkbooks at once."

He chuckled and shook his head. "No. I wish it were a simple matter of failure to pay." He pointed to the file. "Take a look at the yellow papers. Those are original copies of work orders."

She did as she was told. But as she studied the notes about tests administered and failed, remediation of "residential chemical contamination" and certifications secured once the work was done, she wagged her head in confusion.

"Did we build on a toxic waste dump or something?" Marlee had heard her father complain about the Environmental Protection Agency and the costs incurred by following their guidelines her entire life, but building on contaminated land would be a bridge too far, even for Henry.

"No." The older man took a deep breath, then released it with a shuddering sigh. "The Drug Enforcement Agency cut a big swath through this part of the state a couple years ago," he began.

Marlee recalled her father and Jeff talking about the agency's action in Masters and surrounding counties. "Yes. They were looking for people producing methamphetamine, weren't they?"

The older man nodded. "Precisely."

When he said nothing more, she glanced down at the paper in the folder. The puzzle pieces slipped into place. "They were cooking in our houses."

"A number of them, yes." Wendell ruffled a stack of papers with the side of his thumb before proceeding with caution. "When your brother first came to work, your father had put Jeff in charge of overseeing the real estate division."

He let the tidbit of information dangle. Frowning, Marlee slipped her foot out of her pump and swung the shoe on her toes, a nervous habit she'd picked up while being forced to sit through dozens of white tablecloth–draped debutante teas. She flexed her foot faster and faster as she flipped through page after page of documentation. Many of them carried her brother's signature scrawled at the bottom.

"Jeff?" She froze for a moment. "He wasn't involved with drugs, was he?"

Wendell shook his head. "No. The only thing your brother was guilty of was being young and naive." He straightened in his seat. "He acted in good faith, but a number of people around him did not. There were some who escaped prosecution on technicalities. Some, your brother might have considered friends at one time. Adding insult to injury, it galled Jeff to see the real estate division bankrupted on his watch. A fact your father didn't hesitate to remind him of at every opportunity."

Marlee's gut churned and her foot started to twitch again, the leather edges of her pump knocking against the bottom of her heel.

Wendell pushed on, but now he sat still, his gaze fixed on her. "To make amends, he negotiated a deal where they could sell off a chunk of the family's personal property. A parcel earmarked to come to him eventually anyway."

Dread pooled in the depths of her belly. "What property?"

"An attorney representing land development trust made a large offer for several parcels of land out on Sawtooth Lake."

Chapter Seven

Marlee sat at the conference table piled with files. Wendell had abandoned her for a client meeting, so she sat there leafing through countless pages of title transfers, lease agreements and other assorted documentation related to both the sale of the lake property and the remediation of the rental properties in town, wondering what the hell had happened to her hometown in the years since she'd left for college.

In her mind, Pine Bluff was the quintessential small Southern town. They had pancake breakfasts after church on Sundays and parades for almost every holiday. There were ice-cream socials and sewing circles with multiple generations of women from the same family as members. Sure, people moved away, but for some reason or another, a good portion of those people eventually found their way back.

What they didn't have were people who manufactured illicit drugs in their kitchens and massive distribution networks stretching across the state and beyond.

Or so she had thought.

Her mind reeling, she continued flipping pages, trying to focus on the real estate holdings she was supposed to be studying. But here and there she found references to the tenants who were caught up in the legal proceedings stemming from the DEA sting. So many people involved in something she—a Masters from Masters County—had no idea was even happening. It didn't seem possible.

Her father had raised his children to believe their family name made them personally responsible for the health and well-being of every person who lived inside the county lines, but reading through these files, she began to realize her hometown and its surrounding area were not the bucolic microcosms she'd believed them to be.

Some of the statements taken as part of the evictions read like works of fiction. Who would have ever believed Clem Watkins, the man who'd been janitor at the high school as long as anyone could remember, was one of the biggest dealers in town? And he'd been savvy enough to cut a deal with the agency in exchange for a handful of underlings and the name of the man who'd gotten him started in the business.

Clint Young.

But both the agents working the lingering cases and the prosecutor's office had been unable to unearth a shred of evidence to support Clem's claim, and no charges had ever been filed against Clint.

As far as Marlee could see, he'd managed to cover any involvement he might have had so thoroughly, he hadn't even been brought in for formal questioning. Did Ben Kinsella suspect Clint was involved in all this mess, even peripherally? Was he aware Masters County was such an unholy mess when he'd agreed to take the job as sheriff? Were the surrounding counties as much of a mess? Prescott County bordered Sawtooth Lake as well. Who had cleaned up over there? Prescott County's economy was driven by small-crop farmers, some who grew timber to sell to Timber Masters or direct to the paper mills. They didn't have the backing of one solid, stable company. Masters County had Timber Masters and the Masters family. Who was footing the bill for Prescott's recovery?

Closing one file folder, she reached for another labeled Sawtooth Lake Sportsmen's Club and opened it with some trepidation. Wendell had told her Henry had rejected Jeff's idea of selling off parcels of their property out of hand, but in the weeks following her brother's death, he'd reconsidered. Back in the day, there had only been two dwellings on the lake—her family's and the one built by Clint Young's father.

Four bedrooms with adjoining baths, a chef's kitchen and a wraparound deck affording spectacular sunset views made her family's spread a showplace. The extensive use of good Georgia pine and rough-hewn wood accents allowed her father to call it a cabin rather than a lake house—a distinction Henry had found appealing, even if the rest of the family couldn't have cared less.

He primarily used the place for entertaining clients, or loaned it out to people he thought might be influential or beneficial to the business. Her mother had hated it out there and had grudgingly gone only when Henry put his foot down. She and Jeff swam in the lake when they were young, though she preferred a nice chlorinated pool to anything with a mud bottom and slimy grass that wrapped around a person's legs. If she closed her eyes and focused hard, she could conjure up a happy memory or two, but they were sparse.

She couldn't figure out why it upset her so to discover the land adjacent to theirs had been sold. Opening the folder, she inspected the revised plats dividing the property into five sections. The largest belonged to their family. Their closest neighbors were still the Youngs.

Theirs had actually been a cabin. A simple place built by Mr. Young as an escape from his unhappy home life.

There were three other parcels situated on the other side of a cove from the Masters and Young places. They were labeled with names. Pulling the yellow legal pad closer, she noted them.

Thomason, Abernathy and Baker.

She tapped her pen against the pad until something clicked. Abernathy. She'd dated a boy named Bo Abernathy in high school. It was possible his parents had purchased one of the plots, but it didn't seem likely. The family wasn't particularly well-off. Dismissing the name as coincidence, she checked the next. There were three different Baker families in the area, to her recollection. She marked it for further research, then sat staring into space as she ran through her mental map of town. For the life of her, she couldn't place anyone named Thomason but had the niggling suspicion she ought to recognize the name.

Wendell opened the door to the small room where she'd spread out and popped his head in. "Doing all right in here?"

"Is there a Thomason family in town?" She bit her lip as she searched her memory again, trying to place anyone she may have met with the name.

"Family? No." Wendell paused, his expression thoughtful. "You mean other than Will Thomason, right?"

"Who is Will Thomason?"

"Will Thomason," Wendell repeated. "General manager at Timber Masters," he added with a pointed stare.

"I don't know a Will Thomason," Marlee said. "I thought Jeff was the general manager."

"Yes, he was, but..." He let the thought trail off and made a vague circling motion with his hand.

"But Jeff is dead," she concluded flatly. "Will Thomason is the man who took his place."

Wendell rolled his shoulders back, then cocked his head

as he studied her. "Come to think of it, I suppose Will moved while you were in college." He frowned. "I'd have thought your father would have introduced you, but then, you haven't been home long."

"No. I haven't." She closed the file with a sigh. "I guess a lot of things have changed since I've been gone."

"Some things but not everything," Wendell said gently. "You're past due for some lunch. Go walk around town and clear your head a bit. I believe you'll find the onion rings at the Daisy Drive-In are as tasty as they ever were."

She hooked her arm through her handbag and rose, anxious to leave the files behind. "Can I bring you anything?"

"No, thank you. Miss Delia has packed me my no-salt, no-fat, no-flavor lunch, and she reports back to my daughter-in-law if I try to cheat."

She grinned as she imagined the Wingate's five-foot-nothing housekeeper giving the old man what for. "How would she know?"

He chuckled. "Another thing that hasn't changed. Word travels fast around here. She'd sense it if I even dipped a french fry into the ketchup."

Marlee stilled, her hand on the door handle. He was right. The only mill in Masters County that ran faster than her daddy's lumber mill was the rumor mill. It was time to pound the pavement, and possibly press an ear to the ground.

BEN WAS BITING into one of the Daisy Drive-In's famous mile-high club sandwiches when the door to the office swung open and Marlee Masters blew in. He lowered the sandwich to the carryout container and forced himself to chew as she approached. When she drew to a stop in front of his desk, he swallowed with a hard gulp then reached for the cup of sweet tea he'd ordered to go with his lunch, gesturing for his guest to take a seat while he washed the food down.

Holding a to-go cup of her own, Marlee dropped into the wooden guest chair so hard he winced. "Ms. Masters. We meet again," he said, wiping his mouth with one of the inconsequential paper napkins the dairy bar had provided with the meal. "What can I do for you this time?"

Marlee glanced over both shoulders as if she'd only now noticed they weren't alone in the office. Julianne was at home eating her own lunch, but Deputy Mike Schaeffer sat at his desk, his pen frozen in midair. The younger man gaped at Marlee in wide-eyed shock, and it was all Ben could do to suppress a smile. The woman did cause a stir.

"You can go grab your lunch early, Mike," Ben called out to him, his voice genial but the command clear.

He saw the younger man's desire to protest. After all, he'd come on shift only a half hour ago. But Ben had the distinct feeling he shouldn't have an audience around for whatever Ms. Masters wanted from him.

Ben waved his hand in a shooing motion. "It'll keep you from having to run out later." He cast a wistful glance at his uneaten lunch, then carefully closed the lid on the container.

"I'm sorry—I didn't mean to interrupt your lunch," she said. "I figured you'd be done. You must have had a busy morning too." She waved the cup in her hand, indicating she'd been to the Daisy as well. "I opted to drink my lunch. A chocolate malt has everything a girl needs to power through the afternoon." Her cheeks flushed a rosy pink, making her blue eyes appear even brighter. "Please, eat." She waved a hand at the container.

He was about to refuse when his stomach rumbled. Loudly. Marlee laughed, and he felt the heat rise in his own cheeks. "Excuse me," he mumbled. Pushing the sandwich aside, he sat up straighter. "You're going to think all I do is eat."

"Heaven forbid people consume meals at meal times," she countered.

He fixed her with a pointed look. "Is there something I can do for you?"

She scooted forward in her seat and placed her cup on the edge of his desk. "I wanted to ask you a couple of questions, if you don't mind."

Ben nodded, then popped the lip on the container again. "Wanna join the mile-high club with me?" He kept his expression sober but gestured to the quartered club sandwich nestled into a bed of potato chips.

Her lips parted as she looked at him, then down at the sandwich. "You get that from the Daisy?"

"Of course."

He could see she was sorely tempted, but still she refused. "No. Thank you. It looks delicious, though."

He pushed the box closer to her, then picked up the quarter he'd abandoned. "How is your first day going? Did you get a big office and everything?"

"I got farmed out," she said, her lips thinning into a line.

He froze, the stacked sandwich gripped in both hands and his mouth hanging open for a moment. Moving his head to the side, he peered at her around his lunch. "Farmed out?"

"To Wendell Wingate."

She gave a jerky shrug he supposed was meant to be nonchalance, but the tiny furrow between her eyes gave her away. It also annoyed him. Marlee Masters was a woman born to smile, not scowl.

"You've been working with Wendell? Well, I guess that makes sense in a way," he commented, manufacturing his own measure of casualness.

"Sheriff—"

"Ben," he corrected, then sank his teeth into the sandwich.

"I wanted to ask if you knew anything about the sweep the DEA made of this area a couple years ago," she continued.

Ben chewed methodically, examining the question in his mind and checking every angle before deciding how to answer. He swallowed, then took a sip of his tea. His response was nothing more than a cautious, "I do." He then took another healthy bite to buy more time.

She tipped her head to the side, clearly irritated by his succinct answer but prepared to reframe her question in a half dozen other ways.

"Fine. Can you tell me more about the actions surrounding the Drug Enforcement Agency's activities in this area and the fallout from them?"

He nodded again, his mouth full. He watched her practically vibrate with impatience as she waited, and he couldn't resist yanking her chain one more time. Though he acknowledged the necessary role attorneys played in their legal system, as a cop, he wasn't particularly crazy about them. If he was honest with himself, he would admit his willingness to help this one wasn't motivated by a simple desire to see justice served.

"I can." He chewed then swallowed before waving his hand as if telling her to come at him. "Try again, but this time ask in a way that doesn't give me as much wiggle room."

She huffed her indignation, her face alight with a blush. "Fine. What do you know about the raids the DEA staged in this area?"

He tossed the crusts of the sandwich into the box and picked up another segment as he eyed her. "Two years ago, a team of agents undertook an operation to shut down one of the largest methamphetamine networks in the Southeast."

"You were part of the team?"

He ignored her shocked question in favor of getting the pertinent information out of the way. "Most of their operations centered in Masters and Prescott Counties. We made several arrests, turned several more of the operation's key figures into witnesses and shut down the majority of the production in the area."

"The majority but not all?" She nonchalantly picked up a corner of his sandwich and took a bite.

"These people are insidious. You can round up as many as you can, but there will always be others to take their place."

"So you're saying people around here are still producing and distributing methamphetamine?" she pressed, incredulous. "The population of those two counties combined is less than a decent-sized suburb. How many people can be involved?"

"There were over two hundred persons of interest named in the case."

"And you were involved? Working with the DEA?"

He shook his head. "Not directly. I worked for the agency but was assigned elsewhere."

"You were with the DEA?"

"Yes."

"As an agent?"

"Yes."

She gaped at him for a moment, then color rose in her cheeks. "Why are you here, then?" she demanded. "I mean, why did you leave?"

"Personal reasons," he said, though for some reason it

cost him to maintain his usual calm demeanor when she was the person asking the questions.

Marlee's agitation filled the room. The air felt charged. Ionized. Like after a lightning strike. He sniffed, wondering if he'd catch a hint of ozone, but he didn't.

"Does my association with the DEA bother you?" He was taken aback by her reaction to discovering he'd once been a federal agent. Most people were impressed. Her father had been. But Marlee seemed…wary. He changed tactics. "Let me ask this—why does it bother you?"

"It doesn't," she answered a shade too quickly.

He set his section of sandwich aside, then leaned in, folding his arms on the desk. "It does. Why?"

She shot to her feet, and it was all Ben could do not to follow suit. After her morning visit, he'd done nothing but think about her and her brother. He'd even gone so far as to pull Jeffrey Masters's file and compare the notes taken by his predecessor with his own observations of the scene in the Youngs' cabin. They had only two things in common. First, the cause of death, noted as self-inflicted by Mel Schuler on both cases, and Jeff Masters's confirmed by the medical examiner's office in Macon. And second, the fact that both men took their lives in cabins on—

"I want you to come with me out to Sawtooth Lake this evening," Marlee broke into his thoughts.

He was still formulating a response when the office door opened and Mike strode in holding a take-out box of his own. His steps faltered inside the door, and Ben leaned over in his chair to peer around Marlee. "Can you give us a couple minutes more, Mike?"

"I, uh, sure," the younger man said. "I'll go, um…there's a bench in the square."

"Good idea," Ben agreed. "Enjoy some sunshine."

The thermometer had already zipped past the mideighties and was nudging ninety degrees, but Mike didn't protest. He simply left. Straightening, Ben maintained eye contact with Marlee, not speaking until the door closed again.

"Why do I get the feeling you're not asking me on a date?" he said at last.

She colored beautifully at the insinuation but pressed on. "There's something…off about all this. I feel it in my gut."

She pressed her palm flat against her stomach, and Ben lost the battle to maintain eye contact. Her long fingers splayed over her belly. Her fingernails were unpolished. It surprised him for some reason. Probably because most of the women he'd met with her means and social station kept themselves buffed and varnished to a high sheen. But not Marlee. He let his gaze travel over her, taking in the details of her slim skirt and silky blouse as he forced himself to look her in the face again. These clothes were elegant. Simple, but beautifully made and clearly expensive. Unlike the boxy blue suit she'd worn the first time he saw her, these pieces were tailored to nip in at all the key spots and allow for her generous curves in others. He got the distinct impression Marlee had not been the one to select this outfit.

He allowed his curiosity to get the better of him. "Who buys your clothes?"

The question caught her completely off guard. She actually took a small step back, wobbling on her high heels when she bumped into the chair she'd abandoned. "What?"

"Your clothes." He nodded toward her. "Whoever picked out this outfit wasn't the same person who bought the blue suit you wore the other day."

"I—" she started, then stopped. "I'm not a child," she

snapped, fire flashing in her eyes and chagrin adding to the color in her cheeks. “I can dress myself.”

“But the suit—”

“I’d just bought it. I didn’t have time to have it altered,” she explained in a rush. “Are you also the fashion police in these parts?”

“No, I’m a man who makes his living observing people and their actions.” Tired of craning his neck to look up at her, he rose too. “The suit was some kind of a statement. I’m not sure who was supposed to get the message, but it spoke volumes.”

She lifted her chin in defiance. “And what did it say?”

“It said you didn’t want to be here. That you had other plans.” Now staring down at her, he added, “Plans inconveniently interrupted by Clint Young’s death.”

“You think I’m so cold?” she said, slashing the air with her hand. “And Clint’s death has nothing to do with anything.”

“But you told me this morning it did,” he reminded her. “You came trotting in here this morning telling me you think there’s something connecting your brother’s death with Young’s.”

She sucked in a sharp breath, then pressed those lush lips together.

He forced himself to soften his expression and relax his stance. They weren’t on opposing sides of an issue, only on opposite sides of a desk. “Listen, I’ve been in law enforcement most of my adult life,” he said, careful to avoid coming across as condescending. “I started out as military police, got recruited by the agency then came here. I’ve crossed paths and swords with a lot of lawyers in my time, but Miss Marlee, I think we both want the same thing here.”

At least as far as her suspicions went, he amended only

to himself. He was fairly certain Marlee Masters wasn't thinking about him the same way he thought about her.

When she didn't respond to his verbal olive branch, he sighed. "I'm only making observations because I'm trying to figure out the person I'm dealing with."

"By commenting on my clothes?"

"Isn't there some saying about clothes making the man? Or, in this case, woman?" He gestured to the chair she'd vacated, and she crossed her arms over her chest, her expression mulish. Figuring she was dug in, he changed his approach. "Why do you want me to go to the lake with you?"

"I don't think I do anymore."

Ben was sure she'd meant the words as a retort, but they came out with shades of sulkiness. Suddenly, he had absolutely no trouble reconciling the beautiful woman in front of him with the girl who undoubtedly ruled the school. Repressing a chuckle, he reclaimed his seat and reached for his lunch even though he'd lost his appetite.

When he didn't trip all over himself to convince her, she crumbled. "I thought since you saw the scene where Clint…died, you might get something out of seeing my family's cabin."

His brows knit as he wondered what could he gain from seeing the place where yet another young man had decided to end his life? And what could Marlee possibly stand to gain? Didn't she realize she'd have been a prime suspect if there'd been any hint of foul play in her brother's death? Then again, if a woman who had as much to lose as Marlee Masters was asking questions, shouldn't he be paying closer attention?

"Fine," he agreed, even though his brain hadn't quite finished processing her request. Still, he had no desire to take it back. "We can take my truck," he said, picking up another sad excuse for a paper napkin and crumpling it into his palm. "What time should I pick you up?"

Marlee shifted from one foot to the other, clearly surprised by his capitulation. Ben fought the urge to chuckle. He enjoyed keeping her off balance.

But she recovered quickly. "I'll meet you here. Will five thirty work? I want to run home and change." She waited a beat, then flashed him a saucy grin. "I can't wait to hear your breakdown on why I'd choose capris over shorts."

He snorted at her joke, but he wasn't about to let the subject of his picking her up at her home pass. Her refusal of his offer brought out some latent machismo, so he pressed the issue. "I don't mind swinging by to get you."

"I don't want my parents to know I'm looking into this."

Her blunt statement shut him down quite effectively. She didn't want her father to know she was keeping company with him. He couldn't blame her. He'd dealt with enough Henry Masters types to be sure his daughter slumming with a civil servant would stir the man's ire.

And he was all too aware of the strikes against him in the rest of the townspeople's eyes. He was an outsider. An outsider with mixed blood and an excess amount of melanin. A former federal agent to boot. There weren't too many families in Masters or Prescott County who had escaped the agency's dragnet unscathed.

They wanted him here for the same reasons they found him lacking. After the upheaval caused by the DEA raids and adjacent charges, only someone with an unbiased eye and an indisputable reputation could set things to rights. Ben didn't mind being the outsider. He'd never fit in anywhere until he'd joined the agency, and look where he was now. Back on the outside looking in.

"Fine. We'll meet here at five thirty."

She nodded. "Thank you, Sheriff."

"You're welcome, Ms. Masters," he said, slipping back into the formalities as she had.

Without another word, she headed for the door. He watched, admiring the sway of her hips in her slim skirt and imagining the silky feel of her blouse under his fingertips. Because, no matter what their packaging, she was still a beautiful, intriguing woman, and he was undoubtedly a red-blooded man.

Chapter Eight

Ben went back to his place to change as well. Though the jeans and polo shirt weren't any more or less revealing than his uniform, he didn't want to be wearing a badge when he went poking holes in Marlee's theories. She obviously had her hopes pinned on uncovering something at the family's lake house.

When he pulled into the small parking lot adjacent to the municipal building, he spotted her right away. She had chosen cropped pants over shorts, but he couldn't be too disappointed. Though covered in utility pockets and made out of what looked to be parachute sheeting, they fit her perfectly. As did the simple white tank top she'd paired them with.

She stood in a sliver of shade provided by the angle of the sinking sun. For a moment, he wondered if she was hiding so no one would see her meeting up with him. Then he saw her smooth one of the tendrils of hair back up her neck and toward the ponytail she'd fashioned high atop her head. Hot. She was hot. In more ways than one.

The late-afternoon sun baked the cracked cement. Heat rose off the unsheltered pavement in shimmering waves. Drawing to a halt right beside her, he kicked the air-conditioning in the SUV up a notch, then reached for the door handle. He was about to climb out when she yanked open the door and threw herself into the seat.

"Holy Moses, it's hot out there," she complained. Without asking, she reached over and switched the knob to force maximum airflow through the vents. "Air. I need air."

Amused, he drew his leg back in and closed his door again. "I was going to open the door for you."

She snorted, holding up a hand to stave off any other inane offers of assistance he might have offered, and leaned in to let the vent blow directly on her forehead. "Thanks, but I can manage myself."

"So I see." He twisted in his seat to swing an arm over the console. She didn't flinch away, but her movements stilled, like those of an animal scenting the air for danger. "I keep a cooler with some bottled water in here," he explained.

She relaxed visibly as he popped the lid on the plastic ice chest, and he forced himself not to be offended. After all, she was a woman alone in a car with a man who was a virtual stranger. She had every reason and right to be on her guard.

"Here." He wiped the bottom of the dripping bottle on the front of his shirt, then offered it to her. "It's pretty much tepid now, but..."

"Thank you," she said, taking the bottle.

He tried to keep his eyes to himself as she uncapped it and took a long drink, but failed. She was so damn pretty. Not beautiful in the usual blonde Homecoming Queen way, but genuinely pretty. There were freckles on her nose and laugh lines forming at the corners of her eyes. Her hair looked soft and bouncy. He curled his hands into fists on his lap to keep from taking a playful swipe at her ponytail.

Marlee's eyes met his as she lowered the bottle. "What?"

"You should have let me pick you up," he chided gently.

"It's just..." She stopped, clearly torn over explaining. "My mother. She tends to be high-strung, and we're smack dab in the middle of cocktail hour. I didn't want to play twenty questions, so I sort of slipped out of the house."

"I've met your mother."

She shifted to look at him, but Ben thought it best not to reciprocate. He was particularly glad he hadn't when she said, "Then you are aware she's under the influence of...something most of the time. Don't worry. Daddy took the car keys away some time ago." Her voice was sad and wistful. "She never goes anywhere these days anyway."

"Your mother strikes me as a nice lady struggling with her grief."

"Who doesn't?" she said, her half smile self-deprecating. She settled into the seat then let out a huff of oxygen she must have been saving in case of emergency. "I haven't been out there." Apparently, he didn't respond quickly enough to the confession, because she clarified, "To the cabin. It was never my thing, and, well, after..."

"Your family used to own all the land around the lake, right?"

She whipped her head around so fast, her ponytail smacked the passenger window. "How did you find that out?"

He glanced over at her, then refocused on the narrow county road. "It came up in the investigation," he said with a shrug. "Was it a secret?"

"I guess not," she conceded the point grudgingly, then added, "More a surprise. At least for me."

He chanced another look at her. "You weren't aware your father owned the land?"

"No. I knew we owned it." She hesitated, then admitted, "I wasn't aware he'd sold it."

"The other parcels are owned by the Masters County Sportsmen's Club," he informed her.

"Whoever that is," she said peevishly.

She was clearly nettled by not being the only person with the facts at hand. Ben suspected if he let her steer the conversation her way, he might learn something new. "You aren't sure who's behind it?" He was curious to see how much she'd discovered and if she'd share her information with him.

"I guess it was my father's new general manager's idea."

He could feel her watching him closely, and he had to admit, a beautiful woman's scrutiny wasn't entirely unwelcome, regardless of the circumstances. He hadn't dated anyone since walking away from Atlanta with his life and a few haphazardly packed boxes.

"I gather there was quite a bit of…economic fallout after the federal agencies made their presence in the area known."

Her careful wording added fuel to the pride he felt in playing a role in such a successful mission. It beat the tar out of the times when everything went belly-up. "We came short of firebombing the area to flush them out."

"Yes," she said, lifting a hand to indicate the approaching turnoff for the lake. He gave a brusque nod, and she let her hand fall. "I'm sorry. I guess you've been out here." She laced her fingers together in her lap.

"A couple times," he said. "I can get to the lake road, but I may need you to tell me how to get to your place."

"You were at the Youngs' the night they found Clint," she said quietly.

He dipped his head but kept his mouth shut.

"Used to be only our house and the Youngs' out here," she explained. "Follow the lake road about a quarter mile past their place, and you'll see our driveway."

He nodded. "So, your father sold these parcels off to cover real estate expenses?" he prompted, guiding her back on topic as he maneuvered the winding country road that roughly followed the same path as the lake's shoreline.

"Yes. Or so Wendell says," she answered with a shrug. "Seems like swatting a fly with a sledgehammer, but I guess there were costs beyond the actual cleaning and remediation."

"Lost rents and all," he concurred. He fed her a morsel of information in hopes of gaining more. "There were a number of Timber Masters employees involved. I imagine the repercussions went beyond the loss of the current tenants. They may have had a hard time finding new people to move in, given everyone found out what was happening in those houses."

"And my father rents the houses to people who work for the company directly," she added.

Ben bit his lips to keep from smiling. She'd inadvertently confirmed a point Timber Masters's attorneys had danced around in every single interview. There was nothing illegal about choosing to rent to a specific group of people, but there certainly was an issue if they refused to lease a property because they didn't belong to the group. Had pleasant, easygoing old Wendell Wingate been covering for a client who stepped over the line?

But he and Marlee Masters were on the same side of whatever it was they were doing now, he reminded himself sternly. He glanced away from the road as they passed the Youngs' driveway. He caught glimpses of the shake-shingled house through the trees, then drew a deep breath as he refocused on the road ahead of them.

As a member of the law enforcement community, he was so used to viewing lawyers with a jaundiced eye. Marlee had wanted him to come with her to her family's cabin in hopes of uncovering more of the mystery surrounding her brother's untimely death. Nothing more, nothing less.

"Were you close with your brother?"

His question seemed to startle her at first, but she recovered with a short laugh. "I keep forgetting you aren't from around here."

He kept his gaze on the faded yellow lines dividing the two-lane road. "Are you saying yes or no?"

"It's a yes," she said, amusement glinting in her eyes. "We were close." When he darted a look in her direction, she gave a helpless shrug. "I'm sorry. It's only… I got that question pretty often in Atlanta, but I never expected to hear it here in Pine Bluff." She sobered and pointed to a strip of reflectors marking an otherwise-unremarkable lane. "Go left up there."

He did. The *ticktock* of the blinker sounded extra loud in the silence of the car.

"We were close," she said as they started down the winding lane. "All our lives." Her voice caught on the last word. He peered at her, but she was dry-eyed. She motioned for him to pick up the pace again. "I find in families like ours, the kids either band together or go for one another's throats."

"How do you see your family?"

"It's more about how others see us. Families with money, property and some kind of perceived prestige," she said bluntly. "There are the expectations that come with those things."

The road widened as they went around another bend. He nearly swore when the rustic mansion she called a cabin came into view. Letting his foot off the gas, he let the SUV coast into the small gravel parking area. Shifting into Park, he asked, "You think your family's prestige is only perceived?"

"I think prestige is an external value," she said without missing a beat.

"Meaning?"

"It's an arbitrary value placed on someone or something based solely on someone else's say-so."

"I wouldn't say the clout your father wields around here is arbitrary," he countered.

"No, his is real, but it's different. It's power, not prestige," she asserted. "But my mother? Jeff? Me?" She shook her head. "We don't have any real power. We have prestige because other people perceive us as having power by proximity."

"'Power by proximity,'" he repeated.

"It's essentially a marketing tactic," she continued. "I'm not saying I didn't make the most of it back in high school," she admitted, "but Jeff and I…we had no illusions about who holds the power."

He blinked, surprised by her candor. "I see."

"Anyhow, I'm talking too much. I have no idea why I told you all that. We should go in."

But rather than bailing out of the car, Marlee gazed pensively through the windshield. Needing to move past the moment, he threw his shoulder against the door as he opened it. She hadn't stirred by the time he reached the passenger door, so he grabbed the handle and swung it open wide. Marlee's eyebrows rose, and she blinked those big blue eyes.

He glanced down at the ground to see if he'd parked in a puddle or something. "What?"

"You aren't going to offer your hand? What if I injure myself stepping down from here? I might twist an ankle on the gravel or something."

The urge to reach in and haul her out of the truck by her waist was strong, but he restrained himself. She could play semantics with "prestige" and "power," but he couldn't gamble his job on the belief that her goading was playful. After all, she'd admitted to using her position as a Masters once upon a time. What if this whole trip out to the lake was nothing more than some kind of trap?

"I've got this."

He followed her up the natural-stone pathway, mentally kicking himself. Jogging a couple steps to match her long, irritated stride, he huffed in frustration—which seemed to be his primary state around this woman. "Listen, you said yourself your father's power isn't a matter of perception. Who do you think hired me?"

"My father hired you," she said without bothering to look at him.

"And he can fire me."

"I'm not going to get you fired." She paused and heaved a heavy sigh when they reached the bottom of the porch steps. Then she looked up at him, her expression earnest. "Look, I think I just wanted someone to be here with me, and for some reason, you were the person I thought of." She bit her lip, then gave a barely there shrug. "Maybe because you're the sheriff but mostly because I wanted someone…objective to talk things through."

"Maybe you should try talking to your dad."

His cautious response seemed to trip some kind of trigger in her. She spun away from him and headed for the door. "My father and I don't have a relationship conducive to conversation. It's more along the lines of he gives orders, and I do my best to ignore them until I have no other choice."

He laughed. "Is that how he got you back here? He made it so you had no other choice?"

"Essentially." She stooped and flipped back the corner of a welcome mat featuring the Timber Masters logo.

"He's good at getting his way." Holding a key, she sprang up with a grin and an eye roll. "See? Typical Henry. He simply assumes no one would dare break into his house, and guess what? He's right most of the time."

"You're a grown woman. An attorney." He heard the click of tumblers in the lock, and the back of his neck itched. He was there with a legitimate invitation, but instinct had him checking over his shoulder anyway. "I understand you're starting out, fresh from school and all, but surely you could have found some way to keep living life on your own terms."

She stiffened, then said only, "You'd think, right?"

Marlee gave the knob a twist and peered inside, but Ben saw the flash of raw vulnerability streak across her beautiful face. If he drew attention to it, she'd cover it up, so he remained silent as he took in the details of the setting. The trim around the windows had been painted fairly recently. He'd bet the cream-colored enamel hadn't had a full year of weathering. The oak-and-glass door swung on well-oiled hinges. Marlee groped for the light switch, then gasped as the dim interior of the house went from murky and dark to high definition.

Her hand flew to her mouth, and there was no way he could refrain from placing a steadying hand on her shoulder. "Easy. You don't have to go in there."

She turned away from the entry and stalked across the porch. Bracing both hands on the rough-hewn rail, she let her head fall forward as she drew in shuddering breaths.

Ben hung back, giving the interior of the cabin a quick once-over while he had the chance. High-end appliances. The main room was clearly styled to appeal to an outdoorsman but in a tasteful way. No tacky fake fish or mass-produced man cave gewgaws. It was filled with warm neutral colors, textured fabrics thrown about on soft leather furniture and a big, sturdy coffee table with an array of hunting and fishing books and magazines. But where it should have felt homey and comfortable, it fell shy of the mark. Deliberately casual, Ben decided. He would say one thing for Henry Masters—he took good care of his property. Too bad he seemed to be so careless of his kin.

Without a word, he moved to stand next to her. When she shot him a look from under lowered lashes, he leaned in and planted his hands on the rail, mirroring her stance. It was a tactic used in negotiations. And mating rituals. Ben didn't allow himself to dwell on which he thought he was doing. He couldn't, not when the woman beside him was staring intently out at the lake, blinking back tears.

"I'm sorry. The memories must be—"

Marlee twisted to face him, her piercing stare locking on his profile and stopping his attempt at establishing empathy dead in its tracks.

"You don't get it. There are no memories in there. It's been gutted." Her voice was low and quavering, but he didn't have to be a shrink to recognize the source. She wasn't sad—she was angry.

"Excuse me?"

"The whole place. It's totally different. Hell, some of the walls are even gone." A fat tear trickled past her lashes, and she swiped at it with the inside of her wrist. "It's, uh…a whole new house. Like it never happened."

Two more tears followed, and Ben had to tighten his grip on the railing to keep from reaching for her, pulling her into his arms and kissing them away. He looked her in the eye, forcing himself to dig his fingers into the rail and keep his voice even as he replied, "But it did happen."

"Yes."

Her voice broke on the single syllable, and she gazed out at the lake again. He followed her lead. Minutes passed with nothing but the sound of birdcalls and buzzing bees. He heard her draw in a deep breath. The air around them shifted, and Ben could have sworn he felt the planks beneath his feet move too.

"Maybe a complete overhaul was the point of the renovation."

She rolled her shoulders back and looked him in the eye. "My brother didn't kill himself."

She spoke with such quiet conviction, he wanted to believe her, but the evidence—

Marlee interrupted the thought. "He didn't. Except I have no way to prove it."

Straightening away from the rail, he settled his hands on his hips. "There's not one shred of evidence in either case pointing to anything else."

Marlee crossed her arms over her chest, tipped her chin up a notch and stared him down. "He didn't do it."

"Marlee—"

"I know!" she snapped. Forcing herself to settle, she gestured to the lake. "Something about the sale of this property stinks," she continued. He opened his mouth, but she raised a hand to stop him. "Name. Duty. Legacy," she said, counting each word off on her fingers, then holding them high for him to see. "Henry Masters doesn't give up what's his. Certainly not property the family has owned for generations."

Ben nodded, encouraging her to get it all out, even though he believed her suppositions to be wildly baseless. She obviously needed to talk her theories through with someone. Might as well be him.

"The timber around Sawtooth Lake seeded the Timber Masters empire. My great-great-great-grandfather learned the logging trade here on this land as a way of earning his way out of debt." Her chin thrust out, she shifted her gaze to the lake again, blinking furiously. Setting her jaw, she shook her head in sad dismissal. "You see? There was no piece of property in the world that meant as much to my father as these acres. I can't imagine him allowing them to be sold."

"But he did sell them," Ben reminded her gently.

She shook her head again, but this time, her confusion was written all over her beautiful face. "My brother was the one who wanted to sell."

He scowled as he mulled the information over. "Even so, wouldn't your father have had to sign the papers?"

Marlee shrugged. "My father did sign the papers but not until after Jeff died."

"Why then?"

"'Why then?' is the big question."

"Maybe he wanted to follow through on one of your brother's plans?"

"If my father had one ounce of sentimentality, I'd say maybe, but he doesn't. It would take a lot more than some construction costs and lost rents for my father to agree to selling this particular property. There was something else going on, and I'm determined to get to the bottom of it."

"And you want my help," he concluded flatly.

"I *need* your help," she corrected.

Ben blinked, surprised by the blunt admission. Marlee Masters struck him as the sort of woman who prided herself on not needing anyone—which made her request almost irresistible. But not completely. He'd been run out of Atlanta and lost the job he'd once loved. Pine Bluff was supposed to be a respite. A place where he could rest, recuperate and figure out what he was going to do with the rest of his life after his twenty-year plan had been blown to bits. If he crossed swords with Henry Masters, where would he go from there?

Still, he couldn't help wondering what roiled beneath the surface in his new hometown. Here was Marlee Masters herself, giving him an engraved invitation to poke around. "Fine. I'm in. Where do we start?"

Chapter Nine

Marlee gave him a moment to ruminate on whatever it was holding him back, then she placed a hand on his arm to pull him back into the conversation. This time, he was the one to drag both their gazes down to the fingers curled around his bicep.

"Thank you," she said softly.

"You're welcome."

When she didn't withdraw her hand, Ben's heart gave a hard thud. A bad thud. The kind of thud that said, "This way lies danger." Forcing himself to take a step back, he tried not to let the regret he felt when her touch slid away take hold. He couldn't afford to get tangled up with a woman like Marlee Masters.

He cleared his throat. "Listen, uh, I came here to do a job, and I think it's best if I do that job without complications."

The stiff declaration actually startled a laugh out of her. "Are you kidding? You think you can move to a town this small, declare yourself the law and expect to live your life without anyone trying to complicate it?" She scoffed. "You must be a city guy. Small towns don't work the same way."

"You're right. I am a city guy. But I don't care how it works because this may not be a long-term solution for me."

He stopped speaking abruptly. His eyes widened. Whatever he meant, it was a revelation. And one she should probably get a handle on. Trying for cool and unruffled, she forced the corners of her mouth up. This time, she bent over farther, letting her forearms rest atop the smooth wood of the rail, and she squinted at the late-afternoon sun glinting off the water.

"Not a long-term solution," she repeated. "Interesting. I don't suppose you mentioned the bit about Pine Bluff being a pit stop in your job interview?"

"I never said it was a pit stop," he countered.

"But you're not here for the long-term, are you?"

"I want something more permanent but…maybe not here. Are you staying?"

She'd touched a nerve with the sheriff, but she didn't feel obliged to answer his question. Instead, she parried. "How does a big-time federal agent end up getting himself banished to the backwoods anyway?"

"I wasn't banished. I applied for the job."

His attempt to play semantics with her were of no consequence. "You applied and bamboozled my father with your big shotery, I bet."

Her phrasing broke some of the tension. Ben let out a short bark of laughter then bent down to mimic her position. "I'm not sure exactly what big shotery involves, but I can tell you I've never bamboozled anyone."

She'd buy that. This guy was textbook cop. All rugged self-assurance with a side of truth and justice for all thrown in. She smirked at the large man folded nearly in half beside her. She recognized the move for what it was. They'd learned about the psychology behind body language in law school too. No matter how good he looked doing it, no amount of mirroring would make her trust him. Yet. Besides, he was the one on the defensive, and she was the one who had put him there. She needed to move past how insanely attractive she found him and go in for the kill.

"Who did you have to fool to get the job?"

"I wasn't fooling anyone, and from what I hear, the hiring committee was unanimous in its decision."

"The hiring committee comprised of my father and..." She made a circular motion, encouraging him to expound.

"Your father, Wendell Wingate and the county prosecutor, Duane Wade," he said helpfully. "Who, I can assure you, did not live up to the expectations the name might inspire."

The last part threw her off. "What expectations were those?"

He raised a hand to indicate someone who only came up to his shoulder in height. "Little guy. Bet he doesn't break five-ten on a good day."

"Yes, I've met Duane, but what does his height have to do with anything? He's a heck of a prosecutor."

"You don't know who Dwyane Wade is? The NBA player?" he prompted.

Tickled by his obvious impatience, she widened her eyes. "Oh, you mean basketball?" When he snorted a laugh, she chuckled along with him. "Did you actually think you were going to have some all-star athlete interview you to be sheriff in Podunk, Georgia?"

He shrugged. "A guy can hope."

They laughed together, but her laughter quickly faded when the dusk-to-dawn porch light came on. Marlee groaned when she saw they'd left the door to the house wide-open and the lights on. Wouldn't her father love to find his newly renovated lake house infested with mosquitoes?

"Coming out here was a bad idea," she admitted, then pushed from the rail. She stalked over to the door to switch off the lights and lock the place up again. Once she placed the key back under the mat, she brushed her hands together, dusting off the notion of returning to the scene of the…scene.

They walked back to his SUV side by side. She could feel the warmth radiating from him. The fine hairs on her arms stood on end as they navigated the uneven foot path, but still, they didn't touch. When they reached the passenger side of the car, he reached for the door handle and swung it open wide. She stepped around him to enter but drew up short when he thrust out his hand.

She blushed as she placed the tips of her fingers in his open palm. "Why, thank you, kind sir," she cooed as she stepped up into the cab. He closed his fingers, gripping hers firmly, and Marlee sobered as she tried to get a read on his expression. "What?"

"You are exactly the kind of woman I can't risk," he said gruffly. Taken aback by the vehemence in his words, she tried to pull her hand from his, but he held fast. "Women like you…"

He kept squeezing her fingers, but he didn't finish his sentence. She narrowed her eyes. "Women like me, what?"

"You can only be trouble for a man like me," he answered without hesitation or even the slightest hint of remorse. "We come from different worlds."

"I don't recall asking you to do anything—"

"You didn't have to ask," he interrupted. "You with your beauty-queen smiles and steel trap of a mind. You're tuned in to exactly how powerful you are. You use it. You were born knowing how to use it."

She yanked her hand from his, wincing when her elbow jammed into her rib cage. "You think you can read me how?"

"Because I know someone just like you," he said, still crowding the open door. "Or, I should say, I know *of* one."

Despite her irritation, she couldn't help rising to the bait. "Only one? To hear you talk, you'd think we were pretty thick on the ground. Surely you should have more than one former beauty queen under your belt."

"I don't have any under my belt," he said, practically snarling the last words at her.

"But you said you knew one—"

"She was my mother," he said in a growl. Then he stepped back and slammed the car door. The problem was, she wasn't clear if he meant it as a period or an exclamation point.

THEY HARDLY SPOKE to one another as they made their way back into town. Marlee stared out the passenger window, unseeing but seething inside. How dare he presume to understand her? How dare he think he could lump her in with other women? He didn't know the first thing about her, what she was capable of or what she wanted out of life. She was the daughter of the man who ran this tiny town. Everything else he thought he knew about her was pure presumption.

It galled her that he assumed he had her number. What had he meant about his mother? What could she have to do with anything? And how could she have been thinking about kissing a man who was clearly comparing her to his mother? Had her instincts gone completely haywire?

She was still fuming when he pulled to a stop in front of her parents' home. He pressed the brake so hard, the car rocked forward and then back, jolting her from her thoughts. She gaped up at the house looming in the deepening dusk. The windows were ablaze with lights. Her father's enormous car sat parked in the drive rather than pulled into the carriage house beyond the main residence. Heaven forbid the man not be able to make a quick getaway.

Crap. Her father was home, and she was being delivered to the front walk in the sheriff's car. She glanced over at Mrs. Plunkett's house and saw a lace curtain drop back into place. A hot flush of irritation mixed with mortification crept up her neck. By now, everyone who lived in the big old houses lining the block had seen them.

"What are you doing? Why did you bring me here?" she demanded.

"This is where you live, isn't it?" He unfurled his fingers from the steering wheel long enough to gesture to the brick-and-stone mansion built by her great-grandfather.

"Yes, but," she sputtered, "I met you at the station for a reason."

He leveled her with a flat stare. "I'm sorry if you're embarrassed to be seen with me, Marlee, but it's growing dark, and even small towns have their creepers."

Their gazes locked. "Speaking of creepers, he was quiet today." She pulled her phone from one of the pockets of her capris, then scowled when she saw she had five unread messages. She'd forgotten to unmute her notifications after she'd left the office. "Or not," she said, tapping to open the app.

The first message was from her mother wanting her to be home for dinner. Marlee cringed. She hated to worry or inconvenience her mother. It only led to closer scrutiny. She'd simply forgotten how to live under her parents' thumbs. She'd been excited to see Ben, she admitted—only to herself. She pushed aside the morass of mixed feelings and focused on the screen. The four others were from unknown numbers.

"He texted," Ben said flatly.

"I silenced everything when I got to work this morning. I didn't want to give my father any excuse to start in on his 'cell phones are the scourge of man' rant on my first day."

Leaning into the console, she angled the screen so he could see too. The first message read only:

The skirt is good but last nights outfit was better

The next came from an entirely different area code.

Business barbie walking down the street in your sexy shoes sipping your milkshake

She sucked in a sharp breath, wondering how close her stalker had actually gotten to her. She had her answer when she tapped open the next message:

You should be choosier about the company you keep

The last read simply:

Your daddy know you and ben kinsella go out to his lake house to screw around

Ben emitted a low growling sound as he read the last one. Marlee couldn't help wondering if he was more perturbed by the invasion or the insinuation.

"He's too close," Ben said at last. "You need to tell your father about these messages."

"Oh, no," she said with a harsh laugh. "No way."

"Marlee, this guy could be hiding out in your bushes right now," he said heatedly. "This town is small, and Lord knows it seems impossible for you to go unnoticed, but in this case, proximity doesn't mean you're safe."

The residual heat from her embarrassment morphed into a blush of pleasure. Still, telling her father was out of the question. Reaching over, she placed a gentling hand on his thigh. "Ben, I get that you mean well, but telling my father is not a good option. First, he'd insist I bring this to you, which I already have done. Second, I'm not exactly sure who all was involved in this deal with the Sportsmen's Club, but it wouldn't have happened without my father's signing off on the idea. I don't want to show my hand until I can figure out what stinks about it."

He jabbed a finger at her phone. "But this guy isn't talking about the club, or the property, or even your brother. His focus is all on you."

"I understand." She lifted the hand off his leg. "That's why this is my business. Sharing these messages with you or my father or anyone at all is completely my choice. I chose you," she said pointedly. "And Lori," she added after a beat. "I took this directly to my local law enforcement officers for a reason. I am an adult. What my father needs to know about my life is something I decide, not you."

They stared one another down for a moment.

"I want you to be safe," he grumbled at last.

"I appreciate your concern." She lowered her hand again, and this time treated herself to giving his hard, muscled thigh a friendly pat. "In the future, I would appreciate it if you didn't drop me off in front of my house in a marked vehicle for God and all the neighbors to see."

His lips thinned into a line. "I didn't realize you were ashamed to be seen with me."

"I'm not. But all the same, I don't need the ladies at bridge club asking my mother if I got caught shoplifting penny candy from the drugstore again."

The admission coaxed a deep chuckle from him. "'Again'?"

"I was seven, and believe me, I paid for my crime."

His self-deprecating grin set her heart aflutter. "It's a good thing juvenile records are sealed. You might not have passed the background check for the bar."

She caught a movement on the porch and saw her father standing there waiting for her, his hands on his hips. "Oh, boy."

Ben blew out a breath, then said a soft, "Sorry."

She shook her head as she reached for the door handle. "No. It's no problem. If there's one thing I excel at, it's handling my daddy." She hesitated for a moment, then opened the door. Her voice softened as she stepped out of the SUV. "Thanks for going out there with me, Ben."

"It was my pleasure."

Something about the way he said the last word made warmth gather low in her belly. "I'll talk to you tomorrow."

"Hey," he called out to her. "Call me if you hear anything else from your texter."

She nodded. "I will." Then, raising her voice, she said, "Thanks for the lift home, Sheriff. I'll be sure to send a check to the widows-and-orphans fund."

Marlee caught a snatch of his laughter as the heavy door thunked between them. She made her way up the front walk and greeted her father with studied casualness. "Hey, Daddy."

He jerked a chin toward the taillights on Ben's vehicle. "What was that about?"

"What was—" Marlee looked over her shoulder as if she hadn't given a second thought as to how she came to be there. "Oh, he gave me a ride home. I was talking to Lori about Jeff and didn't realize how dark it was."

Her father's expression morphed from suspicious to grim to obvious discomfiture all in the blink of an eye. "Oh."

He couldn't and wouldn't say much more because Marlee had hit on the two topics of conversation her father avoided as much as humanly possible—his lost son and Jeff's relationship with the "Cabrera girl." He hadn't approved of their relationship and made no secret of his opinions.

"Your mother was worried," he admonished as she sauntered past him, determined to reach the safety of her room without too many questions.

Her steps faltered when she crossed the threshold. Guilt plucked at the string of tension in her gut. She glanced back to find her father staring at his own vehicle, stark longing etched into his once-handsome features. For a split second, she felt sorry for him. His only son was gone, and he was losing his wife to pills and alcohol because he couldn't find it in him to share in her grief. But, as quickly as the sympathy flared in her, it died. Smothered by the recollection of how he'd passed her off to Wendell Wingate on her first day.

"I'm heading up. I'll tell Mama I'm sorry about dinner. I guess I'm not used to checking in with anyone."

"Yeah, well, you're not off running wild all around Atlanta anymore," he chided, stepping inside and closing the door behind them. "Around here, people will notice where you are and what you're doing."

She paused at the foot of the ornately carved staircase, her hand tightening on the newel post as she looked back over her shoulder. "Don't forget to add 'who I'm with' to the list."

"That's a given," he said darkly, clearly unamused by her sass.

"Well, you can rest assured I've only been spending time with the esteemed members of our local law enforcement and legal communities today," she said as she started up the stairs, her pace unhurried. It was a tiny show of defiance, but when one was playing on Henry Masters's turf, one took every victory they could get.

At the landing, Marlee glanced back to find her father watching her, a vertical line bisecting his brows. She forced herself to keep to the same measured pace until she gained the top of the stairs. There, she made a beeline for her mother's suite of rooms. Outside Carolee's door, she took a moment to calm her breathing, then pressed an ear to the door. Neither screams nor sobs greeted her. Marlee took the quiet as a good sign. Tapping lightly with her fingernails, she twisted the knob and opened the door an inch or so.

"Mama?"

"That you, Marlee baby?" her mother called from the love seat situated in front of a large flat-screen television. Carolee clasped a tumbler of clear liquid in one hand and the remote control in the other. "You eat somethin'?"

Marlee could tell by the laid-back slur her mother was already well into the evening's allotment of vodka, so she didn't step farther into the room. "I did, Mama."

"You wanna watch *The Matchmaker* with me, sugar?"

Marlee repressed a shudder at the thought of being trapped on Carolee's settee being force-fed trash TV. "Not tonight, Mama. I'm wiped out."

"Sleep well, sugar," her mother called, her attention riveted to the screen.

Marlee smirked as she pulled the door closed. Her mother didn't seem to think there was anything strange about a twenty-five-year-old woman claiming exhaustion at eight in the evening.

In her room, Marlee walked directly to the window, closed the slats and dropped the sheer curtains into place over them. Only then did she switch on the light. Seconds later, her phone buzzed.

Spoilsport.

She made an unladylike hand gesture toward the window, hoping her Peeping Tom might have hung around for the shadow-puppet show.

Chapter Ten

Ben hated to admit it, but he'd spent the better part of the next day hoping to run into her. No such luck. He'd seen her from a distance, though. She'd been driving her father's mammoth SUV rather than her own car, and her mother had been in the passenger seat. He'd whiled away the rest of the day assuming she was tied up with family business. Expectations adjusted, he'd been pleasantly surprised when her name and number appeared on his phone. "Hello?"

"You busy?" Marlee asked without preamble.

He muted his television. "No."

"I can tell you whoever my creeper is, he has a pretty good view of my window," she said grimly.

Stomach knotting, Ben flexed his free hand to keep from balling up a fist. "He texted you?"

She blew out a long, gusty breath. "Yes."

"And you're only telling me now?"

"Yes, because I handled it," she said with exaggerated patience.

"How? How did you handle it?"

"I closed the blinds and drew the curtains."

"But he texted you."

"Yes."

Ben squeezed his eyes shut, quickly tiring of their game of twenty questions. "What did it say?"

A moment later, a text came through. Spoilsport.

Something live and primal growled deep inside him, but Ben bit his tongue. He couldn't give vent to his own fear and anger. His job here was to alleviate hers. "So," he said, keeping his tone neutral, "did he text anything else?"

"Not yet," she admitted.

He ran the flat of his palm over his face. "Do you think he's out there tonight?"

"Do you want me to go out and look?"

The sarcasm behind the question came through loud and clear. "No. I—" He clamped his mouth shut. He was babbling inanities because he couldn't run right over there, yank this bastard out of whatever bush he was hiding in and beat him to a pulp. "I'll call Mike and ask him to spend some extra time patrolling the area."

"I'd appreciate that," she said at last.

"And Marlee?"

"Yeah?"

"It sounds more a game to him. He's scary and annoying, but he doesn't seem to be escalating." He closed his eyes, hoping he was right and not simply fooling the both of them in his attempt to soothe her.

"Right," she said after a beat.

"He wants to rattle you, but I don't think he wants to hurt you." At least, he prayed his instincts were right on this point. A beep sounded in his ear, and he pulled the phone away to see who was calling on the other line. "Oh, hey, Mike is calling. I'll ask him to step up his circuits around your house. You try to get some rest."

"Got it, Officer."

He exhaled, glad to hear some of her sass back. "I'll talk to you later."

He flashed over to Mike. "Hey, what's up?"

"Ben?" the young deputy managed to croak. Dread

slithered down Ben's spine as he listened to Mike's labored breathing on the other end of the line.

"What? What is it?" he demanded.

"I was listening to the scanner earlier, and I heard some of the guys from Prescott County going back and forth concerning a possible 10-56."

Ben sucked in a breath. In all his years as an agent, he'd never had reason to hear the code called. Now, he'd heard it twice in as many weeks. He cringed as he caught on to the one dim bright spot Mike had offered. They wouldn't be handling this case. Whoever the poor victim was, they'd be Prescott County's headache. Still, their jurisdiction overlapped in so many areas, the departments shared a close working relationship.

Exhaling loudly, he scrubbed his right eye with the heel of his hand. "Man, this is rough. Who's on the case?"

"Watson and Rainey," Mike reported. "But that's not the kicker."

Ben lowered his hand, then gripped the arm of the couch to brace himself against what he feared may be a cyclone heading his way. "Let me hear it."

"No ID on the body. The Prescott guys don't recognize him. They want us to come over to see if we can get a visual."

Ben groaned, letting his forehead drop into his palm. He hadn't lived there long enough to give a positive identification on more than a dozen people, tops. Which meant he and one of his deputies had to go and look at another dead body. Then and there, he decided to take Lori. She was made of tough stuff, and Mike was still shaken from seeing Clint Young's body.

"Do they think he's local?"

"Yes. They found him in a half-built house. One of those

fancy architectural places…" Mike took a deep breath, then let it out in a rush. "Out on Sawtooth Lake."

SHE CAUGHT HERSELF holding her phone long after Ben had ended the call. Embarrassed, even though there was no one around to witness her moment of girliness, she tossed it onto the bed and strolled into her bathroom. There, she stripped off her clothes and dropped them onto the floor as she waited for the water in the shower to warm.

Earlier in the evening, she'd driven her mother to a committee meeting at Trudy Skyler's house. She'd sat and dutifully sipped iced tea while the women dithered over what kind of Christmas decorations to order for the town's lampposts. Mostly, she'd thought about Ben and how annoyed she'd been with Wendell for keeping her so busy that she hadn't had a chance to slip over to the municipal building to "drop in" on him. After an evening of screeching, bickering and incessant gossip, Marlee had only wanted to hear his smooth, deep voice.

Holding her hand under the tap to test the water temperature, she hummed softly as she took in her surroundings. The bathroom fittings were old enough to be considered retro. The walls were covered in white-on-white tiles but not the elongated subway-style one saw on all the home-decor shows. Still, the ceramic surfaces gleamed.

She'd missed the old claw-foot tub when she moved away. Her parents had updated it with a rainwater showerhead and charming circular shower curtain, but when she was younger, she'd preferred baths to showers. There were countless evenings when she'd lounge in the tub until the water cooled, reading a book or listening to music.

Only the years of dormitory living as an undergrad and frenetic pace of law school broke her of the habit. She'd grown accustomed to taking nothing more than the necessary five minutes to scrub herself clean and wash her hair. Now, she was home again and not working the sixty-hour weeks most first-year law associates work. She'd have to learn to downshift, take long soaks again. As she drew back the curtain and stepped over the high side of the tub, she made a mental note to pick up some scented bath salts.

Five minutes later, she had a chamois hair towel twisted around her head and a thick bath sheet—one of the ones her mother's housekeeper, Mrs. Franklin, laundered and sprayed with lavender water as they line dried in the sun—wrapped around her body. The long evening hours stretched in front of her. Marlee meticulously applied lotion to every inch of her still-damp skin in a vain attempt to distract herself from the restlessness roiling inside her. Unwinding the hair towel, she finger-combed her hair into wet waves, content to let it air-dry on this warm evening. The steam trapped in the tiled room threatened to make a second shower necessary, so she moved into the cool spaciousness of her bedroom to finish drying off. The house was air-conditioned but built in the days before modern insulation and ductwork. The system worked well enough when it came to sucking the humidity out of the air, but it never felt overly cool.

Holding the knot of the towel, she went straight to the dresser. Her feet skimmed across smooth wood floors. She looked forward to dropping the thick towel and slipping into the cool cotton of one of her brother's old shirts. Wresting a washed-thin Atlanta Braves tee from the bureau, she shook it out, then stopped dead in her tracks.

The sheer curtains had been pushed apart and the slats of the blinds cranked open.

The T-shirt whooshed to the floor at her feet. She blinked twice, unable to believe what she was seeing. But she wasn't imagining it. The slats were angled down. At precisely the correct angle for someone on the street below to see inside.

Clutching her towel tight, she bolted from the room and into the empty hall. She ran to the opposite side of the house, toward her parents' rooms, and skidded to a halt outside her mother's door. The muffled sound of the television leaked out into the hall, but Marlee heard no other noise. Twisting the knob silently, she opened the door enough to see her mother sprawled across the love seat fully dressed, out cold. She held her breath until she caught the rumble of a soft snore, then gently closed the door again.

Her mother wouldn't have been much good in this sort of situation anyway. Making her way to the top of the stairs, Marlee listened for sounds from the first floor. Nothing. Her father might have gone out. But then again, it was also possible she'd run into one of her father's cronies. They came and went at all hours. Usually, they carried important papers and claimed there was some form of business to be discussed, but mostly the men hung out on the back veranda and drank bourbon.

She hesitated, still gripping the oversize towel tightly to her chest. She should go back to her room and dress. She could grab her phone while she was there and…what? Call the sheriff and ask him to come look under her bed?

But she didn't want to go back to her room. Not until she figured out who'd been in there while she'd been in the shower. Grasping the banister with her free hand, she padded down the steps as quietly as century-old wood would allow. The front door was closed, but she'd lay odds it wasn't locked. Biting her lip, Marlee made her way toward the back of the house, pausing for a moment at the partially closed door to her father's study. Two men were talking. One was her father, but she didn't recognize the other man's voice. The last thing she could do was show up at the door to her father's study and expect him to introduce her to whoever it was while she was dressed in only a towel.

Moving as soundlessly as she could, she slipped past the study and tiptoed to the back of the house. The laundry was off the kitchen. She prayed Mrs. Franklin had left something she could slip into in the tiny closet of a room. When she saw the empty hampers and abandoned drying racks, she heaved a heavy sigh. Biting her lip as she gave the towel yet another mournful glance, she consoled herself with the knowledge she could sneak up the narrow back staircase from the kitchen without being seen. She was about to do so when she spotted the canvas bag full of dry cleaning ready to be taken to the cleaners.

"Oh, thank goodness," she said as she abandoned her hold on the towel and began rooting through the bag for something belonging to her. She spotted the black dress she'd worn to Clint Young's visitation and plunged her hand deeper into the bag. The towel came unfurled, but she didn't care. The sides gaped like loosened tent flaps as she shoved her arm into the bag nearly to her shoulder.

"Excuse me, ma'am? Are you all right?"

The question was drawled low. The timbre of his voice conveyed secrecy but failed to mask the speaker's amusement at the sight she must have presented. Yanking her arm from the dry-cleaning bag, she scrambled to get hold of both sides of the bath sheet as it slid another inch down her back. She tugged it all the way up into her armpits, knotted it and shifted the closure so she could pin it in place with her arm. Pushing her now-tangled hair back from her face, she straightened to her full height and faced the intruder head-on.

A tall man with the lithe, athletic build of a distance

runner stood near the kitchen counter, clutching an unopened bottle of bourbon by its neck. His hair was golden blond and about a half inch too long to be considered well-kept. His skin was sun-kissed, and his teeth so white and even, she wondered for a moment if they were caps. She met his frank perusal with a once-over of her own.

"Who are you? And why are you in my kitchen?" She raised her chin a smidge in hopes of coming off more imperious than indecent.

"I'm Will Thomason," he said, brimming with confidence. "You must be Miss Marlee. I keep meanin' to come meet you, but we've been doing some reshuffling of personnel, what with Clint and all..."

The name registered with her, but Marlee wasn't in a giving mood at the moment. She was freaked out, mostly naked, and there was a strange man in her house.

"Have you been in my room?"

Sandy brows shot high. He made a bit of a production out of blinking once, then shook his head. Something about the way he never broke eye contact with her made her mistrust him. It was a tell, a gambit many people misplayed. Oddly enough, the fact that he didn't peek at any other part of her felt like an act of aggression. Was he daring her to question his integrity? If so, she would.

"Were you?"

"Was I in your room?" he parried, still locked in on her eyes.

"Yes."

"Why would I have been in your room? We've only just met." At last, he looked down at the bottle in his hand. "I only came in here to get a fresh bottle for your father. If you want to show me your room, I think we might be better off waiting until your parents aren't home," he said, dropping what she assumed he thought was a playful wink at her.

"It wasn't an invitation. It was a question," she stated through clenched teeth.

"Will, did you find it?"

Marlee closed her eyes and cringed as her father's footsteps rang out against the hardwood floors. "Right above the stove. I keep it up high so—" He stopped on a dime when he spotted her standing in the laundry room door wearing nothing but a towel. "Marlee? What the hell?"

"I think I walked in as Ms. Masters was looking for something in the laundry," Will said, flashing a charmingly sheepish smile at his employer, then her. "I'm afraid we startled each other."

"Why are you running around the house half-naked?" her father demanded.

"I was—" The temptation to use Will Thomason's cover story was tempting, but there was something off about him. She didn't want to give the man the chance to latch on to some kind of rescuer image of himself. "I was in the shower and someone came in my room."

Her father pulled his head back, puzzlement written all over his face. "In your room?"

"While I was taking a shower. Someone was in my room while I was taking a shower." Thankfully, her voice didn't fail her as she stared the two men down. "I came down to see who was in the house."

"You thought whoever it was might be hiding in the hamper?" Will asked, and she decided she loathed the dimple that flashed in his cheek when he chuckled at his own joke.

Now she was too annoyed to be mortified, which, in a way, made Marlee happy. Rolling her shoulders back, she repeated her question. "Was it you?"

"No." He held her gaze in his disconcerting way.

"Why would Will be in your bedroom?" her father demanded.

"I don't have the faintest idea," she said with exaggerated calm. "Why would anyone else be in my room?"

Her father shook his head dismissively. "No one was in your room. If there was anyone, it was your mother," he said. "I've been down here the whole time."

"When did he get here?" she pressed, waving a hand at Will Thomason.

"Will's been here all evening. We're working on an acquisition proposal," her father said impatiently. "He hasn't left my office."

"Except when I went out to my car to get my power cord for my laptop," Will supplied helpfully, a shade too jovial for her liking.

Henry huffed and waved his hand as if her concerns were nothing more than a swarm of gnats. "Yes, well, that's neither here nor there."

"Or in Miss Marlee's room," Will added without missing a beat. He gazed at her, his expression all blank innocence. "Full disclosure, I believe I also availed myself to the powder room a time or two." He hefted the bottle of bourbon. "You see, I wasn't allowed anything more than water until I'd finished my homework."

"Enough," Henry said, annoyed with the disruption of his evening. "You two wanna flirt, do it on your own time."

The mere suggestion that this confrontation with a stranger in her home was a flirtation made Marlee's skin crawl. "We are not flirting."

"I believe Miss Marlee's tastes run more along the lines of the law enforcement type," Will said, his oh-so-casual drawl drawing the observation out to the point of pain.

"Don't be ridiculous," her father said, dismissing the

notion out of hand, despite his earlier display of concern. "We have work to do. Marlee, go on back upstairs. You can't be running around here in nothing but a towel. What would your mother say?"

She wanted to tell him she wouldn't say a thing because she was too busy being passed out at eight in the evening, but her father had already lost interest. Henry snatched the bourbon bottle out of Will Thomason's hand, then gestured for the younger man to precede him.

Will inclined his head to her. "It was a pleasure to meet you." The polite sentiment didn't quite match the predatory gleam in his eyes. Thankfully, he followed her father out of the kitchen and back down the hall.

She crept out of the tiny space she'd backed into and stood for a moment, holding tight to the towel and listening to the low rumble of the two men's voices. Will said something about how pretty she was, and Marlee had to resist the urge to make gagging noises. Then she heard her father say something about how he should have introduced the two of them earlier and how he'd always hoped Will Thomason might "hit it off" with her, and the rough outline of her father's plan began to take shape.

Horrified, she bolted for the back stairs. Bare feet slapped the varnished wood of the upstairs hallway as she stomped her way back to her room. Muttering under her breath, she rushed in. She stuck close to the walls in an effort to avoid walking directly in front of the window, then scooped up the Braves shirt and her phone, retreating to the safety of her bathroom.

Heart pounding, she locked the door behind her and tapped the screen to call Ben. The second the call connected, she slumped against the door, her towel coming unraveled as she sank to the cool tile floor. "You will not believe what happened over here," she began without greeting.

The connection crackled, and she heard Ben speaking, but his words came across garbled.

Frustrated by the delay in relaying her concerns, she interrupted whatever he was trying to tell her. "What? Ben, I can't hear you. Where are you? Can you move to a room with better reception?"

"Not…room," he said, his voice louder but the reception only marginally clearer.

"Where are you?" she repeated.

"I'm…call… Prescott County."

"You're in Prescott County? Why?"

He unleashed a stream of distorted words and heavy breathing. She thought she heard him say the word "body" and might have made a joke about obscene phone calls if he didn't sound so serious. And urgent.

"Why are you huffing and puffing?"

"Trying…hang on…a clearing," he said, the connection clearing at last. "There. Better?"

"Much better. Did you have to climb a hill or something?"

"Or something." Ben inhaled deeply, then said in a rush, "They called me when we got off the phone earlier. They found a body."

Her breath snarled in her throat. Her mouth ran dry. All she could force out was a strangled, "Oh, God."

"We have an ID on the victim, but I can't tell you yet. We're looking into next of kin. Listen, I'm at the scene now, and things are hectic. I have to get back there, but I'm probably going to lose you. It's not terribly developed around here," he said, faltering a bit on the last.

"Most of Prescott County is pretty rural," she managed in a whisper.

"Yeah." His voice softened and he spoke quietly into the phone. "Marlee, can you come see me first thing in the morning?"

"I can stop by when I go for my run. Why? What do you need?"

"They found the body in a half-finished house…on the other side of Sawtooth Lake."

Chapter Eleven

Marlee rolled out of bed, tied her hair up in a messy bun and put on her running shoes. The sun peeped over the horizon. She hadn't slept a wink. Between keeping a watchful eye on her window, replaying the run-in with Will Thomason in her head from every different angle and wondering who'd been found dead on the other side of Sawtooth Lake, she hadn't been able to put her mind on pause long enough to even doze.

Marlee stretched, then took off toward the municipal building at a brisk jog. She'd worked up to a pretty good clip by the time she reached the door to the sheriff's office with the flats of her palms. She looked up and saw Mike Schaeffer's pale, shocked face on the other side of the glass. He raised both hands in surprise, then took a step back so she could enter.

"Hey," she said, breathless. "I'm Marlee Masters. We weren't properly introduced the other day. You're Mike?" She raised her arms over her head in an effort to open her lungs and even out her breathing.

"Um, yes. Yes, ma'am," the deputy stammered.

Swallowing her annoyance, she thrust out a hand. "Not 'ma'am.' Marlee."

He gaped at her for a moment, then gave her hand a brief but firm shake. "Yes, ma—Marlee."

"Marlee?" Ben's deep voice startled Mike into dropping her hand.

"I was goin', but she came runnin' up," the younger man explained in a rush.

Ben nodded his understanding. "She has a way of sneaking up on people. Go on home, Mike. You did good work tonight." The younger man looked unsure, so Ben waved him on. "I'll be leaving here right behind you. Get some rest."

Once the outer door closed, he spoke to Marlee in a hushed rush. "I don't want to talk here."

"But I heard—"

He grasped her elbow and nudged her closer to the door. "I need to talk to you about some stuff, but this is not the time or the place."

She caught his urgency but couldn't follow his logic. They were in the sheriff's office. Another person was dead, and she assumed he might now be giving her suspicions of foul play more credence. What better time? What better place?

His dark eyes bore into her. "Fine," she managed at last. "Where? When?"

"What time do you have to be at the office?"

"I'm going to be working out of Wendell's office. He told me he prefers banker's hours, so not until nine o'clock."

He nodded. "Go run. Meet me at my place. I should be able to shake free from here in about twenty minutes."

"Your place?"

"Yeah. It's a blue house with awnings down the street about—"

"The Larkins' place," she said, pinpointing the house he meant on her internal map.

He nodded. "His daughter rented it to me. He moved to a place in Florida to be closer to her."

She nodded but refused to be distracted by the details. She could get the scoop on the high school's longtime PE teacher later. "Your house. Twenty minutes," she agreed. "And be prepared to spill, because I'm not particularly good at waiting for what I want."

Without another glance, she backed out of the door and forced herself to break into a trot. She'd run for exactly nineteen minutes and forty-six seconds when she hooked a sharp left off the sidewalk and onto the brick walkway leading to the freshly painted front door of the house Ben Kinsella now called home.

More than once, she'd herded Jeff up these porch steps, a bulging trick-or-treat bag bumping against her leg. Mrs. Larkin made the world's most delicious popcorn balls every year. She felt a pang of sadness as she realized that even in Pine Bluff, people probably didn't hand out homemade treats anymore.

Ben opened the door the second her foot hit the top step. Sleep deprived and freaked out about what he might tell her, she had to blink twice at the man framed in the doorway. Unlike any of the Larkins, his head nearly touched the top of the door frame.

"Hey," he said, his voice creaking as he held the screen door open wide in invitation.

She stepped into the dimly lit entry and peered up at him. "Who was it?"

He shook his head, then gently closed the door behind her, cocooning them in the small space. "I think you'd better sit down."

"Who was it?"

"I'm told you were acquainted with the victim." He

drew out his notebook but didn't bother opening it. "The victim's name was Beaufort Abernathy."

Marlee gasped, then pressed her lips together to ward off the hot prickle of tears clogging her throat. "Bo," she managed at last.

"Yes." He fidgeted with the still-unopened notebook. "I'm told the two of you used to date?"

She stared at him uncomprehendingly for a moment. "Date?"

This time, he flipped open the cover on the tiny pad, but his eyes never dropped to the page. "Yes."

"We, uh," she stammered, the fog of shock lifting. "Yeah. In high school. We, um, we went to prom." She scowled when she realized he wasn't taking any of this information down. As a matter of fact, he wasn't even holding a pen. "I take it you knew all this already," she ventured.

"Yes."

His succinct answer made goose bumps rise on her skin, but she refused to lead her own interrogation.

"His wife mentioned you."

"Wife?"

"Kayla Abernathy," he supplied.

She searched her memory. "I don't think I'm familiar with anyone named Kayla."

"She said she was behind you in school."

"Okay," Marlee responded, drawing the word out encouragingly.

"She also says it's your fault he's dead."

Marlee recoiled. "My fault?" She shook her head. "How—why would she…? Wait, Mrs. Brewster said something about a suicide. Did Bo Abernathy shoot himself?"

Ben nodded solemnly. "Single gunshot wound at close range. Weapon at the scene. No sign of a struggle or anything indicating anyone else was there." He hesitated. "Wait, no. I take that back. There was lots of evidence of other people being on the scene, but most of it could be attributed to the construction." A shadow of a smile ghosted across his lips, but it didn't have the oomph to reach his tired eyes. "Let's say the Prescott County deputies were, uh, enthusiastic when they reached the scene." He jerked his head toward the living room. "Come in. I need to sit, or I'll fall over."

Marlee followed him to the floral-print sofa she'd lay odds came with the house. "So, how could it be my fault?"

"Mrs. Abernathy claims the two of you were having an affair."

Her jaw actually dropped. "An affair?" she parroted.

He nodded, his expression somber. "She says he's been talking about you ever since you came back to town."

"Oh, my God," she breathed. "The texts? Do you think they were from Bo?"

"Can't say for certain until we can get a look at the computer and cell phone," he hedged.

"Damn. Bo Abernathy." She gave her head a rueful shake. "I've only spoken to him once since I've been back. It was at…"

She trailed off, and he leaned in. "It was at…" he prompted.

She pressed the tips of her fingers to her lips. "Clint's visitation."

Without prompting, she gave him a brief overview of her relationship with Bo in high school, the last time she'd seen him before she left for college and the hellos they'd exchanged at the funeral home.

Ben nodded, then closed the notebook again, apparently satisfied with her answer. "I'll need to take a statement from you regarding, uh, your whereabouts last night."

"My whereabouts?" she asked distractedly. "You know where I was. I was with you at the lake one night, and the next I drove my mother to a meeting."

He sighed heavily. "Yes, and now our trip to the lake will be part of the records. I'll ask Lori to take it so there's no conflict of interest." His expression grave, he met her eyes. "I'm sorry."

She straightened her shoulders. "Why are you sorry? I'm not ashamed to be with you, Ben."

"I know, but..." He shot her a baleful look. "I don't want to open you up to any gossip."

"Gossip?" She gave a short, bitter laugh. "You know small towns guzzle gossip like gasoline. The talk about me started the day I was born and likely won't die until I do. It's nothing I can't handle."

"I know, but with everything else." He made a circling motion with his hand. "I'm sorry. I understand the text thing has been weighing on you, and hopefully we'll have some answers for that. And I have to tell you, I'm coming around to the way you are thinking about these deaths more and more, but I've been up all day and all night and I am beat."

She nodded. "I didn't sleep well either."

"Did it have something to do with why you called me?"

She started to tell him about her run-in with Will Thomason but stammered to a stop. "It'll keep."

He stared at her, his gaze intense. "Are you sure? I'm not trying to put you off." He held her hand, and she'd swear she felt her bones melt away. "I'm so damn tired."

"I understand."

"We need to talk," he said, lowering her hand with a squeeze and a wistful sigh. "We have to talk about ugly things, and I hate it. I don't want to talk to you about this stuff."

"What do you want to talk about?"

She couldn't help herself. One of them was going to have to give voice to this attraction between them, and she wanted him to speak first. She could no longer play it cool with this man. She wanted to discover exactly what he wanted from her. Then she wanted to find a way to give it to him.

When she looked into his eyes again, he looked so vulnerable, so raw, it scared her. "Anything other than death."

She nodded as they stood. "Get some rest. Maybe we can meet for lunch and fill each other in?"

"Great." His voice cracked with exhaustion.

Then the world caught fire.

He kissed her. Not an accidental brush or a friendly peck but a full-on kiss. His lips were soft but firm. He slid one big hand into her hair, tangling his fingers in the strands caught up in her ponytail and pulling hard enough to extract a soft moan. His other hand found her hip as she wrapped her arms around his waist, clutching at the hard ridges of muscle bracketing his spine. She angled her head, hoping for a better fit, but as quickly as it started, it stopped.

Ben released her so quickly, she stumbled back a step. She touched her fingertips to her tingling lips.

"I'm sorry."

His apology came out rough and ragged. The heat in his eyes told her he was lying. He wasn't sorry. Neither was she. But she couldn't resist baiting him to see if she could make him own it.

"Are you?"

"I shouldn't have."

Her heart fluttered in protest, but she kept her voice steady. "No?"

"No."

"Why not?"

"Because I—" He broke off, running his palm over his hair. She was the one who'd been mussed, but he kept smoothing those close-cropped curls.

She ached to knock his hand away and smooth them herself. Instead, she took her fingers from her lips and pressed them to his mouth. "I wanted you to kiss me."

"I know, but—"

He spoke the protest against her fingers. She laughed and lowered her hand. "Stop with the buts," she ordered. "As a matter of fact, as an attorney, I would advise you to stop speaking altogether. You're sleep-deprived. Crazy, horrible things are happening all around us. But there's nothing you can say to erase that kiss."

"I don't want to erase—"

She pressed her fingertips to his lips again. When his shoulders sagged in capitulation, she pulled her hand down to uncover those warm, delicious lips and cradled his chin in her hand as she rose up to kiss him again. He sighed against her mouth, then gathered her snug against him once more.

This time, she broke the kiss, tipping her head down until she felt his fast, shallow breaths stirring her hair. She sighed happily when he pressed a tender kiss to the top of her head.

"Get some sleep," she said, grasping his strong arms as she pried herself away. "I have to get home and get ready for work."

MARLEE PULLED THE cardigan she'd carried with her into the Wingate Law Firm close around her as she stared down at the open folder in front of her. She'd shivered the previous day away in her silk blouse and pencil skirt. She'd felt much better about today's outfit. The skirt was fuller and longer than its predecessor. Cut in an A-line silhouette, it was at once flattering but more concealing. She'd paired it with a lightweight summer sweater and matching cardigan. Each time the vent above the table whirred to life, she congratulated herself on her forethought.

Dora, Wendell's longtime secretary, poked her head around the door and flaunted her mind-reading skills. "He leaves for court over in Prescott County in ten minutes," she said in a hush. "I gave the thermostat a bump. Hang in there."

Marlee beamed her gratitude. "You're a saint."

Dora rolled her eyes. "I've been freezing my whatsis off for nearly thirty years," she said dryly. "I have a space heater under my desk and a blanket in the bottom file cabinet if you start seeing icicles hanging off the end of your nose."

"I'm good for now. Thank you."

The moment the older woman pulled the door closed, Marlee refocused on the fat file in front of her. To anyone not used to digging through miles of legalese, the work would have seemed tedious, but she found it fascinating.

The endless stream of documents exchanged between attorneys representing two or more parties were nothing more than the movement of legal chess pieces. A proposal, an answer. Counterproposals, demands, refusal, injunctions and subpoenas. These were all small moves made in the course of a larger game. Each party had an objective in mind. Legal wrangling boiled down to what was essentially a footrace run with words.

Her father had been receiving offers for property on Sawtooth Lake for decades. Developer after developer came to him with ever-growing pots of money. Over the years, he'd also fended off the end-around moves made by people hoping to claim that land owned by the Masters family actually belonged to the great state of Georgia. Henry had come out on top each time, thanks in large part to Wendell Wingate's seemingly limitless patience.

Wendell never thrust when he could parry. He raised sidestepping to an art form and wielded a deft hand at drafting motions designed to set his opponents scrambling. The more she read through the files, the greater her respect for her new mentor. She didn't doubt he'd make a fair-minded and highly influential judge.

"How is it coming?"

Wendell stood in the doorway, watching her. "Good," she said automatically. "I'm fine." To her surprise, she realized she was telling the truth. She was fine. Tired and worried, but the work helped. The work made sense. "Off to court?"

"I am." The older man straightened. "This is my last court appearance."

"On this side of the bench," she corrected.

"Precisely. The power of positive thinking."

"When is Simon coming to town?"

"In about a month." Wendell shifted his briefcase from one hand to the other, clearly anxious to be off. "Gives me time to wrap up some other routine matters I have in progress and get you up to speed on your family's pending business. Once he gets here, I'll start campaigning in earnest."

"If you don't mind, I may need you to come with me to the sheriff's office this afternoon. They want a statement regarding where I was last night in conjunction with Bo Abernathy's death."

"A statement? From you?" Wendell's forehead puckered. "I thought they were saying it was self-inflicted."

"They are, but apparently his wife thinks we were carrying on where we left off in high school."

His bushy white eyebrows rose. "Were you?"

"I was with Ben Kinsella at the lake one night. My father was home when he dropped me off," she stated flatly. "I drove my mother to a committee meeting the next night. Plenty of witnesses there."

He digested her recitation, then nodded. "Should be a quick statement, then." He checked his watch. "Okay. I'll meet you here after court. Now, I must go, or I'll be late for my last day."

Marlee stared at the door long after he departed. She'd never thought about Wendell campaigning for his seat on the bench. She'd assumed with her father backing him, the seat as their district's superior court bench would be Wendell's for the taking. She'd forgotten it wasn't an appointment but an elected position. No matter who was backing him, Wendell had to put his name on a ballot and hope people voted for him.

Thanking her lucky stars she had no such ambitions, she pulled the next file in the stack she'd collected to her and flipped open the cover, trying not to think about Bo Abernathy and the text messages she suspected he'd sent. Part of her was glad Wendell hadn't scanned and digitalized most of his old files. Staring at a computer for hours wasn't her idea of fun. Plus, seeing the facts laid out on paper sometimes made things she may have overlooked jump out at her.

Like the names neatly typed at the bottom of a document setting up a partnership agreement. It was for a consulting firm called White, Pinkman, Schrader and McGill. She snorted, then goggled at it, picking each letter out over and over until there was no question in her mind she was reading them correctly.

The names were too distinctive to be a coincidence. But only one person was likely to understand the subtle reference to a television show. Grabbing her phone, she tapped out a quick text to Ben.

Meet me at the Daisy for lunch when you get up. I have something wild to run past you.

Chapter Twelve

Ben stood outside the Daisy Drive-In, pacing back and forth under the short metal awning shading the old dairy bar's order and pick-up windows. It was high noon, and nearly all the now speakerless stalls were filled with people grabbing a quick bite in the air-conditioned comfort of their cars. Every now and then, one of the workers bustling behind the counter would slide open the glass on the pick-up window, shout a name or number through the screen or simply wave and point at a particular car. He'd visited less than a handful of times, but the veteran staff had his favorite menu items pegged. He chose to attribute this phenomenon to their skill. It felt homier than knowing the markings on his truck, the uniform he wore and his *newness* gave him away every time.

"Ben."

He stopped pacing and pivoted on his heel, stalking off in the direction of her voice, desperate to get to her as soon as possible. His gut was telling him Marlee was right when she labeled what was happening around them murder rather than suicide. If she had an inkling as to what tied them together, the knowledge might place her in danger.

"Hey," he said, careful not to reach for her as he stopped on the sidewalk in front of her. "Tenders, sandwich or salad?" He scanned the letter-board menu posted high in the center window. "If you want the chicken-fried chicken, you have to come back on Wednesday. Today the special is catfish."

She elbowed him in the ribs. Darlene, one of the Daisy's longtime staff, watched the byplay between them with an amused smirk.

"Hey, Miss Darlene," Marlee cooed, stooping to peer closer at the woman. "How are you? How's your mama?"

"I'm fine and Mama's ornery as ever." Darlene leaned into the screen, her pencil and order pad at the ready. "Cheeseburger and pineapple shake?"

"Yes, ma'am. And throw in some onion rings," Marlee said cheerfully. "I need to feed the sheriff, stat. We've sure been keeping this poor man busy around here, haven't we?" She gave a pitying shake of her head.

Darlene hummed, then tsked softly. "I promise you, things are usually much quieter around here, Sheriff Ben. These past few years…" She shook her head, a mystified expression on her worry-lined face. "You want a club sandwich and sweet tea, or are you branchin' out today?" She craned her neck to peer up at him through the tiny square screen.

"I'll take a cheeseburger too," he said decisively, peeved to realize he'd fallen into patterns so easily followed. "And sweet tea."

"I'll holler for ya," Darlene promised, then slid the window shut with a thud loud enough to jolt him from his self-chastisement.

Ben shifted, uncomfortable despite the ease between the two women. He never used to be the kind of guy who had a regular order. He'd gotten soft. Or maybe he hadn't cared who followed him out here. Not at first. But now. He'd been careless. Forgetting for whole days he was a man with a target on his back, which was dangerous. Even all the way out here, in backwoods Georgia. He needed to be smarter. For his own sake, and for everyone around him.

"Let's go sit on the wall," Marlee said, tugging on his arm.

He glanced over at the woman beside him and his breath caught. She was the prototypical all-American girl. Her blond hair tumbled in loose waves over her shoulders, pulled back from her face by a narrow band of red elastic. She wore makeup, he was sure, but it didn't obscure the dusting of freckles on the bridge of her nose. The skirt she had on was full and fluffy, falling to her knees in swirling folds. It matched her headband, and the sweater. The sweater she wore was simple but fit snug over her slender figure. She had another long-sleeved sweater looped around her neck. Who wore sweaters tied around their neck in real life?

A strobe burst of memory slowed his steps as she led the way to the cinder block retaining wall encircling the property. White teeth and gold jewelry. His best friend standing in front of the city's biggest thug, holding an assault rifle. Willing to put his body between a stampede of federal agents and a weaselly white guy who wore a tennis sweater around his shoulders.

He could still see Andre's confusion melting away as he realized Ben was the only one who could have given them up to the authorities. But it all went to hell too fast. A blast of automatic-weapon fire on both sides. His weapon in his hand. Andre dropping to his knees, then pitching forward, the light gone from his eyes. They never told him if any of the bullets pulled out of his best friend's body actually came from his weapon, and he never asked.

In the end, all that mattered was Ivan Jones knew his name and his face, and his life in Atlanta was over. Forever.

"Ben?" Marlee called to him.

Shaking off the memory, he picked up the pace again. A smattering of people sat atop the wall in patches of shade provided by nearby trees planted on the neighboring property. He checked their faces. They were vaguely familiar, but there were relatively few people he knew on sight.

They picked a spot a good distance away from a pair of teenagers splitting an order of tater tots smothered in chili and cheese. He automatically reached for Marlee's arm to steady her as she hopped up to sit on the wall.

"Nice sweater," he said, nodding to the cardigan looped around her shoulders.

"Thanks. I had to dress in layers. Wendell keeps the thermostat set at meat locker."

His attention drifted to her bare calves as she crossed her ankles. She wore shiny red high heels. The shoes would definitely have drawn the attention of her secret admirer. If he'd lived to see them.

"Have you received more texts?" He sounded edgy, even to his own ears, but he cut himself some slack. He was running on less than five hours' sleep in the past forty-eight.

"No." She patted the wall beside her. "Sit." She shifted to face him more fully. "I have to tell you something."

"Okay," he replied warily.

"I called you last night to tell you I had a run-in with my dad's minion, Will Thomason, and until this morning, he was number one on my possible creeper list."

"What? Why?" He scowled, pushing down the urge to plant a fist in the guy's face merely on her say-so. "What do you mean, 'run-in'?"

Without a clue about his inner turmoil, Marlee proceeded to tell him about the mystery involving her drapes and how she'd been traipsing around her house in nothing but a towel the previous night.

Ben's hands curled into fists. He looked everywhere but

at her, needing a moment to get a handle on the rage roiling inside him. Marlee would neither welcome nor appreciate any kind of caveman reaction, so he needed to keep the lid clamped down tight.

"Long story, and we'll get to it, but let me tell you what I found this morning."

Ben wanted to bow up at being put off, but she was so obviously bursting to share, he didn't have the heart to disappoint her. "What do you want to tell me?"

"I was going through all these papers, trying to draw some more lines between the members of the Sportsmen's Club and my brother, and I came across a consulting firm with a funny name."

He narrowed his eyes. "Funny how?"

"They set themselves up not long after the furor from the DEA operation died down. They call themselves White, Pinkman, Schrader and McGill."

He shook his head, momentarily confused. "Is this the wild thing you mentioned?" She nodded, and then something clicked. "What were the names again?" He gaped at her as she patiently repeated them.

"White, Pinkman, Schrader and McGill."

"Like the characters from *Breaking Bad*?"

She nodded, pleasure lighting her face. "I knew you'd get it. I imagine a lot of you DEA guys watched that show."

He shrugged. "Some did. It was good television, but to be honest with you, most of us were annoyed they made a sort-of hero out of Walter White."

"Yes, well, I found an offer to buy the land at Sawtooth Lake from this group." She shrugged. "Not the first, but it was the one my brother took to my father."

"And Henry rejected it."

She confirmed his assumption with a brief nod. "Then later reached out to them to accept it. But by then, another party was involved. A real estate investment group represented by Jared Baker. The guy I wanted to go work for in Atlanta."

This was the first he'd heard of any plans Marlee had extending beyond Pine Bluff. Of course it would be Atlanta. The one place in the world he'd never step foot in again. Not even on a layover, if he could help it. "You planned to remain in Atlanta," he said, keeping his voice as even as he could.

She waved a fluttering hand as if her plans were inconsequential. "Yeah, well, the best-laid plans of Masters children and all," she said dismissively.

She was speaking in riddles, and he didn't have the patience to unravel them now. "What kind of law was it?"

"Corporate but medium-sized. Not the flashy stuff." She shrugged. "Doesn't matter. My father made sure I couldn't get an interview, much less the job. This morning I saw Baker's name on the papers."

Ben took a moment to digest the information. "Jared Baker is connected to the Sawtooth Lake Sportsmen's Club, this partnership, and you were supposed to interview for a job with him?"

"Sheriff Ben!" Darlene shouted from the window of the dairy bar.

Marlee nodded and picked up her phone as he slid down from the wall. "You grab the food, and I'll pull up their website and text it to you."

Ben's mind raced, parsing the sentence for pertinent information then filing bits away to be reviewed later. Marlee planned to leave Pine Bluff. That knowledge had to be stowed away for now too. He had to focus on what was happening around Sawtooth Lake. He heard the chime of a text alert as he reached for his wallet to pay for their lunch. "What do I owe you?"

Darlene waved him off. "Nothing. I charged it to Henry's account."

He stared at her, dumbfounded. "You run tabs for people?"

Smirking, she said, "I run a tab for Henry Masters." Then she slid the window shut with a metallic thwack, indicating the end of the conversation.

Clutching their food and drinks, he hurried back to the spot where Marlee sat waiting for him. Upon approach, he wagged his head in exaggerated dismay. "This town is nuttier than a fruitcake."

She beamed as she extracted her milkshake from his hands. "You're only noticing it now?"

He placed the bag between them, then resumed his seat on the wall. "I guess I'm getting used to seeing more instances of nuttiness hanging out with you."

She smiled, then dug into the bag and removed two foil-wrapped burgers along with a paper boat filled with onion rings.

He studied her closely. "You seem to be bearing up well," he observed mildly.

She lowered her sunglasses to peer at him over the frames. "So far, I've lost my brother and two men I've known most of my life." She pushed the glasses up and took a bite of an onion ring, chewing while she let the information sink in. "I can't think too hard about it now."

"Marlee, I—"

"Can we take ten minutes?" Her eyes implored him. "I found the information, and I will talk about it. But I didn't stop to think what it might mean beyond sort of filling in the blanks. And I want—" She broke off. Her gaze dropped to the remaining bite pinched between her fingers. "I want us to eat lunch together like normal people. Maybe talk about something other than death while we do it?" She grimaced. "Do I sound horrible?"

He looked into her big blue eyes, and something inside him uncoiled. "No. I get you," he answered quietly. "Ten minutes isn't going to hurt anyone." He set to work unwrapping his cheeseburger. "I haven't tried a burger yet."

She stared at him, shock widening her eyes as she chewed. "You haven't?"

"There are too many other things. Even I can cook a burger," he said with a shrug.

She snorted and set to work unwrapping her own sandwich. "Not a Daisy burger," she asserted. "You'd better try an onion ring too. They're life changing."

Ben eyed the thick burger. "They are, huh?"

She reached for another of the lightly battered rings and held it so close to his eyes, he could pick out the flecks of pepper in the breading. "You'll swear you saw God this day, Ben Kinsella. Mark my words," she intoned gravely.

Chuckling, he took the onion ring from her and let it dangle from his index finger as he took a big bite of the burger. Juicy, well-seasoned beef made his taste buds sing. He closed his eyes for a moment, then widened them at her as he chewed, letting out an appreciative moan.

Beside him, Marlee laughed and wriggled, delighted by the small triumph. "Told you so. The ring is going to blow your mind."

THEY ATE QUICKLY but kept the conversation mercifully light. Selfishly, she wanted to sit with Ben in the dappled sunlight, eating cheeseburgers and talking about their favorite fried foods. She needed a moment of normalcy, even if it was a bit forced. People cast curious glances in their direction, but she didn't care. She was happy sharing a slice of peace with him.

They split the last onion ring between them. She watched as Ben sucked a bit of burger grease from his finger and thumb, then handed over the remaining, yet wholly inadequate, paper napkin. He took his time wiping his hands. "You ready to talk more now?"

Marlee sighed, a blush warming her cheeks as she balled up her own napkin and tossed it into the paper bag. "Yeah, I guess."

"You're the one who came to me with your suspicions," he reminded her gently. "We aren't the ones making these things happen. If they are connected, if there is something going on, don't you think we owe it to your brother to figure out what it is?"

"Yes."

"We're going to need to have a handle on everything you can unearth about this property deal."

She nodded. "Right. But I think you'd better make it more official. Come to Wendell's office this afternoon. We'll tell him what we suspect and let him decide what he wants to tell my father and when."

The corner of his mouth lifted. "You want me to give your father the chance to lawyer up?"

"My father doesn't need to be any more lawyered up than he already is. Besides, he has as much of an interest in seeing this solved as I do. More, even. He's the one who has had to live with my mother day in and day out since Jeff died," she added quietly. "Maybe it will help him to realize she hasn't been entirely off the mark."

He nodded, then dropped down off the wall. She scrambled to gather her wits and her belongings, but he snatched up their trash in one hand and offered her the other. Grasping her discarded cardigan, she placed her fingertips in his palm and allowed him to steady her as she gained her footing. To her surprise, he closed his fingers around hers, hanging tight to her hand as they made their way toward the trash bins. They'd almost made it past the front bumper of Reverend Mitchell's Buick when he remembered himself.

He tried to drop her hand, but Marlee was having none of his nonsense. She made a show of sliding on the loose gravel at the edge of the pavement and hooked her wrist through his arm. When she flipped her hair back over her shoulder, she tossed a friendly wave toward her family's minister.

"Afternoon, Reverend Mitchell," she called, squeezing Ben's bicep to halt him.

He shot her a glare but obliged as the clergyman rolled his window down.

"Good afternoon," the older man called to them. "It's nice to see you home, Miss Marlee."

"Good to be home," she lied through bared teeth. "I assume you've met Sheriff Kinsella," she added.

"Yes, we have met," the minister said genially. "Sheriff, I hope you're settling in? We'd love to see you some Sunday."

Ben stiffened slightly under her grasp, but he gave the older man a respectful nod. "Kind of you, Reverend. I appreciate the invitation."

"I have to get on back to work," Marlee said, using the hand holding her sweater to wave. "You say hello to Mrs. Mitchell for me."

"You can tell her hello yourself on Sunday," the minister replied. "See you, Miss Marlee." Without waiting for her reply, he grinned and rolled his window up again.

Marlee laughed, hugging Ben's arm to her side as he led the way. "Darn, I walked smack into that trap, didn't I?"

She beamed up at him, but the moment was shattered when her phone dinged to indicate a new text message. A creeping sensation crawled up her spine as she pulled her phone out. Forcing a smile to trigger the device's facial recognition, she stopped dead when she saw the message notification from an unknown number.

No one wants you here, Marlee. Go away!

BEN RESENTED HAVING to return to the sheriff's office. Every minute he spent parted from Marlee made him itchy. Aside from the text that blew his theory out of the water, he wanted to be with her when she shared the information she'd unearthed about the land sale with Wingate so he could gauge the man's reaction. Right now, only the two of them knew about the land, and he wanted to keep it that way for now. What was the old saying? Two people can keep a secret, but three people can only keep one if two of them are dead.

Whether Marlee was aware of it or not, there was inherent risk in sharing her findings with Wendell Wingate. They had no clue who could be mixed up in whatever this was, but Wendell Wingate was aware of the land transactions. If he hadn't already been asking himself questions about the circumstances between Jeff Masters's death and Clint Young's, adding Bo Abernathy's to the mix should certainly set the gears to grinding.

They'd have to watch Wingate carefully. The attorney was too sharp, too skilled a lawyer to have any of the obvious tells. This was where his status as someone new to the area could help. His impressions of Wingate would be fresh and unfiltered.

Sitting at his desk, he scrolled through the Baker Law Firm website, scouring every page for a clue connecting the man to Masters County and Sawtooth Lake. But he found none. The guy was an Atlanta native. Buckhead area, of course. He'd attended Pace Academy, gone north to Harvard for undergrad and law school and then come back to practice. He'd spent only two years as an associate at one of the city's prestigious firms prior to striking out on his own.

From what he could find, the firm's client base was more eclectic than the corporations they represented at his old firm. There were a couple of deep-pocket corporations, of course, but also a mix of financial wizards, athletes, a reality television star and some hotshots from the local rap scene on their client roster. He lingered over an article linking Jared Baker to a gang-connected rapper whose name Ben recognized from the time he spent embedded in the SEATL crew. He closed out of the screen with a growl of frustration.

Spinning away from the computer, he tapped his forefinger to his upper lip as he weighed the possibilities. Also, divulging their suspicions might cause any of the people involved to go to ground—which would be good and bad. Good because it might bring a halt to these horrific scenes but bad because the how or why behind it would remain a mystery.

He sighed and pushed out of his desk chair. He'd stalled as long as he could. He needed to get over to Wingate's offices and start fitting puzzle pieces together. He also needed to talk to Marlee about keeping her nose out of the investigation. There was a time and place for attorneys, but usually, it came later.

Now, he needed to be a cop.

As much as he hated to admit it given the circumstances, for the first time in a long time, it felt good again.

Chapter Thirteen

Wendell sat in his desk chair, his elbows propped on the arms and his fingers steepled beneath his chin, his attention fixed on Ben. Marlee fought the urge to interject facts here and there while Ben methodically laid out the details surrounding the deaths of Jeff Masters, Clint Young and now Bo Abernathy, as well as the connection Marlee had drawn between the three men and the sale of her family's property at Sawtooth Lake. Any information she had in addition to the facts Ben so painstakingly outlined would have been an exercise in gilding the lily. All they had at the moment were three deaths without any evidence pointing to anything beyond suicide and a basket full of supposition, so she kept her mouth shut and let Wendell's sharply honed intellect do the work.

When Ben finished speaking, the older man ran the tips of his interlaced fingers back and forth under his chin. The moment lasted an eternity. He puffed out his cheeks and exhaled a long, weary breath. "Well," he said, his voice creaking from disuse. He cleared his throat and gripped the arm of his chair, sitting straighter. "I don't have to point out your complete lack of evidence," he said meaningfully.

"No, sir," Ben and Marlee said in unrehearsed unison.

They shared a glance, then Ben quickly pinned his attention on the man across the desk. "But you have to admit, there's something off with all this."

Wendell nodded thoughtfully as he stared at Ben, apparently taking the sheriff's measure in a new light. "Here I thought you'd come to Pine Bluff to get away from all this sort of ugliness."

The older man's words were light, but she picked up the mocking edge. Marlee slid forward in her leather club chair and leaned in, ready to put herself between the two men if necessary. But it wasn't necessary. Ben was more than capable of handling himself.

"Masters County has always had its fair share of ugliness, Mr. Wingate." His voice was deep and steady, carrying a clipped note of command. He wasn't easily bullied. "You know it and I knew it when I took the job."

"So you did," Wendell conceded with a nod. Yanking his hands apart, he let his arms fall open, palms-up, in an indication of futility. "You have no evidence."

"Not a bit," Ben confirmed, not backing down.

"What do you propose to do?"

Ben glanced over at Marlee, and she jumped, startled to realize she'd nearly missed her cue. "Uh…" Looking at Ben, she forged ahead. "I saw the parcel where the house was being built was owned by an Abernathy. I assumed it belonged to Bill and Allison Abernathy."

To her surprise, Wendell shook his head. "No, it was young Bo who bought it."

Marlee reared back, shocked by the revelation.

"Bo?" she asked, incredulous. His bushy white brows rose, and she caught the movement of Ben's head out of the corner of her eye, but she couldn't tear her gaze from Wendell. Not until he confirmed they were speaking of the same person.

"Yes, Bo Abernathy. I believe the two of you were an item once, weren't you?"

"Yes. I mean—" She huffed, frustrated with her inability to get her thoughts straight, much less her words. "We dated in high school, is all," she said dismissively. She pushed her point with Wendell. "I saw the sale prices on those parcels. I thought maybe his parents had sold their place in town to move out there or something. Where would Bo get so much money?"

The attorney blinked twice. "I did not handle the closing on each property. They took care of transfer at the Farmers Bank and Trust, but I assume he procured a loan."

She shook her head in disbelief. "But…he's my age. How could he raise the down payment in such a short time? Where does he work?"

This time Wendell didn't bother to hide his amusement. "Bo went to work for Georgia Mutual Insurance after he finished school, I believe. They put him through their training program, and he took over Gary Behrend's agency when he retired. Did you expect he'd dry up into a husk once you left town, Miss Marlee?"

She opened and shut her mouth, outraged by the shot at her ego. It hit too close to home.

"I met this guy," Ben said, breaking the tension of the moment. "Tried to sell me life insurance in the middle of the Piggly Wiggly the first week I moved here."

"Sounds about right," Wendell drawled. "That's where the money is." He paused, then chuckled. "In life insurance, I mean. Not the Piggly Wiggly."

"He bought into this land deal," Marlee interrupted. "Who's the head of this Sportsmen's Club anyway? Do they have a president or something?"

"Yes, they have a nominal president who acts as mediator in any disputes," Wendell said and then pursed his lips enough to give Marlee the impression he didn't approve of the person holding this position or maybe how they were doing their job.

"I suppose it's my father," she said, eyeing him warily.

Wingate shook his head. "No. It isn't. Originally, it was your brother, but after he…passed, Will Thomason took over the job. I suspect he thought it would be too much for your father, given the circumstances and all."

"Will Thomason," Marlee breathed, recoiling in her chair even as she spoke his name.

Wendell maintained his poker face. "Why? Is there an issue with Will?"

"I suspect Bo Abernathy had been sending me creepy text messages since I came back to town," she informed him. If the sudden change of subject threw the older man, he didn't show it. "The texter was using some kind of computer program to send messages from random numbers. His wife must have discovered the plot and immediately jumped to the conclusion we were sleeping together."

"Of course," Wendell said, barely batting an eyelash.

"But up until today, I thought it might have been Will Thomason." She grimaced, shooting Ben a smirk. "We didn't exactly hit it off."

This time, Wendell did raise his bushy eyebrows. "How odd. Most people seem to like Will."

"Yeah, well, I'm not most people." Eager to bypass any possibility of having to tell the towel story again, she plowed ahead. "Apparently, he and my father were doing some work into the evening."

Mr. Wingate steepled his fingers under his chin again. "Not unusual."

Marlee darted a look at Ben. "He was a bit overfamiliar," she said, choosing her words carefully.

"How so?" Ben's voice was a growl.

She shook her head. "Nothing overt. We'd never met, but his comments were fairly laced with innuendo." She met Wendell's eyes because she didn't dare let Ben get a good read on how much Thomason's behavior truly bothered her. "It was disconcerting."

"But you have met him," Wendell insisted, clearly puzzled.

She shook her head. "Not that I recall."

Wendell pursed his lips, then expelled a tired sigh. "Well, it's possible you were never properly introduced, but he was at Jeff's services. He was at your house after we came back from the cemetery. I recall speaking to him while we were in line to fill our plates."

Marlee cast her thoughts back to those horribly muzzy days surrounding her brother's death and interment, but no matter how hard she tried, she could not conjure the vaguest memory of ever having seen Will Thomason. Shaking her head, she said, "If he was there, we were never introduced. He's a good-looking man. I think I would have remembered."

Beside her, Ben made an inarticulate grunt, and she looked over, her lips curving. "What? It was only an observation."

"If you like the type."

She snickered. "Sheriff, I assure you there aren't many women over thirteen or under ninety who'd disagree. The man is empirically handsome. Doesn't make him attractive."

"You said he was, uh, forward with you last night," Wendell interrupted, yanking them back to the crux of the subject.

"Not forward," Marlee said, considering her words carefully. "More along the lines of sly and presumptive."

"This led you to *presume* he is the one sending you

these anonymous messages," he said, tossing her word back at her.

"I thought he might be the one sending them," she admitted. "But now we have reason to believe it was another member of the Sawtooth Lake Sportsmen's Club. We came here because we want to get more information on the sale of the lake property."

The lawyer pounced. "You think they may be connected?"

"I think it's an odd coincidence we've had three apparent suicides in the area in the last year and they have all happened in cabins on Sawtooth Lake," Ben interjected smoothly.

"And all members of this Sportsmen's Club," she added.

"Three suicides," Wendell corrected. "Rulings were made on two of those deaths, and by your own account, we have no reason to suspect anything different will come from the coroner's office on poor Bo." He folded his hands atop his desk and peered at them over the top of his reading glasses. "If you would allow me to play devil's advocate for a moment?"

Ben inclined his head. "You probably won't say anything we're not already thinking, but go ahead."

"Well, I don't want to be a bore," Wendell drawled. "I can tell you if whoever you wanted to accuse came to me for a defense, I would snap the case up in a heartbeat. Big win, easy money and some sensational press to boot." He leaned forward, his expression earnest. "I understand you want a reason for what happened with Jeff, darlin'. We all do. Unfortunately, there's nothing there to justify a formal inquiry."

Marlee persisted. "What's the scoop on the Sportsmen's Club? How did it come to be?"

Wingate sighed as he sank back in his chair. "It's as I

told you. Your brother was overseeing the real estate portion of the family business. Things were pretty rough in all the fallout from the DEA operation." At this, he shot a meaningful look at Ben, who simply met the other man's stare, unflinching and unapologetic. "The Masters land trust needed an infusion of cash, and your father refused to liquidate any of the company's direct holdings."

"Of course. He'd bankrupt himself before jeopardizing the business itself," Marlee said with a hint of acid in her tone.

"Rightly so." Wendell sat up again. "He could use the business to rebuild the family's fortune, but it would be nearly impossible to rebuild the business in this day and age. As it is, he's beating the corporate competition off with a flimsy stick. If word got out we were willing to sell even one inch of Timber Masters acreage, the big boys would have been on him like fire ants."

"They want to buy him out," she concluded.

"When everything went down with the methamphetamine labs, the company was vulnerable for a number of reasons." He rubbed his chin thoughtfully. "Your daddy wondered if maybe some of those operations might have had some form of 'corporate' sponsorship."

His openly questioning gaze landed on Ben. "Do they do that?"

Ben shook his head. "Yes and no. You likely wouldn't have been able to make a direct connection. Most of the profits flowed into or through Atlanta. Most of it was scrubbed. Laundered. It's a chicken-and-egg sort of business model."

"So his suspicions would not have been completely out of left field?" Wendell pressed.

"No more so than Marlee's belief these three deaths may have something more than means and location in common. We need to figure out what the motivation might have been."

Rather than conceding the point, Wendell closed his eyes, drew in a deep breath and held it. He released it with a long hiss. Marlee would swear she could see the man deflating, though he didn't alter his posture one bit. "Motivation is never the difficult part. Most crimes boil down to a handful of motivating factors. Money is probably number one, followed by the misplaced pride we call love," he said with a cynical laugh. "Hell, you can find a list of them in the Bible." He pinned her with a shrewd gaze. "And don't bother arguing gluttony only leads to self-inflicted wounds. I can tell you about the day Betsy Lovell shot her husband of thirty-two years because the man had the gall to eat the last Little Debbie in the box."

Undeterred by the older man's dissertation on the seven deadly sins, Marlee steered the conversation back on course. "The land was purchased by a trust set up in the names of White, Pinkman, Schrader and McGill."

Wendell nodded. "Yes, but I do not believe the attorneys themselves were aware who was funding the trust. I spoke to Jared Baker on the phone, and he said he was excited to be purchasing his lot. Apparently, a friend of his grew up over in Prescott County and he wanted a place for long weekends, or to loan out to special clients during hunting seasons."

He swiveled his chair as he spoke, and the motion seemed to keep the words flowing.

"The land itself has some conservation provisions your grandfather had put in place. Dwellings could be built along the shoreline but only single-family homes. The sale of parcels had to be approved by the Timber Masters board. No commercial development. And there's a whole host of voluntary conservation provisions subject to oversight by the Environmental Protection Agency."

A burst of laughter escaped Marlee so suddenly, Ben jumped in his seat. His head swiveled and she held up a hand in apology. "Sorry," she said, then gasped through the fingers clamped over her mouth.

Wendell chuckled. Finally, he condescended to let Ben in on the joke. "Let's say the timber industry and the EPA have never been bosom buddies. It's been particularly contentious in the past ten years or so." He turned to Marlee. "But your grandpa was a clever one. He tried to hammer out a working relationship with them. Timber Masters survived when so many other companies of comparable size were so twisted up by regulations, they had no choice but to surrender to the conglomerates."

"Whoever bought the land had to agree to work within all these provisions," Ben clarified.

"Exactly. When they came up with the proposal for the Sportsmen's Club, it seemed the perfect solution. The land was already approved for hunting and fishing by the Department of Natural Resources, so as long as the members stayed within the guidelines, it was a natural fit, if you'll pardon the pun."

Marlee sobered as the pieces fell into place for her. "So, after Jeff died, my father agreed to the plan, and Will Thomason took Jeff's place as president."

Since there was no evidence to suggest foul play found at any of the scenes at Sawtooth Lake, Ben couldn't make official inquiries. If anyone was going to talk to Will Thomason about the members of the Sportsmen's Club, it would have to be her. Except she wasn't looking forward to the task. With her lips thinned into a line, she pushed up from her chair. "Thanks for the background. We'll let you get back to your work."

Ben shot to his feet as well. "Thanks for your time." He practically chased Marlee from the room.

To her relief, Wendell didn't attempt to prolong the conversation, and Ben didn't feel the need to say anything more until after they'd left the attorney's inner sanctum and returned to the conference room where she'd been working. The moment she closed the door behind her, though, he shifted into full-on bossy alpha male.

"I don't want you trying to talk to any of these guys."

He was so authoritative, she might have obeyed if she weren't prepared for exactly this sort of order. "I will be talking to them," she replied calmly. "And I'll remind you that you have absolutely no business doing so yourself."

"How can you say I have no business?" he demanded hotly. "I'm the sheriff in this county."

"And as our chief law enforcement officer, you are aware you don't have one sliver of probable cause to ask anyone anything related to these unfortunate and untimely deaths," she said, enunciating the last so pointedly, she was surprised the man didn't start to ooze blood.

"Marlee—"

"I, on the other hand, as the bereaved sister of one of the victims, am free to ask anyone anything I want," she stated officiously.

"These could be dangerous people," he argued. "Hell, you think one of them is keeping tabs on your bedroom window. If you think I'm gonna let you—"

"You don't *'let'* me do anything, Sheriff Kinsella," she said, cutting him off at the knees.

"Damn it, Marlee, you can't drag me into this thing then go off like some small-town Olivia Pope, all badass and ready to 'handle' things," he countered.

She blinked, surprised by the reference to the television show *Scandal* but not displeased by the comparison. "Olivia Pope. Good one. Who doesn't want to be a gladiator in a suit?"

"Stop," he growled.

"You started it," she said, jabbing him in the chest with her index finger.

He grabbed her finger, the heat of his skin sending tingles up her arm, then took hold of her entire hand. When she looked up into his eyes, she found them dark with worry and frustration.

"You can't do anything," she reminded him. "Not in an official capacity. And unofficially, no one is going to talk to you, Ben." She gentled the assertion with a wan smile. "They don't know you."

She winced, seeing the moment the simple truth of her statement hit home with him. He was an outsider and always would be. No matter how welcome they said he was. With a rumbling growl of frustration, he yanked on her hand, pulling her up against the solid wall of his chest.

"Do you always have to be right?"

She raised a shoulder. "I can't help it."

"And I can't help this."

He pressed his mouth to hers, crushing her lips beneath his. She welcomed the punishing force for the thrill it shot through her. When he softened the caress, his lips still clung to hers as he pulled back. They stared at one another, breathless and wanting but all too aware of their surroundings.

"Not sorry," he told her.

"Me either," she answered, lifting her free hand to caress his cheek.

"We're riding on the razor's edge here."

"Yes, we are."

"Marlee, I don't want you anywhere near Will Thomason without me around." He exhaled harshly. "I'm not trying to go all caveman on you. I… I'd be tearing my hair out the whole time."

She slid her hand up to massage his nape. "And it's such nice hair."

"Please," he said, his voice cracking.

She wasn't exactly sure what he was asking her for, but it didn't matter. Marlee was fairly certain they were on the same page. "But I might follow up with Jared Baker, see if maybe he's up for a job interview."

"Please don't."

She sighed. The ache in his voice reminded her the man was running on fumes as it was. She didn't need to add to his anxiety. "I'll let it rest. For today."

"Are you going to tell me about you and this Abernathy guy?"

She brushed his concern aside with a flick of her wrist. "Ancient history. Other than the visitation, I hadn't seen him since we graduated high school. Can't believe he became an insurance salesman, of all things," she added, wrinkling her nose. "Once upon a time, Bo thought he might be destined for a career in mixed martial arts."

Ben raised an interested brow. "He was into martial arts?"

She smirked, but a pang of sadness for the boy she once liked struck her hard. "Nope. He thought he'd learn some moves from one of those video sets they sell on late-night infomercials. I doubt he even made it through the first DVD."

"You two dated steady in high school," he said, completely ignoring any anecdotal color she might throw into the conversation.

"Neither of us expected it to go any further," she assured him. "Once he understood there wasn't a snowball's chance in Hades of me staying here in Pine Bluff and marrying him, he moved on to plan B."

"Which was mixed martial arts," he said, his lips twisting into a sneer.

Marlee shot him a look. "Bo Abernathy was the type of man who was always looking for a shortcut."

Ready to think of anything but Bo, she changed the subject. "Are you free this evening?"

"Yes."

"Interested in spending some time with me?"

"Yes."

She basked in the simplicity of his acceptance. No games. No beating around the bush. He gave her yes after yes. How could any woman resist? "I enjoy spending time with you, Sheriff," she murmured, leaning in for a kiss.

"That may be, but I believe you're operating on my time at the moment," a deep voice drawled from the doorway.

Chapter Fourteen

"Daddy!" Marlee gasped, her hand flying to her throat.

Ben jerked away from Marlee, but not fast enough to complete disentangle himself. "You're not the only one who's surprised," Henry Masters said, his expression foreboding.

But even faced with her father's obvious displeasure, Marlee simply rolled her eyes. "I sincerely doubt you're surprised," she said, dividing a look between her father and himself. "We had lunch together at the Daisy. God and half the town saw us. I'm amazed it took this long for word to make it back to you." She crossed her arms over her chest. "Your network may have some holes in it."

Henry sniffed at the implication. "Please. He wasn't simply giving you a lift home the other night. You all went out to the lake house. Why?"

Marlee shrugged, but for the first time since her father appeared, she avoided his gaze. "I haven't been out there since… Jeff."

Ben could tell she was trying to sound offhanded about it, but something rang hollow. Sure enough, she rolled her shoulders back and drew herself up, then faced Henry directly.

"I wanted to see what you'd done with the place."

"I see." The older man jingled the loose change in

his pocket as he inspected them. "What did you think of it, Sheriff?"

Ben gave his answer a moment of thought. "I think it's a nice house with a sad history."

"Yes." Henry's voice was quiet.

Ben and Marlee exchanged a look. He turned back to Masters, ready to say something, anything, about his intentions toward the man's daughter, but he hadn't the first clue what they were. Marlee might still have plans to return to Atlanta at the first possible opportunity. This sizzle between them could be nothing more than heat. Something to add some spark to the time she was forced to stay here in Pine Bluff. How was he supposed to proclaim his feelings for her to her father when he hadn't the foggiest notion of whether she had feelings for him at all?

Henry spoke again, interrupting his thoughts. "Marlee, the Office of Bar Admissions sent a letter. Congratulations, you passed. You are officially a member of the Georgia Bar."

Marlee blinked. "You opened my mail?"

His eyebrows shot up. "You were okay with me opening the bills for your tuition," Henry said stiffly. "I didn't see how this should be any different."

"But—"

"Your mother and I believe this calls for a celebration. We'll be expecting you home for supper this evening."

Marlee looked like she'd just been hit by a speeding truck. "Yes, sir."

Ben darted a look in her direction, startled by her easy capitulation. Then she added a sunny smile that made the hairs on his arms stand on end.

"Would it be all right if I invited Ben to join us for supper?" she asked, all honeyed sweetness.

Her father rolled his eyes, apparently impervious to her

myriad charms. Finally, he settled an assessing stare on Ben. "Perhaps the sheriff can join us another night. I've already invited Will to eat with us, and I hate to spring too many surprises on your poor mama."

"Oh."

The word slipped out of her, small and soft. Acquiescent. A syllable not at all worthy of Marlee. Hearing the note of uncertainty made his fingers curl into loose fists. He wanted to tell her he didn't care if he had to bring his own bucket of fried chicken to eat, he wasn't going to let her anywhere near Will Thomason without him.

Ben was still casting about for a way to insert himself into whatever setup Henry had going when Marlee swooped in and staged her own rescue.

"Well, Mama invited him when we were all at Mrs. Young's house, so I'm sure she won't mind. I'll call home and make sure Mrs. Franklin is aware we'll be five for supper."

"Good," Henry said with a terse nod. "Now you'd best get back to it. You have a lot to learn and not a lot of time to get up to speed." Done with her, he zeroed in on Ben. "Sheriff, can I walk you out? I have a couple of questions."

Ben looked at Marlee, but she couldn't do much more than give him a shrug. "I'll text you later."

Nodding, he followed her father out of the conference room, feeling like a teenage boy about to be ejected from the parlor for kissing on the couch after curfew. The last thing he wanted to do was give Henry Masters the idea he could control any part of Ben's private life.

"Henry, I—"

The other man gave his head a hard shake, waved to Wendell's ever-vigilant secretary and led them out the door. Ben blinked against the glare of the harsh afternoon sunlight. Shielding his eyes, he drew to an abrupt halt and waited for Masters to realize he was no longer following. The older man was five steps away and still oblivious. Anxious to have his say, and afraid Henry might get himself whipped into a froth, Ben called out to him again—this time, using his most authoritative cop voice.

"Henry, stop."

Masters spun around, surprise lighting his face. He was a man accustomed to giving orders and watching people jump to do his bidding. But Ben had told him from the beginning he wouldn't be one of those people. Now was his time to prove it.

"I want to talk to you about your daughter," he said, closing the distance between them in two strides.

"She'll do everything in her power to get back to Atlanta," Henry informed him without hesitation.

"You plan on keeping her here," Ben countered.

The older man's eyes gleamed, and Ben had a hard time deciphering whether it was respect or challenge he saw there. "Yes, and I also hear tell you can't go back to Atlanta. At least, not if you don't want to end up in a pine box."

But the revelation didn't rattle Ben. His situation was hardly a secret within the agency. It would have surprised him more to discover Masters hadn't uncovered the reason for his decision to switch gears career-wise. "I have absolutely no doubt you think you have a good handle on me, but you don't."

Henry crossed his arms over his chest. "I'm sure you have some hidden depths, but I'm not particularly interested in plumbing them."

Ben stared hard at the shorter man. "You can tell me to back off, but the only person who can make me leave Marlee alone is Marlee herself."

"Why should I? You're the best enticement I have to keep her here," Henry pointed out.

"What do you want to ask me?"

For the first time since he'd met the man, Henry Masters looked uncertain. He pushed his hand through his thinning silver-gold hair, casting a wary glance at the door to Wendell's office. "Do you honestly think there's some deeper connection between my boy's death and these other men?"

Ben shouldn't have been surprised to discover Masters was up to speed on the suspicions Marlee had brought to him. Wendell had probably been on the phone to Henry the second he and Marlee left his office. Ben bristled momentarily but reminded himself Masters was actually Wingate's client and not Marlee or himself. Wendell had been under no obligation to keep their conversation confidential.

"I've taken it into consideration." Ben eyed Henry carefully and was thrown completely off balance when Henry Masters got misty-eyed on him.

"I thought Carolee... She never accepted it. I can't blame her," he said, his voice breaking as he rambled on. "It's unnatural to bury a child. Unbearable to think the boy you loved was so desperately unhappy he'd..." He trailed off, blinking furiously as he stared down at the patch of green lawn in front of Wendell's law offices.

At a loss for what to say, Ben fell back on the most general of platitudes, hoping to buy some time. "No one can ever truly understand what someone else is going through."

"He was happy," Henry insisted. "Well, not unhappy," he amended with a bitter laugh. "He was apprehensive about taking over the company one day, but he planned to have Marlee to help him, and he seemed to genuinely care for the Cabrera girl..."

Again, his words drifted away from him.

"It was such a shock." Clearing his throat, he gave his

head a fierce shake. "Carolee kept insisting there was more to it, but the evidence—"

But the evidence. Those three words kept bouncing around Ben's head. "Yes," he said gruffly. "The evidence."

"But now these others. It can't be a coincidence," he stated firmly. He tossed another uncertain glance Ben's way. "Can it?"

"I don't think it is," Ben told him truthfully. "But it's not much to go on as far as theories go. There's a distinct lack of evidence."

"How can it be?" Masters wondered aloud. "The forensics all pointed to Jeff pulling the trigger himself."

Ben nodded, but his movements were made jerky by a flash of memory. Something Andre had once said to him as they sat on a dirty mattress in a dank southeastern Atlanta flophouse, waiting for members of their crew to return from what Ivan called a "retribution run." He remembered sitting there, staring at the water-stained ceiling and listening to his childhood friend spout some utter nonsense the gang leader believed about how a real man decides when it's his time to live or die.

"Maybe he did, but that doesn't necessarily mean he committed suicide."

"Now you're talking in riddles," Henry said derisively.

"No, I'm saying the cause and effect don't always align the way most people expect them to," Ben retorted. "Life isn't simple."

"So you're thinking someone coerced my son into putting a gun to his head and pulling the trigger?"

Until Henry Masters spoke the words out loud, Ben hadn't allowed himself to go there. But there it was. Plain as day and damn-near impossible to prove. Unless they somehow caught the person responsible in the act. Thanks to Marlee, they had two possible suspects. One of them was coming to supper at Marlee's house.

"Exactly what I'm thinking," Ben confirmed with a short nod. "What time should I be at your house for supper tonight? I have a couple questions for Will Thomason."

Masters blinked twice, a look of resignation setting his features into a grim mask. "Six thirty for cocktails. We'll eat at seven."

"I CAN'T TELL you what a thrill it is to have so many handsome gentlemen at my table," Carolee said, her voice as high and breathy as a girl on her first phone call with a boy. She beamed as she offered Ben the mashed potatoes with a side of fluttering lashes. "Why, when Marlee told me you'd be joining us too, Sheriff, I ran right into the kitchen and told Mrs. Franklin nothing but Mother's English-rose china would do."

Marlee had to hand it to the man. He didn't look the least bit fazed by her mother's flirtation. "I can't tell you how happy I am for a good home-cooked meal, Mrs. Masters." Ben took the proffered dish from her. "And, please, call me Ben."

"Then you must call me Carolee," her mother parried.

"Mrs. Masters is fine," her father grumbled as he placed two slices of Mrs. Franklin's mouthwatering roast beef on his plate.

Marlee's impulse to laugh was stifled when the man beside her spoke up. "And you should call me Will, Marlee."

With barely a glance, she swung a small serving platter his way. "Asparagus, Mr. Thomason?" she asked politely, emphasizing the use of his surname.

He didn't miss the hint. "Thank you, Ms. Masters," he said as he relieved her of the plate. "How are you enjoying your time with Wendell Wingate?"

His delivery was annoyingly congenial. He hadn't even noticed she'd been pointedly rude to him from the moment he walked through the door. Marlee cut him a sharp look. "How do you know I've been working with Mr. Wingate?"

The pause lasted a beat too long. Her question surprised him. The openness of his expressions made her feel more confident. She needed to gauge his reactions when she prodded him about the Sportsmen's Club and the parcels of land surrounding Sawtooth Lake.

"I was the one who suggested you spend time with him first," Thomason said, darting a puzzled look at Henry. "I guess your father didn't mention it."

She shook her head. "Nope. I showed up for my first day at the family business and got foisted off on the trusty family retainer."

Either her word choice or the flippancy captured her father's attention. For the first time since he herded them all from the front parlor into the dining room, Henry looked up from his plate. She saw the deep furrow between his brows and felt an instant stab of remorse. Her mother had always claimed Marlee and Henry butted heads so much because they were too alike. Now, she saw her father's genuine befuddlement.

"'Foisted off'?"

"We thought working with Wendell would be the most logical place for you to start," Thomason cut in smoothly. The silence following his statement stretched a beat too long. Will rushed to fill it on her father's behalf. "Since the plan was for you to come into the administrative end of the business rather than production."

Henry cleared his throat. "Of course, those plans have changed, but it still seemed as good a place to start as any."

A sudden stillness filled the room as even her mother's incessant chatter died away. Marlee scanned her father's face for hints but found him as unreadable as ever. Beside her, Will Thomason tensed, though she had to hand it to him—he didn't let his consternation show. Still, she sensed him gathering his energy in tight, a snake coiling and set to strike.

Intrigued by her father's statement and the closely controlled reaction from the man everyone assumed to be his heir apparent, she placed her fork and knife on the edge of her plate and focused entirely on the man seated at the head of the table. "What do you mean?"

"What I said." Henry's response was sharp and direct. Stripped of his customary bluff and bluster. When all eyes swung to him expectantly, he shrugged their curiosity off. "We'll have to rethink our plans."

"Yes, speaking of, I have plans to order some new curtains for your room, Marlee. I was in there looking at them last night, and I realized it's been forever since I spruced the place up."

Marlee and Ben exchanged a meaningful look. There was one mystery solved. It had been her mother in her room after all. Regardless, she wasn't letting her guard down around Thomason anytime soon.

"I meant our long-range plans," Henry interrupted.

"*Our* long-range plans?" Marlee repeated, emphasizing his choice of pronoun.

"Yes." He fixed her with the same impatient but stubbornly entrenched expression he'd worn when drilling her on multiplication tables.

"You mean *your* plans," she said, choosing the more appropriate pronoun.

"Timber Masters is a family business. You are the last of the line. The company and all of our other interests will one day come to you." Her father didn't break eye contact. "It's my duty to see you are prepared."

Wendell had implied the exact same thing when they first met, but hearing her father lay it out there so bluntly came as a shock. At the opposite end of the table, her mother gasped. Snatching the creamy damask napkin from her lap, Carolee managed to cover her mouth but emitted a strangled sob.

"Mama," Marlee began, half rising in her chair, prepared to usher Carolee from the room if she couldn't rein in her emotions.

"Oh, for the love of—" Henry threw up his hands in surrender. "I dream of getting through one meal without hysterics."

Dropping back onto her seat, Marlee whirled on her father. "Maybe your wife dreams of being able to get through one day without being reminded her only son is gone, but she doesn't have such luxuries."

"He was my son too," Henry fired back.

"Hey, now—" Holding the heavy china platter heaped with steaming slices of succulent beef, Ben tried to step into the fray. But he was no match for a Masters with a full head of steam. They ran over him from all directions.

"He never should have been out there. Jeffrey hated the lake house," Carolee fretted.

Marlee ignored him, choosing instead to gape at her mother. Her eyes widened at what she considered to be a fairly large exaggeration, but she couldn't be bothered with setting her mother straight. Not when she had her father to deal with.

Skipping right over Ben's pleading expression, she leaned into her anger as she spoke to her father. "And he was my brother. Now that we have all our roles assigned, I'd remind you Jeff never wanted to run the business. You bullied him into coming home."

"Bullied," Henry said, tossing his napkin onto the table

with a harsh laugh. "I didn't bully either of you. I simply refused to foot the bill for you not doing your duty to the family." He fixed her with a cold stare. "You and your brother. All you talked about was escaping this town and shirking your responsibilities. You think I was clueless?" His voice shook as it rose in volume. "You don't want anything to do with the company your great-great-grandfather started, but you damn sure don't mind spending the money it makes."

"I had a job lined up, but you shot it down," she reminded him in a harsh whisper.

"A job with a man who—" Henry stopped abruptly, his gaze flying to the opposite end of the table and locking on his wife. "A job with a man who was only speaking to you because your name is Masters."

Awkward silence roared through the room.

Marlee dropped her gaze to her half-filled plate. They hadn't even loaded their plates with roast beef yet and supper was a complete wash. She took two deep breaths and tamped down the urge to howl at the injustice of it all. Everything. Jeff's death. Clint's too. The job in Atlanta she'd thought she wanted. The texts. The jovial jackass seated beside her. The man across the table. How would Ben have fit into the life she'd abandoned in Atlanta? After witnessing the Masters family in their full glory, would he even want anything to do with her?

Beside her plate, her muted phone buzzed once to indicate a new message had arrived. Marlee stiffened. Everyone who might text her was seated at this table. Including Will Thomason. Instinctively, she glanced at the man beside her, but he was carefully selecting a roll from the bread basket. Squirming in her seat, she ignored the tingle of fear that trickled down her spine and steeled her resolve to get to the bottom of his involvement in the land transaction. She'd deal with the texts later.

Wetting her parched lips, she looked up and found Ben staring straight at her, his dark eyes watchful. "Ben?"

"Yes, Marlee?" His gaze didn't waver from hers despite her mother's sniffling and her father's grumbles of displeasure.

"May I have the roast beef, please?"

Still holding her gaze, he offered the platter to her. She took it in both hands then placed it on the table between herself and Will Thomason. Gesturing for their guest to help himself first, she watched as he speared a slice, then served herself and her mother. The potatoes finished making the rounds as well.

Proving her patience and, yes, stubbornness were indeed equal to her father's, she waited until Will had cut off a bite of roast and popped it into his mouth before starting her interrogation. "As president of the Sawtooth Lake Sportsmen's Club, what do you think about losing nearly half your membership in the last year?"

BEN WOULD BE lying if he said he didn't enjoy watching Will Thomason sputter and spin his wheels throughout Marlee's killer line of questioning. She pressed him about how he'd met each of the members, how he'd come to step into the position of president after her brother's death, what all the job entailed. She carried the whole interrogation out while her mother sat sniffling on one end of the table and her father repeatedly tried to intercede from the other. Through it all, Marlee remained utterly unflappable, her performance even more breathtaking than the woman herself.

Sure, some of her angles of attack were a bit awkward and some of her phrasing too close-ended, but he didn't interrupt or try to correct her course. He'd had years of training on how to get the most out of a suspect. She might be newly admitted to the bar, but she cross-examined the squirming man with aplomb. She had the right instincts. The rest would come with time and experience.

Carolee Masters drained her wineglass early in the meal, but no one leaped to fill it for her. By the time Marlee picked up her phone and rose to start clearing plates, Ben almost felt sorry for the poor woman. When Mrs. Masters started to rise too, he set his napkin aside and waved her back into her chair. "No, ma'am. Let me help."

Henry and Will stayed seated, their stunned expressions confirming his suspicion they'd never made such an offer in their lives. Feeling fairly smug for a man carrying a stack of delicate china through the swinging door leading to a surprisingly modern chef's kitchen, he placed the plates he'd collected on the counter next to Marlee's.

"You were magnificent in there," he said quietly.

"I didn't get anything out of him," she said with a huff of disappointment.

"I think you did," he argued.

She lifted her eyes to meet his. "Yeah?"

"Yeah. I think we can agree Will Thomason is ambitious and opportunistic." He lifted his chin. "Check your message."

She closed her eyes for a moment, then beamed the smile to unlock the phone.

No one believes you were with Sheriff Kinsella. You must be paying the man to cover for you.

"Crap," he whispered as Marlee seemed to deflate.

"I could have sworn those texts came from Will. There's something about the way he talks to me." She gave a shudder. "But there's no way he could have unless he schedules them to come at different times. How could he know what I was doing ahead of time, though?"

He had no answer for her. Placing one hand on her shoulder, he rubbed gently as they both read the message again. "Whoever it is, their spelling and punctuation have improved," she said with a forced laugh that fell flat.

He was about to tell her not to fake it with him when something about her observation struck a chord. "Wait. Go back through the others."

Marlee did as he asked, scrolling back to the message she'd received right after she'd returned to town. By the time they got to the last few, one thing became glaringly obvious. This was one case where punctuation counted.

Ben read the message over her shoulder, then pulled out his own phone. He turned away as the call connected. "Mike? I want you to call Judge Warner and ask for a warrant for all electronic devices belonging to Bo or Kayla Abernathy. Then call up to Albany and tell them we need a tech guy down here ASAP."

"Kayla Abernathy?" Marlee asked when he ended the call. "Why?"

"Jealousy?" He shrugged. "She'd have access to his phone or computer or whatever he was using. Only a handful of people know you gave a statement about us being together last night."

Their gazes locked. "I guess."

"He was trying to talk to you. She was trying to scare you away."

"It almost worked."

"God, I hope not." He sighed, then ran a hand over her hair. "We can talk about this later, but for now, we'd better get back." He cast about the kitchen. "You said something about dessert?"

Nodding, she headed for the oven, snagging a dish towel

from the counter along the way. "Grab the ice cream from the freezer."

Ben did his best to keep his gaze aboveboard when she bent, protecting her hands with the towel so she could extract a covered dish from the rack. She set it on the stovetop, then tossed the towel over her shoulder. "Ta-da! Peach cobbler."

"Peach cobbler and a beautiful woman," he said as he pulled a container of ice cream from the freezer. "Proof there is still good in the world."

Chapter Fifteen

The moment they were settled in his car, Marlee turned to him. "Tell me about your parents."

The request startled him. Ben wrapped his hands around the steering wheel and drew in a deep breath, then let it go in a steady stream.

"Come on. You've witnessed mine in all their glory," she cajoled.

He plugged the key into the ignition and cranked the engine, giving it some gas so it roared to life. "Let's take a drive," he said gruffly.

If he was going to tell her a story about a man falling for a girl so far out of his reach that it had ruined him, he sure as hell wasn't going to do it while parked in front of the family mansion.

Without giving it much thought, he wheeled the car around and headed for the highway. "My dad played basketball," he said, beginning at what he considered the man's downfall. "Mostly neighborhood stuff, youth groups, wherever he could." He drummed his fingers on the wheel. "I'm told he was good. So good people from the private high schools came scouting around, looking to recruit some raw talent to add to their rosters."

He didn't bother glancing over at her as he headed down the road that would take them out of the town she would essentially run one day. "My grandmother was ecstatic. All she wanted was for her son to get a good education and get out of the neighborhood. Peachtree Academy was supposed to be the answer to her prayers."

When he fell silent for a moment, she pushed. "What happened?"

"He fell for the Homecoming Queen," he answered without missing a beat. "I guess she was the queen of everything. Blond, blue-eyed, the girl who had everything." He chanced a sidelong look at her. "No telling what she saw in him, exactly. Maybe she thought dating a guy from the 'hood was exotic or something. Probably nothing more than teenage rebellion." He shook his head in disgust. "In the end, she got pregnant and her parents kicked her out."

"Whoa." Instinctively, he let off the gas, but another peek at Marlee told him she wasn't commenting on his driving. "She must have been so scared."

Both annoyed and touched by her compassion for the mother he barely knew, he let the truck coast as they approached the lake road. "Keep going or turn off?"

If Marlee thought the question had two meanings, she didn't let on. She simply gestured to the narrow lane and said, "Go on."

They bumped along the lake road for a minute before Marlee said, "Tell me."

He shrugged. "There isn't a lot more to tell. They moved in with my grandmother. If my mother was scared of anything, it was the neighborhood. It was a fairly hopeless place. Lots of drugs. More than our fair share of thugs to go with them." The truck downshifted to a crawl as he revealed the rest of the story. "Three weeks after I was born, my mother took off. She hadn't lost touch with her old friends. One of them picked her up and drove her back to her parents' house, where I can only assume there was a joyful, mixed baby–free reunion."

"And your dad? He didn't try to go after her?"

He gave a bitter laugh. "My dad. He was still a true believer in those days, I guess. He thought her parents had taken her, so he hitched a ride up to Buckhead and tried to bust her out."

He heard Marlee's sharp intake of breath and let the pause stretch for a moment. "What happened to him?"

"He served ten years for criminal trespass, felony damage to property, kidnapping a person over fourteen years of age," he reported flatly.

"You're kidding me."

He quelled her outrage with a hard look. "Do you think I'm kidding?"

"No, you're not," she said in a horrified whisper.

He could feel her searching look but refused to glance at her. He couldn't let her see the shame and degradation he felt on behalf of his grandmother, a steady, God-fearing woman who'd never done anything to deserve the hardships life piled on her.

"What happened to your parents?"

He shrugged then, out of habit more than necessity, and flipped the signal on to indicate the turn into the drive. "My mother went off to college at Auburn. She couldn't stay anywhere local because *everyone* knew," he said dryly. "She ended up marrying a guy from Mobile."

"And you have never heard from her?"

"I tried to contact her when I was seventeen. I'd signed up for the marines and wanted her to see I wasn't some loser. Wanted to tell her I was going to serve my country and she should be proud of the mutt she'd abandoned."

"Ben—"

Rather than listen to her give him the pep talk he'd

needed then but didn't need anymore, he pressed on with his story. "My dad fell in with a gang while he was inside, continued with them when he got out. My grandmother refused to take the money he made dealing, so we pretty much had nothing. She passed away right after I finished boot camp. Breast cancer."

"What happened to your dad?"

"Oh, he was already dead. Got popped when a drop went south on him. I was a sophomore in high school. The guys he ran with tried to recruit me. Said taking care of Big Benji's family was the least they could do, but my grandmother wouldn't let them come anywhere near me."

"Big Benji," she repeated. "You were named for him."

He nodded. "The last in a long line of losers." He coasted on the approach to the house, the tires crunching on loose gravel as they rolled to a stop. "I'm not even sure why I drove us out here."

Marlee stared bleakly at the house where her brother had died. "Because you were telling me about the mess you lived through, and this is where my mess started." She gestured to the house, her voice quiet and reflective. "This was where Jeff and I cooked up the plan for me to go to law school. He was going to play the game until he took full control of the company, then sell out." She bit her lower lip and let it go when she exhaled. "He didn't want to be like Daddy, and he wasn't." When she looked over at him, her eyes gleamed with unshed tears. "I am."

"Why do you say so?"

She motioned to the house, then to the woods around them. "I can't let it go. Any of it. Jeff's death, this land, the business. I haven't figured out how I'm going to handle it, but I can tell you I won't be selling out. I don't want to live here in Pine Bluff and be the queen of all things Masters, but I won't—I can't—let anyone else do it."

Ben tightened his grip on the steering wheel until his knuckles shone pale against his skin. "I can't let this go any further between us. I won't go down the same path as my father."

"You're afraid getting involved with me will turn you into a gangbanger who deals drugs?"

"I refuse to be a cliché. Nothing good can come out of a guy like me reaching for a woman like you."

"That's the second time you've tried to pigeonhole me," she said, her voice soft and dangerous. "What have I shown you to make you think I think I'm better than you?"

He shook his head, at a complete loss but unable to let go of his convictions too easily. What if he was only seeing what he wanted to see in her? What if she was only putting on a show? Or worse, what if he gave her everything he had and she decided he wasn't what she wanted? After all, his mother had chosen his father once upon a time, but it didn't take long for her to change her mind.

"Forget my looks or whatever," she implored. "Forget who my father is, and pretend my last name is Smith. Would you want to be with me?"

He laughed, but this time there was nothing harsh about it. He laughed because the notion of imagining her in any other way was absurd. She was who she was because she was Marlee Masters of Masters County, Georgia. Her blonde beauty queen looks drew a man in, but she was so much more than an attractive package. Marlee was smart, funny, friendly and, yes, a bit daring. Even then, mere adjectives failed to capture the essence of her. Because above all else, Marlee was genuine. A real person with foibles and fancies but also with feelings. Deep feelings she didn't show to just anyone. But for some reason, she showed them to him, and he'd be damned if he could figure out why.

"It's not a matter of wanting, Marlee," he said at last.

"I want to be with you. Any man with half a brain would, and I have a whole brain. But I can't help but wonder why you keep hanging around me. You can have your pick of men. Why me? What do you want from me?"

For a moment, she looked ready to toss out one of her flippant retorts, but she didn't. Instead, she pressed her lips tight and swallowed hard, then made such intense eye contact with him he felt the urge to draw back.

"Why you?"

Arrested by her, he could only nod in response.

"I could give you a handful of reasons, but to even the playing field, I will skip your looks, the sexy uniform and all other superficial stuff." She stared deep into his eyes, needing to be sure her point hit home. "But don't for one minute think all those things don't work in your favor as well, because they do."

"Noted."

"My father may be a pain in the behind in a lot of ways, Ben, but there's one thing he is and has always been. A man of integrity. As such, he looks for the same in others. He sees what I see in you. A stand-up guy. Someone who will do anything to do the right thing."

"You don't know me."

"Maybe I don't know everything about you, but I think we understand one another. I feel…comfortable with you."

He gave a husky laugh. "The ringing endorsement every guy hopes for."

She could only answer that with a wan smile. "I know, but maybe you'll believe me when I tell you it's a better compliment than it sounds?"

"I believe you."

Her smile widened. "And that, right there. You have a sort of…self-assurance that's compelling."

"You're saying I'm cocky?" he teased.

She shook her head with vehemence. "No. Will is cocky. You're confident. Totally different things."

"Will," Ben said, his inflection dripping with derision.

"I know," she said with a laugh. "I get the feeling Henry was making two points at once in inviting Will tonight." She raised one finger. "To make it absolutely clear to him and everyone else that I am the only person who would be inheriting Timber Masters and everything that goes with it." She took a shuddering breath, reality sinking in. "Two, that all of Will's jostling and positioning himself beside Henry was for nothing. Unless, of course, he decides to marry me."

"Over my dead body," Ben growled.

She tilted her head to the side, then smiled wide and bright. If he had to testify, Ben would swear the sun reappeared in the darkening sky. "So, can you see how the whole 'I can't be involved with you but any other man would have to step over my dead body to get you' thing might be confusing to me?"

"Are you staying or are you going, Marlee?" he asked, his eyes boring into her. "Because Atlanta… Atlanta is not an option for me. It never will be."

"You probably feel the same way about Atlanta as I do about Pine Bluff—"

"No. It's not the same." He grasped both her hands in his and waited until he was sure he had her full attention. "I can never go back to Atlanta because I made a deal in exchange for my life."

"What?"

"I was undercover. Things went bad. Really bad. I crossed a man named Ivan Jones. A really bad dude. The only way I could get out alive was to leave and promise to never come back." He squeezed her hands. "Trust me, the people who work for him are watching."

"How do you know?"

"They send messages every now and then, make it clear they're keeping tabs on where I am and what I'm doing."

"Can't the DEA do anything?"

His expression hardened. "Maybe, but they won't. They let me go when my cover was blown."

"They can't—"

"Yes, they could. Trust me. I broke rules. Most agents who live deep undercover do. It comes back to bite some of us. In my case, they used it for cause."

"But—"

Indignation fired the blue flame in her eyes. He released her hand and pressed his fingertip to her lips. "It's done, Marlee. I've moved on." He gave a laugh, but it sounded tight. "I moved here. The one place you can't stand to be."

"Ben, if it means being with you—"

Whatever she said was cut off by the crackle of the police radio on his dash. "Sheriff? Do you read me?"

It was Lori calling for him, and the jerky cadence of her call told him something was wrong. He snatched the mic from the clip. "Read."

"Can you… I need you to come here. We, uh, we have a situation."

Ben scrubbed his face with the palm of his hand. "What kind of a situation?"

"Uh, I went to the Abernathys' to get their computers and stuff. Mrs. Abernathy tried to refuse to give them up—"

"Did Mike get the warrant?"

"Yes. We had it, and we got the stuff," Lori assured him. "But Mrs. Abernathy is making a stink."

"What kind of stink?" he asked, rubbing his forehead.

"She's telling all the neighbors you're sleeping with

Marlee Masters and that's why she hasn't been arrested for murdering her brother, Clint Young and Bo Abernathy."

WHILE BEN DEALT with the widow Abernathy and her accusations, Marlee cornered her father. She needed answers, and if there was anyone in this town with answers, it would be her father. Thankfully, Will Thomason was nowhere in sight when she got home.

"How did Bo make all his money?" She hadn't bothered to knock on Henry's office door. "I mean, the insurance business is good and all, but his folks didn't have a pot of money. How could he have amassed enough to even buy into the insurance agency?"

Her father opened his hands. "How am I to guess?"

"I understand Mr. Behrend's retired, but they don't hand over an insurance agency to anyone who applies," she continued, pushing away from the door and making her way to the guest chair in front of his antique desk. "When did he get a license? Last I heard, he got his diploma and nothing more. No college, no plans. When we graduated, he had a job changing oil at Hewes Brothers garage. How does Bo Abernathy go from nothing to building a house on the lake?"

"Believe it or not, I don't make a habit of prying into other people's business."

Switching tactics, she nudged a stack of file folders perched on the edge of his desk. "How about Will Thomason? Where'd he come from?"

"I believe his people hail from the Marietta area."

"I didn't mean his family," Marlee said, pinning him with a stare. "How did a guy who didn't even grow up here end up next in line for Jeff's job?"

"He's not next in line for Jeff's job," Henry corrected. "You are."

"You realize he doesn't think so," she said, smirking as she recalled the look on Will's face at dinner. "He's pretty sure he can make you change your mind."

"Then he's mistaken," her father said, folding his hands in front of him.

"I have no intention of marrying him so he can run the family business."

"I won't insult you by pretending the thought hadn't crossed my mind, but I think you've made it clear your interests lie elsewhere."

"How did he end up here?" she persisted. "Most of your managers and foremen are homegrown." She studied her father closely. "How did this guy make it into the inner circle?"

"Through your brother."

"Jeff?" She couldn't mask her surprise. It was hard to imagine her quiet, studious brother being friends with Will Thomason. "Wow."

"I don't think they were close friends," Henry conceded, following the trail of her thoughts easily enough. "Will graduated from UGA a couple years ahead of Jeff. I believe they were in the same fraternity. When he applied for a foreman's position, Jeff confirmed Will had indeed graduated from the Warnell School of Forestry."

"He wanted to be a mill foreman?"

"He didn't want to work for one of the large paper conglomerates," he corrected, sitting up straighter in his leather executive chair. "Believe it or not, lead positions at Timber Masters are highly sought after. We can offer hands-on experience the larger companies cannot."

"As long as you're willing to work at a company with limited opportunity for advancement," she added. "I'm not trying to give offense, Daddy," she said in a rush. "I'm only wondering why a man with other options would choose to climb a ladder with such a low ceiling."

Henry shrugged, slightly mollified but clearly still miffed. "He was unhappy in his previous position and didn't want to go to work for the big boys. With everything happening around here, I was getting dragged into town business more and more. Jeff seemed to trust him, so I was happy to take him."

"So he came here right about the time the whole DEA thing was happening," she concluded.

Henry nodded.

"You don't find the timing odd? That someone would want to move into the area when all the unsavory stuff was happening around here?"

This time, her father gave no more than a jerky shrug. "When you put it in those terms…" He ran his hand over his face again, and her heart slammed into her breastbone. Here, with the light from the desk lamp casting dark shadows across his face, her father looked haggard. Old. For the first time ever, she realized he'd been carrying the weight of their whole world on his shoulders. Her brother's death, her mother's grief and inability to cope, her unwillingness to come home to help.

"It does seem odd the Abernathy boy would fall into such a plum position," he said with a sigh. "I guess… I'm not sure. It's been such a strange time."

Marlee's stomach knotted. The urge to reach across the desk and squeeze his hand had her balling her fingers into a fist. They didn't have a touchy-feely relationship.

"I would think there would have to have been some sort of influence exerted," she mused.

"Excuse me?" Henry pulled himself from his ruminations.

"He couldn't walk in off the street and take over an

agency. There are licenses to be obtained, courses to pass," she said, gesturing impatiently. "Either someone with a good deal of money or influence placed him there.

"Bo was always smart in a sly sort of way," Marlee continued quietly. Her father let out a short laugh, and she couldn't suppress a rueful chuckle herself. "Bright but lazy." A surge of power rushed through her as the bulb went on in her brain. "I told Ben how Bo loved shortcuts. What if he had someone backing him? Someone with some money—"

"Who?" Henry interrupted. "His parents couldn't hang on to two nickels at the same time."

"Maybe he was making some extra money on the side," she postulated. "And Will. How was he able to buy in to the club on a foreman's salary?"

Henry blew out a gusty breath. "I can't say. I assumed he had some family money. He has all sorts of connections in Atlanta. Worked for a sort of a brokerage place. Perhaps he made his money there?"

"And then moved to the sticks to oversee second shift at a lumber mill?" She shook her head. "What was the name of this firm?"

Henry rolled his eyes heavenward, then shrugged again. "I honestly don't recall. I can check his personnel record."

Marlee nodded as she stood. "Yeah. Let's do that first thing. I want to poke around a bit, see if I can follow the paper trail on the land sale."

Her father rose too. "The land sale? Why?"

"Wendell said the firm who acquired the land was a real estate holding company. I want to see who they contracted with as the developer, and who is actually leasing the land to Will, Bo and Jared Baker."

"It seems odd we haven't heard one word from Jared

Baker since all this started," Henry commented. "Then again, he's mainly in contact with Will."

Marlee paused in the open doorway to look back at her father. "Another coincidence." She bit her lip and shook her head. "This place is lousy with them."

"CRYSTAL FOREST CORPORATION," Wendell said as he leafed through a file. They'd all gathered at the attorney's offices bright and early. Even Ben. "The name of the company who actually owns the land at the moment is Crystal Forest Corporation," he clarified. "After Henry called last night, I called in a couple of favors from more technologically adept friends, and they chased it down."

"I thought you said it was some law firm acting on behalf of a trust," Ben chimed in, his confusion evident.

"But the original sale was actually made to White, Pinkman, et al., correct?" Marlee's forehead puckered in a way her mother would surely have chastised.

"Yes. It has gone through a couple more transfers and has now landed with this Crystal Forest Corporation," Wendell confirmed.

"Why does that sound familiar to me?" Henry wondered aloud.

"Didn't Will Thomason work there prior to coming to Timber Masters?" Marlee scrambled to pull the personnel file she'd shoved into her leather tote free. "I read it in here somewhere."

"Crystal Forest," Ben repeated, his eyes focused on something beyond her shoulder. He let out a snort, then said, "No way."

An odd note in his tone caught her attention. "What?"

He dropped his gaze to the polished conference table, but his voice was still distracted when he shifted to sit up taller. "Nothing… The, uh, name struck me."

"Struck you how?" she pressed.

Ben looked up and straight into her eyes. "Crystal meth," he said flatly.

Her jaw dropped as the pieces began to fall into place, but one bit of his conjecture didn't quite fit. "But how would Jeff tie in?" When Ben leveled an unblinking look at her, she shook her head vehemently. "My brother would never get involved in the drug trade."

"People do things they may not want their family—"

"No." She all but spat the word at him as she shot from her chair. "Not Jeff."

"Marlee." Ben rose as well, but she backed away.

"No!" All three men jerked when she shouted the denial. Her voice trembled with rage. "Of all people, you should know."

"Why me 'of all people'?" Ben's voice rose as he circled the end of the table, moving steadily toward her with his ridiculous assumptions.

"Why did you join the military, Ben? What made you want a career with the DEA?" Oblivious to Wendell and her father, she tipped her chin up. "Jeff wasn't the bad guy in this scenario," she hissed. "He was a guy like you—the kid whose parent was half out of it most of the time."

Henry started to rise from his chair. "Now, wait a—"

But Marlee was on a roll, and she wasn't stopping until she knocked over every rock in her path. "You're assuming my mother took up popping pills when my brother passed, but that isn't the case. She's been up and down her whole life—"

"Marlee Kathleen—"

She ignored her father's attempt to interject. "Pour some booze on top and stir in a husband who cared more about his kingdom than he did about his family—"

"Enough!" Henry Masters roared, inserting himself between Marlee and Ben.

The three of them stood in a breathless triangle, tempers high and eyes blazing as they each tried to rein it in.

"I can assure you all Jeffrey was not involved in the drug business." Wendell's voice floated up from behind them, calm and gentle as a spring breeze.

Ben shot the older man a skeptical glance. "How can you be certain?"

"Because I was the one who helped him clean up the mess it left. He loathed what was happening around here." Wendell nodded, then flipped open one of the many files stacked in front of him and hit Marlee with a hard stare. "Now, if you're done bickering amongst yourselves, I can also tell you the Baker Law Firm has handled each of the transactions."

"There's something else," Henry insisted. He ran his hand through his gray-blond hair, then looked directly at Ben. "Jared Baker was the one who gave me your name for the sheriff's job."

Silence fell over the room like a shroud.

Wendell flattened his palms on the polished table. "I would say we seem to have two persons of interest at this point."

Chapter Sixteen

"When we get in there, let me do the talking," Marlee said as they approached the offices of the Baker Law Firm. Her father looked as startled by the demand as she felt. "Right now, we only need to confirm how this all came about, but I have a gut feeling."

Henry frowned at her. "What kind of gut feeling?"

"I'm not entirely sure. Trust me on this?"

He eyed her closely for a long minute, then nodded his assent. Marlee tried her best not to preen as she gestured to the door, but her father's approbation was more rewarding than she had ever expected. "Shall we?"

"Let's get this over with," Henry said impatiently.

Within minutes, they were seated in a sleekly appointed conference room. Marlee mumbled her thanks for the bottle of water placed in front of her by the efficient woman who'd shown them into the room, then took a moment to drink in the industrial-chic surroundings. The exposed brick and conduit made the firm feel hip and edgy to her. Most of the big downtown firms matched their chrome-and-steel furnishings to the skyscrapers housing them or went for a more staid, conservative decor. They screamed establishment. She saw the distressed oak conference table for exactly what it was—set dressing.

"Hello." Jared Baker strode into the room, a broad welcoming smile on his face and his hand outstretched. He shook with her father first, then worked his way around to her. She tried not to bristle at being placed at the bottom of the implied pecking order as he shook her hand. "We finally have a chance to meet." He greeted her smoothly, gesturing for them all to take their seats again. "What can I help you with today?"

Marlee made an effort to relax her shoulders as she maintained eye contact with Baker. "A couple years ago, you handled a land purchase for one of your clients." She flipped open her portfolio and consulted the photocopied page. "Crystal Forest Corporation?"

Jared nodded. "Sounds familiar."

"It ought to. You bought into a leasehold with them." She drew out a sheet of paper with the names of the Sawtooth Lake Sportsmen's Club members listed in a neat column. "We're making an offer to buy the land back."

The other attorney's smile faded by a watt or two. "Excuse me?"

"The land. It's been in my family for generations, and other than setting up a club which has only drawn yourself and people from local families—" she inclined her head "—it can't hold much meaning for your client. I'm sure the Sawtooth Lake property is just another parcel in a vast array of holdings," she continued. "We would agree to honor the existing leaseholds, of course. Including your own."

Baker sat back in his seat, his elbows propped on the arms of his chair. "Hmm." He steepled his fingers beneath his bottom lip, giving the notion his full consideration. "Well, I'm not entirely certain my client would be interested in selling."

"We'd be willing to pay fair market value for the acreage, plus cover any closing costs or other expenses related to the sale." She saw her father stiffen, but thankfully, he remained silent. She flipped to a page in her portfolio, then extracted a proposal she'd typed up and printed on a sheet of Timber Masters letterhead she'd swiped from Wendell's offices. "Here's our offer, but I'm afraid we have a ticking clock on this. The assets we have liquified need to be reinvested by Friday, which means we only have about forty-eight hours to come to an agreement."

"Forty-eight hours?" Jared sat up straighter. "So quick."

"Looking back at the paperwork from the original sale, your clients moved fairly quickly when they decided to invest their money in the property." She leaned in and dropped her voice to a more confidential level. "We're working with an excess of cash on the balance sheet at the moment. Best to keep the money moving. Don't you agree?"

They locked gazes, and a shiver ran down her spine. The look he gave her was speculative but admiring. But rather than feeling gratified by his appreciative stare, Marlee had to curl her toes in her smart black pumps in order to keep from squirming in her chair. She waited without moving a muscle until he picked up the sheet she'd slid across the slick table and took in the numbers. One corner of his mouth twitched upward. It was a tell, but she had no idea if it meant something good or bad.

"I'll make a call today."

"Wonderful." Marlee flipped her portfolio closed and gripped the arms of the chair as she rose, trying to keep the tremors she was feeling on the inside. "We look forward to hearing from you." She thrust her hand across the table, and Jared Baker shook it, an amused gleam in his eyes.

"You've got a go-getter, Henry. I'm sad I couldn't take her on."

Disgusted, Marlee strode from the conference room,

leaving the men to their backslapping and self-congratulations. She couldn't waste time on them now. She needed to get back to Pine Bluff. The trap had been set. Now they had to wait to see which creepy-crawly came out of the woods to take the bait.

"HELLO," BEN SAID when she opened the door to the lake house to admit him.

"Hey." She rose up onto her tiptoes to brush a kiss to his cheek. "Come in."

Sweeping a hand in exaggerated welcome, she moved back to open the door wider. He took the opportunity to peer past her into the house. Part of him was surprised he didn't find Wendell and Henry waiting with her. Another part of him was glad they'd finally be alone. He pulled off the broad-brimmed trooper's hat and stepped through the door.

"I haven't gotten any more text messages," she told him.

"Kayla Abernathy confessed to sending the last few," he informed her. "The tech found the program on Bo's laptop, and, well, you can press charges if you want."

Marlee shook her head. "I don't want to add to her grief."

An awkward silence stretched between them. Ben noted that it was the first time they'd encountered the phenomenon and did his level best to push through it. "I hear you and your father took a trip to Atlanta today," he said, fidgeting with the brim of his hat in his hands as he strolled through the large open-concept living area.

"Yes."

"I wish you would have waited," he grumbled.

"Waited for what?" she pushed. "You can't go there. Besides, what we did today might not even have a direct bearing on the cases you're looking at."

"*We're* looking at," he corrected. He stared directly into those electric-blue eyes. "You're the one who dragged me into this whole thing," he reminded her.

"I did." Her tone was gentle. Conciliatory. He wasn't buying it for a minute.

"So, what did you find out?"

"Nothing specific. I made an offer to buy back the land."

He did a double take. "What?"

"I have no idea if whoever is behind this Crystal Forest land deal will go for it, but it seemed worth a try. If I can recover my family's land… It was worth a try. And it worked. We had a signed agreement in my inbox by the time we got back."

"Congratulations."

"Mostly I wanted to see Jared Baker's face when he saw who his visitors were. He's had dealings with both my father and me. He has about ten fingers in our pie, and I need to figure out why."

"I can tell you why," he said, his voice flat.

"You can?"

"I spoke to one of my friends at the agency today." He gestured toward the sofa. "I think we should sit down."

"I don't care for the sound of this." They sat, their knees briefly touching as he angled toward her. "Why do I need to be sitting down?"

"The suggestion was more for me than for you." He expelled a long breath. "I asked about Crystal Forest or if they had knowledge of any jokers using the *Breaking Bad* names as pseudonyms. The conversation came around to Ivan Jones—"

"The guy who's been after you?" she asked, her voice kicking up an octave. "I thought he was in jail now."

Ben gave a rough snort of laughter. "Jail doesn't mean much to guys like Ivan."

"You're scaring me."

He shook his head. "No need to be scared."

"If you say so."

"I do." He took the opportunity to give her hand a reassuring squeeze. "Crystal Forest is a shell company. They own a lot of smaller businesses they use to launder money. It belonged to Ivan."

"What?" Her eyes widened, then narrowed. "Oh, my God. Forget fingers. This guy is in up to his elbows."

"That's not all."

"Of course not."

He nodded, smiling at her ability to be snarky despite the gravity of their situation. "Ivan and his associates haven't forgotten what the agency did to his business in this area."

"I bet they haven't."

His mouth tightened, and he forced himself to breathe in through his nose before dropping the bigger bombshells on her. "According to my source, Jared Baker was Ivan Jones's attorney of record."

"Really?"

"There's more."

Marlee squeezed her eyes shut. "Stop saying that. I'm not sure how much more I can take."

"Ivan Jones was jumped by some other prisoners about a month ago and beaten into a coma. He died three days ago."

"He's dead?"

He nodded and she bit her bottom lip, white teeth sinking into the tender flesh as she processed the information and the myriad implications.

At last, she released it with a gusty sigh. "Good."

Her single word response to news with the power to alter the course of his whole life coaxed a laugh from him.

"Yeah. Good." He ran a hand over his face. "The man was pure evil. He used to do all sorts of messed-up stuff. Andre told me about this time he made a guy…" He stalled as the story his friend told him in a flophouse a lifetime ago played out in his head.

"What?"

"Why didn't I think of it?"

Ben must have stared into space a minute too long, because Marlee waved a hand in front of his unseeing gaze to get his attention.

"Think of what? Ben? Speak. What are you thinking?"

But he was too busy fitting puzzle pieces into place to let his concentration be broken. "Ivan. Ivan owned Crystal Forest. Will worked for Ivan at Crystal Forest. It was Ivan."

"What was Ivan? How can anything be Ivan?"

"Because everything circles back to that sadistic jackass," he growled.

"But Ben—"

He cut her off before she tried to apply anything as useful as logic to the way Ivan Jones had operated. "Ivan didn't like to get his hands dirty, but he liked to mess with people's heads. One of his favorite things to do was to force people to play Russian roulette."

"What? How?" she asked, her brow crinkling.

He was trying to formulate how to explain when the cabin door flew open and Henry Masters stumbled in.

"I got a voice message from Will Thomason. He's over at his cabin now, but there's something off."

The words were barely out of his mouth when two nearly simultaneous gunshots rang out. Ben and Marlee leaped to their feet, and Henry swung toward the lake. A moment later, the reverberation of a third shot echoed across the still water, but rather than taking cover, Henry Masters set out for his car.

Ben pushed past Marlee and took off after her father. "No, don't!" he shouted as he ran out the door.

He was halfway down the steps when he heard footfalls slapping the deck behind him. "Get back inside," he yelled over his shoulder, sprinting for the Suburban. The engine roared to life, but Henry hadn't shut the driver's door. "No," he barked, reaching into the car and practically dragging the older man from the seat. He switched off the ignition. "What the hell do you think you're doing?"

"We can't—" Henry's voice broke as he struggled in Ben's grip. "I can't let him do it. No more. No more."

The man spoke in a half rant, half sob, but Ben didn't need a translator to understand what he was trying to say. "You think Thomason was planning to kill himself out here tonight?"

"How am I supposed to know?" Henry bellowed. "I can't… Not another one."

Still gripping Henry by the arms, he shoved him toward his county-issued SUV. Opening the rear door, he pushed the older man in. "We're going. I'll take you," he promised. If he convinced the man to get in the back seat, he wouldn't be able to get out without someone to open the door from the outside.

After closing Henry in, he reached for the driver's door and swept the area for Marlee, praying she'd heeded his direction to go back into the house. The second he slid into the seat, he realized he'd given Marlee Masters too much credit when it came to common sense, because she was planted squarely in the passenger seat of his car.

"Marlee, we don't have time—"

She strapped into her seatbelt, then fixed him with the same stubborn glare he'd gotten from her father. "Then maybe you should stop yapping and start driving, Sheriff."

Less than a minute later, they were back on the lake

road. Ben floored the accelerator. Marlee clung to the handle above the door as they sped down the rutted lane cutting through dense forest, but he didn't dare let up. "Grab the mic. Call for backup. Shots fired at Thomason lake house. Officer en route, approaching destination." Marlee dutifully repeated him verbatim. "I'll wait for backup as long as I can, but I need to assess the situation. Request backup from any Prescott County patrols in the area."

She'd hardly gotten the last part out when Ben stomped on the brakes and the SUV skidded to a halt outside the clearing where Will Thomason's house sat. It was a prefabricated home but had the look of a traditional log cabin. One room, or possibly two smaller areas. It was situated in the center of a heavily wooded lot, away from the lakeshore.

Ben squinted through the windshield, trying to make out the details of any entrances and exits in the lowering gloom of the evening storm. The back door had nothing but four wooden steps leading to it, but the entire width of the front had a deck. A pair of camp chairs sat at one end. The rest was bare. Apparently, Thomason wasn't big on homey touches. The second he reached for his door handle, Marlee went for hers. "No," he barked.

"But you can't go in there alone. It will take at least fifteen minutes for backup to get out here," she argued.

"You aren't going in there," he growled.

Henry Masters cleared his throat but spoke in a voice barely louder than a whisper. "Keep it down. Sound carries out here."

"I need you both to stay here," Ben said, infusing his voice with command.

"Not going to happen." Henry was clearly unimpressed. "I'll take Marlee with me and slip around the back, see if we can catch anyone coming or going."

"Whoever is in there is armed," Ben reminded him, twisting in his seat to glare at the older man. "If anyone is even still in there. Whoever it was could be hiding in the woods, waiting to take potshots at us. Stay in the car."

"You have to cover the back one way or another. We'll keep low and close to the house. And we'll arm ourselves," he said, pointing to the firewood stacked in a rack along the side of the house. "We don't have time to wait on anyone else. I promise we won't do anything risky." He slid across the seat and tugged on the handle. When nothing happened, he looked up, incredulous. "Are you kidding me?"

"For the record, either of you step foot out of this car, I'll arrest you. Stay put," he ordered, popping the snap on his gun belt. He opened the car door and stepped onto the forest floor as silently as a thick layer of needles and twigs would allow.

He closed the door and saw Marlee shaking her head, her eyes wide with fear. When the latch caught, she pressed her open palm to the glass. Sparing the cabin a quick glance, he pressed his palm to the exterior of the window. He hoped his gaze conveyed his unspoken promise to return to her and say all the things they needed to say, because he didn't have time to say them now. Unholstering his weapon as he walked, he cautiously made his way toward the door.

He was about to peek through the edge of the first window he came to when he heard the unmistakable sound of a car door opening. He angled his head enough to see Marlee liberating her father from the rear seat of his patrol car and bit back a groan of despair. When she gestured toward the cord of firewood, he gave an impatient wave, trying to shoo them back to the car, but they kept coming.

"Two peas in a pod," he muttered under his breath.

Fixing his attention to the window, he angled for a peek

inside. The place looked to be one big room. The back of a leather sofa served as the dividing line between the living and sleeping areas. He could see the small kitchen in the far corner and a closed door he assumed must be a bathroom. Hoping to get a better look at the living room through the sidelight by the front door, he shuffled his feet along the planks of the wood decking fronting the cabin.

He peeked around the edge of the window and saw a man clad in camouflage hunting pants sprawled on the floor, foot lolling to the side. He blinked, willing his focus to sharpen as he cataloged the other features of the room. The body lay between the big leather sofa and a stone-fireplace hearth. He allowed his gaze to track over the long expanse of leather inch by inch until he found the spot again. Something shiny gleamed in the dull light. No, not shiny. Wet. And dark.

Blood.

The body lay too far away from the sofa for the blood to be his, if he was gauging the distance correctly. The blood had to have come from somewhere else. He was still searching for the source when a hand rose above the sofa. A hand covered in blood. There was someone on that sofa.

Gripping his weapon in both hands, Ben flattened himself against the log wall and shouted, "Masters County Sheriff!"

Thrumming heartbeats passed, then a thin, reedy voice called out, "Help… Help me."

Weapon pointed at the wood deck, he reached out to test the door. Unlocked. The hinges creaked as it swung open. "Masters County Sheriff," he called again. "If you're armed, drop your weapon!"

"Help," the man called, his voice slightly stronger. "Sheriff."

Despite the warm evening, gooseflesh rose on his arms.

Drawing closer, his grip on his gun tightened as he peered through the crack in the door. The man's annoying drawl was all too familiar.

"Thomason, I'm coming in. If you have a weapon, I suggest you drop it."

"Make sure he's dead first," the man said in a ragged whisper.

Galvanized by the response, Ben kicked the door in and burst into the room, his weapon sighted on the sofa. "Drop it now."

Panic raised the other man's voice an octave. "Make… sure."

Ben placed one foot in front of the other, never taking his eyes off the spot where he'd located Will Thomason's bloody hand. "Drop. It."

"He's dead. He has to be dead," Will insisted.

Ben flicked a glance at the man crumpled face-first and bleeding profusely on a cowhide-print rug. In two strides, he loomed over the back of the couch, his gun trained on Thomason. Bright red blood soaked the front of his shirt. He held his left hand to the side of his neck and gripped an old-fashioned revolver in his right. Judging by the man's weakness and the amount of blood seeping through his fingers, Ben worried one of the bullets had at least nicked an artery.

"He's dead," Ben said, willing the injured man on the sofa to drop the damn gun so he could assess the situation better. "Drop it."

Thomason blew out a breath and let the gun fall from his limp hand to the floor.

Then, and only then, did Ben give the other man more than a passing glance. "Who's the corpse?" He eyed the prone body.

"Bake…he did it. He made 'em," Will panted, his voice

weakening to a whisper. “I tried to tell him to stop, but he said…”

His voice trailed off. Circling the end of the couch, he moved closer to Will. With a firm grip on his gun, he nudged his hand under Will’s and took over applying pressure to the wound. The blood flowed warm and steady, and the man’s breathing grew more and more rapid. “He said what?”

“Young, Aberna—” His voice slurred the last syllables together. “Too greedy. Cut.”

“Cut of what? Greedy for what?” Ben’s voice rose as Will’s weakened.

“Made ’em. He made ’em.”

“Made them what?” Ben persisted, moving to place himself directly in front of Thomason’s glassy eyes. “What did he make them do?”

“Roooo-let. Summone taugh him…win…every time,” he mumbled.

“Roolet? Roulette?” Ben’s heart lurched, then sank as the story came full circle. “Russian roulette?”

Ivan Jones had taught his minions his favorite game.

Chapter Seventeen

The creak of hinges caught Ben's attention. Marlee saw his head pop up. A half second later, a gun was pointed in her direction. "Police. Freeze."

"Ben, it's me," Marlee called into the room. "What's happening? Are you hurt? We heard you shouting, then nothing."

"I'm fine. Don't come in here," he snapped, lowering his weapon again. "Go flag down the others. I need an ambulance. And the coroner. Get Schuler," he added.

"Is someone hurt or dead?"

"No! Do not come in," he shouted. "This is an active crime scene!" His voice shook with exertion. Whoever was on the sofa made a gurgling, gaspy sound, regaining Ben's full attention.

"Stay with me, Thomason," he ordered. "I need you to stay with me."

Will. Will Thomason was on the couch and gravely injured. She stood frozen in the doorway, her heart in her throat as she strained to make out what the injured man was saying. "Gree-ee," the other man murmured as his eyes slid shut. "He caugh 'em. Yuhn, Abernaf-ee."

Ben pounced on the gibberish. "He caught them skimming? What about you? Why you? Why Jeff Masters?"

The man's breathing became even more shallow, each

inhalation labored. Ben was losing him. He looked up at Marlee, his gaze imploring. "Ambulance?"

Try as she might, she heard no sirens approaching. The look of desperation on Ben's face spoke volumes. If Thomason went, he'd be taking a whole boatload of secrets with him.

"Hang on," Ben repeated to Will, his voice shredding. "We need you, damn it."

Half a minute passed in deafening silence until, at last, the distant wail of a siren carried on the wind. "Here they come," she reassured him.

Ben's shoulders sagged, and he let out a shuddering breath. "Too late. Damn it," he cursed.

"Ben?" she called out as the blare of multiple sirens drew closer.

"He's dead." The pronouncement came out hard and flat. "And so's Baker."

She flinched when he raised a blood-soaked hand to gesture toward the space between the sofa and the television, but from her angle, Marlee couldn't see anyone else. "Baker?"

"Appears they shot each other."

He rocked back and holstered his weapon, oblivious to the blood. Marlee averted her eyes, her own clean hand flying to her mouth and pressing firmly to trap whatever it was rising up inside her. A scream? A moan? It wasn't important. Ben didn't need to hear it right now. Not when he'd fought so hard to get at least one person out of there alive.

Tires skidded to a halt outside the cabin. Marlee saw a deputy's cruiser and an ambulance parked close to the cabin. She ran for the door, suddenly remembering Ben's car and worried they couldn't get through. Then she spotted the SUV pulled up next to the woodpile. She started toward the approaching vehicles when she spotted her father in the sheriff's SUV, slumped over the steering wheel.

While Lori and the paramedics raced past her to the front door, Marlee picked her way down the prefabricated steps and crossed the thick carpet of fallen pine needles to the SUV. "Daddy? What's wrong?" she called out as she approached. The windows were up; he might not have heard her. Reaching for the door handle, she peered through the tinted glass and her stomach dropped to her toes.

"Daddy?" she cried, yanking the door open. To her relief, Henry fell back against the seat rather than into her arms. She gave him a quick once-over and, seeing no blood, asked again, "What's wrong?"

Henry's mouth moved soundlessly. His eyes were wide and scared. Her stomach sank as she saw the gleam of a thin sheen of perspiration on his forehead. The left side of his face seemed to sag.

"Oh, no," she said, running her hand over his damp forehead. "Oh. Oh, Daddy," she managed, though a hot rush of tears strangled her. Something she'd read in an article somewhere popped into her mind. "Daddy? Can you smile for me?" she prompted, her voice as tremulous as her own attempt to demonstrate.

When only the right corner of his mouth moved, she leaned in and pressed her lips to the slack skin of his left cheek. "Right. Okay. Okay," she whispered. "Don't you move." She made sure he was propped upright in the seat. Keeping her voice as light as she could manage, she nodded a shade too enthusiastically. "Stay here. I'm gonna go get some help."

Closing the door behind her so he couldn't fall out, Marlee sprinted across the scraggy yard for the back door. This time, she didn't stop at the threshold.

"Help. I need help," she cried as she skidded across the laminate floor.

Ben sprang to his feet, reaching out to catch her, but she shied away, freaked out by the blood drying on his hands. "Help. It's Daddy," she panted, shifting her attention to the paramedics who were hovering over Jared Baker's inert body. "I think he's having a stroke." The two men looked at Ben, and she snapped, "He's alive, but he needs help now!"

Ben jerked a nod, and the two men grabbed their equipment and followed her out the back door. Within minutes, they had her father strapped onto a gurney, an oxygen mask over his drooping face, and were wheeling him across the tree roots to the back door of the ambulance. While they were loading him in, Mel Schuler pulled to a halt beside them.

"I thought Lori radioed two dead?" he called out to them. "Miss Marlee, what's going on?"

One of the paramedics waved her into the ambulance. "Two inside. We have a live one, but he's showing signs of stroke, possibly hemorrhagic."

"Good God." Mel threw open his car door and scrambled after Marlee, squinting into the ambulance as the paramedic made sure they were secured for the race to the hospital. "Miss Marlee, is that your daddy?"

She nodded but could make no words come out.

The paramedic shot Mel an annoyed glance as he moved to pull the doors closed behind him. "We have to roll. We're heading straight to Putney Memorial in Albany."

"I'll call someone to get Carolee," the coroner/funeral director called after them.

The door slammed shut, and the man tending to her father called out, "Hit it."

BEN SAT OUT in the general waiting area at Putney Memorial. Hours had passed since the ambulance containing Marlee and her father had sped away. He'd sent Lori ahead to check on them, but he'd been tied up waiting for the crime lab technicians to finish up, giving a statement to the Prescott County Sheriff—since Thomason's land was technically on the other side of the county line bisecting the lake—and waiting for Mel Schuler to transport the bodies.

He'd dragged himself home then, all too aware he looked like an extra from a horror movie and wondering if the sight of him covered in Will Thomason's blood would be the only way Marlee Masters would ever see him now.

For months after the shootout in the abandoned warehouse, he'd only been able to picture the sick glee on Andre's face as he lifted his assault rifle and sprayed the agents swarming through the door with bullets. All traces of the boy he'd loved as a brother were wiped away. All he could see clearly was the expression of stunned betrayal his friend wore when he'd seen Ben's gun pointing at him.

It took over a year for Ben to be able to conjure any other images of his lifelong friend. Still, those gut-wrenching scenes played out in his dreams. Not once did he envision them shooting hoops or hanging out on his grandmother's porch.

Would it be the same for Marlee? Would she look at him and only see blood and destruction? God, he hoped not. But even scrubbed clean and dressed in jeans and a T-shirt, he still felt dirty. Because he was tied into this.

Had their lives been on a collision course? One set off by men driven by greed, power and vengeance?

Propping his elbows on his knees, he rubbed his hands together and let his head fall forward. Would she figure out how long it had taken him to scrub his cuticles clean? If she hugged him, would she smell the coppery scent of blood? His own nostrils were clogged with it.

He'd had to be tested. A Prescott County paramedic had rambled on and on about the dangers of blood-borne pathogens as he poked at Ben's veins. There was no use trying to explain to the kid there'd been no time to pull on a pair of latex gloves, even if he'd had some handy.

"Ben?"

His head jerked up at the sound of her voice. He shot from the chair and covered the ground between them in three long strides. But then he drew up short. She looked worn and worried, and the last thing he wanted was to push himself on her.

"Hey," he croaked. Clearing his throat, he tried again. "How's your dad?"

She drew a shaky breath, then let it go as she flung herself into his arms. He caught her and held her as a hard, wrenching sob broke from her chest. Ben squeezed his eyes shut, his initial rush of relief swallowed up by sympathy as he leaped to the worst-possible conclusion.

Burying his hand in her hair, he gently massaged her nape. "I'm so sorry." He pressed kisses to the top of her head, and she cried harder, tears gushing from her eyes and soaking the front of his clean shirt. "Oh, Marlee," he whispered into her hair. "Marlee."

She pressed into him, and if he could have absorbed all her pain, he would have. Because he loved her in spite of his every effort not to.

"He's okay," she said at last.

Her voice was so muffled by his shirt, for a minute Ben wasn't sure he'd heard her correctly. "Yeah?"

"I mean—" she peeled herself away enough to look up at him "—he will be. We got him here fast, and they were able to get him prepped for treatment on the way. It was ischemic rather than hemorrhagic, so they're treating it intravenously. They think the clot is dissolving."

He hugged her tighter, unwilling to let her go once she'd come to him. "Good. That's good."

"He's asleep now, but he was alert earlier. Seemed to recognize me and my mom. Eleanor Young drove her here," she explained. "They're in with him now."

She tightened her arms around him, and Ben had to bite back a shout of relief. She was holding him as much as he was holding her. "Good. That's good," he repeated. Then, catching himself, he pressed his cheek to her hair and let out a sigh. "Sorry. I'm so glad you were glad to see me," he confessed in a rough voice.

"What?"

She tried to rear back to look at him, but he clamped a hand to her head and pressed her to his chest. "No, don't. Just stay."

Just stay. Two simple, seemingly innocent words. But he wanted her to do more than stay pressed up against his chest. He wanted her to stay here in Pine Bluff. With him.

To his delight, she reclaimed her spot with a hum of pleasure. "I should be asking about what went on out there, but I don't want to," she said, her voice husky. "Not right now."

"We don't have to talk about it. Plenty of time to sort it all out later." He stroked her hair, tangling his fingers in the thick locks and combing them through to the ends. "How's your mother handling things?"

Marlee chuckled as she ran the tips of her fingers up

and down his spine. He curled himself around her, wanting to remain cocooned in the embrace as long as possible.

"She's handling things surprisingly well." She pressed her lips to the base of his throat, and he stilled. "I have a sneaking suspicion she's been waiting for the moment she could be in charge all along."

Snorting, he pressed a kiss to her temple. "I don't doubt it."

She gave his torso another squeeze but didn't relinquish her hold on him. They stood wrapped up in each other in the empty waiting area for several minutes. When they finally broke the silence, they spoke at once.

"Don't go—" he started, his voice low and urgent.

"I've been thinking—" she began.

They laughed, then separated enough to be able to look one another square in the eye. "You first," she said with a nod.

But he'd said all he wanted to say in those two words. He hadn't had a chance to think of a convincing argument beyond them. At least, not one good enough to put to a lawyer.

"No, you go ahead," he prompted. "What have you been thinking?"

"Well," she began, her voice tentative as her hold on his back slipped. "It occurred to me you have more options now. I mean, with Ivan gone, and the others." She ducked her head and cleared her throat. When she looked up at him again, she wore her overbright smile. It clashed with the sadness in her eyes. "You might go back to Atlanta. Maybe get your job back with the agency."

He searched those beautiful blue eyes for a clue as to what was going on behind them, but she wore her poker face. Her lawyer face. She gave nothing away. Then again, if she didn't want him, would she have thrown herself into his arms? Sure, they'd been partners of a sort, but if she were truly done with him, she could have sent him off with a handshake and a hearty, "Thanks for your help, Sheriff."

"I'm not going back to Atlanta." The rough rumble of his voice was unrecognizable to his own ears. "And I don't want you to either."

"You want to stay here?"

He nodded. "Yes. And I want you to stay here. I want you to *want* to stay here," he amended. "I want you to stay with me."

She beamed, and this time her sparkle shone brighter than the summer sun. "You do?"

"I want to stay here. It's nice knowing people's names, and I want them to know mine."

"Well, right now they think your name is Sheriff," she teased.

"That's not how it will be listed on the ballot this fall," he said gruffly. "I'm hoping by then, at least some of them will come to call me Ben."

"I'm sure they will."

Tangling his fingers in her hair, he tugged lightly to get her attention. "Listen, I understand how you've always wanted to get out of here, but I think things could be different than you expect. They are going to be different. Your dad isn't going to be up and at it anytime soon, and with Will—"

She nodded, her expression solemn. "Don't forget, Wendell's retiring and planning to run for a seat on the bench."

"You're needed here, Marlee. I need you here," he stated, laying it all out on the line. "Somehow, I've tripped all over my good intentions and fallen in love with you. Now, I'm going to show you what a selfish jerk I am and ask you to stay here with me. Stay here for me," he said, unable to erase the pleading note from his voice.

A peachy-pink blush tinged her cheeks. He took it as a good sign. Evidence that she approved of what she was hearing. When she tried to burrow back into his chest, he caught her chin and tipped it up so she could look him straight in the eye. "I love you, Marlee Masters."

"I've done nothing but stir up trouble since I came back to town."

"I noticed," he answered gruffly.

"Pine Bluff is a mess. Timber Masters is going to be a mess."

He nodded. "Yes to both messes."

"I shouldn't want any part of this," she argued.

The color in her cheeks deepened, and a surge of heat rushed through him as he realized her eyes were growing bright with unshed tears. "But you do. You want me."

"I do," she said softly.

Gathering her close once more, he fisted his fingers in her hair and planted a long, lingering kiss on her, bending her back to make sure she knew he meant it.

He broke the kiss, breathless. "Do you love me too?"

She gave a huff of a laugh, then kissed him again. "I can't believe you have to ask. I shared my onion rings with you."

"Say the words, Marlee. I need to hear them once. Then you can go on teasing me for the rest of your life."

Unwinding her arms from his waist, she wrapped them around his neck and pulled him down until their foreheads touched. "I love you, Ben Kinsella. And, because I don't want you to feel you have to ask for my love ever again, I plan to give you all the evidence of *that* you'll ever need."

* * * * *

[illegible]

A [illegible] blush tinged her cheeks. He took it as a good sign. [illegible] the [illegible] meeting. [illegible] or [illegible] in the eye. [illegible] Marise [illegible]

[illegible] he answered [illegible]

He nodded. "Yes, to both [illegible]"

* * *

RESCUED BY THE COLTON COWBOY

DEBORAH FLETCHER MELLO

To Carly Silver, the best editor in the whole wide world!

You pushing me out of my comfort zone has made my writing better.

Your patience with me has been affirming. One day, I'll get POV right!

You make me want to keep writing, and for that, I thank you!

Chapter One

Soledad de la Vega brushed her palms against the front of her bib apron, then reached around her waist to undo the ties that wrapped it around her body. As she pulled the twill garment over her head, she stole a quick glance at the smartwatch on her wrist. It was almost midnight and her stomach did a flip, as if the prosciutto and cheese she'd snacked on earlier might come back up.

Working in the bakery after closing rarely unnerved Soledad. Downtown Grave Gulch, Michigan—where her business, Dream Bakes, sat—had always felt safe and she had never given any thought to anyone trying to do her or any of her employees harm. Tonight, though, her anxiety was at an all-time high. She took a deep breath to still her nerves.

She wiped the last remnants of flour from the counter and covered the yeast rolls that needed to rise before going into the oven. She pushed the oversize tray of rolled dough into the center of the table. The morning crew would brush butter across the tops and dust them with sesame and caraway seeds before they baked. Her small staff would hold the bakery down until she returned, and for the first time since starting her own business, Soledad wasn't sure when that would be.

The night wasn't like her usual nights. She wasn't headed home to Melvin, her overweight tabby cat. There was no plan to finish the book on top of the stack that decorated the nightstand next to her bed, no cup of warm tea to soothe her to sleep. In less than an hour, she would be driving her best friend, Annie, to safety. The two had planned every detail of Annie's escape from her abusive husband, Gavin, and Soledad was only minutes from rendezvousing to whisk her and her baby girl, Lyra, away.

She looked at her watch a second time, then reached for the cell phone on the counter behind her. There was no message saying their plans had changed. Making one last sweep of the space to ensure all the ovens were off and the food was put away, she then shut off the lights, exited the building and headed to her car.

Minutes later, Soledad sat in the cul-de-sac near Annie's home with her car running and the headlights off. She had pulled past the driveway and was parked under a massive oak tree. The quiet neighborhood was one of the more prestigious in Grave Gulch, and both she and Annie knew that the security officer who patrolled the neighborhood wouldn't make his next round past the home until twelve thirty. Still, Soledad was praying steadily, every nerve and muscle in her petite body twitching with nervousness. She was scared, everything that could go wrong playing out in her head. Her biggest fear was that Gavin would wake before

Annie could sneak out of the house and their window of opportunity would be lost.

Soledad and Annie had met in high school, the two girls running together on the long-distance track team. They'd been polar opposites, Annie's blond pixie cut, blue eyes and fair skin contrasting starkly with Soledad's blue-black strands, black eyes and olive skin tone. Soledad had been bubbly and effervescent, one of the more popular girls, while Annie had been more reserved and studious. But the two had become fast friends, bonding over the sport, their obsession with boy bands and the soap opera *General Hospital.*

After graduation they'd gone on to Grave Gulch Community College together, Annie wanting to pursue a career in medicine and Soledad unsure of what she wanted to do. It had been Annie who'd encouraged her to turn her love for pastries and baked goods into a career. Annie had pushed her to pursue a degree in business management and Annie had been there with her the day she'd opened Dream Bakes.

Annie had become a nurse practitioner and was considering medical school and pediatric medicine when she'd met Gavin Stone. Gavin, a renowned plastic surgeon fifteen years her senior, had been handsome, charming and obsessed with Annie. So much so that Soledad had gotten a bad feeling about him from the start. He'd been jealous of their friendship, purposely distancing Annie from as many friends and family as he could manage. On their wedding day he'd told Soledad to tell her best friend goodbye, that things would change now that Annie was his. As if Annie were a fragile possession that he planned to tuck away in a drawer far from public view. Soledad had wanted to warn Annie but wasn't sure what to warn her about. And she'd been happy. So much so that Soledad hadn't wanted to do anything to spoil her day or put a damper on the future Annie had seen before her. Soledad had kept her concerns to herself, instead making sure Gavin knew that nothing and no one would ever break the bond the two women shared. No matter how hard he tried.

Gavin's abuse had started slowly, emotional at first and then turning physical. Annie had been made to quit her job at the hospital, Gavin controlling their finances. He told her what she could and could not do and who she could and could not see. He rarely allowed her out of his sight, and even when he was at the hospital working, he would call with regularity to ensure she was home, abiding by his lengthy list of rules. The name-calling had gone from the occasional nasty slur to spitting rages that left Annie in tears. Open-palmed slaps when she had tried to defend her position or said something he didn't like became closed-fist punches that had left her bruised and battered. And each time Gavin had hurt Annie, Soledad had been furious.

With haunting regularity, Annie had cried on Soledad's shoulders, the weight of her problems feeling like a boulder that neither woman could move. Frustration that there was nothing Soledad could say or do to distance Annie from the situation had been devastating. Soledad's suggestions to call the police and report him had fallen on deaf ears, Annie petrified that outside help would only make things worse. She'd been devastated when she'd discovered she was pregnant but had hoped the birth of their child would push Gavin to be a better man. Instead, he'd been furious that their first child together would be a girl when he only wanted a son. He'd proclaimed it Annie's fault, just another in a long list of wrongs he attributed to her.

Soledad's apartment and Dream Bakes had become Annie's sanctuary, the only places where she could run and hide when the abuse became too much. Gavin had tried only once to stall his wife's lifelong friendship with Soledad. It was one of the few times Annie had openly gone toe-to-toe with him, threatening to publicly expose him if he dared impede their bond. Soledad had stood arm in arm with her, ready to show him a world of hurt to protect her friend. Gavin had backed off, but not before leaving Annie with a black eye and bruised clavicle. But Annie had gone back to being a dutiful wife and Soledad had become her refuge. Too often, Soledad had been angry with the world, that Annie was unable to see herself free of the man, and she'd been riddled with guilt that there wasn't something more that she herself could do for her friend.

After the birth of Lyra, Annie had finally agreed to get out of her situation. Soledad knew that the first step was to take Annie as far from her husband as she could run. Therapy and support would follow, and Soledad had put everything in place to ensure as smooth a transition for Annie as she could muster.

Together, they had dedicated weeks to planning each step, considering every fathomable possibility until every detail of Annie's escape plan was committed to memory. Once Annie and the baby were safe inside her Toyota Camry, Soledad would drive them both upstate to a shelter for battered women. The drive would take a few hours and put them at the front door. From there, mother and child would be escorted to their new home and Soledad would be sent on her way to worry about her friend from afar. Cell phones were prohibited, but Annie would be able to call Soledad weekly from a private line in her counselor's office.

Soledad couldn't know her friend's final destination and Annie would be forbidden to disclose her whereabouts, lest she put other sheltered women in danger. Telling anyone of her whereabouts would get Annie evicted from the shelter and the program's many protections. But more important, Gavin wouldn't be able to find her until Annie was ready to be found.

Soledad tapped her hand nervously against her leg, her anxiety beginning to reach peak levels. Annie was ten minutes late. Soledad was tempted to sneak up to the home to peek into the windows, but she didn't want to risk setting off the sensor lights Gavin had installed around the property. They didn't have much time before the security car would make its regularly scheduled drive-by. But there had been contingencies for that, too. Soledad just prayed they wouldn't be necessary.

Panic was just about to set in when the rear passenger door of her car was thrown open and Annie slid inside. She carried little Lyra against her chest and had a designer baby backpack hoisted over her shoulder. She looked like Soledad felt. Scared!

"Drive!" Annie ordered as she slammed the door closed. "Go! Now! Drive!"

Soledad shifted the vehicle into gear and pulled from the makeshift parking space onto the cul-de-sac. Behind her, the Stone family home was suddenly awash with light, looking as if every bulb in every room had come to life. Instinctively knowing that wasn't a good thing, Soledad turned her eyes to the road, hit the gas and peeled off as if someone were already chasing them.

"WE'RE GOING TO stay off the main road until we get into the next county," Soledad said, glancing into her rearview mirror to the back seat. "Hopefully, Gavin will get lost trying to figure out what direction we're headed."

Tears were streaming down Annie's face. It was one of the few times her friend had allowed her vulnerability to show. She looked lost and frightened.

Annie shook her head. "He's going to find us," she whispered.

"He's not," Soledad said firmly. "We won't let him. Did you toss your cell phone?"

Annie nodded. "I left it in the dog food bag."

"Then we're good. Because I wouldn't put it past him to have some sort of tracking device installed to keep up with you. In thirty minutes, we'll be far enough away that there'll be no way he can find you."

Annie forced the slightest smile to her face, but Soledad knew her dear friend wasn't as confident.

Soledad shifted her gaze back and forth between her side mirrors, her rearview mirror, the back seat and the road. Annie had drifted into thought, nuzzling six-month-old Lyra gently beneath her chin, her arms wrapped protectively around the infant. The little girl was wrapped snugly in a cotton blanket, completely oblivious to the lengths her mother and Soledad would go to keep her safe. It was bliss, and Soledad wished she could be so lucky to know that kind of peace and be as unaware.

Annie eased the baby into the infant safety seat, latching it securely around the tiny body before tightening her own seat belt.

They drove in silence for a good little while. The local radio station was playing Shy Carter's newest release. Soledad bobbed her head in time to the beat, singing along with the song that had risen swiftly to the top of the country charts. The service roads were dark, lights nonexistent. Barely a sliver of moonlight peeked through the cover of clouds. It had also begun to drizzle, the threat of heavy rain preceded by a trickle of moisture that was most annoying. And the rising fog was getting thicker with each passing minute.

Annie broke the moment of reverie, her usually poised tone a loud whisper that rippled with tension. "I need you to make me a promise, Soledad."

"Anything. You know that," Soledad responded, shooting her friend a quick glance in the rearview mirror.

"If anything happens to me, I want you to promise

that you'll take care of Lyra. I need you to keep my baby girl safe."

Soledad raised her brows. "Don't talk like that, Annie. Everything is going to be fine. You're going to—"

Annie interrupted her, her voice rising ever so slightly. "Promise me, Soledad. I need you to promise!" Annie's stoic expression was disconcerting, the determination in her eyes feeling almost final.

She nodded. "Whatever you need. You know that!" And Soledad meant that with every fiber of her being as the words slipped past her lips. Soledad understood the fear that gripped her bestie because it rippled down the length of her own spine. It felt corporeal, a thick, viscous energy with the stench of doubt and anger wrapped around it. Stepping into the unknown came with its own set of consequences and proved formidable when you had to worry about someone other than yourself. Annie had her daughter, and fearing for herself was nothing compared to fearing for her child. Soledad was scared for them all.

"I need you to make sure nothing happens to Lyra. That she grows up to be a happy, healthy little girl and a confident young woman. I need you to make sure Gavin doesn't ever get his hands on her. So, please, promise me. I need you to say it!"

"I promise, Annie. I would never let anything happen to Lyra. I'd protect her with my own life!"

"Good," her friend said. "Because I went to see my attorney this week. I left a letter with him to be opened if something happens to me. It details all of Gavin's abuses and points at him if I'm killed. It also names you as Lyra's legal guardian. I've left you two insurance policies, also. One that should be put into trust for Lyra's care. I imagine you'll have to use the other to fight Gavin if he tries to take Lyra from you. It should be more than enough for legal fees or whatever else you might need."

Soledad rolled her eyes skyward to help defuse the tension. "First, please stop being morbid. Things will never get to that point. Nothing is going to happen to you. And, second, you need to stop worrying. I will never let anything happen to my goddaughter. I promised you that, and I will keep that promise."

Annie seemed to breathe a sigh of relief as she gave Soledad a nod. Her eyes shifted to stare out the window at the rain that had started to drop heavily. Another quiet moment passed as Soledad slowed her speed, fighting to see the road that lay ahead of them.

"What happened back at the house?" Soledad asked, her voice rippling through the silence like a pebble skipping across a quiet pond of water.

Annie took a deep breath. Lyra had begun to stir, the faintest squeak rising to a crescendo wail. "She's hungry," her mother muttered softly.

Soledad eyed them in the mirror as Annie lifted the baby from the car seat and undid the top buttons of her blouse. She discreetly covered herself with a blanket as Lyra latched on to her breast to nurse.

"I think he knew," Annie finally said. She shifted her body around to extend her legs so that baby Lyra rested comfortably against her chest. "He'd been ranting all evening about what he would do if I ever thought about leaving him again. He said he had two bullets with my name on them. He said he'd make sure Lyra never knew who I was. That he'd find her a new mother."

"Did you put the sleeping pills in his coffee?"

Annie nodded. "Just like we planned. I made his regular cup after dinner, like I always do. But he barely drank it. When I cleared the dishes away, his cup was still half-full. He was drinking bourbon instead, and you know he rarely drinks. I thought the alcohol affected him harder than I realized, because he fell asleep sooner than I anticipated. I figured he was just drunk enough that he'd be out of it long enough for me to stick to the plan. Once he was snoring, I threw on my clothes, grabbed the diaper bag and Lyra, and sneaked out of the house. But just as I disengaged the house alarm, he was screaming my name. I just ran!"

Soledad realized Annie was crying again, her tears falling on the blanket wrapped around the baby. Annie had tried leaving Gavin once, before Lyra had been born. She'd packed her things and had gone to her mother's, determined to make a go of it without the husband who had promised her the world. Gavin had been relentless in his efforts to get her back. There had been promises of being a better man and trying harder. Assurances they would go to counseling to resolve the problems in their marriage. Every pronouncement had included some lavish gift: huge bouquets of Annie's favorite white roses, gold and diamond baubles, and an excursion to Paris to profess his love. Promises that had held no weight once Annie had given in and gone back to him, every pledge a well-tuned lie.

Despite Soledad's admonishments for Annie to not trust Gavin, nothing she said could convince her friend the good doctor wasn't good at all. Annie desperately wanted to believe him, and Soledad's frustration with the situation increased tenfold. That frustration had been so tangible that Soledad had actually feared the potential demise of their friendship.

Weeks after their reconciliation, Annie discovered she was pregnant. Eight months into her pregnancy, she'd walked in on Gavin and one of his many mistresses in their marital bed. Lyra came days later, and it was as if a perfect storm had converged on her best friend's life. Postpartum depression, a colicky baby and Gavin's emotional battering had left Annie bruised and broken. When Soledad had stepped in with a game plan, pleading with her bestie to choose herself and her daughter, Annie hadn't hesitated. Now here they were, both women questioning if they'd be able to see those plans to fruition. Neither wanting to voice their concerns aloud.

Because Soledad had concerns, starting with the headlights that had been following them for the last few miles. She'd chosen this road because traffic was minimal at that hour. The vehicle behind her tonight, though, seemed to mimic her moves—slowing when she slowed, speeding when she sped. She didn't recognize the vehicle, the car looking like a late-model sedan, a Cadillac, maybe even an Audi, and she was fairly certain it wasn't Gavin. But fairly certain wasn't certain enough. Under any other circumstances, she wouldn't have given it a second thought. However, she knew what they were up against, and whoever followed behind them had her suddenly feeling anxious. Then, almost as if she'd spoken out loud, the distant lights disappeared from her view.

A WAVE OF relief flooded Soledad. Outside, the rain had finally stopped. Lyra had drifted back to sleep and her mother was no longer shaking. They had only been driving some thirty minutes, but it felt like hours had passed.

"We'll be out of the county in a few minutes," Soledad said. "Now that the rain isn't coming down in buckets, I can pick up the speed."

"Don't get another ticket, Soledad."

Soledad joked, "I like my bad driver certificates."

"Well, the state is going to like taking away your license if they have to give you another."

The two women laughed, seeming to relax for the first time since their night had started. The local radio station was digging through its oldie-but-goodie song box, playing Rissi Palmer's popular "Country Girl." By the second verse, they both were singing loudly together, the baby lulled back to sleep by their voices.

For the briefest moment, it felt like old times, lost in a good time. For a split second, Soledad had not a care in the world, letting herself forget why they were traveling in the middle of the night, fleeing from a past that threatened a joyous future. Laughter rang warmly through the space. Then, just like that, their moment was stolen from them.

Chapter Two

The oversize SUV came from out of nowhere, its high beams shining into the back window of the Toyota. The intensity of light was glaring. Soledad depressed her brake, blinded by the onslaught of brightness reflecting off the rearview mirror and into her eyes. When the vehicle behind them slammed into the back of her car, she felt the steering wheel jerk out of her hands as the Camry spun out of control on the wet road. Soledad felt her stomach pitch with fright as she wrestled for control of the steering wheel. She wanted to scream, panic washing over her like a tidal wave, but no sound escaped her lips. Everything inside the car tossed from one side to the other and back again. Annie cried out loudly and the baby began to whimper. The moment was surreal and Soledad held her breath waiting for it to be over.

Gunshots suddenly shattered the rear window. She would never know which shot struck Annie, just that she heard her best friend scream a second time, the harsh sound cut off abruptly and replaced by Lyra's pitiful wail. Even as it was happening, all she could think of was getting them away, needing to protect Annie and Lyra from the danger on their heels. Never in her wildest dreams could she have imagined that she wouldn't be able to do that. Panic gave way to determination. Glancing at her side mirror, Soledad saw Gavin exit his vehicle, advancing on them, his gun raised.

Without a second thought, Soledad threw the car into Reverse and gunned the engine. She knocked him off his feet, then shifted the car into Drive, determined to put as much distance between them as she could muster.

Another round of shots rang out as she pulled away and the engine sputtered and stalled. The Camry rolled off the side of the road, heading for the tree line before slamming into a tall pine and coming to a full stop. Soledad's survival instincts kicked into high gear, her reflexes shifting into overdrive. Stealing another glance behind her, Soledad watched as the man on the ground struggled to get onto his feet, falling on his back as he fought to catch his breath.

"We're going to have to run," Soledad said, turning to eye her friend. But Annie never heard her.

The moment felt like forever as realization settled over her. Soledad felt as if time had come to a standstill, everything spinning in slow motion. Annie was slumped forward, blood streaming down the side of her face. One hand lay protectively over the baby, the cotton blanket clutched tightly between her fingers. Soledad scrambled out of the car and flung the back door open. She muttered her friend's name over and over again, the mantra a loud, pitiful whisper.

"Annie, Annie, Annie, Annie, Annie!" she cried, tears streaming down her face. But Annie was gone, having taken her last breath. Her eyes were open, but the light that had shimmered in the oceanic orbs was gone. "Oh, Annie!" Soledad wailed, her fingers pressed to the dead woman's cheek. She could never have previously imagined the level of hurt that suddenly consumed her now, every ounce of it slicing through her heart like a hot knife through butter. It flooded every vein and blood vessel in her body, like a virus gone awry. She had failed her best friend and she would never again be able to make it right between them. Soledad stifled a sob.

Knowing she had no time to grieve her loss, Soledad snatched the ergonomic baby carrier from the car's floor and wrapped it around her torso. She reached to lift the baby from the car seat and settled the child against her chest.

Gavin's deep baritone suddenly rang out in the darkness. From the corner of her eye, Soledad could see that he'd finally made it onto his feet. His legs were still shaky, but he was snarling like a wounded animal as he stumbled in her direction.

A single gunshot whizzed by Soledad's head, barely missing her as she held tightly to little Lyra. Gavin fired a second and a third shot in her direction, loudly bellowing each time he pulled the trigger. Grabbing the diaper bag, Soledad paused for the briefest moment to squeeze her best friend's hand one last time. Then she took off running into the trees, knowing their lives depended on it.

Behind her, Gavin was still shouting profanities. His rage filled the late-night darkness, haunting the stillness of the cool air. He screamed, his voice eventually fading with each step Soledad put between them. But his final words sent a chill up her spine.

"I'll find you, Soledad! I will find you, and when I do, I'm going to kill you!"

SOLEDAD KNEW ENOUGH from her days as a junior Scout that she was headed north. Beyond that, she didn't have a clue where she was going, but desperation and terror kept her moving forward. Her heart was beating rapidly, feeling like it might burst from her chest, and she sucked in air as if it were her last breath. Tears rained from her eyes and her whole body shook with disbelief and sadness. She felt alone and scared and angry that Gavin had not only taken her best friend from her, but he now had her literally running for her life.

The clouds had cleared, and the stars were shining brightly. The boundary of thick trees began to fade, leading to an open clearing that seemed to go on for miles. With the full moon overhead, there was just enough light that she knew she'd reached farmland.

She slowed her pace, still cradling the baby closely to her. Surprisingly, the steady rhythm of her running had apparently lulled Lyra back to sleep. The infant was out like a light, oblivious to the fact that her whole world had just been ripped to shreds. She would never know her beloved mother, save the stories Soledad would one day share with her. And she'd be sure to also tell her about how Annie could sleep through a storm and never flinch, too.

She couldn't help but wonder what she would tell Lyra about her father. She only hoped that when that time came, Gavin was six feet under or doing a life sentence with no possibility of parole.

Soledad pulled her rain jacket closed, zipping it around herself and her goddaughter. The temperature had dropped considerably with the storm, and the chill in the air felt bone deep. Soledad knew she needed to find refuge to protect Lyra, and herself, from the late-night elements. Off in the distance, Soledad noticed a light—and a light could mean shelter. She snuggled Lyra one last time, took a deep inhalation of air and began a slow jog toward help, praying that assistance would be available when she got them there.

PALMER COLTON SLIPPED his size-twelve feet into his favorite pair of rubber boots, the well-worn footwear years old and as comfortable as walking on air. The storm had finally passed, the downpour gone as quickly as it had risen. He had to make one last check on the animals, most especially Pharaoh, the young Arabian he'd recently acquired. He had purchased the horse to show, Pharaoh's versatility and intelligence making him a natural at a variety of equine sports. Palmer had seen a bright future for the animal, and then Pharaoh had been diagnosed with a case of equine flu, a contagious viral infection. The colt had been quarantined, and Palmer imagined that between the move and now being ill, Pharaoh might be having some difficulty adjusting. He hoped a kind voice and gentle hand would ease the animal's transition to his new home.

Jack, his Bernese mountain dog, suddenly nuzzled his palm and barked.

"What?" Palmer chuckled. "Am I not moving fast enough for you?"

The dog barked a second time.

"Okay, okay. I'm coming!" Palmer said as he stood upright and reached for his jacket.

Jack spun in a circle, his tail wagging excitedly.

Outside there was a distinct chill in the air, the evening temperature feeling more like fall and winter instead of the middle of the summer. There was a full moon, and even in the darkness, Palmer could see farther across the vast expanse of fields than usual.

Jack took off behind the large farmhouse, running at warp speed toward the line of trees that bordered the property. Palmer stared after him, thinking he saw something move in the distance. It was the briefest blip in the dark before it faded into the wave of shadows that danced over the landscape. More than likely a family of white-tailed deer roaming across the land, he thought.

Palmer walked to the barn, turned on the lights. Inside, he moved to the stall where Pharaoh stood, his head hanging just slightly over the stall door. He neighed when Palmer approached and ran his palm down the Arabian's arched neck.

"Hey, big guy. Are you feeling any better?" Palmer said as he stepped inside the stall to give the colt a quick once-over. His nose was running, but the discharge had thinned considerably since his diagnosis. His breathing was only slightly labored, and he had a sporadic cough, his body's natural reflex to the inflammation in his airway. The infection was viral, so there was little that Palmer could do other than keep the animal comfortable and let him get plenty of rest. The vet was scheduled to come back to check on him, so until then, it was a waiting game.

Palmer adjusted the gray blanket he'd thrown over the horse's broad back the night before. "You're going to be just fine," he said, stepping out and securing the stall door behind him.

Pharaoh whinnied again as if in agreement.

A noise at the barn doors suddenly pulled at Palmer's attention. Jack stood there, panting softly.

"Why do you look like trouble?" Palmer questioned, patting Jack's head as the dog moved to his side and lay at his feet.

A bolt of lightning suddenly rippled across the night sky. The rain had returned, beginning to fall steadily. Storms rarely bothered Palmer, but something about the change in the air felt ominous. Things didn't feel right, and he couldn't begin to put his finger on it. Something was coming, but he didn't know what the premonition meant.

"Jack, head to the house," Palmer said, pointing his index finger.

Jack jumped and bolted out the door, heading for the home's back porch. Palmer gave the horse one last pat, wished him a good night and then followed his four-legged friend.

FEAR RIPPLED DEEP in Soledad's midsection as she paused. She came to an abrupt stop when she encountered the family of deer standing still, her presence having interrupted their midnight meal. She hadn't stopped to consider the wild animals that might be in her path as she fled. In fact, there was little she was able to focus on—other than putting distance between them and Gavin. The sounds that emerged from the darkness suddenly felt like a horror movie waiting to write itself.

The dog, though, had been unexpected, a large furry bear of an animal with a tail that wagged nonstop and a tongue that hung lopsidedly out of its mouth. It had come barreling at her, and Soledad had stood defensively, ready to kick if it lunged. Her arms were wrapped protectively around the baby and the carrier, her stance defiant as she presented Fido with her side and back.

The dog had run around her twice, then sat, panting softly, its head cocked to the side as it stared at her. Soledad wasn't sure whether to step or not, but when the large bundle of fur didn't growl or attack, she kept nudging forward, talking to it as it moved in step with her.

"You must be the welcoming committee," she said sarcastically. "I hope your humans are just as kind."

Its tail wagged briskly.

"Do you have a name?" Soledad asked, the question coming as if the animal might actually answer.

The dog suddenly bolted in the direction they'd just

come from. Soledad turned to look where it ran but couldn't see.

Lyra suddenly stirred against her chest and Soledad patted her back gently. "We had company, Lyra," she whispered loudly to the little girl. "I'm not sure where it's run off to," she said. "But you just go back to sleep, baby girl."

Lightning suddenly lit up the dark sky and rain began to fall again slowly. Soledad cursed. "Damn it!" she said as she tucked the blanket and her jacket closer around the baby's body. "I need to find us some shelter before we both catch pneumonia out here in this weather. Or your father catches up to us and keeps his promise to kill me." She began to jog again, the light in the distance much closer. Then, above their heads, the sky opened with a vengeance.

Minutes later, Soledad passed a stone wall that bordered a small garden. She picked up her pace until she reached a large barn. There was a farmhouse a short distance away, but not a single light shone through the windows. From what she could tell in the darkness, the outside of the barn was weathered, reminding her of the old tobacco outbuildings found in the Carolinas. It was rustic and aged, and looked aptly dry.

This will work, Soledad thought. At least until someone found them there. She only hoped whoever that might be would be a friend, and definitely not Gavin. Worst-case scenario, she mused, they would call the police and have her arrested. Best case, she'd be able to get a few minutes of rest so that she could think about what to do next.

Soledad eased the barn door open and slipped inside. Toward the rear of the structure, a single bulb burned from the ceiling, emitting just enough light to hold the darkness at bay. Bales of hay lined one wall, facing four empty stalls. A large black horse stood in the fifth stall, seeming to eye her warily.

"Sorry to be trespassing," Soledad muttered. "But it's an emergency." She wanted to reach out a hand to stroke the horse's neck, but she didn't know the animal and it didn't know her. She also sensed that it might not be well.

She felt like she'd struck gold when she discovered a wooden cabinet filled with blankets, thick and heavy wool coverings to wrap herself and the baby in. She took off her rain jacket and flung one around her shoulders. The baby was still sleeping as if there were nothing in the world for her to worry over, and Soledad was grateful for that small blessing. Preparing a makeshift pallet, she laid Lyra down, ensuring the child wouldn't roll away and hurt herself. She searched the diaper bag and found clean clothes and diapers, as well as a copy of the little girl's birth certificate and other documents Annie had labeled important, and a stack of unopened mail.

Soledad could have kicked herself for not grabbing her cell phone and purse, both now lost in the wreckage of her car. Not that there was anyone she would call under the circumstances. No one she dared put at risk. She'd been thinking about the police, but something told her there was nothing they could do to protect her and Lyra from Gavin. He was intent on doing them harm, and while the law investigated his crimes, he'd be committing just as many more. She wasn't interested in being a casualty of his transgressions. She was safer, she thought, figuring out her next moves on her own, hidden away where Gavin couldn't find her.

But in that moment, she truly wasn't sure she could think straight. The adrenaline that had been fueling her steps had dissipated like air from a popped balloon. She could feel her body beginning to fail her, her eyes wanting to close, sleep anxious to claim her. Her legs had begun to tighten, the muscles fatigued. Her feet hurt; the canvas-bottomed sneakers were not the best running shoes. It was becoming harder to focus and her head hurt, pain throbbing like a drum line behind her eyes.

Soledad leaned back against the bale of hay and pulled at the blanket covering her. Then she saw the blood that saturated her T-shirt and realized for the first time that she'd been shot. She gasped as sanguine fluid gushed over her fingers. That adrenaline had kept the pain at bay, but suddenly it hurt like hell, bringing tears to her eyes. Rising, Soledad went back to the cabinet to grab a roll of gray duct tape from inside it. Back behind the hay bale, she took one of the clean diapers and pressed it tight against the wound. To keep the pressure on, she tightly wrapped the tape around the diaper pressed to her waist and a second against her back where the bullet had made its exit.

Soledad suddenly wanted to cry. Her entire body felt like she'd been hit by a bus and her heart was shredded over the loss of Annie. She patted the baby against her back as she struggled not to sob. She wanted to scream and pull her hair, but she couldn't. She could hear Annie in her ear, reminding her that she had more important things to consider and her pity party would have to wait for another day.

Things weren't looking good and she needed to get herself and Lyra out of the mess she'd dropped into. Trespassing on private property wasn't going to help her situation and keeping Lyra safe would take more than running from the problems she was facing. She needed a plan, but one wasn't coming easily through her fatigue. With a heavy sigh, she pulled the blanket up and around her shoulders. Leaning her head close to Lyra's tiny body, Soledad closed her eyes.

JACK PAWED AT Palmer's leg. He ran in a small circle beside the bed, his exuberance at an all-time high for the late hour. It was close to three o'clock in the morning and not like the animal to be wide-awake and so perky. Palmer opened one eye to stare at the dog. Jack barked and jumped up to paw at him a second time.

"What, Jack? Go to sleep. It's late." He rolled onto his side, his back to the dog.

Jack barked again and ran to the door.

Palmer sighed and rolled to the other side of the bed. He threw his body upward and swung his legs off the side of the mattress. "You've been out all night, Jack. You were acting strange then. What's going on with you, dog?"

Moving down the hall to the front foyer, Palmer slid on his boots. He swung open the front door and took a look out into the dark night. Outside felt like it had dropped another ten degrees, the temperatures clearly out of sync for the time of year. He reached for a jacket and slipped it on. Instinctively, Palmer knew something was amiss as Jack barreled toward the barn, his determination to get inside warning that something wasn't right. Palmer moved down the short flight of steps and followed Jack, suddenly worried that something might be wrong with Pharaoh.

Opening the large doors and stepping inside, Palmer paused to listen, his eyes skating back and forth across the space. Jack sniffed the floor, his tail wagging excitedly, and that was when Palmer noticed the dark spots that trailed across the barn floor. He knelt to take a closer look and saw that it looked like fresh blood. Jack rushed to the back side of the hay bales, but Pharaoh wasn't making a sound, his hindquarters frozen as if he were ready to lurch at something.

Palmer slowly eased toward a corner cabinet and the rifle he kept stashed there for emergencies. He pulled the weapon from inside and slid the bolt back to ensure there was still a round in the chamber. If it were an animal bleeding out, it might feel threatened and attack, so he wasn't going to take any chances. But Jack had taken a seat, seeming unnerved by whatever it was he was staring at.

Easing behind the dog, the barrel of his rifle lifted just in case, Palmer peered around the side of the haystack. His eyes widened in surprise as he was filled with shock and blinked to make sure he wasn't dreaming. Recognition hit him like a sledgehammer slammed against concrete. Palmer knew the woman huddled in the corner of his barn. He knew her and her family. Jack suddenly barked and lunged forward, waking Soledad de la Vega—who was for some reason slumbering peacefully in his barn.

SOLEDAD'S EYES SHOT OPEN, startled from the beginnings of a deep sleep. The dog from earlier was licking her face and sniffing at the wound on her side. He jostled against her, his exuberance palpable, before shifting his attention to Lyra, who'd started to whimper softly.

Instinctively, Soledad pushed to her knees, shooed the animal back and slid her body between the two. The gesture was protective as she threw her arm across the baby's body. Her eyes rose to the handsome man who was staring at her. Shock and awe painted his expression, his eyes wide and his jaw slack.

Soledad was still groggy as she assessed the man and the way he was staring at her. She'd been praying for someone to find them, and now that someone had, she wasn't sure it was a good thing. She realized he might call the police, and she found herself questioning if that was really a good idea.

"You're bleeding," he suddenly said.

She nodded. "I've been shot."

The man took a step forward, his brow furrowing with concern. "Shot?"

"And my best friend was killed," Soledad continued. Her story came quickly. She talked softly and fast, her words emanating from a deep breath that she seemed to be holding in her lungs. They surged like a tidal wave hitting a shoreline, spewing into the late-night air with a vengeance. And when she finished, tears had begun to rain from her eyes, falling against her cheeks. Catching herself, Soledad wiped her eyes with the back of her hand.

"We need to call the police," he said.

Soledad shook her head vehemently. "Please, don't. Don't call the police. I'm begging you!"

"You can't just bleed out in my barn," he said, his tone matter-of-fact. "I could call for a doctor."

"It's a flesh wound. I'll be fine."

"How do you know that? Do you get shot often?" Palmer questioned, a hint of snark in his tone.

"I just know," she replied, not amused. "And you can't call the law. Not until I've figured out what I'm going to do—please!" Soledad pleaded. "Because if her father finds us, he will kill me, and I don't know what will happen to Annie's baby. Please."

Soledad lifted Lyra into her arms and hugged the now awakened little girl close. The baby stared up at Soledad and then in the direction of the man. Her attention dropped to the dog, who was gently nuzzling her little foot. She suddenly laughed, stretching her fingers toward the animal who licked them eagerly.

"Her name's Lyra," Soledad said as she rose. "And I'm Soledad. Soledad de la Vega."

"I know," the man responded. "I'm Palmer. Palmer Colton." He gestured at the dog. "And that's Jack."

Soledad's eyes narrowed ever so slightly. "Colton? Are you related to Stanton Colton?"

"He's my cousin. Our fathers are brothers. He's engaged to your sister."

"Dominique, my twin," she said with a nod of her head.

"We were both at their engagement party last week. You probably don't remember me."

Soledad's eyes skated from side to side as she thought back to that party, remembering her sister's joy. It had been a good time.

Recall suddenly came swiftly and she nodded again. "I do remember you," she said, looking up to meet Palmer's stare. He'd been the most handsome man in a room full of good-looking men. His silk suit had fit him well, despite his apparent dislike of the necktie that he'd kept pulling at awkwardly. There had been a failing effort to tame his tousled blond hair and she'd thought the barest hint of a beard had been sexy as hell. He'd been kind, and polite, and very much a gentleman. The kind of man grandmothers adored and mothers wanted you to marry.

He'd had an intensity about him that had made him quite popular with many of the women. Every single female hedging her bets for a husband had chased him, but it had been obvious to anyone paying an ounce of attention that he wasn't interested in being caught. And Soledad had been paying attention.

She thought back to how she had caught him watching her intently but hadn't made any effort to speak to her. The intensity in his emerald green eyes had been heated. They'd crossed paths a few times that night, but had ignored each other, barely bothering to exchange warm hellos. The little conversation they had shared had been casually polite at best. Each pretending not to notice the other, despite eyeing one another keenly. Heat suddenly flushed her face and warmed her cheeks.

"We need to move you to the house," Palmer said, changing the subject. "I should check out that wound and get you bandaged up properly."

"But you won't call the police, right? If you do, I'll have to leave." There was a hint of attitude in her tone. Just enough to let him know that she meant what she said—that she would not be moved from her decision.

Palmer stared at her, seemingly contemplating how he would make that call without her knowing. How the smart thing for them both to do would be to involve law enforcement if someone was truly intent on harming her. She had been shot, for goodness' sake.

He shook his head. "I won't tell them you're here," he finally said, "but we need to report the accident so they can at least find your friend's body and start investigating the case."

Soledad took a deep breath. She was just about to respond when they heard a car rumble up the length of road that led to the house.

"Are you expecting someone?" Soledad asked.

"No," Palmer answered. "Not at this time of night."

Soledad took a step back, moving into the shadows, out of sight.

"Stay here," Palmer said. "I'll see who it is."

Soledad nodded and cradled the gurgling baby

closer. As Palmer moved to the door, Jack on his heels, she called after him.

"Yes?"

"Thank you," she whispered loudly. "Thank you."

Chapter Three

Palmer peeked out the barn door, watching a man standing outside a black SUV and looking toward the house. He appeared disheveled, as if he'd been run over by a bus. His hands rested on his hips and he was leaning to one side as if his knee or leg hurt.

The man closed his suit jacket, trying to neaten his clothes. Even though it was pitch-black out, save the glow of lights from the house, he pulled a pair of sunglasses from his pocket and put them on his face. He was heading for the home's front porch when Palmer exited the barn, still holding tight to his rifle.

"Can I help you?" he asked, eyeing the man suspiciously.

"My apology for the intrusion, Mr....?"

Palmer didn't bother to acknowledge the question. "This is private property. So I'll ask again—can I help you?"

The intruder bristled, posturing ever so slightly. He reached into his breast pocket and flashed what appeared to be an ID card in Palmer's direction. In the dark, the gesture was more for show than anything else.

Palmer dismissed it as he continued, "My name is Detective Gavin Stone. I'm with the Grave Gulch Police Department. We're looking for a murder suspect. A woman named Soledad de la Vega. We believe she's here in the area and she may have an infant with her."

Palmer recoiled. It didn't take a brain surgeon to know that this was the man Soledad was running from. Him saying her name as he clearly lied had Palmer suddenly on edge. His posture stiffened and he tightened his grip on the rifle. "It's kind of late to be going door to door searching for someone, isn't it?"

Gavin took a deep breath. "We had a tip that she was seen in the neighborhood and we wanted people to be aware that she is armed and dangerous. Fortunately, there aren't a lot of private homes out this far, so I won't be disturbing too many people at this hour."

"Who'd this woman kill?" Palmer questioned.

Gavin's gaze narrowed. He shook his head. "I'm not at liberty to say. Have you seen anyone strange in the area tonight?"

Palmer shook his head. "Just you. There's been no woman here. If there had been, either I or one of the men who works for me would have seen her. We don't usually get a lot of random strangers out this way."

"Are you usually up at this late hour?" Gavin eyed him curiously.

"No. One of my horses is ailing. I came out to check on him."

"There in your barn?" Gavin asked, taking a step in that direction.

Palmer took his own step, blocking the man's way. "Detective Stone, is it?"

"Yes, that's right."

"I haven't seen anyone wandering out here on my property. And definitely not a woman with a baby. But if I do, I will reach out to the police department." But it was more likely he'd call one of his family members at the GGPD to check out Gavin Stone, Palmer thought to himself.

"I'll need to search your barn. In case she may be hiding there." Gavin's pronouncement came with such conviction that Palmer felt himself bristle with indignation. His muscles tensed and his grip tightened around the rifle.

A pregnant pause rose full and thick between them. Unspoken words danced harshly through the late-night air. Both men clearly had things they wanted to say, but neither spoke, waiting to see who would jump first. Palmer suddenly stepped aside and gestured with his free hand. He had learned early in life that the best defense was a good offense, so he was willing to call the man's bluff, knowing he'd never get past his guard dog.

"Help yourself."

Gavin made it as far as the barn door. Jack sat in the entrance, and as Gavin approached, the dog snarled and then snapped.

"Nice doggy!" Gavin said, extending a nervous hand.

Jack growled a second time, his bark threatening.

"He doesn't do well with strangers," Palmer said.

"So, like I told you, it's doubtful any woman with a baby is hiding out anywhere around here."

Gavin took two steps back. He gave Jack one last look and headed slowly toward his SUV.

"If I see this woman, I'll be sure to dial 9-1-1 and get the Grave Gulch police right on out here," Palmer said, working to keep his expression stoic.

Gavin nodded. "I appreciate your time," he said as he slid back into the driver's seat and started the engine. He reversed onto the grass, then pulled forward to head back in the direction from which he'd come. As he pulled off, there was no missing the damage to the front end of his vehicle.

Palmer stood watching until the stranger was out of sight, his taillights disappearing in the distance. A good few minutes passed before he moved. Whoever that man was, he wasn't with the Grave Gulch Police Department. With so much of Palmer's family in law enforcement, there wasn't an officer with the department that he didn't know personally—and there was certainly no Detective Stone. The stranger had lied too easily. Obviously focused on finding Soledad, his intentions had clearly not been in her best interest, just like Soledad had told him.

When Palmer had first laid eyes on her, there had been sheer terror on her face. She'd been petrified and her fear had gleamed from her eyes in a way that tugged at his heartstrings. Despite the story she had told him, he couldn't begin to imagine everything she and her friend had gone through. But he was determined that she would not have to endure any more hurt if he had anything to do with it. He'd initially seen her plea to not involve the police as irrational. And, realistically, it was. But he now had better understanding and her request was making far more sense to him. He blew a loud sigh and turned back toward the barn.

SOLEDAD WAS SHIVERING, fright overriding the cold. The entire time Palmer had stood outside the barn with Gavin, she'd been scared to death Gavin would find her. The conversation between the two men had seemed tense. Wanting to see what was going on, she'd scaled a ladder to the barn's loft, peering out an upper window.

She'd quickly discovered that keeping herself hidden and Lyra quiet was a bigger challenge than she'd anticipated. The baby had been anxious for attention and gurgled constantly. She was a chatterbox without the words to explain herself, but didn't let it slow her down. Soledad had pulled out every trick she knew to keep Lyra quiet, grateful that the little girl was not a crier. It had been nerve-racking at best, to say nothing of the fact that Soledad felt horrible to be putting her through such turmoil to begin with.

She was climbing back down the wooden ladder when Palmer reentered the barn. She noted the quizzical look on his face as he watched her ease down to the main floor, so she gave him the faintest smile.

"We need to move you and the baby to the main house," he said.

"What did Gavin say?"

"Are you certain that was your friend's husband?"

Soledad nodded.

"He asked a lot of questions. Something tells me he didn't get the answers he was hoping for, so he may come back. Then again, he might not. We just need to make sure we're ready if he does. For the time being, though, we need to take care of that wound and then try to figure out what's next."

"I really could use a shower," Soledad said. "And this bundle of joy—" she kissed Lyra's cheek "—needs a diaper change and a bottle."

Palmer nodded. "If it were daylight, I'd probably hide you away in the horse trailer and drive you to the back of the house, so no one sees you."

Soledad shrugged as she considered his comment. She was grateful for his help because he didn't have to be bothered. "Do you think anyone is up this time of the night who might see me?"

He shook his head. "No, and I'm fairly sure your friend is gone. But I'm going to shut down the lights to the house just to be sure. Jack will also give us a heads-up if anyone is out there. Just walk straight ahead. There should be enough moonlight for you to see your way."

"I'll be fine," she said.

Standing in the entrance, he gave a low whistle and Jack shot past him into the darkness. Palmer hesitated momentarily, as if listening for Jack to give him a signal. When the dog didn't return or bark, he gestured for her to follow. Leading the way, he moved swiftly across the property to the path that led straight to the family home. When they reached the front steps, Palmer tossed her a look, concern seeping past his thick lashes.

"Watch your step," he whispered loudly.

"I'm good," Soledad whispered back. She flashed him a grateful smile.

As she took the first step, Palmer eased a protective arm around her waist, his hand resting lightly against her hip, the other cupped under her elbow. His touch was warm, and she was suddenly at ease, comfort washing over her spirit. Soledad hadn't anticipated such a thing ever happening again. The feeling was unexpected, and her stomach did a slight flip. Then her knees began to quiver and her whole body began to shake, threatening to drop her back down to the ground. She held Lyra tighter.

"Are you okay?" Palmer questioned as he pushed open the front door and guided her inside.

Soledad nodded, words stuck deep in her throat. She couldn't bring herself to explain. Despite everything that had happened, feeling like all was lost, being with this man she knew nothing about had her feeling like everything could be well again if she just gave it some time.

"Soledad?"

She lifted her eyes to meet his. He was staring intently, his gaze searching hers, concern seeping from his eyes. Soledad clutched the baby just a little tighter, then dropped to the slate floor and sobbed.

LYRA LAY IN the center of the queen-size bed, pillows propped on either side of her to keep her from rolling off, later that evening. She was warm, her belly was full, and once again she was sleeping as if she didn't have a care in the world. Soledad, on the other hand, looked like she'd taken a swift trip to hell, stopping to battle in the next world war before making the trip back home. She could only imagine what Palmer had thought.

She stared at her reflection in the full-length mirror that decorated the door leading into the private bathroom. Dried blood was splattered in her shoulder-length hair and her tears had left deep streaks in the dirt that painted her face. Her clothes were tattered from the thorny branches they'd caught on and mud caked her shoes and pant legs. She looked wretched and it was a wonder the man hadn't been frightened away by the sight of her. But he hadn't looked at her with fear, just compassion and kindness. And something else that she couldn't quite discern. She only knew that she instinctively trusted it, and him.

Moving to the bathroom, she dropped her top, pants, bra and panties to the tiled floor. She turned on the shower, and when the water was nicely heated, she slid beneath the spray. The warm liquid was a balm to her skin, and she could feel every muscle easing into the comfort of it. She would never have imagined anything being so exhilarating to her spirit, but this was like angels singing in her ears, she thought. Soledad tilted her face into the flow and let it rain over her shoulders and saturate the length of her hair.

As she lathered the strands, she thought about Annie. How Annie would have teased her about always running into a man when she looked like she'd been dragged around and abandoned by a neighborhood cat. Usually, it was baking flour that clung to her clothes and a spattering of chocolate or butter in her hair, depending on whatever she'd put into the ovens at the bakery. Annie would have doubled over with laughter if she'd been there to hear Soledad tell her about being in Palmer's barn. Soledad wasn't ready to laugh about it just yet.

With no sense of time, she stood beneath the warmth until the water began to run cold. The chill was just enough to pull her from the reverie she'd fallen into, thinking about the past and pondering the future. A future that suddenly included a six-month-old and the fight to keep her safe from her father. Motherhood hadn't been on Soledad's to-do list. Not that she didn't want to be a parent. Because she did. But she'd planned on having a husband and father for her child first. She'd been more than satisfied with the role of godmother, able to spoil Lyra senseless. Her sister, Dominique, was also planning to be pregnant as soon as she and Stanton made it down the aisle, so she'd be an auntie sooner than later.

She'd had plans for them that involved excursions for ice cream and visits to the toy stores before returning to their respective parents. Now, assuming she'd get legal custody of Lyra, per Annie's wishes, Soledad had to consider day care and dance classes, doctor's visits, Girl Scouts and whatever else little ones did these days. The fact that Soledad didn't have a clue spoke volumes. She was going to need help with poor little Lyra, she thought.

Stepping out of the shower, Soledad reached for the

oversize white towel Palmer had left for her. He'd been overly concerned with her being comfortable and she appreciated his efforts.

She paused to examine the wound. It looked worse than it was, the abrasion superficial. The bullet had gone in and out, not hitting anything internal or doing any major damage. She'd gotten lucky and she whispered a prayer of gratitude that it wasn't worse. The bleeding had stopped and the wound had looked ghastlier than it was. Admittedly, it had scared her at first, and she realized it had unnerved Palmer, as well. She was just grateful the shots had missed Lyra, Gavin not at all concerned about his child with his felonious behavior. He was lower than graveyard dirt, she thought, knowing she'd never be able to rest well until he was behind bars. She took a deep inhalation and held it for a moment before slowly blowing it back out.

With one last glance in the huge mirror, Soledad made her way from the bathroom back to the bedroom. She suddenly came to an abrupt halt, panic delivering a deep gut punch to her midsection. The bed was in disarray and Lyra was gone.

IT HAD BEEN CRYING, little face beet red as it gasped for air to bellow back out. Palmer had gone to check that both were well when he heard the baby crying and the shower running. He'd hesitated, not quite sure what to do, but then realized Soledad probably couldn't hear the child wailing if she were in the shower. And now it lay in his lap, staring up at him, pale blue gaze eyeing him warily.

Palmer kicked himself for referring to the baby as an it. Even if only in his own head. *It* was a girl. Her name was Lyra. And she wasn't crying anymore. Now she just smelled bad. Like the cow pasture multiplied by ten. He couldn't begin to fathom how such a tiny person could smell so foul. But she reeked, and for the last ten minutes, he'd been trying to get past the stink to put a clean diaper on her bottom.

Palmer had no children, and for the most part, kids were an anomaly. He had friends who had them and, more times than not, he ignored them. His sister had a son, the toddler holding a permanent place in his heart. But he was not a favored godfather or uncle and had never given any thought to being a parent. Fatherhood had not been anything he'd wanted for himself, most especially when he considered the state of the world. His past had also left him jaded when it came to love and family, not that he was interested in rehashing his bad experiences while trying to get beyond toxic sludge oozing past the thigh line of Lyra's diaper. He gagged, fighting not to hurl whatever he'd last eaten onto the floor.

Soledad suddenly barreled into the room wearing nothing but a towel. Her hair was soaked, water trickling down her ringlets. Her warm complexion was pale with fear and fury, the emotion like a stark tattoo across her forehead. Palmer's eyes widened at the sight of her, skating over the curve of her bare shoulders down to the taut muscles of her legs. She was gorgeous, and she took his breath away, even if he did sense a tongue-lashing coming his way.

"What are you doing with her?" Soledad snapped, clutching at the towel she was holding precariously around her lean figure.

He picked up the clean diaper and waved it at her. "She was screaming her head off while you were in the shower. I thought I might be of some help, but it's not going well." Wrinkling his nose, he lifted Lyra up and held her and the diaper at arm's length.

Soledad looked from him to the baby and back again. The wealth of emotion that had led her into the room suddenly dissipated, rising like a morning mist to expose a sky full of sunshine. A smile suddenly pulled at her mouth and she bit her bottom lip to stop herself from laughing outright.

Palmer shook his head. "It's really not funny. What the hell did you feed her?"

Chapter Four

Lyra gurgled contentedly, her little arms flapping at her sides. She sat propped against a fortress of pillows on the family room floor. Jack lay beside her, seeming to ignore the occasional ear pull or kick to his side.

From where he stood in the home's kitchen, Palmer could easily watch them both and finish the meal he had started making. Usually, he would have grabbed a bowl of hot cereal and kept moving, but he thought Soledad might enjoy homemade banana pancakes with a side of bacon.

She had been exhausted, and when sleep had finally claimed her, she hadn't wanted to let it go. After the late night they'd all had, he'd appreciated the few hours of slumber he'd garnered, as well. Lyra's schedule seemed to mimic his own, the little girl waking with the morning sun. Soledad had been grateful when he had offered to take the child with him so she could rest a few more minutes. Now he was watching Jack watch her watching him and, despite the absurdity of it all, was feeling far more comfortable with the situation than he was willing to admit.

Jack shifted his body to lie beside the baby, his tail like a windshield wiper gone awry. He swatted the infant once and then twice, then suddenly yelped when Lyra grabbed him and pulled. The little girl laughed heartily, the wealth of it like the sweetest balm to his heart through the morning air. Jack barked.

"Good dog," Palmer muttered. "Don't take any crap from her. She's trying to steal your heart, pal. Don't let her."

A warm alto responded from the doorway. Palmer turned as Soledad stepped through the entrance. She looked relaxed. Her hair was down and loose, the blue-black strands framing her face. She wore one of his T-shirts and an old pair of shorts he'd found in a closet. Left by one of his sisters, probably Grace, they fit her nicely. Barefoot and comfortable, she was the most beautiful woman he knew, if you excluded his mother, of course. He blushed, feeling his cheeks warm with color.

Soledad laughed. "Really? That's a little cynical, don't you think?"

Palmer had looked up sheepishly as the sound of her voice drew his attention. He felt a wide grin pulling across his face as amusement filled him. "Good morning. I didn't see you standing there."

"Obviously!" She giggled softly. "Good morning to you, too. Lyra wasn't any trouble, was she?" she asked as she moved to the baby's side, a finger tickling her chubby cheek.

He shook his head. "She's been good. No massive explosions. No tantrums. She took a bottle and she's been content lying there ever since. Jack's been in charge, so we've had the situation under control."

Soledad nodded. "Well, thank you." She gave him her own bright smile. "You're good with her," she said as she eased to the center island and took a seat on one of the bar stools.

He ignored the comment, the compliment making him feel uncomfortable since being good with anyone's baby wasn't in his game book. "Would you like a cup of coffee?" Palmer questioned.

"I would love some coffee. And eggs and toast, if you have them."

"I can make that happen. I also have some banana pancakes here. Would you like bacon, too?"

"You must be reading my mind. I'm famished, and those pancakes smell divine."

"You should be. I hadn't realized how far you'd run last night. You were on the south side of my ranch. That's almost ten miles by foot, and most of that property is heavily wooded. How long were you running?"

"I was pacing about ten minutes per mile. Maybe eleven. The added weight slowed me down some." She gestured toward the baby, who was beginning to nod off, her eyes closing and opening and then closing again.

"You're a runner?"

"Since high school. Lyra's mother and I ran track together. That's how we became friends."

"You're lucky you didn't get lost in those woods."

"I was more afraid of the man chasing us than I was a few trees."

Palmer nodded as he cracked half a dozen eggs into a stainless-steel bowl and began to whisk them with salt and pepper and a splash of milk.

"There's a heavy police presence there right now. When I made my morning rounds earlier, I drove past to see for myself. I'm sure it'll be on the news before too long if it isn't already."

"Do you have a remote to that television?" Soledad pointed to the fifty-inch Sony that hung on the family room wall.

Palmer gestured to the corner of the counter, the device resting beside a stack of cookbooks.

Reaching for it, Soledad hit the on button, then sat back against the counter as she flipped the channels to the local news station. There was the briefest commercial and then a familiar newscaster's face filled the screen.

"The big story this morning—an Amber Alert issued for a missing baby and the mother's body found in an abandoned vehicle on Highway 55. The station's Diane Albert reports."

The camera shifted to the roadside where Soledad's white Camry was being pulled out of the ditch by a tow truck. The woman named Diane stared into the camera.

"There is still a lot about this case that detectives are not telling us," Diane said. She was a tall, thin woman, with sharp features, lengthy blond extensions and a hungry glint in her eyes. "What we do know right now is that a young mother is dead, her six-month-old daughter is missing, and the woman's husband and best friend are persons of interest."

Soledad bristled. "A person of interest? How could

they think I hurt Annie? Why am *I* not a missing person, too?"

Palmer reached for the remote and turned off the television. The situation was depressing enough without the two of them scrolling for news that would only make things feel worse. For a split second, Soledad looked as if she wanted to argue. Then she didn't, her shoulders rolling forward as she seemed to sink lower in her seat.

Concern seeped out of Palmer's eyes as he stared at the woman. Sadness had washed over Soledad's face. She took a deep breath and exhaled slowly.

Palmer felt the melancholy that tugged at her spirit. It was corporeal, feeling like clabber and just as foul. He slid a mug across the counter toward her, the warm aroma of Colombian coffee beans wafting through the room. "It's going to be okay," he said, although he wasn't wholeheartedly convinced of that himself. "We're going to figure out what to do. We'll make this right. I promise."

THERE WAS SOMETHING about how he said "we" that lifted Soledad's smile back to her face. Despite the gravity of her situation, she felt comfort in knowing that she wasn't alone. That Palmer Colton, who didn't know anything about her, was willing to promise his assistance and stand by her side meant everything to her.

She tossed a look in Lyra's direction. The child was sleeping soundly, and Jack lay with his head in the baby's lap, her fingers tangled in his fur. She changed the subject. "So, do you have any children of your own, Palmer?"

He tossed her a look before turning to the stove and the pat of butter that had begun to sizzle in the frying pan.

"No. I have neither the time for kids nor the interest in them. I've never wanted to have any."

"Ouch!" Soledad said, her eyes flaring at the comment. Surprise showed on her face, warming her cheeks and furrowing her brow. "That was harsh. Why don't you want kids?"

"I just don't," he said emphatically.

There was a moment of pause as Soledad waited for him to elaborate, but when no explanation came, she persisted. "Do you not like them?" she asked.

"I don't dislike them. I just…well…" He hesitated, visibly thrown off guard as he seemed to search for the right words to explain himself. "I like them well enough," he muttered. "I just don't want my own."

Soledad paused, eyeing him curiously. She finally took a sip of the hot coffee. The silence in the room was thundering, both clearly feeling ill at ease. The moment was awkward, as if neither was sure how they'd gotten there or how to move themselves past it.

Palmer suddenly heaved a heavy sigh. "I'm sorry. I didn't mean to kill the mood," he said, forcing a smile onto his face.

Soledad smiled back, shrugging her shoulders dismissively. "It's all good," she muttered softly.

PALMER TURNED HIS back to her to plate the morning meal. After he loaded the dishes with crisp bacon, pancakes and scrambled eggs, he moved around the counter to take the seat beside her. He watched Soledad take her first bite, her eyes closing as she chewed.

She purred, the low hum moving Palmer to grin broadly. He dropped his eyes to his own plate and began to eat.

"This is so good!" she exclaimed as she took a second bite and then a third. She shifted her gaze to meet his. "You've got skills in the kitchen."

Palmer chuckled. "Thank you."

For the next few minutes, the two ate in silence, nothing but the sound of gnashing teeth and the occasional hum bouncing off the four walls. A grandfather clock ticked loudly from the foyer hallway, and Jack and Lyra were both snoring.

Palmer suddenly broke through the silence. As he began to speak, Soledad lowered her fork and turned to him to listen, giving him her full attention.

"I was adopted into the Colton family. My biological parents had addiction problems and they both died from overdoses. The first time I was removed from their custody, I was two years old. I don't remember a lot from back then, but I do remember constantly being hungry and not always having a bed to sleep in. My mother died when I was three. I had only been back with her for a few weeks when that happened. My father wasn't fit to care for me, and I was put in foster care. Most of the families were decent, but there is always one that gives the system a bad name. I was with that family for two months too long." He took a deep breath, seeming to push the unwanted memories aside. The moment was suddenly awkward as he realized he was sharing more than he'd planned. But he felt an overwhelming sense of ease with the woman who was staring intently in his direction.

A slight grin pulled at his mouth as he continued. "Leanne was volunteering in the last group foster facility I'd been placed in. I thought she was an angel. She was young, only nineteen at the time. And she was beautiful and kind, and she made me feel incredibly special. My first name was her maiden name, so we had an instant connection. I was slightly desperate for attention and would follow her around the home. And she let me. She became *my* angel. I was five when she adopted me. When she married my dad, he adopted me, too."

"Your father's Geoff Colton, right?"

Palmer nodded. "He is."

"I've met him. I sometimes supply fresh-baked bread to Grave Gulch Grill. He has always been genuinely nice to me."

"Dad's a good guy and that restaurant is his pride and joy." He smiled, thinking about his parents bringing him immense joy.

"My past is why I don't want kids, Soledad," he continued. "I've seen the worst of what can happen in families and how children are affected by bad behavior and actions they have no control over. I can't imagine myself putting any child at risk of that."

"But you aren't your parents. And you're not an addict, are you?"

"No, of course not," he said, annoyed at the question. "But we don't know what the future might hold for us. Look at Lyra. Most people would have assumed she had the perfect life with a bright future. Two parents in a beautiful home and a host of possibilities ahead of her. Had her mother anticipated her father turning on them, she surely would have never put her daughter through that. Never!"

"So, you're afraid you'll turn on your family if you have one?" Confusion furrowed Soledad's brow. She sat straighter in her seat as she looked at him intently.

"I'm afraid that life will throw me a curve that I can't control. I wouldn't ever want a child of mine to become lost in the foster system. It's not a pretty place for any kid to be, despite the many professionals and families who care about them and make every effort to make them feel loved."

"That's a bit irrational, don't you think? Especially because I have no doubts that your family would step in to take your kids. Your brother, sisters, even one of your cousins would make sure they weren't put in the care of strangers. Right?"

"I'm sure when your friend had Lyra, she wasn't thinking her daughter would be in the position she's in now."

"Lyra will never go into foster care," Soledad said insistently. "Not as long as I live and breathe. I promised Annie that I would look out for her and I fully intend to keep that promise."

"And that's admirable. But what happens if something happens to you that you can't control? Then what? You can have the perfect family, trust the best people and things still not work out the way you want them to. That's just life, and it will throw you a curve when you least expect." He shrugged his broad shoulders, the gesture dismissive. "Maybe I do sound irrational, but it's how I feel."

Soledad gave him a slow nod. "It's a bit of a reach, but I respect that you've given it so much thought."

"Growing up, it's all I ever thought about. I didn't want any kid of mine to go through a minute of what I went through. Feeling unwanted. Worrying about where my next meal would come from. Desperate for my parents to love me. Then feeling lost when they died and being scared because I didn't have anyone. It was a lot. Granted, I was one of the lucky ones. But there are thousands of kids in the system who'll never get as lucky as I did. And there are twice as many who'll go to hell and back just trying to survive."

SOLEDAD STARED AT HIM. There was intensity in his tone, the wealth of emotion wrapped so tightly around his words that she could just imagine the pledge he had made to himself as a boy. He'd reiterated those words his entire life, until they were so ingrained in his heart that there would be no moving him from his convictions. Tears suddenly formed in her eyes, her own emotions on overload as she imagined the wealth of pain that could have laid that on his spirit.

Soledad had never imagined herself without children. Although there had been no potential father on the horizon, she genuinely believed in the fairy-tale ending. She knew that one day the perfect man would come at the perfect time and, after the perfect engagement and a Disney-worthy wedding, there would be kids. Perfect or imperfect, they would have been hers. Two boys and a girl, and maybe even a beagle named Charlie. She wanted for her own family what she'd had as a girl, she and her sister blessed with an abundance of love and attention from parents who loved each other fiercely and loved their daughters even more.

Now, as she considered the future she hoped to give Lyra, that fairy tale suddenly had an alternate ending she hadn't prepared for.

"I'm sorry," she whispered. "I'm so, so sorry." She fought the sudden urge to reach out and hug him. Instead, she folded her arms across her chest and tucked her hands beneath her armpits. She bit down against her tongue. Hard. Hoping the gesture would stem the rise of feeling that pulled at her.

Palmer shook his head and shrugged.

Another moment of pause rose thickly between them, both refocused on their plates and the last bites of their morning meal.

Soledad found herself thinking about what he'd said, wondering what might happen to little Lyra if something did happen to her. Her emotions were on edge yet again. She took a deep breath and held it deep in her lungs.

Palmer finally spoke, his deep baritone sliding through the silence. "I know how it sounds," he said as he cut his eyes in her direction. "Although I try to be more pragmatic about things, that's the one thing that's like a burr in my side. I hate feeling that way, but it is what it is."

Soledad smiled. "You only sound a *little* off-kilter."

He laughed, a wave of ease washing over him. "I'll take that."

Minutes passed as their conversation shifted gears. Soledad asked questions about the ranch, wanting to know more about the expanse of property. As he answered her questions, pride gleamed from his eyes.

"Colton Ranch is over eight hundred acres of highly productive pasture farm, and I have a great team that helps me manage the property. There's also a good sixty acres of hay fields that we maintain. You ran through the hay fields last night. We have a four hundred cow-and-calf operation, supplying milk around the state. We have a few hundred sheep that we raise for their fleece, their milk and for meat. Our eggs this morning came from my chicken coop, and the hens lay prodigiously, so we eat a lot of them around here."

Soledad laughed. "Your cholesterol levels are probably off the charts."

He shrugged as he continued. "We're pretty self-sufficient. There are also three fully stocked ponds, if you like bass or catfish. We eat a lot of fish, too. And during the fall and winter, you can hunt turkey and white-tailed deer."

"You don't eat Bambi, do you?"

"Why else would we hunt deer?"

Soledad rolled her eyes skyward. "And here I thought you and I could be friends."

Palmer smiled. "It's country living. You spoiled city girls don't know anything about that."

"Spoiled? Obviously, you didn't meet our father. We de la Vega girls were hardly spoiled."

Palmer laughed heartily. Because he had met her father and knew him fairly well. Rigo de la Vega was exceptionally protective of his daughters, wanting nothing but the absolute best for them. When Soledad's twin sister, Dominique, was being threatened, the patriarch had hired Palmer's cousin Stanton to be her bodyguard. There was little their father would not do for them or give to them. They'd been spoiled in the absolute best way, and he imagined her desire to have kids was her wanting that for her own family.

Rising from her seat, Soledad reached for his empty plate. "I'll do the washing up," she said.

"No, you won't," Palmer responded, pulling the dirty dishes from her hands. "You're a guest. Besides, we need to make plans. They'll be looking for the two of you."

For the briefest of moments, Soledad hadn't thought about her predicament, and she'd been grateful for the reprieve. She'd been enjoying his company. She sat, feeling like a ton of weight had been dropped back onto her shoulders. Across the room, Lyra still slept soundly. She sucked her tongue in her sleep and her expression was angelic. The dog hadn't moved, lying protectively beside her. Occasionally, he would lift his head before dozing off.

As Palmer rinsed and loaded the dishwasher, Soledad nosed around the home. The country farmhouse was sizable, almost four thousand square feet of meticulously designed space in a very private setting. The windows were expansive and afforded wonderful views of the pasture, the cattle and the wildlife. The open floor plan included the chef's kitchen and an exceptionally large master suite. There were four bedrooms, each with its own fireplace, six bathrooms total, and Soledad imagined the cream-tinted walls with the pitched ceilings and hardwood floors held many cherished memories of his family's gatherings. She couldn't help but wonder if there'd been someone special who'd been part of the plans for a home so large. A home fit for a family with children and pets.

She liked Palmer. Yet there was something about him that gave her pause, and she found herself wanting to know even more. She was curious about his likes and dislikes and his dreams and goals. She had questions about the women who were important to him, wanting to know more about his mother and sisters and half siblings. She wondered about his past relationships, whether there was someone important in his life who might not be happy about her finding shelter in his family home. She had a multitude of questions, but wasn't sure she should even ask or if she'd ever get the answers.

Soledad was heading toward the family room when she saw a large shadow pass by the front window. Her heart began to race, her breathing suddenly labored as she gasped for air. She sprinted to where Lyra lay, snatching her up so quickly that Jack jumped in alarm and grabbed her by the arm with his teeth. The dog growled. Soledad's eyes widened with fright.

"Jack, no," Palmer said sternly, moving swiftly to her side.

The dog released his grasp and whimpered softly. He sat and then settled at Palmer's feet, his eyes still on the baby as if he dared Soledad to try and run.

"What's wrong?" Palmer questioned, his large hand gently caressing where the dog had just vised her arm in a toothy grip.

"There's someone sneaking around the house," Soledad whispered loudly. "I saw them pass by the front window."

BEFORE PALMER COULD ANSWER, there was a knock on the kitchen door. His heart was suddenly beating as spastically as he imagined hers was, the intensity surprising him. He took a deep breath and pointed to the back of the family home and the master bedroom. "Hide in my bedroom. I'll see who it is," he said firmly.

With a bob of her head, Soledad scurried down the hallway. Palmer watched until she'd closed and locked the bedroom door after herself. Jack had followed Soledad, visibly unhappy when she closed the door in his face, not allowing him into the room with her and Lyra. He lay at the threshold, determined not to be moved.

Palmer walked swiftly to the door, someone knocking a second time for his attention. When he pulled it open, Noé Maldonado stood with his hat clutched in both hands. He was a slim man with a head of jet-black curls and a sepia complexion. The farmhand had been with Palmer for a few years.

"Noé! What's up?" Palmer said, his eyes dancing swiftly across the landscape behind the man's shoulders.

Noé grinned warmly. "*¡Buenos días, jefe!* I'm sorry to interrupt, boss," he said, his accent thick and as rich as warm molasses.

"Not a problem, Noé. What do you need?"

"Just wanted you to know I need to take the big truck into town to pick up supplies. They're behind with the deliveries and we need that last order."

Palmer nodded. "That's not a problem. Who's working the ranch today?"

"It's a small crew, jefe. I have four men working that northern pasture. The fence came down and needs to be replaced. They will not be a problem to you."

"I wasn't concerned," Palmer said. "I know you have it under control. I'll be inside most of the day. I have some paperwork to catch up on. Just call me if you need anything else."

"Yes, sir. Thank you, jefe." Noé backed his way out the door, sliding his hat onto his head. He suddenly hesitated, as if there was something he'd forgotten.

"What is it, Noé?" Palmer asked. "Is something wrong?"

"There was a man on the property earlier. Down by where the horses were grazing. He said he was police, and was asking questions. Said he was looking for a woman. That she had run off with someone else's baby. We told him we hadn't seen anyone, but he said he did not believe us. He said her GPS showed that she was here. When we couldn't tell him anything, he threatened to call ICE on us. But we didn't have anything to tell him, jefe! I told him again that we had not seen any woman and to come talk to you. He said you told him to come talk to us. He made the men nervous. None of them wants any trouble. They are good men, jefe."

"That man lied. I would never send anyone to talk to you or the men, and I certainly wouldn't let anyone threaten you." There was an edge to Palmer's tone, every word wrapped in annoyance and rising rage. Knowing Gavin had violated his property and purposely tried to intimidate his employees had him spitting mad, the emotion wrapped in swells of barbed wire.

"I know, jefe. But not all men are good like you."

"If you see this man again, you call me immediately and I will come to you. And you tell the others they have nothing to be afraid of as long as they are working for me."

"Gracias, jefe," Noé said. "Thank you very much."

Palmer watched until Noé had climbed into the cab of the Ford F-150 and started the engine. Then he closed the door.

He stood quietly for a moment, reflecting on the conversation. Clearly, Soledad's problem was not going to go away, and Lyra's father was laser focused on finding them both—there on the ranch. Palmer had to question why this location and then remembered something

Noé had said. Gavin had told him her "GPS" had put Soledad's location there on the farm. What had Gavin been talking about?

Chapter Five

When Soledad felt safe enough to return to the family room, she found Palmer sitting at the kitchen counter. Lyra's diaper bag lay before him, the contents strewed across the sofa and floor. Concern pulled at the muscles in his face, his brow creased. He lifted his eyes to hers as she entered the room and suddenly Soledad's stomach pitched with fear.

"What?" she said, eyeing him anxiously.

Palmer lifted a small black box from the countertop. It was no bigger than a digital watch face and fit neatly into the palm of his hand. It was nothing Soledad recognized. She gave him a questioning look, asking what it was and why he looked like the world was coming to an end.

"It's a tracking device. It was sewn into the lining of the baby's diaper bag."

Soledad's eyes widened. She had wondered how Gavin had known where they were to pull up on them like he had. She and Annie had considered he might track her through her cell phone, which was why Annie had left hers behind. Neither had considered he would use Lyra to track his wife's whereabouts, much less put a tracking device on anyone. Knowing how abusive he'd been, it shouldn't have surprised her, but Soledad was thrown off guard.

"He knows we're here," she breathed loudly.

Palmer nodded. "It's why he came last night. It's also why he came back this morning."

"He came back?"

"That was one of my ranch hands at the door. He came to tell me that your friend's husband was asking the men questions about you and Lyra. But they didn't know anything and couldn't give him any answers."

Something that felt very much like guilt washed over Soledad's spirit. She suddenly felt responsible for putting Palmer and his employees in harm's way. And she didn't think she could ever forgive herself for Annie's death. Despite her best efforts, she hadn't contemplated every single possibility that could have gone wrong. And the one thing she hadn't considered had gotten her best friend killed.

She hadn't given Gavin's previous bad behavior enough weight. Despite what she did know, she had let her guard down when Annie had trusted her to get it right because she herself had gotten it wrong so many times. Soledad couldn't have been more wrong. She had led Gavin straight to them, and he clearly had no plans to go away until he found her and got his murderous hands on that beautiful baby.

As if he were reading her mind, Palmer shook his head. "This isn't your fault," he said softly, his eyes dancing across her face.

Soledad shook her head, much less confident about him being right. "We need to get out of here," she said, her mind beginning to race. "He can't find us here!" She began to scramble for the baby items that had been tossed to the floor.

Palmer rose from his seat and reached for her, grabbing her arm gently to stall her anxiety. His touch was like an electrical current shooting through her and Soledad's breath caught deep in her chest. She gasped. Loudly.

Palmer snatched his hand away, his eyes wide. "I'm sorry. I didn't mean…" he started, the comment stalling midsentence.

She shook her head vehemently. "No. It's fine. I'm just…"

They were both suddenly stammering, words having slipped into an abyss of emotion that neither had anticipated.

Soledad's heart was beating rapidly. "I'm scared," she whispered loudly, tears welling in her dark eyes. "I've never been so scared."

"It's going to be okay," Palmer responded. He reached for her a second time, his hand gently caressing her forearm. This time she didn't flinch or pull away from him. "I'm not going to let anything happen to you or that baby. But we need to be smart and we need to outsmart him."

Soledad nodded. She felt herself lean into his touch, her knees quivering ever so slightly. She closed her eyes as she considered each word he spoke, feeling her comfort level beginning to revive.

Palmer continued. "Right now, that little device is telling him that you're here. So, we're going to use that to our advantage. I need to go into town to get supplies for you and the baby. When I do, this GPS will put you at the mall, and that's where the tracking device will stay.

"Meanwhile, you need to make some calls. People are worried about you. You need to stay missing, but the authorities need to know you're okay. So, I want you to call my cousin and tell her what happened. You don't have to tell Melissa you're here with me. Just let her know you're safe. Then I think you should call your family. I'm sure they are worried sick."

There was a moment of hesitation as Soledad considered his plan. His cousin Melissa Colton was the chief of the Grave Gulch Police Department. She knew Melissa in passing and had always found her to be pleasant and fair.

She also knew that Melissa already had her hands full with an internal scandal that involved GGPD's former forensic scientist, a man named Randall Bowe. Discovering that Bowe had tampered with evidence in several police cases and allowed a serial killer to go free and kill again had eroded the public's faith in the department. There had been calls for Melissa's resignation and protests had become rampant through the city. Soledad understood that, like people in general, not all cops were good and that a few bad apples in the bunch could make life significantly harder for those who only wanted to do their best under harrowing circumstances. She was sure another investigation, finding killer Len Davison, only added to Melissa's lengthy list of problems. An unnecessary missing persons case added to her list would only hinder the work she needed to be doing. But Soledad still wasn't comfortable with reaching out to the police.

"You can trust her," Palmer assured her.

His voicing the thoughts in her head had begun to give her serious pause. He was overly perceptive, reading her emotions as if they were inked across her forehead. She didn't need to tell him that she would only trust his cousin because he did. She was certain he already knew.

"I don't have my phone," she said softly.

"That's not a problem. I have a burner phone you can use."

Soledad blinked, her lashes batting rapidly. "Why do you have a burner phone?"

"I have a few of them. I buy them in bulk. I employ a lot of migrant workers to work the ranch and sometimes I need to contact them. It also enables them to keep in touch with their families. It just makes things easier for all of us."

"That's actually exceedingly kind of you. I'm sure they appreciate your generosity."

Palmer shrugged. There was suddenly a loud wail from the bedroom and his shoulders rolled back, his head tilting slightly. He gave Soledad a look, concern pulling at his expression.

"That sounds like a diaper overload cry," Soledad said. "Someone's awake and in need of some attention."

"Then that sounds like she's crying for you!" Palmer

responded. He gave her a slight smile. "You go grab the baby and I'll go grab you a phone. Then I need to ride out and check on my men. I won't be long. You'll be safe while I'm gone."

As he turned, Soledad reached for his hand to stall his steps. She slid her fingers between his and held on tightly as he turned back around to meet her gaze. "Why are you doing this for me?" Soledad questioned, staring deep into the look he was giving her.

"Because you need me," he answered. "And I want to help." He gave her hand a warm squeeze, then gestured toward the bedroom and the pitiful cry fervently rising from inside.

AND, AS EXTREME *as it sounds, because I need you*, he thought to himself as she walked away. *Because I need you, too.*

The drive to the north side of the ranch didn't take any time at all. On the way, Palmer thought about the young woman he was harboring in his home. He didn't know if he would ever have the words to explain what it was he was feeling. Mostly because he didn't fully understand it himself.

Palmer had always enjoyed his life. After his adoption, he had wanted for nothing and what he'd received in abundance was love. Yet, despite everything his parents had done for him, trust had always been a major issue he could never overcome.

As an adult, he was content with his choices. He had never imagined himself in a long-term relationship with any woman. He had no need for a wife and preferred casual encounters over lengthy entanglements. It worked for him, and even when it didn't, there was no stress. Women who became attached usually left with their hearts broken, but Palmer never made any promises he wasn't willing to keep. Forever was not something he had ever promised any woman. He was always direct and to the point. They'd known where he'd stood from the start. That level of honesty had always served him well.

Others worried about him being lonely, but even the solitude didn't bother him. He worked hard, rested well, and had never been unhappy with his choices. Or at least he hadn't thought so before Soledad had come barreling into his life. Something about the beautiful woman was creeping beneath his skin and latching on like a wild ivy gone awry. He was genuinely concerned about her well-being and about the baby's. Those bright eyes and that innocent smile had yanked his heart as hard as the little girl sometimes yanked Jack's tail. Like his dog, Palmer was protective of them both. He would move heaven and earth to keep them safe. He was finding a level of joy with Soledad that he'd never known before, and the feeling both surprised and confused him.

SOLEDAD SNAPPED THE onesie closed around the clean diaper, wriggling her nose at Lyra, who was sucking on her fist. The baby smiled and laughed, and Soledad laughed with her.

She started to sing as she lifted Lyra into her arms. Nuzzling her nose into the roll of baby fat beneath Lyra's neck, Soledad inhaled the scent of baby powder deep into her lungs.

"Do you feel better?" Soledad gushed as she kissed the baby's cheek.

Lyra gurgled, pulling her fist back to her mouth.

"You're hungry. Let's go get you something to eat," she said as she settled the child on her hip and headed for the family room.

The burner phone Palmer had promised rested on the kitchen counter. There was also a note that he had already programmed his number and Melissa's cell into the device.

Soledad sighed heavily. Despite her reservations, she had no reason *not* to reach out to let the authorities know she was safe and well. And she definitely needed to put her father and Dominique at ease. Granted, she was scared that Gavin might find her, but she knew no one could find him if they were focused on her and the baby. But that call would have to wait, she thought. Because Lyra was pulling at her shirt and throwing herself backward for Soledad's attention.

Three jars of baby food rested next to the diaper bag. "Look!" Soledad exclaimed, making a face at the little girl. "You can have pears, pears or pears."

Lyra burbled.

"Pears it is," Soledad said excitedly.

She propped Lyra in the corner of the couch, then popped the top on the jar of food. Sitting herself beside the child, she began to feed her, amused as Jack jumped up to sit beside the baby to watch her eat.

"You're a lucky little girl, Lyra," Soledad said as the

infant swirled the puréed fruit around in her mouth. "You have your very own bodyguard. Doesn't she, Jack?"

The dog panted, looking exceptionally happy as he laid his head on Lyra's little legs. The baby giggled, drool sliding down her chin.

Minutes later, finished with her meal, Lyra was chewing on the nipple of her water bottle as she kneaded her fingers through Jack's fur. The dog lay with his eyes closed, not at all bothered by the child's grabby hands.

Soledad loved the bond the two had already formed, thinking that she might have to get Lyra a puppy of her own when they were able to come out of hiding and settle into their fated new life. She was even a little sad that Jack would never have a little person of his own if Palmer stayed true to his convictions about not having children. She couldn't help but hope that he might change his mind. She sensed that he would make an incredible father if he relaxed and just allowed himself to enjoy the experience. He was good with Lyra. She'd even caught him smiling a few times as he'd watched the baby with his dog.

Thinking about Palmer, Soledad had dozens of questions she wanted to ask him, her curiosity increasing tenfold. She wondered about his life between being orphaned and being adopted, and if it were something he ever talked about. It clearly caused him angst.

Appreciating she might better understand if she knew more, she pondered what little she did know.

She assumed from the home's interior decor that

blue was his favorite color, shades enhancing the walls, the floor and the furniture. He was also a fan of Western artwork. Paintings of the Wild West decorated the walls. Her favorite was the cowboy and his horse in the home's front foyer. He clearly loved his animals. They were like family to him, especially the horses. She had eyed the pictures of them that adorned his office walls. She hoped one day to be able to travel down to the stables to see them and maybe even ride with him.

Lyra and the dog suddenly growled at her. She rolled her eyes at the two and sneered. Both seemed to remind her that she and Palmer weren't really friends like that, and she shouldn't be planning future days with the handsome man. Not that a random thought meant she was planning anything.

"You two are no help," Soledad muttered. She leaned to kiss the baby and then the dog as the duo kept playing with each other contentedly.

Moving to the counter, Soledad pulled the burner phone into the palm of her hand. She took a deep breath and pushed the button to dial the police chief. It rang once, twice and then three times before Melissa Colton answered.

"Chief Colton!"

A wave of panic suddenly hit Soledad broadside and she disconnected the call without saying anything. Her hand was shaking; she felt like she might be sick to her stomach. Her gaze shifted to the sofa. The dog was teasing the girl, nuzzling her on one side and then the other. Lyra giggled, her little arms and legs flailing as she tried to grab at the animal. Jack was proving himself to be the best babysitter.

After giving it some thought, Soledad knew she couldn't call to tell Melissa her story without breaking down in tears, and possibly changing her mind about hiding out. Despite her best efforts, she was only holding on by a slim thread. Caring for Lyra was a pleasant diversion and Jack was keeping them both entertained. Her attraction to Palmer was a whole other story. She wasn't yet sure if he was the cherry on an extremely sweet slice of cake or just a necessary distraction through this truly hard time.

Soledad took a deep breath and began to text with her thumbs. The message was direct and to the point.

Melissa, this is Soledad de la Vega. I saw Gavin Stone murder his wife, Annie. He shot me, too, but I am fine. He has threatened to kill me and take Annie's baby, Lyra. We are both safe for now, but I know Gavin is searching for us. We will come out of hiding when he has been caught and is in your custody. I don't mean to be difficult, but I can't risk him finding us. I hope you understand.

She took another deep breath, reread the message once and then again, and then she pushed the button to send.

Minutes later, Melissa responded to her message.

Soledad, I really need you to turn yourself in. We need the details of what happened. I assure you we will do everything in our power to keep you safe, but I cannot have you impeding the investigation. You need to tell me where you are.

Soledad texted back.

No. I don't trust that you can keep me and the baby safe. I'm sorry. Find Gavin and I will tell you where I am. But you will need to arrest Gavin first. You also need to contact Davis Fairbanks. He's Annie's attorney. Annie left information with him that may help you.

There was a lengthy pause before Melissa finally responded. Soledad knew the chief must not be happy with her and could only begin to imagine the rant Melissa was currently waging with herself. Almost thirty minutes passed before Melissa's final text message came through.

Stay safe. We're here for you and will protect you and Lyra when you're ready. Until then, please keep this line open in case I need to reach you. Thank you.

Relief blew past Soledad's lips as she released the breath she'd been holding deep in her lungs. She dropped the phone back to the counter. Stepping up to the large bay window, she looked out over the landscape. The views from the window were stunning, everything about the property already feeling like home. The house was set far off the main road, and she appreciated that it would take some maneuvering for anyone to sneak up on them without being seen or heard.

Palmer had assured her that she and Lyra were safe, and she believed him. With no one knowing they were there, they would not be easily found, not even with Gavin's little tracking device. She trusted that once Palmer disposed of it, not even Gavin would be able to find them. Until life went back to normal, Soledad thought, Palmer Colton might be hard-pressed to rid himself of her and the baby.

PALMER STOOD ON the front porch, pausing to reflect before entering. He'd driven the perimeter of the property, checking the fences and double-checking all the gates and entry points. There were cameras at each location, and he ensured each was functioning and recording. If anyone were to trespass, there'd be a video recording of the infraction. He'd also hired a security team to periodically patrol the property. There was no point in taking any unnecessary risks. Any threat to Soledad would be dealt with vigorously. If he knew what was good for him, Gavin Stone didn't want to come back to Colton Ranch to look for her.

Palmer's act of kindness had become an obsession of sorts. He felt responsible for Soledad and Lyra. The thought of anything happening to them on his watch knotted his stomach and set his teeth on edge.

Truth be told, he'd had a crush on Soledad since forever. He'd often frequented her bakery hoping to catch a glimpse of the beautiful woman as she worked in the back. He was still kicking himself for not taking advantage of the opportunity to speak with her at her sister's engagement party. His brother Troy had teased him about his bachelor lifestyle, encouraging him to go for it, but Palmer had hesitated, fearful of embarrassing himself. Then, just like that, she'd been gone.

Suddenly, with the nearness of her, he found his emotions on overload. Focusing on Soledad's protection enabled him to ignore any other feelings that were trying to surface. Instead of considering what all that sentiment might mean, he focused on keeping her out of harm's way. It was the very least he could do for them both, he thought. If only he could stop himself from wanting to pull her close and kiss her mouth, curious to know how she tasted.

Shaking himself from the reverie he'd fallen into, he reached for the doorknob and stepped inside the home. A bright smile suddenly pulled full and abundant across his face as he took in the view.

Soledad was leading a dance party, twirling the infant around in her arms. She was singing at the top of her lungs, a bad karaoke version of an old Carrie Underwood song sounding through the air. Jack was hopping up and down beside them, an occasional yip thrown in for good measure. The sight of them together seemed to fill his home with joy that he'd only seen on Thanksgiving and Christmas when his sisters had made him host the holiday meal. It was the first time Soledad had looked relaxed since he'd found her hiding in his barn.

She suddenly came to an abrupt stop, spying him standing there watching. She grinned, the wealth of the joy filling her face. Lyra was still laughing excitedly, and this playful Jack was doing more than Palmer had seen Jack do in a very long time.

"Hi," Soledad said, panting ever so slightly. "How long have you been standing there?"

"Not long. Don't let me interrupt. You three look like you're having a grand old time."

"Jack is an excellent dance partner. Isn't he, Lyra?" Soledad nuzzled the baby's cheek.

Lyra yawned in response. Soledad laughed. "That was a yes. He's just worn her out."

"That's Jack."

"Come join us!"

Palmer eyed her with a raised brow. "I think I'll pass. I need to run into town to the store. I figured I'd pick up some things for you and the baby. Since we're not sure how long you're going to be here."

"I appreciate that. In fact, I already made you a list." She gestured toward the counter.

Palmer laughed. "That was slightly presumptuous of you, don't you think?"

Soledad shrugged. "Slightly, but it was either that or Lyra and I would soon be wearing your underwear."

"Makes perfect sense to me," Palmer said with a nod and the faintest of smiles.

He moved to the counter to review her list. It included those things he'd expected: diapers, formula, baby food. As he neared the end of the list, he raised his eyes to hers, a question mark in his stare. Confusion washed over him. "Flour, butter, sugar… What am I missing?"

"I have to bake a cake."

His brows lifted. "A cake?"

Soledad nodded. "I've promised a client a cake, and I need to make good on that promise. My reputation and the reputation of my business is on the line. I've worked too hard to build my business to just throw that away."

"There's no one who works for you that can bake this cake?"

Soledad shook her head. "I have two young women apprenticing with me, but they're not ready for something like this just yet. My other employees are front-end staff. They handle the cash register, bag up the goodies and keep the bakery clean. All of them together can keep things running for a week or so, maybe even two, but it's iffy after that."

"So, you don't think it's going to look strange that the missing woman in a murder and child abduction case suddenly turns up with a cake?"

"I just plan to bake the cake. You're going to get it delivered."

Palmer laughed. "Me?"

"Do you have a better plan?"

"Maybe you don't bake a cake?"

"That's not an option."

Exasperation furrowed Palmer's brow. "Let's be realistic, Soledad. No one is expecting you to bake a cake after everything that's happened."

"No one is going to know I did it. And there's nothing you can say or do that's going to stop me. You're going to make sure it gets there without anyone being able to track it back here to us. I'll let you figure out the logistics of that."

"What if I conveniently forget to buy that half of the list?"

Soledad tossed up a dismissive hand. "Fine. I'll go myself. You stay and watch the baby. If I don't come back, then I'm going to trust you to keep her safe."

A wry smile pulled at Palmer's mouth. His expression was smug. "You are not going to leave that baby. There isn't anyone who knows you who'd believe that."

"Fine," Soledad said defiantly. "I'll take her with me, then."

Palmer rolled his eyes. "I'm missing something. You're really willing to take that risk over some baked goods?"

"I'm willing to do whatever I need to do to keep a promise I made."

"I don't understand." Palmer moved toward her, taking a seat at the counter. He folded his arms across his chest and stared intently. The baby had settled against her shoulder, beginning to doze off. Jack lay with his head against Soledad's foot. Something about the trio made Palmer's heart sing, and he felt a wealth of energy pitch through his midsection, the warmth spreading into his limbs.

"Who did you make a promise to?" he asked. His tone was softer, curiosity tinting his words.

"You're familiar with Randall Bowe and what's going on with the police department, right?"

Palmer nodded. "It's all anyone's talking about. People are even demonstrating downtown in front of the police station. He's made a complete mockery of the judicial system. It's going to take a lot for them to recover from the damage he's caused. But what does all that have to do with this cake?"

"You may have heard about Rachel Montclair?"

His eyes skated back and forth briefly. "I know I've heard the name, but..." He shrugged his shoulders.

"Rachel went to school with me and Annie. She worked as a financial adviser for Grave Gulch Fidelity. Two years ago, she was charged with fraud, theft by false pretenses and embezzlement of funds. She was also charged with the attempted murder of the bank's president. They said she poisoned him when he discovered what she had done. But anyone who knew Rachel knew she didn't rob that bank or poison that man. But she didn't have an alibi the night her boss got sick, nor could she explain her signature being on checks and documents that allowed someone to walk off with a million dollars in bank funds.

"She was convicted on evidence that Randall Bowe manipulated and planted. When they started investigating him, her case came back under review and she was completely exonerated. She's being released from jail tomorrow and I promised to make the cake for her welcome home party. I know I can't be there, but that cake is the least I can do to help celebrate her vindication."

Palmer was still staring at her, noting the strand of blue-black hair that had fallen over her brow and the rise of color that suddenly tinted her cheeks. Her loyalty to her friend was endearing, every ounce of her spirit committed to doing right by those she cared for.

He stood, brushing his palms down his denim slacks. "I don't grocery shop, so we're going to let technology be our friend." He pointed to the laptop that rested on a desk in the corner. "I have an account at Holiday Market. Sign in and order whatever you need. I'll pick it up on my way back. Does that work?"

Soledad nodded. "I can do that."

"There may be a few items already in the cart. It's how I keep up with things I need to remember to shop for. Just add them to whatever you need, please. I know I need cornflakes."

"Cornflakes?"

Palmer shrugged. "I like cornflakes."

Soledad smiled. "Me, too."

"Anything else?"

"You don't have a lot of cookware. I have a business account at the Kitchen Supply House. If I place an order for cake pans, will you pick those up for me, too?"

Palmer gave her a look and shook his head. "Whatever you need," he said, the slightest smile pulling at his lips. "But it might take me a little longer. I'll need to make sure no one is following me. Just in case Dr. Stone gets any brilliant ideas."

"Thank you," Soledad said, nuzzling the baby softly.

"I'll set the house alarm when I leave. Lock yourself and the baby in the bedroom. Just in case. And keep that burner phone close. If there's an emergency, the house alarm will alert me and the authorities. If you need anything, you call me. I'll leave Jack here, too.

He'll make sure no one enters the house who's not supposed to be here."

Soledad eased to his side, her arms still cradled around Lyra. She leaned in as if to whisper something to him, and when he leaned forward, meeting her halfway, she pressed her lips to his cheek in a gentle kiss.

"Thank you," she said again, her voice a loud whisper. "I don't know how I'll ever pay you back for your kindness."

Startled, words caught deep in his chest, he felt his skin burning hot from her touch. "You don't owe me anything," he muttered.

"But I do," Soledad responded. "You don't know how much everything you've done means to me."

Palmer smiled. "You shouldn't have any problems while I'm gone. Just stay inside, please. Away from the windows. I won't be gone long." He pointed to the guest bedroom. "Lock the door," he said as she turned, headed for the back of the house.

He stood watching as she adjusted Lyra against her shoulder and grabbed the laptop. She tossed him one last look as she walked away, the sweetest smile filling her face. Jack followed them and then lay outside the door after Soledad had shut and locked it. Palmer closed his eyes and took a deep breath. He reached for the side of his face and pressed his palm to his cheek, his fingers trembling ever so slightly.

Chapter Six

Soledad and her friend had been traveling on the service road before they'd run into Gavin. Although the route added a few extra miles to any trip, it was the one Palmer had chosen to take to town. He'd driven one last time around the perimeter of the property to double-check that the gates were all locked and secured, and then headed out on his errands.

Rounding the back ridge that bordered the main roadway, he slowed his truck as he approached a police roadblock. Two officers were standing in the middle of the road, checking licenses and asking questions of approaching drivers. Patrol cars were parked on the shoulder. A team of the city's finest was surveying the crime scene, taking measurements and making notes. Soledad's Camry was secure atop a flatbed truck. As Palmer pulled to a stop, he recognized both men in blue. The oldest of the duo called out his name. Loudly.

"Palmer Colton. Surprised to see you here."

"It's good to see you, too, Officer Linwood. What are you guys doing out here?"

Officer Jay Linwood leaned into Palmer's window.

A member of the Grave Gulch police force for as long as Palmer could remember, he was a rotund man with a balding mane and surly attitude. Rarely was he in a good mood when the two men encountered each other. Palmer was genuinely surprised by his buoyant attitude.

"Murder investigation," the man answered. "Found a dead woman on the road out here. Looking for the husband and her baby now," he said unemotionally.

Palmer nodded. Before he could respond, his name was being called a second time. He shook his head, instantly recognizing his sister's voice. Grace was new to the Grave Gulch Police Department and determined to prove her merit.

"You know this rookie?" Linwood questioned sarcastically, eyeing the two of them.

"Since she was in diapers," Palmer answered.

Grace Colton sent her eyes skyward as she came to stand beside the other officer. Linwood winked his eye at her, gave Palmer a nod and moved to the car that had pulled up behind him.

"Where are you headed, big brother?" Grace asked.

"I need to get some errands done. How's it going?"

Grace shook her head. "This one's bad and there's a baby missing. But Melissa has put a gag order on all of us, pending notification to the family."

"I understand."

"Are you coming to dinner this weekend? Mom wants all of us there for Dad's birthday."

Palmer winced. "Is that this weekend?"

"You better show up, Palmer."

"I'll be there," he said with a wry laugh. "How could I miss it? Mom calls to remind me every day."

"Be nice," Grace said. She tapped his forearm as she changed the subject. "You didn't see or hear anything last night, by chance?"

"What would I have heard?" Palmer asked, the little white lie rolling off his tongue. "The house is a few miles from here and it was storming most of the night."

"I told Melissa we should talk to you. The victim was practically shot at your back door."

"You'd be wasting Melissa's time, and mine."

"You don't know that. You might know something and not even realize it. Are you sure you haven't seen any strangers out here?"

Palmer shook his head, dismissing her question. "I need to run," he said. "I'll see you this weekend."

"Stay safe," Grace said.

Palmer grinned. "Love you, too, little sister." He shifted his truck into gear and pulled off down the road.

AN HOUR LATER, Palmer stood in the children's section of a department store, feeling like a deer caught in headlights. Mustering up the courage to come inside had taken longer than necessary, with him worrying about who he might run into and what he would tell them if they asked. He had thought the chore would be easy, but buying clothes for Lyra was proving to be a challenge he hadn't anticipated. He had a fistful of baby onesies in his left hand and garments on hangers in his right. Everything was pink, pink and pink, and he couldn't help but wonder at what age they started making girls' clothes in some other color. He tossed the whole lot into the cart he pushed.

Minutes later, with the help of a sales associate named Berta, he'd added a crib, a change table, bottles, diapers and enough clothes to outfit half the babies in the state.

"Your baby is one lucky little girl!" Berta exclaimed. "You're going to spoil her with all these gifts. I can just imagine what her mother will say."

"I don't..." Palmer started to object, ready to balk at the idea of being anyone's father. But Berta didn't give him a chance to get in a word, suggesting a half dozen other items to add to the stash in his shopping cart.

"Every little girl needs hair bows," she declared, holding up an assortment of ribbons and headbands.

"Fine," Palmer said, feeling his brow crease with anxiety. "I'll take them. That's fine."

Berta clapped her hands excitedly as if she were earning a commission on the sale. Palmer gave her a smile and a wave, then made an about-face. He paused to check out a display of limited-edition teddy bears when he heard his name being called yet again. He winced, feeling like he'd been caught with his hand in the cookie jar, and turned to face his brother.

Troy Colton was grinning broadly as he walked in Palmer's direction. "I thought that was you. What are you doing here?"

The two men shook hands and bumped shoulders in a one-armed embrace.

"Just picking up some things for a friend," Palmer quipped, trying to quickly formulate a lie to explain himself.

Troy scanned his cart, amusement dancing across his face. "That must be some friend. Something you need to tell me, little brother?"

Palmer shrugged dismissively. "It's just a few gifts for one of the farmhands. His wife just had a baby and I'm helping them out."

"That's very generous of you."

"What are you doing here?" Palmer asked, slightly desperate to shift the attention off himself.

"I thought I'd pick up a little gift for Evangeline. To celebrate her new job goals."

"New job? She won't be working for the district attorney's office anymore?"

Troy shook his head. "No. She's decided to go into social work. She wants to help."

"I wish her well. She'll do a great job wherever she lands."

"I think so, too. And I also thought she'd look superb in this," he said, holding up a silk teddy he'd selected from the lingerie department.

Palmer chuckled. "So, exactly who are you buying a present for? Evangeline or you?"

"Trust me, I plan to enjoy it, too."

"I just bet you will." Palmer shook his head, his expression smug. He changed the subject. "You don't have to work today?"

Troy took a deep inhalation of air, filling his lungs

and holding it briefly. "It's my lunch break. I needed some time to clear my head. There's a lot going on."

"I saw Grace on the way here. She said she's working a murder investigation?"

"It's more complicated than that. You haven't heard, have you?"

Palmer's gaze narrowed. "Heard what?"

There was a moment of hesitation as Troy tossed a look over his shoulder. "It's about Soledad de la Vega."

"Soledad? What about Soledad?" Palmer tried to keep his tone even. "Is she okay?"

"She's missing. The woman murdered last night was Soledad's best friend, Annie. Annie's daughter and Soledad haven't been found. The husband is a person of interest, but we haven't been able to find him, either. When I leave here, I'm going to meet Melissa at Soledad's apartment. We're hoping we'll find something there that'll help us locate her."

A wall of silence seemed to rise thick and heavy between the two brothers. Palmer's eyes feigned concern as he tried not to show his hand. He suddenly had an overwhelming need to get back home to check on Soledad and the baby, to make sure both were well and safe. He felt his knees begin to shake, emotion sweeping through him that was both unexpected and surprising.

"I'm sure they'll be fine," he muttered.

Troy eyed him with a raised brow. "That's it? You're not worried?"

"Of course I'm worried. Why wouldn't I be worried? There's just nothing I can do, right?"

Troy nodded. "We're going to find them. And I'm sure she'll be fine."

"I'm sure," Palmer said. "I trust Grave Gulch's finest will do an exceptional job."

"I'm sure you do. Are you sure there's nothing you want to tell me?" Troy prompted. His fingers trailed down the side of the shopping cart.

Palmer gave his brother a stern look. "What's with all the questions? I'm beginning to feel like one of your suspects."

"Probably because of that dopey expression on your face. You look guilty of something. Do you want to talk about it?"

"There's nothing to talk about."

"I saw how you looked at Soledad at the engagement party, remember? You don't have to pretend with me. It's okay if you're worried. I know this is probably a shock for you. It only makes sense that you'd be worried, Palmer. We're all concerned."

"I'm not… I'm just… It's…" Palmer was suddenly feeling completely out of sorts.

Troy tapped him on the arm. "Hey, we Colton men are notorious for not being honest about our feelings. Trust me, I know." He chuckled, seeming to drift off into thought.

Palmer nodded, ready to be done with their conversation. "I'm good. I'm expected back at the ranch, and I'm sure you need to get back to work, too."

Troy stole a quick glance at his wristwatch. "Yeah, I do need to get going."

"Please, let me know if you turn up anything on Soledad," Palmer said softly.

"I definitely will. And when we find her, you need to promise me you'll let her know how you feel about her."

"See, there you go," Palmer chided. "Trying to make it more than it is."

Troy laughed. "It's your lie. Tell it any way you want to."

"Goodbye, Troy," Palmer said with a slight shake of his head.

He watched as Troy gave him a wave and headed for the front of the store. When his brother was finally out of his sight, he grabbed two of the plush toy bears and tossed them on top of the pile in his cart. He took another deep breath to calm his nerves and headed toward the women's department, thinking the day couldn't possibly get any more challenging.

PALMER WAS CERTAIN he'd broken several traffic laws trying to get back to his home, and to Soledad and the baby. He was grateful that traffic was light and the police barricade cleared. He didn't know if he could take running into one more person that he knew. Most especially with the truckload of paraphernalia he was hauling. It wasn't his nature to lie so wantonly; answering the pointed questions he'd gotten this day had him telling many tall tales.

His experience in the women's department had tested every ounce of his fortitude. He'd added T-shirts and shorts to the cart, two-piece pajamas and another pair of sweats. But it was the lingerie section that had done him in and he still couldn't explain it if someone asked.

Bras didn't scare him. He'd grown up with sisters, making slingshots with the garments when he and his brother were bored. As a child, Grace had routinely danced around in nothing but her underwear. He knew how to navigate lingerie, having stripped a few women out of theirs. He hadn't, however, known how to contend with the inquisition that had come as he'd randomly selected items he'd thought Soledad might need.

HE COULD BARELY remember the sales rep's name, but she clearly remembered his, stepping up to him as he selected tank tops he thought Soledad might like. The saleswoman was an employee of the department store, but they had often run into one another in social settings. She was an attractive woman, though not at all Palmer's type. The woman's smile filled her face as she bent to look at his selections with a curious eye.

"Palmer Colton," she cooed, her voice oozing what he imagined it would if she moonlighted as a phone sex operator. "Isn't this a pleasant surprise?"

"Hey. How are you?" His mind raced as he tried to remember if she were a Chelsea, Stacey or Mary. He was grateful when she straightened and he could see the name tag pinned to her blazer. "It's good to see you again, Ms. Robbins."

"Please, call me Stacey. I would hope you and I are on a first-name basis by now." She laughed suggestively.

Palmer chuckled politely, although he wasn't in a jovial mood. "Well, it's good to see you again, *Stacey*."

"I see you're enjoying a shopping spree. Special occasion?" As her gaze narrowed, she rested her palm on the edge of the shopping cart.

"I'm just helping out a friend."

"A close friend?"

"Just someone who needs a helping hand."

She paused, clearly waiting for him to expound on the comment.

The moment, unmistakably awkward, had Palmer wanting to tell her to go away. He obliged her instead.

"She and her children lost everything in a fire," he mumbled.

"Oh, my word!" Stacey exclaimed. "That's horrible."

"They've been devastated," Palmer added. "I just want to make things easier."

"I understand completely." She drew her fingers to the strand of beads around her neck, twirling them anxiously. "How can I help? Because I'd really like to help."

"I just need to get some clothes for her. Clean undergarments, casual wear, that kind of thing."

"Well, those tank tops you're holding are sheer perfection. The fabric is butter-soft against your skin and they can be worn with or without a bra comfortably. They are wonderful layering pieces."

Palmer dropped them atop the merchandise he'd already selected. "I appreciate the recommendation," he said.

"I would also suggest the matching panties," Stacey said. "I absolutely love them. What size is she?"

"Small, I think. She's very petite."

"Small it is." Stacey dropped a half dozen matching colors on top of the tank tops. "How about bras? Do you know her measurements?"

Palmer suddenly imagined his hands cupping Soledad's breasts, the image causing his heart to palpitate and his stomach to twist. Heat rained in his lower extremities and he shifted from side to side to stall the rise of nature threatening to publicly embarrass him. "I don't," he said, shaking his head vehemently. "I think this is enough."

"If I can make a suggestion?" Stacey mused, her brows quirking questioningly.

"Please…"

"Maybe buy her something pretty. You know, to pick up her spirits. We just got these adorable teddies in," she said, holding up a sexy little satin-and-lace set. "I bet this would brighten her day and make her feel very special."

Palmer felt his cheeks flush with heat as he imagined Soledad wearing the set, in his bed, beneath him. It was suddenly too much and he was past ready to be out of the store. He nodded. "Thank you," he said, almost snatching the garment from her hands. "I appreciate all your help."

"Anytime!" Stacey gushed. Her voice dropped two octaves. "And if you need any other assistance," she purred, pressing her business card into the palm of his hand, "don't hesitate to call me. I've written my cell phone number on the back."

With one last nod, Palmer gave the cart a push and hurried toward the registers. As he stood in line to pay, he whispered a silent prayer that the transaction would happen swiftly and that he wouldn't run into anyone else who knew him.

AND EVEN THAT had taken longer than he would have liked, the clerk who'd finally checked him out wanting to gush over the baby clothes, assuming he was a new father who'd gone overboard to prepare for his newborn.

By the time he'd reached the parking lot with his purchases, he was past ready to be done but had one last errand before he could head home. He'd sat for a few minutes, turning the tracking device he'd found in Lyra's diaper bag over in his hands. A part of him had hoped the man with the dark shades and the damaged fender would have shown up while he was in town, but there'd been no sign of him or anyone else following the tracker. Had Palmer seen him, Gavin Stone would have found himself having an unbelievably bad day, because Palmer would have done whatever was necessary to help the man into jail so that Soledad would feel safe again.

Despite the many distractions as he'd shopped, Palmer had still been mindful to keep an eye out for anyone or anything that didn't feel right. Anything that would have triggered his radar and put him on edge. He'd looked around the parking lot one last time, driving slowly up and down each aisle as he'd pretended to look for an empty spot, studying each vehicle instead. As he'd finally pulled out of the lot, he'd driven to the back of the building and the oversize brown dumpsters that serviced the shopping center. He'd pulled up in front of the recycle bins and shut down his truck.

He'd still palmed the small device in his hand, his mind racing as plans formulated in his head about the lengths he would go to just to protect Soledad. He'd debated just how far too far might be.

With one last glance around, he'd stepped out of his truck and leaned in to gather up the empty cups, fast-food bags and stacks of junk. He tossed it all into one half-full dumpster and then headed for the ranch.

Now, turning into the driveway and toward the house, all he could think about was getting back to Soledad.

PALMER HAD BARELY been gone an hour before Soledad was stir-crazy. Being locked away in the bedroom felt as bad as running through the forest in the middle of the night. Every creak and squeak fueled her anxiety, and she was feeling slightly claustrophobic waiting for him to return.

Lyra lay in the center of the bed, doing what Lyra did best. She snored softly and clearly didn't have a care in the world. Soledad wished she could say the same. She pulled open the bedroom door and Jack bounded in, his exuberance steroidal. He ignored Soledad completely, barely letting her pet him on the head before he jumped onto the bed, sniffing and licking the little girl's toes and then settling down beside her.

"Aren't you something," Soledad muttered.

Jack dropped his head to a pillow and closed his eyes, dismissing Soledad with a slight grunt.

She laughed.

Exiting the room, she moved from window to window, peering out in search of Palmer's truck. She wanted to believe that everything was well and that he'd be back without incident. But that wasn't what she was feeling. Every horrible thing she could imagine had run through her head.

She was petrified that Gavin would ambush Palmer, then her, and then disappear with Lyra. She imagined Gavin strangling her or shooting her, or worse, tying her to a stake in the desert for the buzzards to feed on.

Her imagination had devolved into the realm of nightmares with no happy endings for any of them. Imagining Gavin taking a pitchfork or a blowtorch to Palmer had her feeling exceptionally anxious, most especially because Palmer had shown her nothing but kindness since she'd landed on his doorstep. Envisioning Palmer's demise had her nerves on edge. She was anxious for him to return home, to be back safe and secure with her and Lyra.

Soledad debated whether she should call to check on him. Then she imagined he might be put off by her calling when there was no emergency. She tabled the idea, figuring instead that she'd wait at least another hour before sending him a text message if he hadn't returned by then. Until then, she'd have to rein in her doom-and-gloom conjectures.

Soledad took a seat at the counter. With pen and paper in hand, she began to outline Rachel's cake design and to lay out her prep plans. Thinking about business, and what she needed to accomplish, was enough to keep her mind off everything else. She sketched and jotted notes until she felt better about what had to be done.

Time passed and that hour had come and gone, and there was still no sign of Palmer. By hour three, Soledad was beginning to think she needed to be afraid. She pulled the cell phone from the pocket of her pants. She hesitated. *I'm overreacting*, Soledad thought to herself. *This is ridiculous!* Considering everything she had asked him to do, she knew he'd more than likely be gone most of the afternoon. She hadn't thought that one through. Or considered that he might have had his own personal errands to run that she wasn't privy to. Maybe even meeting up with a female friend, someone he wasn't interested in her knowing about. Someone who had his attention, maybe even his heart.

Soledad shook the thought from her head. She was bordering on complete delusion and needed to get a handle on the wealth of emotion consuming her. She palmed the burner phone and began to dial the number committed to memory, assessing the risk versus the necessity. Necessity won out and she tapped her toes as she waited for her twin sister to answer.

"Hello?"

"Dominique, it's me."

"Soledad! Where are you? You've had us worried to death. Whose number is this?"

"I can't tell you. I just want you to know I'm okay."

"*¡Dios mío, chica!* Dad has practically hired the entire US military to search for you. The police won't tell us anything. Stanton hasn't been able to get any information from any of his family. What is going on?"

"Gavin killed Annie. Now he's looking for me."

Dominique gasped loudly. "No. Oh, Soledad. I'm so sorry."

Soledad's eyes misted with tears. "But you can't say anything to anyone, Dom. Not even Dad. It's not safe. Gavin is dangerous and I wouldn't put it past him to try to get to me through my family and friends."

"You need to come home. You know our father would never let anything happen to you. He will keep you safe."

"I know, but I can't risk putting anyone else in danger. This is for the best. I will call you in a day or two to let you know if there's been any change. Meanwhile, tell Dad not to worry, please. I really am doing okay. Lyra and I are fine."

Dominique inhaled swiftly. "That poor baby. I can't even imagine."

"Once the police find Gavin, I'll be able to come out of hiding. Until then, I just don't feel safe to do so."

"This is just too much, Soledad. You need to tell the police so they can protect you."

At that moment, the door flung open and Palmer stepped through the entrance. He and Soledad immediately locked eyes and held on. The intensity of the moment shifted every ounce of air in the atmosphere. Soledad felt something deep in her gut explode, a wave of heat so intense that she began to perspire, moisture puddling in intimate places. It knocked the breath from her and she gasped. Loudly.

"Soledad? You okay?" Dominique questioned, concern ringing in her voice.

"I'm good," Soledad answered. "I have all the protection I need right where I am," she concluded, and then she disconnected the call.

Chapter Seven

Palmer was surprised by the wave of relief that flooded his spirit when he stepped through the door. Laying eyes on Soledad felt like Christmas morning when you still believed in Santa Claus and laid your eyes on your wrapped presents. He was tempted to rub his eyes with his fists to make sure he wasn't dreaming, but he didn't need to. Soledad blessed him with a smile, and just like that, everything he'd gone through earlier at the shopping center was forgotten.

He smiled. "Everything okay?" he asked, trying not to let any anxiety filter through his words.

Soledad nodded. "I took your advice and called my sister to let her know I was okay. I didn't want my father sending out the cavalry looking for me."

"I'm sure the only thing that will stop him from doing that is his laying eyes on you. But I'm glad you let them know you're safe."

"I am, too."

"Where's the baby?"

"Asleep in your room."

"I guess I don't need to ask where Jack is. There

was a time he'd meet me at the door and pretend to be excited that I was home."

Soledad laughed. "I'm sure he's still excited."

"Clearly not as excited about me as he is about Lyra."

"That's true. In fact, I don't think Jack is going to let anyone get between the two of them without a fight."

"Let's hope it never comes down to that," Palmer said. He shook his head. "I'm going to drive around back and start unloading the truck. I think I got everything you needed. But if I didn't and you need anything else, we'll have to order it online and have it delivered. Shopping was painful!"

"Was it that bad?"

"Too many nosy people." He threw up his hands in frustration.

Soledad laughed again. "Grave Gulch definitely has that small-town vibe. Everyone knows everyone and everyone wants to know everyone else's business."

"Well, I'm not used to that many people wanting to know mine."

"Sorry about that."

"Nothing for you to be sorry about."

She blessed him with another bright smile. "Can I help you unpack the car?"

"You can stand at the door and keep out of sight. I stopped and picked up Chinese food for dinner. I'll hand you the food and I would really appreciate it if you would fix me a plate. I haven't eaten anything since I left this morning and I'm starved. I'll eat once I get everything else out the truck, but you feel free to dig in whenever you want."

Soledad rolled her eyes. "That's it?"

"I've got the rest covered. Besides, most of my men will be punching out for the day. They might pass the house on their way out and I don't want anyone to see you."

Palmer gave her a grin of sorts and turned, moving back out the front door. As she watched him walk away, Soledad felt her eyes mist, tears pressing against her lashes. She wiped the back of her hand across her face as her own smile pulled full and wide, something like joy brimming at the edge of her spirit.

HOURS LATER, PALMER stood in the doorway of his guest room. After a quick meal and casual conversation about his shopping experiences, it had taken the two of them very little time to transform the space. He was still in awe that a room that was once part library, part bedroom now looked like a full-scale nursery.

The bright white crib was set up in the corner where a bookcase had once stood. The freshly washed animal-print linens the salesclerk had suggested decorated the tiny mattress. The addition of the changing table and assortment of stuffed animals pulled it all together. Even he was impressed—and that was sometimes hard to accomplish. Soledad had packed away the diapers and baby clothes, and little Lyra had been officially moved in. Under different circumstances, Palmer would have found that amusing. Now he wasn't so sure.

He stood watching as Soledad set the baby down

for the night. She'd had sweet potatoes for her evening meal, preferring them over the peas he had tried to feed her. Now she suckled on a bottle of warm milk, her eyes closing and opening as she settled in for a night's sleep. He watched Soledad, who watched Lyra, in awe of them both. Jack nudging his leg pulled him from the reverie.

"I have to take the dog out and check on the animals," he said softly. "It's time for Pharaoh to get his evening meds."

Soledad shifted to give him a look. She nodded and smiled, then turned her attention back to the baby.

She was a natural when it came to mothering the little girl and Palmer found himself wondering why she didn't already have any children of her own. He hadn't thought to ask her when the two had talked about his own disinterest in fatherhood, but, clearly, he thought, Soledad would make a magnificent mother—and a great wife…to some other guy.

Out in the barn, Pharaoh was resting comfortably, faring far better than he had days earlier. Palmer ensured the horse had fresh bedding, a dose of the medicine the veterinarian had left and a bucket of oats to feed on. He sat with the colt for a good while before tossing a wool blanket on his broad back. The Arabian nuzzled his side and Palmer took that as a good sign the horse was getting better.

Making his regular rounds, Palmer stopped to inspect the fence that had been repaired. He also rode over to the south pasture to check on the cattle. His herd was sizable and seemed to be milling around contentedly together. A few calf stragglers that had strayed from the pack cried out, their mothers mooing in response to guide them. Palmer whistled for Jack, and within a few short minutes, the Bernese was by his side.

"Gather, Jack," Palmer commanded, and the dog shot across the fields to maneuver the dawdlers back into place.

After one last check of the gates, Palmer felt comfortable that all was well and headed back to the house. Usually, the ranch was his happy place, his regular routines giving him a sense of accomplishment and joy. He was proud of what he'd built, and everything about the land and his animals satisfied his sensibilities. This particular night, though, all he wanted was to get back to his home and the woman who was suddenly an anomaly in his life. And nothing about that made an ounce of sense to him. Nothing truly had made sense to him since the night Soledad had turned up in his barn.

SOLEDAD STOOD WITH her hands on her hips, assessing her situation. Lyra had gone to sleep easily, seeming to like her new surroundings. Palmer had outdone himself, buying out half the department store to make them comfortable. She had no idea how she'd ever be able to repay his generosity. He'd made it clear that he didn't expect to be reimbursed, but she knew she could never not repay his benevolence.

There were still dozens of dry goods in shopping

bags for her to sort through, but they would have to wait. She needed to start prepping the cake she'd been contracted to bake, though she was finding it difficult to focus on anything but her situation and Palmer Colton. She kicked herself for being so scattered thinking about a man who was clearly gun-shy. Not that she was interested in a relationship with him—or anyone. Because she wasn't. Or, at least, that was the story she told anyone who asked. She didn't have time to build a relationship with anyone while she built her business. The bakery was currently thriving and usually that would require every ounce of her attention. Any man would have to take a back seat. Now more than ever, though, since she had to reprioritize her life-goals list to place Lyra at the very top.

Soledad sighed softly. She couldn't help but think that maybe she'd made a mistake. If only she had listened to Palmer that first night and gone straight to the police. What if she hadn't overreacted, her concerns more responsive than reactionary. Maybe she'd gotten things overwhelmingly wrong… If only she had chosen differently, she and Lyra could be home, settling into their new routines with each other. She had a lengthy list of if-onlys, what-ifs and maybes, and alternate scenarios with Gavin dropping off the face of the earth. Then she remembered something her father had often said. *If a toad had wings, it wouldn't bump its ass when it hopped.* There was no room for what-ifs. She had to deal with the here and now and the choices she had made.

She had always believed that everything happened

for a reason. Sometimes that reason was easy to see and sometimes fate put a man like Palmer Colton in the way, not caring if it made sense or not. She was overthinking everything and that had never served her well in the past. She needed to shake off all that was clouding her head and to stop thinking about Palmer Colton.

PALMER'S KITCHEN WAS a dream come true. There was enough space for multiple people to cook and prep food comfortably. The Sub-Zero refrigerator and freezer and the Viking gas range were top-of-the-line. Double convection ovens as well as dual sinks would make her tasks easy and Soledad was grateful for it. She had just laid out her ingredients when Palmer and Jack came bounding through the door.

"Hey there," she said, greeting him warmly.

"Hey. You're getting started."

"I have a lot to do before tomorrow."

Palmer moved to the center island, leaning against the counter. He scanned the foodstuffs Soledad had begun to prep. "What are we making?" he questioned.

She gave him a bright smile. "We?"

He shrugged. "Usually, I'd be on the sofa watching CNN until I fell asleep. I thought I might give you a hand instead. Unless I'd be in the way?"

Soledad shook her head. "Not at all. I'd appreciate the company. I spend a lot of time in the bakery after hours working alone, so this will be a nice change."

"So, what are we making?"

"My famous carrot cake with a buttercream filling. I

don't do the usual cream-cheese frosting. It'll have three tiers and be decorated with a stained-glass design."

"Stained glass?"

"It's one of my specialties and I can knock it out fairly quickly."

"Then I'll just sit here and watch you work. If you need help, I'll be close by to give you instruction." He smirked, looking slightly dopey.

Soledad laughed. "The man has jokes."

Palmer laughed with her. "So, walk me through what you're doing," he said, seeming genuinely interested.

"The first thing is to actually bake the carrot cake."

"Easy peasy!"

Soledad's face lit up, amusement dancing in her eyes. "Really?"

He shrugged his broad shoulders. "My mother used to say it all the time. Whenever I thought anything felt like a challenge, she would say it was easy peasy."

"So did mine," Soledad responded. "I haven't heard that in forever." Her smile was wistful as she thought back to the matriarch of her family. Her mother had died five years ago, and the loss still stung. It had left a massive hole in her heart that nothing would ever be able to fill. She and Dominique had moved forward, finding a new normal that revolved around their father and helping him through the devastation. She missed her mother.

"I'm sorry for your loss," Palmer said as if reading her mind. "I remember your father speaking very fondly of her."

"She was the love of his life. They were so happy together. I had hoped to have that for myself someday."

Palmer's brow creased. "You don't anymore?"

"I'm now a single mother. I'm not sure many men are interested in a ready-made family."

"You'd be surprised."

"I would be. The men I've met recently are more interested in their own good time."

"That sounds like a story."

"One day maybe," she said.

The conversation paused as Soledad combined grated carrots and brown sugar together in a bowl. She added raisins and then set the mixture aside. In a second bowl, she beat the eggs until they were lemony yellow. Then she whisked in vanilla, oil and white sugar.

"Did you add enough vanilla?" Palmer questioned lightly. "I'd probably add a bit more."

Soledad giggled. "I'm pretty sure I have enough."

"It's your cake, but if it doesn't taste good, don't say I didn't warn you," he teased. "I'm a professional, so I know these things."

She rolled her eyes skyward, shaking her head slightly as he asked, "How long have you been doing this?"

"Since forever. I have always loved to bake. Cookies, cakes, pastries. I would make doughnuts every weekend in high school, and Dominique and I would eat until we were sick. In college, I really wasn't sure what I wanted to do with my life. It was Annie who convinced me to open the bakery. It was the best decision I've ever made. I leave work every day happy and

I'm excited to go in the next day." There was a moment of hesitation as Soledad thought about her friend. She missed Annie!

Palmer gave her that moment before responding, understanding the pang of loss she was feeling. He nodded, then moved the conversation forward. "That's how I feel about the ranch. I love everything about this cowboy lifestyle."

"Did you always know you wanted to be a rancher?"

"I was hooked the first time my father put me on a horse and taught me to ride. I was eight, maybe nine, at the time."

Soledad smiled, amused that they had both discovered their passions at young ages and had both seen their dreams to fruition.

They paused again as Soledad added crushed pineapple to the egg mixture. She reached for a third bowl and added flour, baking soda, salt and cinnamon. She combined the wet and dry mixtures, then threw in the carrot combination. Her batter was complete with the addition of chopped walnuts.

"That came together fast," Palmer commented as she split the batter between three cake pans she had earlier greased and dusted with flour.

"That's what happens when you know what you're doing. But you know that, being professional and all." She slid the cake pans into the hot oven and set the timer.

Palmer laughed, amused by the hint of snark in her voice. "I, for one, am glad you perfected that doughnut recipe. I admit I'm a fan. I regularly stop at the bakery to get a dozen of your square doughnuts with your signature honey glaze. And the ones with the raspberry filling are to die for."

"The raspberry ones are my personal favorite. The filling is actually my mother's recipe." She grinned, excited to discover that he liked her pastries.

"I've also enjoyed the pecan pie and that twelve-layer chocolate cake with the caramel and nuts. And the cookies! All the cookies are to die for, but the pecan brittle with chocolate glaze are my all-time favorites. I get very excited when you have those in rotation."

Soledad giggled. "How often do you come by the bakery?"

He gave her a wry smile. "Truth?"

"Why would you lie?"

He shrugged. "I wouldn't, but I feel kind of awkward telling you this now." He chuckled softly.

Her forehead furrowed, confusion washing through her. "So, what is it? Have you *never* been to the bakery and you've been sending someone else to pick up your sweets?"

He shook his head, then answered. "I stop by a few times a week. I keep hoping I'll see you there, but you're never out front. Then, of course, I can't leave without buying something, and I try to buy everything because it's all so good." His face was suddenly flushed, color firing his cheeks a deep shade of red.

Soledad felt herself blush, as well, flattered by the compliment. There was an awkward pause that billowed between them. She dropped her gaze to the confectioners' sugar she'd poured into a bowl and took a deep breath. "Why didn't you talk to me at the engagement party the other week?" she asked, still not lifting her eyes to meet his. She prayed the question sounded nonchalant and that curiosity was the only thing he read into it.

Before Palmer could answer, a shrill cry echoed out of the new baby monitor on the counter. Lyra was not happy and wanted them to know it.

Soledad's eyes widened. "Do you mind checking on her?" she asked, finally throwing him a look. She had begun to prep the fondant for her cake, and her hands were full as she kneaded the sugar paste against her palms.

"No problem." Palmer slid off his wooden stool and headed down the hall toward the guest room.

As he left, she mumbled under her breath, *"Saved by the baby!"*

Watching Palmer walk away, Soledad suddenly had new appreciation for the handsome rancher. She realized his rough-and-tough exterior was actually a facade for his soft interior. He was shy and far more introverted than she had realized. She appreciated his effort to come out of his shell to let her in to know him. She imagined that he didn't often have women in his space, ruling his kitchen and practically taking over his home. Had the roles been reversed, she couldn't say with any surety that she would be as accommodating or as pleasant about it.

She moved to the ovens to check on her cakes. It was clear that Palmer didn't use his kitchen often, despite his skills with a scrambled egg. His appliances still had their installation labels, and she didn't think he had ever used his picture-perfect double ovens.

His voice suddenly cooed through the baby monitor and Soledad's smile lifted sweetly as she eavesdropped on his conversation with Lyra.

"HEY, YOU," PALMER SAID, his tone soft and fluffy like cotton candy. "What are you crying for?" He leaned over the crib, untangling the blanket from around Lyra's chubby legs. He reached to pick the baby up into his arms, rocking her gently until her tears eased, leaving her with the hiccups. She pulled a tight fist into her mouth, chewing on her fingers. Jack sat staring up at him, his tail wagging from side to side. The dog barked.

"Easy, boy. I won't drop her. I promise."

Jack barked at him a second time.

Palmer shook his head. He carried Lyra to the changing table and laid her on the platform. She was wet and needed a diaper change. He reached for one of the Huggies he'd purchased. He continued to coo and make faces at the little girl, even blowing bubbles against her belly until she laughed. Minutes later, she had a dry bottom, her tears were gone, and she lay in his arms suckling a bottle of warm milk he'd collected from the kitchen.

Although navigating babies was not his thing, he was fairly decent at the job, he thought. Desiree had given him more than his fair share of practice with his nephew Danny. He thought about the little boy who had given the family a scare when he'd been kidnapped several times. Thinking they might not find his nephew had been devastating. Palmer never wanted to know that feeling again, and the thought of Gavin running off with Lyra felt too similar for any comfort.

Palmer smiled down at the little girl, Lyra's bright eyes dancing across his face as she studied him. She smiled back and a puddle of milk trickled onto her chin. He gently wiped the drool away with the cloth towel tossed over his shoulder.

"You've been through a lot, haven't you, little lady?" His voice was a loud whisper as he stared into her blue eyes. He brushed his hand lightly over her head and tousled the wisps of blond hair. "I'm so sorry about your mommy. My mommy died when I was a little boy, too. But it's going to be okay. I'm not sure what's going to happen, but I don't want you to worry, because that new mommy of yours is a pretty special lady. She is going to love you so hard! And I know she will do everything in her power to make you the happiest little girl in the whole wide world."

Lyra kicked her legs in response and smiled again, another puddle of milk rolling onto her chin.

"We really need to work on that," Palmer said as he dabbed the moisture away. "Try to swallow before you smile at me, kiddo."

Lyra tossed the bottle aside and stretched the length of her body. Lifting her to his shoulder, Palmer gently patted her back until she burped. Loudly.

"That sounded like an old man burp. That's not pretty, kid. Boys will think it's funny when you're nine. But it won't be cute when you're nineteen."

Lyra burped again.

Palmer chuckled softly. He nuzzled his face against her neck, inhaling the sweet scent of baby powder. "Old Jack and I will always be here if you need us, okay? Don't you ever forget that," he whispered against her cheek.

Palmer felt his heart swell and the wealth of emotion surprised him. His concern for the baby's well-being was tangible, building like bricks on a wall. He instinctively knew he would fight tooth and nail to keep her from harm, and nothing and no one would keep him from protecting her.

He sat her on his lap, one large hand supporting her belly and the other gently caressing her back. Together, they were comfortable in the small recliner that decorated the room.

Lyra suddenly screeched, throwing herself toward Jack, who'd dropped his head onto Palmer's thigh. She grabbed two fistfuls of fur and held on, attempting to chew on the animal's ear. Jack licked her face, washing away remnants of milk with his tongue.

"Eww!" Palmer exclaimed, frowning. "Dog drool. Now you need a bath, little girl." He shook his head, holding her upright as she clawed at his dog and the dog nuzzled her in return. He felt a smile, full and expansive, lift his lips and chuckled again. "Something tells me you two are going to be trouble together."

Chapter Eight

Soledad's eyes misted with tears as she tried not to cry into the royal icing she was preparing for the cake. Eavesdropping on Palmer as he'd tended to Lyra had pushed her to the edge of emotional overload. She was surprised by his tenderness with the baby, most especially knowing his disinterest in having children of his own. But he'd been so sweet and funny and entertaining that it had served to remind her of all the good that could be found in people if one just took the time to look.

For a man who was not interested in being anyone's father, Palmer played the role quite well. Had Lyra been blessed with a dad like that, things would be vastly different. Annie would still be alive, her little family at home and happy. Soledad would be in the bakery putting the finishing touches on the next day's orders... and Palmer Colton would only be a fleeting fantasy. She couldn't help but wonder if they would ever have become friends if she hadn't shown up needing to be rescued. She suddenly thought of Gavin and how horrific he had been as a father and as a husband, and her stomach flipped remembering that he was still out there. Still a threat to their safety.

It had gone quiet in the other room, just a low hum echoing out of the speaker. Then Palmer began to sing. He was a pitch-perfect baritone, his voice thick and rich like sorghum molasses. Soledad stopped what she was doing to listen as he serenaded Lyra. It took her a moment to realize he was singing "Can You Feel the Love Tonight?" from Disney's *The Lion King* and singing it quite beautifully. By the time he finished, happy tears were streaming down Soledad's face and she'd ruined a batch of her icing.

PALMER WOKE WITH a start. Lyra lay asleep on his chest, the two of them still sitting in the oversize chair that adorned the room. The little girl actually snored, and her soft snorts made Palmer smile. He took a slow, deep breath. As he blew it out, his chest falling, Lyra jumped ever so slightly. Palmer tapped her gently against her back.

He looked around the room, not knowing what time it was or how long he'd been asleep. So much for being a helping hand in the kitchen, he thought. He could only begin to imagine what Soledad must be thinking about him. Jack was sprawled across the queen-size bed, alone. There was no sign of Soledad.

He shifted forward in the seat, then stood slowly. Moving to the crib, he laid the infant down gently, then draped a cotton receiving blanket over her. He stared down at her, bemused that she could slumber so peacefully. He wondered if she had always been an easy baby or if there had been days and weeks of endless screaming and hours of no sleep for her parents. He brushed the pad of his finger across her forehead, taking a wisp of hair out of her face.

She was a cute little thing. And if she were his, there was no way he'd ever let her out of his sight. How her father could put her at risk baffled him, and then he thought of his own sperm donor and things he had done. Not everyone was meant to be a parent, Palmer thought, and too many folks should never have had kids.

Jack suddenly nuzzled his hand for attention.

"You need to go out, Jack?" Palmer questioned. "Come on, then," he said as the two eased out of the bedroom and headed for the kitchen.

It was dead quiet in the front room. Soledad's carrot cake sat on the counter and it was exquisite. The three tiers had been covered in fondant. She'd piped a floral design in black royal icing, the detailed outline showcasing her talent. He wasn't sure how she'd finished the areas of color that gave the cake its stained-glass effect, but he was duly impressed with her work. He imagined her friend Rachel would be, as well.

Soledad lay on the sofa, her back propped on a mound of pillows. She'd wrapped one of the wool blankets over her torso and was sleeping soundly. Palmer found himself staring, awed by how beautiful she was. Her hair was loose, the length of it framing her face. The warm temperature in the room complemented her olive complexion. She was glowing, and looked as angelic as Lyra when she slept. Jack nuzzled his hand again, more persistent about going outside.

"Okay, dog. Okay," Palmer muttered, tearing his eyes from the young woman. "You're a nuisance, do you know that?"

Jack panted, clearly disinterested in Palmer's opinion. When Palmer opened the door to let him out, he took off running, disappearing into the darkness.

When Palmer turned back around, he was surprised to find Soledad sitting upright, staring at him. She pulled a hand to her eyes and rubbed the sleep away.

"I'm sorry," he said softly. "I didn't mean to wake you."

"I didn't mean to doze off," she answered, giving him a slight smile. "You and Lyra were napping so peacefully I didn't want to wake you. I sat out here to catch my breath and that's all I remember."

"I hadn't planned to fall asleep, either," he said. "I think the stress of the past forty-eight hours finally caught up with us both."

"I'm actually surprised I was able to relax," Soledad said with a soft sigh. "I feel safe here."

Something in her words suddenly had him thinking about the future and what time would eventually bring to them. What would happen when it was all over, and they went back to their own circles? When she no longer needed his protection, and they went back to being passing acquaintances? He was glad she felt safe, but he couldn't let himself forget that it was only temporary. That he couldn't keep either of them forever. A wave of melancholy hit him in the chest and he blew a wistful sigh past his lips. He shook the thoughts from his head and changed the subject as he moved to the refrigerator. "I'm hungry. Can I get you something?"

"What are you having?"

"I have some sliced turkey in the fridge. I can make us sandwiches," he answered.

Soledad nodded as she threw her legs off the sofa. "A turkey sandwich works for me. Do you have any cranberry sauce?"

He grinned. "That's the only way to eat a turkey sandwich."

"It would be sheer perfection if you also had some stuffing."

Palmer laughed. "You're a foodie after my own heart. Tell me you also like grilled cheese."

"I'll have to make you my very special grilled Swiss on rye with bacon and tomato."

"Okay, that does sound good, but not as good as my four-cheese grilled cheese on toasted garlic bread. Or my grilled Brie with ham, caramelized onions and apple compote."

"I do my grilled Brie with candied bacon and apricot jam."

"It sounds like you and I are going to have to have a grilled-cheese runoff to find the best sandwich."

Soledad laughed. "You'll lose. You know that, right?"

"Says you, but I'd put my money on me and my favorite cast-iron grilled-cheese pan. I bet you don't have a pan specifically for grilled cheese."

She giggled. "You might have me beat there."

"The pan is important to the artistry of grilled cheese. Much like your cake pans are important to your cakes."

"Touché!"

He grinned, the smile full and wide. She made him laugh, her quick wit fueling the smart quips. He liked that she didn't take herself, or him, too seriously. He suddenly realized he was going to miss it when she wasn't there anymore, the thought like a punch to his midsection. He took a deep breath and held it.

Palmer suddenly cocked his head to the side. His mood shifted from relaxed to tense in the blink of an eye as he tossed her a look. "Did you hear that?" he breathed loudly as he hurried to the door.

Soledad whispered back, "Hear what?"

As Palmer pulled open the door, the noise was clearer. Jack was barking, making a loud fuss about something. He clearly wasn't happy. And then the dog cried out as if something or someone had caused him pain.

"Bedroom. Now!" Palmer snapped as he shut off the lights, darkening the room. The hall gave off just enough illumination for them both to still see. He reached for the rifle that rested by the door where he'd last placed it and rushed out into the late-night air, slamming the door behind him.

SOLEDAD RAN QUICKLY to the guest bedroom to check on Lyra. The baby was sleeping, undisturbed by whatever was going on. She debated whether she would stay in place and lock the two of them inside but decided fairly quickly that a good defense was an even better offense. Rushing back to the kitchen, she grabbed the largest butcher knife in his knife collection and braced herself for a fight, her eyes dancing between the door and the windows.

Waiting for something to happen, for anything to bring this to an end, was painful at best. It had her head spinning and she was feeling completely out of control. Soledad paced back and forth, then hurried to the door and flung it open. She stared out into the dark, hoping for a glimpse of Palmer, or Jack, or any friendly face that wasn't wanting to cause them harm. She tilted her head to listen for any sound or noise that would calm her nerves and let her know that all was well.

But calm didn't come, terror taking its place instead. Gunshots rang through the air. *Bang! Bang! Bang!* One explosion after another echoed too close for comfort. The shots sounded like they were being fired from a small-caliber handgun, and knowing that pushed her emotions right to the edge. She heard Palmer's rifle fire once, and then hearing it a second time sent her over the edge into an abyss.

The next few minutes felt like an eternity. Panic washed over Soledad in heavy waves. Her mind was mush, every awful thing she could imagine once again playing out like some dark thriller on a big screen. She cursed. Loudly. The level of profanity was the stuff of sailors and adolescent boys discovering they could use their lengthy list of bad words in a complete sentence.

Unable to fathom who was shooting, or what she needed to do, Soledad slammed the door closed. She backed herself against the counter, prepared to knife any stranger who came through the door.

It suddenly felt like a perfect storm had converged around them. Just as Soledad mentally prepared herself for the worst, the house alarm sounded, a deep, loud siren that screeched like fingernails against a chalkboard. Just then, Palmer came barreling through the entrance, shouting her name. Jack limped in beside him, panting heavily. A streak of bright red blood matted the white fur on his chest. The house phone began to ring, and as if on cue, Lyra started crying at the top of her little lungs.

PALMER MOVED TO Soledad's side, pressing a warm palm to her cheek. "Are you okay?" he asked, his gaze skipping over her face as concern seeped from his eyes.

She shook her head, tears beginning to rise in her eyes. "No. You scared me. I thought you were dead!" She tossed the knife in her hand onto the marble counter.

He smiled. "I don't plan to go down that easy. Besides, I still need to get myself right with God. Maybe go to church a time or two," he joked.

Soledad rolled her eyes skyward, not at all amused at his attempt at humor. She was Catholic and you didn't play when it came to the Father, the Son, and the Holy Spirit. "Was it Gavin? Was it him shooting at you?"

Palmer shrugged. "Probably, but I'm not sure. They were too far away for me to see exactly, but they shot first and I shot back! I think I hit whoever it was. He's bleeding, I know that." He moved to the alarm box and entered in the passcode to stop the siren. Lyra was still crying, her wails having transitioned to a full-scale sob.

The phone had stopped ringing but began again. "That's the alarm service," Palmer said. "I'm sure they've already dispatched the police. You'll need to stay out of sight unless you're ready to come out of hiding."

"No," she answered with a shake of her head.

"Then my bedroom is the safest place. Lock the door. The room is soundproof, so even if Lyra cries, they won't hear you."

Soledad eyed him oddly. "Why is your master bedroom soundproof?"

"I'm a screamer when I orgasm," he said nonchalantly.

Soledad blinked, her lashes batting up and down as she stared at him. "Are you serious?"

He laughed. "No. I just thought it would lighten the moment."

She shook her head. She bit back her snarky response as Lyra's cries got louder, the baby girl on the verge of hysteria.

Soledad shook her head. "My poor baby. I need to settle Lyra down," she said as she scurried down the length of the hallway to the guest bedroom.

Palmer finally answered the phone. "This is Palmer Colton… Yes…yes…the code is 547893… Yes…there was an intruder… I think I shot him… Yes…thank you." He hung up, his eyes turning toward Jack, who looked like he'd just gone ten rounds in a heavyweight fight.

"Hey, big boy," he said, grabbing a dishrag from the counter and dropping to the floor to inspect the dog's injuries. He swiped at the blood on the dog's fur, grateful that it wasn't his. Jack licked his hand, then lay against the tiled floor and closed his eyes. Giving in to the exhaustion, he began to snore softly.

Outside, the first police car was pulling onto the property. The car lights were flashing, and the siren sounded. Palmer stood as two additional patrol cars followed behind it.

Soledad rushed into the kitchen, to the refrigerator. She grabbed a bottle of milk from inside. Lyra was in her arms, no longer crying. The baby looked around, trying to make sense of the moment. Palmer pressed his hand to Soledad's arm and leaned in to kiss the child's forehead. Lyra grabbed at his chin and giggled.

"Do you need to warm that?" he asked, gesturing at the baby bottle.

Soledad shook her head as she stole a quick glance out the bay window. "I'll run it under hot water in the bathroom. It'll warm quickly."

He nodded. "Just lock the door. I'll do my best to keep them out of the house," he said softly. He gave her a gentle pat against her back, his touch like the sweetest balm. Then he headed outside to meet with the officers.

PALMER WASN'T PREPARED when the silver Honda Accord pulled in line with the Grave Gulch police cars in front of his home. He had already given a statement to the first officers who'd arrived on-site. They had confiscated his rifle and were now canvasing the property for signs of the intruder who had fired on him and possibly taken a bullet for his efforts. The line of flashlights waving about in the distance was formidable. Their bright glow against the dark canvas was slightly eerie. But whoever had breached the property had come in on foot, not having the code to unlock the gates, and the officers were walking the fields to make sure there was no body there.

He wasn't surprised when Troy stepped out of the driver's side of the car, but he had not anticipated his cousin Stanton's exit from the passenger side. He groaned, not in the mood for what he knew would come. The two men hurried to his side and it started as soon as he greeted them.

"Detective Colton. Mr. Colton. I'm surprised to see you two. What brings you here this time of night?" he said facetiously.

"We were enjoying a late dinner with Evangeline and Dominique when we heard the call on Troy's police scanner," Stanton answered.

"Are you okay?" Troy asked as the two men embraced.

"I've been better," Palmer answered. "It's not every day someone is shooting at you on your own property."

"No, it's not. Did you see who it was? Was it anyone you recognized?"

Palmer shrugged. "It was too dark. Someone was firing at me and I fired back. Two shots. And whoever it was kicked my dog. But I think one of my shots landed. Either that or Jack bit a good chunk out of him and made him bleed."

Troy laughed. "I was wondering where Jack was. He's usually right by your side."

"He was traumatized. He's in the house, shaking it off."

Stanton shook his head. "Do you think this was personal? Did you piss someone off?"

"No," Palmer said firmly. "I don't think it has anything at all to do with me."

Troy nodded. "You might be right. We heard from Soledad today. She witnessed that shooting last night. She's scared and won't come in. We've had teams out looking for the husband most of the day. We think he might still be in the area and we're sure he's looking for Soledad, too. Someone trashed her apartment before we got there this afternoon."

"You think it might have been him?" Palmer asked.

"I don't think it's coincidental. And I don't think she should go back there until we apprehend him."

"Do you think it was him shooting at me?"

"You never know. There are only two or three homes close to where the murder happened. Yours happens to be one of them. He might have hedged his bet that Soledad was here. Your neighbors reported a strange man pretending to be police coming to question them about her. Did he stop here, by chance?"

"Yeah, as a matter of fact. It was late. I was in the barn, tending to my new horse, when he drove up."

"And you didn't say something?"

"No one asked and I've had other things on my mind."

"Like buying baby clothes for an employee and his family?" There was a hint of sarcasm in Troy's voice.

Palmer's gaze narrowed. The static vibrating in the air between the two brothers had become dense.

Palmer took a deep breath. "Just cut to the chase. Should I be worried?"

"That depends," Troy said smugly. "Are you harboring our witness?"

Stanton laughed, amused by the two brothers as they stared each other down.

There was a moment of pause before Palmer responded. "And if I were?"

Troy heaved a heavy sigh. "Then I have to trust you'll do whatever you need to do to keep her safe. Just don't tell Melissa," he said, his voice dropping an octave as he tossed a look over his shoulder. "Chief Colton is not happy about all this."

"Melissa has a lot on her shoulders right now," Stanton answered. "She'd probably have problems with it, but it wouldn't be personal. I doubt she'd arrest you or anything."

"Oh, she'd arrest him. In a heartbeat. You know Melissa doesn't play when it comes to the law. She'd hem you up on obstructing an investigation without even blinking," Troy quipped.

Palmer shook his head. He knew his brother was right about their cousin, but he wasn't willing to put Soledad or Lyra in harm's way. Not even for family he trusted. Maybe it was obstruction, but they'd get over it. "Then I guess if I were harboring your witness, I wouldn't go out of my way to let you or my cousin know about it."

"That might be wise," Stanton said with a hearty chuckle.

"Excuse me for a minute," Troy interjected. "Let me find out where they are with their search. I'll be back as soon as I know what's going on."

Palmer watched his brother walk away, seeking the officer who'd taken his initial statement.

"So, are you harboring the witness?" Stanton questioned when it was just the two of them standing together. "Because Dominique is worried sick about her sister."

"I need you to do me a favor," Palmer said, ignoring the question.

"What's that?"

"Come by later today and pick up a package for me. I'll tell you where to deliver it then."

"Is it important?"

Palmer nodded. "Yeah, very important, and I don't feel comfortable leaving the house right now. I'll owe you one if you do this for me."

"I got you," Stanton responded. "Ten o'clock too early?"

"That'll work. I'll see you at ten. Thank you."

The two continued to chat, the conversation casual. His arms folded over his chest, Palmer thought about his brother's question and knew his face had probably given him away. He was good, but not that good. He rarely lied and had never had much of a poker face. Any one of his siblings asking too many questions had always been his downfall. It had been that way since they were children. Keeping Soledad and Lyra's whereabouts a secret was more for him than them, he mused. Admittedly, he didn't want to risk losing them. He hated keeping the truth from his family, but it was well worth the repercussions he knew would come later.

Troy returned minutes later. "They found blood on the south gate. And tire tracks. It looks like someone sped off in a hurry. We'll send a team out at daybreak when they're able to see more. Our forensic experts will also come by."

Palmer nodded. "Do you need anything else from me?"

"No. Unless you have something you'd like to share?"

"I don't," Palmer said smugly. "I can't tell you any more than you already know."

The two men exchanged a look and Troy nodded. "We'll step up our patrols at each of your entrances. I'll order a car to sit at the main gate. Just in case. Meanwhile, they've already put in a call to the hospital and medical clinics to look out for anyone showing up with a gunshot wound. Or a dog bite. I spoke to Stavros personally," Troy concluded. "If he shows up while he's on duty, we'll know about it instantly." Stavros Makris was their sister Desiree's fiancé and an emergency room physician.

"Well, if you need anything more, you know where to find me," Palmer said. "I'm going to go turn in. I've got a long day tomorrow. I need some sleep."

Troy gave him a nod. "You're good. My guys will

be out of here momentarily and you can get back to whatever it was you were doing." He paused. "What were you doing?"

Palmer smiled. "Minding my own business. You?"

The other two men chuckled.

"If you can think of anything else that you want to tell us, you know where I am," Troy said, heading back to his car. "Until then, please don't let anything happen to our witness."

Stanton gave Palmer a fist bump as he winked. "See you at ten, cousin." As he turned away, Palmer called his name one last time.

"Yeah?"

"Tell Dominique she doesn't have to worry. Soledad is safe."

MINUTES LATER, PALMER stood in his kitchen as Soledad peppered him with questions about all that had happened. She wanted every detail of what had been said and who had said it. Palmer obliged her to the best of his ability, understanding that she was feeling out of the loop with everything going on. Answering her queries also helped him to sort the pieces to make sense of it all.

She suddenly went silent, seeming to fall into thoughts that didn't include him. It was only when their eyes connected again that he realized maybe whatever she was thinking did, in fact, have something to do with the two of them. Then again, he mused as she looked away, maybe it was all just wishful thinking on his part.

"Palmer, are you okay?" Soledad asked, the question shaking him from his thoughts.

"My brother knows you're here."

"Your brother the detective? You told him?"

"He asked and I didn't deny it. He also said you shouldn't go home. Someone trashed your apartment. They think it was Gavin Stone."

"He was in my home? Going through my things?" She suddenly began to shake.

"They're going to find him, Soledad. You just have to be patient."

Soledad wrapped her arms around her torso, her head waving from side to side. She blew a soft sigh. "So, what now? Are they going to come arrest me? Or take Lyra away?"

"No, I don't think so." Palmer wanted to pull her into his arms and hold her close. He fought the urge, clenching his fists tightly as they stared at one another.

"This is such a mess," she muttered.

As Palmer watched her, something he didn't recognize crossed her face. She no longer looked frightened or even angry. There was something like a quiet resolve in her eyes, determination and focus gleaming in her stare.

"I'm exhausted," she said. "I think I'm going to call it a night."

Palmer nodded. "Are *you* okay?" he questioned, not sure what else to ask, or if he should ask anything at all.

Soledad shrugged. "I'm not sure what I am besides tired. I'm just ready for this to be over so Lyra and I can go home."

Palmer didn't like how she was feeling but he understood it. He was as exhausted with it all as she was, yet, deep down, he didn't want her to go. He actually enjoyed having her around. But he couldn't tell her that and he wasn't sure he should even be thinking it.

"Sleep well, Soledad," he said instead.

She gave him the faintest smile as she stepped past him. "You, too, Palmer."

SLEEP DIDN'T COME quick enough. Soledad lay staring at the ceiling, trying to make sense out of the nonsense that had become her life. She missed her routines, her bakery and her cat. She trusted that Dominique would step in to care for the feline while she was gone, but it wasn't enough. She just wanted to feel normal again, whatever that looked like. She just knew it didn't look like she was a fugitive on the run, hiding out with a man she would have enjoyed getting to know more had their circumstances been different.

There was a part of her that wanted to be angry with Palmer, but with all that he had done and continued to do to keep her safe, she couldn't find enough energy to give him attitude. She instinctively knew that his telling his brother was all about him being honest and upstanding and nothing about him trying to hurt her. She was just bothered by him sharing a secret that was supposed to have been kept between the two of them. She knew that even that thought was irrational on her part.

The more she thought about Palmer, the more Soledad knew he would never purposely cause her an ounce of pain. He would do everything in his power to protect her. She realized that, other than her father, there had been no man before him she could have said that about. And still, in all honesty, she didn't have a clue if he was genuinely interested in her or was just standing by her side because it was the right thing to do. And, if he was nothing else, Palmer was honorable. She had questions for him and wondered if he had answers he was willing to give.

LYING TO HIS family wasn't something Palmer did. He didn't always tell them everything, but he never lied outright. Troy discovering that Soledad was there had been inevitable when the two had run into each other at the department store. His cart full of baby items had been telling, and even he hadn't believed his own explanation.

He rolled from one side of his king-size bed to the other. Jack slept at his feet, lifting his head briefly to give Palmer a look before settling down. Palmer was finding sleep to be elusive, too much spinning around in his head.

Palmer wished things were different and wondered if they would have been if he had asked Soledad to dinner the night of the engagement party. If they could have had a relationship had he not been a coward, given the number of times he'd gone to the bakery hoping to see her. If he'd had a great pickup line or two or three and been smoother, like his brother and cousins. He wished they'd gotten to know each other over bottles of good wine and questionable Netflix movies. He had a lengthy wish list when it came to Soledad de la Vega.

Chapter Nine

An hour later, a knock sounded at Palmer's bedroom door and surprised him. Startled, he jumped, thinking something might be wrong. When he snatched the door open, Soledad stood on the other side. Her eyes were wide, her expression anxious. She was wearing his T-shirt, the oversize garment draped like a dress around her petite frame. Her legs and feet were bare, her toes painted a brilliant shade of bright pink. She'd pulled her hair up into a messy bun and her skin was makeup free and flawless. She was gorgeous and he felt a wave of heat shift every muscle in his lower quadrant. She bit down against her bottom lip as she met his stare.

"What's wrong?" he asked, curiosity painting his expression.

Soledad shook her head. "Nothing. I couldn't sleep and I wanted to ask you something. Did I wake you?"

Relief flooded Palmer's spirit and he felt his whole body sink into the calm. He shook his head. "No. I couldn't sleep, either. I've had a lot on my mind."

"Me, too," she said as she pushed past him. She moved to the king-size bed and took a seat, folding her legs beneath her. She carried the baby monitor in her hand. "Do you mind?" she asked, gesturing with her free hand as she set the monitor on the nightstand.

Palmer shrugged. "If you're comfortable, I'm fine." He moved to the other side of the bed and took his own seat, leaning against the multitude of pillows. Extending his legs, he pulled a pillow into his lap. "What's bothering you?"

"At the engagement party, I felt like there might have been a connection between us, but then you wouldn't speak to me. In fact, I thought you were avoiding me. What was going on? I really need to know."

She was staring at him intently, and Palmer's cheeks warmed with color. The temperature in the room had suddenly risen tenfold.

Palmer was a pro at deflection. He changed the conversation. "Do you know you are the only woman who has ever been in my bedroom and my bed?" He shot her a quick look, then dropped his eyes to the bedclothes.

The words had slipped past his lips before he could catch them. It had not been his intention to share that tidbit of information. No matter how true it was. He hadn't planned to explain that his home and that bedroom had been built with his future wife in mind. Even though he no longer considered marriage to be on the table, the space was sacred, never intended for any random woman he'd been inclined to bed.

Soledad blinked, her lengthy lashes fluttering. It looked as if the comment had surprised her, totally unexpected, and the faintest hint of amusement flickered in her eyes. "I find that very difficult to believe."

He laughed. "Why?"

"You're handsome, intelligent, kind, generous..." She paused. "You're what most people consider a good catch," she concluded. "I find it difficult to believe that not one woman has been able to capture your attention and hold it long enough to make it into your bed."

He hesitated, reflecting on her words. Finally, he said, "One woman has."

Soledad's brows lifted. "This woman must be pretty special."

"I think so. It's why she's sitting on my bed in the middle of the night interrogating me."

Soledad's lips rose in the sweetest smile, spreading full and wide across her face. She laughed. "I asked a question. One question is hardly an interrogation."

"It feels like an interrogation."

"That's because I still can't believe there haven't been many women in your life or your bed."

"I've had to be protective of my personal space. That's why I rarely bring any woman to my home. My home is my sanctuary, and I haven't wanted that to be disrupted. And I've been selfish. I like my peace, and when there's someone else in your space, you have to be considerate of their wants and needs."

"Then along came me and Lyra."

He smiled. "You two have actually been a very pleasant disruption. Of sorts."

"And other women haven't?"

He shrugged. "Too many I've known have wanted a long-term relationship. I don't do long-term. I'm always clear about that. I let anyone I date know up front what will and what won't happen, and I typically don't do any relationship longer than a week. It keeps a woman from becoming too attached and then wanting to move in and be married."

"Just to be clear, they call that a one-night stand. And, instead of being a good catch, that kind of makes you a jerk."

"Maybe, but I'm honest," he replied. "You know what you'll get with me from jump."

"And a woman won't get marriage and children?"

"She'll get friendship, companionship and appreciation. I've never been able to promise anything else."

SOLEDAD HEAVED A deep sigh. She lay back against the mattress, pulling her arms up and over her head. She realized there was still so much about Palmer that she didn't know, but what she was certain of was believing what he told her. She'd dated more than her fair share of men who said what they meant and meant what they said, and she hadn't wanted to believe them. Not believing them, or thinking she could change their minds, had only gotten her heart broken. She wasn't interested in Palmer Colton breaking her heart.

"So, tell me again why you ignored me at the party?" she persisted.

Palmer crossed his legs at the ankles, shifting in his seat. "Because I overheard a conversation you were having with your sister about being thirty and your biological clock starting to tick. It was clear you wanted the dream—the husband, kids, dog and house with the picket fence. I knew I couldn't give that to you, so there was no point in me wasting your time."

The quiet in the room was suddenly stifling. Soledad was trying to reconcile how a man could have convictions so severe that they would potentially leave him alone and unhappy in his old age. Her heart suddenly hurt for Palmer. That he would want that for himself was devastating. Because, she thought, he was a man who deserved so much more.

Rolling onto her stomach, Soledad lifted herself onto her elbows. She stared at him, searching for the words that would make sense of it all, but she had none. The hurt in Palmer's heart had to be unfathomable. She reached for one of his pillows and pulled it beneath her head instead.

PALMER SHIFTED ONTO his side to face her. He reached out his hand to brush her hair from her face. She was hauntingly beautiful, and he imagined many men had fallen head over heels in love with her. He knew that if he wasn't careful, falling for her would be easy to do. He snatched his hand back, clutching his fingers as if he'd been burned.

"What was your first happy memory as a child?" Soledad asked.

The question was unexpected. He paused to consider his answer before he spoke. "It was my first birthday after my adoption was finalized," he said finally. "I had riding lessons, and it was the best time. There was ice cream and chocolate cake and all my friends. That was a good day."

"Sounds like someone wanted you to feel very special that day."

"My mother made every day feel special," Palmer said as he slipped into thought, memories placing a smile across his face. He suddenly yawned.

"Don't do that. It's contagious," Soledad said as she yawned with him.

"I think I've finally hit my wall," he said. "I'm having a hard time keeping my eyes open."

"I know the feeling." Soledad settled comfortably against the mattress. "I should probably go back to my room…" she said but didn't move.

"Don't leave on my account," Palmer muttered, losing his own struggle to stay awake.

"I wasn't," Soledad said with the slightest giggle.

Palmer smiled, his body beginning to give in to the slumber that was suddenly determined to drag him into a deep sleep. "Good night, Soledad," he muttered. "Sweet dreams."

Chapter Ten

Soledad was laughing hysterically when Palmer entered the kitchen later that morning. Lyra was on the family room floor propped against her pillows and Jack was playing his version of peekaboo with her. There were squeals and barks, and a joy so immense that Palmer immediately smiled. The energy in the room reminded him of those days when he, Troy, Desiree, Annalise and Grace were kids, and their home was everything any child could have wanted. When life was simple, and easy, and he couldn't have imagined wanting anything else for himself. Before the days of adulthood and responsibility and the fear of failure existed.

Soledad's grin was canyon wide as she greeted him. "Good morning."

"Good morning. How long have you been up?"

"I only got about two hours of sleep before Lyra woke me up. You were out like a light, so I didn't bother you."

"I should have gotten up when you did. I'm late for my morning rounds."

"Coffee?" she asked, holding up an overlarge mug.

He nodded. “Black coffee, please. And it needs to be superstrong.”

“I’ve got you covered.” Soledad filled the mug and placed it in front of him as he took a seat at the counter. She slid a plate of freshly baked muffins toward him, as well. “Did you know you have blueberries growing out by the barn?” she said.

Palmer shrugged. “I know the ranch hands sometimes pick them. I also have apple and pear trees on the other side of the west pasture. I don’t bother with those, either. Why were you outside?”

“Lyra had fallen back to sleep and I needed to clear my head. Since the baby monitor was still in the bedroom with you, I knew you’d hear her if she woke up again, so I took a quick walk. No one saw me.”

“You sure about that?”

“I don’t think anyone saw me,” she said.

“You hope no one saw you,” Palmer countered. “I don’t like you taking risks like that, Soledad. What if something had happened to you?” His words were steeped in concern, his tone reprimanding. “You can’t be too careful.”

She eyed him with a raised brow. “I appreciate your concern, but I was fine, Palmer.”

“This time,” he quipped as he took a bite of the blueberry muffin. He suddenly hummed, licking his fingers and grabbing for another muffin. “These are really good.”

“I know. It’s the fresh blueberries,” Soledad said, her expression smug as she giggled softly.

Palmer shook his head, amusement lifting his own

smile. The look she gave him was teasing and he couldn't help but wonder if she tasted as sweet as the blueberry treats she was plying him with. Needing a distraction before he did or said something that might get him in trouble, he shifted his attention from Soledad to the dynamic duo on the floor.

Jack was acting like he was still a pup with endless energy. He would bounce and bark, and Lyra would burst with giggles. Palmer couldn't help but laugh with her.

"Soledad, look!" he suddenly exclaimed. Excitement burst across his face and his chest pushed forward with undeniable pride.

She turned to see that Lyra had pulled herself forward and was sitting upright all on her own, without any assistance. The little girl reached for the dog, trying to grab his tail, and then she toppled over, falling like the pins at the end of a bowling lane. Palmer shot Soledad a glance and the two busted out laughing.

Soledad rushed to the baby's side. Lyra struggled to sit upright as Jack nudged her, trying to help. "Look at you, sweet pea. Such a big girl," Soledad soothed.

Lyra responded with a bloodcurdling scream followed by hysterical giggles.

Palmer swallowed the last bite of his muffin, then moved to the floor to join the trio. For the next few minutes, they all played together effortlessly. Palmer cooed with Soledad, and Lyra bobbed up and down like a windup toy gone awry. He found himself in awe of the ease with which they felt like a family. Like *his* family.

Lyra suddenly fell back against the pillows, clearly ready to be done with them all. "Babababa ba…" she sputtered.

"You want a bottle, don't you, sweet pea? And I think you need a fresh diaper," Soledad said softly.

Palmer wriggled his nose. "I'll grab that bottle. You can have the diaper."

"Chicken."

"Damn right," he returned. "She's like a miniature toxic waste dump. It's downright scary. Jack's not even that bad."

Soledad laughed as she scooped Lyra up into her arms and nuzzled her nose into the folds of the baby's neck. "Stinky butt!" She laid the child on a vinyl pad and reached for a dry diaper.

"Told you."

"Can you still deliver my cake for me today?" Soledad questioned.

"I can't, but I've made arrangements for it to be delivered."

Her eyes widened. "Arrangements with who?"

"Someone I trust. In fact, he'll be here at ten."

"That's in five minutes."

Palmer shrugged. "Okay. Is it not ready to go?"

"It's ready. I just…well…" She shrugged. "This is especially important to me. I don't want to trust it to just anyone."

"Because it's important to you, it's important to me, and since you entrusted me with getting the task done, I'm going to make that happen."

"But who did you—" Soledad started to ask when there was a knock on the door, interrupting their conversation.

Panic washed over her. She started down the hallway, Lyra held tightly to her chest, when Palmer stopped her. He pressed his hand against her forearm, his fingers teasing her skin. "It'll be okay," he said. "You don't have to hide. It's your delivery guy."

Soledad looked confused as she came to an abrupt stop. She watched as Palmer stepped up to the door and pulled it open. But he was shocked when Dominique de la Vega came barreling into the room, Stanton following sheepishly behind her.

"What the hell?" Palmer snapped, giving his cousin a narrowed side-eye. "Who else did you tell?"

"He only told me," Dominique answered. "We would never do anything to put my sister in harm's way."

Soledad practically threw herself into her sister's arms, the two women hugging tightly. Lyra was clutched between them, looking from one to the other as she tried to decipher what was going on and breathe at the same time.

Palmer and Stanton stood side by side, each giving the other a look. Stanton shrugged his shoulders. "I couldn't not tell her, Palmer. They are sisters. And, besides, she always knows when I'm lying, or keeping something from her. I had to tell her. She wasn't going to stop worrying until she could lay eyes on Soledad."

Palmer gave him an eye roll as he gestured with his head. "Come on in. Looks like you're going to be here for a minute."

Dominique kissed her sister's cheek, then took the baby from her arms. "You've had me scared to death!" she exclaimed.

"Sorry. I didn't want to risk putting anyone else in harm's way. Gavin is dangerous."

"I am so sorry that you had to go through that, but you really need to come home. You know Dad isn't going to let anything happen to you. Right now, you're out here in the middle of nowhere. That can't be a good thing with that psycho looking for you."

"I really am good, Dominique. I feel safe here."

Dominique tossed Palmer a look. "He's not holding you hostage, is he?"

Soledad laughed. "He's been a real champ about the whole thing."

Her sister looked him up and down. "I just bet he has," she said snidely. "Maybe we should give him a cookie for all his hard work. Maybe one of those ones with the cream filling and chocolate icing on top that you make for special occasions?"

The two men exchanged a look. Stanton shook his head, fighting not to laugh out loud.

Palmer was not amused. Their teasing had him feeling out of sorts. When it came to sisters, it was usually him and his brother making light work of the girls, not the girls besting them. Dominique and Soledad had him feeling like he was in a tag-team match with no one to tag him out and he was losing. "I think this would be a good time for me to go make my rounds. I shouldn't be too long," he said, excusing himself from the room.

"I think I'll make those rounds with you," Stanton said, following on his cousin's heels as he moved toward the door.

"That's a very good idea. You two should do that," Dominique called after the duo. She laughed heartily as they quickly made their escape.

WHEN THE MEN were out of sight, Dominique began to walk through the home, taking it all in. "Give me a tour," she said.

Soledad shook her head as she followed her sister from room to room. "You are so nosy."

"I am," Dominique responded. "And he's got a very nice place."

Soledad nodded in agreement. "It's been very comfortable. He's been such a blessing to me and Lyra."

Her sister paused in the guest bedroom. "Isn't this cute. He did all this?"

"He did," Soledad answered. "Palmer went on a full-scale shopping spree to make us comfortable."

"Hmm." Dominique gave Soledad a look as she moved on to the master bedroom. "This is very nice. Have you poked around?"

"Of course not. Why would I poke around in the man's stuff? I'm not trying to get thrown out."

Dominique's expression brimmed with exasperation. "To make sure he's on the up-and-up. That's why." She moved to the nightstand and pulled open the drawer to peek inside.

"Your journalistic claws are showing. You're like one of those writers from a supermarket tabloid going through people's trash to get a story. Don't do that. It's not pretty."

Dominique laughed. "I do whatever I need to do to get the story." She pulled a firearm from the drawer, a Smith & Wesson .45 semiautomatic pistol. After checking to see if it was loaded, she slid it back where she'd found it. "FYI, he keeps one in the chamber," she said.

Soledad was still shaking her head.

Dominique suddenly grinned, pulling a blue box from inside the drawer. "'Trojan Bareback Lubricated Condoms. Size large,'" she read, waving the container at her sister. "And it hasn't been opened. So, either he goes through them quickly or he doesn't use them often. It should be interesting for you to find out."

Soledad felt her face flush with color. "You need to stop invading the man's privacy before you get me evicted. Put those back."

Dominique laughed as she slid the box into the drawer and closed it. "You'd be amazed what you can find out about a man by going through his things."

"I can't believe you," Soledad said as she led the way out of the room.

Dominique was still chuckling, amusement dancing across her face. Soledad laughed with her sister, shaking her head as her twin settled on the couch, cuddling Lyra in her lap. She took the seat beside her twin. "So, why were you giving Stanton and Palmer a hard time?"

"It keeps them on their toes. Stanton never knows what to expect. That's how I keep the romance alive in our relationship." She winked at her sister.

"How are the wedding plans going?" Soledad asked.

"They'd be going better if my maid of honor was around to help me with them."

Soledad sighed. "Sorry," she said as she leaned back against the sofa. "I hate that this is happening. My whole life is on hold. I barely know what day it is, and I haven't accomplished a third of the things I need to accomplish. I'm sure my business is falling apart, and I don't have a clue when I'll be able to get myself back on track or what I'll need to be doing to make that happen."

"What can I do to help?" Dominique asked.

"I'd really appreciate it if you could run by the bakery to check on how things are going. I'm sure they're okay for the time being, but it can't last much longer."

"I'll swing by to see how they're doing. And if you aren't home by next week, then I suggest you close shop temporarily. We can put a sign on the door that says you're away for vacation."

"Actually, that's not a bad idea. I think I should just do that anyway. I only have one big order due this weekend and then nothing after that I need to be worried about. So it would be the perfect time for a vacation."

"Consider it done. What about the employees? Are you going to lay them off?"

Soledad shook her head. "No, I'd rather give them two weeks' paid vacation."

"Can you afford that?"

"I'll pull it from my savings. It's not their fault that this is happening."

"Anything else?" Dominique prompted.

"When they shut down, make sure they take any leftovers to the food bank for distribution. Please, tell them not to let it go to waste."

Dominique nodded.

"Have they made arrangements for Annie yet?" Soledad asked, her voice dropping an octave. "I know I probably can't go to the funeral, but I want to pay my respects and maybe send some flowers."

"I'll make that happen. You just keep your head down, please. I'd hate for you to go to all this trouble and then do something that exposes you. At least let them catch the killer first. Promise me."

Soledad smiled. "I promise. Besides, Palmer's keeping a close eye on me."

"Speaking of the devil… What's going on with you two? You look very cozy together."

Soledad felt herself blush. She shook her head. "It's not like that. He's just been exceedingly kind."

Dominique chortled. "You usually aren't that naive. That man is head over heels for you."

Soledad laughed with her sister. "Now I know Dad dropped you on your skull when we were babies. You've completely lost your mind if you think that. He's just a really nice—"

"Just a really nice guy…" Dominique mocked, reminiscent of when they'd been younger.

"Well, he is!" Soledad exclaimed, tossing up her hands. "And he's been supersweet to Lyra and me."

For thirty minutes, Soledad clued her sister in on all that had happened since arriving in Palmer's barn. The twins laughed heartily, cried, bickered, and their time together felt like it always did. Soledad found it unfathomable that despite how close they were, their routines kept them from each other for long periods of time. So focused on their respective careers, they seldom realized how much they missed each other until they were together again. She was beyond grateful for the opportunity to spend some time together.

Lyra lay sleeping on Dominique's shoulder.

"You look good with a baby in your arms," Soledad said.

"I do, don't I?" Dominique answered, her expression telling. "I can't wait to have Stanton's babies."

"They'll be cute babies."

"So, what about you? Are you ready for this responsibility? Lyra's a doll, but even dolls can be a handful."

Soledad shrugged. "Honestly, I don't have a clue what's going to happen. Annie's attorney has her codicil naming me Lyra's guardian, but I'm sure Gavin is going to fight that with everything he can if it comes down to it. I just know that I promised Annie I would take care of her daughter, and I won't break that promise."

"Well, you know you'll have all the support in the world. I know Dad will be over the moon when he finds out. He can't wait to be a grandfather."

Soledad trailed her hand down Lyra's back, her touch whisper soft. "Palmer doesn't want kids. He doesn't want to be a father and says he's not interested in marriage."

"He told you this?"

Soledad nodded. "He survived some childhood traumas and, because of them, decided he never wanted children. The level of hurt he was made to endure just breaks my heart."

Dominique stared at her sister. "You do *like* him, don't you?"

Soledad stared at her sister, considering the question. Yes, she did like Palmer. She liked him more than she'd realized, and admitting it would force her to acknowledge feelings she was trying desperately to ignore. "Does it really matter?" Soledad said with a shrug. "There's no way I'd ever consider being in a relationship with a man who didn't want a family with me. Being a wife and mother has always been on my bucket list. I'm not willing to give that up for anyone. And now that I'm a mother by default, I could never be with a man who isn't willing to accept Lyra. Going forward, she and I are a package deal."

A wave of sadness went through Soledad and her twin reached out to give her a hug.

"YOU DO KNOW those two are a package deal, right?" Stanton asked from the passenger seat.

Palmer shot his cousin a look as he maneuvered his truck across the fields. "What two?"

"Soledad and her sister. If you marry one, you automatically get the other by default. Whether you want her or not. It's some twin thing they have going on. It's a good thing they're fraternal, because I imagine that could be a problem if they were identical."

Palmer laughed, his cousin's expression too serious for the conversation.

"Someone who gets my sense of humor!" Stanton exclaimed. "Seriously, though, those two are super close. You need to be ready for it."

"We're not dating. Right now, I'm just helping her out, and when she goes back home, I hope that we'll remain friends." Palmer said the words but even he didn't believe them. What he was feeling for Soledad was far more than friendship and he found himself hoping that her going home would never happen.

"Then you need to stop looking at her the way you do," Stanton chuckled.

"What do you mean? How do I look at her?"

"Like you're hopelessly in love."

"You're seeing things."

"You get those sad puppy-dog eyes, and you start sweating around the collar. It's so obvious. Everyone saw it at our engagement party."

"No one saw anything they weren't imagining."

Stanton shrugged. "Okay. If you don't believe me, ask your brother. He was talking about it on the ride back last night. How you've been fantasizing about you and her since forever. How you've been too nervous to ask her out and tell her how you feel. He said you're like a walking Hallmark card, the way you wear your heart on your sleeve."

"Remind me to kill my brother the next time I see him." Palmer felt his face flush, knowing his cheeks were tinted a rich bright red.

Stanton eyed him, his expression serious. "Life's short. If she's the one, don't let her get away. Why spend your life regretting lost love when you can have a lifetime of happiness instead?"

"So, you're an expert now?"

"Look, it took a lot to get me to this headspace. Dominique worked overtime to help me see the error of my ways. That's why I love her as much as I do. She knows what she wants and she's fearless about going after it. She's got fight and I love that she challenges me."

"Well, Soledad and I are on different pages. She wants children and marriage, and that has never been in my playbook."

"Sounds like you may want to rewrite some of those plays, or even get you a new book. Women like the de la Vega sisters don't come calling every day, and the fact that she likes you is half your battle."

Palmer sighed. "Whatever, man. Right now, all I can focus on is her safety. Protecting her and that baby are the best I can do."

"I hear you. But think about it. If I were you, I wouldn't want to lose her."

Palmer shook his head. "We need to get back. You need to make that delivery for me."

"What's the package?"

"A cake for a client's party tonight."

"A cake?"

"Yeah, Soledad had a cake order that she was determined to fill. I was going to deliver it myself, but I don't want to leave her alone or risk anyone else figuring out she's here with me."

"You could wear a disguise. Maybe a wig and hat to conceal your identity?"

Palmer gave his cousin a look, not at all amused by his suggestion. "Would you focus, please?"

Stanton laughed and shrugged. "Have you tasted this cake? Is it any good? You know I really like cake."

"I swear, cousin, if anything happens to that damn cake and you mess this up for me, I will rip you to shreds. Don't even think about showing your face around here again."

Stanton laughed, the wealth of it gut deep. "Sure, you're not in love," he said facetiously. "It's your lie, cousin, but tell it any way that makes you happy!"

WHEN THE TWO men returned, Soledad and her sister were seated at the counter. Soledad was giving Dominique explicit instructions for delivering and setting up the cake for her client.

Dominique rolled her eyes, clearly done with the conversation. "Who worked for free the first summer you were open, helping with every position in that damn bakery?"

"You did."

"Who set up the Pinkney wedding cake all by her lonesome when you broke your foot?"

"You did—but I directed you."

"No, you didn't."

"Yes, I did. I kept calling you to tell you what to do."

"You kept calling to be a nuisance and I still managed to get that monstrosity of a wedding cake onto the table without it falling apart. It was stunning when I walked out of there."

"Because I make wonderful cakes."

Dominique tossed Stanton a look. "It was fifteen tiers and had to be delivered in sections and set up on-site. I earned the salary I wasn't making that day."

"You make that sound like I have never pulled an all-nighter editing one of your articles," Soledad retorted. "Without snacks and coffee."

"You got snacks."

"A stale bag of peanuts from some flight you'd taken does not count."

Dominique shrugged. "You didn't complain then."

"I was hungry."

The two women laughed, enjoying the banter that came naturally.

"Is there anything I need to know or do?" Stanton asked, looking from one to the other.

"No, honey. I think I have it under control," Dominique answered. "My sister just doesn't want to give me my due credit."

"I've got your back, baby," Stanton said as he leaned to kiss his fiancée's cheek.

"You just get your girl and that cake to their destination, in one piece, please. You just do that." Palmer gave his cousin a narrowed stare.

Jack suddenly barked and they all turned to look at the same time. Lyra had taken a nosedive into a mound of pillows and was struggling to right herself. Soledad noticed how Palmer made it to her side in three swift steps, lifting the small bundle into his arms.

"Did that bad doggy push you?" he said, snuggling the infant. "You have to be easy with the baby, Jack. You can't bowl her over like one of your play toys."

Soledad chuckled. Amusement danced across her face as she watched Palmer with the baby, the tenderness he showed the little girl like a warm blanket. "Don't yell at Jack. He didn't do anything. She keeps trying to grab his ears, and when she misses, she falls over. When she hits her target, she tries to drag the poor dog. She's going to be a terror when she starts walking."

Palmer was cooing and making silly faces at the baby. Lyra was giggling as she grabbed at Palmer's face, trying to chew his chin. The two were quite a pair, and watching them, she couldn't help but smile.

Soledad and her sister exchanged a look, the duo having a silent conversation that no one else was privy to. Doing that thing twins did when they shut out the world and it was just them. Dominique's eyes lifted, her brow furrowed. Her expression was inquisitive and the slightest smile pulled at her lips. Soledad responded with her own wide-eyed stare, batting her lashes rapidly.

Watching the man and the baby together, Soledad realized Palmer Colton was a natural, despite his assertions that fatherhood was not for him. In that moment, Soledad couldn't help but wonder if she'd ever find a man like Palmer, who was both tender and protective of her and that baby girl. Would there ever be someone who looked at her like he sometimes did? Would she want him as much as she found herself suddenly wanting Palmer? As if reading her mind, Dominique reached for her hand, the two interlocking their fingers and holding tightly to each other.

Chapter Eleven

Staring out the large bay window, Soledad watched as Dominique and Stanton drove away with her cake delivery. She stared until she could no longer see the car, and she was still staring minutes after. An air of melancholy had filled the room, no hint of the laughter that had been there just an hour earlier. Watching her, Palmer felt as if he'd taken a punch to his gut, unable to catch his breath and make things well.

She caught him staring, noticing his reflection in the glass, and she turned to meet his gaze. He opened his mouth to speak, but she held up her hand, stalling his words. "Please, don't ask me if I'm okay, because I'm not. I'm not okay," she snapped, shaking her head vehemently. Her tone was short and riddled with emotion. "I'm so over this. I want my life back."

Palmer nodded politely. "Are you ready to go to the police?" he asked.

There was a hint of hesitation before she answered. "No. I'm sure if I do, they're just going to put me in hiding somewhere else and maybe even take Lyra from me. For all I know, they might even put me in jail for taking the baby. I can't let that happen. I still feel safer here. With you."

Palmer reflected on her comment as Soledad turned back to the window, her forlorn expression like a knife in his heart. He understood why she felt the way she did and knew there was little he could do to make her feel better. What surprised Palmer was that he found himself wishing that Soledad wanting to remain in his home could be more about her wanting *him* and less about her simply feeling safe. He released the breath he'd been holding, allowing the warm air to blow softly past his lips.

"Why don't I make us some dinner?" he said, moving to the refrigerator. "I don't know about you, but I'm hungry."

Soledad turned back around and gave him a smile. "Thank you," she said. "You've been so kind to me, and I realize I probably sounded ungrateful just then. But I hope you know how much I appreciate everything you've done for me. I'll probably never be able to repay you for everything, but I hope I'm able to come close."

"You don't owe me anything, Soledad."

"And there you go being sweet again. Which is why I'm going to make you dinner." Her smile widened. "Grilled cheese?"

Palmer laughed. "Grilled cheese works for me."

AN HOUR LATER, Soledad and Palmer stood side by side in the kitchen, prepping their evening meal. Lyra was sound asleep and Jack lay beneath her crib, keeping a watchful eye out for any threats.

As Soledad cut vegetables for a salad, Palmer slid their favorite sandwich together, layering three different cheeses with fresh spinach on a thick crusty bread. He topped off the bread with a light garlic-butter spread and then laid it in a warm cast-iron pan.

Palmer had turned on the stereo, and as they worked, someone's jazz played softly in the background. The music was soft and easy, and filled the space with warm energy. The conversation between them was casual, the two chatting comfortably together. Soledad discovered he had a penchant for old black-and-white films and country music. He learned she liked roller coasters and NASCAR racing. Both enjoyed a good James Patterson novel and were members of the mile-high club. Time had revived the laughter in the home, the two chuckling together like old friends who knew each other's darkest secrets. They were comfortable with one another, and that spoke volumes to Soledad.

After checking on Lyra, they sat to eat, and their conversation continued. The discussion was heated, the two debating the popular television series *The Blacklist*.

"How can you not like Raymond Reddington?" Palmer questioned. "The man is ultracool."

"The man is a criminal who wears nice suits and has a poetic tongue. But he's still a criminal."

Palmer laughed. "I see watching television with you is going to be interesting."

"Especially if you won't even acknowledge when you're wrong." A slow smile spread across her face.

Shaking his head, Palmer began to clear away the dirty dishes. "I'll wash if you dry."

"I can do that," Soledad responded. "I hate washing dishes. That's what a dishwasher's for."

"It's two plates, Soledad."

"Two or twenty. What difference does it make?"

"You're funny."

"I'm told you like women with a sense of humor."

Palmer gave her a look out of the corner of his eye. "And who told you that?"

"I have my sources."

"Sounds like my cousin's been talking out of turn again."

"Maybe. Maybe not." Soledad grabbed the dish towel to wipe the moisture from the plate he passed to her.

Palmer chuckled.

"I'm glad your sister came," he said after a few minutes of silence between them. "I know you hated to see her leave, but it was nice you two could spend some time together. I think it was good for you."

"It was good. I needed that time more than I realized. And I'm sorry again if I was acting like a brat before."

"You're forgiven. I was told you could be a little high-strung."

"You were not," Soledad quipped, her voice rising to a high squeal. Shock registered; she was surprised that anyone would think such a thing about her. A nervous giggle blew past her lips.

"Yes, I was."

"There is no one who would tell you something like that about me. Because I am not high-strung. Not all the time, anyway." She smiled.

"Maybe. Maybe not." He smirked, his wide smile like a beam in the center of his face.

Soledad gave him an eye roll.

Palmer changed the subject. "So, Stanton mentioned Dominique has been working on articles about the Grave Gulch Police Department. How is that going for her?"

Soledad nodded. "She is. But she says her exposé is more about the forensic scientist that duped them."

"Was that Randall Bowe? The subject of that manhunt?"

"Yes, him. Dominique says she's uncovered information she thinks will change public opinion of the Grave Gulch PD. That the full scope of what he did and how he did it is eye-opening."

"I've read a few of her articles. Dominique's a talented writer."

"Yes, she is. She's a stickler for details and she believes in getting her facts right. She has a way with words, and I'm always impressed with her ability to manipulate them into pretty sentences."

"Much like you manipulate dough into cookies?"

Soledad smiled. "Very much like that."

"Speaking of cookies…" Palmer's eyebrows rose, his eyes bright. "Since you now have my secret grilled-cheese recipe, maybe you can show me how to make those oatmeal cookies with the nuts and Craisins that taste kind of like spice cake. I really like those."

"You want them tonight or tomorrow?" Soledad asked.

Palmer moved to the cupboard and began to pull out the flour and oatmeal and any other ingredient he thought she might need. He dropped everything onto the counter. "No hurry," he said. "I don't want you to think I'm rushing you or anything."

Soledad laughed. "I think you're the one that's funny, Palmer Colton. Just too funny."

Palmer laughed with her. "I will own that," he answered. "For your cookies, I will own it and wear it proudly. Would you like to see my stand-up?" he asked as he winked at her.

She eyed him warmly. He turned back to the pantry, beginning to pull out the baking pans. Muscles rippled beneath the T-shirt he wore and his denim jeans hugged his backside nicely. She bit down against her bottom lip, thinking she'd love to see his stand-up—and anything else he was interested in showing her.

SOLEDAD SCOOPED THE last of the cookie dough onto a sheet, twelve evenly arranged balls of doughy goodness. She slid the pan into the oven and the mixing bowl into the sink. It was the last batch of three dozen. The first dozen was cooling on a wire rack on the counter, and the second dozen had a few more minutes in the other oven.

Palmer had left the kitchen to answer the cries of a

six-month-old. Lyra had begun crying after they had tossed all the ingredients into the bowl and he had yet to return. Eavesdropping via the baby monitor, she knew the little girl now had a dry diaper, a full tummy, and she was currently being lulled back to sleep with an Irish lullaby. Palmer's voice was liquid gold and the sweetest caress to her ears.

The smell of sugar and spice filled the air. Fresh-baked cookies were the best balm and absolutely made her heart sing. She hadn't realized just how much she'd missed her work at the bakery. The art of sifting flour and whipping butter gave her immense joy. Folding in steel-cut oats, chopped nuts and a host of spices that teased her senses brought her immeasurable delight.

The time Palmer had spent measuring the ingredients had been great fun. She found herself enjoying the moments they shared. Soledad had to admit to a few moments of flirtation, the innuendos overt and heated. Palmer was a tease and he seemed to take a great deal of pleasure in making her blush.

She suddenly thought about her sister and the comment she'd made about Palmer being in love with her. Maybe she was naive, Soledad thought, because she couldn't see it. Yes, he was kind and generous and had blessed her immensely. Soledad didn't think him being sweet to her had anything at all to do with his feelings for her. But she liked him. She liked him more than she'd been willing to admit out loud, and the more she thought about him, the more she would have given almost anything for him to return the sentiment. She imagined that what he was feeling had more to do with pity than anything else. And even if it wasn't, nothing could come of it, if Palmer wasn't interested in a family and children.

Leaning across the counter, she reached for a warm cookie and took a large bite.

LYRA HAD FINALLY drifted off to sleep. She'd eaten and played and been thoroughly entertained. Palmer had made silly faces and strange noises to make the baby giggle and laugh. Amazingly, Lyra had him in full "daddy" mode, and he was still in awe of how easily he'd fallen into the role.

The entire evening had been one of the best experiences he'd had in some time. He couldn't remember the last time he'd laughed as much or as hard or been that happy. But Soledad had him walking on cloud nine and Lyra was the pot of gold at the end of a bright rainbow.

Palmer was reluctant to give it a name. He just knew it was bigger than a schoolboy crush and next to impossible to pursue because he couldn't wrap his mind around the concept of forever. Not even with a woman he wanted as much as he wanted Soledad.

He groaned heavily, a gust of air escaping past his thin lips. The weight of all the emotion he was feeling fell away, leaving him to question what might come next if he opened himself to the possibility. He knew the life Soledad wanted. He just couldn't see himself being the one to give it to her. He knew his attitude about marriage and children sounded irrational, but he couldn't help how he felt, and he had no plans to apologize for his feelings.

He had been here before. Dating women who wanted more than he was willing to give. He'd always walked away, unconcerned with what anyone thought. As he spent more time with Soledad, he suddenly couldn't see himself walking away from her. But then he remembered they weren't dating, and he had no idea how Soledad felt about him.

"It shouldn't be so hard," Palmer whispered softly, blowing his words into the palm of Lyra's little hand. "Any advice for me, kiddo?" He paused, drawing the pads of his fingers over the roundness of her chubby cheek. "No? I didn't think so." He chuckled softly as he lifted the baby from his lap and lowered her into the crib.

He stood there for a few minutes, staring down at the little girl. Watching her sleep brought him a sense of peace. He relished the peace. Inhaling the scent of cinnamon, nutmeg and sugar, he craved a cookie. One of Soledad's. As he exited the room, he couldn't help but think of the sophomoric joke hidden in that thought.

HOURS LATER, SOLEDAD and Palmer were still noshing on oatmeal cookies and cups of hot caramel lattes. There was little they hadn't talked about; he'd found a level of comfort with her that felt as natural as breathing.

"Why aren't you married already?" Palmer questioned. He took a sip of his beverage.

Soledad shrugged. "I've spent the past two years completely focused on building my brand. The bakery is my whole life and it has required all of my attention."

"So, you're all work and no play?" he asked, wondering what it would take to get her to play games with him.

"Very little play, but then, you know all about that."

Palmer nodded. "I do. This ranch requires everything I have to give."

"So, tell me what you actually do. What's an average day in the life of Palmer Colton, rancher extraordinaire?"

"Not sure that I'm a rancher extraordinaire," Palmer asserted with a grin, "but I am fully committed to what I do. I supervise all the operations that keep this machine running.

"An average day starts ultra early," he continued. "The animals have to be fed and watered, and the stables need to be cleaned. I tend the herds, deciding when to rotate stock, and I make decisions about breeding. Sometimes we will gather semen from the cattle to sell to continue the stronger bloodlines. Then, of course, I tend to any of the animals that might be sick. There's also the maintenance of the outbuildings and ensuring all the fencing is intact. And let's not forget the fields and crops. That's a Monday. Tuesdays I do that and the paperwork, and start over again on Wednesdays."

Soledad giggled. "But you have help, right?"

"And a lot of it. It takes a whole football team to keep this place running. I employ a great group to help me out."

"I really look forward to getting a tour one day. Maybe I can help out somewhere."

"Whenever you're ready. I like to show the ranch off. I'm proud of what I've built here."

"You should be proud. It's impressive." Soledad suddenly yawned. She pulled her closed fist to her lips. "Excuse me. I'm suddenly exhausted."

"You should go get some rest. We can resume this conversation in the morning over coffee and cookies."

She laughed. "I think I'm all cookied out."

"Never! I will never get enough of your cookies."

Soledad's brow quirked as she eyed him.

"I mean your cookie cookies. I mean…you know…" he stammered, feeling like he'd put his foot in his mouth and not the mashup of oatmeal and sweet raisins he'd been eating.

"I can't believe you're actually blushing."

"You've got me feeling like a grade-schooler who told a dirty joke. Or heard one."

She stood up, her head shaking slightly. "Well, just for the record…" Soledad moved slowly toward the guest bedroom. "If you want a taste of my cookies, you'll have to ask me nicely." She tossed him one last look over her shoulder, a wry smile lifting her lush mouth.

Chapter Twelve

It was still dark out when Palmer's bedside alarm sounded. After depressing the stop button to silence the annoying chime, he threw his legs off the side of the bed and sat upright. He was stiff and felt heavy, needing a few more hours of sleep, but such was not a luxury he could enjoy. Hanging out half the night enjoying Soledad's company had come with a price, and he would have to pay it over the next few hours as he went about his chores.

He was headed to the bathroom when he heard noises coming from the kitchen. Jack hadn't left the room where little Lyra slept, and Palmer couldn't imagine that Soledad was awake if she didn't have to be. He suddenly couldn't remember if he'd set the house alarm, so distracted by Soledad and those darn oatmeal cookies. His heart began to race, anxiety rising with a vengeance. Easing to his nightstand, he removed the loaded firearm from its lockbox, then crept out the door and down the hallway.

As he moved into the room, he lowered his weapon, a smile creeping across his face. Soledad stood staring into the refrigerator. He couldn't help but notice her bra-style top and the boy-cut shorts that complemented the length of her legs. She'd pulled her hair up into a ponytail that swung back and forth behind her. He cleared his throat and she looked up to meet his gaze.

"Good morning," she chimed cheerily. Her tone changed slightly as her eyes dropped to the weapon in his hand. "Everything okay? Should I be scared?"

Palmer nodded. "Everything's good. I heard someone out here and was coming to make sure they belonged." He engaged the safety and went to tuck the weapon into the waistband of his sleep pants when he realized he was standing there in nothing but his underwear. His eyes widened and his cheeks turned a nice shade of embarrassed when he realized Soledad was staring at his bare chest.

"I like your tighty-whiteys." She giggled.

He ignored the comment. "What's got you up so early?"

"I thought I'd make you breakfast before you headed out. I saw you had four hours blocked off on your calendar to volunteer this morning?" She pointed to the planner that rested on the counter.

His brow lifted as he answered. "Yeah. I volunteer with the Grave Gulch Children's Home. It's a group foster facility for boys. I sponsor a program called Rough Riders, where we bring a group of kids here every week for a dude-ranch event."

"That sounds like fun. What do you all do?"

"We give them the full cowboy experience. The kids take horseback riding lessons and go on trail rides. They also learn what's involved in caring for the horses. Throughout the year, we bring in guests to demonstrate rodeo games. Sometimes I'll take them to fish down at the ponds, which I keep fully stocked so everyone can catch at least one.

"We also do nature walks, and the older boys learn archery and rifle shooting and how to handle each responsibly. During the fall and winter months, there are hayrides and cookouts. We sometimes camp in the woods and sit around the campfire just talking. Many of the boys who participate are about to age out of the foster-care system, so I try to give them some direction and hope about what will happen after they leave. We even make them learn how to square-dance!"

Soledad chuckled. "That's very cool. I'm impressed."

"I've enjoyed it. It's been very rewarding."

"Maybe I can whip up some cookies for them?"

Palmer laughed. "I don't know if I want to share your cookies with anyone else."

Soledad tossed him a lopsided smirk. "You need to be nice. They're kids. I'll save my special cookies just for you," she teased.

"I may collect on that," he said.

"I hope you do," Soledad answered, her voice dropping an octave. She bit down against her bottom lip as they eyed each other intently. She finally gave in, her shoulders rising in a lighthearted shrug. "Anyway, I thought, since I kept you up all night, that the least I could do was make you a good breakfast. So, why don't you go take your shower? By the time you get back, I should have the food ready."

"Thank you," Palmer said. "That's very sweet of you." He turned and headed back to his room.

Soledad called his name, stepping from behind the counter to stand at the end of the hallway.

"Yes?"

"I really do hope you'll take me up on that cookie," she said, blessing him with another bright smile. "I really, really do."

As he walked away, he could feel her staring at his backside, her gaze throwing heat deep into the core of his body.

EITHER ONE OF two things had happened, Soledad thought. If Palmer was not interested in what she had offered, then she had just made a complete fool of herself. Or her suggestive quip had opened the door for them to move their relationship in a whole other direction. Despite it feeling like the former, she was willing to bank on the latter. When she'd said what she'd said, there was nothing for her to lose and everything to gain.

She had spent most of the night thinking about him. Playing their conversations over in her head. Remembering the gentleness of his touch. How he was with Lyra. How he made her laugh. He was magical. There was something special about him that had her wishing for more. She knew that he might not be her forever, but why shouldn't she take advantage of the right now? Soledad firmly believed in fate and knew there was a reason Palmer had come into her life in the way he had. That he knew her, and had been interested, was a bonus—and much for her to consider. She wanted it to be love, but just being honest about that was taking her completely out of her comfort zone.

She refocused on the popovers she was prepping for breakfast. Blending flour, milk, eggs and butter until she had a batter the consistency of heavy cream. She half filled the cups of the pan and popped it in a hot oven.

By the time Palmer returned, crisp bacon, scrambled eggs and hot popovers with raspberry butter were waiting for him.

She gasped as he walked toward her. He was wearing denim. Dark denim jeans with a matching denim shirt, steel-toed boots and a wide-brimmed, brown-leather Stetson. He looked delicious and she suddenly wanted him more than she wanted the meal she'd fixed.

"Wow!" she exclaimed. "You clean up nice."

"As opposed to how I look any other time?"

"As in, you look yummy," she said teasingly. "If I were a jealous woman, I'd wonder who you were all dressed up for."

"I'm glad you're not a jealous woman," he said, "because you'd be sorely disappointed. She's almost eighty. Her name is Grandma Butler and she's one of the house mothers at the foster home."

Laughter rang sweetly.

"Seriously, though," Soledad said, as she passed him a plate of food. "You look very nice."

"Thank you."

"Can you come back just before lunch to pick up the cookies? I'm going to start baking right after Lyra wakes up and I get her settled."

He nodded. "You really don't need to do that, but I'm sure the boys will appreciate the gesture."

"It's not like I have a lot to do. I just want to keep busy, so I don't drive myself crazy thinking about everything."

"Does that include me?" Palmer asked. He avoided her eyes as he took a bite of his popover.

"I like thinking about you," Soledad said softly.

He cut an eye in her direction and gave her a slight nod. "I like thinking about you, too. And I think about you all the time."

"Is this weird?" Soledad queried. "You and me? I know we joke a lot, but..." She let her words trail off.

"It's not necessarily normal. Whatever *normal* is," he said, making air quotes with his fingers.

"I just don't want our unusual circumstances to blind us to what our reality is."

"I agree. All jokes aside, I want whatever happens between us to be about what feels right to us both. And I want it to be for the right reasons." He stole a quick glance at his wristwatch. "I hate to cut our conversation short, but I have to run. Can we talk more later?"

"Of course." Soledad nodded. "I didn't mean to hold you up."

"Thank you for breakfast. Those popovers were good." He rose from his seat, moving to the sink with his plate. "I'll be back to check on you. And I'll set the house alarm when I leave. In case you need it, my gun is in the nightstand." He paused. "I guess I should ask if you know how to use a gun."

Soledad gave him a smile. "Since I was twelve. Our father made sure Dominique and I were comfortable with a wide range of weapons. I can wield a mean bow and arrow if I need to."

"I'll have to see that for myself one day," he responded, duly impressed.

He continued. "Melissa's got a patrol car positioned at all the main gates, and one of them will do a drive-by every hour. If you need anything, you just call me. I'll still be right here on the property, and I can be back in seconds."

"We'll be fine. Jack will keep an eye out for us."

"Jack will save Lyra. It's the rest of us who might be in trouble!"

Soledad laughed as Palmer sauntered toward the door. There was a moment of hesitation as he stood with his hand on the doorknob, seeming to fall into thought. She took a step forward as he turned around, their gazes connecting across the room. She felt her pulse begin to race, her heart beating rapidly.

Then Palmer hurried to where she stood and pressed a kiss to her forehead, his lips lingering for only a moment as his hand cupped her face. His touch was heated, and she felt her breath catch deep in her chest. Without another word, he hurried back to the door and made his exit.

WHEN PALMER PULLED into the pasture, his lips were still tingling from that kiss. Her skin had been warm and soft as silk, and he only regretted that there hadn't been time to see if one kiss could have become two. He couldn't help but wonder what Soledad was thinking about the brazenness of the act. He only wished he had time to reflect back on the moment for a little longer, but the bus from the children's home was already there.

The boys had exited the vehicle and were milling around in the field, waiting for something to happen. There were twenty of them, ranging in age from ten to seventeen. Most had visited before and were visibly excited to see what would come this visit. The newbies tried to appear indifferent, and Palmer knew that was their way of protecting themselves from disappointment if the day didn't pan out the way they hoped.

Noé hurried to his side as he parked his truck. The man's enthusiasm was corporeal, bubbling up like water in a fountain. Most of the men who worked for Palmer looked forward to helping out during the Rough Rider events. They all felt good about giving back to the community and the kids who simply needed a kind hand to support and nurture them.

"*¡Buenos días, jefe!*"

"Good morning, Noé. Sorry I'm late."

"Is everything well, jefe?" Concern blanketed the farmhand's face, seeping like mist from his eyes. "Are there problems?"

Palmer nodded. "Everything's fine," he said, a little white lie slipping past his lips. Because everything wasn't fine. In fact, everything was far from fine as he thought about Soledad, wishing he was back at the house with her. He missed her. Missed her laughter and the snarky comments that always gave him pause. He'd kissed her, and truth be told, all he could think about was sweeping her up into his arms, laying her across his bed and ravaging her with pleasure. He thought about the places his hands would lead and his mouth would follow. Fantasizing about her and him together suddenly felt like an obsession he couldn't control, and Palmer hated not being in control. He shook the thoughts from his head and turned his attention back to his friend. "I apologize for being late."

"You are never late. And you don't miss any days. We thought you might be sick when we did not see you yesterday."

"I just had a ton of paperwork to finish," he said, the little white lie catching in his throat. He coughed into his elbow and blamed it on his allergies. "Excuse me," he said. "The pollen is high today."

"¡Salud!" Noé said.

"Thank you."

"Most of the boys have been here before. We will have our regular four groups today."

"That works. I'll take the older boys who already have riding experience to the stable. They're predicting record-high heat today, so it might be a good idea to take the younger boys to the pond. Let them fish and play in the water. We'll have lunch in the old barn on the west side of the ranch."

"Not the one closest to the house?" Noé questioned.

"No. I'm going to move all of our activities to the other barn permanently. I've arranged to have the space renovated. We'll add classrooms and recreational space specifically for our volunteer programs. They'll start the work in the next few weeks, and it should be finished before the summer is over."

"The boys are very lucky to have you, jefe! You are very good to them."

"They just need to know we care, Noé," Palmer said, thinking back to when he'd been in the system and how he'd been desperate to know that someone cared about his well-being and wanted him to be happy. Leanne showing him attention and supporting him had been everything he wanted when he'd needed to feel loved.

The man nodded. "Everyone is waiting for you, boss."

"Give me one minute," Palmer said. "I need to make a quick telephone call before we get started."

"Very good," Noé said. "We will wait."

As Noé walked away, Palmer leaned back against his truck and took out his cell phone. He wanted to call the house to speak with Soledad, to just hear her voice. He was missing her already and feeling completely out of sorts because of it.

Soledad's presence in his life was a distraction, albeit a pleasant one, but still a distraction that was already proving to be problematic. It wasn't like him to show up to anything late, and he hadn't missed a day of work since before he had closed on the property. Now not wanting to leave Soledad's side and being unable to stop thinking about her had him slacking on the job. How quickly things had changed, he thought.

He sighed, slipping his cell into the back pocket of his jeans. He would see her in an hour or so to pick up those cookies. Until then, he would have to settle for the memory of a kiss he wished he had planted on her lips instead.

"YOU OWN ALL THIS?" one of the boys challenged.

His name was Tyler, and Palmer thought he looked like a miniature version of Jimmy Kimmel but with red hair. Skepticism filled the boy's face as he eyed Palmer with reservation.

"I do," Palmer answered. "This is all mine."

"I don't want no farm," a second little boy interjected. "I plan to live in a penthouse apartment in a big city like New York or Miami."

"That's good," Palmer said. "It's good to have goals. You can accomplish anything you put your mind to."

"I plan to be a race-car driver," a third child added.

"I love your ambition," Palmer answered. And he was proud of them. They were good kids who'd been dealt bad hands, but most of them were willing to bet the bank on themselves succeeding. He admired their perseverance, determination seeming like it was ingrained in their DNA.

"These are some good cookies," another little boy chimed in. "Where you buy them cookies?"

Palmer laughed. "I didn't buy them. A friend made them especially for you boys."

"I like your friend."

"I like her, too," Palmer said as he bit into his own chocolate-chip cookie that Soledad had made with chunks of dark chocolate and trickles of caramel across the top. He found himself hoping that how much he liked Soledad didn't show on his face.

Running back home to pick up the freshly baked cookies had come with its own challenges. Soledad had been playing with Jack and the baby when he'd arrived, the trio dancing around his living room again. The cookies had been packed in a plastic container and waiting for him on the counter. He had only been able to stay for a quick second, Noé sitting in the truck outside waiting for him to return.

Despite his nervousness, Soledad hadn't had anything to say about that kiss or their previous conversation. It was almost as if he'd dreamed it, nothing at all having happened between them. He had rushed in and rushed back out, cookies in hand and thoughts of Soledad in his head.

The boys' conversation shifted to the latest video game and some girl named Paloma. Paloma's "breast game" had all their attention, someone declaring that she'd moved from training bras to ones with real cups and lace. From the gist of the conversation, Palmer surmised Paloma was much older, closer to fourteen and at least three to five years out of their league.

Despite his efforts to keep the conversation on track, it would split off in a dozen different directions as quickly as a random thought crossed one of their young minds. Those thoughts spoken aloud kept Palmer and the rest of the chaperones on their toes.

Grandma Butler chastised two of the youngsters for inappropriate language and Palmer gave her a smile, nodding his head. "Get them, Grandma!" he said.

One of the new kids sat with his hand raised, waving it eagerly. Palmer gave him a nod. "Yes, Charlie?"

"Can I come back here next time?"

Palmer smiled, his head bobbing up and down. "As long as you keep your grades up and do what you're supposed to do, you'll be able to come back every time."

"Cool. I like this place," he said. "I like riding the horses."

One of the older boys rolled his eyes, less than impressed. He scowled, leaning back in his chair, the front legs lifted off the floor. "Man, this place bites," he grumbled. "Why do we have to muck the horse stalls?"

"David, we have this same conversation every week," Palmer said. "Mucking the stalls is necessary to maintain the health and well-being of the horses. If you want to ride, you also have to be responsible for their care. Those are the rules."

The young man shrugged. "Whatever."

"What's happened?" Palmer questioned. "Why are you in a mood today? This isn't like you." And it wasn't, Palmer thought. David pretended to be hard, a coping mechanism to protect his feelings. Deep down, he was a good kid, kind, compassionate and eager to be of help to others. He had rarely been a problem, so his sour disposition and belligerent attitude were completely out of character.

Since David's first visit to the ranch, Palmer had wanted to see him excel. He'd taken the young man under his wing, personally overseeing his training around the property. Palmer saw a lot of himself in

David and he knew the right attention could be a springboard for his success. He asked him again. "Do you want to talk about it?"

David looked away, not bothering to offer Palmer an explanation. His bad mood seemed to intensify when he punched one of the younger kids in the shoulder for stepping on his sneakers.

Palmer stood. "We're not going to do that. Get up," he snapped.

David gave him a defiant stare, visibly debating his options before finally standing.

"Now apologize," Palmer ordered. "We don't resolve any issue with our fists. Not for any reason."

The boy tried to stare Palmer down but gave in when he quickly realized it was a battle he would not win. "Sorry," he muttered under his breath.

Palmer corrected him. "'I apologize. I should not have hit you.' Now say it. Clearly and with conviction, and look him in the eye when you do."

David snarled, wishing he could sit back down and forget the conversation altogether. A minute passed before he finally turned to the boy he'd bullied and repeated what Palmer had instructed him to say.

"I apologize. I should not have hit you."

The other boy laughed. "You're a punk!"

"We're not going to do that, either," Palmer said, pointing a finger at the child. He shook his head as he turned back to David. "Walk with me," he said, guiding the boy toward the door.

Minutes later, the two sat atop the fence that bordered the pasture where the horses were grazing.

Palmer knew that David enjoyed riding and that the quarter horse named Majestic was one of his favorites. This was his third or fourth year in the program and he had always been one of the promising students and successes.

"Talk to me, buddy. What's going on with you?" Palmer asked.

David shrugged his shoulders, staring out across the landscape. His eyes swung back and forth, and Palmer sensed he was trying not to cry.

"It's okay," he persisted. "You can talk to me. Did something happen?"

"It's my birthday next week."

"Happy birthday to you!" Palmer exclaimed. "When you consider the alternative, that's a good thing."

"I'll be eighteen. I'll have to leave the foster home and my aunt said I can't come live with her. She's got a new boyfriend and he's got two daughters, so he says I can't stay there with them. I don't have no place to go."

Palmer heaved a heavy sigh. The number of children who aged out of the foster-care system each year was astronomical. Far too many became instantly homeless. Even more were unemployable. And some suffered with mental-health issues that would never be treated. It had become a vicious cycle, and even David knew he was about to become lost within it.

"What does your social worker say?"

"I might be able to stay at the center until the end of the summer, as long as they don't need the bed. Then I'll be able to move into the dorm at the college."

"You were accepted?"

"I got into the University of Michigan, Michigan State and Wayne."

"Dude! Congratulations! Have you decided where you're going?"

"I got a full scholarship to Wayne State. And I like their engineering program. It'll also pay for housing if I can get through the summer."

"That's good news. I'm proud of you."

David shrugged his shoulders again. "I don't know if I'm going to be able to go. I'll need to find a job to support myself. My aunt is the only family I have left, and she just tossed me over for some guy named Larry."

Palmer could sense the boy's deflation, every ounce of his spirit feeling bruised and battered by the hand life had dealt him. As he shared, tears rained down David's cheeks.

Palmer sat staring out over the landscape. His own frustration was palpable. Too many boys would feel like David did. They would commit to the work, turn their lives around and then get kicked down on their way out the door. "Let me talk to your social worker. We'll figure something out. You won't be homeless. I promise."

"You'd do that for me?"

"Yes, I would. Just remember, though, one day, I'm going to need you to pay it forward and do something good for someone else. Understood?"

David nodded. "Yeah!"

"Good. Now stop beating up on the younger kids. You need to be an example for them to emulate."

"Yes, sir."

"We need to head back. It's almost time for your bus to pull out."

"Thanks, Mr. Colton," David said, throwing himself off the side of the fence to the ground. "Thanks a lot."

As the yellow school bus pulled off the property, Palmer and his men watched, waving goodbye at the boys who were waving at them.

Noé gestured for Palmer's attention.

"We didn't have any problems, did we?" Palmer asked.

"No, boss. Just the usual with them. For the most part, all the boys were good today."

"Yes, they were! I was impressed by their ingenuity and the effort they all put into the team-building exercises. It was a good session this week."

"We have new livestock being delivered tomorrow," Noé reminded him. "I've scheduled more hands on deck to help get them tagged. Is there anything else you need me to do?"

"What time's that truck due?"

"Early morning. He came before eleven the last time."

"We'll be ready. Anything else?"

"No, jefe. We are good."

"Then I'm headed back to the house. I will see you in the morning."

"Thank you, boss. You have a good night."

"You, too, Noé. And thank you for all your help today."

As Palmer headed back to his truck, he smiled. It

had been a good day and another successful event for the kids. He thought about David, making a mental note to give his social worker a call first thing in the morning. The young man was headed toward a bright future, and he wasn't willing to let anyone or anything impede his journey. He felt responsible for David in a way that awed him. Palmer couldn't help but think if he had a son he would go to bat for him in the same way. But he didn't have a son, and he didn't want to worry about someone being there for his child if he couldn't be.

He blew a soft sigh, suddenly wondering if he was being irrational about not wanting children. Because he was there and able to do whatever was necessary. Starting his day with Soledad and Lyra had him rethinking every aspect of his life, and he found himself enjoying the experience of family. It took him back to his days after being adopted. And those had been great days! What if he could have what his parents had and not be afraid that it might blow up on him? Palmer suddenly realized he had more soul-searching to do. Until then, he looked forward to his evening, he thought, pulling his truck out of its parking spot. The night couldn't help but be good once he was back with Soledad.

Chapter Thirteen

Soledad was putting the final touches on five dozen cupcakes as Palmer sat at the table and rocked Lyra to sleep. This was the only other order that she was determined to fulfill. Palmer had promised to take it to her sister, who would deliver the order to her client.

The mother of the bride had ordered lemon cupcakes hand-decorated with vanilla-buttercream flowers and leaves. They were layered and tiered, and Soledad was certain each cupcake, individually wrapped in a green, tulip-cut paper baking cup, would make for a stunning presentation. This was one of those custom orders that would solidify her position in the local culinary scene—and bring in a dozen more orders from those present at the party.

Looking up, she watched as Palmer pulled his index finger to his lips, shushing the dog. Jack had begun to whine for his attention, not impressed that he had rocked the baby to sleep. The dog had apparently wanted to snuggle with the little girl by his lonesome, seeming irritated by Palmer's presence.

"Stop, Jack," Palmer whispered loudly. The little

girl shifted against his shoulder, turning her head to stare down at the dog nuzzling her foot. She leaned and reached a small hand out, muttering something that Palmer couldn't begin to decipher.

"You woke the baby, Jack," Palmer said, rising and shaking his head.

Soledad laughed. "Actually, if you just go put her down in the crib, she'll fall asleep. You rocking her to sleep is spoiling her."

"I like spoiling her," Palmer said.

"You do know, then, that you'll have to come over every night to get her to sleep when we go home, right?"

"Or you could just stay here," he mumbled under his breath.

"Excuse me?" Soledad said, her voice rising slightly. "I didn't catch that."

"I didn't say anything." He blushed, turning toward the makeshift nursery to lay the baby down to sleep.

Soledad laughed. She'd already been prepping the cupcakes when he'd come back from his volunteer event. Lyra had been napping, Jack keeping a watchful eye on her. Palmer had lumbered through the door with a rowdy *Honey, I'm home*, and the laughter between them had started all over again.

After a quick shower, he'd taken a seat at the counter for a quick lesson on the art of cupcake making and then he'd shared the events of his day. As the cupcakes had baked and cooled, they'd eaten a light dinner, still chatting about their day. Everything between them had felt comfortable and natural. Almost *too* comfortable, Soledad had thought.

Although she enjoyed their time together and the banter between them was as easy as breathing, Soledad couldn't help but worry that maybe she was becoming too close to the man. Palmer didn't want a family and she couldn't let herself want a family with someone who didn't want what she did.

Minutes later, Palmer walked back into the kitchen and resumed his seat at the table. "Those look incredible," he said, eyeing the artwork she'd crafted atop each dessert.

Soledad placed one on a saucer and passed it to him. "I made a few extra for us. Tell me how they taste."

Palmer took a big bite, his eyes widening. He hummed his appreciation. "This is really good, Soledad."

"Thank you. It's one of our more popular flavor combinations."

"I think the salted caramel that you make is probably my favorite."

Soledad gave him a look, one hand falling to her hip. "You really did spend a lot of time at my bakery, didn't you?"

"You didn't believe me? I told you I was there almost every day hoping to catch a glimpse of you. How come you never come out front?"

She laughed. "I do sometimes, but depending on what orders I need to fulfill, I have to be in the kitchen most of the time. Had you *asked* for me, I would have gladly come to the front to see you."

He tossed up his hands. "Now you tell me!"

Soledad shook her head. "Seriously, though, why didn't you ask me out?"

"Because I am painfully shy if I don't know you. And truth be told, I really didn't think I had a chance with you."

Oh, you had a chance! she thought to herself. She smiled and said out loud, "You may have been right." Soledad teased. "It's not like you're my type."

"You have a type?"

"Don't you?"

"Don't change the subject. What's your type?"

"I like my men tall, handsome and intelligent."

Palmer blinked. "You're right. I might not be your type. I'm probably an inch shy of tall," he said smugly.

Soledad laughed, the beauty of it ringing warmly through the room. "So, what's your type?" she asked after catching her breath.

"Beautiful inside, beautiful inside and beautiful inside," he answered.

"You're not hard to please, I see."

"You'd be surprised." He finished off the last bite of a second cupcake and licked the icing from his fingers.

A significant pause swelled thick and full between them as each dropped silently into self-thought. Palmer eventually spoke first, shattering the quiet that had fallen over the room.

"What's going on with us, Soledad?"

She shrugged her shoulders as she placed the last of the dirty dishes into his dishwasher. "I've been thinking about that most of the day. I worry that what's happening is just us reacting to our being thrown together in what looks like an impossible situation."

Palmer nodded. "I've thought that, too. But I also know that I've had a crush on you since forever. But it's like I told you before—I didn't pursue it because I knew we were on different pages. I didn't think I could give you what I knew you wanted for your future."

"And now?"

He hesitated briefly. "And now I think about you all the time. I don't want to leave your side because I'm enjoying your company so much. I want to see where we can take this if we put effort into it."

"I feel the same way..." Soledad responded, her voice trailing to a whisper. Her eyes skated across his face, noting the tiny scar above his top lip. One eye was just a hair smaller than the other and his cheeks dimpled if he smiled just so.

Palmer smiled. "There's a *but* there..."

She shrugged again, smiling back. "But... I can't help but wonder..." She struggled to find the right words to convey what she was thinking, but nothing came. She shrugged a third time.

"You and I are very similar," Palmer said. "We don't do anything that doesn't make sense. We are desperately trying to make sense of all this. Of what's happening. What might happen. Our feelings about everything. About each other. It's a lot. Maybe even too much. Maybe we should shelve this until another time, after you go back to your life?"

"Is that what you really want?" Soledad questioned, her eyes still dancing over his face. Because it wasn't what she wanted, she thought to herself. She wanted forever, and she found herself wanting forever with him and being afraid that she couldn't have it.

Palmer answered without hesitating. "Not at all," he said. "What I really want is you."

With the stealth of an animal on the African plain, Palmer slipped to Soledad's side. He stood before her, the heat between them rising swiftly, easing them into a dance that had them both panting heavily. He placed one arm around her waist and pulled her to him. Soledad slid her own arms around his neck, still staring into his eyes. Then she stood on the tips of her toes and kissed his mouth with a fervor she had never known before.

As soon as he did it, Palmer knew that kissing Soledad had quickly become his most favorite thing in the world to do. His mouth fit over hers with near perfection. She tasted sweet, her lips sugared from the cupcake icing. When she'd parted her lips and had granted him permission to enter, his tongue had slipped past the line of her teeth to tangle sweetly with hers. He'd tightened his hold around her waist, pulling her pelvis to his, and every muscle in his lower extremities had tautened with a vengeance. In that moment, he knew there'd be no way in hell that he would ever kiss anyone else again.

Soledad suddenly pressed her palms to his broad chest and pushed him back gently to break their connection. Her breathing labored, she was gasping for air.

"I'm sorry," Palmer apologized, still panting softly.

He took a deep breath and held it momentarily before blowing it back out slowly. He was unable to read the emotion that seeped from her eyes.

"N-no," she sputtered. "Everything…everything is…fine." She gasped, inhaling deeply.

Confusion washed through him. "What is it?"

"I can't make love to you. Not tonight."

Palmer felt a slow smile creep across his face. He saw the bewilderment that washed over hers. And he understood it. She could take all the time in the world, because he was willing to wait for her no matter how long it took for her to be ready and things to be fine between them. "Okay…"

"I don't want you to think I'm easy. Because I'm not. I need to make you work for it."

"Okay," he chuckled. "Is that how dating works now?"

"I don't know. I just know it's what my mother always told me and my sister when we were growing up. She'd say, 'Don't just give a man your sugar dish. Make him earn that privilege. He'll work for it if he really wants a taste.'"

"Sugar dish?"

"Sugar dish, cookie jar, goodies… Take your pick."

Palmer smiled at her. "I just want to kiss you, but we can take things as slow or as fast as you want."

"And I want to kiss you, too, but I'm also ready to come right out of my clothes, and I haven't shaved anything since before I got here. The fur on my legs alone might scare you away."

"Fur?" Palmer howled with laughter. "Really?"

"It's not pretty," Soledad said.

He leaned forward and pecked at her lips. His heart swelled full of excitement and anticipation. He couldn't begin to tell her that everything about her brought him pure joy. Even the "fur" she feared he might see.

"And if you keep kissing me, I'm sure I'm going to be embarrassed at some point."

He shook his head. "I doubt there's anything I will ever see that you need to be embarrassed about. You set the pace, Soledad," he said. "We'll make love when you're ready, not one second before. Okay?"

Soledad nodded, her eyes still dancing with his. Her lips parted ever so slightly, warm breath blowing softly. "Kiss me," she whispered.

Palmer slid his fingers into the length of her hair and dropped his mouth to hers, kissing her hungrily.

As if to resist the sensations of his touch, Soledad fell against his body and kissed him back. Sweeping her up and into his arms, Palmer carried her down the short length of the hallway to his bedroom. He laid her gently across the bed, then stood back to stare down at her. She was the most exquisite woman he had ever known. Her hair fell in wisps around her face and there was the faintest dusting of baking flour across her cheek. Her lips had swollen slightly from his ministrations, leaving her with a picture-perfect pout.

HE REACHED FOR the hem of his T-shirt and pulled the garment up and over his head. He looked like he'd been pumping weights, his muscles like sculpted marble beneath his taut skin. He had a near-perfect six-pack, his hard body the result of the manual labor he did around the ranch. Soledad's eyes dropped to his narrowed waist and the lines that V'd downward. She bit her bottom lip and the gesture sent a wave of heat into the pit of his abdomen and then rippled up the length of his spine.

Soledad reached for him and her fingers crept slowly against his skin. As he lowered his body to hers, settling in the eave of her parted legs, his mouth reclaimed hers. Every ounce of air felt as if it were being sucked from the room as she slid her hands into the back of his sweatpants and grabbed the round of his ass.

Palmer whispered her name, muttering it over and over again as if in prayer, and then, without warning, Lyra's tiny voice cried out from the baby monitor and Jack barked for their attention.

SOLEDAD SHOOK HER HEAD, laughing as Palmer pulled away from her. He adjusted himself in his pants as he blew a heavy sigh.

"Well, it looks like we have our very own personal chaperones," he muttered, visibly flustered.

"I'll go check on her," Soledad said as she pulled herself upright.

"I've got her," Palmer answered.

"Are you sure?"

He nodded. "Jack probably needs to go out, so Lyra and I will walk him to the door." He winked at her as he turned and headed for the other room.

Soledad tossed him a smile as she slid to the edge of the bed and adjusted her clothes. She'd been one kiss from welcoming him to her most private place, excited to spread herself open to him. Everything about him felt like home, and she had wanted to give him the key and have him claim her. She laughed out loud, pulling her knees to her chest and wrapping her arms around her legs.

She could hear him cooing, trying to calm Lyra down, but her wails moved from the bedroom to the kitchen and back.

Palmer suddenly called Soledad's name, a hint of anxiety in his tone.

He called her a second time. "Soledad!"

"What's wrong?"

"Lyra has a fever. Do you have a baby thermometer?"

Soledad hurried to his side, pressing her hand to Lyra's forehead and cheek. "She is warm," she said as she reached for the diaper bag.

Annie had packed everything she'd thought her daughter would need, including a digital thermometer and children's ibuprofen. Palmer sat with the baby in his arms, Lyra clinging to him like her life depended on it. Twice, Soledad tried to pick her up, but the little girl wasn't having it. She only wanted Palmer, her tears dripping onto his bare chest as he cradled her against him. Outside, Jack was barking to get back inside.

Soledad shook her head. "If you would take her temperature, please, while I go let Jack back in."

Palmer nuzzled his cheek next to the baby's. Lyra clutched his facial hair in a tight fist, still whimpering steadily. Soledad ran her hand down the child's back before going to the kitchen to let Jack back inside.

After securing the door, she warmed a bottle of milk for the baby, hoping meds and a full belly would help Lyra to feel better. Heaven forbid, Soledad thought, that something serious was wrong with Lyra. She didn't want the child to be ill, but if she was, Soledad hoped it was a simple virus or a cold that Lyra could fight off on her own. Anything more serious would put them in the hospital emergency room, where Gavin might find them.

There was a moment of quiet panic as Soledad tried to fathom what she would need to do and how she would do it if something were seriously wrong with Lyra. Would a doctor allow Soledad to be responsible for the baby's treatment? Would the hospital insist on calling her only living parent? Would they call the police? Truth be told, Lyra had always been such a healthy baby that Soledad hadn't considered illness an option she would have to contend with. Now she didn't have a clue what she needed to do, and she was worried that she might lose Lyra.

She moved to the computer, pulled up Google and typed in Lyra's symptoms. The lengthy list of search results suddenly had her even more anxious, her stomach twisting nervously. She suddenly felt as if she were failing Parenting for Dummies, being thrown a curve she hadn't prepped for.

Back in the room, Lyra had finally stopped crying. She still clung to Palmer, her head resting against his shoulder. She stared at Soledad, but wasn't moved by the woman's efforts to comfort her.

"Her temperature is high," Palmer said, "but it's not high enough that I think there's something seriously wrong. I gave her a dose of that ibuprofen. She should feel better in no time."

"I thought she might want a bottle," Soledad said, handing it to him.

She watched as Palmer shifted the infant in his arms and fed her the warm milk. Lyra's eyes traveled between the two adults, then stopped to linger on Palmer's face.

I like him, too, Soledad thought, amused by the look of awe Lyra was giving him. *I like him, too!*

Chapter Fourteen

WHEN THE ALARM sounded, Palmer woke with a start, feeling like he'd been run over by a truck. It had been a long night, neither he nor Soledad getting much sleep. When the night had started, he'd imagined that making love to Soledad would have kept him up till the midmorning, the two of them savoring the sensual exploration that came with the first time. Neither had imagined a sick baby usurping the moment. Lyra had fussed on and off well into the early morning. Then, just like that, she'd fallen into a sound sleep, leaving the two of them to wonder what they'd done right and why they hadn't done it sooner.

Once they'd realized it was going to be a long night, Palmer had insisted they all climb into his bed. The television had played in the background, reruns of some investigative criminal show Palmer was a fan of. They had passed Lyra back and forth between them, depending on whose arms she showed preference for. To Soledad's chagrin, Jack had licked her tears away, but even she couldn't complain when the dog seemed able to calm her down when they couldn't.

Despite it all, what Palmer had found most interesting was how natural it felt to him: waking up to Soledad in his bed, the baby asleep atop a pillow between them and Jack snoring at their feet. The only other time in his life when something had felt so right, so amazingly perfect, was when his mother Leanne had gone above and beyond to adopt him. When he'd discovered the love of family for the first time and that family was all his. It felt like that again, with Soledad and Lyra. It was inexplicable joy, and Palmer realized it was something he'd been missing, and he wasn't ready to let it go.

He sat watching the two of them. Soledad mumbled in her sleep, only a word here or there that he could recognize. Her breathing was steady, her chest rising and falling rhythmically. Her face was flushed, and one fist was clenched tightly around the bedclothes.

He smiled. He'd often heard friends complain about children changing the trajectory of their sex lives, and now he fully understood it. Any other time, he would have made love to Soledad until his body failed him, exhausted from their loving. Lyra had successfully blocked that effort, his erection withering with her cries. But there was still that ache of need and desire through his pelvic floor, that tingling in his appendages as he thought about the two of them together.

Rising, he headed into the shower, needing the spray of cool water to help him open his eyes and get his day started.

When Soledad opened her eyes, Lyra was sound asleep beside her and Jack lay on her other side. The sound of running water told her Palmer was in the adjoining bathroom. As she thought about him, that shower suddenly felt like it was calling her name. It had been an exceptionally long night and Soledad knew it was probably going to be a long day, as well. She imagined that Lyra would sleep until she was well rested. Then she'd be wide-awake and in need of attention.

Soledad eased her body off the bed, careful not to disturb the sleeping child. Jack lifted his head to give her a look, then nuzzled himself even closer to the baby. They were quite a pair, she thought, remembering how Lyra had given her a side-eye when she'd tried to move Jack to the floor. They had claimed each other and refused to be moved from the comfort they found in their affection for one another. Soledad found herself a little envious of their connection.

She suddenly thought about Palmer again. They had been one orgasm from the tide of their relationship shifting. The intimacy between them had been unexpected and everything Soledad had ever wished for. She had wanted him more than she had ever wanted any man in her life and knew the feeling had been mutual. She could feel it in the hardened lines of every muscle that had risen in his body and in hers. In fact, she still wanted him, that desire so intense that it felt like a gulf had opened up in the pit of her stomach, threatening to swallow her from the inside. The heat was so vast that she imagined herself combusting internally.

Nothing about their situation made an ounce of sense, but in the insanity of it, something beautiful was blooming between them. Something so precious that it gave immense value to the future she wanted for herself. And what she wanted for herself was him.

Sliding open the nightstand drawer, she carefully opened that new box of condoms and palmed one in her hand.

Easing off the bed so as not to wake the baby or the dog, she headed toward the bathroom. With each step, Soledad second-guessed her decision. It was a momentary hesitation as she questioned if she was doing the right thing. Instinctively, she kept moving forward, faith in everything that felt right about him and her together guiding her steps.

As she stepped into the bathroom, Soledad dropped a trail of clothes onto the tiled floor. The room was warm and moist, steam from the hot water painting the walls. Palmer stood behind the frosted glass doors, his head tilted back as the water washed over him. He looked startled when Soledad slid the shower door open.

Neither spoke, words unnecessary as they each admired the view. Soap streaked his torso and the patch of pubic hair was lathered with bubbles. His breathing was suddenly labored and she watched as his erection grew, seeming to beckon her to him. She lifted her eyes to his, moisture laced through his lashes.

The prophylactic in her palm spoke volumes. She watched as he took it from her and sheathed himself quickly. He extended his hand toward her and pulled her forward. As the palms of her hands pressed against his chest, Palmer crushed his mouth to hers in a kiss that stole her breath and had her curling her toes.

They were suddenly an amalgamation of hands and fingers, mouths and tongues. He lifted her against the tiled wall as she wrapped her legs around him. Heat coursed between them with a mind of its own, the magnitude sweeping through the entirety of the bathroom.

When his body entered hers, Soledad cried out, her nails digging into the flesh across his back. The walls of her most private place pulsed with fervor around his male member, welcoming him home. She met him stroke for stroke as he pushed and pulled against her. Their loving was intense and swift, its power like a tidal wave of energy neither could control. It was a sweet dance of give and take, back and forth, round and round. Soledad climaxed first, her entire body convulsing with pleasure as she clung to him. Palmer followed, the intensity of their interaction making her feel like she'd been thrown from a cliff and was flying sky-high. His legs shook as he eased himself and her to the shower floor, collapsing beneath the sheer beauty of the moment.

PALMER SENT NOÉ a text message to let him know he would be late. Again. It was becoming a bad habit that he was going to have to break before it became problematic. He could only begin to imagine what the ranch hands were whispering about him. In the past, they could set their clocks by his punctuality; missing a full day of work on the ranch was completely out of the question. Lately, he'd been late with some regularity, even not showing up multiple days in a row. Heaven forbid his family found out.

He stared at his reflection in the bathroom mirror. There was something in his face he didn't recognize. Something that put a shimmer in his eyes and deepened the dimples in his cheeks. He liked the change, although he would never admit it to anyone aloud. A wide grin filled his face, the smile spreading from ear to ear.

Making love to Soledad had left him exhilarated. The first time had been fast and furious, only about the physical act necessary to release the sexual tension that had grown between them before Lyra had interrupted them. The second time had been more emotional, the sensual act bringing them both to tears. The third time had been about exploration, about discovering each other's bodies and idiosyncrasies. Like finding that sweet spot just behind her ear that had Soledad writhing with ecstasy whenever he nuzzled his lips and tongue against it.

There would have been a fourth time if Lyra hadn't interrupted them again. She was a demanding little thing, he thought, her sweet smile deceiving if you didn't know better. Palmer shook his head, trying to fathom how parents managed to have two, three and four kids when the first never let them enjoy the act of procreation. He laughed out loud as he wrapped a bath sheet around his waist.

Walking into the bedroom, he was surprised to find Jack lying in the middle of the bed alone. Soledad and the baby had disappeared into another room.

"What? The girls abandoned you and now you want to hang out with me?"

Jack grunted at him, disinterest written all over his muzzle. He jumped from the bed and padded slowly out the door.

"So much for loyalty and appreciation," Palmer muttered. He laughed, moving to the closet to find his clothes.

When he stepped into the kitchen minutes later, Soledad stood in the center of the room, her hands on her hips as she stared at the television set. There was a commercial playing and she seemed to be waiting for something, one foot tapping anxiously against the hardwood floor. She made him smile and he imagined what every day could be for them with her and the baby there.

Lyra sat propped against Jack, who opened one eye to give him a look that dared Palmer to take the little girl from him. His dog had officially become a monster, Palmer thought.

The local station returned to the morning news. There was a clear shot of downtown, the camera spanning the length of Grave Gulch Boulevard toward the police station and town hall. The streets were lined with protesters holding signs and chanting, their voices ringing out in unison. The newscaster's voice narrated over the images.

"Folks also took to the streets in downtown Grave Gulch today to peacefully protest ongoing concerns with local police chief Melissa Colton and what some are calling a clear lack of accountability and leadership within the ranks. Protesters tell us this issue is particularly concerning in light of the recent discovery that forensic scientist Randall Bowe manipulated evidence in numerous cases, resulting in prejudicial outcomes. Bowe is currently wanted for questioning and a warrant has been issued for his arrest."

The camera then panned to two protesters, a robust woman who was the spitting image of Dolly Parton and an African American man who owned a local business on the protest route.

"All police aren't bad," the woman was saying. "My father is a retired police chief. The problem is the good cops lack the support and resources to do their jobs successfully. We have an issue with that."

The shop owner was less enthusiastic. "Corruption within the police ranks is rampant, and until those in charge are held to a higher standard, it's not going to get better. We need a police chief who isn't afraid to push the status quo and demand better from his team!" he admonished.

The camera went back to the line of protesters, capturing their chants a second time. The newscaster continued.

"The Grave Gulch Police Department took to social media today, posting its response to the protests and calls for Chief Colton's resignation. To read their full statement, go to our website."

The cameras shot back to the newsroom and the newscaster. She was an attractive brunette who looked pageant-ready with her overbright smile and bouffant hairstyle.

"New this morning, authorities are looking for a missing Michigan woman who may have been in Grave Gulch prior to her disappearance, and they need your help."

Soledad's picture suddenly filled the screen. It was a promotional photo she'd had taken when she'd opened the bakery. One of the few pictures that she liked of herself. The on-air personality resumed.

"Grave Gulch Police Department said thirty-year-old Soledad de la Vega was reported missing when she failed to show up for work at her local business, Dream Bakes. De la Vega is believed to have last been in the company of Annie Stone, whose body was discovered days ago. Dr. Gavin Stone is considered a person of interest in the investigation. However, Ms. de la Vega's disappearance is considered suspicious, police said. Anyone with information about the whereabouts of Soledad de la Vega should contact the Grave Gulch police. There is currently a five-thousand-dollar reward for information leading to her whereabouts. When we return..."

Palmer reached for the television remote and depressed the off button. Soledad spun toward him, her eyes wild.

"That doesn't make any sense," she started. "Why would they report me missing?"

Palmer shook his head. "I'm not going to venture to guess," he said as he pulled his cell phone out of his back pocket and dialed. The number rang three times before his brother answered.

"What's wrong?" Troy questioned.

"Is that how you say hello?"

"Under the circumstances, I have to be concerned."

"Local police reported Soledad missing. Do you know anything about that?"

"Technically, she is missing. Melissa was afraid that if it didn't look like we were looking for her or concerned about her whereabouts, Dr. Stone would figure out we knew where she was and maybe figure out where she is himself. We don't want to take any chances he'll find her before we find him."

"And the reward?"

"We wanted to make it look good."

Palmer nodded into the receiver, bobbing his head as if Troy could see him. "Any leads on where Stone might be?"

"The investigation is still ongoing. He's got money and connections, which is making our job harder. Melissa thinks he may have left the state, but there have been one or two tips that have come in, saying he's been spotted here in Grave Gulch."

"You people need to find him," Palmer said.

"You just take care of our witness," Troy answered.

"You need to step up the patrols around my property. Just in case," Palmer quipped. "Please," he added.

"Done," Troy responded.

Disconnecting the call, Palmer shared the information with Soledad. She shook her head, suddenly feeling completely out of sorts. She moved back to the kitchen and the sink full of dishes. Frustration pulled her mouth into a frown, and her eyes narrowed as she felt her brow crease with worry.

"I have to ask," Palmer said. "Are you okay?"

Soledad shrugged her shoulders. "I let my guard down. I let myself forget why Lyra and I are here. Then I started playing house with you like this is some fairy tale with a happy ending."

"It can be."

She shook her head. "I'm not safe as long as Gavin is out there. And me just being here puts you in danger, too."

Palmer shook his head, seeming to fall into thought as he pondered her comment. "No, not as long as I'm here and you trust me. Five minutes from now things will feel like normal again and I will still be doing everything within my power to protect you and Lyra. Nothing is going to happen to you on my watch. Nothing."

Soledad took a deep breath and let it out slowly. She finally gave him a quick nod, her gaze clinging to him as if her life depended on it. Because in many ways, it did.

Something in the oven had filled the room with the aroma of cinnamon and sugar. Soledad took a peek inside the appliance, then moved back to the sink. Palmer shook his head as he eased up behind her. He dropped his hands to the curve of her hips and pressed a damp kiss to her neck. She purred in response, then turned her face to be kissed, grateful to be distracted from those feelings of dread.

"Hungry?" she asked.

"For you."

Soledad giggled. "I made cinnamon rolls. They should be ready any minute now."

"The ones you sell at the bakery with the thick cream-cheese icing?"

She nodded. "Yep. Those ones."

"Let me grab a very large cup of coffee," he said as he kissed her one last time. "Or I'll need a nap when I'm finished with breakfast."

"You're going to be late, aren't you?"

"You mean I'm already late, don't you? If someone hadn't been holding me hostage in the shower..."

Soledad laughed. "You are not going to blame me because you got greedy."

"Greedy? If you weren't giving it away, all willy-nilly like. I am a man, after all."

"Willy-nilly?"

Palmer waved his hand in the air. "I am just calling it like I see it."

"And that sounds just like it might be the last time you get to see it," she joked.

Palmer didn't miss the innuendo. He laughed with her, chuckling heartily. Sliding his arms around her torso, he hugged her close, feeling her body settle against his. He kissed her cheeks, the tip of her nose, her forehead.

"It's going to be okay," he whispered softly. "I promise."

Soledad nodded as she lifted her face to his, easing into the vow against his lips. The kiss they shared was furtive, tongues doing a brazen two-step. He snaked a hand beneath her T-shirt, his fingers pulling at the rock-hard nipple that had blossomed beneath his touch. The moment stalled abruptly when Lyra began crying for attention.

Palmer lifted his gaze, amusement in his eyes. “Baby girl,” he said, as he shifted himself from Soledad. “We really need to work on your timing, princess.”

FEELING COMPLETELY OUT of control at having to stay indoors, Soledad was ready to run screaming into the fields and pull her hair out. She was frustrated and ready to take out her anguish on the first person who looked at her the wrong way. Although she loved Palmer's home, the four walls were starting to feel too close for comfort. She wasn't sure how much more she could take.

Beside her, Lyra gurgled and cooed in her baby seat. Soledad was grateful that the child had no clue what was going on or that what was going on was beginning to get to her. Lyra was happy and the smile on her face could melt icebergs. She was a great source of joy, and Soledad still worried that, with everything going on, she wouldn't be able to keep the child safe.

She hadn't wanted Palmer to see how frightened she was. Because it wasn't Gavin who frightened her. It wasn't Gavin who had her heart racing, thinking about what would happen when things were over and her life went back to normal. Gavin didn't have anything to do with her concerns about where things would stand with Palmer when there was no one and nothing for him to protect her from.

Palmer was trying so hard to ease her mind and to

convince her that everything was going to be well. He was also doing a darn good job keeping her distracted. Every time he was near, the heat from their bodies merging, she had a hard time thinking straight. Because Palmer Colton was sexy as hell and damn near perfection in bed! Everything about the man made her heart sing. Taking that step with him had been more than she could have ever wished for. He was definitely some bright sunshine on a dark day.

Soledad suddenly thought about Annie. How she and Annie would have huddled together over the details and a bottle of wine. How Annie would have alleviated her fears and encouraged her to take a risk if it meant she would be happy. How Annie would have been thrilled that she'd found someone she could love. Someone who would love her back.

Annie would have also given her a hard time about jumping into bed with a man she hadn't known longer than a minute. Under normal circumstances, what had happened between them would have been more of a one-night stand. Annie would have helped her make sense of everything she was feeling, though. She would have made sense out of the nonsense. Soledad missed her best friend.

Lyra giggled, seeming to read her mind. She made Soledad laugh and Soledad had seriously needed the laughter. The baby suddenly scrunched up her face as if to cry, but pulled her big toe into her mouth. Drool trickled down her foot.

Soledad chuckled. "Okay, kiddo, I'm limber, but I'm not that limber. Why are you showing off?"

Lyra looked at her with wide eyes and the slightest pout. Her face twisted a second time, and then she kicked her legs and pitched her body backward.

"Well, that's not very ladylike. What's going on, sweet pea?"

Lyra went back to chewing on that toe and her clenched fist. Soledad grabbed a cloth diaper and wiped at the spit that puddled over the baby's chin. That was when she saw the beginnings of a new tooth piercing Lyra's upper gum.

"Someone's teething. Look at that! Poor baby! No wonder you had a bad night!"

Lyra gurgled and chewed.

Soledad leaned to give the baby a kiss on her forehead. Everything about Lyra brought her immense joy. She fully understood Annie's commitment to the infant because she now, too, would lay down her own life to keep the child safe. Her love knew no limits and she imagined it was what Palmer's mother felt for him when he'd been adopted.

She suddenly had a light-bulb moment. "I need to bake you some teething cookies," she thought out loud. "In fact, I'm going to bake cookies for you and for Palmer. Palmer likes my cookies."

Lyra didn't look all that impressed, which made Soledad laugh.

Chapter Fifteen

Whether or not Palmer showed up on time, Colton Ranch still operated like an efficient machine. Between the miles of fencing, irrigation systems, corrals for holding the sheep and cattle, the loading chutes and trailers, his crew was quite able to keep things running smoothly. With the new shipment of cattle that had arrived the day before, they now had to be branded with the ranch logo.

Palmer was fortunate in his ranch hands. Between the animals, the land, the machines and dozens of other jobs that needed to be performed, his workers were loyal, giving him 110 percent of themselves. As he pulled up to the site, Noé was already in place, ensuring the branding process went off without a hitch.

Gone were the days of traditional branding, where an animal was captured and thrown to the ground, its legs tied together and a fire-heated branding iron applied to its hindquarters. Palmer and his crew herded the animals through a chute instead, where they ran into a confined area and could be safely secured while the brand was being applied with an electric iron. By the time Palmer reached the pasture, more than half the cows had been marked.

"Good job," Palmer said, extending his hand to shake Noé's. "I can't tell you how much I appreciate you."

"All the men are doing great," Noé said, gesturing at one of the workers with his hand. "This is a good crew."

Palmer nodded. "Then I'm going to leave you to it. I'll head over to the north fields. We need to finish the repairs on those irrigation pipes. It'll probably be dusk when we get done."

"I'll head over to help when we are done here, jefe."

Palmer shook his head. "No, I need you to move the cattle to the other pasture, so they don't start overgrazing here. Tomorrow we're going to need to cut the hay, so we'll need to check the haying equipment tonight to make sure everything's in good working order."

Noé gave him a nod, then went back to focusing on the job at hand.

Jumping back into his truck, Palmer drove to the other side of the ranch. He parked his vehicle and got out, pulling on a pair of leather gloves as he made his exit. A handful of men, already in place, had started to dig out the ditches that needed to be repaired. Grabbing his own shovel from the bed of the truck, Palmer leaped in to give them a hand.

An hour later his shirt was stained with sweat, his face was streaked with mud, and every muscle in his body hurt. The work wasn't easy and only a select few were able to do it and do it well. These were some of the strongest men he'd ever known, and he was honored to call most of them friends.

Lunch came quickly and they were past the point of readiness when they were finally able to take a break. Most fell to the ground to rest and enjoy packed lunches and bottles of ice water from the cooler in the bed of Palmer's truck. Laughter was abundant and Palmer took a bit of ribbing from the men who'd known him longest. Shortly after lunch, Noé and two of the other men joined them, helping to knock the job out quickly.

Palmer was first to see the young man in the distance. He was coming from the direction of the main road. He was alone and walking at a good pace toward the crew. As he got closer, Palmer saw that he was fairly young, more boy than man, with dark curls, large eyes and a lanky frame. He wore denim jeans, a white T-shirt, and carried a backpack. He wasn't the first stranger to pass through the farmland and probably wouldn't be the last, but given everything going on with Soledad, Palmer didn't trust anyone he didn't know.

Noé seemed to sense his concern as he stepped beside him.

"Do you recognize him?" Palmer asked.

Noé shook his head. "No, jefe. I have never seen him before."

"Do me a favor and check him out. If he doesn't feel right to you, send him on his way."

Palmer watched as Noé met the boy down the road. The two stood in conversation for a brief moment, then began to walk together toward Palmer and the work crew. As tests went, it looked like he had passed the first one. Getting past Palmer's number two in charge wasn't an easy thing to do.

When the two reached his side, Noé gave his boss a nod as he sauntered past, leaving him and the boy standing together.

"How can I help you?" Palmer asked.

He extended his hand. "Good afternoon, sir. My name's Benjamin Harris. I heard you might be hiring and I'm looking for a job."

"Palmer Colton," he said as he shook the boy's hand. "How old are you, Benjamin Harris? You look awful young."

"I'll be eighteen in the fall."

"Have you ever worked on a ranch before? Or done any kind of manual labor?"

"Not really, but I'm willing to learn. My father was a jack-of-all-trades and he taught me a lot before he died."

"I'm sorry for your loss."

The young man shrugged. "Thank you."

"So, why should I hire you?"

"I have a strong work ethic. I'll work hard. I'm a fast learner and I like getting my hands dirty. You won't be disappointed."

Palmer stared at the kid. There was something in his eyes that Palmer recognized. A deep hunger that seeped past his lashes. A look that reminded Palmer of himself at that age. Determined to have his dreams, to accomplish a lengthy list of goals and to be the best person he could possibly be. What he saw in the young man named Benjamin had been the same drive he himself had possessed when he had wanted to make his parents proud.

"What about school?" Palmer asked. "Have you graduated?"

"Yes, sir. This past spring."

"What about college? Are you going in the fall?"

"I don't know if school is what I want to do with my life right now. That's why I need a job."

"Do you know anything about horses?"

"Some. My dad taught me how to ride, but we never owned one."

Palmer turned to eye the crew, who'd just replaced the last length of pipe that needed to be repaired. The trenches were being filled in and the crew was ready to be done for the day. He turned back to Benjamin.

"If you're willing to learn, I'm willing to give you a shot. Be here tomorrow at dawn. The work is going to be dirty. You'll be mucking horse stalls and cleaning stables. Whether or not we keep you will depend on how well you do."

Benjamin grinned. "Thank you, sir. Thank you. I really appreciate it."

Palmer held out his hand a second time. "Call me Palmer."

Benjamin nodded. "Palmer, thank you. And you can call me Ben."

"Well, Ben, aren't you going to ask me how much you'll be making?"

Ben shrugged. "I know it'll be a fair wage. Your reputation precedes you, sir."

As he headed back to the house, Palmer had a lot on his mind. A few times, he thought his head might explode, too many thoughts vying for his attention—Soledad taking center stage with most of them. He had missed her. Even as he'd dug piles of dirt and torn up his hands cinching pipe, she had been on his mind. All he could think of was getting to the end of the day and getting back to her.

There was so much for him to process and unpack. Soledad was his dream come true, but he had to be rational about their situation. Soledad had known what she'd wanted. But had she wanted what had happened between them because she'd desired him or because she'd needed a diversion from the stress of the situation? And why was he suddenly doubtful about them being together, second-guessing if taking that jump had been a good thing? Because, deep down, he knew that what they'd shared was honest and genuine, and everything he had ever wanted. He just wasn't certain that Soledad felt the same way, and that actually scared him more than anything else.

As he pulled in, his cell phone rang. He glanced at the incoming number before he answered the call.

"I could use some good news," he said to the caller, not bothering with "hello."

"So could I. Do you have any for me?" Melissa Colton asked.

"I wish. How are you doing, beautiful?"

"I've been better. I'm sure you've heard about the protests. They're calling for my head on a platter."

"I hate that you have to go through this."

"It may well be the end for me. I know the city council is considering a special meeting to discuss whether or not I am fit to continue in my position."

"Whatever you need from me, you know you have it, right?"

"I appreciate that. Right now, though, I need to know about my witness."

"Obviously, I'm not doing a good job keeping her hidden if you're asking about her."

"Quite the opposite. I wouldn't know where she was if you hadn't told Troy."

"He's such a tattletale."

"He's a good cop. We excuse the rest because he's family."

Palmer chuckled. "So, where are you with finding Gavin Stone?"

"That's why I'm calling. I want you to know I've stepped up the patrols in your area. We've had two credible sightings. He is definitely still in the area, and for some reason, he seems to be focused on that end of town."

"Good. I have something for him if he shows up."

Melissa took a deep breath. "I want to move Soledad and the baby to a safe house. I think it would be best."

Palmer paused, considering the comment. Personally, he didn't agree with his cousin. He wasn't ready for Soledad or Lyra to leave him, and he was willing to do whatever was necessary to keep her there, safe and sound under his watch. He said, "I'll discuss it with her, but I doubt she'll do it. Under the circumstances, she's not very trusting."

"Look, I get it, but I still think it would be in her best interest."

"I don't want to risk her running. I'll see what she says, but if the answer is no, I'll keep a watchful eye on her. You can trust that."

"You just be careful, please. Stone is a dangerous man and there's no telling what he might do if he feels cornered. He's hell-bent on getting his hands on Soledad and his baby, and there's no telling what he might do."

"Does he have a legal claim to Lyra?" Palmer questioned.

Melissa took a deep breath. "Legally, the court would have to consider any claims he may have, since he is her biological father, but Annie was very clear about where she wanted the child to be placed. I highly doubt he's planning to take any legal route to get custody of Lyra."

Palmer sighed, a heavy breath blowing past his lips. "I'll call you once I talk to Soledad. But I wouldn't get my hopes up if I were you," he said.

"Thanks, cousin. Love you!"

Palmer disconnected the call. He didn't have to ask Soledad the question to know the answer. She wasn't going to leave if she didn't have to, and he didn't want her to go. He couldn't keep her safe if she were somewhere else, and he didn't have the heart to tell Melissa that he wasn't so trusting of the Grave Gulch Police Department himself. He knew most of the officers through his family. Some he liked, others he didn't. Trust didn't come just because they wore a badge and carried a gun. Many were a fine lot of officers and most just wanted to do the best job they could possibly do. It was the few who weren't as committed that worried him. The ones who didn't wear a sign that said they might be dirty, on the take or just plain lazy about their responsibilities. So, no, he thought. Soledad and Lyra weren't going anywhere if he had anything to say about it.

From where he sat, he saw Soledad peeking out past the wooden blinds that decorated his windows. He waved his hand so that she would know he was fine. He had one more phone call to make before he went inside, and he was dialing as she blew him a kiss through the glass.

Geoff Colton answered on the first ring. "Where are you, son? We were expecting you here an hour ago."

"Hey, Pop. Happy birthday."

"Thank you."

"I ran into some problems here on the ranch. It's taking me longer to get them resolved than I anticipated."

"I hate to hear that. Do you need us to come give you a hand?"

Palmer chuckled. "No, sir. I can handle it. You just enjoy your birthday party. I'm sorry I can't be there, but I'll make it up to you." And Palmer was sorry, wishing he could be there and wishing Soledad and Lyra could be there with him.

He finally understood what his father had meant when he'd been a boy, professing that your family was your greatest blessing. How he'd been a stern disciplinarian, ensuring they all stayed on a straight and narrow path. He often found himself sounding like his dad when he spoke with the boys in his program. And his time with baby Lyra brought memories of his father's adoration for his sisters. Geoff Colton was the epitome of what a father should be, and Palmer was discovering just how much he wanted to follow in those footsteps.

There was a rumbling on the other end and Palmer could hear Grace's muffled voice. He didn't have to be there to know that she was fussing, or that his father had covered the receiver with his hand, hoping that he wouldn't hear her complaining.

Geoff cleared his throat. "Your sister is already making faces. Do you want to talk to her?"

"Oh, hell no. Tell Grace there is only one woman who gets to discipline me, and her name is Leanne Colton."

Geoff laughed. "Well, Mom is loving on little Danny. Your nephew is quite the ladies' man."

"I'm sure Desiree doesn't want to hear that."

"Your sister will have to get over it. When you have pretty babies, they grow up to be pretty adults. Danny will be a heartbreaker like his grandpa."

Palmer laughed. "Well, I hate to miss all the fun, but I'll run by the house to see you both soon."

"Not to worry, son. God willing, there'll be more birthday parties for you to celebrate with me. I plan to get good and old."

"I love you, Dad."

"We love you, too, son."

WHEN PALMER WALKED through the door, Soledad stood with Lyra in her arms, the two of them smiling brightly. Amusement flitted across their faces.

"What?" he said, eyeing them both anxiously. "What did I do?" He tossed a look over both shoulders in jest.

"We need a taste tester," Soledad announced.

Lyra suddenly flung a biscuit across the room. Jack bounded in that direction and eagerly scooped up the treat.

"Naughty girl." Soledad's scold brimmed with amusement. "Stop doing that."

Confusion danced through Palmer. "What are you three up to?"

"I tried to make teething biscuits for Lyra. But she doesn't like them, and every time I give her one, she flings it across the room for Jack to eat."

"That's not saying much. Jack is a canine vacuum cleaner. He'll eat pretty much anything and everything."

"I think they taste good. There's no accounting for her taste buds. You get to be the deciding vote," Soledad said as she pointed to the plate of cookies on the counter.

Palmer shook his head as he stepped forward to take one. He eyed the cookie cautiously, his brow lifted and his face squinched. "It doesn't look very appetizing. There aren't any chocolate chips or nuts or caramel… Nothing."

"It's a teething biscuit."

He took a nibble and then a bigger bite. A second later, he flung the cookie across the room and Jack happily retrieved it. Lyra laughed robustly, the wealth of it so heartwarming that Soledad and Palmer couldn't help but laugh with her.

"You two are no help at all," Soledad said.

Palmer leaned in to kiss her lips. "They taste like paste with a hint of vanilla."

"Paste? They are not that bad!"

Palmer took Lyra from Soledad's arms. "Oh, yes, they are. Isn't that right, princess?"

Soledad rolled her eyes at the ceiling. "How was your day?"

"Long and exhausting. I need a shower, something to eat and your good cookies." He gave her a suggestive wink.

Soledad felt herself blush, her cheeks warming rapidly.

"Not those cookies," Palmer said teasingly. "Your *other* cookies."

Soledad moved to stand behind the counter. "Well, go grab that shower. By the time you get back, the food will be ready and we can discuss my cookies after Lyra goes down for the night. Considering that food review, I'm not sure you're going to get any more of my cookies."

"Do you see how your mommy does me?" Palmer said teasingly. He nuzzled his face against Lyra's as the little girl grabbed both his cheeks. "She's not being a very nice mommy."

"You're not winning any points, Mr. Colton. You might want to quit while you're ahead."

Palmer sat Lyra in her high chair. He eased around the counter to press himself against Soledad, cradling his body against hers. She was warm and soft and smelled of cardamom and ginger. He pressed a damp kiss to her neck and felt her body jump ever so slightly.

Dessert couldn't come fast enough, Palmer thought. He kissed her one last time, then headed down the hall to the bedroom.

Chapter Sixteen

"No!" Soledad said emphatically. "If Melissa insists, Lyra and I'll take off and find somewhere else to hide out, but I'm not going into witness protection with the local police department."

"I told her you probably wouldn't agree, but I promised I'd ask," Palmer responded.

The two sat side by side on the family room sofa. Palmer was finishing off a bottle of beer and she sipped on a glass of white wine. Lyra had gone down for the night and they hoped with fingers crossed that she would sleep through most of it. Jack had gone out the door ten minutes earlier, racing across the fields toward goodness knew what. He would come in when Palmer made his late-night rounds to check on the animals.

"Unless you'd prefer we leave?" Soledad said. She shifted in her seat to face him.

"Not at all. You are welcome to stay here for as long as you need."

"And that's kind of you, but how do you really feel about us being here?" Soledad questioned.

Palmer paused for a split second. "It would break

my heart if you left," he finally said softly. "I want you here, with me." He leaned to kiss her cheek, allowing his lips to linger sweetly against her skin.

Soledad let go of the breath she'd been holding as she waited for him to answer. She took a sip of her wine. "Did she say anything about Gavin?"

Palmer pushed his shoulders toward the ceiling. "They're still looking," he muttered, not bothering to elaborate because he really had nothing new to add to the conversation.

"Maybe he has left town," Soledad said. "Maybe this will be over soon and then things can go back to normal for the both of us."

"What's normal?"

"You'll get your life back and you won't have to babysit me and Lyra anymore."

"Who's babysitting you?"

"Didn't you have a party to go to tonight? You mentioned it the other day."

"Yeah, it was a birthday party for my father. There'll be other ones," Palmer said.

"I hate that you had to miss it. You know you could have gone. Lyra and I would have been fine."

"I didn't want to go. I wanted to spend the evening with you."

"But your family…"

"My family celebrates something every other week. Hopefully, when they have the next party, you'll be able to go with me." Palmer shifted in his seat. Things were different between them now and he knew he couldn't consider a future that didn't include her and the baby.

More important, Palmer knew he didn't want to. He frequently wished a quiet prayer that she was feeling the same way.

"Do you think about what will happen with us when this is over, Palmer?"

"I do. All the time. I imagine you'll go back to the bakery and forget all about me," he said facetiously.

"I was thinking the same thing about you and your ranch."

"I could never forget about you, Soledad." Palmer gave her a smile as he slid his empty beer bottle across the table. "You've left quite an impression on me."

"You say that now. But we'll see."

"I'm sure we will," Palmer laughed and then changed the subject. "I'm going to be gone most of the day tomorrow. I have to catch up on some maintenance work. Noé has to take a few days off, so I'll need to step up and act like I own this place."

"One of your employees came to the door today. At least, I think it was one of your employees."

"Here at the house?"

Soledad nodded. "He was a young guy. He wore jeans and a T-shirt, and he carried a backpack. He rang the bell first and then he went into the barn. Later I saw him with the other guys, sitting in the bed of the truck. That's why I assumed he worked for you."

"He was in the barn?"

"Yeah, and then he walked that way." She pointed a finger toward where Palmer and his crew had been working.

Palmer's eyes shifted as he pondered that tidbit of

news. He had to wonder who had trespassed and why, although he was fairly certain he knew who it had been. But why, he wondered, was his new employee poking around the property?

"Did he see you?" Palmer prodded.

"No, I don't think so. When he came to the door, he was trying to peek through the sidelights, but Lyra and I were in the bedroom. I only knew he went into the barn because he was coming out of it when I finally came out to see who it was."

"Interesting..."

"Does he not work for you?"

"If we're talking about the same young man, I actually hired him today."

"So, he's new and he was nosing around?"

"I was just thinking the same thing," Palmer said. "I have some questions for him tomorrow. If I don't like the answers, his career here may come to a quick end."

"I didn't get the impression that he was up to anything malicious. Just that maybe he was looking for you."

"Let's hope that's all it was. Because I really liked him. He seemed like a good kid and I thought he had potential. He reminded me a lot of myself."

Soledad reached her hand out and tapped his thigh. The gesture was gentle and comforting. Palmer dropped his own atop hers and tangled his fingers with her fingers. They sat together for a few minutes, listening to the jazz that played on his stereo.

"I need to make my rounds," Palmer finally said. He pressed a kiss to her cheek.

"Find that babysitter of ours while you're out there," Soledad said. "And I'll go get your cookies ready."

Palmer laughed and kissed her again.

PALMER STOOD IN the center of the barn and looked around. Although Soledad was certain the young man who'd told Palmer his name was Ben Harris had been there, there was nothing amiss or out of place that gave Palmer any pause. They had been able to move Pharaoh back with the other horses the day before, so this barn was empty, housing nothing but old tools and farm equipment. He didn't bother to check the cabinets because he had moved all the guns from the space the night he'd been shot at. Giving any possible intruders easy access to a weapon didn't seem prudent.

Jack suddenly barked as he came barreling into the barn. He was panting heavily, like he'd just run a marathon. Palmer filled a metal trough with water, and the dog drank, practically plunging his whole head into the container. "What's up, big guy? What are you chasing?"

Jack barked again excitedly, spinning around Palmer's feet. He raced to the farmhouse and back again.

"Okay! Okay! We're going back inside. Just be patient. Down, Jack," he commanded.

Jack lay at his feet, feigning patience. He made Palmer laugh as he tried not to jump up and down.

Minutes later, the Bernese was sound asleep under the crib in the guest bedroom. Lyra slept as soundly, out like a light. The kitchen was clean, and Soledad had dimmed the lights. He could hear soft music coming from the bedroom. After double-checking that all the doors were closed and locked, and then setting the alarm, he made his way to the master bedroom.

He stilled in the doorway. Excitement rained through his body like a downpour in the middle of a summer day. Soledad lay naked across the bed. Her head rested against the palm of her hand, her elbow propping up her torso. Her legs were crossed at the ankles and a plate of chocolate-chip cookies rested in front of her pubic area. The smile on her face was pure gold.

"Cookies!" Palmer exclaimed. "May I have one?"

He watched as she bit down on her bottom lip, widened her eyes and gave the slightest shrug of her shoulder.

Palmer reached for one of the treats, pulled it to his mouth and took a bite. He chewed slowly, observing her as she slid her top leg up the length of the other and back down.

He reached his hand down a second time to caress her long hair, twirling a strand around his finger. Soledad trailed her index finger across the back of his hand. Her touch was teasing, and every muscle in his body quivered for attention.

Palmer swallowed the last bite of his treat, then bent to kiss her mouth. Their lips met in a gentle touch, gliding like velvet against silk. Their tongues danced sweetly, flirted nonchalantly.

He finally took a step back. He began a slow striptease, pulling his T-shirt over his head and flinging it to the side. His pants followed, boxers and all, as he slid them to his ankles and kicked them after his discarded shirt. Soledad rolled back against the pillows, apparently admiring the sight as Palmer lifted one knee onto the mattress and then the other.

Picking up the plate, Palmer eased it onto the nightstand. He grabbed Soledad by the ankle and parted her legs. Before she could exhale a breath, he pressed his mouth against her, his tongue darting back and forth over her mons.

He could sense the sheer pleasure rippling through her, every nerve obviously firing sweetly as he gently spread her open like a flower, exposing the petals of her sex as his tongue lashed at her hungrily.

Soledad slid her hand against the back of his head and pushed herself into his face. She moaned, and when he found her most sensitive spot, his tongue wrapping around it as he sucked her juices, she arched her back and he heard her call out his name.

Palmer clutched the round of her buttocks and rolled, pulling her above him, his mouth still locked tightly around her. Her arms flailed as she began to ride his face, thrusting her pubis back and forth against his lips and tongue.

She came quickly, her orgasm hitting with a vengeance. Her body quivered and shook as he held her, refusing to let her move from him as his mouth and tongue continued their ministrations. Then Palmer shifted gears, sliding her downward until she dropped against him, his sheathed dick like solid steel piercing her feminine spirit.

They made the sweetest love, his hands wrapped around her body as he cupped her buttocks beneath his palms and guided her ministrations. He felt her muscles grab his member, her insides pulsing rhythmically around him. It was almost more than he could bear as she leaned forward to kiss his chest, his neck and that sweet spot beneath his chin.

Palmer pumped himself into and out of her, over and over again. He grabbed one bouncing breast and then the other as he fondled the dark nubs that had hardened beneath his touch. Fluids mingled, time stood still and then every nerve in both their bodies exploded in unison. It was pure bliss, paradise on steroids, pleasure beyond belief. As Soledad collapsed against him, Palmer wrapped her in his arms and hugged her tightly against him, vowing to never let her go.

Sleep came quickly to them both, but not before he whispered her name and told her that he loved her. When Soledad closed her eyes, a smile graced her face and joy blessed her heart.

THERE HAD TO be some law against the things she and Palmer had done in his bed, Soledad thought. In the back of her mind, she swore that she had heard her mother's voice admonishing her to be a good girl because only bad girls behaved so wantonly. Annie's voice had superseded the matriarch's, her bestie praising her and giving her a high five for being able to get both legs up over her head. Him saying he loved her was icing on some very sweet, sweet cake!

Making love to Palmer was truly an out-of-body experience, and Soledad was certain Saint Peter would hose her down, make her recite a decade's worth of

Hail Marys and then maybe, just maybe, consider giving her a ticket to enter through the pearly gates.

"We're going straight to hell," she said out loud.

Palmer laughed. "You don't go to hell for great sex, Soledad."

"Well, you definitely don't get into heaven doing what we just did."

"Correct me if I'm wrong, but I think they call that purgatory."

"Exactly. We're going straight to hell. Because what we just did can't possibly be any good for anyone."

He tightened his arms around her, her head resting on his chest.

"Do you regret being with me, Soledad?" Palmer asked. "Because you're starting to make me feel some kind of way."

"No. Not at all. If I had to make the decision again, I would do it each and every time. What about you?"

"I might not do a repeat of that cramp I caught in my thigh, but I would happily give you a repeat performance of everything else."

Soledad giggled. They had made love, slept and then woken to repeat their performance over again. Now, lying together as the sun was starting to find its rightful seat in the sky, both were wide-awake and she was feeling reflective.

"We happened fast. Under extenuating circumstances," Soledad continued.

"Which makes our being together even more special."

"Some people would say we've only set ourselves up for failure."

"What do you say?"

"I don't want us to fail," she said. And she didn't, because Soledad had come to accept that she loved Palmer. She loved him with every fiber of her being and she never wanted to let him go. She lifted her gaze to his, her eyes saying everything that was in her heart.

"Then we won't. But you're doing what I often do. You're overthinking things and you need to stop. Can't we just enjoy being together without questioning every little detail?"

Soledad paused, thinking about his question. "No, of course not," she finally answered. "Where's the fun in that? Especially since that now means we have a daughter to consider and little girls come with a whole other set of problems!"

Palmer laughed again. "I'm going to grab a quick nap. Then I'm going to make love to you one more time before I have to get up and go to work. I'd suggest you do the same." He curled his body around hers, his pelvis against her buttocks, his chest to her back, his arms crossed over her breasts. He cuddled close to her and blew a kiss against the back of her neck.

"Hey," Soledad said minutes later. "I love you, too, Palmer Colton." And then she giggled softly, because Palmer was sound asleep and hadn't heard a word she said.

SOLEDAD JUMPED, A loud noise in the kitchen scaring her awake. She lay there for a moment, listening. Except for what had dropped in the distance, it was quiet. Eerily quiet. She reached a hand over to the other side of the bed and it was empty. Palmer was gone. And so was the baby monitor that had rested on the nightstand. If Lyra had cried, she wouldn't have heard a thing. She took a deep breath to calm her nerves.

Rising, she grabbed the clothes she'd discarded the night before and threw them on to cover her nakedness. Pulling her hair back, she twisted the lengthy strands into a bun. Still uncertain, Soledad hurried down the hall to the other bedroom to check for Lyra, but the baby wasn't there. She rushed to the kitchen.

Palmer sat at the counter, sipping on a cup of coffee. He was jotting notes onto a sheet of paper. Lyra was in her high chair, gumming one of the teething cookies from the night before. Soledad felt her entire body smile at the sight of them.

"Good morning," she said softly.

Palmer looked up, not having expected her to be there. "Good morning," he answered. "You're up. I was going to let you sleep until I had to leave."

"I heard a loud noise."

"I dropped that big pot trying to put it into the cabinet. I apologize."

"No apology necessary. Are you late?"

He shook his head. "No, right on schedule, actually."

"You must be exhausted. You didn't get a whole lot of sleep last night."

"I got enough. I feel invigorated."

"That probably won't last long. You'll be dragging by lunch."

"Then I'll come home and you can put me to bed."

"Me putting you to bed is why you didn't get any sleep last night," she said with a hearty laugh.

Palmer chuckled with her. "That's what I was counting on."

"Do I have time to grab a shower before you have to leave?"

He nodded. "You do if it's a quick one. I'm going to finish my coffee and read the headlines to Lyra."

"Aren't you a lucky little girl," Soledad said as she moved to give the baby a kiss.

Lyra gurgled, still gnawing on that cookie.

"What did you do to get her to eat that?"

"I smeared a little grape jelly on it," Palmer said. "I thought about peanut butter, but since we don't know if she has any allergies, grape jelly won out."

Soledad shook her head. "Seriously, they were not that bad."

He laughed. "You're right, but with jelly and peanut butter, they are much better."

Chapter Seventeen

Palmer stopped digging the trench to take a quick breather. The sun had finally disappeared behind a multitude of clouds, giving them a few minutes of reprieve. He gulped air and stretched his tired muscles. At the other end of the expanse, Benjamin was still wielding his shovel, breaking the soil and slinging dirt behind him. He'd been shoveling for as long as Palmer, only pausing for water once or twice. Palmer still had concerns about the boy's motives, questions unanswered about why he'd gone to the house and into the barn. He trusted the answers would come, and as he watched him work so steadily, Palmer was impressed with his fortitude and told him so.

"You're doing a good job, Ben," he said as he stepped over to where the boy was working. "You tired yet?"

Benjamin stopped and stood upright. He swept dirt from his hands onto his face as he wiped away the sweat pooling on his forehead. "Thank you, sir. I'm just trying to keep up with you."

"That could get you hurt. You just focus on doing what you can do, son."

"Yes, sir."

"You ready to grab some lunch?"

Benjamin shrugged. "I didn't bring anything to eat, so I can just keep working."

"Don't worry about that. I'll gladly share mine. But you need to take a break. You can't keep pushing your body like that without risking an injury."

"Yes, sir. Thank you, sir."

"Come on. We're done here for the day. I need to make my rounds. Then, after we eat something, I'm going to teach you how to muck the stables. You'll do that for the rest of the day. It's dirty work but necessary."

"Whatever you need, sir."

"And stop 'sir-ing' me. Call me Palmer."

"Yes, sir."

Palmer gave the kid a look, then burst out laughing. "Let's ride," he said, gesturing toward his truck.

Gathering the shovels, Benjamin followed Palmer to his vehicle. They placed the tools in the bed and hopped into the cab. Palmer started the ignition and a gust of cool air rushed out of the vents.

"Air-conditioning!" Benjamin said with a chuckle.

"It can be a workingman's best friend," Palmer said.

Palmer twiddled with the radio dial until the local country station came in loud and clear. A Trace Adkins song billowed out of the speakers, and both men began to bob their heads in time to the music.

"There's nothing like a cool breeze and a good country song," Palmer said.

"Maybe throw in a bottle of pop," Benjamin added.

"A cool breeze, a good country song and your favorite beverage. Sounds like heaven to me," Palmer laughed.

"My father used to say heaven was a good meal, a good woman and good loving. If a man had that, he didn't need anything else."

"Tell me about your father," Palmer said as he drove toward the pastures to check on the cattle. He wanted to know more about the kid, still not sure if he could be trusted. In the back of his mind something about the boy was eating at him. Something that said he needed to be wary, most especially since he had to protect Soledad and Lyra with every resource available to him.

"He was a great guy. He and my mother adopted me when I was a kid. According to my adoption records, they didn't know who my sperm donor was, and my biological mother just abandoned me at the local hospital. They never found her and I was put in foster care for a few years.

"The Harris family was the fourth or fifth family to take me in. I wasn't an easy kid. I had rage issues. But they were great. My mom was so patient with me. I remember how she used to just sit and hold me and sing to me until I calmed down. She died when I was twelve years old. She had breast cancer. After that, it was just me and my dad. He became my mother and my father. He was the best. He said that they had once wanted to adopt more children, but never got the chance, and when my mom died, he thought it best that I get all his attention, so I never had any siblings. It was just me and him. He gave me a good life. A really good life."

"If you don't mind me asking, what happened to him?" Palmer asked, cutting his eye toward the young man. "I know you said he died recently."

"He was murdered. You know that serial killer Len Davison, who's been in the news for getting away with murder because of that dude who threw away all the evidence?"

Palmer nodded. "Yeah, Randall Bowe."

"My dad was one of his victims. I didn't have anyone after that, and now I'm here."

Palmer released a heavy sigh. "I'm sorry that it's been hard for you, kid. I was in foster care, too. I was five years old when my family adopted me. I'm blessed to still have them. I know everyone's not that lucky and I don't take it for granted."

Palmer felt the young man staring at him. "You were lucky," the kid said, his tone almost wistful.

Palmer smiled. "We were both lucky. Don't ever think differently. We had family who loved us. Not all the kids in foster care will have that."

Benjamin muttered something under his breath.

"Excuse me?" Palmer said. "I didn't catch that."

Benjamin shook his head. "It was nothing. I was just agreeing with you." He changed the subject. "Do you have any kids?"

Palmer shook his head. "No. I really wasn't interested in having kids, but...well..." He hesitated, suddenly realizing that, since Lyra and Soledad, everything he had thought he'd wanted and everything he'd believed about himself had changed. He was a different man and life had taken on a whole other meaning.

It had happened so quickly that he hadn't even seen it coming. "No," he concluded, "I don't have any children yet." He took a deep inhalation of air, allowing the wealth of emotion he was feeling to envelop him.

"I thought you had a wife and kid," Benjamin was saying. "I saw them at your house when I was there."

Palmer's brow creased. "When were you at my house?"

"Yesterday, when I walked in from the road. One of the work crews pointed me toward the house, but no one answered when I rang the bell. I looked in the barn for you, but when you weren't there, I kept walking until I ran into you."

Palmer nodded his head as he took the information in, but didn't respond. Why had Benjamin been looking for him?

"You're not upset with me, are you?" Benjamin continued. "I know I was trespassing, but I didn't mean your family any harm. And I don't think she even saw me. I just wanted to ask about a job."

"No, it's fine," Palmer said finally. But it wasn't, something still laying a brick wall of doubt around him. He ignored the comment as he pondered the ramifications of Ben's admission, his answers feeling ready before the questions were even asked.

The two had finally made it to the other side of the property by the ponds. Palmer parked the truck and gestured for Benjamin to follow him. He grabbed a picnic basket from the rear and began to walk. Two massive rock formations bordered one side of the watery pool. The landing at the top of each was flat and

Palmer climbed up a set of steps that looked like they'd been carved into the towers. He took a seat. Benjamin climbed up after him and they settled down to enjoy their lunch.

"This is pretty cool," Benjamin said as he looked out over the water, enjoying the view.

"This was one reason why I purchased the property. The previous owner was a friend of my father's, and my brother and I would come play here when we were little. This spot here has become my personal sanctuary when I need to think and clear my head. Because I have been where you are now and I understand how you feel, I thought you could use a space like this. You're welcome to come sit anytime. And if you ever need someone to talk to, I'm here for you." Palmer gave the young man a compassionate smile.

"Thank you," Benjamin responded. "I appreciate the kindness. You know when you're a foster kid that people aren't always kind to you."

Palmer nodded. "It's a broken system, and sadly, there are some who are so broken themselves that all they know how to do is hurt others."

Seeming to fall into thought, Benjamin shifted his gaze back over the landscape.

Palmer carried on. "You were blessed to have been spared the hardships of the foster system. I'm grateful every day that I was showed so much love by my adoptive family. Just as I'm sure you appreciate yours."

"Yeah," Benjamin said, "it was a blessing."

Palmer flipped the lid open on the lunch basket he'd carried to the top with them. Soledad had packed him two sandwiches and he passed one to Benjamin. The bread was homemade. It was a focaccia topped with fresh rosemary, olive oil and flaky sea salt. She had layered the bread with Genoa salami and provolone topped with thinly sliced onion, lettuce, pepperoncino and tomatoes, then drizzled with olive oil and vinegar.

Benjamin took a bite, chewing slowly. He suddenly hummed his appreciation. "This is really good," he said.

Palmer grinned. "One of my new favorites."

He pulled a penknife from his back pocket and sliced an apple in two. There were also three cookies, one of which he gave to Benjamin. "These were made special just for me. I can't share them as generously."

Benjamin laughed. "I wouldn't share, either. They're even better than the sandwich."

The men continued to chat easily. The more Palmer learned about Benjamin, the more he saw himself and the more he wanted to help the kid.

"There's a program I sponsor every month for children in Grave Gulch group homes. I'd like it if you'd think about volunteering and helping out. I think you'd be an inspiration to them. Especially the older boys who are looking for role models."

"Me? A role model?"

"Of course. Why not?"

"Why would anyone want to look up to me?" Benjamin asked.

"Because you're doing the work to better yourself

and it's important that other kids see that the hard work is necessary for success."

"You sound like one of those pamphlets they give you when you age out of the system."

"I don't know about all that. I was actually thinking I just sounded a lot like my father," Palmer said with a soft chuckle.

SOLEDAD LISTENED AS Palmer told her about his day. He was excited, his new employee having made quite an impression on him. She found his exuberance heartwarming. They were falling into an easy pattern with each other. Their love language felt natural and easy as the fresh air blowing through the trees outside. She felt confident in the decisions they would make together, and she trusted him with her and Lyra's lives. She reached for his hand and squeezed his fingers.

"I think he just needs to know there are people out there who care about him," Palmer told her. "He's carrying a lot of baggage. I also get the impression there's something else weighing on his spirit. He may still be mourning the loss of his father. Or having a difficult time processing his dad's death."

"It's so heartbreaking. It's almost like he's had two families stolen from him." Soledad shook her head. "That may be a lot for you to take on. Are you certain you can handle what might get thrown at you?"

"I'm not sure, and I won't know until I'm in the situation. I just know I want to try." Palmer raised Lyra to his shoulder and gently patted her back. She'd polished off a full bottle of milk and the burp that erupted from her sounded like a truck backfiring.

"Whoa!" Palmer exclaimed. "That one was award worthy."

"She's going to give the boys a good run for their money." Soledad snickered as she rose from her seat, removing the used dishes from the kitchen table. Dinner had been a large salad topped with sautéed shrimp. It had been a quick and easy meal. "So what's on your agenda tonight?"

"I have some paperwork I need to finish. Then I'm all yours. Why? What do you have in mind?"

"Shall we Netflix and chill?"

"You've been dying to say that, haven't you?"

Soledad giggled. "Yeah."

"Just don't pick a romance movie and I'll be good. Give me something with a little action in it. Maybe a drama."

"Check. Action and drama. I think I can handle that. Meanwhile, I want to go pick the last of those blueberries. I'd like to make a tart."

Palmer tossed a glance over his shoulder to the clock on the wall. "Most of the men have gone for the day. I don't think there's anyone still around. If you want, I can do my rounds early just to be sure."

"I think I'll be good. And I'll be careful. It shouldn't take too long. They're past ready to be picked, so it should be quick."

"Do your thing, honey. I'll watch Lyra while you do."

"I love it when a plan comes together." Soledad went to the cupboard to take out a large ceramic bowl.

Palmer moved to the front door, the baby still in his arms. He looked out and, when it was clear, gestured for Soledad to head for the barn.

Hurrying across the walkway, Soledad slipped into the barn and out the far door.

The bushes on the back side of the barn were sizable, each shrub loaded with berries. Soledad began filling her bowl with the ripe fruit, excited as she began to plan how she would use them. That tart, more muffins, maybe even a cobbler or scones. Her bowl was almost full when she suddenly felt like she wasn't alone. She looked up and around, but saw nothing. A tight knot formed in the pit of her stomach. She couldn't help but wonder if she would always be afraid that Gavin was lurking somewhere in the wings, determined to do them harm. Afraid that the wrong move or a bad choice would take Lyra and Palmer from her.

Fear was a funny emotion, she suddenly thought. There was little she'd been afraid of as a child and even less as an adult. Now the slightest noise could leave her shaking like a withered leaf, her own shadow giving her reason to pause. She took a deep breath and held on tighter to the bowl.

Just as she was moving back toward the barn door, it flung open and Palmer stepped through. Lyra, cradled high in his arms, squealed excitedly at being outside.

Soledad pulled her hand to her chest, breathing a sigh of relief. "It's just you."

"Were you expecting someone else?" he teased, his eyes shining sweetly.

"No. I just…well… It was like…" She faltered, suddenly unable to explain what it was she was feeling.

"You okay?" Palmer asked. Concern washed over his face.

She shook her head. "I've been better. I think I'm ready to go back inside."

"It's okay," he said as he shifted to her side. Reaching for the large bowl, he passed her the baby and wrapped an arm around her waist to guide her back toward the house.

THEY HAD JUST made it to the steps of the farmhouse when Benjamin called out his name. Palmer turned abruptly, surprised by the young man walking hurriedly in their direction. "Go inside," he snapped, his voice a loud whisper. He gave Soledad a gentle shove. "And lock the door."

As she and the baby stepped over the threshold, the door closing securely behind them, Palmer turned.

Benjamin stopped in front of him at the bottom of the stairs.

"What's going on? Why are you still here?" Palmer asked.

"I missed my ride. I went back to the pond to sit and think about some things and I lost track of time. I was walking out to the main road to hitchhike home when I saw you. I didn't mean to interrupt you and your friend." He gestured toward the house and Soledad, who was standing behind the closed door, eyeing him with reservation.

"If you want, I can give you a ride," Palmer said. "Just let me get my wallet."

"I don't want to be any trouble."

"It's not a problem," Palmer said as he turned, took the steps and bounded into the house. But it was a problem, because something still didn't feel right, and Palmer always trusted his gut.

SOLEDAD COULD FEEL the young man watching her intently through the glass door. He seemed innocent enough and Palmer was willing to vouch for him, but that knot in the middle of her belly was only getting tighter. There was just…something about the way he looked at her that made her uncomfortable. She took a step back from the door and out of his view.

"I shouldn't be too long," Palmer said as he kissed her cheek. "I feel like there's something going on with him and I'd like to try to figure out what it is. Will you be okay?"

Soledad forced a smile to her face. "We'll be fine. I have the alarm, the dog and your gun. Besides, I doubt Gavin is planning to just come out of the shadows without some kind of fanfare. He likes attention too much. But if he does, he'll regret it."

"I'm sure he will. But I'll still lock the door and set the alarm. Just to be safe, you and Lyra should hang out in my bedroom until I get back."

"Lyra and I are making a blueberry tart. We'll be fine."

Palmer kissed her again. "Just keep that burner in your pocket in case you need to call me or 9-1-1 for help."

PALMER DROPPED BEN off downtown, on the corner of Market and Holland streets. Home was a friend's sofa, and the friend, a young woman named Hadley, hadn't finished her shift at the local McDonald's. Palmer learned that Hadley had also been a foster kid until she hadn't been, returned to her mother when she'd been fifteen.

Palmer couldn't put his finger on it, but something about Benjamin was starting to bother him. The kid just showing up at his front door was problematic, despite the young man's assertions that he meant no ill will.

On the ride to town, they'd had a lengthy conversation about boundaries and him being respectful of them, but Palmer couldn't say with certainty that Benjamin understood or even cared. He sometimes talked too fast and had an explanation for everything Palmer threw at him. There was also something in his demeanor that gave Palmer pause whenever they talked about family. He couldn't help but wonder if the boy was dealing with issues bigger than Palmer was prepared to handle.

After some thoughtful consideration, the more he reflected on what he knew about the kid, the more uncertain Palmer suddenly felt. He turned his truck onto Grave Gulch Boulevard and headed for the police station.

THE PATH LEADING into the building was crowded with protesters. Their chants for police reform and Melissa Colton's dismissal were loud and caustic. Store owners had begun to board up their neighboring buildings, fearful that the protests would turn violent and agitators would destroy their town. Watching it on television had been one thing. Seeing it up close and personal was something totally different.

The main entrance to the building was gated. Inside, a receptionist at the front desk would point visitors to where they needed to go. The receptionist's name was Mary and behind her stern business demeanor was a sweet, bubbly personality. She was well-liked by everyone and greeted Palmer warmly.

"Mr. Colton. How are you?"

"I'm well, Mary."

"So what can I do for you today?"

"I was hoping to see Troy. Is he here, by chance?"

"I believe he is," she answered. "Let me call him up for you."

"Thank you, Mary."

Minutes later, Troy came from the back of the building. He looked frustrated, despite his efforts to hide his emotion. "Hey, what's up? What brings you here?" Troy asked, extending his hand to shake his brother's.

"I'm headed home, but I need you to do me a favor," Palmer said, dropping his voice slightly as the two stepped outside.

"What's going on?"

"I need you to run a background check on a new hire for me."

"Something out of sync?"

"Something, but I can't put my finger on it. He says his father was murdered and was one of the Len Davison victims. I like the kid and I want to believe him, but I need to be careful with Soledad and the baby."

Palmer handed his brother a Post-it note with Benjamin's personal information written on it.

"Do you have a picture of him?"

"No. Do you need one?"

"That would have been nice."

Palmer shrugged. "He looks like he could be Zayn Malik's little brother."

"Zayn who?"

Palmer laughed. "He was a singer in that boy band One Direction."

"How do you know this?" Troy asked, his incredulous expression spurring Palmer to laughter. "When do you have time to follow a boy band?"

"Seriously, how have things been going here with you?"

"Busy."

"Busy is good, though, right?"

Troy shrugged. "Depends on how you look at it."

"You sound frustrated."

"I am. The protests are starting to wear on my nerves. I get it. People have the right to express their frustration. In fact, it's their civic duty to bring attention to issues the community needs to be aware of. But the timing right now couldn't be worse. I'm afraid the protests are going to distract my officers from closing these cases. We have a serial killer to find, a murderer to catch so Soledad can go home, and Bowe is still out there wreaking havoc. It's a lot and it doesn't help that they're gunning for Melissa when she's been working her ass off to do right by this department and this city."

"How can I support you? If I can, I really want to help."

"You're letting me vent. I can't tell you how much that means to me." He shrugged.

"Well, anytime you need an ear, you know I'm here, right?"

"Yeah, but I need to get back to work." Troy gestured with that piece of paper. "I'll run this and give you a call when I find out something."

"Thanks, and you stay safe out there, please!"

Chapter Eighteen

Soledad split the last slice of blueberry tart in two, taking a sliver for herself and plating the other for Palmer. It had been two days since she had picked the fresh berries, and the sweet treats she'd made had finally run their course. She and Palmer had also had their fill of blueberries. What they hadn't had their fill of was each other.

Everything about their time together was beginning to feel like forever. Enjoying everything about Palmer was as natural as breathing. Where days earlier she'd had doubts about the two of them, she could now see them having a brilliant future together. Or maybe it was just wishful thinking? Whatever it was, Soledad thought, she planned to enjoy every bit of it for as long as she could.

She carried the dessert plates on a wooden tray into the family room and took the seat beside Palmer. He sat with Lyra on his chest, the little girl having fallen asleep right after dinner. "I'm going to go put her in her crib," Soledad said as she gently took the child out of his arms.

"I'll find us a movie while you're gone," Palmer responded.

"Let's not do a movie," Soledad said. "I'd much rather we chat and cuddle. I know you have to be up bright and early in the morning, and that way we can get to bed early."

"That sounds like you're trying to seduce me," Palmer teased.

"Do I need to try?" Soledad teased back. "I thought seducing you was as easy as dropping my clothes."

Palmer laughed. "Says the woman who is clearly sex-crazed!"

She laughed. "I am not. Just because we've made love every day…"

"Two and three times per day…"

"…doesn't make me sex-crazed."

"If you say so, but I'm good with going to bed early, if you are."

Thirty minutes later, the tart demolished, teeth brushed and pajamas on, Soledad and Palmer were cuddled together in the center of his bed, catching up on the day.

"It was a good day today," Palmer said. "We're finally finished with the irrigation repairs. Fencing is complete and I'll be able to finalize the renovations on the large barn this week."

"I had a good day, too," Soledad said. "I've created two new cupcake recipes and tested four bread-pudding recipes. I think tomorrow I may try my hand at making a banana pudding."

Palmer made a face. "Banana pudding?"

"It'll be some of the best banana pudding you will ever have. I put rum in the cream and I make my vanilla wafers from scratch."

"Why does that sound like we need to order groceries?"

"Probably because we do," Soledad said with a giggle.

"You're missing the bakery, aren't you?"

There was a moment of pause as Soledad considered her answer. "I am. I really am. I've been thinking that maybe I just need to go back to my life. That may bring Gavin out of hiding and they'll be able to arrest him."

"It may also put you at risk for him to do you harm."

"At some point I may very well have to take that risk. I'd rather do it sooner than later. I don't want to get so comfortable that I make Lyra and myself targets because I've done something silly, believing that I'm safe."

Palmer nodded. "Well, if you think you're ready, we can put a plan in place. We can think about security for you and the baby. Maybe a team at the bakery? Definitely at your apartment?"

Soledad agreed, though hearing him talk about her going home suddenly felt very final and not something she wanted to consider. And definitely not as she lay content in his arms as they traded easy caresses. But they had not discussed her staying, and she didn't think it was her place to ask. But she wanted to stay, to make his home her home. She was excited to wake up with him in the mornings and go to bed with him at night. She liked that they could agree to disagree when they didn't share the same opinion about things. She loved that he so willingly supported those things that brought her joy. She blew a soft sigh.

Palmer captured her lips, kissing her sweetly. He tasted like minty toothpaste. His kisses became more intense, his touches passionate. Their bodies responded in kind to the ministrations, and soon they were making love as easily as they breathed. Both believed their bodies were meant for each other, and they swayed across the mattress, perspiration puddling in secret places, panting softly and whispering sweetly in one another's ear.

PALMER HAD RIGGED a pulley system to lift the oversize beams to the open loft of the barn. As he yanked on the thick rope, he was joined by Noé and Benjamin, both standing behind him and pulling in unison. The work was hard, and care needed to be taken to ensure no accidents happened. Palmer appreciated the teamwork, the guys coming together to get the job done. And he trusted Noé, even if he wasn't as confident about Benjamin.

As the last beam fell into place, the two men cheered, sounding like a squad at a homecoming event.

"It's been a good day, guys. I hope you two know how much I appreciate you."

"¡Gracias, jefe!"

"Thanks!"

Palmer gave them both a nod. "Noé, if you'd please go pass out payroll, then dismiss the crew. We're going to call it a day."

"Yes, boss," Noé said. He took the stack of envelopes Palmer passed to him, jumped into the pickup truck and headed for the pasture where a crew was herding cattle.

Palmer handed Benjamin a single envelope. "You've really impressed me these past few days. And I'll be honest. I've had my doubts about you. But you've worked hard, taken the advice given to you and stepped up when you were needed. I appreciate having you here. Good job!"

"Thanks, boss! I sometimes get ahead of myself, so it means a lot to me that you were willing to give me a chance. And I apologize again if I overstepped. I just wanted to make a good impression."

Palmer nodded. "As long as you're honest with me, we can make things work," he said.

"Thank you." Benjamin peeked into the mailer and quickly counted his money. "Wow!" he exclaimed. "Wow. I wasn't expecting this."

"You earned it. Keep up the good work and there'll be more where that came from. You have a good night."

Benjamin left the barn. When he was out of sight, Palmer checked his phone for any missed calls. He was still waiting to hear back from his brother since Soledad was talking more and more about going home.

He hadn't been able to express how he felt about that and it bothered him. He didn't want her to go. Although there wasn't anything they still felt uncomfortable talking about, he wasn't ready to consider that she might not want to be there with him anymore. That would have broken his heart. So much had changed between them. With *him*. He wanted something different and he hadn't yet verbalized that to himself, so telling Soledad wasn't something he was prepared to do.

Fatherhood was actually a consideration. He adored Lyra, had grown to love caring for her. She would need a father, and for the first time in his life, he felt capable and ready to be that for her.

Palmer was putting away tools and futzing around when Benjamin came strolling back into the space. He looked anxious, moisture beading his brow.

"Hey, what are you still doing here? I thought you'd left."

"I did. I was hoping to catch a ride with Noé, but he didn't have any more room. I was wondering if you might be able to give me a ride home. I hate to ask, but I'm supposed to meet my roommate tonight before she heads to work, and if I have to walk, I'm not going to make it in time."

Palmer looked at his watch. He had planned a date night for him and Soledad. Since a sitter wasn't possible, Lyra and Jack were going to be their third and fourth wheels, and he was hopeful that both would go down early for the night.

A private event planner was currently in the small barn by the house, transforming the space into a light-filled wonderland complete with white linens and gold chairs. Dinner had been ordered from Soledad's favorite food truck and staff had been hired to serve and clean up. He was planning to wear the only tuxedo he owned, and a flower delivery would be arriving soon with a few dozen white roses. There would be a scavenger hunt after dessert, and if all went well, Palmer planned to make love to Soledad well into the next morning. Leaving the ranch to give anyone a ride had not been on the list of things he needed to do.

"Hey, it's not a problem," Benjamin said, seeming to read his mind. "I can walk. Really. And my roomie will understand. Since I have a job, she's thinking about letting me live with her permanently so that I can go to school."

"That's great news. It's good to hear."

Benjamin smiled. "Thank you. I'll get out of your way."

"Look, I have something planned myself tonight, but if you can give me a few minutes, I can give you a ride." Palmer sighed, his jaw tightening as he clenched his back teeth together. He wanted to help the kid, but he couldn't shake the feeling that something was amiss. Giving him a ride took him off the property and far from his family.

Benjamin's smile widened. "Thank you. I really appreciate that. I can't tell you how much this means to me."

"Not a problem. Hop in the truck. I need to stop by the house first and then we can take off. That good?"

"It sure is! Thank you again."

Palmer made a quick stop to let Soledad know where he was headed.

"You've had to give him a ride practically every day since he got here. That's not cool."

"I need to talk to him about it. He's been doing so well that I don't want to make an issue of it when it's really not that big a deal. I'll be back in plenty of time to get dressed and escort you to dinner."

Soledad shrugged. "Well, just be careful, please. I don't know what you've got planned, but I'm excited about dressing up and spending the evening with you." And she was, a new dress hanging against the bedroom door. Palmer had excellent taste, and she was excited to wear the purchase he had gifted her earlier in the day.

He kissed her lips. "You know the routine. Lock the doors and set the alarm. There's no reason for anyone to come into the house. For anything."

She gave him a salute. "Yes, captain," she said teasingly.

"I'm serious, Soledad. Don't do anything to put yourself at risk."

Palmer quickly walked from the house to the small barn to pop his head in and check that things were going smoothly. The party planner was gone, so he knew setup was complete. The catering people weren't due for another hour, so he had some time.

As he passed by his Ford F-150, Benjamin was on his cell phone, seeming to be in a heated conversation with someone. Minutes later, satisfied that everything was on track, Palmer jumped into his truck and took off for the main road.

"Everything okay?" he asked, sensing that Benjamin's mood had shifted drastically.

"Sorry, my roommate is just tripping."

"Anything I can help with?" Palmer asked.

"No," Benjamin answered, shaking his head. "I just need to show her I can be responsible and take care of myself. I still don't know if it'll work out, but if it means I'll have a home, I want to try to make it work."

"I'm proud of you, Ben. I want you to know that. This isn't easy and you can easily get distracted. I'm proud that you're focused on doing what you need to do."

"Really?"

"Why wouldn't I be?"

He shrugged, his shoulders rolling forward as he fell into thought. Minutes passed before either spoke again. They were parked in traffic, an accident keeping them from their destination. Palmer kept watching the clock, time not being a good friend to him.

Benjamin broke through the quiet. "I've made some bad choices. Some of them I can't take back," he said, his voice a loud whisper. "But I'm not really a bad person. At least, I'm not trying to be."

"You're still finding your way. Your confusion now is not a bad thing. You'll get my age and still be learning about yourself. Trust that."

Benjamin turned to stare out the window, his brow creased with thought. For a split second, Palmer thought he might cry, but he didn't, seeming to pull himself together.

"Are you sure you don't want to talk about it?"

Benjamin shook his head, words catching in his throat. Before either man could say anything more, Palmer's cell phone rang, his brother's image popping up on the screen.

"Sorry, I need to take this," Palmer said as he answered the call. "Hey, what's up?"

"I think you've got a problem."

"What do you mean?" Palmer felt every nerve in his body bristle with tension.

"What's the deal with this kid? Is he working for you?"

Palmer shifted his cell phone to his other ear. He shot Benjamin a look, the boy still staring intently out the window. "Yeah. Why?"

"Benjamin Harris is Benjamin Harris Monroe. Monroe is his legal last name. He is eighteen years old, but he was never adopted by anyone named Harris. In fact, he bounced from foster home to foster home, starting when he was five years old. He was labeled problematic, has been arrested four times for various misdemeanors and has one felony conviction for assault. His last place of residence was a group home in Detroit before being incarcerated at the juvenile detention center here in Grave Gulch. He aged out of the foster-care system six months ago."

"Well, that's definitely not the story I was told."

"There's more," Troy noted. "He has no connection to Len Davison. There was no father who was a victim of Davison's, but he does have a connection to Dr. Gavin Stone. Stone volunteered at the detention center as part of his own community service for assaulting a woman three years ago. He took a plea deal that gave him community service in exchange for his record being expunged once completed."

"Are you sure about that?"

"I just spoke to Benjamin's parole officer. Dr. Stone vouched for him and wrote a letter of recommendation for his release from the detention center. They would seem to know each other very well."

The traffic inched forward a single car length. Palmer had broken out into a sweat, perspiration like a faucet left running. A quiet rage suddenly swept through him. "Troy, hold on," he snapped as he dropped his cell phone into his lap. Abruptly making a three-point turn, he aimed the truck in the opposite direction and sped off back toward the ranch.

"I think we have a bigger problem," Palmer suddenly snapped as he pulled the phone back to his ear. "Send units to my house now!"

SOLEDAD LOVED THAT Lyra always slept when she needed her to. She was the best baby, and even in the short time they'd been with Palmer, the little girl had grown exponentially. Her mother would have been very proud.

Stepping out of the shower, Soledad peeked into the nursery as she made her way to her room. Lyra was sleeping peacefully, and Jack had taken up his guardian position beneath the crib.

The dress that lay across the bed had been in a box lined with tissue paper. An exquisite off-the-shoulder, midi-length dress with ruched mesh, it was the most stunning design she'd seen in a long time. And it fit her figure like a glove. She couldn't begin to explain how excited she was to wear it, even if their date night only started and stopped in the kitchen. She just knew that it wasn't a meal she had to cook or dishes she had to clean, and the entire evening was devoted to her and Palmer. The flurry of activity that was happening in the barn only served to heighten her excitement, and she couldn't wait to see what he'd been up to.

She didn't want to admit it, but tension had risen between them. It was like a layer of frustration that neither was willing to address. Despite wanting a future together, they'd been reluctant to express what that future might look like when she was free to go home. Would they start to date like normal people did? Would they bounce from his place to hers and back? Would there be mornings when they didn't wake up to each other, or nights when they went to bed alone?

Soledad knew Palmer cared about her. He'd even told her it was love. But did he care about her enough to want to marry her? Or would his love for her fade into a casual friendship with benefits? Most important, was he still opposed to being a father, and would he turn his back on Lyra when he no longer felt responsible for her?

Suddenly, once again, Soledad had more questions than answers, and even as she admired her reflection in the pretty dress, there was still far too much that she didn't know about how Palmer was feeling when it came down to their relationship.

The sound of glass breaking in the kitchen startled her from her thoughts. She reached for the remote for the bedroom stereo and lowered the volume. She stood as still as stone. Jack had jumped from where he rested and he eased his way to the door, moving as if he were hunting prey. The sound of rubber-soled shoes on the hardwood floor moved the dog to growl. Instinctively,

Soledad knew someone was in the house and it wasn't Palmer who had come home.

She hurried into the bathroom and turned the shower back on. Leaving the door partially closed, she moved to the crib and lifted Lyra into her arms. The baby barely noticed as she rested her head on Soledad's shoulder and continued to snore softly.

Soledad tiptoed to the bed and set the infant down in its center. She had to think fast and, knowing that there was nowhere for her to run, fast meant putting up a good fight to protect the little girl she loved with every fiber of her being.

She grabbed a fire poker from the fireplace and stood behind the door. Seeing his shadow before she saw him, she knew she was cornered. There was nowhere to run, no escaping the inevitable, and so she braced herself, prepared to give Gavin Stone the worst day of his life.

PALMER WAS SHOUTING, his calm having dissipated into thin air. "What did you do? What does he have planned?" He didn't care about the traffic laws he was breaking as he zigzagged between the cars to get back to his ranch.

"I don't know," Benjamin shouted back. "He just asked me to get you out of the house. He said that woman kidnapped his daughter and he just wanted to get her back."

Palmer was ready to commit murder himself, his frustration level miles high. He had let his guard down and put Soledad in danger. If anything happened to her, he thought, he would never forgive himself and he would make it his mission to destroy everyone who'd had anything to do with her being harmed—starting with Benjamin.

"I trusted you!" Palmer snapped. "Did he send you to spy for him?"

"He wasn't sure where she was and he needed me to confirm if I saw her."

"So you came and asked for a job?"

"Yes, and I'm sorry!"

Rage washed over Palmer's face. "You'll be sorry if he does anything to her. He killed his wife. Did you know that? Soledad's hiding because she witnessed him commit murder."

Shock registered in Benjamin's expression. He had no words as his gaze dropped to the floor, apparently struggling to make sense of what Palmer was telling him.

Palmer took a hard right turn into the southern entrance of the Colton Ranch property. He barreled straight through the closed gate, not bothering to wait for the metal fencing to open. He depressed the accelerator, speeding up the F-150 as he barreled down the dirt road, turning left toward home.

His heart was racing and he was finding it difficult to breathe, but all he could think of was getting to Soledad and the baby as quickly as he could. In the distance, he heard the sound of sirens and wished a silent prayer that they all could get to them in time.

Chapter Nineteen

As Gavin moved into the room, his eyes focused on the baby lying on the bed, Soledad swung the fire poker with every ounce of energy that she possessed. Due to the height differential, she missed his head, striking him in the shoulder instead. Gavin bellowed in pain, which was just enough of a diversion for Jack to lunge for his neck. As he struggled to get the dog off him, he managed to fire off a shot from the gun in his hand, the bullet missing Soledad and shattering the dresser mirror instead.

Soledad grabbed the baby and ran, Jack racing them both to the front door. A second shot zoomed past her head. Flinging the door open, Soledad bolted onto the front porch and down the steps. With nowhere else to run, she headed for the small barn beside the house to hide, hopeful that Palmer hadn't made too many changes and the bales of hay would still afford them a modicum of shelter.

As HE NEARED his home, Palmer saw Soledad bolt across the yard toward the barn. Though the siren sounds were getting closer, there was no sign of any of the patrol cars.

Gavin Stone came limping out of the house and off the porch, clearly determined to give chase. Palmer just missed hitting the murderer with his truck, throwing the vehicle into Park as Gavin jumped out of his way.

Then everything seemed to happen in slow motion, like a scene in a bad movie.

Palmer grabbed the Glock he kept in the glove box and threw himself from the truck. Gavin fired his weapon as Palmer ducked behind the rear of the vehicle. As he did, they exchanged fire, both determined to bring the fight to an end.

Palmer didn't know when or how, but Jack was suddenly standing between them, baring his teeth at Stone. Palmer watched as the man raised his gun arm.

Palmer shouted and Jack shifted gears, turning toward him.

In that split second, Palmer lost focus, his firearm wavering. Gavin aimed and fired, and from out of nowhere, Benjamin threw himself between the two men, taking a bullet that wasn't meant for him. As both men watched the boy's body fall, Palmer fired once and then a second time, hitting his target squarely in the chest with both shots.

The moment was surreal, everything seeming to happen in slow motion. Palmer felt his stomach pitch with tension, and concern for Benjamin rose with a vengeance. The kid has purposely put himself in the line of fire and saved his life. Seconds later, his body was flooded with relief.

He stood tall as Gavin Stone fell to the ground.

The shooting finally stopped. Lyra was crying. Jack was barking. Outside, it sounded as if sirens were surrounding the building. Voices shouted and Palmer was screaming Soledad's name. But in that moment, all Soledad could see were the miniature lights that sparkled around the room. There was a dinner table set for two, with white linens, gold-trimmed dinner plates, crystal wineglasses and flickering battery-powered candles. It was the most amazing presentation that she had ever seen.

Soledad came out from behind the hay bales in the loft. She had scaled the ladder with Lyra in her arms, determined that Gavin would never get his hands on the baby. Retreating to ground level proved to be more of a challenge, and she'd just planted her bare feet on the wooden planks when Palmer barreled into the barn. Melissa Colton and his brother Troy were both on his heels.

It was only when Palmer pulled her into his arms that Soledad realized tears streamed down her face. Her pretty dress was torn down the side and dirt covered her face and hands. But Palmer Colton kissed her like she was the prettiest girl in the whole wide world.

"I was so scared," he muttered against her lips as his eyes skated easily back and forth over hers. "Are you okay?"

She shook her head. "I didn't know what to do. I just knew I had to fight and keep Lyra safe."

Palmer kissed her again, pulling his hand through her hair as he wrapped his other arm around her and the baby.

"Where is he?" she asked, still shaking.

"He's dead," Palmer muttered. "You never have to worry about him again." Something dark and sad spilled from his eyes.

"What?" Soledad questioned, concern wafting like a cool breeze between them.

"I shot him," Palmer said, his voice a loud whisper. The magnitude of everything that had happened suddenly hit him. He'd killed a man and he didn't take that lightly. Whether or not he'd find atonement for that sin was yet to be seen. He tightened the grip he had on Soledad and the baby.

Melissa interjected. "The ambulance is transporting Mr. Monroe to the hospital now. EMS says it doesn't look like the bullet hit any vital organs, so they anticipate he'll survive his injuries."

Soledad looked confused. "Who's Mr. Monroe?"

"Benjamin Harris," Palmer said matter-of-factly, filling her in on the connection between him and Gavin.

"I'm so sorry," she whispered. "I know how much you wanted to help him. You put a lot of faith into him succeeding."

"I did and I'm still processing how I got that wrong."

"He'll be charged with conspiracy," Troy added. "I imagine he's going to do some time in an adult jail this time."

Palmer shook his head. "He saved my life. He didn't have to do that, but he did."

His brother shrugged. "He'll still be charged. What he did was criminal."

Soledad brushed her palm against Palmer's back, gliding her hand up and down the length of his spine.

"I need EMS to check that you and the baby are okay," Melissa said. "Then you and Palmer will need to come down to the station to give us statements. I'm glad that you're all right, Soledad, and you can have your life back."

Soledad smiled. "Thank you. And thank you for supporting my decision to hide out here."

Melissa grinned. "I don't know anything about that. I'm just happy we were able to find you safe and sound."

They all watched as Melissa turned and exited the barn.

"Do you two need anything else from me?" Troy asked.

Palmer shook his head for a second time. "I think we're good."

Troy glanced around the barn. "It sure is pretty in here. Looks like a great place to ask someone to marry you."

Palmer shook his head yet again and snapped, "Go away!"

Troy chuckled heartily as he gave Soledad a wave and made his way out of the building.

Palmer pulled Soledad back into his arms. He kissed her and then bent his head to give Lyra a kiss, too. The baby was staring in awe, completely mesmerized by the lights.

"My date-night plans were ruined," Palmer said. "I

don't even know if the caterer has been able to make it onto the property with all the police cars out there."

"You outdid yourself."

"Well, my brother was right about one thing," he said. "I was determined to have a pretty place to ask you to be my wife." He reached into his pocket and pulled a stunning diamond ring from inside.

Soledad's mouth fell open and her eyes widened. Surprise seeped from her eyes.

Palmer dropped to one knee, taking Soledad's hand into his. "Soledad de la Vega, I love you. I am so in love with you that I almost lost my mind at the very thought of something happening to you. I never want to lose you. Or Lyra. You and that beautiful baby girl have become my entire life, and I want to spend every day from now until eternity making you happy. Will you marry me? And will you allow me to adopt Lyra, so that she is officially our baby girl?"

Soledad pressed her hand to Palmer's face, her eyes dancing a beautiful two-step with his. He loved her. He wanted her. And he wanted the life she envisioned for herself and for Lyra. She smiled. "Oh, hell yes!" she exclaimed. "I didn't know if you would ever ask."

THE GRAVE GULCH Police Department was buzzing with reporters hoping to get an exclusive interview with Soledad. News of the shooting that ended the hunt for Annie Stone's murderer had broken on the evening news. Both Soledad and Palmer had endured hours of questioning by numerous detectives until they'd been satisfied that the case could be closed. Dominique and

Stanton had rushed to the home and were waiting there with Lyra until they returned.

The magistrate had also granted Soledad temporary custody of Lyra pending a formal hearing and the reading of Annie's last will and testament. There was no doubt from anyone involved that her mother's last wishes were for Lyra to remain in the care of Soledad.

Soledad held tight to Palmer's hand as Troy walked them to a side exit. They paused when he was stopped by K-9 detective Brett Shea.

"Sorry to interrupt, partner," the man said. He gave Palmer and Soledad a look, apologizing for the interruption. "We've gotten a tip on Randall Bowe. It's credible and I'm headed to check it out. I thought you might want to take the ride with me."

Troy nodded. "Let me grab my stuff and I'll be right there." He turned to his brother. "I'll check on you two tomorrow unless you need something else?"

Palmer shook his head. "We're good. I need to go feed my woman and we need to check on our baby girl."

"That's important."

"Is he new? I don't recognize him," Palmer said, gesturing after the officer who'd just rushed out the door.

Troy nodded. "That's Brett Shea."

"He's intense," Soledad observed. "He obviously takes his work seriously."

"He was recently transferred here from Lansing. He's fighting some demons and he's got trust issues. One of his best friends was arrested for a crime he didn't commit. Brett struggled because he couldn't help him, even though he knew he wasn't guilty. The friend served some time, but was eventually exonerated."

"That's horrible!" Soledad exclaimed.

Troy nodded. "I often think that when the department is able to regain Brett's trust, I'll know we've won back the community's trust, as well."

Palmer nodded. "You be safe out there, big brother."

"We Coltons don't go down easy," Troy said with a wink.

The couple watched as he hurried after his partner, one more case needing to be solved.

Soledad lifted her gaze to Palmer's. "Can we go home? I want to dance cheek to cheek in the barn, under the pretty lights."

Palmer laughed. "Soledad, I adore you. And for you, my darling, whatever you wish for is yours. There's only one problem with that wish, though."

"What's that?"

"I can't dance."

Soledad laughed. "I still love you!"

* * * * *